PENGUIN BOOKS

A Capote Reader

TRUMAN CAPOTE was born in New Orleans in 1924 and was raised in various parts of the South, his family spending winters in New Orleans and summers in Alabama and New Georgia. He left school when he was fifteen and subsequently worked for the *New Yorker* which provided his first – and last – regular job. In 1948 his first novel, *Other Voices, Other Rooms*, was published to international critical acclaim, assuring Capote a place among the prominent postwar American writers. His other works include *The Grass Harp* (1951), *Breakfast at Tiffany's* (1958), *In Cold Blood* (1965), which immediately became the centre of a storm of controversy on its publication, *Music for Chameleons* (1980) and *Answered Prayers* (1986). *Summer Crossing*, Capote's first novel, was sold at Sotheby's, New York, in 2004, and published for the first time in the UK by Penguin Classics in 2005. Truman Capote died in August 1984.

TRUMAN CAPOTE

A CAPOTE READER

PENGUIN BOOKS

PENGUIN BOOKS

Published by the Penguin Group
Penguin Books Ltd, 80 Strand, London WC2R 0RL, England
Penguin Putnam Inc., 375 Hudson Street, New York, New York 10014, USA
Penguin Books Australia Ltd, 250 Camberwell Road, Camberwell, Victoria 3124, Australia
Penguin Books Canada Ltd, 10 Alcorn Avenue, Toronto, Ontario, Canada M4V 3B2
Penguin Books India (P) Ltd, 11 Community Centre, Panchsheel Park, New Delhi – 110 017, India
Penguin Books (NZ) Ltd, Cnr Rosedale and Airborne Roads, Albany, Auckland, New Zealand
Penguin Books (South Africa) (Pty) Ltd, 24 Sturdee Avenue, Rosebank 2196, South Africa

Penguin Books Ltd, Registered Offices: 80 Strand, London WC2R 0RL, England

www.penguin.com

First published in Great Britain by Hamish Hamilton,
by arrangement with Random House, Inc. 1987
Published in Penguin Books 1993
Reprinted in Penguin Classics 2002

9

Copyright © Alan U. Schwartz, 1987
All rights reserved

Printed in England by Clays Ltd, St Ives plc

ISBN-13: 978–0–141–18530–9
ISBN-10: 0–141–18530–9

CONTENTS

CONTENTS

SHORT
STORIES

Miriam

(1945)

FOR SEVERAL YEARS, MRS. H. T. MIL-
ler had lived alone in a pleasant apart-
ment (two rooms with kitchenette) in a remodeled brownstone near the
East River. She was a widow: Mr. H. T. Miller had left a reasonable
amount of insurance. Her interests were narrow, she had no friends to
speak of, and she rarely journeyed farther than the corner grocery. The
other people in the house never seemed to notice her: her clothes were
matter-of-fact, her hair iron-gray, clipped and casually waved; she did not
use cosmetics, her features were plain and inconspicuous, and on her last
birthday she was sixty-one. Her activities were seldom spontaneous: she
kept the two rooms immaculate, smoked an occasional cigarette, prepared
her own meals and tended a canary.

Then she met Miriam. It was snowing that night. Mrs. Miller had
finished drying the supper dishes and was thumbing through an afternoon
paper when she saw an advertisement of a picture playing at a neighborhood theater. The title sounded good, so she struggled into her beaver coat,
laced her galoshes and left the apartment, leaving one light burning in the
foyer: she found nothing more disturbing than a sensation of darkness.

The snow was fine, falling gently, not yet making an impression on the
pavement. The wind from the river cut only at street crossings. Mrs. Miller
hurried, her head bowed, oblivious as a mole burrowing a blind path. She
stopped at a drugstore and bought a package of peppermints.

3

A long line stretched in front of the box office; she took her place at the end. There would be (a tired voice groaned) a short wait for all seats. Mrs. Miller rummaged in her leather handbag till she collected exactly the correct change for admission. The line seemed to be taking its own time and, looking around for some distraction, she suddenly became conscious of a little girl standing under the edge of the marquee.

Her hair was the longest and strangest Mrs. Miller had ever seen: absolutely silver-white, like an albino's. It flowed waist-length in smooth, loose lines. She was thin and fragilely constructed. There was a simple, special elegance in the way she stood with her thumbs in the pockets of a tailored plum-velvet coat.

Mrs. Miller felt oddly excited, and when the little girl glanced toward her, she smiled warmly. The little girl walked over and said, "Would you care to do me a favor?"

"I'd be glad to, if I can," said Mrs. Miller.

"Oh, it's quite easy. I merely want you to buy a ticket for me; they won't let me in otherwise. Here, I have the money." And gracefully she handed Mrs. Miller two dimes and a nickel.

They went over to the theater together. An usherette directed them to a lounge; in twenty minutes the picture would be over.

"I feel just like a genuine criminal," said Mrs. Miller gaily, as she sat down. "I mean, that sort of thing's against the law, isn't it? I do hope I haven't done the wrong thing. Your mother knows where you are, dear? I mean she does, doesn't she?"

The little girl said nothing. She unbuttoned her coat and folded it across her lap. Her dress underneath was prim and dark blue. A gold chain dangled about her neck, and her fingers, sensitive and musical-looking, toyed with it. Examining her more attentively, Mrs. Miller decided the truly distinctive feature was not her hair, but her eyes; they were hazel, steady, lacking any childlike quality whatsoever and, because of their size, seemed to consume her small face.

Mrs. Miller offered a peppermint. "What's your name, dear?"

"Miriam," she said, as though, in some curious way, it were information already familiar.

"Why, isn't that funny—my name's Miriam, too. And it's not a terribly common name either. Now, don't tell me your last name's Miller!"

"Just Miriam."

"But isn't that funny?"

"Moderately," said Miriam, and rolled the peppermint on her tongue.

Mrs. Miller flushed and shifted uncomfortably. "You have such a large vocabulary for such a little girl."

"Do I?"

"Well, yes," said Mrs. Miller, hastily changing the topic to: "Do you like the movies?"

4

"I really wouldn't know," said Miriam. "I've never been before."

Women began filling the lounge; the rumble of the newsreel bombs exploded in the distance. Mrs. Miller rose, tucking her purse under her arm. "I guess I'd better be running now if I want to get a seat," she said. "It was nice to have met you."

Miriam nodded ever so slightly.

It snowed all week. Wheels and footsteps moved soundlessly on the street, as if the business of living continued secretly behind a pale but impenetrable curtain. In the falling quiet there was no sky or earth, only snow lifting in the wind, frosting the window glass, chilling the rooms, deadening and hushing the city. At all hours it was necessary to keep a lamp lighted, and Mrs. Miller lost track of the days: Friday was no different from Saturday and on Sunday she went to the grocery: closed, of course.

That evening she scrambled eggs and fixed a bowl of tomato soup. Then, after putting on a flannel robe and cold-creaming her face, she propped herself up in bed with a hot-water bottle under her feet. She was reading the *Times* when the doorbell rang. At first she thought it must be a mistake and whoever it was would go away. But it rang and rang and settled to a persistent buzz. She looked at the clock: a little after eleven; it did not seem possible, she was always asleep by ten.

Climbing out of bed, she trotted barefoot across the living room. "I'm coming, please be patient." The latch was caught; she turned it this way and that way and the bell never paused an instant. "Stop it," she cried. The bolt gave way and she opened the door an inch. "What in heaven's name?"

"Hello," said Miriam.

"Oh . . . why, hello," said Mrs. Miller, stepping hesitantly into the hall. "You're that little girl."

"I thought you'd never answer, but I kept my finger on the button; I knew you were home. Aren't you glad to see me?"

Mrs. Miller did not know what to say. Miriam, she saw, wore the same plum-velvet coat and now she had also a beret to match; her white hair was braided in two shining plaits and looped at the ends with enormous white ribbons.

"Since I've waited so long, you could at least let me in," she said.

"It's awfully late. . . ."

Miriam regarded her blankly. "What difference does that make? Let me in. It's cold out here and I have on a silk dress." Then, with a gentle gesture, she urged Mrs. Miller aside and passed into the apartment.

She dropped her coat and beret on a chair. She was indeed wearing a silk dress. White silk. White silk in February. The skirt was beautifully pleated and the sleeves long; it made a faint rustle as she strolled about the room. "I like your place," she said. "I like the rug, blue's my favorite color." She touched a paper rose in a vase on the coffee table. "Imitation," she commented wanly. "How sad. Aren't imitations sad?" She seated herself on the sofa, daintily spreading her skirt.

"What do you want?" asked Mrs. Miller.

"Sit down," said Miriam. "It makes me nervous to see people stand."

Mrs. Miller sank to a hassock. "What do you want?" she repeated.

"You know, I don't think you're glad I came."

For a second time Mrs. Miller was without an answer; her hand motioned vaguely. Miriam giggled and pressed back on a mound of chintz pillows. Mrs. Miller observed that the girl was less pale than she remembered; her cheeks were flushed.

"How did you know where I lived?"

Miriam frowned. "That's no question at all. What's your name? What's mine?"

"But I'm not listed in the phone book."

"Oh, let's talk about something else."

Mrs. Miller said, "Your mother must be insane to let a child like you wander around at all hours of the night—and in such ridiculous clothes. She must be out of her mind."

Miriam got up and moved to a corner where a covered birdcage hung from a ceiling chain. She peeked beneath the cover. "It's a canary," she said. "Would you mind if I woke him? I'd like to hear him sing."

"Leave Tommy alone," said Mrs. Miller anxiously. "Don't you dare wake him."

"Certainly," said Miriam. "But I don't see why I can't hear him sing." And then, "Have you anything to eat? I'm starving! Even milk and a jam sandwich would be fine."

"Look," said Mrs. Miller, arising from the hassock, "look—if I make some nice sandwiches will you be a good child and run along home? It's past midnight, I'm sure."

"It's snowing," reproached Miriam. "And cold and dark."

"Well, you shouldn't have come here to begin with," said Mrs. Miller, struggling to control her voice. "I can't help the weather. If you want anything to eat, you'll have to promise to leave."

Miriam brushed a braid against her cheek. Her eyes were thoughtful, as if weighing the proposition. She turned toward the birdcage. "Very well," she said, "I promise."

How old is she? Ten? Eleven? Mrs. Miller, in the kitchen, unsealed a jar of strawberry preserves and cut four slices of bread. She poured a glass of milk and paused to light a cigarette. *And why has she come?* Her hand shook as

6

she held the match, fascinated, till it burned her finger. The canary was singing; singing as he did in the morning and at no other time. "Miriam," she called, "Miriam, I told you not to disturb Tommy." There was no answer. She called again; all she heard was the canary. She inhaled the cigarette and discovered she had lighted the cork-tip end and—oh, really, she mustn't lose her temper.

She carried the food in on a tray and set it on the coffee table. She saw first that the birdcage still wore its night cover. And Tommy was singing. It gave her a queer sensation. And no one was in the room. Mrs. Miller went through an alcove leading to her bedroom; at the door she caught her breath.

"What are you doing?" she asked.

Miriam glanced up and in her eyes there was a look that was not ordinary. She was standing by the bureau, a jewel case opened before her. For a minute she studied Mrs. Miller, forcing their eyes to meet, and she smiled. "There's nothing good here," she said. "But I like this." Her hand held a cameo brooch. "It's charming."

"Suppose—perhaps you'd better put it back," said Mrs. Miller, feeling suddenly the need of some support. She leaned against the door frame; her head was unbearably heavy; a pressure weighted the rhythm of her heartbeat. The light seemed to flutter defectively. "Please, child—a gift from my husband . . ."

"But it's beautiful and I want it," said Miriam. *"Give it to me."*

As she stood, striving to shape a sentence which would somehow save the brooch, it came to Mrs. Miller there was no one to whom she might turn; she was alone; a fact that had not been among her thoughts for a long time. Its sheer emphasis was stunning. But here in her own rŏom in the hushed snow-city were evidences she could not ignore or, she knew with startling clarity, resist.

Miriam ate ravenously, and when the sandwiches and milk were gone, her fingers made cobweb movements over the plate, gathering crumbs. The cameo gleamed on her blouse, the blond profile like a trick reflection of its wearer. "That was very nice," she sighed, "though now an almond cake or a cherry would be ideal. Sweets are lovely, don't you think?"

Mrs. Miller was perched precariously on the hassock, smoking a cigarette. Her hairnet had slipped lopsided and loose strands straggled down her face. Her eyes were stupidly concentrated on nothing and her cheeks were mottled in red patches, as though a fierce slap had left permanent marks.

"Is there a candy—a cake?"

Mrs. Miller tapped ash on the rug. Her head swayed slightly as she tried to focus her eyes. "You promised to leave if I made the sandwiches," she said.

"Dear me, did I?"

"It was a promise and I'm tired and I don't feel well at all."

"Mustn't fret," said Miriam. "I'm only teasing."

She picked up her coat, slung it over her arm, and arranged her beret in front of a mirror. Presently she bent close to Mrs. Miller and whispered, "Kiss me good night."

"Please—I'd rather not," said Mrs. Miller.

Miriam lifted a shoulder, arched an eyebrow. "As you like," she said, and went directly to the coffee table, seized the vase containing the paper roses, carried it to where the hard surface of the floor lay bare, and hurled it downward. Glass sprayed in all directions and she stamped her foot on the bouquet.

Then slowly she walked to the door, but before closing it, she looked back at Mrs. Miller with a slyly innocent curiosity.

Mrs. Miller spent the next day in bed, rising once to feed the canary and drink a cup of tea; she took her temperature and had none, yet her dreams were feverishly agitated; their unbalanced mood lingered even as she lay staring wide-eyed at the ceiling. One dream threaded through the others like an elusively mysterious theme in a complicated symphony, and the scenes it depicted were sharply outlined, as though sketched by a hand of gifted intensity: a small girl, wearing a bridal gown and a wreath of leaves, led a gray procession down a mountain path, and among them there was unusual silence till a woman at the rear asked, "Where is she taking us?" "No one knows," said an old man marching in front. "But isn't she pretty?" volunteered a third voice. "Isn't she like a frost flower . . . so shining and white?"

Tuesday morning she woke up feeling better; harsh slats of sunlight, slanting through Venetian blinds, shed a disrupting light on her unwholesome fancies. She opened the window to discover a thawed, mild-as-spring day; a sweep of clean new clouds crumpled against a vastly blue, out-of-season sky; and across the low line of rooftops she could see the river and smoke curving from tugboat stacks in a warm wind. A great silver truck plowed the snow-banked street, its machine sound humming on the air.

After straightening the apartment, she went to the grocer's, cashed a check and continued to Schrafft's, where she ate breakfast and chatted happily with the waitress. Oh, it was a wonderful day—more like a holiday—and it would be so foolish to go home.

She boarded a Lexington Avenue bus and rode up to Eighty-sixth Street; it was here that she had decided to do a little shopping.

She had no idea what she wanted or needed, but she idled along, intent only upon the passers-by, brisk and preoccupied, who gave her a disturbing sense of separateness.

It was while waiting at the corner of Third Avenue that she saw the man: an old man, bowlegged and stooped under an armload of bulging packages; he wore a shabby brown coat and a checkered cap. Suddenly she realized they were exchanging a smile: there was nothing friendly about this smile, it was merely two cold flickers of recognition. But she was certain she had never seen him before.

He was standing next to an El pillar, and as she crossed the street he turned and followed. He kept quite close; from the corner of her eye she watched his reflection wavering on the shopwindows.

Then in the middle of the block she stopped and faced him. He stopped also and cocked his head, grinning. But what could she say? Do? Here, in broad daylight, on Eighty-sixth Street? It was useless and, despising her own helplessness, she quickened her steps.

Now Second Avenue is a dismal street, made from scraps and ends; part cobblestone, part asphalt, part cement; and its atmosphere of desertion is permanent. Mrs. Miller walked five blocks without meeting anyone, and all the while the steady crunch of his footfalls in the snow stayed near. And when she came to a florist's shop, the sound was still with her. She hurried inside and watched through the glass door as the old man passed; he kept his eyes straight ahead and didn't slow his pace, but he did one strange, telling thing: he tipped his cap.

"Six white ones, did you say?" asked the florist. "Yes," she told him, "white roses." From there she went to a glassware store and selected a vase, presumably a replacement for the one Miriam had broken, though the price was intolerable and the vase itself (she thought) grotesquely vulgar. But a series of unaccountable purchases had begun, as if by prearranged plan: a plan of which she had not the least knowledge or control.

She bought a bag of glazed cherries, and at a place called the Knickerbocker Bakery she paid forty cents for six almond cakes.

Within the last hour the weather had turned cold again; like blurred lenses, winter clouds cast a shade over the sun, and the skeleton of an early dusk colored the sky; a damp mist mixed with the wind and the voices of a few children who romped high on mountains of gutter snow seemed lonely and cheerless. Soon the first flake fell, and when Mrs. Miller reached the brownstone house, snow was falling in a swift screen and foot tracks vanished as they were printed.

. . .

The white roses were arranged decoratively in the vase. The glazed cherries shone on a ceramic plate. The almond cakes, dusted with sugar, awaited a hand. The canary fluttered on its swing and picked at a bar of seed.

At precisely five the doorbell rang. Mrs. Miller *knew* who it was. The hem of her housecoat trailed as she crossed the floor. "Is that you?" she called.

"Naturally," said Miriam, the word resounding shrilly from the hall. "Open this door."

"Go away," said Mrs. Miller.

"Please hurry . . . I have a heavy package."

"Go away," said Mrs. Miller. She returned to the living room, lighted a cigarette, sat down and calmly listened to the buzzer; on and on and on. "You might as well leave. I have no intention of letting you in."

Shortly the bell stopped. For possibly ten minutes Mrs. Miller did not move. Then, hearing no sound, she concluded Miriam had gone. She tiptoed to the door and opened it a sliver; Miriam was half-reclining atop a cardboard box with a beautiful French doll cradled in her arms.

"Really, I thought you were never coming," she said peevishly. "Here, help me get this in, it's awfully heavy."

It was not spell-like compulsion that Mrs. Miller felt, but rather a curious passivity; she brought in the box, Miriam, the doll. Miriam curled up on the sofa, not troubling to remove her coat or beret, and watched disinterestedly as Mrs. Miller dropped the box and stood trembling, trying to catch her breath.

"Thank you," she said. In the daylight she looked pinched and drawn, her hair less luminous. The French doll she was loving wore an exquisite powdered wig and its idiot glass eyes sought solace in Miriam's. "I have a surprise," she continued. "Look into my box."

Kneeling, Mrs. Miller parted the flaps and lifted out another doll; then a blue dress which she recalled as the one Miriam had worn that first night at the theater; and of the remainder she said, "It's all clothes. Why?"

"Because I've come to live with you," said Miriam, twisting a cherry stem. "Wasn't it nice of you to buy me the cherries . . .?"

"But you can't! For God's sake go away—go away and leave me alone!"

". . . and the roses and the almond cakes? How really wonderfully generous. You know, these cherries are delicious. The last place I lived was with an old man; he was terribly poor and we never had good things to eat. But I think I'll be happy here." She paused to snuggle her doll closer. "Now, if you'll just show me where to put my things . . ."

Mrs. Miller's face dissolved into a mask of ugly red lines; she began to cry, and it was an unnatural, tearless sort of weeping, as though, not having wept for a long time, she had forgotten how. Carefully she edged backward till she touched the door.

She fumbled through the hall and down the stairs to a landing below. She pounded frantically on the door of the first apartment she came to; a short, redheaded man answered and she pushed past him. "Say, what the hell is this?" he said. "Anything wrong, lover?" asked a young woman who appeared from the kitchen, drying her hands. And it was to her that Mrs. Miller turned.

"Listen," she cried, "I'm ashamed behaving this way but—well, I'm Mrs. H. T. Miller and I live upstairs and . . ." She pressed her hands over her face. "It sounds so absurd. . . ."

The woman guided her to a chair, while the man excitedly rattled pocket change. "Yeah?"

"I live upstairs and there's a little girl visiting me, and I suppose that I'm afraid of her. She won't leave and I can't make her and—she's going to do something terrible. She's already stolen my cameo, but she's about to do something worse—something terrible!"

The man asked, "Is she a relative, huh?"

Mrs. Miller shook her head. "I don't know who she is. Her name's Miriam, but I don't know for certain who she is."

"You gotta calm down, honey," said the woman, stroking Mrs. Miller's arm. "Harry here'll tend to this kid. Go on, lover." And Mrs. Miller said, "The door's open—5A."

After the man left, the woman brought a towel and bathed Mrs. Miller's face. "You're very kind," Mrs. Miller said. "I'm sorry to act like such a fool, only this wicked child . . ."

"Sure, honey," consoled the woman. "Now, you better take it easy."

Mrs. Miller rested her head in the crook of her arm; she was quiet enough to be asleep. The woman turned a radio dial; a piano and a husky voice filled the silence and the woman, tapping her foot, kept excellent time. "Maybe we oughta go up too," she said.

"I don't want to see her again. I don't want to be anywhere near her."

"Uh huh, but what you shoulda done, you shoulda called a cop."

Presently they heard the man on the stairs. He strode into the room frowning and scratching the back of his neck. "Nobody there," he said, honestly embarrassed. "She musta beat it."

"Harry, you're a jerk," announced the woman. "We been sitting here the whole time and we woulda seen . . ." she stopped abruptly, for the man's glance was sharp.

"I looked all over," he said, "and there just ain't nobody there. Nobody, understand?"

"Tell me," said Mrs. Miller, rising, "tell me, did you see a large box? Or a doll?"

"No, ma'am, I didn't."

And the woman, as if delivering a verdict, said, "Well, for cryinoutloud. . . ."

Mrs. Miller entered her apartment softly; she walked to the center of the room and stood quite still. No, in a sense it had not changed: the roses, the cakes, and the cherries were in place. But this was an empty room, emptier than if the furnishings and familiars were not present, lifeless and petrified as a funeral parlor. The sofa loomed before her with a new strangeness: its vacancy had a meaning that would have been less penetrating and terrible had Miriam been curled on it. She gazed fixedly at the space where she remembered setting the box and, for a moment, the hassock spun desperately. And she looked through the window; surely the river was real, surely snow was falling—but then, one could not be certain witness to anything: Miriam, so vividly there—and yet, where was she? Where, where?

As though moving in a dream, she sank to a chair. The room was losing shape; it was dark and getting darker and there was nothing to be done about it; she could not lift her hand to light a lamp.

Suddenly, closing her eyes, she felt an upward surge, like a diver emerging from some deeper, greener depth. In times of terror or immense distress, there are moments when the mind waits, as though for a revelation, while a skein of calm is woven over thought; it is like a sleep, or a supernatural trance; and during this lull one is aware of a force of quiet reasoning: well, what if she had never really known a girl named Miriam? that she had been foolishly frightened on the street? In the end, like everything else, it was of no importance. For the only thing she had lost to Miriam was her identity, but now she knew she had found again the person who lived in this room, who cooked her own meals, who owned a canary, who was someone she could trust and believe in: Mrs. H. T. Miller.

Listening in contentment, she became aware of a double sound: a bureau drawer opening and closing; she seemed to hear it long after completion —opening and closing. Then gradually, the harshness of it was replaced by the murmur of a silk dress and this, delicately faint, was moving nearer and swelling in intensity till the walls trembled with the vibration and the room was caving under a wave of whispers. Mrs. Miller stiffened and opened her eyes to a dull, direct stare.

"Hello," said Miriam.

My Side of
the Matter

(1945)

I KNOW WHAT IS BEING SAID ABOUT
me and you can take my side or theirs,
that's your own business. It's my word against Eunice's and Olivia-Ann's,
and it should be plain enough to anyone with two good eyes which one
of us has their wits about them. I just want the citizens of the U.S.A. to
know the facts, that's all.

The facts: On Sunday, August 12, this year of our Lord, Eunice tried to
kill me with her papa's Civil War sword and Olivia-Ann cut up all over
the place with a fourteen-inch hog knife. This is not even to mention lots
of other things.

It began six months ago when I married Marge. That was the first thing
I did wrong. We were married in Mobile after an acquaintance of only four
days. We were both sixteen and she was visiting my cousin Georgia. Now
that I've had plenty of time to think it over, I can't for the life of me figure
how I fell for the likes of her. She has no looks, no body and no brains
whatsoever. But Marge is a natural blonde and maybe that's the answer.
Well, we were married going on three months when Marge ups and gets
pregnant; the second thing I did wrong. Then she starts hollering that she's
got to go home to Mama—only she hasn't got no mama, just these two
aunts. Eunice and Olivia-Ann. So she makes me quit my perfectly swell
position clerking at the Cash 'n' Carry and move here to Admiral's Mill,
which is nothing but a damn gap in the road any way you care to consider
it.

The day Marge and I got off the train at the L&N depot it was raining cats and dogs and do you think anyone came to meet us? I'd shelled out forty-one cents for a telegram, too! Here my wife's pregnant and we have to tramp seven miles in a downpour. It was bad on Marge, as I couldn't carry hardly any of our stuff on account of I have terrible trouble with my back. When I first caught sight of this house I must say I was impressed. It's big and yellow and has real columns out in front and japonica trees, both red and white, lining the yard.

Eunice and Olivia-Ann had seen us coming and were waiting in the hall. I swear I wish you could get a look at these two. Honest, you'd die! Eunice is this big old fat thing with a behind that must weigh a tenth of a ton. She troops around the house, rain or shine, in this real old-fashioned nightie, calls it a kimono, but it isn't anything in this world but a dirty flannel nightie. Furthermore she chews tobacco and tries to pretend so ladylike, spitting on the sly. She keeps gabbing about what a fine education she had, which is her way of attempting to make me feel bad, although, personally, it never bothers me so much as one whit, as I know for a fact she can't even read the funnies without she spells out every single, solitary word. You've got to hand her one thing, though—she can add and subtract money so fast that there's no doubt but what she could be up in Washington, D.C., working where they make the stuff. Not that she hasn't got plenty of money! Naturally she says she hasn't but I know she has because one day, accidentally, I happened to find close to a thousand dollars hidden in a flowerpot on the side porch. I didn't touch one cent, only Eunice says I stole a hundred-dollar bill, which is a venomous lie from start to finish. Of course anything Eunice says is an order from headquarters, as not a breathing soul in Admiral's Mill can stand up and say he doesn't owe her money and if she said Charlie Carson (a blind ninety-year-old invalid who hasn't taken a step since 1896) threw her on her back and raped her, everybody in this county would swear the same on a stack of Bibles.

Now, Olivia-Ann is worse, and that's the truth! Only she's not so bad on the nerves as Eunice, for she is a natural-born half-wit and ought really to be kept in somebody's attic. She's real pale and skinny and has a mustache. She squats around most of the time whittling on a stick with her fourteen-inch hog knife, otherwise she's up to some devilment, like what she did to Mrs. Harry Steller Smith. I swore not ever to tell anyone that, but when a vicious attempt has been made on a person's life, I say the hell with promises.

Mrs. Harry Steller Smith was Eunice's canary named after a woman from Pensacola who makes home-made cure-all that Eunice takes for the gout. One day I heard this terrible racket in the parlor and upon investigating, what did I find but Olivia-Ann shooing Mrs. Harry Steller Smith out an open window with a broom and the door to the birdcage wide. If I hadn't walked in at exactly that moment, she might never have been caught. She got scared that I would tell Eunice and blurted out the whole thing, said it wasn't fair to keep one of God's creatures locked up that way, besides which she couldn't stand Mrs. Harry Steller Smith's singing. Well, I felt kind of sorry for her and she gave me two dollars, so I helped her cook up a story for Eunice. Of course I wouldn't have taken the money except I thought it would ease her conscience.

The very *first* words Eunice said when I stepped inside this house were, "So this is what you ran off behind our back and married, Marge?"

Marge says, "Isn't he the best-looking thing, Aunt Eunice?"

Eunice eyes me u-p and d-o-w-n and says, "Tell him to turn around."

While my back is turned, Eunice says, "You sure must've picked the runt of the litter. Why, this isn't any sort of man at all."

I've never been so taken back in my life! True, I'm slightly stocky, but then, I haven't got my full growth yet.

"He is too," says Marge.

Olivia-Ann, who's been standing there with her mouth so wide the flies could buzz in and out, says, "You heard what Sister said. He's not any sort of a man whatsoever. The very idea of this little runt running around claiming to be a man! Why, he isn't even of the male sex!"

Marge says, "You seem to forget, Aunt Olivia-Ann, that this is my husband, the father of my unborn child."

Eunice made a nasty sound like only she can and said, "Well, all I can say is I most certainly wouldn't be bragging about it."

Isn't that a nice welcome? And after I gave up my perfectly swell position clerking at the Cash 'n' Carry.

But it's not a drop in the bucket to what came later that same evening. After Bluebell cleared away the supper dishes, Marge asked, just as nice as she could, if we could borrow the car and drive over to the picture show at Phoenix City.

"You must be clear out of your head," says Eunice, and, honest, you'd think we'd asked for the kimono off her back.

"You must be clear out of your head," says Olivia-Ann.

"It's six o'clock," says Eunice, "and if you think I'd let that runt drive my just-as-good-as-brand-new 1934 Chevrolet as far as the privy and back, you must've gone clear out of your head."

Naturally such language makes Marge cry.

"Never you mind, honey," I said, "I've driven pulenty of Cadillacs in my time."

"Humf," says Eunice.

"Yeah," says I.

Eunice says, "If he's ever so much as driven a plow, I'll eat a dozen gophers fried in turpentine."

"I won't have you refer to my husband in any such manner," says Marge. "You're acting simply outlandish! Why, you'd think I'd picked up some absolutely strange man in some absolutely strange place."

"If the shoe fits, wear it!" says Eunice.

"Don't think you can pull the sheep over our eyes," says Olivia-Ann in that braying voice of hers so much like the mating call of a jackass you can't rightly tell the difference.

"We weren't born just around the corner, you know," says Eunice.

Marge says, "I'll give you to understand that I'm legally wed till death do us part to this man by a certified justice of the peace as of three and one-half months ago. Ask anybody. Furthermore, Aunt Eunice, he is free, white and sixteen. Furthermore, George Far Sylvester does not appreciate hearing his father referred to in any such manner."

George Far Sylvester is the name we've planned for the baby. Has a strong sound, don't you think? Only the way things stand I have positively no feelings in the matter now whatsoever.

"How can a girl have a baby with a girl?" says Olivia-Ann, which was a calculated attack on my manhood. "I do declare there's something new every day."

"Oh, shush up," says Eunice. "Let us hear no more about the picture show in Phoenix City."

Marge sobs, "Oh-h-h, but it's Judy Garland."

"Never mind, honey," I said, "I most likely saw the show in Mobile ten years ago."

"That's a deliberate falsehood," shouts Olivia-Ann. "Oh, you are a scoundrel, you are. Judy hasn't been in the pictures ten years." Olivia-Ann's never seen not even one picture show in her entire fifty-two years (she won't tell anybody how old she is but I dropped a card to the capitol in Montgomery and they were very nice about answering), but she subscribes to eight movie books. According to Postmistress Delancey, it's the only mail she ever gets outside of the Sears & Roebuck. She has this positively morbid crush on Gary Cooper and has one trunk and two suitcases full of his photos.

So we got up from the table and Eunice lumbers over to the window and looks out to the chinaberry tree and says, "Birds settling in their roost —time we went to bed. You have your old room, Marge, and I've fixed a cot for this gentleman on the back porch."

It took a solid minute for that to sink in.

I said, "And what, if I'm not too bold to ask, is the objection to my sleeping with my lawful wife?"

Then they both started yelling at me.

So Marge threw a conniption fit right then and there. "Stop it, stop it, stop it! I can't stand any more. Go on, babydoll—go on and sleep wherever they say. Tomorrow we'll see. . . ."

Eunice says, "I swanee if the child hasn't got a grain of sense, after all."

"Poor dear," says Olivia-Ann, wrapping her arm around Marge's waist and herding her off, "poor dear, so young, so innocent. Let's us just go and have a good cry on Olivia-Ann's shoulder."

May, June and July and the best part of August I've squatted and sweltered on that damn back porch without an ounce of screening. And Marge—she hasn't opened her mouth in protest, not once! This part of Alabama is swampy, with mosquitoes that could murder a buffalo, given half a chance, not to mention dangerous flying roaches and a posse of local rats big enough to haul a wagon train from here to Timbuctoo. Oh, if it wasn't for that little unborn George, I would've been making dust tracks on the road, way before now. I mean to say I haven't had five seconds alone with Marge since that first night. One or the other is always chaperoning and last week they like to have blown their tops when Marge locked herself in her room and they couldn't find me nowhere. The truth is I'd been down watching the niggers bale cotton but just for spite I let on to Eunice like Marge and I'd been up to no good. After that they added Bluebell to the shift.

And all this time I haven't even had cigarette change.

Eunice has hounded me day in and day out about getting a job. "Why don't the little heathen go out and get some honest work?" says she. As you've probably noticed, she never speaks to me directly, though more often than not I am the only one in her royal presence. "If he was any sort of man you could call a man, he'd be trying to put a crust of bread in that girl's mouth instead of stuffing his own off my vittles." I think you should know that I've been living almost exclusively on cold yams and leftover grits for three months and thirteen days and I've been down to consult Dr. A. N. Carter twice. He's not exactly sure whether I have the scurvy or not.

And as for my not working, I'd like to know what a man of my abilities, a man who held a perfectly swell position with the Cash 'n' Carry, would find to do in a fleabag like Admiral's Mill? There is all of one store here and Mr. Tubberville, the proprietor, is actually so lazy its painful for him to have to sell anything. Then we have the Morning Star Baptist Church but they already have a preacher, an awful old turd named Shell whom Eunice drug over one day to see about the salvation of my soul. I heard him with my own ears tell her I was too far gone.

But it's what Eunice has done to Marge that really takes the cake. She has turned that girl against me in the most villainous fashion that words could not describe. Why, she even reached the point when she was sassing me back, but I provided her with a couple of good slaps and put a stop to that. No wife of mine is ever going to be disrespectful to me, not on your life!

The enemy lines are stretched tight: Bluebell, Olivia-Ann, Eunice,

Marge and the whole rest of Admiral's Mill (pop. 342). Allies: none. Such was the situation as of Sunday, August 12, when the attempt was made upon my very life.

Yesterday was quiet and hot enough to melt rock. The trouble began at exactly two o'clock. I know because Eunice has one of those fool cuckoo contraptions and it scares the daylights out of me. I was minding my own personal business in the parlor, composing a song on the upright piano, which Eunice bought for Olivia-Ann and hired her a teacher to come all the way from Columbus, Georgia, once a week. Postmistress Delancey, who was my friend till she decided that it was maybe not so wise, says that the fancy teacher tore out of this house one afternoon like old Adolf Hitler was on his tail and leaped in his Ford coupé, never to be heard from again. Like I say, I'm trying to keep cool in the parlor not bothering a living soul when Olivia-Ann trots in with her hair all twisted up in curlers and shrieks, "Cease that infernal racket this very instant! Can't you give a body a minute's rest? And get off my piano right smart. It's not your piano, it's my piano, and if you don't get off it right smart, I'll have you in court like a shot the first Monday in September."

She's not anything in this world but jealous on account of I'm a natural-born musician and the songs I make up out of my own head are absolutely marvelous.

"And just look what you've done to my genuine ivory keys, Mr. Sylvester," says she, trotting over to the piano, "torn nearly every one of them off right at the roots for purentee meanness, that's what you've done."

She knows good and well that the piano was ready for the junk heap the moment I entered this house.

I said, "Seeing as you're such a know-it-all, Miss Olivia-Ann, maybe it would interest you to know that I'm in the possession of a few interesting tales myself. A few things that maybe other people would be very grateful to know. Like what happened to Mrs. Harry Steller Smith, as for instance."

Remember Mrs. Harry Steller Smith?

She paused and looked at the empty birdcage. "You gave me your oath," says she and turned the most terrifying shade of purple.

"Maybe I did and again maybe I didn't," says I. "You did an evil thing when you betrayed Eunice that way but if some people will leave other people alone, then maybe I can overlook it."

Well, sir, she walked out of there just as *nice* and *quiet* as you please. So I went and stretched out on the sofa, which is the most horrible piece of furniture I've ever seen and is part of a matched set Eunice bought in Atlanta in 1912 and paid two thousand dollars for, cash—or so she claims. This set is black and olive plush and smells like wet chicken feathers on a damp day. There is a big table in one corner of the parlor which supports two pictures of Miss E and O-A's mama and papa. Papa is kind of handsome but just between you and me I'm convinced he has black blood in him from somewhere. He was a captain in the Civil War and that is one thing I'll never forget on account of his sword, which is displayed over the mantel and figures prominently in the action yet to come. Mama has that hang-dog, half-wit look like Olivia-Ann, though I must say Mama carries it better.

So I had just dozed off when I heard Eunice bellowing, "Where is he? Where is he?" And the next thing I know she's framed in the doorway with her hands planted plumb on those hippo hips and the whole pack scrunched up behind her: Bluebell, Olivia-Ann and Marge.

Several seconds passed with Eunice tapping her big old bare foot just as fast and furious as she could and fanning her fat face with this cardboard picture of Niagara Falls.

"Where is it?" says she. "Where's my hundred dollars that he made away with while my trusting back was turned?"

"*This* is the straw that broke the camel's back," says I, but I was too hot and tired to get up.

"That's not the only back that's going to be broke," says she, her bug eyes about to pop clear out of their sockets. "That was my funeral money and I want it back. Wouldn't you know he'd steal from the dead?"

"Maybe he didn't take it," says Marge.

"You keep your mouth out of this, missy," says Olivia-Ann.

"He stole my money sure as shooting," says Eunice. "Why, look at his eyes—black with guilt!"

I yawned and said, "Like they say in the courts—if the party of the first part falsely accuses the party of the second part, then the party of the first part can be locked away in jail even if the State Home is where they rightfully belong for the protection of all concerned."

"God will punish him," says Eunice.

"Oh, Sister," says Olivia-Ann, "let us not wait for God."

Whereupon Eunice advances on me with this most peculiar look, her dirty flannel nightie jerking along the floor. And Olivia-Ann leeches after her and Bluebell lets forth this moan that must have been heard clear to Eufala and back while Marge stands there wringing her hands and whimpering.

"Oh-h-h," sobs Marge, "please give her back that money, babydoll."

I said, "Et tu Brute?" which is from William Shakespeare.

"Look at the likes of him," says Eunice, "lying around all day not doing so much as licking a postage stamp."

"Pitiful," clucks Olivia-Ann.

"You'd think he was having a baby instead of that poor child." Eunice speaking.

Bluebell tosses in her two cents, "Ain't it the truth?"

"Well, if it isn't the old pots calling the kettle black," says I.

"After loafing here for three months, does this runt have the audacity to cast aspersions in my direction?" says Eunice.

I merely flicked a bit of ash from my sleeve and not the least bit fazed said, "Dr. A. N. Carter has informed me that I am in a dangerous scurvy condition and can't stand the least excitement whatsoever—otherwise I'm liable to foam at the mouth and bite somebody."

Then Bluebell says, "Why don't he go back to that trash in Mobile, Miss Eunice? I'se sick and tired of carryin' his ol' slop jar."

Naturally that coal-black nigger made me so mad I couldn't see straight.

So just as calm as a cucumber I arose and picked up this umbrella off the hat tree and rapped her across the head with it until it cracked smack in two.

"My real Japanese silk parasol!" shrieks Olivia-Ann.

Marge cries, "You've killed Bluebell, you've killed poor old Bluebell!"

Eunice shoves Olivia-Ann and says, "He's gone clear out of his head, Sister! Run! Run and get Mr. Tubberville!"

"I don't like Mr. Tubberville," says Olivia-Ann staunchly. "I'll go get my hog knife." And she makes a dash for the door, but seeing as I care nothing for death, I brought her down with a sort of tackle. It wrenched my back something terrible.

"He's going to kill her!" hollers Eunice loud enough to bring the house down. "He's going to murder us all! I warned you, Marge. Quick, child, get Papa's sword!"

So Marge gets Papa's sword and hands it to Eunice. Talk about wifely devotion! And, if that's not bad enough, Olivia-Ann gives me this terrific knee punch and I had to let go. The next thing you know we hear her out in the yard bellowing hymns.

> Mine eyes have seen the glory of the
> coming of the Lord;
> He is trampling out the vintage where
> the grapes of wrath are stored. . . .

Meanwhile, Eunice is sashaying all over the place, wildly thrashing Papa's sword, and somehow I've managed to clamber atop the piano. Then Eunice climbs up on the piano stool and how that rickety contraption survived a monster like her I'll never be the one to tell.

"Come down from there, you yellow coward, before I run you through," says she and takes a whack and I've got a half-inch cut to prove it.

By this time Bluebell has recovered and skittered away to join Olivia-Ann holding services in the front yard. I guess they were expecting my body and God knows it would've been theirs if Marge hadn't passed out cold.

That's the only good thing I've got to say for Marge.

What happened after that I can't rightly remember except for Olivia-Ann reappearing with her fourteen-inch hog knife and a bunch of the neighbors. But suddenly Marge was the star attraction and I suppose they carried her to her room. Anyway, as soon as they left I barricaded the parlor door.

I've got all those black and olive plush chairs pushed against it and that big mahogany table that must weigh a couple of tons and the hat tree and lots of other stuff. I've locked the windows and pulled down the shades. Also I've found a five-pound box of Sweet Love candy and this very minute I'm munching a juicy, creamy, chocolate cherry. Sometimes they come to the door and knock and yell and plead. Oh, yes, they've started singing a song of a very different color. But as for me—I give them a tune on the piano every now and then just to let them know I'm cheerful.

A Tree
of Night

(1945)

It was winter. A string of naked
light bulbs, from which it seemed all
warmth had been drained, illuminated the little depot's cold, windy platform. Earlier in the evening it had rained, and now icicles hung along the
station-house eaves like some crystal monster's vicious teeth. Except for a
girl, young and rather tall, the platform was deserted. The girl wore a gray
flannel suit, a raincoat and a plaid scarf. Her hair, parted in the middle and
rolled up neatly on the sides, was rich blondish-brown; and, while her face
tended to be too thin and narrow, she was, though not extraordinarily so,
attractive. In addition to an assortment of magazines and a gray suede purse
on which elaborate brass letters spelled Kay, she carried conspicuously a
green Western guitar.

When the train, spouting steam and glaring with light, came out of the
darkness and rumbled to a halt, Kay assembled her paraphernalia and
climbed up into the last coach.

The coach was a relic with a decaying interior of ancient red-plush seats,
bald in spots, and peeling iodine-colored woodwork. An old-time copper
lamp, attached to the ceiling, looked romantic and out of place. Gloomy
dead smoke sailed the air; and the car's heated closeness accentuated the
stale odor of discarded sandwiches, apple cores and orange hulls: this
garbage, including Lily cups, soda-pop bottles and mangled newspapers,
littered the long aisle. From a water cooler, embedded in the wall, a steady

stream trickled to the floor. The passengers, who glanced up wearily when Kay entered, were not, it seemed, at all conscious of any discomfort.

Kay resisted a temptation to hold her nose and threaded her way carefully down the aisle, tripping once, without disaster, over a dozing fat man's protruding leg. Two nondescript men turned an interested eye as she passed; and a kid stood up in his seat, squalling, "Hey, Mama, look at de banjo! Hey, lady, lemme play ya banjo!" till a slap from Mama quelled him.

There was only one empty place. She found it at the end of the car in an isolated alcove occupied already by a man and woman who were sitting with their feet settled lazily on the vacant seat opposite. Kay hesitated a second, then said, "Would you mind if I sat here?"

The woman's head snapped up as if she had not been asked a simple question, but stabbed with a needle, too. Nevertheless, she managed a smile. "Can't say as I see what's to stop you, honey," she said, taking her feet down and also, with a curious impersonality, removing the feet of the man who was staring out the window, paying no attention whatsoever.

Thanking the woman, Kay took off her coat, sat down, and arranged herself with purse and guitar at her side, magazines in her lap: comfortable enough, though she wished she had a pillow for her back.

The train lurched; a ghost of steam hissed against the window; slowly the dingy lights of the lonesome depot faded past.

"Boy, what a jerkwater dump," said the woman. "No town, no nothin'."

Kay said, "The town's a few miles away."

"That so? Live there?"

No. Kay explained she had been at the funeral of an uncle. An uncle who, though she did not of course mention it, had left her nothing in his will but the green guitar. Where was she going? Oh, back to college.

After mulling this over, the woman concluded, "What'll you ever learn in a place like that? Let me tell you, honey, I'm plenty educated and I never saw the inside of no college."

"You didn't?" murmured Kay politely and dismissed the matter by opening one of her magazines. The light was dim for reading and none of the stories looked in the least compelling. However, not wanting to become involved in a conversational marathon, she continued gazing at it stupidly till she felt a furtive tap on her knee.

"Don't read," said the woman. "I need somebody to talk to. Naturally, it's no fun talking to *him.*" She jerked a thumb toward the silent man. "He's afflicted: deaf and dumb, know what I mean?"

Kay closed the magazine and looked at her more or less for the first time. She was short; her feet barely scraped the floor. And like many undersized people she had a freak of structure, in her case an enormous, really huge head. Rouge so brightened her sagging, fleshy-featured face it was difficult even to guess at her age: perhaps fifty, fifty-five. Her big sheep eyes squinted, as if distrustful of what they saw. Her hair was an obviously dyed red, and twisted into parched, fat corkscrew curls. A once-elegant lavender hat of impressive size flopped crazily on the side of her head, and she was kept busy brushing back a drooping cluster of celluloid cherries sewed to the brim. She wore a plain, somewhat shabby blue dress. Her breath had a vividly sweetish gin smell.

"You do wanna talk to me, don't you, honey?"

"Sure," said Kay, moderately amused.

"Course you do. You bet you do. That's what I like about a train. Bus people are a close-mouthed buncha dopes. But a train's the place for putting your cards on the table, that's what I always say." Her voice was cheerful and booming, husky as a man's. "But on accounta *him,* I always try to get us this here seat; it's more private, like a swell compartment, see?"

"It's very pleasant," Kay agreed. "Thanks for letting me join you."

"Only too glad to. We don't have much company; it makes some folks nervous to be around him."

As if to deny it, the man made a queer, furry sound deep in his throat and plucked the woman's sleeve. "Leave me alone, dear-heart," she said, as if she were talking to an inattentive child. "I'm okay. We're just having us a nice little ol' talk. Now behave yourself or this pretty girl will go away. She's very rich; she goes to college." And winking, she added, "He thinks I'm drunk."

The man slumped in the seat, swung his head sideways and studied Kay intently from the corners of his eyes. These eyes, like a pair of clouded milky-blue marbles, were thickly lashed and oddly beautiful. Now, except for a certain remoteness, his wide, hairless face had no real expression. It was as if he were incapable of experiencing or reflecting the slightest emotion. His gray hair was clipped close and combed forward into uneven bangs. He looked like a child aged abruptly by some uncanny method. He wore a frayed blue serge suit, and he had anointed himself with a cheap, vile perfume. Around his wrist was strapped a Mickey Mouse watch.

"He thinks I'm drunk," the woman repeated. "And the real funny part is, I am. Oh, shoot—you gotta do something, ain't that right?" She bent closer. "Say, ain't it?"

Kay was still gawking at the man; the way he was looking at her made her squeamish, but she could not take her eyes off him. "I guess so," she said.

"Then let's us have us a drink," suggested the woman. She plunged her hand into an oilcloth satchel and pulled out a partially filled gin bottle. She began to unscrew the cap, but seeming to think better of this, handed the bottle to Kay. "Gee, I forgot about you being company," she said. "I'll go get us some nice paper cups."

So, before Kay could protest that she did not want a drink, the woman had risen and started none too steadily down the aisle toward the water cooler.

Kay yawned and rested her forehead against the windowpane, her fingers idly strumming the guitar: the strings sang a hollow, lulling tune, as monotonously soothing as the Southern landscape, smudged in darkness, flowing past the window. An icy winter moon rolled above the train across the night sky like a thin white wheel.

And then, without warning, a strange thing happened: the man reached out and gently stroked Kay's cheek. Despite the breathtaking delicacy of this movement, it was such a bold gesture Kay was at first too startled to know what to make of it: her thoughts shot in three or four fantastic directions. He leaned forward till his queer eyes were very near her own; the reek of his perfume was sickening. The guitar was silent while they exchanged a searching gaze. Suddenly, from some spring of compassion, she felt for him a keen sense of pity; but also, and this she could not suppress, an overpowering disgust, an absolute loathing: something about him, an elusive quality she could not quite put a finger on, reminded her of—of what?

After a little, he lowered his hand solemnly and sank back in the seat, an asinine grin transfiguring his face, as if he had performed a clever stunt for which he wished applause.

"Giddyup! Giddyup! my little bucker-ROOS . . ." shouted the woman. And she sat down, loudly proclaiming to be, "Dizzy as a witch! Dog tired! Whew!" From a handful of Lily cups she separated two and casually thrust the rest down her blouse. "Keep 'em safe and dry, ha ha ha. . . ." A coughing spasm seized her, but when it was over, she appeared calmer. "Has my boy friend been entertaining?" she asked, patting her bosom reverently. "Ah, he's so sweet." She looked as if she might pass out. Kay rather wished she would.

"I don't want a drink," Kay said, returning the bottle. "I never drink: I hate the taste."

"Mustn't be a killjoy," said the woman firmly. "Here now, hold your cup like a good girl."

"No, please . . ."

"Formercysake, hold it still. Imagine, nerves at your age! Me, I can shake like a leaf. I've got reasons. Oh, Lordy, have I got 'em."

"But . . ."

A dangerous smile tipped the woman's face hideously awry. "What's the matter? Don't you think I'm good enough to drink with?"

"Please, don't misunderstand," said Kay, a tremor in her voice. "It's just that I don't like being forced to do something I don't want to. So look, couldn't I give this to the gentleman?"

"Him? No sirree: he needs what little sense he's got. Come on, honey, down the hatch."

Kay, seeing it was useless, decided to succumb and avoid a possible scene. She sipped and shuddered. It was terrible gin. It burned her throat till her eyes watered. Quickly, when the woman was not watching, she emptied the cup into the sound hole of the guitar. It happened, however, that the man saw; and Kay, realizing it, recklessly signaled to him with her eyes a plea not to give her away. But she could not tell from his clear-blank expression how much he understood.

"Where you from, kid?" resumed the woman presently.

For a bewildered moment, Kay was unable to provide an answer. The names of several cities came to her all at once. Finally, from this confusion, she extracted: "New Orleans. My home is in New Orleans."

The woman beamed. "N.O.'s where I wanna go when I kick off. One time, oh, say 1923, I ran me a sweet little fortune-telling parlor there. Let's see, that was on St. Peter Street." Pausing, she stooped and set the empty gin bottle on the floor. It rolled into the aisle and rocked back and forth with a drowsy sound. "I was raised in Texas—on a big ranch—my papa was rich. Us kids always had the best; even Paris, France, clothes. I'll bet you've got a big swell house, too. Do you have a garden? Do you grow flowers?"

"Just lilacs."

A conductor entered the coach, preceded by a cold gust of wind that rattled the trash in the aisle and briefly livened the dull air. He lumbered along, stopping now and then to punch a ticket or talk with a passenger. It was after midnight. Someone was expertly playing a harmonica. Someone else was arguing the merits of a certain politician. A child cried out in his sleep.

"Maybe you wouldn't be so snotty if you knew who we was," said the woman, bobbing her tremendous head. "We ain't nobodies, not by a long shot."

Embarrassed, Kay nervously opened a pack of cigarettes and lighted one. She wondered if there might not be a seat in a car up ahead. She could not bear the woman, or, for that matter, the man, another minute. But she had never before been in a remotely comparable situation. "If you'll excuse me now," she said, "I have to be leaving. It's been very pleasant, but I promised to meet a friend on the train. . . ."

With almost invisible swiftness the woman grasped the girl's wrist. "Didn't your mama ever tell you it was sinful to lie?" she stage-whispered. The lavender hat tumbled off her head but she made no effort to retrieve it. Her tongue flicked out and wetted her lips. And, as Kay stood up, she increased the pressure of her grip. "Sit down, dear . . . there ain't any friend . . . Why, we're your only friends and we wouldn't have you leave us for the world."

"Honestly, I wouldn't lie."

"Sit down, dear."

Kay dropped her cigarette and the man picked it up. He slouched in the corner and became absorbed in blowing a chain of lush smoke rings that mounted upward like hollow eyes and expanded into nothing.

"Why, you wouldn't want to hurt his feelings by leaving us, now, would you, dear?" crooned the woman softly. "Sit down—down—now, that's a good girl. My, what a pretty guitar. What a pretty, pretty guitar . . ." Her voice faded before the sudden whooshing, static noise of a second train. And for an instant the lights in the coach went off; in the darkness the passing train's golden windows winked black-yellow-black-yellow-black-yellow. The man's cigarette pulsed like the glow of a firefly, and his smoke rings continued rising tranquilly. Outside, a bell pealed wildly.

When the lights came on again, Kay was massaging her wrist where the woman's strong fingers had left a painful bracelet mark. She was more puzzled than angry. She determined to ask the conductor if he would find her a different seat. But when he arrived to take her ticket, the request stuttered on her lips incoherently.

"Yes, miss?"

"Nothing," she said.

And he was gone.

The trio in the alcove regarded one another in mysterious silence till the woman said, "I've got something here I wanna show you, honey." She rummaged once more in the oilcloth satchel. "You won't be so snotty after you get a gander at this."

What she passed to Kay was a handbill, printed on such yellowed, antique paper it looked as if it must be centuries old. In fragile, overly fancy lettering, it read:

LAZARUS

The Man Who Is Buried Alive

A Miracle

SEE FOR YOURSELF

Adults 25¢—Children 10¢

"I always sing a hymn and read a sermon," said the woman. "It's awful sad: some folks cry, especially the old ones. And I've got me a perfectly elegant costume: a black veil and a black dress, oh, very becoming. *He* wears a gorgeous made-to-order bridegroom suit and a turban and lotsa talcum on his face. See, we try to make it as much like a bona fide funeral as we can. But shoot, nowadays you're likely to get just a buncha smart

27

alecks come for laughs—so sometimes I'm real glad he's afflicted like he is on accounta otherwise his feelings would be hurt, maybe."

Kay said, "You mean you're with a circus or a sideshow or something like that?"

"Nope, us alone," said the woman as she reclaimed the fallen hat. "We've been doing it for years and years—played every tank town in the South: Singasong, Mississippi—Spunky, Louisiana—Eureka, Alabama . . ." these and other names rolled off her tongue musically, running together like rain. "After the hymn, after the sermon, we bury him."

"In a coffin?"

"Sort of. It's gorgeous, it's got silver stars painted all over the lid."

"I should think he would suffocate," said Kay, amazed. "How long does he stay buried?"

"All told it takes maybe an hour—course that's not counting the lure."

"The lure?"

"Uh huh. It's what we do the night before a show. See, we hunt up a store, any ol' store with a big glass window'll do, and get the owner to let *him* sit inside this window, and, well, hypnotize himself. Stays there all night stiff as a poker and people come and look: scares the livin' hell out of 'em. . . ." While she talked she jiggled a finger in her ear, withdrawing it occasionally to examine her find. "And one time this ol' bindlestiff Mississippi sheriff tried to . . ."

The tale that followed was baffling and pointless: Kay did not bother to listen. Nevertheless, what she had heard already inspired a reverie, a vague recapitulation of her uncle's funeral; an event which, to tell the truth, had not much affected her, since she had scarcely known him. And so, while gazing abstractedly at the man, an image of her uncle's face, white next the pale silk casket pillow, appeared in her mind's eye. Observing their faces simultaneously, both the man's and uncle's, as it were, she thought she recognized an odd parallel: there was about the man's face the same kind of shocking, embalmed, secret stillness, as though, in a sense, he were truly an exhibit in a glass cage, complacent to be seen, uninterested in seeing.

"I'm sorry, what did you say?"

"I said: I sure wish they'd lend us the use of a regular cemetery. Like it is now we have to put on the show wherever we can . . . mostly in empty lots that are nine times outa ten smack up against some smelly fillin' station, which ain't exactly a big help. But like I say, we got us a swell act, the best. You oughta come see it if you get a chance."

"Oh, I should love to," Kay said, absently.

"Oh, I should love to," mimicked the woman. "Well, who asked you? Anybody ask you?" She hoisted up her skirt and enthusiastically blew her nose on the ragged hem of a petticoat. "Bu-leeve me, it's a hard way to turn a dollar. Know what our take was last month? Fifty-three bucks! Honey, you try living on that sometime." She sniffed and rearranged her skirt with considerable primness. "Well, one of these days my sweet boy's sure enough going to die down there; and even then somebody'll say it was a gyp."

At this point the man took from his pocket what seemed to be a finely shellacked peach seed and balanced it on the palm of his hand. He looked across at Kay and, certain of her attention, opened his eyelids wide and began to squeeze and caress the seed in an undefinably obscene manner.

Kay frowned. "What does he want?"

"He wants you to buy it."

"But what is it?"

"A charm," said the woman. "A love charm."

Whoever was playing the harmonica stopped. Other sounds, less unique, became at once prominent: someone snoring, the gin bottle seesaw rolling, voices in sleepy argument, the train wheels' distant hum.

"Where could you get love cheaper, honey?"

"It's nice. I mean it's cute. . . ." Kay said, stalling for time. The man rubbed and polished the seed on his trouser leg. His head was lowered at a supplicating, mournful angle, and presently he stuck the seed between his teeth and bit it, as if it were a suspicious piece of silver. "Charms always bring me bad luck. And besides . . . please, can't you make him stop acting that way?"

"Don't look so scared," said the woman, more flat-voiced than ever. "He ain't gonna hurt you."

"Make him stop, damn it!"

"What can I do?" asked the woman, shrugging her shoulders. "You're the one that's got money. You're rich. All he wants is a dollar, one dollar."

Kay tucked her purse under her arm. "I have just enough to get back to school," she lied, quickly rising and stepping out into the aisle. She stood there a moment, expecting trouble. But nothing happened.

The woman, with rather deliberate indifference, heaved a sigh and closed her eyes; gradually the man subsided and stuck the charm back in his pocket. Then his hand crawled across the seat to join the woman's in a lax embrace.

Kay shut the door and moved to the front of the observation platform. It was bitterly cold in the open air, and she had left her raincoat in the alcove. She loosened her scarf and draped it over her head.

Although she had never made this trip before, the train was traveling through an area strangely familiar: tall trees, misty, painted pale by malicious moonshine, towered steep on either side without a break or clearing. Above, the sky was a stark, unexplorable blue thronged with stars that faded here and there. She could see streamers of smoke trailing from the train's engine like long clouds of ectoplasm. In one corner of the platform a red kerosene lantern cast a colorful shadow.

She found a cigarette and tried to light it: the wind snuffed match after match till only one was left. She walked to the corner where the lantern burned and cupped her hands to protect the last match: the flame caught, sputtered, died. Angrily she tossed away the cigarette and empty folder; all the tension in her tightened to an exasperating pitch and she slammed the wall with her fist and began to whimper softly, like an irritable child.

The intense cold made her head ache, and she longed to go back inside the warm coach and fall asleep. But she couldn't, at least not yet; and there was no sense in wondering why, for she knew the answer very well. Aloud, partly to keep her teeth from chattering and partly because she needed the reassurance of her own voice, she said: "We're in Alabama now, I think, and tomorrow we'll be in Atlanta and I'm nineteen and I'll be twenty in August and I'm a sophomore. . . ." She glanced around at the darkness, hoping to see a sign of dawn, and finding the same endless wall of trees, the same frosty moon. "I hate him, he's horrible and I hate him. . . ." She stopped, ashamed of her foolishness and too tired to evade the truth: she was afraid.

Suddenly she felt an eerie compulsion to kneel down and touch the lantern. Its graceful glass funnel was warm, and the red glow seeped through her hands, making them luminous. The heat thawed her fingers and tingled along her arms.

She was so preoccupied she did not hear the door open. The train wheels roaring clickety-clack-clackety-click hushed the sound of the man's footsteps.

It was a subtle zero sensation that warned her finally; but some seconds passed before she dared look behind.

He was standing there with a mute detachment, his head tilted, his arms dangling at his sides. Staring up into his harmless, vapid face, flushed brilliant by the lantern light, Kay knew of what she was afraid: it was a memory, a childish memory of terrors that once, long ago, had hovered above her like haunted limbs on a tree of night. Aunts, cooks, strangers— each eager to spin a tale or teach a rhyme of spooks and death, omens, spirits, demons. And always there had been the unfailing threat of the wizard man: stay close to the house, child, else a wizard man'll snatch and eat you alive! He lived everywhere, the wizard man, and everywhere was danger. At night, in bed, hear him tapping at the window? Listen!

Holding on to the railing, she inched upward till she was standing erect. The man nodded and waved his hand toward the door. Kay took a deep breath and stepped forward. Together they went inside.

The air in the coach was numb with sleep: a solitary light now illuminated the car, creating a kind of artificial dusk. There was no motion but the train's sluggish sway, and the stealthy rattle of discarded newspapers.

The woman alone was wide awake. You could see she was greatly excited: she fidgeted with her curls and celluloid cherries, and her plump little legs, crossed at the ankles, swung agitatedly back and forth. She paid no attention when Kay sat down. The man settled in the seat with one leg tucked beneath him and his arms folded across his chest.

In an effort to be casual, Kay picked up a magazine. She realized the man was watching her, not removing his gaze an instant: she knew this though she was afraid to confirm it, and she wanted to cry out and waken everyone in the coach. But suppose they did not hear? What if they were not really *asleep?* Tears started in her eyes, magnifying and distorting the print on a page till it became a hazy blur. She shut the magazine with fierce abruptness and looked at the woman.

"I'll buy it," she said. "The charm, I mean. I'll buy it, if that's all—just all you want."

The woman made no response. She smiled apathetically as she turned toward the man.

As Kay watched, the man's face seemed to change form and recede before her like a moon-shaped rock sliding downward under a surface of water. A warm laziness relaxed her. She was dimly conscious of it when the woman took away her purse, and when she gently pulled the raincoat like a shroud above her head.

Jug of
Silver

(1945)

A FTER SCHOOL I USED TO WORK IN
the Valhalla drugstore. It was owned
by my uncle, Mr. Ed Marshall. I call him Mr. Marshall because everybody,
including his wife, called him Mr. Marshall. Nevertheless he was a nice
man.

This drugstore was maybe old-fashioned, but it was large and dark and
cool: during summer months there was no pleasanter place in town. At the
left, as you entered, was a tobacco-magazine counter behind which, as a
rule, sat Mr. Marshall: a squat, square-faced, pink-fleshed man with looping, manly, white mustaches. Beyond this counter stood the beautiful soda
fountain. It was very antique and made of fine, yellowed marble, smooth
to the touch but without a trace of cheap glaze. Mr. Marshall bought it at
an auction in New Orleans in 1910 and was plainly proud of it. When you
sat on the high, delicate stools and looked across the fountain you could
see yourself reflected softly, as though by candlelight, in a row of ancient
mahogany-framed mirrors. All general merchandise was displayed in glass-
doored, curio-like cabinets that were locked with brass keys. There was
always in the air the smell of syrup and nutmeg and other delicacies.

The Valhalla was the gathering place of Wachata County till a certain
Rufus McPherson came to town and opened a second drugstore directly
across the courthouse square. This old Rufus McPherson was a villain; that
is, he took away my uncle's trade. He installed fancy equipment such as

electric fans and colored lights; he provided curb service and made grilled-cheese sandwiches to order. Naturally, though some remained devoted to Mr. Marshall, most folks couldn't resist Rufus McPherson.

For a while, Mr. Marshall chose to ignore him: if you were to mention McPherson's name, he would sort of snort, finger his mustaches and look the other way. But you could tell he was mad. And getting madder. Then one day toward the middle of October I strolled into the Valhalla to find him sitting at the fountain playing dominoes and drinking wine with Hamurabi.

Hamurabi was an Egyptian and some kind of dentist, though he didn't do much business, as the people hereabouts have unusually strong teeth, due to an element in the water. He spent a great deal of his time loafing around the Valhalla and was my uncle's chief buddy. He was a handsome figure of a man, this Hamurabi, being dark-skinned and nearly seven feet tall; the matrons of the town kept their daughters under lock and key and gave him the eye themselves. He had no foreign accent whatsoever, and it was always my opinion that he wasn't any more Egyptian than the man in the moon.

Anyway, there they were swigging red Italian wine from a gallon jug. It was a troubling sight, for Mr. Marshall was a renowned teetotaler. So naturally, I thought: Oh, golly, Rufus McPherson has finally got his goat. That was not the case, however.

"Here, son," said Mr. Marshall, "come have a glass of wine."

"Sure," said Hamurabi, "help us finish it up. It's store-bought, so we can't waste it."

Much later, when the jug was dry, Mr. Marshall picked it up and said, "Now we shall see!" And with that disappeared out into the afternoon.

"Where's he off to?" I asked.

"Ah," was all Hamurabi would say. He liked to devil me.

A half-hour passed before my uncle returned. He was stooped and grunting under the load he carried. He set the jug atop the fountain and stepped back, smiling and rubbing his hands together. "Well, what do you think?"

"Ah," purred Hamurabi.

"Gee . . ." I said.

It was the same wine jug, God knows, but there was a wonderful difference; for now it was crammed to the brim with nickels and dimes that shone dully through the thick glass.

"Pretty, eh?" said my uncle. "Had it done over at the First National. Couldn't get in anything bigger-sized than a nickel. Still, there's lotsa money in there, let me tell you."

"But what's the point, Mr. Marshall?" I said. "I mean, what's the idea?"

Mr. Marshall's smile deepened to a grin. "This here's a jug of silver, you might say . . ."

"The pot at the end of the rainbow," interrupted Hamurabi.

". . . and the idea, as you call it, is for folks to guess how much money is in there. For instance, say you buy a quarter's worth of stuff—well, then you get to take a chance. The more you buy, the more chances you get. And I'll keep all guesses in a ledger till Christmas Eve, at which time whoever comes closest to the right amount will get the whole shebang."

Hamurabi nodded solemnly. "He's playing Santa Claus—a mighty crafty Santa Claus," he said. "I'm going home and write a book: *The Skillful Murder of Rufus McPherson.*" To tell the truth, he sometimes did write stories and send them out to the magazines. They always came back.

It was surprising, really like a miracle, how Wachata County took to the jug. Why, the Valhalla hadn't done so much business since Station Master Tully, poor soul, went stark raving mad and claimed to have discovered oil back of the depot, causing the town to be overrun with wildcat prospectors. Even the poolhall bums who never spent a cent on anything not connected with whiskey or women took to investing their spare cash in milk shakes. A few elderly ladies publicly disapproved of Mr. Marshall's enterprise as a kind of gambling, but they didn't start any trouble and some even found occasion to visit us and hazard a guess. The schoolkids were crazy about the whole thing, and I was very popular because they figured I knew the answer.

"I'll tell you why all this is," said Hamurabi, lighting one of the Egyptian cigarettes he bought by mail from a concern in New York City. "It's not for the reason you may imagine; not, in other words, avidity. No. It's the mystery that's enchanting. Now you look at those nickels and dimes and what do you think: ah, so much! No, no. You think: ah, *how* much? And that's a profound question, indeed. It can mean different things to different people. Understand?"

And oh, was Rufus McPherson wild! When you're in trade, you count on Christmas to make up a large share of your yearly profit, and he was hard pressed to find a customer. So he tried to imitate the jug; but being such a stingy man he filled his with pennies. He also wrote a letter to the editor of the *Banner,* our weekly paper, in which he said that Mr. Marshall ought to be "tarred and feathered and strung up for turning innocent little children into confirmed gamblers and sending them down the path to Hell!" You can imagine what kind of laughingstock he was. Nobody had anything for McPherson but scorn. And so by the middle of November he just stood on the sidewalk outside his store and gazed bitterly at the festivities across the square.

. . . .

At about this time Appleseed and sister made their first appearance.

He was a stranger in town. At least no one could recall ever having seen him before. He said he lived on a farm a mile past Indian Branches; told us his mother weighed only seventy-four pounds and that he had an older brother who would play the fiddle at anybody's wedding for fifty cents. He claimed that Appleseed was the only name he had and that he was twelve years old. But his sister, Middy, said he was eight. His hair was straight and dark yellow. He had a tight, weather-tanned little face with anxious green eyes that had a very wise and knowing look. He was small and puny and high-strung; and he wore always the same outfit: a red sweater, blue denim britches and a pair of man-sized boots that went clop-clop with every step.

It was raining that first time he came into the Valhalla; his hair was plastered round his head like a cap and his boots were caked with red mud from the country roads. Middy trailed behind as he swaggered like a cowboy up to the fountain, where I was wiping some glasses.

"I hear you folks got a bottle fulla money you fixin' to give 'way," he said, looking me square in the eye. "Seein' as you-all are givin' it away, we'd be obliged iffen you'd give it to us. Name's Appleseed, and this here's my sister, Middy."

Middy was a sad, sad-looking kid. She was a good bit taller and older-looking than her brother: a regular bean pole. She had tow-colored hair that was chopped short, and a pale pitiful little face. She wore a faded cotton dress that came way up above her bony knees. There was something wrong with her teeth, and she tried to conceal this by keeping her lips primly pursed like an old lady.

"Sorry," I said, "but you'll have to talk with Mr. Marshall."

So sure enough he did. I could hear my uncle explaining what he would have to do to win the jug. Appleseed listened attentively, nodding now and then. Presently he came back and stood in front of the jug and, touching it lightly with his hand, said, "Ain't it a pretty thing, Middy?"

Middy said, "Is they gonna give it to us?"

"Naw. What you gotta do, you gotta guess how much money's inside there. And you gotta buy two bits' worth so's even to get a chance."

"Huh, we ain't got no two bits. Where you 'spec we gonna get us two bits?"

Appleseed frowned and rubbed his chin. "That'll be the easy part, just leave it to me. The only worrisome thing is: I can't just take a chance and guess . . . I gotta *know*."

Well, a few days later they showed up again. Appleseed perched on a stool at the fountain and boldly asked for two glasses of water, one for him and one for Middy. It was on this occasion that he gave out the information about his family: ". . . then there's Papa Daddy, that's my mama's papa, who's a Cajun, an' on accounta that he don't speak English good. My brother, the one what plays the fiddle, he's been in jail three times. . . . It's on accounta him we had to pick up and leave Louisiana. He cut a fella bad in a razor fight over a woman ten years older'n him. She had yellow hair."

Middy, lingering in the background, said nervously, "You oughtn't to be tellin' our personal private fam'ly business thataway, Appleseed."

"Hush now, Middy," he said, and she hushed. "She's a good little gal," he added, turning to pat her head, "but you can't let her get away with much. You go look at the picture books, honey, and stop frettin' with your teeth. Appleseed here's got some figurin' to do."

This figuring meant staring hard at the jug, as if his eyes were trying to eat it up. With his chin cupped in his hand, he studied it for a long period, not batting his eyelids once. "A lady in Louisiana told me I could see things other folks couldn't see 'cause I was born with a caul on my head."

"It's a cinch you aren't going to see how much there is," I told him. "Why don't you just let a number pop into your head, and maybe that'll be the right one."

"Uh, uh," he said, "too darn risky. Me, I can't take no sucha chance. Now, the way I got it figured, there ain't but one sure-fire thing and that's to count every nickel and dime."

"Count!"

"Count what?" asked Hamurabi, who had just moseyed inside and was settling himself at the fountain.

"This kid says he's going to count how much is in the jug," I explained.

Hamurabi looked at Appleseed with interest. "How do you plan to do that, son?"

"Oh, by countin'," said Appleseed matter-of-factly.

Hamurabi laughed. "You better have X-ray eyes, son, that's all I can say."

"Oh, no. All you gotta do is be born with a caul on your head. A lady in Louisiana told me so. She was a witch; she loved me and when my ma wouldn't give me to her she put a hex on her and now my ma don't weigh but seventy-four pounds."

"Ve-ry in-ter-esting," was Hamurabi's comment as he gave Appleseed a queer glance.

Middy sauntered up, clutching a copy of *Screen Secrets*. She pointed out a certain photo to Appleseed and said: "Ain't she the nicest-lookin' lady? Now you see, Appleseed, you see how pretty her teeth are? Not a one outa joint."

"Well, don't you fret none," he said.

After they left, Hamurabi ordered a bottle of orange Nehi and drank it slowly, while smoking a cigarette. "Do you think maybe that kid's okay upstairs?" he asked presently in a puzzled voice.

Small towns are best for spending Christmas, I think. They catch the mood quicker and change and come alive under its spell. By the first week in December house doors were decorated with wreaths, and store windows were flashy with red paper bells and snowflakes of glittering isinglass. The kids hiked out into the woods and came back dragging spicy evergreen trees. Already the women were busy baking fruit cakes, unsealing jars of mincemeat and opening bottles of blackberry and scuppernong wine. In the courthouse square a huge tree was trimmed with silver tinsel and colored electric bulbs that were lighted up at sunset. Late of an afternoon you could hear the choir in the Presbyterian church practicing carols for their annual pageant. All over town the japonicas were in full bloom.

The only person who appeared not the least touched by this heartwarming atmosphere was Appleseed. He went about his declared business of counting the jug-money with great, persistent care. Every day now he came to the Valhalla and concentrated on the jug, scowling and mumbling to himself. At first we were all fascinated, but after a while, it got tiresome and nobody paid him any mind whatsoever. He never bought anything, apparently having never been able to raise the two bits. Sometimes he'd talk to Hamurabi, who had taken a tender interest in him and occasionally stood treat to a jawbreaker or a penny's worth of licorice.

"Do you still think he's nuts?" I asked.

"I'm not so sure," said Hamurabi. "But I'll let you know. He doesn't eat enough. I'm going to take him over to the Rainbow Café and buy him a plate of barbecue."

"He'd appreciate it more if you'd give him a quarter."

"No. A dish of barbecue is what he needs. Besides, it would be better if he never was to make a guess. A high-strung kid like that, so unusual, I wouldn't want to be the one responsible if he lost. Say, it would be pitiful."

I'll admit that at the time, Appleseed struck me as being just funny. Mr. Marshall felt sorry for him, and the kids tried to tease him, but had to give it up when he refused to respond. There you could see him plain as day sitting at the fountain with his forehead puckered and his eyes fixed forever on that jug. Yet he was so withdrawn you sometimes had this awful creepy feeling that, well, maybe he didn't exist. And when you were pretty much convinced of this he'd wake up and say something like, "You know, I hope a 1913 buffalo nickel's in there. A fella was tellin' me he saw where a 1913 buffalo nickel's worth fifty dollars." Or, "Middy's gonna be a big lady in the picture shows. They make lotsa money, the ladies in the picture shows do, and then we ain't gonna never eat another collard green as long as we live. Only Middy says she can't be in the picture shows 'less her teeth look good."

Middy didn't always tag along with her brother. On those occasions when she didn't come, Appleseed wasn't himself; he acted shy and left soon.

Hamurabi kept his promise and stood treat to a dish of barbecue at the café. "Mr. Hamurabi's nice, all right," said Appleseed afterward, "but he's got peculiar notions: has a notion that if he lived in this place named Egypt, he'd be a king or somethin'."

And Hamurabi said, "That kid has the most touching faith. It's a beautiful thing to see. But I'm beginning to despise the whole business." He gestured toward the jug. "Hope of this kind is a cruel thing to give anybody, and I'm damned sorry I was ever a party to it."

Around the Valhalla the most popular pastime was deciding what you would buy if you won the jug. Among those who participated were: Solomon Katz, Phoebe Jones, Carl Kuhnhardt, Puly Simmons, Addie Foxcroft, Marvin Finkle, Trudy Edwards and a colored man named Erskine Washington. And these were some of their answers: a trip to and a permanent wave in Birmingham, a second-hand piano, a Shetland pony, a gold bracelet, a set of *Rover Boys* books and a life insurance policy.

Once Mr. Marshall asked Appleseed what he would get. "It's a secret," was the reply, and no amount of prying could make him tell. We took it for granted that whatever it was, he wanted it real bad.

Honest winter, as a rule, doesn't settle on our part of the country till late January, and then is mild, lasting only a short time. But in the year of which I write we were blessed with a singular cold spell the week before Christmas. Some still talk of it, for it was so terrible: water pipes froze solid; many folks had to spend the days in bed snuggled under their quilts, having neglected to lay in enough kindling for the fireplace; the sky turned that strange dull gray as it does just before a storm, and the sun was pale as a waning moon. There was a sharp wind: the old dried-up leaves of last fall fell on the icy ground, and the evergreen tree in the courthouse square was twice stripped of its Christmas finery. When you breathed, your breath made smoky clouds. Down by the silk mill where the very poor people lived, the families huddled together in the dark at night and told tales to keep their minds off the cold. Out in the country the farmers covered their delicate plants with gunnysacks and prayed; some took advantage of the weather to slaughter their hogs and bring the fresh sausage to town. Mr. R. C. Judkins, our town drunk, outfitted himself in a red cheesecloth suit and played Santa Claus at the five 'n' dime. Mr. R. C. Judkins was the father of a big family, so everybody was happy to see him sober enough to earn a dollar. There were several church socials, at one of which Mr. Marshall came face to face with Rufus McPherson: bitter words were passed but not a blow was struck.

Now, as has been mentioned, Appleseed lived on a farm a mile below Indian Branches; this would be approximately three miles from town; a mighty long and lonesome walk. Still, despite the cold, he came every day to the Valhalla and stayed till closing time, which, as the days had grown short, was after nightfall. Once in a while he'd catch a ride partway home with the foreman from the silk mill, but not often. He looked tired, and there were worry lines about his mouth. He was always cold and shivered a lot. I don't think he wore any warm drawers underneath his red sweater and blue britches.

It was three days before Christmas when out of the clear sky, he announced: "Well, I'm finished. I mean I know how much is in the bottle." He claimed this with such grave, solemn sureness it was hard to doubt him.

"Why, say now, son, hold on," said Hamurabi, who was present. "You can't know anything of the sort. It's wrong to think so: you're just heading to get yourself hurt."

"You don't need to preach to me, Mr. Hamurabi. I know what I'm up to. A lady in Louisiana, she told me . . ."

"Yes yes yes—but you got to forget that. If it were me, I'd go home and stay put and forget about this goddamned jug."

"My brother's gonna play the fiddle at a wedding over in Cherokee City tonight and he's gonna give me the two bits," said Appleseed stubbornly. "Tomorrow I'll take my chance."

So the next day I felt kind of excited when Appleseed and Middy arrived. Sure enough, he had his quarter: it was tied for safekeeping in the corner of a red bandanna.

The two of them wandered hand in hand among the showcases, holding a whispery consultation as to what to purchase. They decided finally on a thimble-sized bottle of gardenia cologne, which Middy promptly opened and partly emptied on her hair. "I smells like . . . Oh, darlin' Mary, I ain't never smelled nothin' as sweet. Here, Appleseed, honey, let me douse some on your hair." But he wouldn't let her.

Mr. Marshall got out the ledger in which he kept his records, while Appleseed strolled over to the fountain and cupped the jug between his hands, stroking it gently. His eyes were bright and his cheeks flushed from excitement. Several persons who were in the drugstore at that moment crowded close. Middy stood in the background quietly scratching her leg and smelling the cologne. Hamurabi wasn't there.

Mr. Marshall licked the point of his pencil and smiled. "Okay, son, what do you say?"

Appleseed took a deep breath. "Seventy-seven dollars and thirty-five cents," he blurted.

In picking such an uneven sum, he showed originality, for the run-of-the-mill guess was a plain round figure. Mr. Marshall repeated the amount solemnly as he copied it down.

"When'll I know if I won?"

"Christmas Eve," someone said.

"That's tomorrow, huh?"

"Why, so it is," said Mr. Marshall, not surprised. "Come at four o'clock."

During the night the thermometer dropped even lower, and toward dawn there was one of those swift, summerlike rainstorms, so that the following day was bright and frozen. The town was like a picture postcard of a Northern scene, what with icicles sparkling whitely on the trees and frost flowers coating all windowpanes. Mr. R. C. Judkins rose early and, for no clear reason, tramped the streets ringing a supper bell, stopping now and then to take a swig of whiskey from a pint which he kept in his hip pocket. As the day was windless, smoke climbed lazily from various chimneys straightway to the still, frozen sky. By mid-morning the Presbyterian choir was in full swing; and the town kids (wearing horror masks, as at Halloween) were chasing one another round and round the square, kicking up an awful fuss.

Hamurabi dropped by at noon to help us fix up the Valhalla. He brought along a fat sack of Satsumas, and together we ate every last one, tossing the hulls into a newly installed potbellied stove (a present from Mr. Marshall to himself) which stood in the middle of the room. Then my uncle took the jug off the fountain, polished and placed it on a prominently situated table. He was no help after that whatsoever, for he squatted in a chair and spent his time tying and retying a tacky green ribbon around the jug. So Hamurabi and I had the rest to do alone: we swept the floor and washed the mirrors and dusted the cabinets and strung streamers of red and green crepe paper from wall to wall. When we were finished it looked very fine and elegant.

But Hamurabi gazed sadly at our work, and said: "Well, I think I better be getting along now."

"Aren't you going to stay?" asked Mr. Marshall, shocked.

"No, oh, no," said Hamurabi, shaking his head slowly. "I don't want to see that kid's face. This is Christmas and I mean to have a rip-roaring time. And I couldn't, not with something like that on my conscience. Hell, I wouldn't sleep."

"Suit yourself," said Mr. Marshall. And he shrugged, but you could see he was really hurt. "Life's like that—and besides, who knows, he might win."

Hamurabi sighed gloomily. "What's his guess?"

"Seventy-seven dollars and thirty-five cents," I said.

"Now I ask you, isn't that fantastic?" said Hamurabi. He slumped in a chair next to Mr. Marshall and crossed his legs and lit a cigarette. "If you got any Baby Ruths, I think I'd like one; my mouth tastes sour."

As the afternoon wore on, the three of us sat around the table feeling terribly blue. No one said hardly a word and, as the kids had deserted the square, the only sound was the clock tolling the hour in the courthouse steeple. The Valhalla was closed to business, but people kept passing by and peeking in the window. At three o'clock Mr. Marshall told me to unlock the door.

Within twenty minutes the place was jam full; everyone was wearing his Sunday best, and the air smelled sweet, for most of the little silk-mill girls had scented themselves with vanilla flavoring. They scrunched up against the walls, perched on the fountain, squeezed in wherever they could; soon the crowd had spread to the sidewalk and stretched into the road. The square was lined with team-drawn wagons and Model T Fords that had carted farmers and their families into town. There was much laughter and shouting and joking—several outraged ladies complained of the cursing and the rough, shoving ways of the younger men, but nobody left. At the side entrance a gang of colored folks had formed and were having the most fun of all. Everybody was making the best of a good thing. It's usually so quiet around here: nothing much ever happens. It's safe to say that nearly all of Wachata County was present, but invalids and Rufus McPherson. I looked around for Appleseed but didn't see him anywhere.

Mr. Marshall harrumphed, and clapped for attention. When things quieted down and the atmosphere was properly tense, he raised his voice like an auctioneer, and called: "Now listen, everybody, in this here envelope you see in my hand"—he held a manila envelope above his head—"well, in it's the *answer*—which nobody but God and the First National Bank knows up to now, ha, ha. And in this book"—he held up the ledger with his free hand—"I've got written down what you folks guessed. Are there any questions?" All was silence. "Fine. Now, if we could have a volunteer . . ."

Not a living soul budged an inch: it was as if an awful shyness had overcome the crowd, and even those who were ordinarily natural-born show-offs shuffled their feet, ashamed. Then a voice, Appleseed's, hollered, "Lemme by . . . Outa the way, please, ma'am." Trotting along behind as he pushed forward were Middy and a lanky, sleepy-eyed fellow who was evidently the fiddling brother. Appleseed was dressed the same as usual, but his face was scrubbed rosy clean, his boots polished and his hair slicked back skintight with Stacomb. "Did we get here in time?" he panted.

But Mr. Marshall said, "So you want to be our volunteer?"

Appleseed looked bewildered, then nodded vigorously.

"Does anybody have an objection to this young man?"

Still there was dead quiet. Mr. Marshall handed the envelope to Appleseed, who accepted it calmly. He chewed his under lip while studying it a moment before ripping the flap.

In all that congregation there was no sound except an occasional cough and the soft tinkling of Mr. R. C. Judkins' supper bell. Hamurabi was leaning against the fountain, staring up at the ceiling; Middy was gazing blankly over her brother's shoulder, and when he started to tear open the envelope she let out a pained little gasp.

Appleseed withdrew a slip of pink paper and, holding it as though it was very fragile, muttered to himself whatever was written there. Suddenly his face paled and tears glistened in his eyes.

"Hey, speak up, boy," someone hollered.

Hamurabi stepped forward and all but snatched the slip away. He cleared his throat and commenced to read when his expression changed most comically. "Well, Mother o' God . . ." he said.

"Louder! Louder!" an angry chorus demanded.

"Buncha crooks!" yelled Mr. R. C. Judkins, who had a snootful by this time. "I smell a rat and he smells to high heaven!" Whereupon a cyclone of catcalls and whistling rent the air.

Appleseed's brother whirled round and shook his fist. "Shuddup, shuddup 'fore I bust every one of your goddamn heads together so's you got knots the size a musk melons, hear me?"

"Citizens," cried Mayor Mawes, "citizens—I say, this is Christmas . . . I say . . ."

And Mr. Marshall hopped up on a chair and clapped and stamped till a minimum of order was restored. It might as well be noted here that we later found out Rufus McPherson had paid Mr. R. C. Judkins to start the rumpus. Anyway, when the outbreak was quelled, who should be in possession of the slip but me . . . don't ask how.

Without thinking, I shouted, "Seventy-seven dollars and thirty-five cents." Naturally, due to the excitement, I didn't at first catch the meaning; it was just a number. Then Appleseed's brother let forth with his whooping yell, and so I understood. The name of the winner spread quickly, and the awed, murmuring whispers were like a rainstorm.

Oh, Appleseed himself was a sorry sight. He was crying as though he was mortally wounded, but when Hamurabi lifted him onto his shoulders so the crowd could get a gander, he dried his eyes with the cuffs of his sweater and began grinning. Mr. R. C. Judkins yelled, "Gyp! Lousy gyp!" but was drowned out by a deafening round of applause.

Middy grabbed my arm. "My teeth," she squealed. "Now I'm gonna get my teeth."

"Teeth?" said I, kind of dazed.

"The false kind," says she. "That's what we're gonna get us with the money—a lovely set of white false teeth."

But at that moment my sole interest was in how Appleseed had known. "Hey, tell me," I said desperately, "tell me, how in God's name did he know there was just exactly seventy-seven dollars and thirty-five cents?"

Middy gave me this *look*. "Why, I thought he told you," she said, real serious. "He counted."

"Yes, but how—how?"

"Gee, don't you even know how to count?"

"But is that all he did?"

"Well," she said, following a thoughtful pause, "he did do a little praying, too." She started to dart off, then turned back and called, "Besides, he was born with a caul on his head."

And that's the nearest anybody ever came to solving the mystery. Thereafter, if you were to ask Appleseed "How come?" he would smile strangely and change the subject. Many years later he and his family moved to somewhere in Florida and were never heard from again.

But in our town his legend flourishes still; and, till his death a year ago last April, Mr. Marshall was invited each Christmas Day to tell the story of Appleseed to the Baptist Bible class. Hamurabi once typed up an account and mailed it around to various magazines. It was never printed. One editor wrote back and said that "If the little girl really turned out to be a movie star, then there might be something to your story." But that's not what happened, so why should you lie?

The
Headless
Hawk

(1946)

*They are of those that rebel against the
light; they know not the ways thereof, nor
abide in the paths thereof. In the dark they
dig through houses, which they had
marked for themselves in the daytime:
they know not the light. For the morning
is to them as the shadow of death: if one
know them, they are in the terrors of the
shadow of death.*

—JOB 24: 13, 16, 17

VINCENT SWITCHED OFF THE LIGHTS
in the gallery. Outside, after locking the
door, he smoothed the brim of an elegant Panama, and started toward
Third Avenue, his umbrella-cane tap-tap-tapping along the pavement. A
promise of rain had darkened the day since dawn, and a sky of bloated
clouds blurred the five o'clock sun; it was hot, though, humid as tropical
mist, and voices, sounding along the gray July street, sounding muffled and
strange, carried a fretful undertone. Vincent felt as though he moved below
the sea. Buses, cruising crosstown through Fifty-seventh Street, seemed

44

like green-bellied fish, and faces loomed and rocked like wave-riding masks. He studied each passer-by, hunting one, and presently he saw her, a girl in a green raincoat. She was standing on the downtown corner of Fifty-seventh and Third, just standing there smoking a cigarette, and giving somehow the impression she hummed a tune. The raincoat was transparent. She wore dark slacks, no socks, a pair of huaraches, a man's white shirt. Her hair was fawn-colored, and cut like a boy's. When she noticed Vincent crossing toward her, she dropped the cigarette and hurried down the block to the doorway of an antique store.

Vincent slowed his step. He pulled out a handkerchief and dabbed his forehead; if only he could get away, go up to the Cape, lie in the sun. He bought an afternoon paper, and fumbled his change. It rolled in the gutter, dropped silently out of sight down a sewer grating. "Ain't but a nickel, bub," said the newsdealer, for Vincent, though actually unaware of his loss, looked heartbroken. And it was like that often now, never quite in contact, never sure whether a step would take him backward or forward, up or down. Very casually, with the handle of the umbrella hooked over an arm, and his eyes concentrated on the paper's headlines—but what did the damn thing say?—he continued downtown. A swarthy woman carrying a shopping bag jostled him, glared, muttered in coarsely vehement Italian. The ragged cut of her voice seemed to come through layers of wool. As he approached the antique store where the girl in the green raincoat waited, he walked slower still, counting one, two, three, four, five, six—at six he halted before the window.

The window was like a corner of an attic; a lifetime's discardings rose in a pyramid of no particular worth: vacant picture frames, a lavender wig, Gothic shaving mugs, beaded lamps. There was an Oriental mask suspended on a ceiling cord, and wind from an electric fan whirring inside the shop revolved it slowly round and round. Vincent, by degrees, lifted his gaze, and looked at the girl directly. She was hovering in the doorway so that he saw her greenness distorted wavy through double glass; the elevated pounded overhead and the window trembled. Her image spread like a reflection on silverware, then gradually hardened again: she was watching him.

He hung an Old Gold between his lips, rummaged for a match and, finding none, sighed. The girl stepped from the doorway. She held out a cheap little lighter; as the flame pulsed up, her eyes, pale, shallow, cat-green, fixed him with alarming intensity. Her eyes had an astonished, a shocked look, as though, having at one time witnessed a terrible incident, they'd locked wide open. Carefree bangs fringed her forehead; this boy haircut emphasized the childish and rather poetic quality of her narrow, hollow-cheeked face. It was the kind of face one sometimes sees in paintings of medieval youths.

Letting the smoke pour out his nose, Vincent, knowing it was useless to ask, wondered, as always, what she was living on and where. He flipped away the cigarette, for he had not wanted it to begin with, and then, pivoting, crossed rapidly under the El; as he approached the curb he heard a crash of brakes, and suddenly, as if cotton plugs had been blasted from his ears, city noises crowded in. A cab driver hollered: "Fa crissake, sistuh, get the lead outa yuh pants!" but the girl did not even bother turning her head; trance-eyed, undisturbed as a sleepwalker, and staring straight at Vincent, who watched dumbly, she moved across the street. A colored boy wearing a jazzy purple suit took her elbow. "You sick, Miss?" he said, guiding her forward, and she did not answer. "You look mighty funny, Miss. If you sick, I . . ." then, following the direction of her eyes, he released his hold. There was something here which made him all still inside. "Uh —yeah," he muttered, backing off with a grinning display of tartar-coated teeth.

So Vincent began walking in earnest, and his umbrella tapped codelike block after block. His shirt was soaked through with itchy sweat, and the noises, now so harsh, banged in his head: a trick car horn hooting "My Country 'Tis of Thee," electric spray of sparks crackling bluely off thundering rails, whiskey laughter hiccuping through gaunt doors of beer-stale bars where orchid juke machines manufactured U.S.A. music—"I got spurs that jingle jangle jingle. . . ." Occasionally he caught a glimpse of her, once mirrored in the window of Paul's Seafood Palace, where scarlet lobsters basked on a beach of flaked ice. She followed close with her hands shoved into the pockets of her raincoat. The brassy lights of a movie marquee blinked, and he remembered how she loved movies: murder films, spy chillers, Wild West shows. He turned into a side street leading toward the East River; it was quiet here, hushed like Sunday: a sailor-stroller munching an Eskimo Pie, energetic twins skipping rope, an old velvet lady with gardenia-white hair lifting aside lace curtains and peering listlessly into rain-dark space—a city landscape in July. And behind him the soft insistent slap of sandals. Traffic lights on Second Avenue turned red; at the corner a bearded midget, Ruby the Popcorn Man, wailed, "Hot buttered popcorn, big bag, yah?" Vincent shook his head, and the midget looked very put out, then: "Yuh see?" he jeered, pushing a shovel inside the candlelit cage, where bursting kernels bounced like crazy moths. "Yuh see, de girlie knows popcorn's nourishin'." She bought a dime's worth, and it was in a green sack matching her raincoat, matching her eyes.

This is my neighborhood, my street, the house with the gateway is where I live. To remind himself of this was necessary, inasmuch as he'd substituted for a sense of reality a knowledge of time, and place. He glanced gratefully at sourfaced, faded ladies, at the pipe-puffing males squatting on the surrounding steps of brownstone stoops. Nine pale little girls shrieked round a corner flower cart begging daisies to pin in their hair, but the peddler said "Shoo!" and, fleeing like beads of a broken bracelet, they circled in the street, the wild ones leaping with laughter, and the shy ones, silent and isolated, lifting summer-wilted faces skyward: the rain, would it never come?

Vincent, who lived in a basement apartment, descended several steps and took out his keycase; then, pausing behind the hallway door, he looked back through a peephole in the paneling. The girl was waiting on the sidewalk above; she leaned against a brownstone banister, and her arms fell limp—and popcorn spilled snowlike round her feet. A grimy little boy crept slyly up to pick among it like a squirrel.

2

For Vincent it was a holiday. No one had come by the gallery all morning, which, considering the arctic weather, was not unusual. He sat at his desk devouring tangerines, and enjoying immensely a Thurber story in an old *New Yorker.* Laughing loudly, he did not hear the girl enter, see her cross the dark carpet, notice her at all, in fact, until the telephone rang. "Garland Gallery, hello." She was odd, most certainly, that indecent haircut, those depthless eyes—"Oh, Paul. *Comme ci, comme ça* and you?"—and dressed like a freak: no coat, just a lumberjack's shirt, navy-blue slacks and—was it a joke?—pink ankle socks, a pair of huaraches. "The ballet? Who's dancing? Oh, her!" Under an arm she carried a flat parcel wrapped in sheets of funny-paper—"Look, Paul, what say I call back? There's someone here . . ." and, anchoring the receiver, assuming a commercial smile, he stood up. "Yes?"

Her lips, crusty with chap, trembled with unrealized words as though she had possibly a defect of speech, and her eyes rolled in their sockets like loose marbles. It was the kind of disturbed shyness one associates with children. "I've a picture," she said. "You buy pictures?"

At this, Vincent's smile became fixed. "We exhibit."

"I painted it myself," she said, and her voice, hoarse and slurred, was Southern. "My picture—I painted it. A lady told me there were places around here that bought pictures."

Vincent said, "Yes, of course, but the truth is"—and he made a helpless gesture—"the truth is I've no authority whatever. Mr. Garland—this is his gallery, you know—*is* out of town." Standing there on the expanse of fine carpet, her body sagging sideways with the weight of her package, she looked like a sad rag doll. "Maybe," he began, "maybe Henry Krueger up the street at Sixty-five . . ." but she was not listening.

"I did it myself," she insisted softly. "Tuesdays and Thursdays were our painting days, and a whole year I worked. The others, they kept messing it up, and Mr. Destronelli . . ." Suddenly, as though aware of an indiscretion, she stopped and bit her lip. Her eyes narrowed. "He's not a friend of yours?"

"Who?" said Vincent, confused.

"Mr. Destronelli."

He shook his head, and wondered why it was that eccentricity always excited in him such curious admiration. It was the feeling he'd had as a child toward carnival freaks. And it was true that about those whom he'd loved there was always a little something wrong, broken. Strange, though, that this quality, having stimulated an attraction, should, in his case, regularly end it by destroying it. "Of course I haven't any authority," he repeated, sweeping tangerine hulls into a wastebasket, "but, if you like, I suppose I could look at your work."

A pause; then, kneeling on the floor, she commenced stripping off the funny-paper wrapping. It originally had been, Vincent noticed, part of the New Orleans *Times-Picayune*. "From the South, aren't you?" he said. She did not look up, but he saw her shoulders stiffen. "No," she said. Smiling, he considered a moment, decided it would be tactless to challenge so transparent a lie. Or could she have misunderstood? And all at once he felt an intense longing to touch her head, finger the boyish hair. He shoved his hands in his pockets and glanced at the window. It was spangled with February frost, and some passer-by had scratched on the glass an obscenity. "There," she said.

A headless figure in a monklike robe reclined complacently on top a tacky vaudeville trunk; in one hand she held a fuming blue candle, in the other a miniature gold cage, and her severed head lay bleeding at her feet: it was the girl's, this head, but here her hair was long, very long, and a snowball kitten with crystal spitfire eyes playfully pawed, as it would a spool of yarn, the sprawling ends. The wings of a hawk, headless, scarlet-breasted, copper-clawed, curtained the background like a nightfall sky. It was a crude painting, the hard pure colors molded with male brutality, and, while there was no technical merit evident, it had that power often seen in something deeply felt, though primitively conveyed. Vincent reacted as he did when occasionally a phrase of music surprised a note of inward recognition, or a cluster of words in a poem revealed to him a secret concerning himself: he felt a powerful chill of pleasure run down his spine. "Mr. Garland is in Florida," he said cautiously, "but I think he should see it; you couldn't leave it for, say, a week?"

"I had a ring and I sold it," she said, and he had the feeling she was talking in a trance. "It was a nice ring, a wedding ring—not mine—with writing on it. I had an overcoat, too." She twisted one of her shirt buttons, pulled till it popped off and rolled on the carpet like a pearl eye. "I don't want much—fifty dollars; is that unfair?"

"Too much," said Vincent, more curtly than he intended. Now he wanted her painting, not for the gallery, but for himself. There are certain works of art which excite more interest in their creators than in what they have created, usually because in this kind of work one is able to identify something which has until that instant seemed a private inexpressible perception, and you wonder: who is this that knows me, and how? "I'll give thirty."

For a moment she gaped at him stupidly, and then, sucking her breath, held out her hand, palm up. This directness, too innocent to be offensive, caught him off guard. Somewhat embarrassed, he said, "I'm most awfully afraid I'll have to mail a check. Could you . . . ?" The telephone interrupted, and, as he went to answer, she followed, her hand outstretched, a frantic look pinching her face. "Oh, Paul, may I call back? Oh, I see. Well, hold on a sec." Cupping the mouthpiece against his shoulder, he pushed a pad and pencil across the desk. "Here, write your name and address."

But she shook her head, the dazed, anxious expression deepening.

"*Check*," said Vincent, "I have to mail a check. Please, your name and address." He grinned encouragingly when at last she began to write.

"Sorry, Paul . . . Whose party? Why, the little bitch, she didn't invite . . . Hey!" he called, for the girl was moving toward the door. "Please, hey!" Cold air chilled the gallery, and the door slammed with a glassy rattle. Hellohellohello. Vincent did not answer; he stood puzzling over the curious information she'd left printed on his pad: D.J.—Y.W.C.A. Hellohellohello.

It hung above his mantel, the painting, and on those nights when he could not sleep he would pour a glass of whiskey and talk to the headless hawk, tell it the stuff of his life: he was, he said, a poet who had never written poetry, a painter who had never painted, a lover who had never loved (absolutely)—someone, in short, without direction, and quite headless. Oh, it wasn't that he hadn't tried—good beginnings, always, bad endings, always. Vincent, white, male, age thirty-six, college graduate: a man in the sea, fifty miles from shore; a victim, born to be murdered, either by himself or another; an actor unemployed. It was there, all of it, in the painting, everything disconnected and cockeyed, and who was she that she should know so much? Inquiries, those he'd made had led nowhere; not another dealer knew of her, and to search for a D.J. living in, presumably, a Y.W.C.A. seemed absurd. Then, too, he'd quite expected she would reappear, but February passed, and March. One evening, crossing the square which fronts the Plaza, he had a queer thing happen. The archaic hansom drivers who line that location were lighting their carriage lamps, for it was dusk, and lamplight traced through moving leaves. A hansom pulled from the curb and rolled past in the twilight. There was a single occupant, and this passenger, whose face he could not see, was a girl with chopped fawn-colored hair. So he settled on a bench, and whiled away time talking with a soldier, and a fairy colored boy who quoted poetry, and a man out airing a dachshund: night characters with whom he waited—but the carriage, with the one for whom he waited, never came back. Again he saw her (or supposed he did) descending subway stairs, and this time lost her in the tiled tunnels of painted arrows and Spearmint machines. It was as if her face were imposed upon his mind; he could no more dispossess it than could, for example, a dead man rid his legendary eyes of the last image seen. Around the middle of April he went up to Connecticut to spend a weekend with his married sister; keyed-up, caustic, he wasn't, as she complained, at all like himself. "What is it, Vinny darling—if you need money . . ." "Oh, shut up!" he said. "Must be love," teased his brother-in-law. "Come on, Vinny, 'fess up; what's she like?" And all this so annoyed him he caught the next train home. From a booth in Grand Central he called to apologize, but a sick nervousness hummed inside him, and he hung up while the operator was still trying to make a connection. He wanted a drink. At the Commodore Bar he spent an hour or so downing four daiquiris—it was Saturday, it was nine, there was nothing to do unless he did it alone, he was feeling sad for himself. Now in the park behind the Public Library sweethearts moved whisperingly under trees, and drinking-fountain water bubbled softly, like their voices, but for all the white April evening meant to him, Vincent, drunk a little and wandering, might as well have been old, like the old bench-sitters rasping phlegm.

In the country, spring is a time of small happenings happening quietly, hyacinth shoots thrusting in a garden, willows burning with a sudden frosty fire of green, lengthening afternoons of long flowing dusk, and midnight rain opening lilac; but in the city there is the fanfare of organ-grinders, and odors, undiluted by winter wind, clog the air; windows long closed go up, and conversation, drifting beyond a room, collides with the jangle of a peddler's bell. It is the crazy season of toy balloons and roller skates, of courtyard baritones and men of freakish enterprise, like the one who jumped up now like a jack-in-the-box. He was old, he had a telescope and a sign: 25¢ See the Moon! See the Stars! 25¢. No stars could penetrate a city's glare, but Vincent saw the moon, a round, shadowed whiteness, and then a blaze of electric bulbs: Four Roses, Bing Cro——. He was moving through caramel-scented staleness, swimming through oceans of cheese-pale faces, neon and darkness. Above the blasting of a jukebox, bullet-fire boomed, a cardboard duck fell plop, and somebody screeched: "Yay Iggy!" It was a Broadway funhouse, a penny arcade, and jammed from wall to wall with Saturday splurgers. He watched a penny movie (*What The Bootblack Saw*), and had his fortune told by a wax witch leering behind glass: "Yours is an affectionate nature" . . . but he read no further, for up near the jukebox there was an attractive commotion. A crowd of kids, clapping in time to jazz music, had formed a circle around two dancers. These dancers were both colored, both girls. They swayed together slow and easy, like lovers, rocked and stamped and rolled serious savage eyes, their muscles rhythmically attuned to the ripple of a clarinet, the rising harangue of a drum. Vincent's gaze traveled round the audience, and when he saw her a bright shiver went through him, for something of the dance's violence was reflected in her face. Standing there beside a tall ugly boy, it was as if she were the sleeper and the Negroes a dream. Trumpet-drum-piano, bawling on behind a black girl's froggy voice, wailed toward a rocking finale. The clapping ended, the dancers parted. She was alone now; though Vincent's instinct was to leave before she noticed, he advanced, and, as one would gently waken a sleeper, lightly touched her shoulder. "Hello," he said, his voice too loud. Turning, she stared at him, and her eyes were clear-blank. First terror, then puzzlement replaced the dead lost look. She took a step backward, and, just as the jukebox commenced hollering again, he seized her wrist: "You remember me," he prompted, "the gallery? Your painting?" She blinked, let the lids sink sleepily over those eyes, and he could feel the slow relaxing of tension in her arm. She was thinner than he recalled, prettier, too, and her hair, grown out somewhat, hung in casual disorder. A little Christmas ribbon dangled sadly from a stray lock. He started to say, "Can I buy you a drink?" but she leaned against him, her head resting on his chest like a child's, and he said: "Will you come home with me?" She lifted her face; the answer, when it came, was a breath, a whisper: "Please," she said.

Vincent stripped off his clothes, arranged them neatly in the closet, and admired his nakedness before a mirrored door. He was not so handsome as he supposed, but handsome all the same. For his moderate height he was excellently proportioned; his hair was dark yellow, and his delicate, rather snub-nosed face had a fine, ruddy coloring. The rumble of running water broke the quiet; she was in the bathroom preparing to bathe. He dressed in loose-fitting flannel pajamas, lit a cigarette, said, "Everything all right?" The water went off, a long silence, then: "Yes, thank you." On the way home in a cab he'd made an attempt at conversation, but she had said nothing, not even when they entered the apartment—and this last offended him, for, taking rather female pride in his quarters, he'd expected a complimentary remark. It was one enormously high-ceilinged room, a bath and kitchenette, a backyard garden. In the furnishings he'd combined modern with antique and produced a distinguished result. Decorating the walls were a trio of Toulouse-Lautrec prints, a framed circus poster, D.J.'s

painting, photographs of Rilke, Nijinsky and Duse. A candelabra of lean
blue candles burned on a desk; the room, washed in their delirious light,
wavered. French doors led into the yard. He never used it much, for it was
a place impossible to keep clean. There were a few dead tulip stalks dark
in the moonshine, a puny heaven tree, and an old weather-worn chair left
by the last tenant. He paced back and forth over the cold flagstones, hoping
that in the cool air the drugged drunk sensation he felt would wear off.
Nearby a piano was being badly mauled, and in a window above there was
a child's face. He was thumbing a blade of grass when her shadow fell long
across the yard. She was in the doorway. "You mustn't come out," he said,
moving toward her. "It's turned a little cold."

There was about her now an appealing softness; she seemed somehow
less angular, less out of tune with the average, and Vincent, offering a glass
of sherry, was delighted at the delicacy with which she touched it to her
lips. She was wearing his terry-cloth robe; it was by yards too large. Her
feet were bare, and she tucked them up beside her on the couch. "It's like
Glass Hill, the candlelight," she said, and smiled. "My Granny lived at
Glass Hill. We had lovely times, sometimes; do you know what she used
to say? She used to say, 'Candles are magic wands; light one and the world
is a story book.'"

"What a dreary old lady she must've been," said Vincent, quite drunk.
"We should probably have hated each other."

"Granny would've loved you," she said. "She loved any kind of man,
every man she ever met, even Mr. Destronelli."

"Destronelli?" It was a name he'd heard before.

Her eyes slid slyly sideways, and this look seemed to say: There must
be no subterfuge between us, we who understand each other have no need
of it. "Oh, you know," she said with a conviction that, under more commonplace circumstances, would have been surprising. It was, however, as
if he'd abandoned temporarily the faculty of surprise. "Everybody knows
him."

He curved an arm around her, and brought her nearer. "Not me, I
don't," he said, kissing her mouth, neck; she was not responsive especially,
but he said—and his voice had gone adolescently shaky—"Never met Mr.
Whoozits." He slipped a hand inside her robe, loosening it away from her
shoulders. Above one breast she had a birthmark, small and star-shaped. He
glanced at the mirrored door, where uncertain light rippled their reflections, made them pale and incomplete. She was smiling. "Mr. Whoozits,"
he said, "what does he look like?" The suggestion of a smile faded, a small
monkeylike frown flickered on her face. She looked above the mantel at
her painting, and he realized that this was the first notice she'd shown it;
she appeared to study in the picture a particular object, but whether hawk

or head he could not say. "Well," she said quietly, pressing closer to him, "he looks like you, like me, like most anybody."

It was raining; in the wet noon light two nubs of candle still burned, and at an open window gray curtains tossed forlornly. Vincent extricated his arm; it was numb from the weight of her body. Careful not to make a noise, he eased out of bed, blew out the candles, tiptoed into the bathroom, and doused his face with cold water. On the way to the kitchenette he flexed his arms, feeling, as he hadn't for a long time, an intensely male pleasure in his strength, a healthy wholeness of person. He made and put on a tray orange juice, raisin-bread toast, a pot of tea; then, so inexpertly that everything on the tray rattled, he brought the breakfast in and placed it on a table beside the bed.

She had not moved; her ruffled hair spread fanwise across the pillow, and one hand rested in the hollow where his head had lain. He leaned over and kissed her lips, and her eyelids, blue with sleep, trembled. "Yes, yes, I'm awake," she murmured, and rain, lifting in the wind, sprayed against the window like surf. He somehow knew that with her, there would be none of the usual artifice: no avoidance of eyes, no shame-faced, accusing pause. She raised herself on her elbow; she looked at him, Vincent thought, as if he were her husband, and, handing her the orange juice, he smiled his gratitude.

"What is today?"

"Sunday," he told her, bundling under the quilt, and settling the tray across his legs.

"But there are no church bells," she said. "And it's raining."

Vincent divided a piece of toast. "You don't mind that, do you? Rain —such a peaceful sound." He poured tea. "Sugar? Cream?"

She disregarded this, and said, "Today is Sunday what? What month, I mean?"

"Where have you been living, in the subway?" he said, grinning. And it puzzled him to think she was serious. "Oh, April . . . April something-or-other."

"April," she repeated. "Have I been here long?"

"Only since last night."

"Oh."

Vincent stirred his tea, the spoon tinkling in the cup like a bell. Toast crumbs spilled among the sheets, and he thought of the *Tribune* and the *Times* waiting outside the door, but they, this morning, held no charms; it was best lying here beside her in the warm bed, sipping tea, listening to the rain. Odd, when you stopped to consider, certainly very odd. She did not know his name, nor he hers. And so he said, "I still owe you thirty dollars, do you realize that? Your own fault, of course—leaving such a damn-fool address. And D.J., what is that supposed to mean?"

"I don't think I'd better tell you my name," she said. "I could make up one easy enough: Dorothy Jordan, Delilah Johnson; see? There are all kinds of names I could make up, and if it wasn't for him, I'd tell you right."

Vincent lowered the tray to the floor. He rolled over on his side, and, facing her, his heartbeat quickened. "Who's him?" Though her expression was calm, anger muddied her voice when she said, "If you don't know him, then tell me, why am I here?"

Silence, and outside the rain seemed suddenly suspended. A ship's horn moaned in the river. Holding her close, he combed his fingers through her hair, and, wanting so much to be believed, said, "Because I love you."

She closed her eyes. "What became of them?"

"Who?"

"The others you've said that to."

It commenced again, the rain spattering grayly at the window, falling on hushed Sunday streets; listening, Vincent remembered. He remembered his cousin, Lucille, poor, beautiful, stupid Lucille, who sat all day embroidering silk flowers on scraps of linen. And Allen T. Baker—there was the winter they'd spent in Havana, the house they'd lived in, crumbling rooms of rose-colored rock; poor Allen, he'd thought it was to be forever. Gordon too. Gordon, with the kinky yellow hair, and a head full of old Elizabethan ballads. Was it true he'd shot himself? And Connie Silver, the deaf girl, the one who had wanted to be an actress—what had become of her? Or Helen, Louise, Laura? "There was just one," he said, and to his own ears this had a truthful ring. "Only one, and she's dead."

Tenderly, as if in sympathy, she touched his cheek "I suppose he killed her," she said, her eyes so close he could see the outline of his face imprisoned in their greenness. "He killed Miss Hall, you know. The dearest woman in the world, Miss Hall, and so pretty your breath went away. I had piano lessons with her, and when she played the piano, when she said hello and when she said good-bye—it was like my heart would stop." Her voice had taken on an impersonal tone, as though she were talking of matters belonging to another age, and in which she was not concerned directly. "It was the end of summer when she married him—September, I think. She went to Atlanta, and they were married there, and she never came back. It was just that sudden." She snapped her fingers. "Just like that. I saw a picture of him in the paper. Sometimes I think if she'd known how much I loved her—why are there some you can't ever tell?—I think maybe she wouldn't have married; maybe it would've all been different, like I wanted it." She turned her face into the pillow, and if she cried, there was no sound.

. . .

On May twentieth she was eighteen; it seemed incredible—Vincent had thought her many years older. He wanted to introduce her at a surprise party, but had finally to admit that this was an unsuitable plan. First off, though the subject was always there on the tip of his tongue, not once had he ever mentioned D.J. to any of his friends; secondly, he could visualize discouragingly well the entertainment provided them at meeting a girl about whom, while they openly shared an apartment, he knew nothing, not even her name. Still the birthday called for some kind of treat. Dinner and the theater were hopeless. She hadn't, through no fault of his, a dress of any sort. He'd given her forty-odd dollars to buy clothes, and here is what she spent it on: a leather windbreaker, a set of military brushes, a raincoat, a cigarette lighter. Also, her suitcase, which she'd brought to the apartment, had contained nothing but hotel soap, a pair of scissors she used for pruning her hair, two Bibles and an appalling color-tinted photograph. The photograph showed a simpering middle-aged woman with dumpy features. There was an inscription: Best Wishes and Good Luck from Martha Lovejoy Hall.

Because she could not cook they had their meals out; his salary and the limitations of her wardrobe confined them mostly to the Automat—her favorite: the macaroni was so delicious!—or one of the bar-grills along Third. And so the birthday dinner was eaten in an Automat. She'd scrubbed her face until the skin shone red, trimmed and shampooed her hair, and with the messy skill of a six-year-old playing grown-up, varnished her nails. She wore the leather windbreaker, and on it pinned a sheaf of violets he'd given her; it must have looked amusing, for two rowdy girls sharing their table giggled frantically. Vincent said if they didn't shut up . . .

"Oh, yeah, who you think you are?"

"Superman. Jerk thinks he's superman."

It was too much, and Vincent lost his temper. He shoved back from the table, upsetting a ketchup jar. "Let's get the hell out of here," he said, but D.J., who had paid the fracas no attention whatever, went right on spooning blackberry cobbler; furious as he was, he waited quietly until she finished, for he respected her remoteness, and yet wondered in what period of time she lived. It was futile, he'd discovered, to question her past; still, she seemed only now and then aware of the present, and it was likely the future didn't mean much to her. Her mind was like a mirror reflecting blue space in a barren room.

"What would you like now?" he said, as they came into the street. "We could ride in a cab through the park."

She wiped off with her jacket-cuff flecks of blackberry staining the corners of her mouth, and said, "I want to go to a picture show."

The movies. Again. In the last month he'd seen so many films, snatches of Hollywood dialogue rumbled in his dreams. One Saturday at her insistence they'd bought tickets to three different theaters, cheap places where smells of latrine disinfectant poisoned the air. And each morning before leaving for work he left on the mantel fifty cents—rain or shine, she went to a picture show. But Vincent was sensitive enough to see why; there had been in his own life a certain time of limbo when he'd gone to movies every day, often sitting through several repeats of the same film; it was in its way like religion, for there, watching the shifting patterns of black and white, he knew a release of conscience similar to the kind a man must find confessing to his father.

"Handcuffs," she said, referring to an incident in *The Thirty-Nine Steps,* which they'd seen at the Beverly in a program of Hitchcock revivals. "That blond woman and the man handcuffed together—well, it made me think of something else." She stepped into a pair of his pajamas, pinned the corsage of violets to the edge of her pillow, and folded up on the bed. "People getting caught like that, locked together."

Vincent yawned. "Uh huh," he said, and turned off the lights. "Again, happy birthday, darling, it *was* a happy birthday?"

She said, "Once I was in this place, and there were two girls dancing; they were so free—there was just them and nobody else, and it was beautiful like a sunset." She was silent a long while; then, her slow Southern voice dragging over the words: "It was mighty nice of you to bring me violets."

"Glad—like them," he answered sleepily.

"It's a shame they have to die."

"Yes, well, good night."

"Good night."

Close-up. Oh, but John, it isn't for my sake after all we've the children to consider a divorce would ruin their lives! Fadeout. The screen trembles; rattle of drums, flourish trumpets: R.K.O. PRESENTS . . .

Here is a hall without exit, a tunnel without end. Overhead, chandeliers sparkle, and wind-bent candles float on currents of air. Before him is an old man rocking in a rocking chair, an old man with yellow-dyed hair, powdered cheeks, kewpie-doll lips: Vincent recognizes Vincent. Go away, screams Vincent, the young and handsome, but Vincent, the old and horrid, creeps forward on all fours, and climbs spiderlike onto his back. Threats, pleas, blows, nothing will dislodge him. And so he races with his shadow, his rider jogging up and down. A serpent of lightning blazes, and all at once the tunnel seethes with men wearing white tie and tails, women costumed in brocaded gowns. He is humiliated; how gauche they must think him appearing at so elegant a gathering carrying on his back, like Sinbad, a sordid old man. The guests stand about in petrified pairs, and there is no conversation. He notices then that many are also saddled with malevolent semblances of themselves, outward embodiments of inner decay. Just beside him a lizardlike man rides an albino-eyed Negro. A man is coming toward him, the host; short, florid, bald, he steps lightly, precisely in glacé shoes; one arm, held stiffly crooked, supports a massive headless hawk whose talons, latched to the wrist, draw blood. The hawk's wings unfurl as its master struts by. On a pedestal there is perched an old-time phonograph. Winding the handle, the host supplies a record: a tinny worn-out waltz vibrates the morning-glory horn. He lifts a hand, and in a soprano voice announces: "Attention! The dancing will commence." The host with his hawk weaves in and out as round and round they dip, they turn. The walls widen, the ceiling grows tall. A girl glides into Vincent's arms, and a cracked, cruel imitation of his voice says: "Lucille, how divine; that exquisite scent, is it violet?" This is Cousin Lucille, and then, as they circle the room, her face changes. Now he waltzes with another. "Why, Connie, Connie Silver! How marvelous to see you," shrieks the voice, for Connie is quite deaf. Suddenly a gentleman with a bullet-bashed head cuts in: "Gordon, forgive me, I never meant . . ." but they are gone, Gordon and Connie, dancing together. Again, a new partner. It is D.J., and she too has a figure barnacled to her back, an enchanting auburn-haired child; like an emblem of innocence, the child cuddles to her chest a snowball kitten. "I am heavier than I look," says the child, and the terrible voice retorts, "But I am heaviest of all." The instant their hands meet he begins to feel the weight upon him diminish; the old Vincent is fading. His feet lift off the floor, he floats upward from her embrace. The victrola grinds away loud as ever, but he is rising high, and the white receding faces gleam below like mushrooms on a dark meadow.

The host releases his hawk, sends it soaring. Vincent thinks, no matter, it is a blind thing, and the wicked are safe among the blind. But the hawk wheels above him, swoops down, claws foremost; at last he knows there is to be no freedom.

And the blackness of the room filled his eyes. One arm lolled over the bed's edge, his pillow had fallen to the floor. Instinctively he reached out, asking mother-comfort of the girl beside him. Sheets smooth and cold; emptiness, and the tawdry fragrance of drying violets. He snapped up straight: "You, where are you?"

The French doors were open. An ashy trace of moon swayed on the threshold, for it was not yet light, and in the kitchen the refrigerator purred like a giant cat. A stack of paper rustled on the desk. Vincent called again, softly this time, as if he wished himself unheard. Rising, he stumbled forward on dizzy legs, and looked into the yard. She was there, leaning, half-kneeling, against the heaven tree. "What?" and she whirled around. He could not see her well, only a dark substantial shape. She came closer. A finger pressed her lips.

"What is it?" he whispered.

She rose on tiptoe, and her breath tingled in his ear. "I warn you, go inside."

"Stop this foolishness," he said in a normal voice. "Out here barefooted, you'll catch . . ." but she clamped a hand over his mouth.

"I saw him," she whispered. "He's here."

Vincent knocked her hand away. It was hard not to slap her. "Him! Him! Him! What's the matter with you? Are you"—he tried too late to prevent the word—"crazy?" There, the acknowledgment of something he'd known, but had not allowed his conscious mind to crystallize. And he thought: Why should this make a difference? A man cannot be held to account for those he loves. Untrue. Feeble-witted Lucille weaving mosaics on silk, embroidering his name on scarves; Connie, in her hushed deaf world, listening for his footstep, a sound she would surely hear; Allen T. Baker thumbing his photograph, still needing love, but old now, and lost —all betrayed. And he'd betrayed himself with talents unexploited, voyages never taken, promises unfulfilled. There had seemed nothing left him until—oh, why in his lovers must he always find the broken image of himself? Now, as he looked at her in the aging dawn, his heart was cold with the death of love.

She moved away, and under the tree. "Leave me here," she said, her eyes scanning tenement windows. "Only a moment."

Vincent waited, waited. On all sides windows looked down like the doors of dreams, and overhead, four flights up, a family's laundry whipped a washline. The setting moon was like the early moon of dusk, a vaporish cartwheel, and the sky, draining of dark, was washed with gray. Sunrise wind shook the leaves of the heaven tree, and in the paling light the yard assumed a pattern, objects a position, and from the roofs came the throaty morning rumble of pigeons. A light went on. Another.

And at last she lowered her head; whatever she was looking for, she had not found it. Or, he wondered as she turned to him with tilted lips, had she?

"Well, you're home kinda early, aren't you, Mr. Waters?" It was Mrs. Brennan, the super's bowlegged wife. "And, well, Mr. Waters—lovely weather, ain't it?—you and me got sumpin' to talk about."

"Mrs. Brennan"—how hard it was to breathe, to speak; the words grated his hurting throat, sounded loud as thunderclaps—"I'm rather ill, so if you don't mind . . ." and he tried to brush past her.

"Say, that's a pity. Ptomaine, must be ptomaine. Yessir, I tell you a person can't be too careful. It's them Jews, you know. They run all them delicatessens. Uh uh, none of that Jew food for me." She stepped before the gate, blocking his path, and pointed an admonishing finger: "Trouble with you, Mr. Waters, is you don't lead no kinda *normal* life."

A knot of pain was set like a malignant jewel in the core of his head; each aching motion made jeweled pinpoints of color flare out. The super's wife babbled on, but there were blank moments when, fortunately, he could not hear at all. It was like a radio—the volume turned low, then full blast. "Now I know she's a decent Christian lady, Mr. Waters, or else what would a gentleman like you be doing with—hm. Still, the fact is, Mr. Cooper don't tell lies, and he's a real calm man, besides. Been gas meter man for this district I don't know how long." A truck rolled down the street spraying water, and her voice, submerged below its roar, came up again like a shark. "Mr. Cooper had every reason to believe she meant to kill him—well, you can imagine, her standin' there with them scissors, and shoutin'. She called him an Eyetalian name. Now all you got to do is look at Mr. Cooper to know he ain't no Eyetalian. Well, you can see, Mr. Waters, such carryings-on are bound to give the house a bad . . ."

Brittle sunshine plundering the depths of his eyes made tears, and the super's wife, wagging her finger, seemed to break into separate pieces: a nose, a chin, a red, red eye. "Mr. Destronelli," he said. "Excuse me, Mrs. Brennan, I mean excuse me." She thinks I'm drunk, and I'm sick, and can't she see I'm sick? "My guest is leaving. She's leaving today, and she won't be back."

"Well, now, you don't say," said Mrs. Brennan, clucking her tongue. "Looks like she needs a rest, poor little thing. So pale, sorta. Course I don't want no more to do with them Eyetalians than the next one, but imagine thinking Mr. Cooper was an Eyetalian. Why, he's white as you or me." She tapped his shoulder solicitously. "Sorry you feel so sick, Mr. Waters; ptomaine, I tell you. A person can't be too care . . ."

The hall smelled of cooking and incinerator ashes. There was a stairway which he never used, his apartment being on the first floor, straight ahead. A match snapped fire, and Vincent, groping his way, saw a small boy— he was not more than three or four—squatting under the stairwell; he was playing with a big box of kitchen matches, and Vincent's presence appeared not to interest him. He simply struck another match. Vincent could not make his mind work well enough to phrase a reprimand, and as he waited there, tongue-tied, a door, his door, opened.

Hide. For if she saw him, she would know something was wrong, suspect something. And if she spoke, if their eyes met, then he would never be able to go through with it. So he pressed into a dark corner behind the little boy, and the little boy said, "Whatcha doin', Mister?" She was coming

—he heard the slap of her sandals, the green whisper of her raincoat. "Whatcha doin', Mister?" Quickly, his heart banging in his chest, Vincent stooped and, squeezing the child against him, pressed his hand over its mouth so it could not make a sound. He did not see her pass; it was later, after the front door clicked, that he realized she was gone. The little boy sank back on the floor. "Whatcha doin', Mister?"

Four aspirins, one right after the other, and he came back into the room; the bed had not been tidied for a week, a spilt ashtray messed the floor, odds and ends of clothing decorated improbable places, lampshades and such. But tomorrow, if he felt better, there would be a general cleaning; perhaps he'd have the walls repainted, maybe fix up the yard. Tomorrow he could begin thinking about his friends again, accept invitations, entertain. And yet this prospect, tasted in advance, was without flavor: all he'd known before seemed to him now sterile and spurious. Footsteps in the hall; could she return this soon, the movie over, the afternoon gone? Fever can make time pass so queerly, and for an instant he felt as though his bones were floating loose inside him. Clop-clop, a child's sloppy shoefall, the footsteps passed up the stairs, and Vincent moved, floated toward the mirrored closet. He longed to hurry, knowing he must, but the air seemed thick with gummy fluid. He brought her suitcase from the closet, and put it on the bed, a sad cheap suitcase with rusty locks and a warped hide. He eyed it with guilt. Where would she go? How would she live? When he'd broken with Connie, Gordon, all the others, there had been about it at least a certain dignity. Really, though—and he'd thought it out—there was no other way. So he gathered her belongings. Miss Martha Lovejoy Hall peeked out from under the leather windbreaker, her music-teacher's face smiling an oblique reproach. Vincent turned her over, face down, and tucked in the frame an envelope containing twenty dollars. That would buy a ticket back to Glass Hill, or wherever it was she came from. Now he tried to close the case, and, too weak with fever, collapsed on the bed. Quick yellow wings glided through the window. A butterfly. He'd never seen a butterfly in this city, and it was like a floating mysterious flower, like a sign of some sort, and he watched with a kind of horror as it waltzed in the air. Outside, somewhere, the razzledazzle of a beggar's grind-organ started up; it sounded like a broken-down pianola, and it played *La Marseillaise*. The butterfly lighted on her painting, crept across crystal eyes and flattened its wings like a ribbon bow over the loose head. He fished about in the suitcase until he found her scissors. He first purposed to slash the butterfly's wings, but it spiraled to the ceiling and hung there like a star. The scissors stabbed the hawk's heart, ate through canvas like a ravening steel mouth, scraps of picture flaking the floor like cuttings of stiff hair. He went on his knees, pushed the pieces into a pile, put them in the suitcase, and slammed the lid shut. He was crying. And through the tears the butterfly magnified on the ceiling, huge as a bird, and there were more: a flock of lilting, winking yellow; whispering lonesomely, like surf sucking a shore. The wind from their wings blew the room into space. He heaved forward, the suitcase banging his leg, and threw open the door. A match flared. The little boy said: "Whatcha doin', Mister?" And Vincent, setting the suitcase in the hall, grinned sheepishly. He closed the door like a thief, bolted the safety lock and, pulling up a chair, tilted it under the knob. In the still room there was only the subtlety of shifting sunlight and a crawling butterfly; it drifted downward like a tricky scrap of crayon paper, and landed on a candlestick. *Sometimes he is not a man at all*—she'd told him that, huddling here on the bed, talking swiftly in the minutes before dawn —*sometimes he is something very different: a hawk, a child, a butterfly.* And then she'd said: *At the place where they took me there were hundreds of old ladies, and young men, and one of the young men said he was a pirate, and one of the old ladies—she was near ninety—used to make me feel her stomach. "Feel," she'd say, "feel how strong he kicks?" This old lady took painting class, too, and her paintings looked like crazy quilts. And naturally he was in this place. Mr. Destronelli. Only he called himself Gum. Doctor Gum. Oh, he didn't fool me, even though he wore a gray wig, and made himself up to look real old and kind, I knew. And then one day I left, ran clear away, and hid under a lilac bush, and a man came along in a little red car, and he had a little mouse-haired mustache, and little cruel eyes. But it was him. And when I told him who he was he made me get out of his car. And then another man, that was in Philadelphia, picked me up in a café and took me into an alley. He talked Italian, and had tattoo pictures all over. But it was him. And the next man, he was the one who painted his toenails, sat down beside me in a movie because he thought I was a boy, and when he found out I wasn't he didn't get mad but let me live in his room, and cooked pretty things for me to eat. But he wore a silver locket and one day I looked inside and there was a picture of Miss Hall. So I knew it was him, so I had this feeling she was dead, so I knew he was going to murder me. And he will. He will.* Dusk, and nightfall, and the fibers of sound called silence wove a shiny blue mask. Waking, he peered through eyeslits, heard the frenzied pulsebeat of his watch, the scratch of a key in a lock. Somewhere in this hour of dusk a murderer separates himself from shadow and with a rope follows the flash of silk legs up doomed stairs. And here the dreamer staring through his mask dreams of deceit. Without investigating, he knows the suitcase is missing, that she has come, that she has gone; why, then, does he feel so little the pleasure of safety, and only cheated, and small—small as the night when he searched the moon through an old man's telescope?

3

Like fragments of an old letter, scattered popcorn lay trampled flat, and she, leaning back in a watchman's attitude, allowed her gaze to hunt among it, as if deciphering here and there a word, an answer. Her eyes shifted discreetly to the man mounting the steps, Vincent. There was about him the freshness of a shower, shave, cologne, but dreary blue circled his eyes, and the crisp seersucker into which he'd changed had been made for a heavier man: a long month of pneumonia, and wakeful burning nights had lightened his weight a dozen pounds, and more. Each morning, evening, meeting her here at his gate, or near the gallery, or outside the restaurant where he lunched, a nameless disorder took hold, a paralysis of time and identity. The wordless pantomime of her pursuit contracted his heart, and there were comalike days when she seemed not one, but all, a multiple person, and her shadow in the street every shadow, following and followed. And once they'd been alone together in an automatic elevator, and he'd screamed: "I am not him! Only me, only me!" But she smiled as she'd smiled telling of the man with painted toenails, because after all, she knew.

It was suppertime, and, not knowing where to eat, he paused under a street lamp that, blooming abruptly, fanned complex light over stone; while he waited there came a clap of thunder, and all along the street every face but two, his and the girl's, tilted upward. A blast of river breeze tossed the children's laughter as they, linking arms, pranced like carousel ponies, and carried the mama's voice who, leaning from a window, howled: rain, Rachel, rain—gonna rain gonna rain! And the gladiola, ivy-filled flower cart jerked crazily as the peddler, one eye slanted skyward, raced for shelter. A potted geranium fell off, and the little girls gathered the blooms and tucked them behind their ears. The blending spatter of running feet and raindrops tinkled on the xylophone sidewalks—the slamming of doors, the lowering of windows, then nothing but silence, and rain. Presently, with slow scraping steps, she came below the lamp to stand beside him, and it was as if the sky were a thunder-cracked mirror, for the rain fell between them like a curtain of splintered glass.

Shut a
Final Door

(1947)

"WALTER, LISTEN TO ME: IF EVERY-
one dislikes you, works against you,
don't believe they do so arbitrarily; you create these situations for yourself."

Anna had said that, and, though his healthier side told him she intended
nothing malicious (if Anna was not a friend, then who was?), he'd despised
her for it, had gone around telling everybody how much he despised Anna,
what a bitch she was. That woman! he said, don't trust that Anna. This
plainspoken act of hers—nothing but a cover-up for all her repressed
hostility; terrible liar, too, can't believe a word she says: dangerous, my
God! And naturally all he said went back to Anna, so that when he called
about a play-opening they'd planned attending together, she told him:
"Sorry, Walter, I can't afford you any longer. I understand you very well,
and I have a certain amount of sympathy. It's very compulsive, your
malice, and you aren't too much to blame, but I don't want ever to see you
again because I'm not so well myself that I can afford it." But why? And
what had he done? Well, sure, he'd gossiped about her, but it wasn't as
though he'd meant it, and after all, as he said to Jimmy Bergman (now there
was a two-face if ever there was one), what was the use of having friends
if you couldn't discuss them objectively?

He said you said they said we said round and round. Round and round,
like the paddle-bladed ceiling fan wheeling above; turning and turning,

stirring stale air ineffectively, it made a watch-tick sound, counted seconds in the silence. Walter inched to a cooler part of the bed and closed his eyes against the dark little room. At seven that evening he'd arrived in New Orleans, at seven-thirty he'd registered in this hotel, an anonymous, side-street place. It was August, and it was as though bonfires burned in the red night sky, and the unnatural Southern landscape, observed so assiduously from the train, and which, trying to sublimate all else, he retraced in memory, intensified a feeling of having traveled to the end, the falling off.

But why he was here in this stifling hotel in this faraway town he could not say. There was a window in the room, but he could not seem to get it open, and he was afraid to call the bellboy (what queer eyes that kid had!), and he was afraid to leave the hotel, for what if he got lost? and if he got lost, even a little, then he would be lost altogether. He was hungry; he hadn't eaten since breakfast, so he found some peanut-butter crackers left over from a package he'd bought in Saratoga, and washed them down with a finger of Four Roses, the last. It made him sick. He vomited in the wastebasket, collapsed back on the bed, and cried until the pillow was wet. After a while he just lay there in the hot room, shivering, just lay there and watched the slow-turning fan; there was no beginning to its action, and no end; it was a circle.

An eye, the earth, the rings of a tree, everything is a circle, and all circles, Walter said, have a center. It was crazy for Anna to say what had happened was his own doing. If there was anything wrong with him really, then it had been made so by circumstances beyond his control, by, say, his churchly mother, or his father, an insurance official in Hartford, or his older sister, Cecile, who'd married a man forty years her senior. "I just wanted to get out of the house." That was her excuse, and, to tell the truth, Walter had thought it reasonable enough.

But he did not know where to begin thinking about himself, did not know where to find the center. The first telephone call? No, that had been only three days ago and, properly speaking, was the end, not the beginning. Well, he could start with Irving, for Irving was the first person he'd known in New York.

Now Irving was a sweet little Jewish boy with a remarkable talent for chess and not much else: he had silky hair, and pink baby cheeks, and looked about sixteen. Actually he was twenty-three, Walter's age, and they'd met at a bar in the Village. Walter was alone and very lonesome in New York, and so when this sweet little Irving was friendly he decided maybe it would be a good idea to be friendly, too—because you never can tell. Irving knew a great many people, and everyone was very fond of him, and he introduced Walter to all his friends.

And there was Margaret. Margaret was more or less Irving's girl friend. She was only so-so-looking (her eyes bulged, there was always a little lipstick on her teeth, she dressed like a child of ten), but she had a hectic brightness which Walter found attractive. He could not understand why she bothered with Irving at all. "Why do you?" he said, on one of the long walks they'd begun taking together in Central Park.

"Irving is sweet," she said, "and he loves me very purely, and who knows: I might just as well marry him."

"A damn-fool thing to do," he said. "Irving could never be your husband because he's really your little brother. Irving is everyone's little brother."

Margaret was too bright not to see the truth in this. So one day when Walter asked if he might not make love to her she said, all right, she didn't mind if he did. They made love often after that.

Eventually, Irving heard about it, and one Monday there was a nasty scene in, curiously enough, the same bar where they'd met. There had been that evening a party in honor of Kurt Kuhnhardt (Kuhnhardt Advertising), Margaret's boss, and she and Walter had gone together, afterward stopping by this bar for a nightcap. Except for Irving and a couple of girls in slacks the place was empty. Irving was sitting at the bar, his cheeks quite pink, his eyes rather glazed. He looked like a little boy playing grown-up, for his legs were too short to reach the stool's footrest; they dangled doll-like. The instant Margaret recognized him she tried to turn around and walk out, but Walter wouldn't let her. And anyway, Irving had seen them: never taking his eyes from them, he put down his whiskey, slowly climbed off the stool, and, with a kind of sad, ersatz toughness, strutted forward.

"Irving, dear," said Margaret, and stopped, for he'd given her a terrible look.

His chin was trembling. "You go away," he said, and it was as though he were denouncing some childhood tormentor, "I hate you." Then, almost in slow motion, he swung out and, as if he clutched a knife, struck Walter's chest. It was not much of a blow, and when Walter did nothing but smile, Irving slumped against a jukebox, screaming: "Fight me, you damned coward; come on, and I'll kill you, I swear before God I will." So that was how they left him.

Walking home, Margaret began to cry in a soft tired way. "He'll never be sweet again," she said.

And Walter said, "I don't know what you mean."

"Oh, yes, you do," she told him, her voice a whisper. "Yes, you do; the two of us, we've taught him how to hate. Somehow I don't think he ever knew before."

Walter had been in New York now four months. His original capital of five hundred dollars had fallen to fifteen, and Margaret lent him money to pay his January rent at the Brevoort. Why, she wanted to know, didn't he move someplace cheaper? Well, he told her, it was better to have a good address. And what about a job? When was he going to start working? Or was he? Sure, he said, sure, as a matter of fact he thought about it a good deal. But he didn't intend fooling around with just any little jerkwater thing that came along. He wanted something good, something with a future, something in, say, advertising. All right, said Margaret, maybe she could help him; at any rate, she'd speak with her boss, Mr. Kuhnhardt.

2

The K.K.A., so-called, was a middle-sized agency, but, as such things go, very good, the best. Kurt Kuhnhardt, who'd founded it in 1925, was a curious man with a curious reputation: a lean, fastidious German, a bachelor, he lived in an elegant black house on Sutton Place, a house interestingly furnished with, among other things, three Picassos, a superb music box, South Sea Island masks and a burly Danish youngster, the houseboy. He invited occasionally some one of his staff in to dinner, whoever was favorite at the moment, for he was continually selecting protégés. It was a dangerous position, these alliances being, as they were, whimsical and uncertain: the protégé found himself checking the want ads when, just the evening previous, he'd dined most enjoyably with his benefactor. During his second week at the K.K.A., Walter, who had been hired as Margaret's assistant, received a memorandum from Mr. Kuhnhardt asking him to lunch, and this, of course, excited him unspeakably.

"Kill-joy?" said Margaret, straightening his tie, plucking lint off a lapel. "Nothing of the sort. It's just that—well, Kuhnhardt's wonderful to work for so long as you don't get too involved—or you're likely not to be working—period."

Walter knew what she was up to; she didn't fool him a minute; he felt like telling her so, too, but restrained himself; it wasn't time yet. One of these days, though, he was going to have to get rid of her, and soon. It was degrading, his working for Margaret. And besides, the tendency from now on would be to keep him down. But nobody could do that, he thought, looking into Mr. Kuhnhardt's sea-blue eyes, nobody could keep Walter down.

"You're an idiot," Margaret told him. "My God, I've seen these little friendships of K.K.'s a dozen times, and they don't mean a damn. He used to palsy-walsy around with the switchboard operator. All K.K. wants is someone to play the fool. Take my word, Walter, there aren't any shortcuts: what matters is how you do your job."

He said: "And have you complaints on that score? I'm doing as well as could be expected."

"It depends on what you mean by expected," she said.

One Saturday not long afterward he made a date to meet her in Grand Central. They were going up to Hartford to spend the afternoon with his family, and for this she'd bought a new dress, new hat and shoes. But he did not show up. Instead, he drove out on Long Island with Mr. Kuhnhardt, and was the most awed of three hundred guests at Rosa Cooper's debut ball. Rosa Cooper (née Kuppermann) was heiress to the Cooper Dairy Products: a dark, plump, pleasant child with an unnatural British accent, the result of four years at Miss Jewett's. She wrote a letter to a friend named Anna Stimson, who subsequently showed it to Walter: "Met the divinest man. Danced with him six times, a divine dancer. He is an Advertising Executive, and is terribly divinely good-looking. We have a date—dinner and the theater!"

Margaret did not mention the episode, nor did Walter. It was as though nothing had happened, except that now, unless there was office business to discuss, they never spoke, never saw each other. One afternoon, knowing she would not be at home, he went to her apartment and used a passkey given him long ago; there were things he'd left here, clothes, some books, his pipe; rummaging around collecting all this, he discovered a photograph of himself scrawled red with lipstick: it gave him for an instant the sensation of falling in a dream. He also came across the only gift he'd ever given her, a bottle of L'Heure Bleue, still unopened. He sat down on the bed, and, smoking a cigarette, stroked his hand over the cool pillow, remembering the way her head had lain there, remembering, too, how they used to lie here Sunday mornings reading the funnies aloud, Barney Google and Dick Tracy and Joe Palooka.

He looked at the radio, a little green box; they'd always made love to music, any kind, jazz, symphonies, choir programs: it had been their signal, for whenever she'd wanted him, she'd said, "Shall we listen to the radio, darling?" Anyway, it was finished, and he hated her, and that was what he needed to remember. He found the bottle of perfume again, and put it in his pocket: Rosa might like a surprise.

In the office the next day he stopped by the water cooler and Margaret was standing there. She smiled at him fixedly, and said: "Well, I didn't know you were a thief." It was the first overt disclosure of the hostility between them. And suddenly it occurred to Walter he hadn't in all the office a single ally. Kuhnhardt? He could never count on him. And everyone else was an enemy: Jackson, Einstein, Fischer, Porter, Capehart, Ritter, Villa, Byrd. Oh, sure, they were all smart enough not to tell him point-blank, not so long as K.K.'s enthusiasm continued.

Well, dislike was at least positive, and the one thing he could not tolerate was vague relations, possibly because his own feelings were so indecisive, ambiguous. He was never certain whether he liked X or not. He needed

X's love, but was incapable of loving. He could never be sincere with X, never tell him more than fifty percent of the truth. On the other hand, it was impossible for him to permit X these same imperfections: somewhere along the line Walter was sure he'd be betrayed. He was afraid of X, terrified. Once in high school he'd plagiarized a poem, and printed it in the school magazine; he could not forget its final line, *All our acts are acts of fear.* And when his teacher caught him out, had anything ever seemed to him more unjust?

3

He spent most of the early summer weekends at Rosa Cooper's Long Island place. The house was, as a rule, well staffed with hearty Yale and Princeton undergraduates, which was irritating, for they were the sort of boys who, around Hartford, made green birds fly in his stomach, and seldom allowed him to meet them on their own ground. As for Rosa herself, she was a darling; everyone said so, even Walter.

But darlings are rarely serious, and Rosa was not serious about Walter. He didn't mind too much. He was able on these weekends to make a good many contacts: Taylor Ovington, Joyce Randolph (the starlet), E. L. McEvoy, a dozen or so people whose names cast considerable glare in his address book. One evening he went with Anna Stimson to see a film featuring the Randolph girl, and before they were scarcely seated everyone for aisles around knew she was a Friend of his, knew she drank too much, was immoral, and not nearly so pretty as Hollywood made her out to be. Anna told him he was an adolescent female. "You're a man in only one respect, sweetie," she said.

It was through Rosa that he'd met Anna Stimson. An editor on a fashion magazine, she was almost six feet tall, wore black suits, affected a monocle, a walking cane and pounds of jingling Mexican silver. She'd been married twice, once to Buck Strong, the horse-opera idol, and she had a child, a fourteen-year-old son who'd had to be put away in what she called a "corrective academy."

"He was a nasty child," she said. "He liked to take potshots out the window with a .22, and throw things, and steal from Woolworth's: awful brat, just like you."

Anna was good to him, though, and in her less depressed, less malevolent moments listened kindly while he groaned out his problems, while he explained why he was the way he was. All his life some cheat had been dealing him the wrong cards. Attributing to Anna every vice but stupidity, he liked to use her as a kind of confessor: there was nothing he could tell her of which she might legitimately disapprove. He would say: "I've told Kuhnhardt a lot of lies about Margaret; I suppose that's pretty rotten, but she would do the same for me; and anyway, my idea is not for him to fire her, but maybe transfer her to the Chicago office."

Or, "I was in a bookshop, and a man was standing there and we began talking: a middle-aged man, rather nice, very intelligent. When I went outside he followed, a little ways behind: I crossed the street, he crossed the street, I walked fast, he walked fast. This kept up six or seven blocks, and when I finally figured out what was going on I felt tickled, I felt like kidding him on. So I stopped at the corner and hailed a cab; then I turned around and gave this guy a long, long look, and he came rushing up, all smiles. And I jumped in the cab, and slammed the door and leaned out the window and laughed out loud: the look on his face, it was awful, it was like Christ. I can't forget it. And tell me, Anna, why did I do this crazy thing? It was like paying back all the people who've ever hurt me, but it was something else, too." He would tell Anna these stories, go home and go to sleep. His dreams were clear blue.

Now the problem of love concerned him, mainly because he did not consider it a problem. Nevertheless, he was conscious of being unloved. This knowledge was like an extra heart beating inside him. But there was no one. Anna, perhaps. Did Anna love him? "Oh," said Anna, "when was anything ever what it seemed to be? Now it's a tadpole, now it's a frog. It looks like gold but you put it on your finger and it leaves a green ring. Take my second husband: he looked like a nice guy, and turned out to be just another heel. Look around this very room: why, you couldn't burn incense in that fireplace, and those mirrors, they give space, they tell a lie. Nothing, Walter, is ever what it seems to be. Christmas trees are cellophane, and snow is only soap chips. Flying around inside us is something called the Soul, and when you die you're never dead; yes, and when we're alive we're never alive. And so you want to know if I love you? Don't be dumb, Walter, we're not even friends. . . ."

4

Listen, the fan: turning wheels of whisper: he said you said they said we said round and round fast and slow while time recalled itself in endless chatter. Old broken fan breaking silence: August the third the third the third!

August the third, a Friday, and it was there, right in Winchell's column, his own name: "Big shot Ad exec Walter Ranney and dairy heiress Rosa Cooper are telling intimates to start buying rice." Walter himself had given the item to a friend of a friend of Winchell's. He showed it to the counter boy at the Whelan's where he ate breakfast. "That's me," he said, "I'm the guy," and the look on the boy's face was good for his digestion.

It was late when he reached the office that morning, and as he walked down the aisle of desks a small gratifying flurry among the typists preceded him. No one said anything, however. Around eleven, after a pleasant hour of doing nothing but feel exhilarated, he went to the drugstore downstairs for a cup of coffee. Three men from the office, Jackson, Ritter and Byrd, were there, and when Walter came in, Jackson poked Byrd, and Byrd poked Ritter, and all of them turned around. "Whatcha say, big shot?" said Jackson, a pink man prematurely bald, and the other two laughed. Acting as if he hadn't heard, Walter stepped quickly into a phone booth. "Bastards," he said, pretending to dial a number. And finally, after waiting a long while for them to leave, he made a real call. "Rosa, hello, did I wake you up?"

"No."

"Say, did you see Winchell?"

"Yes."

Walter laughed. "Where do you suppose he gets that stuff?"

Silence.

"What's the matter? You sound kind of funny."

"Do I?"

"Are you mad or something?"

"Just disappointed."

"About what?"

Silence. And then: "It was a cheap thing to do, Walter, pretty cheap."

"I don't know what you mean."

"Good-bye, Walter."

On the way out he paid the cashier for a cup of coffee he'd forgotten to have. There was a barbershop in the building. He said he wanted a shave; no—make it a haircut; no—a manicure; and suddenly, seeing himself in the mirror, where his face reflected as pale almost as the barber's bib, he knew he did not know what he wanted. Rosa had been right, he was cheap. He'd always been willing to confess his faults, for, by admitting them, it was as if he made them no longer to exist. He went back upstairs, and sat at his desk, and felt as though he were bleeding inside, and wished very much to believe in God. A pigeon strutted on the ledge outside his window. For some time he watched the shimmering sunlit feathers, the wobbly sedateness of its movements; then, before realizing it, he'd picked up and thrown a glass paperweight: the pigeon climbed calmly upward, the paperweight careened like a giant raindrop: suppose, he thought, listening for a faraway scream, suppose it hits someone, kills them? But there was nothing. Only the ticking fingers of typists, a knocking at the door! "Hey, Ranney, K.K. wants to see you."

"I'm sorry," said Mr. Kuhnhardt, doodling with a gold pen. "And I'll write a letter for you, Walter. Any time."

Now in the elevator the enemy, all submerging with him, crushed Walter between them; Margaret was there wearing a blue hair-ribbon. She looked at him, and her face was different from other faces, not vacant as theirs were, and sterile: here still was compassion. But as she looked at him, she looked through him, too. This is my dream: he must not allow himself to believe otherwise; and yet under his own arm he carried the dream's contradiction, a manila envelope stuffed with all the personals saved from his desk. When the elevator emptied into the lobby, he knew he must speak with Margaret, ask her to forgive him, beg her protection, but she was slipping swiftly toward an exit, losing herself among the enemy. I love you, he said, running after her, I love you, he said, saying nothing.

"Margaret! Margaret!"

She turned around. The blue hair-ribbon matched her eyes, and her eyes, gazing up at him, softened, became rather friendly. Or pitying.

"Please," he said, "I thought we could have a drink together, go over to Benny's, maybe. We used to like Benny's, remember?"

She shook her head. "I've got a date, and I'm late already."

"Oh."

"Yes—well, I'm late," she said, and began to run. He stood watching as she raced down the street, her ribbon streaming, shining in the darkening summer light. And then she was gone.

His apartment, a one-room walk-up near Gramercy Park, needed an airing, a cleaning, but Walter, after pouring a drink, said to hell with it and stretched out on the couch. What was the use? No matter what you did or how hard you tried, it all came finally to zero; everyday everywhere everyone was being cheated, and who was there to blame? It was strange, though; lying here sipping whiskey in the dusk-graying room, he felt calmer than he had for God knows how long. It was like the time he'd failed algebra and felt so relieved, so free: failure was definite, a certainty, and there is always peace in certainties. Now he would leave New York, take a vacation trip; he had a few hundred dollars, enough to last until fall.

And, wondering where he should go, he all at once saw, as if a film had commenced running in his head, silk caps, cherry-colored and lemon, and little wise-faced men wearing exquisite polka-dot shirts. Closing his eyes, he was suddenly five years old, and it was delicious remembering the cheers, the hot dogs, his father's big pair of binoculars. Saratoga! Shadows masked his face in the sinking light. He turned on a lamp, fixed another drink, put a rumba record on the phonograph, and began to dance, the soles of his shoes whispering on the carpet: he'd often thought that with a little training he could've been a professional.

Just as the music ended, the telephone rang. He simply stood there, afraid somehow to answer, and the lamplight, the furniture, everything in the room went quite dead. When at last he thought it had stopped, it commenced again; louder, it seemed, and more insistent. He tripped over a footstool, picked up the receiver, dropped and recovered it, said: "Yes?"

Long-distance: a call from some town in Pennsylvania, the name of which he didn't catch. Following a series of spasmic rattlings, a voice, dry and sexless and altogether unlike any he'd ever heard before, came through: "Hello, Walter."

"Who is this?"

No answer from the other end, only a sound of strong orderly breathing; the connection was so good it seemed as though whoever it was was standing beside him with lips pressed against his ear. "I don't like jokes. Who is this?"

"Oh, you know me, Walter. You've known me a long time." A click, and nothing.

5

It was night and raining when the train reached Saratoga. He'd slept most of the trip, sweating in the hot dampness of the car, and dreamed of an old castle where only old turkeys lived, and dreamed a dream involving his father, Kurt Kuhnhardt, someone no-faced, Margaret and Rosa, Anna Stimson and a queer fat lady with diamond eyes. He was standing on a long, deserted street; except for an approaching procession of slow, black, funeral-like cars there was no sign of life. Still, he knew, eyes unseen observed his nakedness from every window, and he hailed frantically the first of the limousines; it stopped and a man, his father, invitingly held open the door. Daddy, he yelled, running forward, and the door slammed shut, mashing off his fingers, and his father, with a great belly laugh, leaned out the window to toss an enormous wreath of roses. In the second car was Margaret, in the third the lady with the diamond eyes (wasn't this Miss Casey, his old algebra teacher?), in the fourth Mr. Kuhnhardt and a new protégé, the no-faced creature. Each door opened, each closed, all laughed, all threw roses. The procession rolled smoothly away down the silent street. And with a terrible scream Walter fell among the mountain of roses: thorns tore wounds, and a sudden rain, a gray cloudburst, shattered the blooms, and washed pale blood bleeding over the leaves.

By the fixed stare of a woman sitting opposite, he realized at once he'd yelled aloud in his sleep. He smiled at her sheepishly, and she looked away with, he imagined, some embarrassment. She was a cripple; on her left foot she wore a giant shoe. Later, in the Saratoga station, he helped with her luggage, and they shared a taxi; there was no conversation: each sat in his corner looking at the rain, the blurred lights. In New York a few hours before, he'd withdrawn from the bank all his savings, locked the door of his apartment, and left no messages; furthermore, there was in this town not a soul who knew him. It was a good feeling.

The hotel was filled: not to mention the racing crowd, there was, the desk clerk told him, a medical convention. No, sorry, he didn't know of a room anywhere. Maybe tomorrow.

So Walter found the bar. As long as he was going to stay up all night, he might as well do it drunk. The bar, very large, very hot and noisy, was brilliant with summer-season grotesques: sagging silver-fox ladies, and little stunted jockeys, and pale loud-voiced men wearing cheap fantastic checks. After a couple of drinks, though, the noise seemed faraway. Then, glancing around, he saw the cripple. She was alone at a table, where she sat primly sipping a crème de menthe. They exchanged a smile. Rising, Walter went to join her. "It's not like we were strangers," she said, as he sat down. "Here for the races, I suppose?"

"No," he said, "just a rest. And you?"

She pursed her lips. "Maybe you noticed I've got a clubfoot. Oh, sure now, don't look surprised: you noticed, everybody does. Well, see," she said, twisting the straw in her glass, "see, my doctor's going to give a talk at this convention, going to talk about me and my foot on account of I'm pretty special. Gee, I'm scared. I mean I'm going to have to show off my foot."

Walter said he was sorry, and she said, oh, there was nothing to be sorry about; after all, she was getting a little vacation out of it, wasn't she? "And I haven't been out of the city in six years. It was six years ago I spent a week at the Bear Mountain Inn." Her cheeks were red, rather mottled, and her eyes, set too closely together, were lavender-colored, intense: they seemed never to blink. She wore a gold band on her wedding finger; play-acting, to be sure: it would not have fooled anybody.

"I'm a domestic," she said, answering a question. "And there's nothing wrong with that. It's honest and I like it. The people I work for have the cutest kid, Ronnie. I'm better to him than his mother, and he loves me more; he's told me so. That one, she stays drunk all the time."

It was depressing to listen to, but Walter, afraid suddenly to be alone, stayed and drank and talked in the way he'd once talked to Anna Stimson. Shh! she said at one point, for his voice had risen too high, and a good many people were staring. Walter said the hell with them, he didn't care; it was as if his brain were made of glass, and all the whiskey he'd drunk had turned into a hammer; he could feel the shattered pieces rattling in his head, distorting focus, falsifying shape; the cripple, for instance, seemed not one person, but several: Irving, his mother, a man named Bonaparte, Margaret, all those and others: more and more he came to understand experience is a circle of which no moment can be isolated, forgotten.

6

The bar was closing. They went Dutch on the check and, while waiting for change, neither spoke. Watching him with her unblinking lavender eyes, she seemed quite controlled, but there was going on inside, he could tell, some subtle agitation. When the waiter returned they divided the change, and she said: "If you want to, you can come to my room." A rashlike blush covered her face. "I mean, you said you didn't have any place to sleep. . . ." Walter reached out and took her hand: the smile she gave him was touchingly shy.

Reeking with dime-store perfume, she came out of the bathroom wearing only a sleazy flesh-colored kimono, and the monstrous black shoe. It was then that he realized he could never go through with it. And he'd never felt so sorry for himself: not even Anna Stimson would ever have forgiven him this. "Don't look," she said, and there was a trembling in her voice, "I'm funny about anybody seeing my foot."

He turned to the window, where pressing elm leaves rustled in the rain, and lightning, too far off for sound, winked whitely. "All right," she said. Walter did not move.

"All right," she repeated anxiously. "Shall I put out the light? I mean, maybe you like to get ready—in the dark."

He came to the edge of the bed, and, bending down, kissed her cheek. "I think you're so very sweet, but . . ."

The telephone interrupted. She looked at him dumbly. "Jesus God," she said, and covered the mouthpiece with her hand, "it's long-distance! I'll bet it's about Ronnie! I'll bet he's sick, or—hello—what?—Ranney? Gee, no. You've got the wrong . . ."

"Wait," said Walter, taking the receiver. "This is me, this is Walter Ranney."

"Hello, Walter."

The voice, dull and sexless and remote, went straight to the pit of his stomach. The room seemed to seesaw, to buckle. A mustache of sweat sprouted on his upper lip. "Who is this?" he said so slowly the words did not connect coherently.

"Oh, you know me, Walter. You've known me a long time." Then silence: whoever it was had hung up.

"Gee," said the woman, "now how do you suppose they knew you were in my room? I mean—say, was it bad news? You look kind of . . ."

Walter fell across her, clutching her to him, pressing his wet cheek against hers. "Hold me," he said, discovering he could still cry. "Hold me, please."

"Poor little boy," she said, patting his back. "My poor little boy: we're awfully alone in this world, aren't we?" And presently he went to sleep in her arms.

But he had not slept since, nor could he now, not even listening to the lazy lull of the fan; in its turning he could hear train wheels: Saratoga to New York, New York to New Orleans. And New Orleans he'd chosen for no special reason, except that it was a town of strangers, and a long way off. Four spinning fan blades, wheels and voices, round and round; and after all, as he saw it now, there was to this network of malice no ending, none whatever.

Water flushed down wall pipes, steps passed overhead, keys jangled in the hall, a news commentator rumbled somewhere beyond, next door a little girl said, why? Why? WHY? Yet in the room there was a sense of silence. His feet shining in the transom-light looked like amputated stone: the gleaming toenails were ten small mirrors, all reflecting greenly. Sitting up, he rubbed sweat off with a towel; now more than anything the heat frightened him, for it made him know tangibly his own helplessness. He threw the towel across the room, where, landing on a lampshade, it swung back and forth. At this moment the telephone rang. And rang. And it was ringing so loud he was sure all the hotel could hear. An army would be pounding at his door. So he pushed his face into the pillow, covered his ears with his hands, and thought: Think of nothing things, think of wind.

Master
Misery

(1949)

Her high heels, clacking across
the marble foyer, made her think of ice
cubes rattling in a glass, and the flowers, those autumn chrysanthemums
in the urn at the entrance, if touched they would shatter, splinter, she was
sure, into frozen dust; yet the house was warm, even somewhat overheated,
but cold, and Sylvia shivered, but cold, like the snowy swollen wastes of
the secretary's face: Miss Mozart, who dressed all in white, as though she
were a nurse. Perhaps she really was; that, of course, could be the answer.
Mr. Revercomb, you are mad, and this is your nurse; she thought about
it for a moment: well, no. And now the butler brought her scarf. His beauty
touched her: slender, so gentle, a Negro with freckled skin and reddish,
unreflecting eyes. As he opened the door, Miss Mozart appeared, her
starched uniform rustling dryly in the hall. "We hope you will return,"
she said, and handed Sylvia a sealed envelope. "Mrs. Revercomb was most
particularly pleased."

Outside, dusk was falling like blue flakes, and Sylvia walked crosstown
along the November streets until she reached the lonely upper reaches of
Fifth Avenue. It occurred to her then that she might walk home through
the park: an act of defiance almost, for Henry and Estelle, always insistent
upon their city wisdom, had said over and again, Sylvia, you have no idea
how dangerous it is, walking in the park after dark; look what happened
to Myrtle Calisher. This isn't Easton, honey. That was the other thing they

said. And said. God, she was sick of it. Still, and aside from a few of the other typists at SnugFare, an underwear company for which she worked, who else in New York did she know? Oh, it would be all right if only she did not have to live with them, if she could afford somewhere a small room of her own; but there in that chintz-cramped apartment she sometimes felt she would choke them both. And why did she come to New York? For whatever reason, and it was indeed becoming vague, a principal cause of leaving Easton had been to rid herself of Henry and Estelle; or rather, their counterparts, though in point of fact Estelle was actually from Easton, a town north of Cincinnati. She and Sylvia had grown up together. The real trouble with Henry and Estelle was that they were so excruciatingly married. Nambypamby, bootsytotsy, and everything had a name: the telephone was Tinkling Tillie, the sofa, Our Nelle, the bed, Big Bear; yes, and what about those His-Her towels, those He-She pillows? Enough to drive you loony. "Loony!" she said aloud, the quiet park erasing her voice. It was lovely now, and she was right to have walked here, with wind moving through the leaves, and globe lamps, freshly aglow, kindling the chalk drawings of children, pink birds, blue arrows, green hearts. But suddenly, like a pair of obscene words, there appeared on the path two boys: pimple-faced, grinning, they loomed in the dusk like menacing flames, and Sylvia, passing them, felt a burning all through her, quite as though she'd brushed fire. They turned and followed her past a deserted playground, one of them bump-bumping a stick along an iron fence, the other whistling: these sounds accumulated around her like the gathering roar of an oncoming engine, and when one of the boys, with a laugh, called, "Hey, whatsa hurry?" her mouth twisted for breath. Don't, she thought, thinking to throw down her purse and run. At that moment, a man walking a dog came up a sidepath, and she followed at his heels to the exit. Wouldn't they feel gratified, Henry and Estelle, wouldn't they we-told-you-so if she were to tell them? and, what is more, Estelle would write it home and the next thing you knew it would be all over Easton that she'd been raped in Central Park. She spent the rest of the way home despising New York: anonymity, its virtuous terror; and the squeaking drainpipe, all-night light, ceaseless footfall, subway corridor, numbered door (3C).

"Shh, honey," Estelle said, sidling out of the kitchen, "Bootsy's doing his homework." Sure enough, Henry, a law student at Columbia, was hunched over his books in the living room, and Sylvia, at Estelle's request, took off her shoes before tiptoeing through. Once inside her room, she threw herself on the bed and put her hands over her eyes. Had today really happened? Miss Mozart and Mr. Revercomb, were they really there in the tall house on Seventy-eighth Street?

"So, honey, what happened today?" Estelle had entered without knocking.

Sylvia sat up on her elbow. "Nothing. Except that I typed ninety-seven letters."

"About what, honey?" asked Estelle, using Sylvia's hairbrush.

"Oh, hell, what do you suppose? SnugFare, the shorts that safely support our leaders of Science and Industry."

"Gee, honey, don't sound so cross. I don't know what's wrong with you sometimes. You sound so cross. Ouch! Why don't you get a new brush? This one's just knotted with hair. . . ."

"Mostly yours."

"What did you say?"

"Skip it."

"Oh, I thought you said something. Anyway, like I was saying, I wish you didn't have to go to that office and come home every day feeling cross and out of sorts. Personally, and I said this to Bootsy just last night and he agreed with me one hundred percent, I said, Bootsy, I think Sylvia ought to get married: a girl high-strung like that needs her tensions relaxed. There's no earthly reason why you shouldn't. I mean maybe you're not pretty in the ordinary sense, but you have beautiful eyes, and an intelligent, really sincere look. In fact you're the sort of girl any professional man would be lucky to get. And I should think you would want to . . . Look what a different person I am since I married Henry. Doesn't it make you lonesome seeing how happy we are? I'm here to tell you, honey, that there is nothing like lying in bed at night with a man's arms around you and . . ."

"Estelle! For Christ's sake!" Sylvia sat bolt upright in bed, anger on her cheeks like rouge. But after a moment she bit her lip and lowered her eyelids. "I'm sorry," she said, "I didn't mean to shout. Only I wish you wouldn't talk like that."

"It's all right," said Estelle, smiling in a dumb, puzzled way. Then she went over and gave Sylvia a kiss. "I understand, honey. It's just that you're plain worn out. And I'll bet you haven't had anything to eat either. Come on in the kitchen and I'll scramble you some eggs."

When Estelle set the eggs before her, Sylvia felt quite ashamed; after all, Estelle was trying to be nice; and so then, as though to make it all up, she said: "Something did happen today."

Estelle sat down across from her with a cup of coffee, and Sylvia went on: "I don't know how to tell about it. It's so odd. But—well, I had lunch at the Automat today, and I had to share the table with these three men. I might as well have been invisible because they talked about the most personal things. One of the men said his girl friend was going to have a baby and he didn't know where he was going to get the money to do anything about it. So one of the other men asked him why didn't he sell something. He said he didn't have anything to sell. Whereupon the third man (he was rather delicate and didn't look as if he belonged with the others) said yes, there was something he could sell: *dreams.* Even I laughed, but the man shook his head and said very seriously: no, it was perfectly true, his wife's aunt, Miss Mozart, worked for a rich man who bought dreams, regular night-time dreams—from anybody. And he wrote down the man's name and address and gave it to his friend; but the man simply left it lying on the table. It was too crazy for him, he said."

"Me, too," Estelle put in a little righteously.

"I don't know," said Sylvia, lighting a cigarette. "But I couldn't get it out of my head. The name written on the paper was A. F. Revercomb and the address was on East Seventy-eighth Street. I only glanced at it for a moment, but it was . . . I don't know, I couldn't seem to forget it. It was beginning to give me a headache. So I left the office early . . ."

Slowly and with emphasis, Estelle put down her coffee cup. "Honey, listen, you don't mean you went to see him, this Revercomb nut?"

"I didn't mean to," she said, immediately embarrassed. To try and tell about it she now realized was a mistake. Estelle had no imagination, she would never understand. So her eyes narrowed, the way they always did when she composed a lie. "And, as a matter of fact, I didn't," she said flatly. "I started to; but then I realized how silly it was, and went for a walk instead."

"That was sensible of you," said Estelle as she began stacking dishes in the kitchen sink. "Imagine what might have happened. Buying dreams! Whoever heard! Uh uh, honey, this sure isn't Easton."

Before retiring, Sylvia took a Seconal, something she seldom did; but she knew otherwise she would never rest, not with her mind so nimble and somersaulting; then, too, she felt a curious sadness, a sense of loss, as though she'd been the victim of some real or even moral theft, as though, in fact, the boys encountered in the park had snatched (abruptly she switched on the light) her purse. The envelope Miss Mozart had handed her: it was in the purse, and until now she had forgotten it. She tore it open. Inside there was a blue note folded around a bill; on the note there was written: *In payment of one dream,* $5. And now she believed it; it was true, and she had sold Mr. Revercomb a dream. Could it be really so simple as that? She laughed a little as she turned off the light again. If she were to sell a dream only twice a week, think of what she could do: a place somewhere all her own, she thought, deepening toward sleep; ease, like firelight, wavered over her, and there came the moment of twilit lantern slides, deeply deeper. His lips, his arms: telescoped, descending; and distastefully she kicked away the blanket. Were these cold man-arms the arms Estelle had spoken of? Mr. Revercomb's lips brushed her ear as he leaned far into her sleep. Tell me? he whispered.

It was a week before she saw him again, a Sunday afternoon in early

December. She'd left the apartment intending to see a movie, but somehow, and as though it had happened without her knowledge, she found herself on Madison Avenue, two blocks from Mr. Revercomb's. It was a cold, silver-skied day, with winds sharp and catching as hollyhock; in store windows icicles of Christmas tinsel twinkled amid mounds of sequined snow: all to Sylvia's distress, for she hated holidays, those times when one is most alone. In one window she saw a spectacle which made her stop still. It was a life-sized, mechanical Santa Claus; slapping his stomach, he rocked back and forth in a frenzy of electrical mirth. You could hear beyond the thick glass his squeaky uproarious laughter. The longer she watched the more evil he seemed, until, finally, with a shudder, she turned and made her way into the street of Mr. Revercomb's house. It was, from the outside, an ordinary town house, perhaps a trifle less polished, less imposing than some others, but relatively grand all the same. Winter-withered ivy writhed about the leaded windowpanes and trailed in octopus ropes over the door; at the sides of the door were two small stone lions with blind, chipped eyes. Sylvia took a breath, then rang the bell. Mr. Revercomb's pale and charming Negro recognized her with a courteous smile.

On the previous visit, the parlor in which she had awaited her audience with Mr. Revercomb had been empty except for herself. This time there were others present, women of several appearances, and an excessively nervous, gnat-eyed young man. Had this group been what it resembled, namely, patients in a doctor's anteroom, he would have seemed either an expectant father or a victim of St. Vitus. Sylvia was seated next to him, and his fidgety eyes unbuttoned her rapidly: whatever he saw apparently intrigued him very little, and Sylvia was grateful when he went back to his twitchy preoccupations. Gradually, though, she became conscious of how interested in her the assemblage seemed; in the dim, doubtful light of the plant-filled room their gazes were more rigid than the chairs upon which they sat; one woman was particularly relentless. Ordinarily, her face would have had a soft commonplace sweetness, but now, watching Sylvia, it was ugly with distrust, jealousy. As though trying to tame some creature which might suddenly spring full-fanged, she sat stroking a flea-bitten neck fur, her stare continuing its assault until the earthquake footstep of Miss Mozart was heard in the hall. Immediately, and like frightened students, the group, separating into their individual identities, came to attention. "You, Mr. Pocker," accused Miss Mozart, "you're next!" and Mr. Pocker, wringing his hands, jittering his eyes, followed after her. In the dusk-room the gathering settled again like sun motes.

It began then to rain; melting window reflections quivered on the walls, and Mr. Revercomb's young butler, seeping through the room, stirred a fire in the grate, set tea things upon a table. Sylvia, nearest the fire, felt drowsy with warmth and the noise of rain; her head tilted sideways, she closed her eyes, neither asleep nor really awake. For a long while only the crystal swingings of a clock scratched the polished silence of Mr. Revercomb's house. And then, abruptly, there was an enormous commotion in the hall, capsizing the room into a fury of sound: a bull-deep voice, vulgar as red, roared out: "Stop Oreilly? The ballet butler and who else?" The owner of this voice, a tub-shaped, brick-colored little man, shoved his way to the parlor threshold, where he stood drunkenly seesawing from foot to foot. "Well, well, well," he said, his gin-hoarse voice descending the scale, "and all these ladies before me? But Oreilly is a gentleman, Oreilly waits his turn."

"Not here, he doesn't," said Miss Mozart, stealing up behind him and seizing him sternly by the collar. His face went even redder and his eyes bubbled out: "You're choking me," he gasped, but Miss Mozart, whose green-pale hands were as strong as oak roots, jerked his tie still tighter, and propelled him toward the door, which presently slammed with shattering effect: a teacup tinkled, and dry dahlia leaves tumbled from their heights. The lady with the fur slipped an aspirin into her mouth. "Dis*gusting,*" she said, and the others, all except Sylvia, laughed delicately, admiringly, as Miss Mozart strode past dusting her hands.

It was raining thick and darkly when Sylvia left Mr. Revercomb's. She looked around the desolate street for a taxi; there was nothing, however, and no one; yes, someone, the drunk man who had caused the disturbance. Like a lonely city child, he was leaning against a parked car and bouncing a rubber ball up and down. "Lookit, kid," he said to Sylvia, "lookit, I just found this ball. Do you suppose that means good luck?" Sylvia smiled at him; for all his bravado, she thought him rather harmless, and there was a quality in his face, some grinning sadness suggesting a clown minus make-up. Juggling his ball, he skipped along after her as she headed toward Madison Avenue. "I'll bet I made a fool of myself in there," he said. "When I do things like that I just want to sit down and cry." Standing so long in the rain seemed to have sobered him considerably. "But she ought not to have choked me that way; damn, she's too rough. I've known some rough women: my sister Berenice could brand the wildest bull; but that other one, she's the roughest of the lot. Mark Oreilly's word, she's going to end up in the electric chair," he said, and smacked his lips. "They've got no cause to treat me like that. It's every bit his fault anyhow. I didn't have an awful lot to begin with, but then he took it every bit, and now I've got *niente,* kid, *niente.*"

"That's too bad," said Sylvia, though she did not know what she was being sympathetic about. "Are you a clown, Mr. Oreilly?"

"Was," he said.

By this time they had reached the avenue, but Sylvia did not even look for a taxi; she wanted to walk on in the rain with the man who had been a clown. "When I was a little girl I only liked clown dolls," she told him. "My room at home was like a circus."

"I've been other things besides a clown. I have sold insurance, too."

"Oh?" said Sylvia, disappointed. "And what do you do now?"

Oreilly chuckled and threw his ball especially high; after the catch his head still remained tilted upward. "I watch the sky," he said. "There I am with my suitcase traveling through the blue. It's where you travel when you've got no place else to go. But what do I do on this planet? I have stolen, begged, and sold my dreams—all for purposes of whiskey. A man cannot travel in the blue without a bottle. Which brings us to a point: how'd you take it, baby, if I asked for the loan of a dollar?"

"I'd take it fine," Sylvia replied, and paused, uncertain of what she'd say next. They wandered along so slowly, the stiff rain enclosing them like an insulating pressure; it was as though she were walking with a childhood doll, one grown miraculous and capable; she reached and held his hand: dear clown traveling in the blue. "But I haven't got a dollar. All I've got is seventy cents."

"No hard feelings," said Oreilly. "But honest, is that the kind of money he's paying nowadays?"

Sylvia knew whom he meant. "No, no—as a matter of fact, I didn't sell him a dream." She made no attempt to explain; she didn't understand it herself. Confronting the graying invisibility of Mr. Revercomb (impeccable, exact as a scale, surrounded in a cologne of clinical odors; flat gray eyes planted like seed in the anonymity of his face and sealed within steel-dull lenses), she could not remember a dream, and so she told of two thieves who had chased her through the park and in and out among the swings of a playground. "Stop, he said for me to stop; there are dreams and dreams, he said, but that is not a real one, that is one you are making up. Now how do you suppose he knew that? So I told him another dream; it was about him, of how he held me in the night with balloons rising and moons falling all around. He said he was not interested in dreams concerning himself." Miss Mozart, who transcribed the dreams in shorthand, was told to call the next person. "I don't think I will go back there again," she said.

"You will," said Oreilly. "Look at me, even I go back, and he has long since finished with me, Master Misery."

"Master Misery? Why do you call him that?"

They had reached the corner where the maniacal Santa Claus rocked and bellowed. His laughter echoed in the rainy squeaking street, and a shadow of him swayed in the rainbow lights of the pavement. Oreilly, turning his back upon the Santa Claus, smiled and said: "I call him Master Misery on account of that's who he is. Master Misery. Only maybe you call him something else; anyway, he is the same fellow, and you must've known him. All mothers tell their kids about him: he lives in hollows of trees, he comes down chimneys late at night, he lurks in graveyards and you can hear his step in the attic. The sonofabitch, he is a thief and a threat: he will take everything you have and end by leaving you nothing, not even a dream. Boo!" he shouted, and laughed louder than Santa Claus. "Now do you know who he is?"

Sylvia nodded. "I know who he is. My family called him something else. But I can't remember what. It was long ago."

"But you remember him?"

"Yes, I remember him."

"Then call him Master Misery," he said, and, bouncing his ball, walked away from her. "Master Misery," his voice trailed to a mere moth of sound, "Mas-ter Mis-er-y . . ."

It was hard to look at Estelle, for she was in front of a window, and the window was filled with windy sun, which hurt Sylvia's eyes, and the glass rattled, which hurt her head. Also, Estelle was lecturing. Her nasal voice sounded as though her throat were a depository of rusty razor blades. "I wish you could see yourself," she was saying. Or was that something she'd said a long while back? Never mind. "I don't know what's happened to you: I'll bet you don't weigh a hundred pounds, I can see every bone and vein, and your hair! You look like a poodle."

Sylvia passed a hand over her forehead. "What time is it, Estelle?"

"It's four," she said, interrupting herself long enough to look at her watch. "But where is your watch?"

"I sold it," said Sylvia, too tired to lie. It did not matter. She had sold so many things, including her beaver coat and gold mesh evening bag.

Estelle shook her head. "I give up, honey, I plain give up. And that was the watch your mother gave you for graduation. It's a shame," she said, and made an old-maid noise with her mouth, "a pity and a shame. I'll never understand why you left us. That is your business, I'm sure; only how could you have left us for this . . . this . . . ?"

"Dump," supplied Sylvia, using the word advisedly. It was a furnished room in the East Sixties between Second and Third avenues. Large enough for a daybed and a splintery old bureau with a mirror like a cataracted eye, it had one window, which looked out on a vast vacant lot (you could hear the tough afternoon voices of desperate running boys), and in the distance, like an exclamation point for the skyline, there was the black smokestack of a factory. This smokestack occurred frequently in her dreams; it never failed to arouse Miss Mozart: "Phallic, phallic," she would mutter, glancing up from her shorthand. The floor of the room was a garbage pail of books begun but never finished, antique newspapers, even orange hulls, fruit cores, underwear, a spilled powder box.

Estelle kicked her way through this trash, and sat down on the daybed. "Honey, you don't know, but I've been worried crazy. I mean I've got pride and all that and if you don't like me, well okay; but you've got no right to stay away like this and not let me hear from you in over a month. So today I said to Bootsy, Bootsy, I've got a feeling something terrible has happened to Sylvia. You can imagine how I felt when I called your office and they told me you hadn't worked there for the last four weeks. What happened, were you fired?"

"Yes, I was fired." Sylvia began to sit up. "Please, Estelle—I've got to get ready; I've got an appointment."

"Be still. You're not going anywhere till I know what's wrong. The landlady downstairs told me you were found sleepwalking. . . ."

"What do you mean talking to her? Why are you spying on me?"

Estelle's eyes puckered, as though she were going to cry. She put her hand over Sylvia's and petted it gently. "Tell me, honey, is it because of a man?"

"It's because of a man, yes," said Sylvia, laughter at the edge of her voice.

"You should have come to me before," Estelle sighed. "I know about men. That is nothing for you to be ashamed of. A man can have a way with a woman that kind of makes her forget everything else. If Henry wasn't the fine upstanding potential lawyer that he is, why, I would still love him, and do things for him that before I knew what it was like to be with a man would have seemed shocking and horrible. But honey, this fellow you've mixed up with, he's taking advantage of you."

"It's not that kind of relationship," said Sylvia, getting up and locating a pair of stockings in the furor of her bureau drawers. "It hasn't got anything to do with love. Forget about it. In fact, go home and forget about me altogether."

Estelle looked at her narrowly. "You scare me, Sylvia; you really scare me." Sylvia laughed and went on getting dressed. "Do you remember a long time ago when I said you ought to get married?"

"Uh huh. And now you listen." Sylvia turned around; there was a row of hairpins spaced across her mouth; she extracted them one at a time all the while she talked. "You talk about getting married as though it were the answer absolute; very well, up to a point I agree. Sure, I want to be loved; who the hell doesn't? But even if I was willing to compromise, where is the man I'm going to marry? Believe me, he must've fallen down a man-hole. I mean it seriously when I say there are no men in New York—and even if there were, how do you meet them? Every man I ever met here who seemed the slightest bit attractive was either married, too poor to get married, or queer. And anyway, this is no place to fall in love; this is where you ought to come when you want to get over being in love. Sure, I suppose I could marry somebody; but do I want that? Do I?"

Estelle shrugged. "Then what do you want?"

"More than is coming to me." She poked the last hairpin into place, and smoothed her eyebrows before the mirror. "I have an appointment, Estelle, and it is time for you to go now."

"I can't leave you like this," said Estelle, her hand waving helplessly around the room. "Sylvia, you were my childhood friend."

"That is just the point: we're not children anymore; at least, I'm not. No, I want you to go home, and I don't want you to come here again. I just want you to forget about me."

Estelle fluttered at her eyes with a handkerchief, and by the time she reached the door she was weeping quite loudly. Sylvia could not afford remorse: having been mean, there was nothing to be but meaner. "Go on," she said, following Estelle into the hall, "and write home any damn non-sense about me you want to!" Letting out a wail that brought other roomers to their doors, Estelle fled down the stairs.

After this Sylvia went back into her room and sucked a piece of sugar to take the sour taste out of her mouth: it was her grandmother's remedy for bad tempers. Then she got down on her knees and pulled from under the bed a cigar box she kept hidden there. When you opened the box it played a homemade and somewhat disorganized version of "Oh, How I Hate to Get Up in the Morning." Her brother had made the music box and given it to her on her fourteenth birthday. Eating the sugar, she'd thought of her grandmother, and hearing the tune, she thought of her brother; the rooms of the house where they had lived rotated before her, all dark and she like a light moving among them: up the stairs, down, out and through, spring sweet and lilac shadows in the air and the creaking of a porch swing. All gone, she thought, calling their names, and now I am absolutely alone. The music stopped. But it went on in her head; she could hear it bugling above the child-cries of the vacant lot. And it interfered with her reading. She was reading a little diarylike book she kept inside the box. In this book she wrote down the essentials of her dreams; they were endless now, and it was so hard to remember. Today she would tell Mr. Revercomb about the three blind children. He would like that. The prices he paid varied, and she was sure this was at least a ten-dollar dream. The cigar-box anthem followed her down the stairs and through the streets and she longed for it to go away.

In the store where Santa Claus had been there was a new and equally unnerving exhibit. Even when she was late to Mr. Revercomb's, as now, Sylvia was compelled to pause by the window. A plaster girl with intense glass eyes sat astride a bicycle pedaling at the maddest pace; though its wheel spokes spun hypnotically, the bicycle of course never budged: all that effort and the poor girl going nowhere. It was a pitifully human situation, and one that Sylvia could so exactly identify with herself that she always felt a real pang. The music box rewound in her head: the tune, her brother, the house, a high-school dance, the house, the tune! Couldn't Mr. Revercomb hear it? His penetrating gaze carried such dull suspicion. But he seemed pleased with her dream, and, when she left, Miss Mozart gave her an envelope containing ten dollars.

"I had a ten-dollar dream," she told Oreilly, and Oreilly, rubbing his hands together, said, "Fine! Fine! But that's just my luck, baby—you should've got here sooner 'cause I went and did a terrible thing. I walked into a liquor store up the street, snatched a quart and ran." Sylvia didn't believe him until he produced from his pinned-together overcoat a bottle of bourbon, already half gone. "You're going to get in trouble some day," she said, "and then what would happen to me? I don't know what I would do without you." Oreilly laughed and poured a shot of the whiskey into a water glass. They were sitting in an all-night cafeteria, a great glaring food depot alive with blue mirrors and raw murals. Although to Sylvia it seemed a sordid place, they met there frequently for dinner; but even if she could have afforded it, she did not know where else they could go, for together they presented a curious aspect: a young girl and a doddering, drunken man. Even here people often stared at them; if they stared long enough, Oreilly would stiffen with dignity and say: "Hello, hot lips, I remember you from way back. Still working in the men's room?" But usually they were left to themselves, and sometimes they would sit talking until two and three in the morning.

"It's a good thing the rest of Master Misery's crowd don't know he gave you that ten bucks. One of them would say you stole the dream. I had that happen once. Eaten up, all of 'em, never saw such a bunch of sharks, worse than actors or clowns or businessmen. Crazy, if you think about it: you worry whether you're going to go to sleep, if you're going to have a dream, if you're going to remember the dream. Round and round. So you get a couple of bucks, so you rush to the nearest liquor store—or the nearest sleeping-pill machine. And first thing you know, you're roaming your way up outhouse alley. Why, baby, you know what it's like? It's just like life."

"No, Oreilly, that's what it isn't like. It hasn't anything to do with life. It has more to do with being dead. I feel as though everything were being taken from me, as though some thief were stealing me down to the bone. Oreilly, I tell you I haven't an ambition, and there used to be so much. I don't understand it and I don't know what to do."

He grinned. "And you say it isn't like life? Who understands life and who knows what to do?"

"Be serious," she said. "Be serious and put away that whiskey and eat your soup before it gets stone cold." She lighted a cigarette, and the smoke, smarting her eyes, intensified her frown. "If only I knew what he wanted with those dreams, all typed and filed. What does he do with them? You're right when you say he is Master Misery. . . . He can't be simply some silly quack; it can't be so meaningless as that. But why does he want dreams? Help me, Oreilly, think, think: what does it mean?"

Squinting one eye, Oreilly poured himself another drink; the clownlike twist of his mouth hardened into a line of scholarly straightness. "That is a million-dollar question, kid. Why don't you ask something easy, like how to cure the common cold? Yes, kid, what does it mean? I have thought about it a good deal. I have thought about it in the process of making love to a woman, and I have thought about it in the middle of a poker game." He tossed the drink down his throat and shuddered. "Now a sound can start a dream; the noise of one car passing in the night can drop a hundred sleepers into the deep parts of themselves. It's funny to think of that one car racing through the dark, trailing so many dreams. Sex, a sudden change of light, a pickle, these are little keys that can open up our insides, too. But most dreams begin because there are furies inside of us that blow open all the doors. I don't believe in Jesus Christ, but I do believe in people's souls; and I figure it this way, baby: dreams are the mind of the soul and the secret truth about us. Now Master Misery, maybe he hasn't got a soul, so bit by bit he borrows yours, steals it like he would steal your dolls or the chicken wing off your plate. Hundreds of souls have passed through him and gone into a filing case."

"Oreilly, be serious," she said again, annoyed because she thought he was making more jokes. "And look, your soup is . . ." She stopped abruptly, startled by Oreilly's peculiar expression. He was looking toward the entrance. Three men were there, two policemen and a civilian wearing a clerk's cloth jacket. The clerk was pointing toward their table. Oreilly's eyes circled the room with trapped despair; he sighed then, and leaned back in his seat, ostentatiously pouring himself another drink. "Good evening, gentlemen," he said, when the official party confronted him, "will you join us for a drink?"

"You can't arrest him," cried Sylvia, "you can't arrest a clown!" She threw her ten-dollar bill at them, but the policemen did not pay any attention, and she began to pound the table. All the customers in the place were staring, and the manager came running up, wringing his hands. The police said for Oreilly to get to his feet. "Certainly," Oreilly said, "though I do think it shocking you have to trouble yourselves with such petty crimes as mine when everywhere there are master thieves afoot. For instance, this pretty child"—he stepped between the officers and pointed to Sylvia—"she is the recent victim of a major theft: poor baby, she has had her soul stolen."

For two days following Oreilly's arrest Sylvia did not leave her room: sun on the window, then dark. By the third day she had run out of cigarettes, so she ventured as far as the corner delicatessen. She bought a package of cupcakes, a can of sardines, a newspaper and cigarettes. In all this time she'd not eaten and it was a light, delicious, sharpening sensation; but the climb back up the stairs, the relief of closing the door, these so exhausted her she could not quite make the daybed. She slid down to the floor and did not move until it was day again. She thought afterward that she'd been there about twenty minutes. Turning on the radio as loud as it would go, she dragged a chair up to the window and opened the newspaper on her lap: *Lana Denies, Russia Rejects, Miners Conciliate:* of all things this was saddest, that life goes on: if one leaves one's lover, life should stop for him, and if one disappears from the world, then the world should stop, too; and it never did. And that was the real reason for most people getting up in the morning: not because it would matter but because it wouldn't. But if Mr. Revercomb succeeded finally in collecting all the dreams out of every head, perhaps—the idea slipped, became entangled with radio and newspaper. *Falling Temperatures.* A snowstorm moving across Colorado, across the West, falling upon all the small towns, yellowing every light, filling every footfall, falling now and here; but how quickly it had come, the snowstorm: the roofs, the vacant lot, the distance deep in white and deepening, like sheep. She looked at the paper and she looked at the snow. But it must have been snowing all day. It could not have just started. There was no sound of traffic; in the swirling wastes of the vacant lot children circled a bonfire; a car, buried at the curb, winked its headlights: help, help! silent, like the heart's distress. She crumbled a cupcake and sprinkled it on the windowsill: north-birds would come to keep her company. And she left the window open for them; snow-wind scattered flakes that dissolved on the floor like April-fool jewels. *Presents Life Can Be Beautiful:* turn down that radio! The witch of the woods was tapping at her door: Yes, Mrs. Halloran, she said, and turned off the radio altogether. Snow-quiet, sleep-silent, only the fun-fire faraway songsinging of children; and the room was blue with cold, colder than the cold of fairy tales: lie down my heart among the igloo flowers of snow. Mr. Revercomb, why do you wait upon the threshold? Ah, do come inside, it is so cold out there.

But her moment of waking was warm and held. The window was closed, and a man's arms were around her. He was singing to her, his voice gentle but jaunty: *cherryberry, moneyberry, happyberry pie, but the best old pie is a loveberry pie* . . .

"Oreilly, is it—is it really you?"

He squeezed her. "Baby's awake now. And how does she feel?"

"I had thought I was dead," she said, and happiness winged around inside her like a bird lamed but still flying. She tried to hug him and she was too weak. "I love you, Oreilly; you are my only friend and I was so frightened. I thought I would never see you again." She paused, remembering. "But why aren't you in jail?"

Oreilly's face got all tickled and pink. "I was never in jail," he said mysteriously. "But first, let's have something to eat. I brought some things up from the delicatessen this morning."

She had a sudden feeling of floating. "How long have you been here?"

"Since yesterday," he said, fussing around with bundles and paper plates. "You let me in yourself."

"That's impossible. I don't remember it at all."

"I know," he said, leaving it at that. "Here, drink your milk like a good kid and I'll tell you a real wicked story. Oh, it's wild," he promised, slapping his sides gladly and looking more than ever like a clown. "Well, like I said, I never was in jail and this bit of fortune came to me because there I was being hustled down the street by those bindlestiffs when who should I see come swinging along but the gorilla woman: you guessed it, Miss Mozart. Hi, I says to her, off to the barbershop for a shave? It's about time you were put under arrest, she says, and smiles at one of the cops. Do your duty, Officer. Oh, I says to her, I'm not under arrest. Me, I'm just on my way to the station house to give them the lowdown on you, you dirty communist. You can imagine what sort of holler she set up then; she grabbed hold of me and the cops grabbed hold of her. Can't say I didn't warn them: careful, boys, I said, she's got hair on her chest. And she sure did lay about her. So I just sort of walked off down the street. Never have believed in standing around watching fistfights the way people do in this city."

Oreilly stayed with her in the room over the weekend. It was like the most beautiful party Sylvia could remember; she'd never laughed so much, for one thing, and no one, certainly no one in her family, had ever made her feel so loved. Oreilly was a fine cook, and he fixed delicious dishes on the little electric stove; once he scooped snow off the windowsill and made sherbet flavored with strawberry syrup. By Sunday she was strong enough to dance. They turned on the radio and she danced until she fell to her knees, windless and laughing. "I'll never be afraid again," she said. "I hardly know what I was afraid of to begin with."

"The same things you'll be afraid of the next time," Oreilly told her quietly. "That is a quality of Master Misery: no one ever knows what he is—not even children, and they know mostly everything."

Sylvia went to the window; an arctic whiteness lay over the city, but the snow had stopped, and the night sky was as clear as ice: there, riding above the river, she saw the first star of evening. "I see the first star," she said, crossing her fingers.

"And what do you wish when you see the first star?"

"I wish to see another star," she said. "At least that is what I usually wish."

"But tonight?"

She sat down on the floor and leaned her head against his knee. "Tonight I wished that I could have back my dreams."

"Don't we all?" Oreilly said, stroking her hair. "But then what would you do? I mean what would you do if you could have them back?"

Sylvia was silent a moment; when she spoke her eyes were gravely distant. "I would go home," she said slowly. "And that is a terrible decision, for it would mean giving up most of my other dreams. But if Mr. Revercomb would let me have them back, then I would go home tomorrow."

Saying nothing, Oreilly went to the closet and brought back her coat. "But why?" she asked as he helped her on with it. "Never mind," he said, "just do what I tell you. We're going to pay Mr. Revercomb a call, and you're going to ask him to give you back your dreams. It's a chance."

Sylvia balked at the door. "Please, Oreilly, don't make me go. I can't, please, I'm afraid."

"I thought you said you'd never be afraid again."

But once in the street he hurried her so quickly against the wind she did not have time to be frightened. It was Sunday, stores were closed and the traffic lights seemed to wink only for them, for there were no moving cars along the snow-deep avenue. Sylvia even forgot where they were going, and chattered of trivial oddments: right here at this corner is where she'd seen Garbo, and over there, that is where the old woman was run over. Presently, however, she stopped, out of breath and overwhelmed with sudden realization. "I can't, Oreilly," she said, pulling back. "What can I say to him?"

"Make it like a business deal," said Oreilly. "Tell him straight out that you want your dreams, and if he'll give them to you, you'll pay back all the money: on the installment plan, naturally. It's simple enough, kid. Why the hell couldn't he give them back? They are all right there in a filing case."

This speech was somehow convincing and, stamping her frozen feet, Sylvia went ahead with a certain courage. "That's the kid," he said. They separated on Third Avenue, Oreilly being of the opinion that Mr. Revercomb's immediate neighborhood was not for the moment precisely safe. He confined himself in a doorway, now and then lighting a match and singing aloud: *but the best old pie is a whiskeyberry pie!* Like a wolf, a long thin dog came padding over the moon-slats under the elevated, and across the street there were the misty shapes of men ganged around a bar: the idea of maybe cadging a drink in there made him groggy.

Just as he had decided on perhaps trying something of the sort, Sylvia appeared. And she was in his arms before he knew that it was really her. "It can't be so bad, sweetheart," he said softly, holding her as best he could. "Don't cry, baby; it's too cold to cry: you'll chap your face." As she strangled for words, her crying evolved into a tremulous, unnatural laugh. The air was filled with the smoke of her laughter. "Do you know what he said?" she gasped. "Do you know what he said when I asked for my dreams?" Her head fell back, and her laughter rose and carried over the street like an abandoned, wildly colored kite. Oreilly had finally to shake her by the shoulders. "He said—I couldn't have them back because—because he'd used them all up."

She was silent then, her face smoothing into an expressionless calm. She put her arm through Oreilly's, and together they moved down the street; but it was as if they were friends pacing a platform, each waiting for the other's train, and when they reached the corner he cleared his throat and said: "I guess I'd better turn off here. It's as likely a spot as any."

Sylvia held on to his sleeve. "But where will you go, Oreilly?"

"Traveling in the blue," he said, trying a smile that didn't work out very well.

She opened her purse. "A man cannot travel in the blue without a bottle," she said, and kissing him on the cheek, slipped five dollars in his pocket.

"Bless you, baby."

It did not matter that it was the last of her money, that now she would have to walk home, and alone. The pilings of snow were like the white waves of a white sea, and she rode upon them, carried by winds and tides of the moon. I do not know what I want, and perhaps I shall never know, but my only wish from every star will always be another star; and truly I am not afraid, she thought. Two boys came out of a bar and stared at her; in some park some long time ago she'd seen two boys and they might be the same. Truly I am not afraid, she thought, hearing their snowy footsteps following her; and anyway, there was nothing left to steal.

Children on
Their Birthdays

(1949)

YESTERDAY AFTERNOON THE SIX-o'clock bus ran over Miss Bobbit. I'm not sure what there is to be said about it; after all, she was only ten years old, still I know no one of us in this town will forget her. For one thing, nothing she ever did was ordinary, not from the first time that we saw her, and that was a year ago. Miss Bobbit and her mother, they arrived on that same six-o'clock bus, the one that comes through from Mobile. It happened to be my cousin Billy Bob's birthday, and so most of the children in town were here at our house. We were sprawled on the front porch having tutti-frutti and devil cake when the bus stormed around Deadman's Curve. It was the summer that never rained; rusted dryness coated everything; sometimes when a car passed on the road, raised dust would hang in the still air an hour or more. Aunt El said if they didn't pave the highway soon, she was going to move down to the seacoast; but she'd said that for such a long time. Anyway, we were sitting on the porch, tutti-frutti melting on our plates, when suddenly, just as we were wishing that something would happen, something did; for out of the red road dust appeared Miss Bobbit. A wiry little girl in a starched lemon-colored party dress, she sassed along with a grown-up mince, one hand on her hip, the other supporting a spinsterish umbrella. Her mother, lugging two cardboard valises and a wind-up victrola, trailed in the background. She was a gaunt shaggy woman with silent eyes and a hungry smile.

All the children on the porch had grown so still that when a cone of wasps started humming, the girls did not set up their usual holler. Their attention was too fixed upon the approach of Miss Bobbit and her mother, who had by now reached the gate. "Begging your pardon," called Miss Bobbit in a voice that was at once silky and childlike, like a pretty piece of ribbon, and immaculately exact, like a movie star or a schoolmarm, "but might we speak with the grown-up persons of the house?" This, of course, meant Aunt El; and, at least to some degree, myself. But Billy Bob and all the other boys, no one of whom was over thirteen, followed down to the gate after us. From their faces you would have thought they'd never seen a girl before. Certainly not like Miss Bobbit. As Aunt El said, whoever heard tell of a child wearing make-up? Tangee gave her lips an orange glow, her hair, rather like a costume wig, was a mass of rosy curls, and her eyes had a knowing, penciled tilt; even so, she had a skinny dignity, she was a lady, and, what is more, she looked you in the eye with manlike directness. "I'm Miss Lily Jane Bobbit, Miss Bobbit from Memphis, Tennessee," she said solemnly. The boys looked down at their toes, and, on the porch, Cora McCall, whom Billy Bob was courting at the time, led the girls into a fanfare of giggles. "*Country* children," said Miss Bobbit with an understanding smile, and gave her parasol a saucy whirl. "My mother"—and this homely woman allowed an abrupt nod to acknowledge herself—"my mother and I have taken rooms here. Would you be so kind as to point out the house? It belongs to a Mrs. Sawyer." Why, sure, said Aunt El, that's Mrs. Sawyer's, right there across the street. The only boardinghouse around here, it is an old tall dark place with about two dozen lightning rods scattered on the roof: Mrs. Sawyer is scared to death in a thunderstorm.

Coloring like an apple, Billy Bob said, please, ma'am, it being such a hot day and all, wouldn't they rest a spell and have some tutti-frutti? and Aunt El said yes, by all means, but Miss Bobbit shook her head. "Very fattening, tutti-frutti; but *merci* you kindly," and they started across the road, the mother half-dragging her parcels in the dust. Then, and with an earnest expression, Miss Bobbit turned back; the sunflower yellow of her eyes darkened, and she rolled them slightly sideways, as if trying to remember a poem. "My mother has a disorder of the tongue, so it is necessary that I speak for her," she announced rapidly and heaved a sigh. "My mother is a very fine seamstress; she has made dresses for the society of many cities and towns, including Memphis and Tallahassee. No doubt you have noticed and admired the dress I am wearing. Every stitch of it was hand-sewn by my mother. My mother can copy any pattern, and just recently she won a twenty-five-dollar prize from the *Ladies' Home Journal.* My mother can also crochet, knit and embroider. If you want any kind of sewing done, please come to my mother. Please advise your friends and family. Thank you." And then, with a rustle and a swish, she was gone.

Cora McCall and the girls pulled their hair-ribbons nervously, suspiciously, and looked very put out and prune-faced. I'm *Miss* Bobbit, said Cora, twisting her face into an evil imitation, and I'm Princess Elizabeth, that's who I am, ha, ha, ha. Furthermore, said Cora, that dress was just as tacky as could be; personally, Cora said, all my clothes come from Atlanta; plus a pair of shoes from New York, which is not even to mention my silver turquoise ring all the way from Mexico City, Mexico. Aunt El said they ought not to behave that way about a fellow child, a stranger in the town, but the girls went on like a huddle of witches, and certain boys, the sillier ones that liked to be with the girls, joined in and said things that made Aunt El go red and declare she was going to send them all home and tell their daddies, to boot. But before she could carry forward this threat Miss Bobbit herself intervened by traipsing across the Sawyer porch, costumed in a new and startling manner.

The older boys, like Billy Bob and Preacher Star, who had sat quiet while the girls razzed Miss Bobbit, and who had watched the house into which she'd disappeared with misty, ambitious faces, they now straightened up and ambled down to the gate. Cora McCall sniffed and poked out her lower lip, but the rest of us went and sat on the steps. Miss Bobbit paid us no mind whatever. The Sawyer yard is dark with mulberry trees and it is planted with grass and sweet shrub. Sometimes after a rain you can smell the sweet shrub all the way into our house; and in the center of this yard there is a sundial which Mrs. Sawyer installed in 1912 as a memorial to her Boston bull, Sunny, who died after having lapped up a bucket of paint. Miss Bobbit pranced into the yard toting the victrola, which she put on the sundial; she wound it up, and started a record playing, and it played the Court of Luxemborg. By now it was almost nightfall, a firefly hour, blue as milkglass; and birds like arrows swooped together and swept into the folds of trees. Before storms, leaves and flowers appear to burn with a private light, color, and Miss Bobbit, got up in a little white skirt like a powderpuff and with strips of gold-glittering tinsel ribboning her hair, seemed, set against the darkening all around, to contain this illuminated quality. She held her arms arched over her head, her hands lily-limp, and stood straight up on the tips of her toes. She stood that way for a good long while, and Aunt El said it was right smart of her. Then she began to waltz around and around, and around and around she went until Aunt El said, why, she was plain dizzy from the sight. She stopped only when it was time to rewind the victrola; and when the moon came rolling down the ridge, and the last supper bell had sounded, and all the children had gone home, and the night iris was beginning to bloom, Miss Bobbit was still there in the dark turning like a top.

We did not see her again for some time. Preacher Star came every morning to our house and stayed straight through to supper. Preacher is a rail-thin boy with a butchy shock of red hair; he has eleven brothers and sisters, and even they are afraid of him, for he has a terrible temper, and is famous in these parts for his green-eyed meanness: last Fourth of July he whipped Ollie Overton so bad that Ollie's family had to send him to the hospital in Pensacola; and there was another time he bit off half a mule's ear, chewed it and spit it on the ground. Before Billy Bob got his growth, Preacher played the devil with him, too. He used to drop cockleburrs down his collar, and rub pepper in his eyes, and tear up his homework. But now they are the biggest friends in town: talk alike, walk alike; and occasionally they disappear together for whole days, Lord knows where to. But during these days when Miss Bobbit did not appear they stayed close to the house. They would stand around in the yard trying to slingshot sparrows off telephone poles; or sometimes Billy Bob would play his ukulele, and they would sing so loud Uncle Billy Bob, who is Judge for this county, claimed he could hear them all the way to the courthouse: *send me a letter, send it by mail, send it in care of the Birming-ham jail.* Miss Bobbit did not hear them; at least she never poked her head out the door. Then one day Mrs. Sawyer, coming over to borrow a cup of sugar, rattled on a good deal about her new boarders. You know, she said, squinting her chicken-bright eyes, the husband was a crook, uh huh, the child told me herself. Hasn't an ounce of shame, not a mite. Said her daddy was the dearest daddy and the sweetest singing man in the whole of Tennessee. . . . And I said, honey, where is he? and just as offhand as you please she says, Oh, he's in the penitentiary and we don't hear from him no more. Say, now, does that make your blood run cold? Uh huh, and I been thinking, her mama, I been thinking she's some kinda foreigner: never says a word, and sometimes it looks like she don't understand what nobody says to her. And you know, they eat everything *raw*. *Raw* eggs, *raw* turnips, carrots—no meat whatsoever. For reasons of health, the child says, but ho! she's been straight out on the bed running a fever since last Tuesday.

That same afternoon, Aunt El went out to water her roses, only to discover them gone. These were special roses, ones she'd planned to send to the flower show in Mobile, and so naturally she got a little hysterical. She rang up the Sheriff, and said, listen here, Sheriff, you come over here right fast. I mean somebody's got off with all my Lady Anne's that I've devoted myself to heart and soul since early spring. When the Sheriff's car pulled up outside our house, all the neighbors along the street came out on their porches, and Mrs. Sawyer, layers of cold cream whitening her face, trotted across the road. Oh shoot, she said, very disappointed to find no one had been murdered, oh shoot, she said, nobody's stole them roses. Your Billy Bob brought them roses over and left them for little Bobbit. Aunt El did not say one word. She just marched over to the peach tree, and cut herself a switch. Ohhh, Billy Bob, she stalked along the street calling his name, and then she found him down at Speedy's garage, where he and Preacher were watching Speedy take a motor apart. She simply lifted him by the hair and, switching blueblazes, towed him home. But she couldn't make him say he was sorry and she couldn't make him cry. And when she was finished with him he ran into the backyard and climbed high into the tower of a pecan tree and swore he wasn't ever going to come down. Then his daddy stood at the window and called to him: Son, we aren't mad with you, so come down and eat your supper. But Billy Bob wouldn't budge. Aunt El went and leaned against the tree. She spoke in a voice soft as the gathering light. I'm sorry, son, she said, I didn't mean whipping you so hard like that. I've fixed a nice supper, son, potato salad and boiled ham and deviled eggs. Go away, said Billy Bob, I don't want no supper, and I hate you like all-fire. His daddy said he ought not to talk like that to his mother, and she began to cry. She stood there under the tree and cried, raising the hem of her skirt to dab at her eyes. I don't hate you, son. . . . If I didn't love you, I wouldn't whip you. The pecan leaves began to rattle; Billy Bob slid slowly to the ground, and Aunt El, rushing her fingers through his hair, pulled him against her. Aw, Ma, he said, Aw, Ma.

After supper Billy Bob came and flung himself on the foot of my bed. He smelled all sour and sweet, the way boys do, and I felt very sorry for him, especially because he looked so worried. His eyes were almost shut with worry. You're s'posed to send sick folks flowers, he said righteously. About this time we heard the victrola, a lilting faraway sound, and a night moth flew through the window, drifting in the air delicate as the music. But it was dark now, and we couldn't tell if Miss Bobbit was dancing. Billy Bob, as though he were in pain, doubled up on the bed like a jackknife; but his face was suddenly clear, his grubby boy-eyes twitching like candles. She's so cute, he whispered, she's the cutest dickens I ever saw, gee, to hell with it, I don't care, I'd pick all the roses in China.

Preacher would have picked all the roses in China, too. He was as crazy about her as Billy Bob. But Miss Bobbit did not notice them. The sole communication we had with her was a note to Aunt El thanking her for the flowers. Day after day she sat on her porch, always dressed to beat the band, and doing a piece of embroidery, or combing curls in her hair, or reading a Webster's dictionary—formal, but friendly enough; if you said good-day to her, she said good-day to you. Even so, the boys never could seem to get up the nerve to go over and talk with her, and most of the time she simply looked through them, even when they tomcatted up and down the street trying to get her eye. They wrestled, played Tarzan, did fool-headed bicycle tricks. It was a sorry business. A great many girls in town strolled by the Sawyer house two and three times within an hour just on the chance of getting a look. Some of the girls who did this were: Cora McCall, Mary Murphy Jones, Janice Ackerman. Miss Bobbit did not show any interest in them either. Cora would not speak to Billy Bob anymore. The same was true with Janice and Preacher. As a matter of fact, Janice wrote Preacher a letter in red ink on lace-trimmed paper in which she told him he was vile beyond all human beings and words, that she considered their engagement broken, that he could have back the stuffed squirrel he'd given her. Preacher, saying he wanted to act nice, stopped her the next time she passed our house, and said, well, hell, she could keep that old squirrel if she wanted to. Afterward, he couldn't understand why Janice ran away bawling the way she did.

Then one day the boys were being crazier than usual; Billy Bob was sagging around in his daddy's World War khakis, and Preacher, stripped to the waist, had a naked woman drawn on his chest with one of Aunt El's old lipsticks. They looked like perfect fools, but Miss Bobbit, reclining in a swing, merely yawned. It was noon, and there was no one passing in the street, except a colored girl, baby-fat and sugarplum-shaped, who hummed along carrying a pail of blackberries. But the boys, teasing at her like gnats, joined hands and wouldn't let her go by, not until she paid a tariff. I ain't studyin' no tariff, she said, what kinda tariff you talkin' about, mister? A party in the barn, said Preacher, between clenched teeth, mighty nice party in the barn. And she, with a sulky shrug, said, huh, she intended studyin' no barn parties. Whereupon Billy Bob capsized her berry pail, and when she, with despairing, piglike shrieks, bent down in futile gestures of rescue, Preacher, who can be mean as the devil, gave her behind a kick which sent her sprawling jellylike among the blackberries and the dust. Miss Bobbit came tearing across the road, her finger wagging like a metronome; like a schoolteacher she clapped her hands, stamped her foot, said: "It is a well-known fact that gentlemen are put on the face of this earth for the protection of ladies. Do you suppose boys behave this way in towns like Memphis, New York, London, Hollywood or Paris?" The boys hung back and shoved their hands in their pockets. Miss Bobbit helped the colored girl to her feet; she dusted her off, dried her eyes, held out a handkerchief and told her to blow. "A pretty pass," she said, "a fine situation when a lady can't walk safely in the public daylight."

Then the two of them went back and sat on Mrs. Sawyer's porch; and for the next year they were never far apart, Miss Bobbit and this baby elephant, whose name was Rosalba Cat. At first, Mrs. Sawyer raised a fuss about Rosalba being so much at her house. She told Aunt El that it went against the grain to have a nigger lolling smack there in plain sight on her front porch. But Miss Bobbit had a certain magic, whatever she did she did it with completeness, and so directly, so solemnly, that there was nothing to do but accept it. For instance, the tradespeople in town used to snicker when they called her *Miss* Bobbit; but by and by she was Miss Bobbit, and they gave her stiff little bows as she whirled by spinning her parasol. Miss Bobbit told everyone that Rosalba was her sister, which caused a good many jokes; but like most of her ideas, it gradually seemed natural, and when we would overhear them calling each other Sister Rosalba and Sister Bobbit, none of us cracked a smile. But Sister Rosalba and Sister Bobbit did some queer things. There was the business about the dogs. Now there are a great many dogs in this town, rat terriers, bird dogs, bloodhounds; they trail along the forlorn noon-hot streets in sleepy herds of six to a dozen, all waiting only for dark and the moon, when straight through the lonesome hours you can hear them howling: someone is dying, someone is dead. Miss Bobbit complained to the Sheriff; she said that certain of the dogs always planted themselves under her window, and that she was a light sleeper to begin with; what is more, and as Sister Rosalba said, she did not believe they were dogs at all, but some kind of devil. Naturally the Sheriff did nothing; and so she took the matter into her own hands. One morning, after an especially loud night, she was seen stalking through the town with Rosalba at her side, Rosalba carrying a flower basket filled with rocks; whenever they saw a dog they paused while Miss Bobbit scrutinized him. Sometimes she would shake her head, but more often she said, "Yes, that's one of them, Sister Rosalba," and Sister Rosalba, with ferocious aim, would take a rock from her basket and crack the dog between the eyes.

Another thing that happened concerns Mr. Henderson. Mr. Henderson has a back room in the Sawyer house; a tough runt of a man who formerly was a wildcat oil prospector in Oklahoma, he is about seventy years old and, like a lot of old men, obsessed by functions of the body. Also, he is a terrible drunk. One time he had been drunk for two weeks; whenever he heard Miss Bobbit and Sister Rosalba moving around the house, he would charge to the top of the stairs and bellow down to Mrs. Sawyer that there were midgets in the walls trying to get at his supply of toilet paper. They've already stolen fifteen cents' worth, he said. One evening, when the two girls were sitting under a tree in the yard, Mr. Henderson, sporting nothing more than a nightshirt, stamped out after them. Steal all my toilet paper, will you? he hollered, I'll show you midgets. . . . Somebody come help me, else these midget bitches are liable to make off with every sheet in town. It was Billy Bob and Preacher who caught Mr. Henderson and held him until some grown men arrived and began to tie him up. Miss Bobbit, who had behaved with admirable calm, told the men they did not know how to tie a proper knot, and undertook to do so herself. She did such a good job that all the circulation stopped in Mr. Henderson's hands and feet and it was a month before he could walk again.

It was shortly afterward that Miss Bobbit paid us a call. She came on Sunday and I was there alone, the family having gone to church. "The odors of a church are so offensive," she said, leaning forward and with her hands folded primly before her. "I don't want you to think I'm a heathen, Mr. C.; I've had enough experience to know that there is a God and that there is a Devil. But the way to tame the Devil is not to go down there to church and listen to what a sinful mean fool he is. No, love the Devil like you love Jesus: because he is a powerful man, and will do you a good turn if he knows you trust him. He has frequently done me good turns, like at dancing school in Memphis. . . . I always called in the Devil to help me get the biggest part in our annual show. That is common sense; you see, I knew Jesus wouldn't have any truck with dancing. Now, as a matter of fact, I have called in the Devil just recently. He is the only one who can help me get out of this town. Not that I live here, not exactly. I think always about somewhere else, somewhere else where everything is dancing, like people dancing in the streets, and everything is pretty, like children on their birthdays. My precious papa said I live in the sky, but if he'd lived more in the sky, he'd be rich like he wanted to be. The trouble with my papa was he did not love the Devil, he let the Devil love him. But I am very smart in that respect; I know the next best thing is very often the best. It was the next best thing for us to move to this town; and since I can't pursue my career here, the next best thing for me is to start a little business on the side. Which is what I have done. I am sole subscription agent in this county for an impressive list of magazines, including *Reader's Digest, Popular Mechanics, Dime Detective* and *Child's Life.* To be sure, Mr. C., I'm not here to sell you anything. But I have a thought in mind. I was thinking those two boys that are always hanging around here, it occurred to me that they are men, after all. Do you suppose they would make a pair of likely assistants?"

Billy Bob and Preacher worked hard for Miss Bobbit, and for Sister Rosalba, too. Sister Rosalba carried a line of cosmetics called Dewdrop, and it was part of the boys' job to deliver purchases to her customers. Billy Bob used to be so tired in the evening he could hardly chew his supper. Aunt El said it was a shame and a pity, and finally one day when Billy Bob came down with a touch of sunstroke she said, all right, that settled it, Billy Bob would just have to quit Miss Bobbit. But Billy Bob cussed her out until his daddy had to lock him in his room; whereupon he said he was going to kill himself. Some cook we'd had told him once that if you ate a mess of collards all slopped over with molasses, it would kill you sure as shooting; and so that is what he did. I'm dying, he said, rolling back and forth on his bed, I'm dying and nobody cares.

Miss Bobbit came over and told him to hush up. "There's nothing wrong with you, boy," she said. "All you've got is a stomachache." Then she did something that shocked Aunt El very much: she stripped the covers off Billy Bob and rubbed him down with alcohol from head to toe. When

Aunt El told her she did not think that was a nice thing for a little girl to do, Miss Bobbit replied: "I don't know whether it's nice or not, but it's certainly very refreshing." After which Aunt El did all she could to keep Billy Bob from going back to work for her, but his daddy said to leave him alone, they would have to let the boy lead his own life.

Miss Bobbit was very honest about money. She paid Billy Bob and Preacher their exact commission, and she would never let them treat her, as they often tried to do, at the drugstore or to the picture show. "You'd better save your money," she told them. "That is, if you want to go to college. Because neither one of you has got the brains to win a scholarship, not even a football scholarship." But it was over money that Billy Bob and Preacher had a big falling-out; that was not the real reason, of course: the real reason was that they had grown cross-eyed jealous over Miss Bobbit. So one day, and he had the gall to do this right in front of Billy Bob, Preacher said to Miss Bobbit that she'd better check her accounts carefully because he had more than a suspicion that Billy Bob wasn't turning over to her *all* the money he collected. That's a damned lie, said Billy Bob, and with a clean left hook he knocked Preacher off the Sawyer porch and jumped after him into a bed of nasturtiums. But once Preacher got a hold on him, Billy Bob didn't stand a chance. Preacher even rubbed dirt in his eyes. During all this, Mrs. Sawyer, leaning out an upper-story window, screamed like an eagle, and Sister Rosalba, fatly cheerful, ambiguously shouted, Kill him! Kill him! Kill him! Only Miss Bobbit seemed to know what she was doing. She plugged in the lawn hose, and gave the boys a close-up, blinding bath. Gasping, Preacher staggered to his feet. Oh, honey, he said, shaking himself like a wet dog, honey, you've got to decide. "Decide *what?*" said Miss Bobbit, right away in a huff. Oh, honey, wheezed Preacher, you don't want us boys killing each other. You got to decide who is your real true sweetheart. "Sweetheart, my eye," said Miss Bobbit. "I should've known better than to get myself involved with a lot of country children. What sort of businessman are you going to make? Now, you listen here, Preacher Star: I don't want a sweetheart, and if I did, it wouldn't be you. As a matter of fact, you don't even get up when a lady enters the room."

Preacher spit on the ground and swaggered over to Billy Bob. Come on, he said, just as though nothing had happened, she's a hard one, she is, she don't want nothing but to make trouble between two good friends. For a moment it looked as if Billy Bob was going to join him in a peaceful togetherness; but suddenly, coming to his senses, he drew back and made a gesture. The boys regarded each other a full minute, all the closeness between them turning an ugly color: you can't hate so much unless you love, too. And Preacher's face showed all of this. But there was nothing for him to do except go away. Oh, yes, Preacher, you looked so lost that day that for the first time I really liked you, so skinny and mean and lost going down the road all by yourself.

They did not make it up, Preacher and Billy Bob; and it was not because they didn't want to, it was only that there did not seem to be any straight way for their friendship to happen again. But they couldn't get rid of this friendship: each was always aware of what the other was up to; and when Preacher found himself a new buddy, Billy Bob moped around for days, picking things up, dropping them again, or doing sudden wild things, like purposely poking his finger in the electric fan. Sometimes in the evenings Preacher would pause by the gate and talk with Aunt El. It was only to torment Billy Bob, I suppose, but he stayed friendly with all of us, and at Christmastime he gave us a huge box of shelled peanuts. He left a present for Billy Bob, too. It turned out to be a book of Sherlock Holmes; and on the flyleaf there was scribbled, "Friends Like Ivy On the Wall Must Fall." That's the corniest thing I ever saw, Billy Bob said. Jesus, what a dope he is! But then, and though it was a cold winter day, he went in the backyard and climbed up into the pecan tree, crouching there all afternoon in the blue December branches.

But most of the time he was happy, because Miss Bobbit was there, and she was always sweet to him now. She and Sister Rosalba treated him like a man; that is to say, they allowed him to do everything for them. On the other hand, they let him win at three-handed bridge, they never questioned his lies, nor discouraged his ambitions. It was a happy while. However, trouble started again when school began. Miss Bobbit refused to go. "It's ridiculous," she said, when one day the principal, Mr. Copland, came around to investigate, "really ridiculous; I can read and write and there are *some* people in this town who have every reason to know that I can count money. No, Mr. Copland, consider for a moment and you will see neither of us has the time nor energy. After all, it would only be a matter of whose spirit broke first, yours or mine. And besides, what is there for you to teach me? Now, if you knew anything about dancing, that would be another matter; but under the circumstances, yes, Mr. Copland, under the circumstances, I suggest we forget the whole thing." Mr. Copland was perfectly willing to. But the rest of the town thought she ought to be whipped. Horace Deasley wrote a piece in the paper which was titled "A Tragic Situation." It was, in his opinion, a tragic situation when a small girl could defy what he, for some reason, termed the Constitution of the United States. The article ended with a question: *Can she get away with it?* She did; and so did Sister Rosalba. Only she was colored, so no one cared. Billy Bob was not as lucky. It was school for him, all right; but he might as well have stayed home for the good it did him. On his first report card he got three F's, a record of some sort. But he is a smart boy. I guess he just couldn't live through those hours without Miss Bobbit; away from her he always seemed half-asleep. He was always in a fight, too; either his eye was black or his lip was split or his walk had a limp. He never talked about these fights, but Miss Bobbit was shrewd enough to guess the reason why. "You are a dear, I know, I know. And I appreciate you, Billy Bob. Only don't fight with people because of me. Of course they say mean things about me. But do you know why that is, Billy Bob? It's a compliment, kind of. Because deep down they think I'm absolutely wonderful."

And she was right: if you are not admired, no one will take the trouble to disapprove. But actually we had no idea of how wonderful she was until there appeared the man known as Manny Fox. This happened late in February. The first news we had of Manny Fox was a series of jovial placards posted up in the stores around town: Manny Fox Presents the Fan Dancer Without the Fan; then, in smaller print: Also, Sensational Amateur Program Featuring Your Own Neighbors—First Prize, A Genuine Hollywood Screen Test. All this was to take place the following Thursday. The tickets were priced at one dollar each, which around here is a lot of money; but it is not often that we get any kind of flesh entertainment, so everybody shelled out their money and made a great to-do over the whole thing. The drugstore cowboys talked dirty all week, mostly about the fan dancer without the fan, who turned out to be Mrs. Manny Fox. They stayed down the highway at the Chucklewood Tourist Camp; but they were in town all day, driving around in an old Packard which had Manny Fox's full name stenciled on all four doors. His wife was a deadpan pimento-tongued redhead with wet lips and moist eyelids; she was quite large actually, but compared to Manny Fox she seemed rather frail, for he was a fat cigar of a man.

They made the pool hall their headquarters, and every afternoon you could find them there, drinking beer and joking with the town loafs. As it developed, Manny Fox's business affairs were not restricted to theatrics. He also ran a kind of employment bureau: slowly he let it be known that for a fee of $150 he could get for any adventurous boys in the county high-class jobs working on fruit ships sailing from New Orleans to South America. The chance of a lifetime, he called it. There are not two boys around here who readily lay their hands on so much as five dollars; nevertheless, a good dozen managed to raise the money. Ada Willingham took all she'd saved to buy an angel tombstone for her husband and gave it to her son, and Acey Trump's papa sold an option on his cotton crop.

But the night of the show! That was a night when all was forgotten: mortgages, and the dishes in the kitchen sink. Aunt El said you'd think we were going to the opera, everybody so dressed up, so pink and sweet-smelling. The Odeon had not been so full since the night they gave away the matched set of sterling silver. Practically everybody had a relative in the show, so there was a lot of nervousness to contend with. Miss Bobbit was the only contestant we knew real well. Billy Bob couldn't sit still; he kept telling us over and over that we mustn't applaud for anybody but Miss Bobbit; Aunt El said that would be very rude, which sent Billy Bob off into a state again; and when his father bought us all bags of popcorn he wouldn't touch his because it would make his hands greasy, and please, another thing, we mustn't be noisy and eat ours while Miss Bobbit was performing. That she was to be a contestant had come as a last-minute surprise. It was logical enough, and there were signs that should've told us; the fact, for instance, that she had not set foot outside the Sawyer house in how many days? And the victrola going half the night, her shadow whirling on the window shade, and the secret, stuffed look on Sister Rosalba's face whenever asked after Sister Bobbit's health. So there was her name on the program, listed second, in fact, though she did not appear for a long while. First came Manny Fox, greased and leering, who told a lot of peculiar jokes, clapping his hands, ha, ha. Aunt El said if he told another joke like that, she was going to walk straight out: he did, and she didn't. Before Miss Bobbit came on, there were eleven contestants, including Eustacia Bernstein, who imitated movie stars so that they all sounded like Eustacia, and there was an extraordinary Mr. Buster Riley, a jug-eared old wool-hat from way in the back country who played "Waltzing Matilda" on a saw. Up to that point, he was the hit of the show; not that there was any marked difference in the various receptions, for everybody applauded generously, everybody, that is, except Preacher Star. He was sitting two rows ahead of us, greeting each act with a donkey-loud boo. Aunt El said she was never going to speak to him again. The only person he ever applauded was Miss Bobbit. No doubt the Devil was on her side, but she deserved it. Out she came, tossing her hips, her curls, rolling her eyes. You could tell right away it wasn't going to be one of her classical numbers. She tapped across the stage, daintily holding up the sides of a cloud-blue skirt. That's the cutest thing I ever saw, said Billy Bob, smacking his thigh, and Aunt El had to agree that Miss Bobbit looked real sweet. When she started to twirl the whole audience broke into spontaneous applause; so she did it all over again, hissing, "Faster, faster," at poor Miss Adelaide, who was at the piano doing her Sunday-school best. "I was born in China, and raised in Jaypan . . ." We had never heard her sing before, and she had a rowdy sandpaper voice. ". . . if you don't like my peaches, stay away from my can, o-ho o-ho!" Aunt El gasped; she gasped again when Miss Bobbit, with a bump, up-ended her skirt to display blue-lace underwear, thereby collecting most of the whistles the boys had been saving for the fan dancer without the fan, which was just as well, as it later turned out, for that lady, to the tune of "An Apple for the Teacher" and cries of gyp gyp, did her routine attired in a bathing suit. But showing off her bottom was not Miss Bobbit's final triumph. Miss Adelaide commenced an ominous thundering in the darker keys, at which point Sister Rosalba, carrying a lighted Roman candle, rushed onstage and handed it to Miss Bobbit, who was in the midst of a full split; she made it, too, and just as she did the Roman candle burst into fiery balls of red, white and blue, and we all had to stand up because she was singing "The Star-Spangled Banner" at the top of her lungs. Aunt El said afterward that it was one of the most gorgeous things she'd ever seen on the American stage.

Well, she surely did deserve a Hollywood screen test and, inasmuch as she won the contest, it looked as though she were going to get it. Manny Fox said she was: honey, he said, you're real star stuff. Only he skipped town the next day, leaving nothing but hearty promises. Watch the mails, my friends, you'll all be hearing from me. That is what he said to the boys whose money he'd taken, and that is what he said to Miss Bobbit. There are three deliveries daily, and this sizable group gathered at the post office for all of them, a jolly crowd growing gradually joyless. How their hands trembled when a letter slid into their mailbox. A terrible hush came over them as the days passed. They all knew what the other was thinking, but no one could bring himself to say it, not even Miss Bobbit. Postmistress Patterson said it plainly, however: the man's a crook, she said, I knew he was a crook to begin with, and if I have to look at your faces one more day I'll shoot myself.

Finally, at the end of two weeks, it was Miss Bobbit who broke the spell. Her eyes had grown more vacant than anyone had ever supposed they might, but one day, after the last mail was up, all her old sizzle came back. "Okay, boys, it's lynch law now," she said, and proceeded to herd the whole troupe home with her. This was the first meeting of the Manny Fox Hangman's Club, an organization which, in a more social form, endures to this day, though Manny Fox has long since been caught and, so to say, hung. Credit for this went quite properly to Miss Bobbit. Within a week she'd written over three hundred descriptions of Manny Fox and dispatched them to Sheriffs throughout the South; she also wrote letters to papers in the larger cities, and these attracted wide attention. As a result, four of the robbed boys were offered good-paying jobs by the United Fruit Company, and late this spring, when Manny Fox was arrested in Uphigh, Arkansas, where he was pulling the same old dodge, Miss Bobbit was presented with a Good Deed Merit award from the Sunbeam Girls of America. For some reason, she made a point of letting the world know that this did not exactly thrill her. "I do not approve of the organization," she said. "All that rowdy bugle blowing. It's neither good-hearted nor truly feminine. And anyway, what is a good deed? Don't let anybody fool you, a good deed is something you do because you want something in return." It would be reassuring to report she was wrong, and that her just reward, when at last it came, was given out of kindness and love. However, this is not the case. About a week ago the boys involved in the swindle all received from Manny Fox checks covering their losses, and Miss Bobbit, with clodhopping determination, stalked into a meeting of the Hangman's Club, which is now an excuse for drinking beer and playing poker every Thursday night. "Look, boys," she said, laying it on the line, "none of you ever thought to see that money again, but now that you have, you ought to invest it in something practical—like me." The proposition was that they should pool their money and finance her trip to Hollywood; in return, they would get ten percent of her life's earnings which, after she was a star, and that would not be very long, would make them all rich men. "At least," as she said, "in this part of the country." Not one of the boys wanted to do it: but when Miss Bobbit looked at you, what was there to say?

Since Monday, it has been raining buoyant summer rain shot through with sun, but dark at night and full of sound, full of dripping leaves, watery chimings, sleepless scuttlings. Billy Bob is wide-awake, dry-eyed, though everything he does is a little frozen and his tongue is as stiff as a bell tongue. It has not been easy for him, Miss Bobbit's going. Because she'd meant more than that. Than what? Than being thirteen years old and crazy in love. She was the queer things in him, like the pecan tree and liking books and caring enough about people to let them hurt him. She was the things he was afraid to show anyone else. And in the dark the music trickled through the rain: won't there be nights when we will hear it just as though it were really there? And afternoons when the shadows will be all at once confused, and she will pass before us, unfurling across the lawn like a pretty piece of ribbon? She laughed to Billy Bob; she held his hand, she even kissed him. "I'm not going to die," she said. "You'll come out there, and we'll climb a mountain, and we'll all live there together, you and me and Sister Rosalba." But Billy Bob knew it would never happen that way, and so when the music came through the dark he would stuff the pillow over his head.

Only there was a strange smile about yesterday, and that was the day she was leaving. Around noon the sun came out, bringing with it into the air all the sweetness of wisteria. Aunt El's yellow Lady Anne's were blooming again, and she did something wonderful, she told Billy Bob he could pick them and give them to Miss Bobbit for good-bye. All afternoon Miss Bobbit sat on the porch surrounded by people who stopped by to wish her well. She looked as though she were going to Communion, dressed in white and with a white parasol. Sister Rosalba had given her a handkerchief, but she had to borrow it back because she couldn't stop blubbering. Another little girl brought a baked chicken, presumably to be eaten on the bus; the only trouble was she'd forgotten to take out the insides before cooking it. Miss Bobbit's mother said that was all right by her, chicken was chicken; which is memorable because it is the single opinion she ever voiced. There was only one sour note. For hours Preacher Star had been hanging around down at the corner, sometimes standing at the curb tossing a coin, and sometimes hiding behind a tree, as if he didn't want anyone to see him. It made everybody nervous. About twenty minutes before bus time he sauntered up and leaned against our gate. Billy Bob was still in the garden picking roses; by now he had enough for a bonfire, and their smell was as heavy as wind. Preacher stared at him until he lifted his head. As they looked at each other the rain began again, falling fine as sea spray and colored by a rainbow. Without a word, Preacher went over and started helping Billy Bob separate the roses into two giant bouquets: together they carried them to the curb. Across the street there were bumblebees of talk, but when Miss Bobbit saw them, two boys whose flower-masked faces were like yellow moons, she rushed down the steps, her arms outstretched. You could see what was going to happen; and we called out, our voices like lightning in the rain, but Miss Bobbit, running toward those moons of roses, did not seem to hear. That is when the six-o'clock bus ran over her.

A Diamond
Guitar

(1950)

THE NEAREST TOWN TO THE PRISON
farm is twenty miles away. Many forests
of pine trees stand between the farm and the town, and it is in these forests
that the convicts work; they tap for turpentine. The prison itself is in a
forest. You will find it there at the end of a red rutted road, barbed wire
sprawling like a vine over its walls. Inside, there live one hundred and nine
white men, ninety-seven Negroes and one Chinese. There are two sleep
houses—great green wooden buildings with tar-paper roofs. The white
men occupy one, the Negroes and the Chinese the other. In each sleep
house there is one large potbellied stove, but the winters are cold here, and
at night with the pines waving frostily and a freezing light falling from the
moon, the men, stretched on their iron cots, lie awake with the fire colors
of the stove playing in their eyes.

The men whose cots are nearest the stove are the important men—those
who are looked up to or feared. Mr. Schaeffer is one of these. Mr. Schaeffer
—for that is what he is called, a mark of special respect—is a lanky,
pulled-out man. He has reddish, silvering hair, and his face is attenuated,
religious; there is no flesh to him; you can see the workings of his bones,
and his eyes are a poor, dull color. He can read and he can write, he can
add a column of figures. When another man receives a letter, he brings it
to Mr. Schaeffer. Most of these letters are sad and complaining; very often
Mr. Schaeffer improvises more cheerful messages and does not read what

107

is written on the page. In the sleep house there are two other men who can read. Even so, one of them brings his letters to Mr. Schaeffer, who obliges by never reading the truth. Mr. Schaeffer himself does not receive mail, not even at Christmas; he seems to have no friends beyond the prison, and actually he has none there—that is, no particular friend. This was not always true.

One winter Sunday some winters ago Mr. Schaeffer was sitting on the steps of the sleep house carving a doll. He is quite talented at this. His dolls are carved in separate sections, then put together with bits of spring wire; the arms and legs move, the head rolls. When he has finished a dozen or so of these dolls, the Captain of the farm takes them into town, and there they are sold in a general store. In this way Mr. Schaeffer earns money for candy and tobacco.

That Sunday, as he sat cutting out the fingers for a little hand, a truck pulled into the prison yard. A young boy, handcuffed to the Captain of the farm, climbed out of the truck and stood blinking at the ghostly winter sun. Mr. Schaeffer only glanced at him. He was then a man of fifty, and seventeen of those years he'd lived at the farm. The arrival of a new prisoner could not arouse him. Sunday is a free day at the farm, and other men who were moping around the yard crowded down to the truck. Afterward, Pick Axe and Goober stopped by to speak with Mr. Schaeffer.

Pick Axe said, "He's a foreigner, the new one is. From Cuba. But with yellow hair."

"A knifer, Cap'n says," said Goober, who was a knifer himself. "Cut up a sailor in Mobile."

"Two sailors," said Pick Axe. "But just a café fight. He didn't hurt them boys none."

"To cut off a man's ear? You call that not hurtin' him? They give him two years, Cap'n says."

Pick Axe said, "He's got a guitar with jewels all over it."

It was getting too dark to work. Mr. Schaeffer fitted the pieces of his doll together and, holding its little hands, set it on his knee. He rolled a cigarette; the pines were blue in the sundown light, and the smoke from his cigarette lingered in the cold, darkening air. He could see the Captain coming across the yard. The new prisoner, a blond young boy, lagged a pace behind. He was carrying a guitar studded with glass diamonds that cast a starry twinkle, and his new uniform was too big for him; it looked like a Halloween suit.

"Somebody for you, Schaeffer," said the Captain, pausing on the steps of the sleep house. The Captain was not a hard man; occasionally he invited Mr. Schaeffer into his office, and they would talk together about things they had read in the newspaper. "Tico Feo," he said as though it were the name of a bird or a song, "this is Mr. Schaeffer. Do like him, and you'll do right."

Mr. Schaeffer glanced up at the boy and smiled. He smiled at him longer than he meant to, for the boy had eyes like strips of sky—blue as the winter evening—and his hair was as gold as the Captain's teeth. He had a fun-loving face, nimble, clever; and, looking at him, Mr. Schaeffer thought of holidays and good times.

"Is like my baby sister," said Tico Feo, touching Mr. Schaeffer's doll. His voice with its Cuban accent was soft and sweet as a banana. "She sit on my knee also."

Mr. Schaeffer was suddenly shy. Bowing to the Captain, he walked off into the shadows of the yard. He stood there whispering the names of the evening stars as they opened in flower above him. The stars were his pleasure, but tonight they did not comfort him; they did not make him remember that what happens to us on earth is lost in the endless shine of eternity. Gazing at them—the stars—he thought of the jeweled guitar and its worldly glitter.

It could be said of Mr. Schaeffer that in his life he'd done only one really bad thing: he'd killed a man. The circumstances of that deed are unimportant, except to say that the man deserved to die and that for it Mr. Schaeffer was sentenced to ninety-nine years and a day. For a long while—for many years, in fact—he had not thought of how it was before he came to the farm. His memory of those times was like a house where no one lives and where the furniture has rotted away. But tonight it was as if lamps had been lighted through all the gloomy dead rooms. It had begun to happen when he saw Tico Feo coming through the dusk with his splendid guitar. Until that moment he had not been lonesome. Now, recognizing his loneliness, he felt alive. He had not wanted to be alive. To be alive was to remember brown rivers where the fish run, and sunlight on a lady's hair.

Mr. Schaeffer hung his head. The glare of the stars had made his eyes water.

The sleep house usually is a glum place, stale with the smell of men and stark in the light of two unshaded electric bulbs. But with the advent of Tico Feo it was as though a tropic occurrence had happened in the cold room, for when Mr. Schaeffer returned from his observance of the stars, he came upon a savage and garish scene. Sitting cross-legged on a cot, Tico Feo was picking at his guitar with long swaying fingers and singing a song that sounded as jolly as jingling coins. Though the song was in Spanish, some of the men tried to sing it with him, and Pick Axe and Goober were dancing together. Charlie and Wink were dancing too, but separately. It was nice to hear the men laughing, and when Tico Feo finally put aside his guitar, Mr. Schaeffer was among those who congratulated him.

"You deserve such a fine guitar," he said.

"Is diamond guitar," said Tico Feo, drawing his hand over its vaudeville dazzle. "Once I have a one with rubies. But that one is stole. In Havana my sister work in a, how you say, where make guitar; is how I have this one."

Mr. Schaeffer asked him if he had many sisters, and Tico Feo, grinning, held up four fingers. Then, his blue eyes narrowing greedily, he said, "Please, mister, you give me doll for my two little sister?"

The next evening Mr. Schaeffer brought him the dolls. After that he was Tico Feo's best friend and they were always together. At all times they considered each other.

Tico Feo was eighteen years old and for two years had worked on a freighter in the Caribbean. As a child, he'd gone to school with nuns, and he wore a gold crucifix around his neck. He had a rosary too. The rosary he kept wrapped in a green silk scarf that also held three other treasures: a bottle of Evening in Paris cologne, a pocket mirror and a Rand McNally map of the world. These and the guitar were his only possessions, and he would not allow anyone to touch them. Perhaps he prized his map the most. At night, before the lights were turned off, he would shake out his map and show Mr. Schaeffer the places he'd been—Galveston, Miami, New Orleans, Mobile, Cuba, Haiti, Jamaica, Puerto Rico, the Virgin Islands—and the places he wanted to go to. He wanted to go almost everywhere, especially Madrid, especially the North Pole. This both charmed and frightened Mr. Schaeffer. It hurt him to think of Tico Feo on the seas and in far places. He sometimes looked defensively at his friend and thought, "You are just a lazy dreamer."

It is true that Tico Feo was a lazy fellow. After that first evening he had to be urged even to play his guitar. At daybreak when the guard came to rouse the men, which he did by banging a hammer on the stove, Tico Feo would whimper like a child. Sometimes he pretended to be ill, moaned and rubbed his stomach; but he never got away with this, for the Captain would send him out to work with the rest of the men. He and Mr. Schaeffer were put together on a highway gang. It was hard work, digging at frozen clay and carrying croker sacks filled with broken stone. The guard had always to be shouting at Tico Feo, for he spent most of the time trying to lean on things.

Each noon, when the dinner buckets were passed around, the two friends sat together. There were some good things in Mr. Schaeffer's bucket, as he could afford apples and candy bars from the town. He liked giving these things to his friend, for his friend enjoyed them so much, and he thought, "You are growing; it will be a long time until you are a grown man."

Not all the men liked Tico Feo. Because they were jealous, or for more subtle reasons, some of them told ugly stories about him. Tico Feo himself seemed unaware of this. When the men gathered around him, and he played his guitar and sang his songs, you could see that he felt he was loved. Most of the men did feel a love for him; they waited for and depended upon the hour between supper and lights out. "Tico, play your box," they would say. They did not notice that afterward there was a deeper sadness than there had ever been. Sleep jumped beyond them like a jack rabbit, and their eyes lingered ponderingly on the firelight that creaked behind the grating of the stove. Mr. Schaeffer was the only one who understood their troubled feeling, for he felt it too. It was that his friend had revived the brown rivers where the fish run, and ladies with sunlight in their hair.

Soon Tico Feo was allowed the honor of having a bed near the stove and next to Mr. Schaeffer. Mr. Schaeffer had always known that his friend was a terrible liar. He did not listen for the truth in Tico Feo's tales of adventure, of conquests and encounters with famous people. Rather, he took pleasure in them as plain stories, such as you would read in a magazine, and it warmed him to hear his friend's tropic voice whispering in the dark.

Except that they did not combine their bodies or think to do so, though such things were not unknown at the farm, they were as lovers. Of the seasons, spring is the most shattering: stalks thrusting through the earth's winter-stiffened crust, young leaves cracking out on old left-to-die branches, the falling-asleep wind cruising through all the newborn green. And with Mr. Schaeffer it was the same, a breaking up, a flexing of muscles that had hardened.

It was late January. The friends were sitting on the steps of the sleep house, each with a cigarette in his hand. A moon thin and yellow as a piece of lemon rind curved above them, and under its light, threads of ground frost glistened like silver snail trails. For many days Tico Feo had been drawn into himself—silent as a robber waiting in the shadows. It was no good to say to him, "Tico, play your box." He would only look at you with smooth, under-ether eyes.

"Tell a story," said Mr. Schaeffer, who felt nervous and helpless when he could not reach his friend. "Tell about when you went to the racetrack in Miami."

"I not ever go to no racetrack," said Tico Feo, thereby admitting to his wildest lie, one involving hundreds of dollars and a meeting with Bing Crosby. He did not seem to care. He produced a comb and pulled it sulkily through his hair. A few days before, this comb had been the cause of a fierce quarrel. One of the men, Wink, claimed that Tico Feo had stolen the comb from him, to which the accused replied by spitting in his face. They had wrestled around until Mr. Schaeffer and another man got them separated. "Is my comb. You tell him!" Tico Feo had demanded of Mr. Schaeffer. But Mr. Schaeffer with quiet firmness had said no, it was not his friend's comb —an answer that seemed to defeat all concerned. "Aw," said Wink, "if he wants it so much, Christ's sake, let the sonofabitch keep it." And later, in a puzzled, uncertain voice, Tico Feo had said, "I thought you was my friend." "I am," Mr. Schaeffer had thought, though he said nothing.

"I not go to no racetrack, and what I said about the widow woman, that is not true also." He puffed up his cigarette to a furious glow and looked at Mr. Schaeffer with a speculating expression. "Say, you have money, mister?"

"Maybe twenty dollars," said Mr. Schaeffer hesitantly, afraid of where this was leading.

"Not so good, twenty dollar," Tico said, but without disappointment. "No important, we work our way. In Mobile I have my friend Frederico. He will put us on a boat. There will not be trouble," and it was as though he were saying that the weather had turned colder.

There was a squeezing in Mr. Schaeffer's heart; he could not speak.

"Nobody here can run to catch Tico. He run the fastest."

"Shotguns run faster," said Mr. Schaeffer in a voice hardly alive. "I'm too old," he said, with the knowledge of age churning like nausea inside him.

Tico Feo was not listening. "Then, the world. The world, *el mundo,* my friend." Standing up, he quivered like a young horse; everything seemed to draw close to him—the moon, the callings of screech owls. His breath came quickly and turned to smoke in the air. "Should we go to Madrid? Maybe someone teach me to bullfight. You think so, mister?"

Mr. Schaeffer was not listening either. "I'm too old," he said. "I'm too damned old."

For the next several weeks Tico Feo kept after him—the world, *el mundo,* my friend; and he wanted to hide. He would shut himself in the toilet and hold his head. Nevertheless, he was excited, tantalized. What if it could come true, the race with Tico across the forests and to the sea? And he imagined himself on a boat, he who had never seen the sea, whose whole life had been land-rooted. During this time one of the convicts died, and in the yard you could hear the coffin being made. As each nail thudded into place, Mr. Schaeffer thought, "This is for me, it is mine."

Tico Feo himself was never in better spirits; he sauntered about with a dancer's snappy, gigolo grace, and had a joke for everyone. In the sleep house after supper his fingers popped at the guitar like firecrackers. He taught the men to cry *olé,* and some of them sailed their caps through the air.

When work on the road was finished, Mr. Schaeffer and Tico Feo were moved back into the forests. On Valentine's Day they ate their lunch under a pine tree. Mr. Schaeffer had ordered a dozen oranges from the town and he peeled them slowly, the skins unraveling in a spiral; the juicier slices he gave to his friend, who was proud of how far he could spit the seeds—a good ten feet.

It was a cold beautiful day, scraps of sunlight blew about them like butterflies, and Mr. Schaeffer, who liked working with the trees, felt dim and happy. Then Tico Feo said, "That one, he no could catch a fly in his mouth." He meant Armstrong, a hog-jowled man sitting with a shotgun propped between his legs. He was the youngest of the guards and new at the farm.

"I don't know," said Mr. Schaeffer. He'd watched Armstrong and noticed that, like many people who are both heavy and vain, the new guard moved with a skimming lightness. "He might could fool you."

"I fool him, maybe," said Tico Feo, and spit an orange seed in Armstrong's direction. The guard scowled at him, then blew a whistle. It was the signal for work to begin.

Sometime during the afternoon the two friends came together again; that is, they were nailing turpentine buckets onto trees that stood next to each other. At a distance below them a shallow bouncing creek branched through the woods. "In water no smell," said Tico Feo meticulously, as though remembering something he'd heard. "We run in the water; until dark we climb a tree. Yes, mister?"

Mr. Schaeffer went on hammering, but his hand was shaking, and the hammer came down on his thumb. He looked around dazedly at his friend. His face showed no reflection of pain, and he did not put the thumb in his mouth, the way a man ordinarily might.

Tico Feo's blue eyes seemed to swell like bubbles, and when in a voice quieter than the wind sounds in the pinetops he said, "Tomorrow," these eyes were all that Mr. Schaeffer could see.

"Tomorrow, mister?"

"Tomorrow," said Mr. Schaeffer.

The first colors of morning fell upon the walls of the sleep house, and Mr. Schaeffer, who had rested little, knew that Tico Feo was awake too. With the weary eyes of a crocodile he observed the movements of his friend in the next cot. Tico Feo was unknotting the scarf that contained his treasures. First he took the pocket mirror. Its jellyfish light trembled on his face. For a while he admired himself with serious delight, and combed and slicked his hair as though he were preparing to step out to a party. Then he hung the rosary about his neck. The cologne he never opened, nor the map. The last thing he did was to tune his guitar. While the other men were dressing, he sat on the edge of his cot and tuned the guitar. It was strange, for he must have known he would never play it again.

Bird shrills followed the men through the smoky morning woods. They walked single file, fifteen men to a group, and a guard bringing up the rear of each line. Mr. Schaeffer was sweating as though it were a hot day, and he could not keep in marching step with his friend, who walked ahead, snapping his fingers and whistling at the birds.

A signal had been set. Tico Feo was to call, "Time out," and pretend to go behind a tree. But Mr. Schaeffer did not know when it would happen.

The guard named Armstrong blew a whistle, and his men dropped from the line and separated to their various stations. Mr. Schaeffer, though going about his work as best he could, took care always to be in a position where he could keep an eye on both Tico Feo and the guard. Armstrong sat on a stump, a chew of tobacco lopsiding his face, and his gun pointing into the sun. He had the tricky eyes of a cardsharp; you could not really tell where he was looking.

Once another man gave the signal. Although Mr. Schaeffer had known at once that it was not the voice of his friend, panic had pulled at his throat like a rope. As the morning wore on there was such a drumming in his ears he was afraid he would not hear the signal when it came.

The sun climbed to the center of the sky. "He is just a lazy dreamer. It will never happen," thought Mr. Schaeffer, daring for a moment to believe this. "But first we eat," said Tico Feo with a practical air as they set their dinner pails on the bank above the creek. They ate in silence, almost as though each bore the other a grudge, but at the end of it Mr. Schaeffer felt his friend's hand close over his own and hold it with a tender pressure.

"Mister Armstrong, time out . . ."

Near the creek Mr. Schaeffer had seen a sweet gum tree, and he was thinking it would soon be spring and the sweet gum ready to chew. A razory stone ripped open the palm of his hand as he slid off the slippery embankment into the water. He straightened up and began to run; his legs were long, he kept almost abreast of Tico Feo, and icy geysers sprayed around them. Back and forth through the woods the shouts of men boomed hollowly like voices in a cavern, and there were three shots, all highflying, as though the guard were shooting at a cloud of geese.

Mr. Schaeffer did not see the log that lay across the creek. He thought he was still running, and his legs thrashed about him; it was as though he were a turtle stranded on its back.

While he struggled there, it seemed to him that the face of his friend, suspended above him, was part of the white winter sky—it was so distant, judging. It hung there but an instant, like a hummingbird, yet in that time he'd seen that Tico Feo had not wanted him to make it, had never thought he would, and he remembered once thinking that it would be a long time before his friend was a grown man. When they found him, he was still lying in the ankle-deep water as though it were a summer afternoon and he were idly floating on the stream.

Since then three winters have gone by, and each has been said to be the coldest, the longest. Two recent months of rain washed deeper ruts in the clay road leading to the farm, and it is harder than ever to get there, harder to leave. A pair of searchlights has been added to the walls, and they burn there through the night like the eyes of a giant owl. Otherwise, there have not been many changes. Mr. Schaeffer, for instance, looks much the same, except that there is a thicker frost of white in his hair, and as the result of a broken ankle he walks with a limp. It was the Captain himself who said that Mr. Schaeffer had broken his ankle attempting to capture Tico Feo. There was even a picture of Mr. Schaeffer in the newspaper, and under it this caption: "Tried to Prevent Escape." At the time he was deeply mortified, not because he knew the other men were laughing, but because he thought of Tico Feo seeing it. But he cut it out of the paper anyway, and keeps it in an envelope along with several clippings pertaining to his friend: a spinster woman told the authorities he'd entered her home and kissed her, twice he was reported seen in the Mobile vicinity, finally it was believed that he had left the country.

No one has ever disputed Mr. Schaeffer's claim to the guitar. Several months ago a new prisoner was moved into the sleep house. He was said to be a fine player, and Mr. Schaeffer was persuaded to lend him the guitar. But all the man's tunes came out sour, for it was as though Tico Feo, tuning his guitar that last morning, had put a curse upon it. Now it lies under Mr. Schaeffer's cot, where its glass diamonds are turning yellow; in the night his hand sometimes searches it out, and his fingers drift across the strings: then, the world.

House
of Flowers

(1952)

OTTILIE SHOULD HAVE BEEN THE happiest girl in Port-au-Prince. As Baby said to her, Look at all the things that can be put to your credit. Like what? said Ottilie, for she was vain and preferred compliments to pork or perfume. Like your looks, said Baby: you have a lovely light color, even almost blue eyes, and such a pretty, sweet face—there is no girl on the road with steadier customers, every one of them ready to buy you all the beer you can drink. Ottilie conceded that this was true, and with a smile continued to total her fortunes: I have five silk dresses and a pair of green satin shoes, I have three gold teeth worth thirty thousand francs, maybe Mr. Jamison or someone will give me another bracelet. But, Baby, she sighed, and could not express her discontent.

Baby was her best friend; she had another friend too: Rosita. Baby was like a wheel, round, rolling; junk rings had left green circles on several of her fat fingers, her teeth were dark as burnt tree stumps, and when she laughed you could hear her at sea, at least so the sailors claimed. Rosita, the other friend, was taller than most men, and stronger; at night, with the customers on hand, she minced about, lisping in a silly doll voice, but in the daytime she took spacious, loping strides and spoke out in a military baritone. Both of Ottilie's friends were from the Dominican Republic, and considered it reason enough to feel themselves a cut above the natives of this darker country. It did not concern them that Ottilie was a native. You have brains, Baby told her, and certainly what Baby doted on was a good brain. Ottilie was often afraid that her friends would discover that she could neither read nor write.

The house where they lived and worked was rickety, thin as a steeple, and frosted with fragile, bougainvillaea-vined balconies. Though there was no sign outside, it was called the Champs Elysées. The proprietress, a spinsterish, smothered-looking invalid, ruled from an upstairs room, where she stayed locked away rocking in a rocking chair and drinking ten to twenty Coca-Colas a day. All counted, she had eight ladies working for her; with the exception of Ottilie, no one of them was under thirty. In the evening, when the ladies assembled on the porch, where they chatted and flourished paper fans that beat the air like delirious moths, Ottilie seemed a delightful dreaming child surrounded by older, uglier sisters.

Her mother was dead, her father was a planter who had gone back to France, and she had been brought up in the mountains by a rough peasant family, the sons of whom had each at a young age lain with her in some green and shadowy place. Three years earlier, when she was fourteen, she had come down for the first time to the market in Port-au-Prince. It was a journey of two days and a night, and she'd walked carrying a ten-pound sack of grain; to ease the load she'd let a little of the grain spill out, then a little more, and by the time she had reached the market there was almost none left. Ottilie had cried because she thought of how angry the family would be when she came home without the money for the grain; but these tears were not for long: such a jolly nice man helped her dry them. He bought her a slice of coconut, and took her to see his cousin, who was the proprietress of the Champs Elysées. Ottilie could not believe her good luck; the jukebox music, the satin shoes and joking men were as strange and marvelous as the electric light-bulb in her room, which she never tired of clicking on and off. Soon she had become the most talked-of girl on the road, the proprietress was able to ask double for her, and Ottilie grew vain; she could pose for hours in front of a mirror. It was seldom that she thought of the mountains; and yet, after three years, there was much of the mountains still with her: their winds seemed still to move around her, her hard, high haunches had not softened, nor had the soles of her feet, which were rough as lizard's hide.

When her friends spoke of love, of men they had loved, Ottilie became sulky: How do you feel if you're in love? she asked. Ah, said Rosita with swooning eyes, you feel as though pepper has been sprinkled on your heart, as though tiny fish are swimming in your veins. Ottilie shook her head; if Rosita was telling the truth, then she had never been in love, for she had never felt that way about any of the men who came to the house.

This so troubled her that at last she went to see a Houngan who lived in the hills above town. Unlike her friends, Ottilie did not tack Christian pictures on the walls of her room; she did not believe in God, but many gods: of food, light, of death, ruin. The Houngan was in touch with these gods; he kept their secrets on his altar, could hear their voices in the rattle of a gourd, could dispense their power in a potion. Speaking through the gods, the Houngan gave her this message: You must catch a wild bee, he said, and hold it in your closed hand . . . if the bee does not sting, then you will know you have found love.

On the way home she thought of Mr. Jamison. He was a man past fifty, an American connected with an engineering project. The gold bracelets chattering on her wrists were presents from him, and Ottilie, passing a fence snowy with honeysuckle, wondered if, after all, she was not in love with Mr. Jamison. Black bees festooned the honeysuckle. With a brave thrust of her hand she caught one dozing. Its stab was like a blow that knocked her to her knees; and there she knelt, weeping until it was hard to know whether the bee had stung her hand or her eyes.

It was March, and events were leading toward carnival. At the Champs Elysées the ladies were sewing on their costumes; Ottilie's hands were idle, for she had decided not to wear a costume at all. On rah-rah weekends, when drums sounded at the rising moon, she sat at her window and watched with a wandering mind the little bands of singers dancing and drumming their way along the road; she listened to the whistling and the laughter and felt no desire to join in. Somebody would think you were a thousand years old, said Baby, and Rosita said: Ottilie, why don't you come to the cockfight with us?

She was not speaking of an ordinary cockfight. From all parts of the island contestants had arrived bringing their fiercest birds. Ottilie thought she might as well go, and screwed a pair of pearls into her ears. When they arrived the exhibition was already under way; in a great tent a sea-sized crowd sobbed and shouted, while a second crowd, those who could not get in, thronged on the outskirts. Entry was no problem to the ladies from the Champs Elysées: a policeman friend cut a path for them and made room on a bench by the ring. The country people surrounding them seemed embarrassed to find themselves in such stylish company. They looked shyly at Baby's lacquered nails, the rhinestone combs in Rosita's hair, the glow of Ottilie's pearl earrings. However, the fights were exciting, and the ladies were soon forgotten; Baby was annoyed that this should be so, and her eyes rolled about searching for glances in their direction. Suddenly she nudged Ottilie. Ottilie, she said, you've got an admirer: see that boy over there, he's staring at you like you were something cold to drink.

At first she thought he must be someone she knew, for he was looking at her as though she should recognize him; but how could she know him when she'd never known anyone so beautiful, anyone with such long legs, little ears? She could see that he was from the mountains: his straw country hat and the worn-out blue of his thick shirt told her as much. He was a ginger color, his skin shiny as a lemon, smooth as a guava leaf, and the tilt of his head was as arrogant as the black-and-scarlet bird he held in his hands. Ottilie was used to boldly smiling at men; but now her smile was fragmentary, it clung to her lips like cake crumbs.

Eventually there was an intermission. The arena was cleared, and all who could crowded into it to dance and stamp while an orchestra of drums and strings sang out carnival tunes. It was then that the young man approached Ottilie; she laughed to see his bird perched like a parrot on his shoulder. Off with you, said Baby, outraged that a peasant should ask Ottilie to dance, and Rosita rose menacingly to stand between the young man and her friend. He only smiled, and said: Please, madame, I would like to speak with your daughter. Ottilie felt herself being lifted, felt her hips meet against his to the rhythm of music, and she did not mind at all, she let him lead her into the thickest tangle of dancers. Rosita said: Did you hear that, he thought I was her mother? And Baby, consoling her, grimly said: After all, what do you expect? They're only natives, both of them: when she comes back we'll just pretend we don't know her.

As it happened, Ottilie did not return to her friends. Royal, this was the young man's name, Royal Bonaparte, he told her, had not wanted to dance. We must walk in a quiet place, he said, hold my hand and I will take you. She thought him strange, but did not feel strange with him, for the mountains were still with her, and he was of the mountains. With her hands together, and the iridescent cock swaying on his shoulder, they left the tent and wandered lazily down a white road, then along a soft lane, where birds of sunlight fluttered through the greenness of leaning acacia trees.

I have been sad, he said, not looking sad. In my village Juno is a champion, but the birds here are strong and ugly, and if I let him fight, I would only have a dead Juno. So I will take him home and say that he won. Ottilie, will you have a dip of snuff?

She sneezed voluptuously. Snuff reminded her of her childhood, and mean as those years had been, nostalgia touched her with its far-reaching wand. Royal, she said, be still a minute, I want to take off my shoes.

Royal himself did not have shoes; his golden feet were slender and airy, and the prints they left were like the track of a delicate animal. He said: How is it that I find you here, in all the world here, where nothing is good, where the rum is bad and the people thieves? Why do I find you here, Ottilie?

Because I must make my way, the same as you, and here there is a place for me. I work in a—oh, kind of hotel.

We have our own place, he said. All the side of a hill, and there at the top of the hill is my cool house. Ottilie, will you come and sit inside it?

Crazy, said Ottilie, teasing him, crazy, and she ran between the trees, and he was after her, his arms out as though he held a net. The bird Juno flared his wings, crowed, flew to the ground. Scratchy leaves and fur of moss thrilled the soles of Ottilie's feet as she lilted through the shade and shadows; abruptly, into a veil of rainbow fern, she fell with a thorn in her heel. She winced when Royal pulled out the thorn; he kissed the place where it had been, his lips moved to her hands, her throat, and it was as though she were among drifting leaves. She breathed the odor of him, the dark, clean smell that was like the roots of things, of geraniums, of heavy trees.

Now that's enough, she pleaded, though she did not feel that this was so: it was only that after an hour of him her heart was about to give out. He was quiet then, his tickly-haired head rested above her heart, and shoo she said to the gnats that clustered about his sleeping eyes, shush she said to Juno, who pranced around crowing at the sky.

While she lay there, Ottilie saw her old enemy, the bees. Silently, in a line like ants, the bees were crawling in and out of a broken stump that stood not far from her. She loosened herself from Royal's arms, and smoothed a place on the ground for his head. Her hand was trembling as she lay it in the path of the bees, but the first that came along tumbled onto her palm, and when she closed her fingers it made no move to hurt her. She counted ten, just to be sure, then opened her hand, and the bee, in spiraling arcs, climbed the air with a joyful singing.

The proprietress gave Baby and Rosita a piece of advice: Leave her alone, let her go, a few weeks and she will be back. The proprietress spoke in the calm of defeat: to keep Ottilie with her, she'd offered the best room in the house, a new gold tooth, a Kodak, an electric fan, but Ottilie had not wavered, she had gone right on putting her belongings in a cardboard box. Baby tried to help, but she was crying so much that Ottilie had to stop her: it was bound to be bad luck, all those tears falling on a bride's possessions. And to Rosita she said: Rosita, you ought to be glad for me instead of standing there wringing your hands.

It was only two days after the cockfight that Royal shouldered Ottilie's cardboard box and walked her in the dusk toward the mountains. When it was learned that she was no longer at the Champs Elysées many of the customers took their trade elsewhere; others, though remaining loyal to the old place, complained of a gloom in the atmosphere: some evenings there was hardly anyone to buy the ladies a beer. Gradually it began to be felt that Ottilie after all would not come back; at the end of six months the proprietress said: She must be dead.

. . .

Royal's house was like a house of flowers; wisteria sheltered the roof, a curtain of vines shaded the windows, lilies bloomed at the door. From the windows one could see far, faint winkings of the sea, as the house was high up a hill; here the sun burned hot but the shadows were cold. Inside, the house was always dark and cool, and the walls rustled with pasted pink and green newspapers. There was only one room; it contained a stove, a teetering mirror on top a marble table, and a brass bed big enough for three fat men.

But Ottilie did not sleep in this grand bed. She was not allowed even to sit upon it, for it was the property of Royal's grandmother, Old Bonaparte. A charred, lumpy creature, bowlegged as a dwarf and bald as a buzzard, Old Bonaparte was much respected for miles around as a maker of spells. There were many who were afraid to have her shadow fall upon them; even Royal was wary of her, and he stuttered when he told her that he'd brought home a wife. Motioning Ottilie to her, the old woman bruised her here and there with vicious little pinches, and informed her grandson that his bride was too skinny: She will die with her first.

Each night the young couple waited to make love until they thought Old Bonaparte had gone to sleep. Sometimes, stretched on the straw moonlit pallet where they slept, Ottilie was sure that Old Bonaparte was awake and watching them. Once she saw a gummy, star-struck eye shining in the dark. There was no use complaining to Royal, he only laughed: What harm was there in an old woman who had seen so much of life wanting to see a little more?

Because she loved Royal, Ottilie put away her grievances and tried not to resent Old Bonaparte. For a long while she was happy; she did not miss her friends or the life in Port-au-Prince; even so, she kept her souvenirs of those days in good repair: with a sewing basket Baby had given her as a wedding gift she mended the silk dresses, the green silk stockings that now she never wore, for there was no place to wear them: only men congregated at the café in the village, at the cockfights. When women wanted to meet they met at the washing stream. But Ottilie was too busy to be lonesome. At daybreak she gathered eucalyptus leaves to start a fire and begin their meals; there were chickens to feed, a goat to be milked, there was Old Bonaparte's whining for attention. Three and four times a day she filled a bucket of drinking water and carried it to where Royal worked in the cane fields a mile below the house. She did not mind that on these visits he was gruff with her: she knew that he was showing off before the other men who worked in the fields, and who grinned at her like split watermelons. But at night, when she had him home, she'd pull his ears and pout that he treated her like a dog until, in the dark of the yard where the fireflies flamed, he would hold her and whisper something to make her smile.

They had been married about five months when Royal began doing the things he'd done before his marriage. Other men went to the café in the evenings, stayed whole Sundays at a cockfight—he couldn't understand why Ottilie should carry on about it; but she said he had no right behaving the way he did, and that if he loved her, he wouldn't leave her alone day and night with that mean old woman. I love you, he said, but a man has to have his pleasures, too. There were nights when he pleasured himself until the moon was in the middle of the sky; she never knew when he was coming home, and she would lie fretting on the pallet, imagining she could not sleep without his arms around her.

But Old Bonaparte was the real torment. She was about to worry Ottilie out of her mind. If Ottilie was cooking, the terrible old woman was sure to come poking around the stove, and when she did not like what there was to eat she would take a mouthful and spit it on the floor. Every mess she could think of she made: she wet the bed, insisted on having the goat in the room, whatever she touched was soon spilled or broken, and to Royal she complained that a woman who couldn't keep a nice house for her husband was worthless. She was underfoot the whole day, and her red, remorseless eyes were seldom shut; but the worst of it, the thing that finally made Ottilie threaten to kill her, was the old woman's habit of sneaking up from nowhere and pinching her so hard you could see the fingernail marks. If you do that one more time, if you just dare, I'll snatch that knife and cut out your heart! Old Bonaparte knew Ottilie meant it, and though she stopped the pinching, she thought of other jokes: for instance, she made a point of walking all over a certain part of the yard, pretending she did not know that Ottilie had planted a little garden there.

One day two exceptional things happened. A boy came from the village bringing a letter for Ottilie; at the Champs Elysées postcards had once in a while arrived from sailors and other traveling men who had spent pleasant moments with her, but this was the first letter she'd ever received. Since she could not read it, her first impulse was to tear it up: there was no use having it hang around to haunt her. Of course there was a chance that someday she would learn to read; and so she went to hide it in her sewing basket.

When she opened the sewing basket, she made a sinister discovery: there, like a gruesome ball of yarn, was the severed head of a yellow cat. So, the miserable old woman was up to new tricks! She wants to put a spell, thought Ottilie, not in the least frightened. Primly lifting the head by one of its ears, she carried it to the stove and dropped it into a boiling pot: at noon Old Bonaparte sucked her teeth and remarked that the soup Ottilie had made for her was surprisingly tasty.

The next morning, just in time for the midday meal, she found twisting in her basket a small green snake, which, chopping fine as sand, she sprinkled into a serving of stew. Each day her ingenuity was tested: there were spiders to bake, a lizard to fry, a buzzard's breast to boil. Old Bonaparte ate several helpings of everything. With a restless glittering her eyes followed Ottilie as she watched for some sign that the spell was taking hold. You don't look well, Ottilie, she said, mixing a little molasses in the vinegar of her voice. You eat like an ant: here now, why don't you have a bowl of this good soup?

Because, answered Ottilie evenly, I don't like buzzard in my soup; or spiders in my bread, snakes in the stew: I have no appetite for such things.

Old Bonaparte understood; with swelling veins and a stricken, powerless tongue, she rose shakily to her feet, then crashed across the table. Before nightfall she was dead.

Royal summoned mourners. They came from the village, from the neighboring hills and, wailing like dogs at midnight, laid siege to the house. Old women beat their heads against the walls, moaning men prostrated themselves: it was the art of sorrow, and those who best mimicked grief were much admired. After the funeral everyone went away, satisfied that they'd done a good job.

Now the house belonged to Ottilie. Without Old Bonaparte's prying and her mess to clean, she had more spare time, but she did not know what to do with it. She sprawled on the great brass bed, she loafed in front of the mirror; monotony hummed in her head, and to drive away its fly-buzz sound she would sing the songs she'd learned from the jukebox at the Champs Elysées. Waiting in the twilight for Royal, she would remember that at this hour her friends in Port-au-Prince were gossiping on the porch and waiting for the turning headlights of a car; but when she saw Royal ambling up the path, his cane cutter swinging at his side like a crescent moon, she forgot such thoughts and ran with a satisfied heart to meet him.

One night as they lay half-drowsing, Ottilie felt suddenly another presence in the room. Then, gleaming there at the foot of the bed, she saw, as she had seen before, a watching eye; thus she knew what for some time she had suspected: that Old Bonaparte was dead but not gone. Once, when she was alone in the house, she'd heard a laugh, and once again, out in the yard, she'd seen the goat gazing at someone who was not there and twinkling his ears as he did whenever the old woman scratched his skull.

Stop shaking the bed, said Royal, and Ottilie, with a finger raised at the eye, whisperingly asked him if he could not see it. When he replied that she was dreaming, she reached for the eye and screamed at feeling only air. Royal lighted a lamp; he cuddled Ottilie on his lap and smoothed her hair while she told him of the discoveries she'd made in her sewing basket, and of how she had disposed of them. Was it wrong what she'd done? Royal did not know, it was not for him to say, but it was his opinion that she would have to be punished; and why? because the old woman wanted it, because she would otherwise never leave Ottilie in peace: that was the way with haunts.

In accordance with this, Royal fetched a rope the next morning and proposed to tie Ottilie to a tree in the yard: there she was to remain until dark without food or water, and anyone passing would know her to be in a state of disgrace.

But Ottilie crawled under the bed and refused to come out. I'll run away, she whimpered. Royal, if you try to tie me to that old tree, I'll run away.

Then I'd have to go and get you, said Royal, and that would be the worse for you.

He gripped her by an ankle and dragged her squealing from under the bed. All the way to the yard she caught at things, the door, a vine, the goat's beard, but none of these would hold her, and Royal was not detained from tying her to the tree. He made three knots in the rope, and went off to work sucking his hand where she had bit him. She hollered to him all the bad words she'd ever heard until he disappeared over the hill. The goat, Juno and the chickens gathered to stare at her humiliation; slumping to the ground, Ottilie stuck out her tongue at them.

Because she was almost asleep, Ottilie thought it was a dream when, in the company of a child from the village, Baby and Rosita, wobbling on high heels and carrying fancy umbrellas, tottered up the path calling her name. Since they were people in a dream, they probably would not be surprised to find her tied to a tree.

My God, are you mad? shrieked Baby, keeping her distance as though she feared that indeed this must be the case. Speak to us, Ottilie!

Blinking, giggling, Ottilie said: I'm just happy to see you. Rosita, please untie me so that I can hug you both.

So this is what the brute does, said Rosita, tearing at the ropes. Wait till I see him, beating you and tying you in the yard like a dog.

Oh no, said Ottilie. Royal never beats me. It's just that today I'm being punished.

You wouldn't listen to us, said Baby. And now you see what's come of it. That man has plenty to answer for, she added, brandishing her umbrella.

Ottilie hugged her friends and kissed them. Isn't it a pretty house? she said, leading them toward it. It's like you picked a wagon of flowers and built a house with them: that is what I think. Come in out of the sun. It's cool inside and smells so sweet.

Rosita sniffed as though what she smelled was nothing sweet, and in her well-bottom voice declared that yes, it was better that they stay out of the sun, as it seemed to be affecting Ottilie's head.

It's a mercy that we've come, said Baby, fishing inside an enormous purse. And you can thank Mr. Jamison for that. Madame said you were dead, and when you never answered our letter we thought it must be so. But Mr. Jamison, that's the loveliest man you'll ever know, he hired a car for me and Rosita, your dearest loving friends, to come up here and find out what had happened to our Ottilie. Ottilie, I've got a bottle of rum here in my purse, so get us a glass and we'll all have a round.

The elegant foreign manners and flashing finery of the city ladies had intoxicated their guide, a little boy whose peeking black eyes bobbed at the window. Ottilie was impressed, too, for it was a long time since she'd seen painted lips or smelled bottle perfume, and while Baby poured the rum she got out her satin shoes, her pearl earrings. Dear, said Rosita when Ottilie had finished dressing up, there's no man alive that wouldn't buy you a whole keg of beer; to think of it, a gorgeous piece like you suffering far away from those who love you.

I haven't been suffering so much, said Ottilie. Just sometimes.

Hush now, said Baby. You don't have to talk about it yet. It's all over anyway. Here, dear, let me see your glass again. A toast to old times, and those to be! Tonight Mr. Jamison is going to buy champagne for everybody: Madame is letting him have it at half-price.

Oh, said Ottilie, envying her friends. Well, she wanted to know, what did people say of her, was she remembered?

Ottilie, you have no idea, said Baby; men nobody ever laid eyes on before have come into the place asking where is Ottilie, because they've heard about you way off in Havana and Miami. As for Mr. Jamison, he doesn't even look at us other girls, just comes and sits on the porch drinking by himself.

Yes, said Ottilie wistfully. He was always sweet to me, Mr. Jamison.

Presently the sun was slanting, and the bottle of rum stood three-quarters empty. A thunderburst of rain had for a moment drenched the hills that now, seen through the windows, shimmered like dragonfly wings, and a breeze, rich with the scent of rained-on flowers, roamed the room rustling the green and pink papers on the walls. Many stories had been told, some of them funny, a few that were sad; it was like any night's talk at the Champs Elysées, and Ottilie was happy to be a part of it again.

But it's getting late, said Baby. And we promised to be back before midnight. Ottilie, can we help you pack?

Although she had not realized that her friends expected her to leave with them, the rum stirring in her made it seem a likely assumption, and with a smile she thought: I told him I would go away. Only, she said aloud, it's not like I would have even a week to enjoy myself: Royal will come right down and get me.

Both her friends laughed at this. You're so silly, said Baby. I'd like to see that Royal when some of our men got through with him.

I wouldn't stand for anybody hurting Royal, said Ottilie. Besides, he'd be even madder when we got home.

Baby said: But, Ottilie, you wouldn't be coming back here with him.

Ottilie giggled, and looked about the room as though she saw something invisible to the others. Why, sure I would, she said.

Rolling her eyes, Baby produced a fan and jerked it in front of her face. That's the craziest thing I've ever heard, she said between hard lips. Isn't that the craziest thing you've ever heard, Rosita?

It's that Ottilie's been through so much, said Rosita. Dear, why don't you lie down on the bed while we pack your things?

Ottilie watched as they commenced piling her possessions. They scooped her combs and pins, they wound up her silk stockings. She took off her pretty clothes, as if she were going to put on something finer still; instead, she slipped back into her old dress; then, working quietly, and as though she were helping her friends, she put everything back where it belonged. Baby stamped her foot when she saw what was happening.

Listen, said Ottilie. If you and Rosita are my friends, please do what I tell you: tie me in the yard just like I was when you came. That way no bee is ever going to sting me.

Stinking drunk, said Baby; but Rosita told her to shut up. I think, said Rosita with a sigh, I think Ottilie is in love. If Royal wanted her back, she would go with him, and this being the way things were, they might as well go home and say that Madame was right, that Ottilie was dead.

Yes, said Ottilie, for the drama of it appealed to her. Tell them that I am dead.

So they went into the yard; there, with heaving bosoms and eyes as round as the daytime moon scudding above, Baby said she would have no part in tying Ottilie to the tree, which left Rosita to do it alone. On parting, it was Ottilie who cried the most, though she was glad to see them go, for she knew that as soon as they were gone she would not think of them again. Teetering on their high heels down the dips of the path, they turned to wave, but Ottilie could not wave back, and so she forgot them before they were out of sight.

Chewing eucalyptus leaves to sweeten her breath, she felt the chill of twilight twitch the air. Yellow deepened the daytime moon, and roosting birds sailed into the darkness of the tree. Suddenly, hearing Royal on the path, she threw her legs akimbo, let her neck go limp, lolled her eyes far back into their sockets. Seen from a distance, it would look as though she had come to some violent, pitiful end; and, listening to Royal's footsteps quicken to a run, she happily thought: This will give him a good scare.

Among the
Paths to Eden

(1960)

ONE SATURDAY IN MARCH, AN OCCA-
sion of pleasant winds and sailing
clouds, Mr. Ivor Belli bought from a Brooklyn florist a fine mass of jonquils
and conveyed them, first by subway, then foot, to an immense cemetery
in Queens, a site unvisited by him since he had seen his wife buried there
the previous autumn. Sentiment could not be credited with returning him
today, for Mrs. Belli, to whom he had been married twenty-seven years,
during which time she had produced two now grown and matrimonially
settled daughters, had been a woman of many natures, most of them trying:
he had no desire to renew so unsoothing an acquaintance, even in spirit.
No; but a hard winter had just passed, and he felt in need of exercise, air,
a heart-lifting stroll through the handsome, spring-prophesying weather;
of course, rather as an extra dividend, it was nice that he would be able to
tell his daughters of a journey to their mother's grave, especially so since
it might a little appease the elder girl, who seemed resentful of Mr. Belli's
too comfortable acceptance of life as lived alone.

The cemetery was not a reposeful, pretty place; was, in fact, a damned
frightening one: acres of fog-colored stone spilled across a sparsely grassed
and shadeless plateau. An unhindered view of Manhattan's skyline provided the location with beauty of a stage-prop sort—it loomed beyond the
graves like a steep headstone honoring these quiet folk, its used-up and very
former citizens: the juxtaposed spectacle made Mr. Belli, who was by

127

profession a tax accountant and therefore equipped to enjoy irony however sadistic, smile, actually chuckle—yet, oh God in heaven, its inferences chilled him, too, deflated the buoyant stride carrying him along the cemetery's rigid, pebbled paths. He slowed until he stopped, thinking: "I ought to have taken Morty to the zoo"; Morty being his grandson, aged three. But it would be churlish not to continue, vengeful: and why waste a bouquet? The combination of thrift and virtue reactivated him; he was breathing hard from hurry when, at last, he stooped to jam the jonquils into a rock urn perched on a rough gray slab engraved with Gothic calligraphy declaring that

SARAH BELLI

1901–1959

had been the

DEVOTED WIFE OF IVOR
BELOVED MOTHER OF IVY AND REBECCA

Lord, what a relief to know the woman's tongue was finally stilled. But the thought, pacifying as it was, and though supported by visions of his new and silent bachelor's apartment, did not relight the suddenly snuffed-out sense of immortality, of glad-to-be-aliveness, which the day had earlier kindled. He had set forth expecting such good from the air, the walk, the aroma of another spring about to be. Now he wished he had worn a scarf; the sunshine was false, without real warmth, and the wind, it seemed to him, had grown rather wild. As he gave the jonquils a decorative pruning, he regretted he could not delay their doom by supplying them with water; relinquishing the flowers, he turned to leave.

A woman stood in his way. Though there were few other visitors to the cemetery, he had not noticed her before, or heard her approach. She did not step aside. She glanced at the jonquils; presently her eyes, situated behind steel-rimmed glasses, swerved back to Mr. Belli.

"Uh. Relative?"

"My wife," he said, and sighed as though some such noise was obligatory.

She sighed, too; a curious sigh that implied gratification. "Gee, I'm sorry."

Mr. Belli's face lengthened. "Well."

"It's a shame."

"Yes."

"I hope it wasn't a long illness. Anything painful."

"No-o-o," he said, shifting from one foot to the other. "In her sleep." Sensing an unsatisfied silence, he added, "Heart condition."

"Gee. That's how I lost my father. Just recently. Kind of gives us something in common. Something," she said, in a tone alarmingly plaintive, "something to talk about."

"—know how you must feel."

"At least they didn't suffer. That's a comfort."

The fuse attached to Mr. Belli's patience shortened. Until now he had kept his gaze appropriately lowered, observing, after his initial glimpse of her, merely the woman's shoes, which were of the sturdy, so-called sensible type often worn by aged women and nurses. "A great comfort," he said, as he executed three tasks: raised his eyes, tipped his hat, took a step forward.

Again the woman held her ground; it was as though she had been employed to detain him. "Could you give me the time? My old clock," she announced, self-consciously tapping some dainty machinery strapped to her wrist, "I got it for graduating high school. That's why it doesn't run so good anymore. I mean, it's pretty old. But it makes a nice appearance."

Mr. Belli was obliged to unbutton his topcoat and plow around for a gold watch embedded in a vest pocket. Meanwhile, he scrutinized the lady, really took her apart. She must have been blond as a child, her general coloring suggested so: the clean shine of her Scandinavian skin, her chunky cheeks, flushed with peasant health, and the blueness of her genial eyes—such honest eyes, attractive despite the thin silver spectacles surrounding them; but the hair itself, what could be discerned of it under a drab felt hat, was poorly permanented frizzle of no particular tint. She was a bit taller than Mr. Belli, who was five-foot-eight with the aid of shoe lifts, and she may have weighed more; at any rate, he couldn't imagine that she mounted scales too cheerfully. Her hands: kitchen hands; and the nails: not only nibbled ragged, but painted with a pearly lacquer queerly phosphorescent. She wore a plain brown coat and carried a plain black purse. When the student of these components recomposed them he found they assembled themselves into a very decent-looking person whose looks he liked; the nail polish was discouraging; still he felt that here was someone you could trust. As he trusted Esther Jackson, Miss Jackson, his secretary. Indeed, that was who she reminded him of, Miss Jackson; not that the comparison was fair—to Miss Jackson, who possessed, as he had once in the course of a quarrel informed Mrs. Belli, "intellectual elegance and elegance otherwise." Nevertheless, the woman confronting him seemed imbued with that quality of good-will he appreciated in his secretary, Miss Jackson, Esther (as he'd lately, absent-mindedly, called her). Moreover, he guessed them to be about the same age: rather on the right side of forty.

"Noon. Exactly."

"Think of that! Why, you must be famished," she said, and unclasped her purse, peered into it as though it were a picnic hamper crammed with sufficient treats to furnish a smörgåsbord. She scooped out a fistful of peanuts. "I practically live on peanuts since Pop—since I haven't anyone to cook for. I must say, even if I do say so, I miss my own cooking; Pop always said I was better than any restaurant he ever went to. But it's no pleasure cooking just for yourself, even when you *can* make pastries light as a leaf. Go on. Have some. They're fresh-roasted."

Mr. Belli accepted; he'd always been childish about peanuts and, as he sat down on his wife's grave to eat them, only hoped his friend had more. A gesture of his hand suggested that she sit beside him; he was surprised to see that the invitation seemed to embarrass her; sudden additions of pink saturated her cheeks, as though he'd asked her to transform Mrs. Belli's bier into a love bed.

"It's okay for you. A relative. But me. Would she like a stranger sitting on her—resting place?"

"Please. Be a guest. Sarah won't mind," he told her, grateful the dead cannot hear, for it both awed and amused him to consider what Sarah, that vivacious scene-maker, that energetic searcher for lipstick traces and stray blond strands, would say if she could see him shelling peanuts on her tomb with a woman not entirely unattractive.

And then, as she assumed a prim perch on the rim of the grave, he noticed her leg. Her left leg; it stuck straight out like a stiff piece of mischief with which she planned to trip passers-by. Aware of his interest, she smiled, lifted the leg up and down. "An accident. You know. When I was a kid. I fell off a roller coaster at Coney. Honest. It was in the paper. Nobody knows why I'm alive. The only thing is I can't bend my knee. Otherwise it doesn't make any difference. Except to go dancing. Are you much of a dancer?"

Mr. Belli shook his head; his mouth was full of peanuts.

"So that's something else we have in common. Dancing. I *might* like it. But I don't. I like music, though."

Mr. Belli nodded his agreement.

"And flowers," she added, touching the bouquet of jonquils; then her fingers traveled on and, as though she were reading Braille, brushed across the marble lettering on his name. "Ivor," she said, mispronouncing it. "Ivor Belli. My name is Mary O'Meaghan. But I wish *I* were Italian. My sister is; well, she married one. And oh, he's full of fun; happy-natured and outgoing, like all Italians. He says my spaghetti's the best he's ever had. Especially the kind I make with seafood sauce. You ought to taste it."

Mr. Belli, having finished the peanuts, swept the hulls off his lap. "You've got a customer. But he's not Italian. Belli sounds like that. Only I'm Jewish."

She frowned, not with disapproval, but as if he had mysteriously daunted her.

"My family came from Russia; I was born there."

This last information restored her enthusiasm, accelerated it. "I don't care what they say in the papers. I'm sure Russians are the same as everybody else. Human. Did you see the Bolshoi Ballet on TV? Now didn't that make you proud to be a Russian?"

He thought: she means well; and was silent.

"Red cabbage soup—hot or cold—with sour cream. Hmnn. See," she said, producing a second helping of peanuts, "you *were* hungry. Poor fellow." She sighed. "How you must miss your wife's cooking."

It was true, he did; and the conversational pressure being applied to his appetite made him realize it. Sarah had set an excellent table: varied, on time, and well flavored. He recalled certain cinnamon-scented feast days. Afternoons of gravy and wine, starchy linen, the "good" silver; followed by a nap. Moreover, Sarah had never asked him to dry a dish (he could hear her calmly humming in the kitchen), had never complained of housework; and she had contrived to make the raising of two girls a smooth series of thought-out, affectionate events; Mr. Belli's contribution to their upbringing had been to be an admiring witness; if his daughters were a credit to him (Ivy living in Bronxville, and married to a dental surgeon; her sister the wife of A. J. Krakower, junior partner in the law firm of Finnegan, Loeb and Krakower), he had Sarah to thank; they were her accomplishment. There was much to be said for Sarah, and he was glad to discover himself thinking so, to find himself remembering not the long hell of hours she had spent honing her tongue on his habits, supposed poker-playing, woman-chasing vices, but gentler episodes: Sarah showing off her self-made hats, Sarah scattering crumbs on snowy windowsills for winter pigeons: a tide of visions that towed to sea the junk of harsher recollections. He felt, was all at once happy to feel, mournful, sorry he had not been sorry sooner; but, though he did genuinely value Sarah suddenly, he could not pretend regret that their life together had terminated, for the current arrangement was, on the whole, preferable by far. However, he wished that, instead of jonquils, he had brought her an orchid, the gala sort she'd always salvaged from her daughters' dates and stored in the icebox until they shriveled.

"—aren't they?" he heard, and wondered who had spoken until, blinking, he recognized Mary O'Meaghan, whose voice had been playing along unlistened to: a shy and lulling voice, a sound strangely small and young to come from so robust a figure.

"I said they must be cute, aren't they?"

"Well," was Mr. Belli's safe reply.

"Be modest. But I'm sure they are. If they favor their father; ha ha, don't take me serious, I'm joking. But, seriously, kids just slay me. I'll trade any kid for any grown-up that ever lived. My sister has five, four boys and a girl. Dot, that's my sister, she's always after me to baby-sit now that I've got the time and don't have to look after Pop every minute. She and Frank, he's my brother-in-law, the one I mentioned, they say Mary, nobody can handle kids like *you*. At the same time have fun. But it's so easy; there's nothing like hot cocoa and a mean pillow fight to make kids sleepy. Ivy," she said, reading aloud the tombstone's dour script. "Ivy and Rebecca. Sweet names. And I'm sure you do your best. But two little girls without a mother."

"No, no," said Mr. Belli, at last caught up. "Ivy's a mother herself. And Becky's expecting."

Her face restyled momentary chagrin into an expression of disbelief. "A grandfather? You?"

Mr. Belli had several vanities: for example, he thought he was *saner* than other people; also, he believed himself to be a walking compass; his digestion, and an ability to read upside down, were other ego-enlarging items. But his reflection in a mirror aroused little inner applause; not that he disliked his appearance; he just knew that it was very so-what. The harvesting of his hair had begun decades ago; now his head was an almost barren field. While his nose had character, his chin, though it made a double effort, had none. His shoulders were broad; but so was the rest of him. Of course he was neat: kept his shoes shined, his laundry laundered, twice a day scraped and talcumed his bluish jowls; but such measures failed to camouflage, actually they emphasized, his middle-class, middle-aged ordinariness. Nonetheless, he did not dismiss Mary O'Meaghan's flattery; after all, an undeserved compliment is often the most potent.

"Hell, I'm fifty-one," he said, subtracting four years. "Can't say I feel it." And he didn't; perhaps it was because the wind had subsided, the warmth of the sun grown more authentic. Whatever the reason, his expectations had reignited, he was again immortal, a man planning ahead.

"Fifty-one. That's nothing. The prime. Is if you take care of yourself. A man your age needs tending so. Watching after."

Surely in a cemetery one was safe from husband stalkers? The question, crossing his mind, paused midway while he examined her cozy and gullible face, tested her gaze for guile. Though reassured, he thought it best to remind her of their surroundings. "Your father. Is he"—Mr. Belli gestured awkwardly—"nearby?"

"Pop? Oh, no. He was very firm; absolutely refused to be buried. So he's at home." A disquieting image gathered in Mr. Belli's head, one that her next words, "His ashes are," did not fully dispel. "Well," she shrugged, "that's how he wanted it. Or—I see—you wondered why *I'm* here? I don't live too far away. It's somewhere to walk, and the view . . ." They both turned to stare at the skyline, where the steeples of certain buildings flew pennants of cloud, and sun-dazzled windows glittered like a million bits of mica. Mary O'Meaghan said, "What a perfect day for a parade!"

Mr. Belli thought, *You're a very nice girl;* then he said it, too, and wished he hadn't, for naturally she asked him why. "Because. Well, that was nice what you said. About parades."

"See? So many things in common! I never miss a parade," she told him triumphantly. "The bugles. I play the bugle myself; used to, when I was at Sacred Heart. You said before—" She lowered her voice, as though approaching a subject that required grave tones. "You indicated you were a music lover. Because I have thousands of old records. Hundreds. Pop was in the business and that was his job. Till he retired. Shellacking records in a record factory. Remember Helen Morgan? She slays me, she really knocks me out."

"*Jesus* Christ," he whispered. Ruby Keeler, Jean Harlow: those had been keen but curable infatuations; but Helen Morgan, albino-pale, a sequined wraith shimmering beyond Ziegfeld footlights—truly, truly he had loved her.

"Do you believe it? That she drank herself to death? On account of a gangster?"

"It doesn't matter. She was lovely."

"Sometimes, like when I'm alone and sort of fed up, I pretend I'm her. Pretend I'm singing in a nightclub. It's fun; you know?"

"Yes, I know," said Mr. Belli, whose own favorite fantasy was to imagine the adventures he might have if he were invisible.

"May I ask: would you do me a favor?"

"If I can. Certainly."

She inhaled, held her breath as if she were swimming under a wave of shyness; surfacing, she said: "Would you listen to my imitation? And tell me your honest opinion?" Then she removed her glasses: the silver rims had bitten so deeply their shape was permanently printed on her face. Her eyes, nude and moist and helpless, seemed stunned by freedom; the skimpily lashed lids fluttered like long-captive birds abruptly let loose. "There: everything's soft and smoky. Now you've got to use your imagination. So pretend I'm sitting on a piano—gosh, for*give* me, Mr. Belli."

"Forget it. Okay. You're sitting on a piano."

"I'm sitting on a piano," she said, dreamily drooping her head backward until it assumed a romantic posture. She sucked in her cheeks, parted her lips; at the same moment Mr. Belli bit into his. For it was a tactless visit that glamour made on Mary O'Meaghan's filled-out and rosy face; a visit that should not have been paid at all; it was the wrong address. She waited, as though listening for music to cue her; then, "*Don't ever leave me, now that you're here! Here is where you belong. Everything seems so right when you're near, When you're away it's all wrong.*" And Mr. Belli was shocked, for what he was hearing was exactly Helen Morgan's voice, and the voice, with its vulnerable sweetness, refinement, its tender quaver toppling high notes, seemed not to be borrowed, but Mary O'Meaghan's own, a natural expression of some secluded identity. Gradually she abandoned theatrical poses, sat upright, singing with her eyes squeezed shut: *"I'm so dependent, When I need comfort, I always run to you. Don't ever leave me! 'Cause if you do, I'll have no one to run to."* Until too late, neither she nor Mr. Belli noticed the coffin-laden entourage invading their privacy: a black caterpillar composed of sedate Negroes who stared at the white couple as though they had stumbled upon a pair of drunken grave robbers—except one mourner, a dry-eyed little girl who started laughing and couldn't stop; her hiccuplike hilarity resounded long after the procession had disappeared around a distant corner.

"If that kid was mine," said Mr. Belli.

"I feel so ashamed."

"Say, listen. What for? That was beautiful. I mean it; you can sing."

"Thanks," she said; and, as though setting up a barricade against impending tears, clamped on her spectacles.

"Believe me, I was touched. What I'd like is, I'd like an encore."

It was as if she were a child to whom he'd handed a balloon, a unique balloon that kept swelling until it swept her upward, danced her along with just her toes now and then touching ground. She descended to say: "Only not here. Maybe," she began, and once more seemed to be lifted, lilted through the air, "maybe sometime you'll let me cook you dinner. I'll plan it really Russian. And we can play records."

The thought, the apparitional suspicion that had previously passed on tiptoe, returned with a heavier tread, a creature fat and foursquare that Mr. Belli could not evict. "Thank you, Miss O'Meaghan. That's something to look forward to," he said. Rising, he reset his hat, adjusted his coat. "Sitting on cold stone too long, you can catch something."·

"When?"

"Why, never. You should *never* sit on cold stone."

"When will you come to dinner?"

Mr. Belli's livelihood rather depended upon his being a skilled inventor of excuses. "Any time," he answered smoothly. "Except any time soon. I'm a tax man; you know what happens to us fellows in March. Yes sir," he said, again hoisting out his watch, "back to the grind for me." Still he couldn't—could he?—simply saunter off, leave her sitting on Sarah's grave? He owed her courtesy; for the peanuts, if nothing more, though there was more—perhaps it was due to her that he had remembered Sarah's orchids withering in the icebox. And anyway, she *was* nice, as likable a woman, stranger, as he'd ever met. He thought to take advantage of the weather, but the weather offered none: clouds were fewer, the sun exceedingly visible. "Turned chilly," he observed, rubbing his hands together. "Could be going to rain."

"Mr. Belli. Now I'm going to ask you a very personal question," she said, enunciating each word decisively. "Because I wouldn't want you to think I go about inviting just anybody to dinner. My intentions are—" Her eyes wandered, her voice wavered, as though the forthright manner had been a masquerade she could not sustain. "So I'm going to ask you a very personal question. Have you considered marrying again?"

He hummed, like a radio warming up before it speaks; when he did, it amounted to static: "Oh, at *my* age. Don't even want a dog. Just give me TV. Some beer. Poker once a week. Hell. Who the hell would want me?" he said; and, with a twinge, remembered Rebecca's mother-in-law, Mrs. A. J. Krakower, Sr., Dr. Pauline Krakower, a female dentist (retired) who had been an audacious participant in a certain family plot. Or what about Sarah's best friend, the persistent "Brownie" Pollock? Odd, but as long as Sarah lived he had enjoyed, upon occasion taken advantage of, Brownie's admiration; afterward—finally he had *told* her not to telephone him anymore (and she had shouted: "Everything Sarah ever said, she was right. You fat little *hairy* little bastard"). Then; and then there was Miss Jackson. Despite Sarah's suspicions, her in fact devout conviction, nothing untoward, very untoward, had transpired between him and the pleasant Esther, whose hobby was bowling. But he had always surmised, and in recent months known, that if one day he suggested drinks, dinner, a workout in some bowling alley . . . He said: "I *was* married. For twenty-seven years. That's enough for any lifetime"; but as he said it, he realized that, in just this moment, he had come to a decision, which was: he *would* ask Esther to dinner, he would take her bowling and buy her an orchid, a gala purple one with a lavender ribbon-bow. And where, he wondered, do couples honeymoon in April? At the latest May. Miami? Bermuda? Bermuda! "No, I've never considered it. Marrying again."

One would have assumed from her attentive posture that Mary O'Meaghan was raptly listening to Mr. Belli—except that her eyes played hookey, roamed as though she were hunting at a party for a different, more promising face. The color had drained from her own face; and with it had gone most of her healthy charm. She coughed.

He coughed. Raising his hat, he said: "It's been very pleasant meeting you, Miss O'Meaghan."

"Same here," she said, and stood up. "Mind if I walk with you to the gate?"

He did, yes; for he wanted to mosey along alone, devouring the tart nourishment of this spring-shiny parade-weather, be alone with his many thoughts of Esther, his hopeful, zestful, live-forever mood. "A pleasure," he said, adjusting his stride to her slower pace and the slight lurch her stiff leg caused.

"But it *did* seem like a sensible idea," she said argumentatively. "And

135

there was old Annie Austin: the living proof. Well, nobody had a *better* idea. I mean, everybody was at me: Get married. From the day Pop died, my sister and everybody was saying: Poor Mary, what's to become of her? A girl that can't type. Take shorthand. With her leg and all; can't even wait on table. What happens to a girl—a *grown* woman—that doesn't know anything, never done anything? Except cook and look after her father. All I heard was: Mary, you've got to get married."

"So. Why fight that? A fine person like you, you ought to be married. You'd make some fellow very happy."

"Sure I would. But *who?*" She flung out her arms, extended a hand toward Manhattan, the country, the continents beyond. "So I've looked; I'm not lazy by nature. But honestly, frankly, how does anybody ever find a husband? If they're not very, very pretty; a terrific dancer. If they're just —oh, ordinary. Like me."

"No, no, not at all," Mr. Belli mumbled. "Not ordinary, no. Couldn't you make something of your talent? Your voice?"

She stopped, stood clasping and unclasping her purse. "Don't poke fun. Please. My life is at stake." And she insisted: "I *am* ordinary. So is old Annie Austin. And she says the place for me to find a husband—a decent, comfortable man—is in the obituary column."

For a man who believed himself a human compass, Mr. Belli had the anxious experience of feeling he had lost his way; with relief he saw the gates of the cemetery a hundred yards ahead. "She does? She says that? Old Annie Austin?"

"Yes. And she's a very practical woman. She feeds six people on fifty-eight dollars and seventy-five cents a week: food, clothes, everything. And the way she explained it, it certainly *sounded* logical. Because the obituaries are full of unmarried men. Widowers. You just go to the funeral and sort of introduce yourself: sympathize. Or the cemetery: come here on a nice day, or go to Woodlawn, there are always widowers walking around. Fellows thinking how much they miss home life and maybe wishing they were married again."

When Mr. Belli understood that she was in earnest, he was appalled; but he was also entertained: and he laughed, jammed his hands in his pockets and threw back his head. She joined him, spilled a laughter that restored her color, that, in skylarking style, made her rock against him. "Even I—" she said, clutching at his arm, "even *I* can see the humor." But it was not a lengthy vision; suddenly solemn, she said: "But that is how Annie met her husbands. Both of them: Mr. Cruikshank, and then Mr. Austin. So it *must* be a practical idea. Don't you think?"

"Oh, I do think."

She shrugged. "But it hasn't worked out too well. Us, for instance. *We* seemed to have such a lot in common."

"One day," he said, quickening his steps. "With a livelier fellow."

"I don't know. I've met some grand people. But it always ends like this. Like us . . ." she said, and left unsaid something more, for a new pilgrim, just entering through the gates of the cemetery, had attached her interest: an alive little man spouting cheery whistlings and with plenty of snap to his walk. Mr. Belli noticed him, too, observed the black band sewn round the sleeve of the visitor's bright green tweed coat, and commented: "Good luck, Miss O'Meaghan. Thanks for the peanuts."

Mojave

(1975)

A<small>T 5 P.M. THAT WINTER AFTERNOON</small>
she had an appointment with Dr. Bent-
sen, formerly her psychoanalyst and currently her lover. When their relationship had changed from the analytical to the emotional, he insisted, on
ethical grounds, that she cease to be his patient. Not that it mattered. He
had not been of much help as an analyst, and as a lover—well, once she
had watched him running to catch a bus, two hundred and twenty pounds
of shortish, fiftyish, frizzly-haired, hip-heavy, myopic Manhattan Intellectual, and she had laughed: how was it possible that she could love a man
so ill-humored, so ill-favored as Ezra Bentsen? The answer was she didn't;
in fact, she disliked him. But at least she didn't associate him with resignation and despair. She feared her husband; she was not afraid of Dr. Bentsen.
Still, it was her husband she loved.

She was rich; at any rate, had a substantial allowance from her husband,
who was rich, and so could afford the studio-apartment hideaway where
she met her lover perhaps once a week, sometimes twice, never more. She
could also afford gifts he seemed to expect on these occasions. Not that he
appreciated their quality: Verdura cuff links, classic Paul Flato cigarette
cases, the obligatory Cartier watch, and (more to the point) occasional
specific amounts of cash he asked to "borrow."

He had never given *her* a single present. Well, one: a mother-of-pearl
Spanish dress comb that he claimed was an heirloom, a mother-treasure.

Of course, it was nothing she could wear, for she wore her own hair, fluffy and tobacco-colored, like a childish aureole around her deceptively naïve and youthful face. Thanks to dieting, private exercises with Joseph Pilatos, and the dermatological attentions of Dr. Orentreich, she looked in her early twenties; she was thirty-six.

The Spanish comb. Her hair. That reminded her of Jaime Sanchez and something that had happened yesterday. Jaime Sanchez was her hair-dresser, and though they had known each other scarcely a year, they were, in their own way, good friends. She confided in him somewhat; he confided in her considerably more. Until recently she had judged Jaime to be a happy, almost overly blessed young man. He shared an apartment with an attractive lover, a young dentist named Carlos. Jaime and Carlos had been schoolmates in San Juan; they had left Puerto Rico together, settling first in New Orleans, then New York, and it was Jaime, working as a beautician, a talented one, who had put Carlos through dental school. Now Carlos had his own office and a clientele of prosperous Puerto Ricans and blacks.

However, during her last several visits she had noticed that Jaime Sanchez's usually unclouded eyes were somber, yellowed, as though he had a hangover, and his expertly articulate hands, ordinarily so calm and capable, trembled a little.

Yesterday, while scissor-trimming her hair, he had stopped and stood gasping, gasping—not as though fighting for air, but as if struggling against a scream.

She had said: "What is it? Are you all right?"

"No."

He had stepped to a washbasin and splashed his face with cold water. While drying himself, he said: "I'm going to kill Carlos." He waited, as if expecting her to ask him why; when she merely stared, he continued: "There's no use talking anymore. He understands nothing. My words mean nothing. The only way I can communicate with him is to kill him. Then he will understand."

"I'm not sure that I do, Jaime."

"Have I ever mentioned to you Angelita? My cousin Angelita? She came here six months ago. She has always been in love with Carlos. Since she was, oh, twelve years old. And now Carlos is in love with her. He wants to marry her and have a household of children."

She felt so awkward that all she could think to ask was: "Is she a nice girl?"

"Too nice." He had seized the scissors and resumed clipping. "No, I mean that. She is an excellent girl, very petite, like a pretty parrot, and much too nice; her kindness becomes cruel. Though she doesn't under-stand that she is being cruel. For example . . ." She glanced at Jaime's face moving in the mirror above the washbasin; it was not the merry face that had often beguiled her, but pain and perplexity exactly reflected. "Angelita and Carlos want me to live with them after they are married, all of us together in one apartment. It was her idea, but Carlos says yes! yes! we must all stay together and from now on he and I will live like brothers. That is the reason I have to kill him. He could never have loved me, not if he could ignore my enduring such hell. He says, 'Yes, I love you, Jaime; but Angelita—this is different.' There is no difference. You love or you do not. You destroy or you do not. But Carlos will never understand that. Nothing reaches him, nothing can—only a bullet or a razor."

She wanted to laugh; at the same time she couldn't because she realized he was serious and also because she well knew how true it was that certain persons could only be made to recognize the truth, be made to *understand*, by subjecting them to extreme punishment.

Nevertheless, she did laugh, but in a manner that Jaime would not interpret as genuine laughter. It was something comparable to a sympathetic shrug. "You could never kill anyone, Jaime."

He began to comb her hair; the tugs were not gentle, but she knew the anger implied was against himself, not her. "Shit!" Then: "No. And that's the reason for most suicides. Someone is torturing you. You want to kill them, but you can't. All that pain is because you love them, and you can't kill them because you love them. So you kill yourself instead."

Leaving, she considered kissing him on the cheek, but settled for shaking his hand. "I know how trite this is, Jaime. And for the moment certainly no help at all. But remember—there's always somebody else. Just don't look for the same person, that's all."

The rendezvous apartment was on East Sixty-fifth Street; today she walked to it from her home, a small town house on Beekman Place. It was windy, there was leftover snow on the sidewalk and a promise of more in the air, but she was snug enough in the coat her husband had given her for Christmas—a sable-colored suede coat that was lined with sable.

A cousin had rented the apartment for her in his own name. The cousin, who was married to a harridan and lived in Greenwich, sometimes visited the apartment with his secretary, a fat Japanese woman who drenched herself in nose-boggling amounts of Mitsouko. This afternoon the apartment reeked of the lady's perfume, from which she deduced that her cousin had lately been dallying here. That meant she would have to change the sheets.

She did so, then prepared herself. On a table beside the bed she placed a small box wrapped in shiny cerulean paper; it contained a gold toothpick she had bought at Tiffany, a gift for Dr. Bentsen, for one of his unpleasing habits was constantly picking his teeth, and, moreover, picking them with an endless series of paper matches. She had thought the gold pick might make the whole process a little less disagreeable. She put a stack of Lee Wiley and Fred Astaire records on a phonograph, poured herself a glass of cold white wine, undressed entirely, lubricated herself and stretched out on the bed, humming, singing along with the divine Fred and listening for the scratch of her lover's key at the door.

To judge from appearances, orgasms were agonizing events in the life of Ezra Bentsen: he grimaced, he ground his dentures, he whimpered like a frightened mutt. Of course, she was always relieved when she heard the whimper; it meant that soon his lathered carcass would roll off her, for he was not one to linger, whispering tender compliments: he just rolled right off. And today, having done so, he greedily reached for the blue box, knowing it was a present for him. After opening it, he grunted.

She explained: "It's a gold toothpick."

He chuckled, an unusual sound coming from him, for his sense of humor was meager. "That's kind of cute," he said, and began picking his teeth. "You know what happened last night? I slapped Thelma. But good. And I punched her in the stomach, too."

Thelma was his wife; she was a child psychiatrist, and by reputation a fine one.

"The trouble with Thelma is you can't talk to her. She doesn't understand. Sometimes that's the only way you can get the message across. Give her a fat lip."

She thought of Jaime Sanchez.

"Do you know a Mrs. Roger Rhinelander?" Dr. Bentsen said.

"Mary Rhinelander? Her father was my father's best friend. They owned a racing stable together. One of her horses won the Kentucky Derby. Poor Mary, though. She married a real bastard."

"So she tells me."

"Oh? Is Mrs. Rhinelander a new patient?"

"Brand-new. Funny thing. She came to me for more or less the particular reason that brought you; her situation is almost identical."

The particular reason? Actually, she had a number of problems that had contributed to her eventual seduction on Dr. Bentsen's couch, the principal one being that she had not been capable of having a sexual relationship with her husband since the birth of their second child. She had married when she was twenty-four; her husband was fifteen years her senior. Though they had fought a lot, and were jealous of each other, the first five years of their marriage remained in her memory as an unblemished vista. The difficulty started when he asked her to have a child; if she hadn't been so much in love with him, she would never have consented—she had been afraid of children when she herself was a child, and the company of a child still made her uneasy. But she had given him a son, and the experience of pregnancy had traumatized her: when she wasn't actually suffering, she imagined she was, and after the birth she descended into a depression that continued more than a year. Every day she slept fourteen hours of Seconal sleep; as for the other ten, she kept awake by fueling herself with amphetamines. The second child, another boy, had been a drunken accident—though she suspected that really her husband had tricked her. The instant she knew she was pregnant again she had insisted on having an abortion; he had told her that if she went ahead with it, he would divorce her. Well, he had lived to regret that. The child had been born two months prematurely, had nearly died, and because of massive internal hemorrhaging, so had she; they had both hovered above an abyss through months of intensive care. Since then, she had never shared a bed with her husband; she wanted to, but she couldn't, for the naked presence of him, the thought of his body inside hers, summoned intolerable terrors.

Dr. Bentsen wore thick black socks with garters, which he never removed while "making love"; now, as he was sliding his gartered legs into a pair of shiny-seated blue serge trousers, he said: "Let's see. Tomorrow is Tuesday. Wednesday is our anniversary . . ."

"Our anniversary?"

"Thelma's! Our twentieth. I want to take her to . . . Tell me the best restaurant around now?"

"What does it matter? It's very small and very smart and the owner would never give you a table."

His lack of humor asserted itself: "That's a damn strange thing to say. What do you mean, he wouldn't give me a table?"

"Just what I said. One look at you and he'd know you had hairy heels. There are *some* people who won't serve people with hairy heels. He's one of them."

Dr. Bentsen was familiar with her habit of introducing unfamiliar lingo, and he had learned to pretend he knew what it signified; he was as ignorant of her ambience as she was of his, but the shifting instability of his character would not allow him to admit it.

"Well, then," he said, "is Friday all right? Around five?"

She said: "No, thank you." He was tying his tie and stopped; she was still lying on the bed, uncovered, naked; Fred was singing "By Myself." "No, thank you, darling Dr. B. I don't think we'll be meeting here anymore."

She could see he was startled. Of course he would miss her—she was beautiful, she was considerate, it never bothered her when he asked her for money. He knelt beside the bed and fondled her breast. She noticed an icy mustache of sweat on his upper lip. "What is this? Drugs? Drink?"

She laughed and said: "All I drink is white wine, and not much of that. No, my friend. It's simply that you have hairy heels."

Like many analysts, Dr. Bentsen was quite literal-minded; just for a second she thought he was going to strip off his socks and examine his feet. Churlishly, like a child, he said: "I *don't* have hairy heels."

"Oh, yes you do. Just like a horse. All ordinary horses have hairy heels. Thoroughbreds don't. The heels of a well-bred horse are flat and glistening. Give my love to Thelma."

"Smart-ass. Friday?"

The Astaire record ended. She swallowed the last of the wine.

"Maybe. I'll call you," she said.

As it happened, she never called, and she never saw him again—except once, a year later, when she sat on a banquette next to him at La Grenouille; he was lunching with Mary Rhinelander, and she was amused to see that Mrs. Rhinelander signed the check.

The promised snow had arrived by the time she returned, again on foot, to the house on Beekman Place. The front door was painted pale yellow and had a brass knocker shaped like a lion's claw. Anna, one of four Irishwomen who staffed the house, answered the door and reported that the children, exhausted from an afternoon of ice-skating at Rockefeller Center, had already had their supper and been put to bed.

Thank God. Now she wouldn't have to undergo the half hour of playtime and tale-telling and kiss-goodnight that customarily concluded her children's day; she may not have been an affectionate mother, but she was a dutiful one—just as her own mother had been. It was seven o'clock, and her husband had phoned to say he would be home at seven-thirty; at eight they were supposed to go to a dinner party with the Sylvester Hales, friends from San Francisco. She bathed, scented herself to remove memories of Dr. Bentsen, remodeled her make-up, of which she wore the most modest quantity, and changed into a gray silk caftan and gray silk slippers with pearl buckles.

She was posing by the fireplace in the library on the second floor when she heard her husband's footsteps on the stairs. It was a graceful pose, inviting as the room itself, an unusual octagonal room with cinnamon lacquered walls, a yellow lacquered floor, brass bookshelves (a notion borrowed from Billy Baldwin), two huge bushes of brown orchids ensconced in yellow Chinese vases, a Marino Marini horse standing in a corner, a South Seas Gauguin over the mantel, and a delicate fire fluttering in the fireplace. French windows offered a view of a darkened garden, drifting snow and lighted tugboats floating like lanterns on the East River. A voluptuous couch, upholstered in mocha velvet, faced the fireplace, and in front of it, on a table lacquered the yellow of the floor, rested an ice-filled silver bucket; embedded in the bucket was a carafe brimming with pepper-flavored red Russian vodka.

Her husband hesitated in the doorway, and nodded at her approvingly: he was one of those men who truly noticed a woman's appearance, gathered at a glance the total atmosphere. He was worth dressing for, and it was one of her lesser reasons for loving him. A more important reason was that he resembled her father, a man who had been, and forever would be, the man in her life; her father had shot himself, though no one ever knew why, for he was a gentleman of almost abnormal discretion. Before this happened, she had terminated three engagements, but two months after her father's death she met George, and married him because in both looks and manners he approximated her great lost love.

She moved across the room to meet her husband halfway. She kissed his cheek, and the flesh against her lips felt as cold as the snowflakes at the window. He was a large man, Irish, black-haired and green-eyed, handsome even though he had lately accumulated considerable poundage and had gotten a bit jowly, too. He projected a superficial vitality; both men and women were drawn to him by that alone. Closely observed, however, one sensed a secret fatigue, a lack of any real optimism. His wife was severely aware of it, and why not? She was its principal cause.

She said: "It's such a rotten night out, and you look so tired. Let's stay home and have supper by the fire."

"Really, darling—you wouldn't mind? It seems a mean thing to do to the Haleses. Even if she is a cunt."

"*George!* Don't use that word. You know I hate it."

"Sorry," he said; he was, too. He was always careful not to offend her, just as she took the same care with him: a consequence of the quiet that simultaneously kept them together and apart.

"I'll call and say you're coming down with a cold."

"Well, it won't be a lie. I think I am."

While she called the Haleses, and arranged with Anna for a soup and soufflé supper to be served in an hour's time, he chug-a-lugged a dazzling dose of the scarlet vodka and felt it light a fire in his stomach; before his wife returned, he poured himself a respectable shot and stretched full length on the couch. She knelt on the floor and removed his shoes and began to massage his feet: God knows, *he* didn't have hairy heels.

He groaned. "Hmm. That feels good."

"I love you, George."

"I love you, too."

She thought of putting on a record, but no, the sound of the fire was all the room needed.

"George?"

"Yes, darling."

"What are you thinking about?"

"A woman named Ivory Hunter."

"You really know somebody named Ivory Hunter?"

"Well. That was her stage name. She'd been a burlesque dancer."

She laughed. "What is this, some part of your college adventures?"

"I never knew her. I only heard about her once. It was the summer after I left Yale."

He closed his eyes and drained his vodka. "The summer I hitchhiked out to New Mexico and California. Remember? That's how I got my nose broke. In a bar fight in Needles, California." She liked his broken nose, it offset the extreme gentleness of his face; he had once spoken of having it rebroken and reset, but she had talked him out of it. "It was early September, and that's always the hottest time of the year in Southern California; over a hundred almost every day. I ought to have treated myself to a bus ride, at least across the desert. But there I was like a fool, deep in the Mojave, hauling a fifty-pound knapsack and sweating until there was no sweat in me. I swear it was a hundred and fifty in the shade. Except there wasn't any shade. Nothing but sand and mesquite and this boiling blue sky. Once a big truck drove by, but it wouldn't stop for me. All it did was kill a rattlesnake that was crawling across the road.

"I kept thinking something was bound to turn up somewhere. A garage. Now and then cars passed, but I might as well have been invisible. I began to feel sorry for myself, to understand what it means to be helpless, and to understand why it's a good thing that Buddhists send out their young monks to beg. It's chastening. It rips off that last layer of baby fat.

"And then I met Mr. Schmidt. I thought maybe it was a mirage. An old white-haired man about a quarter mile up the highway. He was standing by the road with heat waves rippling around him. As I got closer I saw that he carried a cane and wore pitch-black glasses, and he was dressed as if headed for church—white suit, white shirt, black tie, black shoes.

"Without looking at me, and while some distance away, he called out: 'My name is George Schmidt.'

"I said: 'Yes. Good afternoon, sir.'

"He said: '*Is* it afternoon?'

"'After three.'

"'Then I must have been standing here two hours or more. Would you mind telling me where I am?'

"'In the Mojave Desert. About eighteen miles west of Needles.'

"'Imagine that,' he said. 'Leaving a seventy-year-old blind man stranded alone in the desert. Ten dollars in my pocket, and not another rag to my name. Women are like flies: they settle on sugar or shit. I'm not saying I'm sugar, but she's sure settled for shit now. My name is George Schmidt.'

"I said: 'Yes, sir, you told me. I'm George Whitelaw.' He wanted to know where I was going, what I was up to, and when I said I was hitchhiking, heading for New York, he asked if I would take his hand and help him along a bit, maybe until we could catch a ride. I forgot to mention that he had a German accent and was extremely stout, almost fat; he looked as if he'd been lying in a hammock all his life. But when I held his hand I felt the roughness, the immense strength of it. You wouldn't have wanted a pair of hands like that around your throat. He said: 'Yes, I have strong hands. I've worked as a masseur for fifty years, the last twelve in Palm Springs. You got any water?' I gave him my canteen, which was still half full. And he said: 'She left me here without even a drop of water. The whole thing took me by surprise. Though I can't say it should have, knowing Ivory good as I did. That's my wife. Ivory Hunter, she was. A stripper; she played the Chicago World's Fair, 1932, and she would have been a star if it hadn't been for that Sally Rand. Ivory invented this fan-dance thing and that Rand woman stole it off her. So Ivory said. Probably just more of her bullshit. Uh-oh, watch out for that rattler, he's over there someplace, I can hear him really singing. There's two things I'm scared of. Snakes and women. They have a lot in common. One thing they have in common is: the last thing that dies is their tail.'

"A couple of cars passed and I stuck out my thumb and the old man tried to flag them down with his stick, but we must have looked too peculiar— a dirty kid in dungarees and a blind fat man dressed in his city best. I guess we'd still be out there if it hadn't been for this truck driver. A Mexican. He was parked by the road fixing a flat. He could speak about five words of Tex-Mex, all of them four-letter, but I still remembered a lot of Spanish from the summer with Uncle Alvin in Cuba. So the Mexican told me he was on his way to El Paso, and if that was our direction, we were welcome aboard.

"But Mr. Schmidt wasn't too keen. I had practically to drag him into the caboose. 'I hate Mexicans. Never met a Mexican I liked. If it wasn't for a Mexican . . . Him only nineteen and her I'd say from the touch of her skin, I'd say Ivory was a woman way past sixty. When I married her a couple of years ago, she said she was fifty-two. See, I was living in this trailer camp out on Route III. One of those trailer camps halfway between Palm Springs and Cathedral City. Cathedral City! Some name for a dump that's nothing but honky-tonks and pool halls and fag bars. The only thing you can say about it is Bing Crosby lives there. If that's saying something. Anyway, living next to me in this other trailer is my friend Hulga. Ever since my wife died—she died the same day Hitler died—Hulga had been driving me to work; she works as a waitress at this Jew club where I'm the masseur. All the waiters and waitresses at the club are big blond Germans. The Jews like that; they really keep them stepping. So one day Hulga tells me she has a cousin coming to visit. Ivory Hunter. I forget her legal name, it was on the marriage certificate, but I forget. She had about three husbands before; she probably didn't remember the name she was born with. Anyway, Hulga tells me that this cousin of hers, Ivory, used to be a famous dancer, but now she's just come out of the hospital and she's lost her last husband on account of she's spent a year in the hospital with TB. That's why Hulga asked her out to Palm Springs. Because of the air. Also, she didn't have any place else to go. The first night she was there, Hulga invited me over, and I liked her cousin right away; we didn't talk much, we listened to the radio mostly, but I liked Ivory. She had a real nice voice, real slow and gentle, she sounded like nurses ought to sound; she said she didn't smoke or drink and she was a member of the Church of God, same as me. After that, I was over at Hulga's almost every night.' "

George lit a cigarette, and his wife tilted out a jigger more of the pepper vodka for him. To her surprise, she poured one for herself. A number of things about her husband's narrative had accelerated her ever-present but usually Librium-subdued anxiety; she couldn't imagine where his memoir was leading, but she knew there was some destination, for George seldom rambled. He had graduated third in his class at Yale Law School, never practiced law but had gone on to top his class at Harvard Business School; within the past decade he had been offered a presidential Cabinet post, and an ambassadorship to England or France or wherever he wanted. However, what had made her feel the need for red vodka, a ruby bauble burning in the firelight, was the disquieting manner in which George Whitelaw had become Mr. Schmidt; her husband was an exceptional mimic. He could imitate certain of their friends with infuriating accuracy. But this was not casual mimicry; he seemed entranced, a man fixed in another man's mind.

" 'I had an old Chevy nobody had driven since my wife died. But Ivory got it tuned up, and pretty soon it wasn't Hulga driving me to work and bringing me home, but Ivory. Looking back, I can see it was all a plot between Hulga and Ivory, but I didn't put it together then. Everybody around the trailer park, and everybody that met her, all they said was what a lovely woman she was, big blue eyes and pretty legs. I figured it was just good-heartedness, the Church of God—I figured that was why she was spending her evenings cooking dinner and keeping house for an old blind man. One night we were listening to the *Hit Parade* on the radio, and she kissed me and rubbed her hand along my leg. Pretty soon we were doing it twice a day—once before breakfast and once after dinner, and me a man of sixty-nine. But it seemed like she was as crazy about my cock as I was about her cunt—' "

She tossed her vodka into the fireplace, a splash that made the flames hiss and flourish; but it was an idle protest: Mr. Schmidt would not be re-proached.

" 'Yes, sir, Ivory was all cunt. Whatever way you want to use the word. It was exactly one month from the day I met her to the day I married her. She didn't change much, she fed me good, she was always interested to hear about the Jews at the club, and it was me that cut down on the sex —*way* down, what with my blood pressure and all. But she never com-plained. We read the Bible together, and night after night she would read aloud from magazines, good magazines like *Reader's Digest* and *The Satur-day Evening Post,* until I fell asleep. She was always saying she hoped she died before I did because she would be heartbroken and destitute. It was true I didn't have much to leave. No insurance, just some bank-savings that I turned into a joint account, and I had the trailer put in her name. No, I can't say there was a harsh word between us until she had the big fight with Hulga.

" 'For a long time I didn't know what the fight was about. All I knew was that they didn't speak to each other anymore, and when I asked Ivory what was going on, she said: "Nothing." As far as she was concerned, she hadn't had any falling-out with Hulga: "But you know how much she drinks." That was true. Well, like I told you, Hulga was a waitress at the club, and one day she comes barging into the massage room. I had a customer on the table, had him there spread out buck-naked, but a lot she cared—she smelled like a Four Roses factory. She could hardly stand up. She told me she had just got fired, and suddenly she started swearing and pissing. She was hollering at me and pissing all over the floor. She said everybody at the trailer park was laughing at me. She said Ivory was an old whore who had latched on to me because she was down and out and couldn't do any better. And she said what kind of a chowderhead was I? Didn't I know my wife was fucking the balls off Freddy Feo since God knows when?

" 'Now, see, Freddy Feo was an itinerant Tex-Mex kid—he was just out of jail somewhere, and the manager of the trailer park had picked him up in one of those fag bars in Cat City and put him to work as a handyman. I don't guess he could have been one-hundred-percent fag because he was giving plenty of the old girls around there a tickle for their money. One of them was Hulga. She was loop-de-do over him. On hot nights him and Hulga used to sit outside her trailer on her swing-seat drinking straight tequila, forget the lime, and he'd play the guitar and sing spic songs. Ivory described it to me as a green guitar with his name spelled out in rhinestone letters. I'll say this, the spic could sing. But Ivory always claimed she couldn't stand him; she said he was a cheap little greaser out to take Hulga for every nickel she had. Myself, I don't remember exchanging ten words with him, but I didn't like him because of the way he smelled. I have a nose like a bloodhound and I could smell him a hundred yards off, he wore so much brilliantine in his hair, and something else that Ivory said was called Evening in Paris.

" 'Ivory swore up and down it wasn't so. Her? *Her* let a Tex-Mex monkey like Freddy Feo put a finger on her? She said it was because Hulga had been dumped by this kid that she was crazy and jealous and thought he was humping everything from Cat City to Indio. She said she was insulted that I'd listen to such lies, even though Hulga was more to be pitied than reviled. And she took off the wedding ring I'd given her—it had belonged to my first wife, but she said that didn't make any difference because she knew I'd loved Hedda and that made it all the better—and she handed it to me and she said if I didn't believe her, then here was the ring and she'd take the next bus going anywhere. So I put it back on her finger and we knelt on the floor and prayed together.

" 'I did believe her; at least I thought I did; but in some way it was like a seesaw in my head—yes, no, yes, no. And Ivory had lost her looseness; before, she had an easiness in her body that was like the easiness in her voice. But now it was all wire—tense, like those Jews at the club that keep whining and scolding because you can't rub away all their worries. Hulga got a job at the Miramar, but out at the trailer park I always turned away when I smelled her coming. Once she sort of whispered up beside me: "Did you know that sweet wife of yours gave the greaser a pair of gold earrings! But his boyfriend won't let him wear them." I don't know. Ivory prayed every night with me that the Lord would keep us together, healthy in spirit and body. But I noticed . . . Well, on those warm summer nights when Freddy Feo would be out there somewhere in the dark, singing and playing his guitar, she'd turn off the radio right in the middle of Bob Hope or Edgar Bergen or whatever, and go sit outside and listen. She said she was looking at the stars: "I bet there's no place in the world you can see the stars like here." But suddenly it turned out she hated Cat City and the Springs. The whole desert, the sandstorms, summers with temperatures up to a hundred thirty degrees, and nothing to do if you wasn't rich and belonged to the Racquet Club. She just announced this one morning. She said we should pick up the trailer and plant it down anywhere where the air was cool. Wisconsin. Michigan. I felt good about the idea; it set my mind to rest as to what might be going on between her and Freddy Feo.

" 'Well, I had a client there at the club, a fellow from Detroit, and he said he might be able to get me on as a masseur at the Detroit Athletic Club; nothing definite, only one of them maybe deals. But that was enough for Ivory. Twenty-three skidoo, and she's got the trailer uprooted, fifteen years of planting strewn all over the ground, the Chevy ready to roll, and all our savings turned into traveler's checks. Last night she scrubbed me top to bottom and shampooed my hair, and this morning we set off a little after daylight.

" 'I realized something was wrong, and I'd have known what it was if I hadn't dozed off soon as we hit the highway. She must have dumped sleeping pills in my coffee.

" 'But when I woke up, I smelled him. The brilliantine and the dime-store perfume. He was hiding in the trailer. Coiled back there somewhere like a snake. What I thought was: Ivory and the kid are going to kill me and leave me for the buzzards. She said: "You're awake, George." The way she said it, the slight fear, I could tell she knew what was going on in my head. That I'd guessed it all. I told her, *Stop the car.* She wanted to know what for? Because I had to take a leak. She stopped the car, and I could hear she was crying. As I got out, she said: "You been good to me, George, but I didn't know nothing else to do. And you got a profession. There'll always be a place for you somewhere."

" 'I got out of the car, and I really did take a leak, and while I was standing there the motor started up and she drove away. I didn't know where I was until you came along, Mr. . . . ?'

" 'George Whitelaw.' And I told him: 'Jesus, that's just like murder. Leaving a blind man helpless in the middle of nowhere. When we get to El Paso we'll go to the police station.'

"He said: 'Hell, no. She's got enough trouble without the cops. She settled on shit—leave her to it. Ivory's the one out in nowhere. Besides, I love her. A woman can do you like that, and still you love her.' "

George refilled his vodka; she placed a small log on the fire, and the new rush of flame was only a little brighter than the furious red suddenly flushing her cheeks.

"That *women* do," she said, her tone aggressive, challenging. "Only a crazy person . . . Do you think I could do something like that?"

The expression in his eyes, a certain visual silence, shocked her and made her avert her eyes, withdrawing the question. "Well, what happened to him?"

"Mr. Schmidt?"

"Mr. Schmidt."

He shrugged. "The last I saw of him he was drinking a glass of milk in a diner, a truck stop outside El Paso. I was lucky; I got a ride with a trucker all the way to Newark. I sort of forgot about it. But for the last few months I find myself wondering about Ivory Hunter and George Schmidt. It must be age; I'm beginning to feel old myself."

She knelt beside him again; she held his hand, interweaving her fingers with his. "Fifty-two? And you feel *old*?"

He had retreated; when he spoke, it was the wondering murmur of a man addressing himself. "I always had such confidence. Just walking the street, I felt such a *swing*. I could feel people looking at me—on the street, in a restaurant, at a party—envying me, wondering who is that guy. Whenever I walked into a party, I knew I could have half the women in the room if I wanted them. But that's all over. Seems as though old George Whitelaw has become the invisible man. Not a head turns. I called Mimi Stewart twice last week, and she never returned the calls. I didn't tell you, but I stopped at Buddy Wilson's yesterday, he was having a little cocktail thing. There must have been twenty fairly attractive girls, and they all looked right through me; to them I was a tired old guy who smiled too much."

She said: "But I thought you were still seeing Christine."

"I'll tell you a secret. Christine is engaged to that Rutherford boy from Philadelphia. I haven't seen her since November. He's okay for her; she's happy and I'm happy for her."

"Christine! Which Rutherford boy? Kenyon or Paul?"

"The older one."

"That's Kenyon. You knew that and didn't tell me?"

"There's so much I haven't told you, my dear."

Yet that was not entirely true. For when they had stopped sleeping together, they had begun discussing together—indeed, collaborating on— each of his affairs. Alice Kent: five months; ended because she'd demanded he divorce and marry her. Sister Jones: terminated after one year when her husband found out about it. Pat Simpson: a *Vogue* model who'd gone to Hollywood, promised to return and never had. Adele O'Hara: beautiful, an alcoholic, a rambunctious scenemaker; he'd broken that one off himself. Mary Campbell, Mary Chester, Jane Vere-Jones. Others. And now Christine.

A few he had discovered himself; the majority were "romances" she herself had stage-managed, friends she'd introduced him to, confidantes she had trusted to provide him with an outlet but not to exceed the mark.

"Well," she sighed. "I suppose we can't blame Christine. Kenyon Rutherford's rather a catch." Still, her mind was running, searching like the flames shivering through the logs: a name to fill the void. Alice Combs: available, but too dull. Charlotte Finch: too rich, and George felt emasculated by women—or men, for that matter—richer than himself. Perhaps the Ellison woman? The soigné Mrs. Harold Ellison, who was in Haiti getting a swift divorce . . .

He said: "Stop frowning."

"I'm not frowning."

"It just means more silicone, more bills from Orentreich. I'd rather see the human wrinkles. It doesn't matter whose fault it is. We all, sometimes, leave each other out there under the skies, and we never understand why."

. . .

An echo, caverns resounding: Jaime Sanchez and Carlos and Angelita; Hulga and Freddy Feo and Ivory Hunter and Mr. Schmidt; Dr. Bentsen and George, George and herself, Dr. Bentsen and Mary Rhinelander . . .

He gave a slight pressure to their interwoven fingers, and with his other hand, raised her chin and insisted on their eyes meeting. He moved her hand up to his lips and kissed its palm.

"I love you, Sarah."

"I love you, too."

But the touch of his lips, the insinuated threat, tautened her. Below stairs, she heard the rattle of silver on trays: Anna and Margaret were ascending with the fireside supper.

"I love you, too," she repeated with pretended sleepiness, and with a feigned languor moved to draw the window draperies. Drawn, the heavy silk concealed the night river and the lighted riverboats, so snow-misted that they were as muted as the design in a Japanese scroll of winter night.

"George?" An urgent plea before the supper-laden Irishwomen arrived, expertly balancing their offerings: *"Please,* darling. We'll think of somebody."

NOVELLAS

The
Grass Harp

(1951)

WHEN WAS IT THAT FIRST I HEARD of the grass harp? Long before the autumn we lived in the China tree; an earlier autumn, then; and of course it was Dolly who told me, no one else would have known to call it that, a grass harp.

If on leaving town you take the church road, you soon will pass a glaring hill of bonewhite slabs and brown burnt flowers: this is the Baptist cemetery. Our people, Talbos, Fenwicks, are buried there; my mother lies next to my father, and the graves of kinfolk, twenty or more, are around them like the prone roots of a stony tree. Below the hill grows a field of high Indian grass that changes color with the seasons: go to see it in the fall, late September, when it has gone red as sunset, when scarlet shadows like firelight breeze over it and the autumn winds strum on its dry leaves sighing human music, a harp of voices.

Beyond the field begins the darkness of River Woods. It must have been on one of those September days when we were there in the woods gathering roots that Dolly said: Do you hear? that is the grass harp, always telling a story—it knows the stories of all the people on the hill, of all the people who ever lived, and when we are dead it will tell ours, too.

After my mother died, my father, a traveling man, sent me to live with his cousins, Verena and Dolly Talbo, two unmarried ladies who were sisters. Before that, I'd not ever been allowed into their house. For reasons no one ever got quite clear, Verena and my father did not speak. Probably Papa asked Verena to lend him some money, and she refused; or perhaps she did make the loan, and he never returned it. You can be sure that the trouble was over money, because nothing else would have mattered to them so much, especially Verena, who was the richest person in town. The drugstore, the drygoods store, a filling station, a grocery, an office building, all this was hers, and the earning of it had not made her an easy woman.

Anyway, Papa said he would never set foot inside her house. He told such terrible things about the Talbo ladies. One of the stories he spread, that Verena was a morphadite, has never stopped going around, and the ridicule he heaped on Miss Dolly Talbo was too much even for my mother: she told him he ought to be ashamed, mocking anyone so gentle and harmless.

I think they were very much in love, my mother and father. She used to cry every time he went away to sell his Frigidaires. He married her when she was sixteen; she did not live to be thirty. The afternoon she died Papa, calling her name, tore off all his clothes and ran out naked into the yard.

It was the day after the funeral that Verena came to the house. I remember the terror of watching her move up the walk, a whip-thin, handsome woman with shingled pepper-salt hair, black, rather virile eyebrows and a dainty cheek-mole. She opened the front door and walked right into the house. Since the funeral, Papa had been breaking things, not with fury, but quietly, thoroughly: he would amble into the parlor, pick up a china figure, muse over it a moment, then throw it against the wall. The floor and stairs were littered with cracked glass, scattered silverware; a ripped nightgown, one of my mother's, hung over the banister.

Verena's eyes flicked over the debris. "Eugene, I want a word with you," she said in that hearty, coldly exalted voice, and Papa answered: "Yes, sit down, Verena. I thought you would come."

That afternoon Dolly's friend Catherine Creek came over and packed my clothes, and Papa drove me to the impressive, shadowy house on Talbo Lane. As I was getting out of the car he tried to hug me, but I was scared of him and wriggled out of his arms. I'm sorry now that we did not hug each other. Because a few days later, on his way up to Mobile, his car skidded and fell fifty feet into the Gulf. When I saw him again there were silver dollars weighting down his eyes.

Except to remark that I was small for my age, a runt, no one had ever paid any attention to me; but now people pointed me out, and said wasn't it sad? that poor little Collin Fenwick! I tried to look pitiful because I knew it pleased people: every man in town must have treated me to a Dixie Cup or a box of Cracker Jack, and at school I got good grades for the first time. So it was a long while before I calmed down enough to notice Dolly Talbo.

And when I did I fell in love.

Imagine what it must have been for her when first I came to the house, a loud and prying boy of eleven. She skittered at the sound of my footsteps or, if there was no avoiding me, folded like the petals of shy-lady fern. She was one of those people who can disguise themselves as an object in the room, a shadow in the corner, whose presence is a delicate happening. She wore the quietest shoes, plain virginal dresses with hems that touched her ankles. Though older than her sister, she seemed someone who, like myself, Verena had adopted. Pulled and guided by the gravity of Verena's planet, we rotated separately in the outer spaces of the house.

In the attic, a slipshod museum spookily peopled with old display dummies from Verena's drygoods store, there were many loose boards, and by inching these, I could look down into almost any room. Dolly's room, unlike the rest of the house, which bulged with fat dour furniture, contained only a bed, a bureau, a chair: a nun might have lived there, except for one fact: the walls, everything was painted an outlandish pink, even the floor was this color. Whenever I spied on Dolly, she usually was to be seen doing one of two things: she was standing in front of a mirror snipping with a pair of garden shears her yellow and white, already brief hair; either that, or she was writing in pencil on a pad of coarse Kress paper. She kept wetting the pencil on the tip of her tongue, and sometimes she spoke aloud a sentence as she put it down: *Do not touch sweet foods like candy and salt will kill you for certain.* Now I'll tell you, she was writing letters. But at first this correspondence was a puzzle to me. After all, her only friend was Catherine Creek, she saw no one else and she never left the house, except once a week when she and Catherine went to River Woods, where they gathered the ingredients of a dropsy remedy Dolly brewed and bottled. Later I discovered she had customers for this medicine throughout the state, and it was to them that her many letters were addressed.

Verena's room, connecting with Dolly's by a passage, was rigged up like an office. There was a rolltop desk, a library of ledgers, filing cabinets. After supper, wearing a green eyeshade, she would sit at her desk totaling figures and turning the pages of her ledgers until even the street lamps had gone out. Though on diplomatic, political terms with many people, Verena had no close friends at all. Men were afraid of her, and she herself seemed to be afraid of women. Some years before, she had been greatly attached to a blond jolly girl called Maudie Laura Murphy, who worked for a bit in the post office here and who finally married a liquor salesman from St. Louis. Verena had been very bitter over this and said publicly that the man was no-account. It was therefore a surprise when, as a wedding present, she gave the couple a honeymoon trip to the Grand Canyon. Maudie and her husband never came back; they opened a filling station nearby Grand Canyon, and from time to time sent Verena Kodak snapshots of themselves. These pictures were a pleasure and a grief. There were nights when she never opened her ledgers, but sat with her forehead leaning in her hands, and the pictures spread on the desk. After she had put them away, she would pace around the room with the lights turned off, and presently there would come a hurt rusty crying sound as though she'd tripped and fallen in the dark.

That part of the attic from which I could have looked down into the kitchen was fortified against me, for it was stacked with trunks like bales of cotton. At that time it was the kitchen I most wanted to spy upon; this was the real living room of the house, and Dolly spent most of the day there chatting with her friend Catherine Creek. As a child, an orphan, Catherine Creek had been hired out to Mr. Uriah Talbo, and they had all grown up together, she and the Talbo sisters, there on the old farm that has since become a railroad depot. Dolly she called Dollyheart, but Verena she called That One. She lived in the backyard in a tin-roofed silvery little house set among sunflowers and trellises of butterbean vine. She claimed to be an Indian, which made most people wink, for she was dark as the angels of Africa. But for all I know it may have been true: certainly she dressed like an Indian. That is, she had a string of turquoise beads, and wore enough rouge to put out your eyes; it shone on her cheeks like votive taillights. Most of her teeth were gone; she kept her jaws jacked up with cotton wadding, and Verena would say Dammit Catherine, since you can't make a sensible sound, why in creation won't you go down to Doc Crocker and let him put some teeth in your head? It was true that she was hard to understand: Dolly was the only one who could fluently translate her friend's muffled, mumbling noises. It was enough for Catherine that Dolly understood her: they were always together and everything they had to say they said to each other: bending my ear to an attic beam, I could hear the tantalizing tremor of their voices flowing like sapsyrup through the old wood.

To reach the attic, you climbed a ladder in the linen closet, the ceiling of which was a trapdoor. One day, as I started up, I saw that the trapdoor was swung open and, listening, heard above me an idle sweet humming, like the pretty sounds small girls make when they are playing alone. I would have turned back, but the humming stopped, and a voice said: "Catherine?"

"Collin," I answered, showing myself.

The snowflake of Dolly's face held its shape; for once she did not dissolve. "This is where you come—we wondered," she said, her voice frail and crinkling as tissue paper. She had the eyes of a gifted person, kindled, transparent eyes, luminously green as mint jelly: gazing at me through the attic twilight they admitted, timidly, that I meant her no harm. "You play games up here—in the attic? I told Verena you would be lonesome." Stooping, she rooted around in the depths of a barrel. "Here now," she said, "you can help me by looking in that other barrel. I'm hunting for a coral castle; and a sack of pearl pebbles, all colors. I think Catherine will like that, a bowl of goldfish, don't you? For her birthday. We used to have a bowl of tropical fish—devils, they were: ate each other up. But I remember when we bought them; we went all the way to Brewton, sixty miles. I never went sixty miles before, and I don't know that I ever will again. Ah see, here it is, the castle." Soon afterward I found the pebbles; they were like kernels of corn or candy, and: "Have a piece of candy," I said, offering the sack. "Oh thank you," she said, "I love a piece of candy, even when it tastes like a pebble."

We were friends, Dolly and Catherine and me. I was eleven, then I was sixteen. Though no honors came my way, those were the lovely years.

I never brought anyone home with me, and I never wanted to. Once I took a girl to the picture show, and on the way home she asked couldn't she come in for a drink of water. If I'd thought she was really thirsty, I would've said all right; but I knew she was faking just so she could see inside the house the way people were always wanting to, and so I told her she better wait until she got home. She said: "All the world knows Dolly Talbo's gone, and you're gone too." I liked that girl well enough, but I gave her a shove anyway, and she said her brother would fix my wagon, which he did: right here at the corner of my mouth I've still got a scar where he hit me with a Coca-Cola bottle.

I know: Dolly, they said, was Verena's cross, and said, too, that more went on in the house on Talbo Lane than a body cared to think about. Maybe so. But those were the lovely years.

On winter afternoons, as soon as I came in from school, Catherine hustled open a jar of preserves, while Dolly put a foot-high pot of coffee on the stove and pushed a pan of biscuits into the oven; and the oven, opening, would let out a hot vanilla fragrance, for Dolly, who lived off sweet foods, was always baking a pound cake, raisin bread, some kind of cookie or fudge: never would touch a vegetable, and the only meat she liked was the chicken brain, a pea-sized thing gone before you've tasted it. What with a woodstove and an open fireplace, the kitchen was warm as a cow's tongue. The nearest winter came was to frost the windows with its zero blue breath. If some wizard would like to make me a present, let him give me a bottle filled with the voices of that kitchen, the ha ha ha and fire whispering, a bottle brimming with its buttery sugary bakery smells— though Catherine smelled like a sow in the spring. It looked more like a cozy parlor than a kitchen; there was a hook rug on the floor, rocking chairs; ranged along the walls were pictures of kittens, an enthusiasm of Dolly's; there was a geranium plant that bloomed, then bloomed again all year round, and Catherine's goldfish, in a bowl on the oilcloth-covered table, fanned their tails through the portals of the coral castle. Sometimes we worked jigsaw puzzles, dividing the pieces among us, and Catherine would hide pieces if she thought you were going to finish your part of the puzzle before she finished hers. Or they would help with my homework; that was a mess. About all natural things Dolly was sophisticated; she had the subterranean intelligence of a bee that knows where to find the sweetest flower: she could tell you of a storm a day in advance, predict the fruit of the fig tree, lead you to mushrooms and wild honey, a hidden nest of guinea hen eggs. She looked around her, and felt what she saw. But about homework Dolly was as ignorant as Catherine. "America must have been called America before Columbus came. It stands to reason. Otherwise, how would he have known it was America?" And Catherine said: "That's correct. America is an old Indian word." Of the two, Catherine was the worst: she insisted on her infallibility, and if you did not write down exactly what she said, she got jumpy and spilled the coffee or something. But I never listened to her again after what she said about Lincoln: that he was part Negro and part Indian and only a speck white. Even I knew this was not true. But I am under special obligation to Catherine; if it had not been for her, who knows whether I would have grown to ordinary human size? At fourteen I was not much bigger than Biddy Skinner, and people told how he'd had offers from a circus. Catherine said don't worry yourself honey, all you need is a little stretching. She pulled at my arms, legs, tugged at my head as though it were an apple latched to an unyielding bough. But it's the truth that within two years she'd stretched me from four feet nine to five feet seven, and I can prove it by the breadknife notches on the pantry door, for even now when so much has gone, when there is only wind in the stove and winter in the kitchen, those growing-up scars are still there, a testimony.

Despite the generally beneficial effect Dolly's medicine appeared to have on those who sent for it, letters once in a while came saying Dear Miss Talbo we won't be needing any more dropsy cure on account of poor Cousin Belle (or whoever) passed away last week bless her soul. Then the kitchen was a mournful place; with folded hands and nodding heads my two friends bleakly recalled the circumstances of the case, and Well, Catherine would say, we did the best we could Dollyheart, but the good Lord had other notions. Verena, too, could make the kitchen sad, as she was always introducing a new rule or enforcing an old one: do, don't, stop, start: it was as though we were clocks she kept an eye on to see that our time jibed with her own, and woe if we were ten minutes fast, an hour slow: Verena went off like a cuckoo. That One! said Catherine, and Dolly would go hush now! hush now! as though to quiet not Catherine but a mutinous inner whispering. Verena in her heart wanted, I think, to come into the kitchen and be a part of it; but she was too like a lone man in a house full of women and children, and the only way she could make contact with us was through assertive outbursts: Dolly, get rid of that kitten, you want to aggravate my asthma? Who left the water running in the bathroom? which one of you broke my umbrella? Her ugly moods sifted through the house like a sour yellow mist. That One. Hush now, hush.

Once a week, Saturdays mostly, we went to River Woods. For these trips, which lasted the whole day, Catherine fried a chicken and deviled a dozen eggs, and Dolly took along a chocolate layer cake and a supply of divinity fudge. Thus armed, and carrying three empty grain sacks, we walked out the church road past the cemetery and through the field of Indian grass. Just entering the woods, there was a double-trunked China tree, really two trees, but their branches were so embraced that you could step from one into the other; in fact, they were bridged by a tree house: spacious, sturdy, a model of a tree house, it was like a raft floating in the sea of leaves. The boys who built it, provided they are still alive, must by now be very old men; certainly the tree house was fifteen or twenty years old when Dolly first found it and that was a quarter of a century before she showed it to me. To reach it was easy as climbing stairs; there were footholds of gnarled bark and tough vines to grip; even Catherine, who was heavy around the hips and complained of rheumatism, had no trouble. But Catherine felt no love for the tree house; she did not know, as Dolly knew and made me know, that it was a ship, that to sit up there was to sail along the cloudy coastline of every dream. Mark my word, said Catherine, them boards are too old, them nails are slippery as worms, gonna crack in two, gonna fall and bust our heads don't I know it.

Storing our provisions in the tree house, we separated into the woods, each carrying a grain sack to be filled with herbs, leaves, strange roots. No one, not even Catherine, knew altogether what went into the medicine, for it was a secret Dolly kept to herself, and we were never allowed to look at the gatherings in her own sack: she held tight to it, as though inside she had captive a blue-haired child, a bewitched prince. This was her story: "Once, back yonder when we were children (Verena still with her baby teeth and Catherine no higher than a fence post) there were gypsies thick as birds in a blackberry patch—not like now, when maybe you see a few straggling through each year. They came with spring: sudden, like the dogwood pink, there they were—up and down the road and in the woods around. But our men hated the sight of them, and daddy, that was your great-uncle Uriah, said he would shoot any he caught on our place. And so I never told when I saw the gypsies taking water from the creek or stealing old winter pecans off the ground. Then one evening, it was April and falling rain, I went out to the cowshed, where Fairybell had a new little calf; and there in the cowshed were three gypsy women, two of them old and one of them young, and the young one was lying naked and twisting on the cornshucks. When they saw that I was not afraid, that I was not going to run and tell, one of the old women asked would I bring a light. So I went to the house for a candle, and when I came back the woman who had sent me was holding a red hollering baby upside down by its feet, and the other woman was milking Fairybell. I helped them wash the baby in the warm milk and wrap it in a scarf. Then one of the old women took my hand and said: Now I am going to give you a gift by teaching you a rhyme. It was a rhyme about evergreen bark, dragonfly fern—and all the other things we come here in the woods to find: *Boil till dark and pure if you want a dropsy cure.* In the morning they were gone; I looked for them in the fields and on the road; there was nothing left of them but the rhyme in my head."

Calling to each other, hooting like owls loose in the daytime, we worked all morning in opposite parts of the woods. Toward afternoon, our sacks fat with skinned bark, tender, torn roots, we climbed back into the green web of the China tree and spread the food. There was good creek water in a mason jar, or if the weather was cold, a thermos of hot coffee, and we wadded leaves to wipe our chicken-stained, fudge-sticky fingers. Afterward, telling fortunes with flowers, speaking of sleepy things, it was as though we floated through the afternoon on the raft in the tree; we belonged there, as the sun-silvered leaves belonged, the dwelling whippoorwills.

About once a year I go over to the house on Talbo Lane, and walk around in the yard. I was there the other day, and came across an old iron tub lying overturned in the weeds, like a black fallen meteor: Dolly—Dolly, hovering over the tub dropping our grain-sack gatherings into boiling water and stirring, stirring with a sawed-off broomstick the brown-as-tobacco-spit brew. She did the mixing of the medicine alone while Catherine and I stood watching like apprentices to a witch. We all helped later with the bottling of it and, because it produced a fume that exploded ordinary corks, my particular job was to roll stoppers of toilet paper. Sales averaged around six bottles a week, at two dollars a bottle. The money, Dolly said, belonged to the three of us, and we spent it fast as it came in. We were always sending away for stuff advertised in magazines: Take Up Woodcarving, Parcheesi: the game for young and old, Anyone Can Play A Bazooka. Once we sent away for a book of French lessons: it was my idea that if we got to talk French, we would have a secret language that Verena or nobody would understand. Dolly was willing to try, but "Passez-moi a spoon" was the best she ever did, and after learning "Je suis fatigué," Catherine never opened the book again: she said that was all she needed to know.

Verena often remarked that there would be trouble if anyone ever got poisoned, but otherwise she did not show much interest in the dropsy cure. Then one year we totaled up and found we'd earned enough to have to pay an income tax. Whereupon Verena began asking questions: money was like a wildcat whose trail she stalked with a trained hunter's muffled step and an eye for every broken twig. What, she wanted to know, went into the medicine? and Dolly, flattered, almost giggling, nonetheless waved her hands and said Well this and that, nothing special.

Verena seemed to let the matter die; yet very often, sitting at the supper table, her eyes paused ponderingly on Dolly, and once, when we were gathered in the yard around the boiling tub, I looked up and saw Verena in a window watching us with uninterrupted fixity: by then, I suppose, her plan had taken shape, but she did not make her first move until summer.

Twice a year, in January and again in August, Verena went on buying trips to St. Louis or Chicago. That summer, the summer I reached sixteen, she went to Chicago and after two weeks returned accompanied by a man called Dr. Morris Ritz. Naturally everyone wondered who was Dr. Morris Ritz? He wore bow ties and sharp jazzy suits; his lips were blue and he had gaudy small swerving eyes; altogether, he looked like a mean mouse. We heard that he lived in the best room at the Lola Hotel and ate steak dinners at Phil's Café. On the streets he strutted along bobbing his shiny head at every passer-by; he made no friends, however, and was not seen in the company of anyone except Verena, who never brought him to the house and never mentioned his name until one day Catherine had the gall to say, "Miss Verena, just who is this funny-looking little Dr. Morris Ritz?" and Verena, getting white around the mouth, replied: "Well now, he's not half so funny-looking as some I could name."

Scandalous, people said, the way Verena was carrying on with that little Jew from Chicago: and him twenty years younger. The story that got around was that they were up to something out in the old canning factory the other side of town. As it developed, they were; but not what the gang at the poolhall thought. Most any afternoon you could see Verena and Dr. Morris Ritz walking out toward the canning factory, an abandoned blasted brick ruin with jagged windows and sagging doors. For a generation no one had been near it except schoolkids who went there to smoke cigarettes and get naked together. Then early in September, by way of a notice in the *Courier*, we learned for the first time that Verena had bought the old canning factory; but there was no mention as to what use she was planning to make of it. Shortly after this, Verena told Catherine to kill two chickens, as Dr. Morris Ritz was coming to Sunday dinner.

During the years that I lived there, Dr. Morris Ritz was the only person ever invited to dine at the house on Talbo Lane. So for many reasons it was an occasion. Catherine and Dolly did a spring cleaning: they beat rugs, brought china from the attic, had every room smelling of floorwax and lemon polish. There was to be fried chicken and ham, English peas, sweet potatoes, rolls, banana pudding, two kinds of cake and tutti-fruitti ice cream from the drugstore. Sunday noon Verena came in to look at the table: with its sprawling centerpiece of peach-colored roses and dense fancy stretches of silverware, it seemed set for a party of twenty; actually, there were only two places. Verena went ahead and set two more, and Dolly, seeing this, said weakly, Well, it was all right if Collin wanted to eat at the table, but that she was going to stay in the kitchen with Catherine. Verena put her foot down: "Don't fool with me, Dolly. This is important. Morris is coming here expressly to meet you. And what is more, I'd appreciate it if you'd hold up your head: it makes me dizzy, hanging like that."

Dolly was scared to death: she hid in her room, and long after our guest had arrived I had to be sent to fetch her. She was lying in the pink bed with a wet washrag on her forehead, and Catherine was sitting beside her. Catherine was all sleeked up, rouge on her cheeks like lollipops and her jaws jammed with more cotton than ever; she said, "Honey, you ought to get up from there—you're going to ruin that pretty dress." It was a calico dress Verena had brought from Chicago; Dolly sat up and smoothed it, then immediately lay down again: "If Verena knew how sorry I am," she said helplessly, and so I went and told Verena that Dolly was sick. Verena said she'd see about that, and marched off leaving me alone in the hall with Dr. Morris Ritz.

Oh he was a hateful thing. "So you're sixteen," he said, winking first one, then the other of his sassy eyes. "And throwing it around, huh? Make the old lady take you next time she goes to Chicago. Plenty of good stuff there to throw it at." He snapped his fingers and jiggled his razzle-dazzle, dagger-sharp shoes as though keeping time to some vaudeville tune: he might have been a tapdancer or a soda-jerk, except that he was carrying a briefcase, which suggested a more serious occupation. I wondered what kind of doctor he was supposed to be; indeed, was on the point of asking when Verena returned, steering Dolly by the elbow.

The shadows of the hall, the tapestried furniture failed to absorb her; without raising her eyes, she lifted her hand, and Dr. Ritz gripped it so ruggedly, pumped it so hard she went nearly off balance. "Gee, Miss Talbo; am I honored to meet you!" he said, and cranked his bow tie.

We sat down to dinner, and Catherine came around with the chicken. She served Verena, then Dolly, and when the doctor's turn came he said, "Tell you the truth, the only piece of chicken I care about is the brain: don't suppose you'd have that back in the kitchen, mammy?"

Catherine looked so far down her nose she got almost cross-eyed; and with her tongue all mixed up in the cotton wadding she told him that "Dolly's took those brains on her plate."

"These Southern accents, Jesus," he said, genuinely dismayed.

"She says I have the brains on my plate," said Dolly, her cheeks red as Catherine's rouge. "But please let me pass them to you."

"If you're sure you don't mind . . ."

"She doesn't mind a bit," said Verena. "She only eats sweet things anyway. Here, Dolly: have some banana pudding."

Presently Dr. Ritz commenced a fit of sneezing. "The flowers, those roses, old allergy . . ."

"Oh dear," said Dolly, who, seeing an opportunity to escape into the kitchen, seized the bowl of roses: it slipped, crystal crashed, roses landed in gravy and gravy landed on us all. "You see," she said, speaking to herself and with tears teetering in her eyes, "you see, it's hopeless."

"Nothing is hopeless, Dolly; sit down and finish your pudding," Verena advised in a substantial, chin-up voice. "Besides, we have a nice little surprise for you. Morris, show Dolly those lovely labels."

Murmuring "No harm done," Dr. Ritz stopped rubbing gravy splotches off his sleeve, and went into the hall, returning with his briefcase. His fingers buzzed through a sheaf of papers, then lighted on a large envelope, which he passed down to Dolly.

There were gum-stickers in the envelope, triangular labels with orange lettering: Gypsy Queen Dropsy Cure: and a fuzzy picture of a woman wearing a bandana and gold earloops. "First class, huh?" said Dr. Ritz. "Made in Chicago. A friend of mine drew the picture: real artist, that guy," Dolly shuffled the labels with a puzzled, apprehensive expression until Verena asked: "Aren't you pleased?"

The labels twitched in Dolly's hands. "I'm not sure I understand."

"Of course you do," said Verena, smiling thinly. "It's obvious enough. I told Morris that old story of yours and he thought of this wonderful name."

"Gypsy Queen Dropsy Cure: very catchy, that," said the doctor. "Look great in ads."

"*My* medicine?" said Dolly, her eyes still lowered. "But I don't need any labels, Verena. I write my own."

Dr. Ritz snapped his fingers. "Say, that's good! We can have labels printed like her own handwriting: personal, see?"

"We've spent enough money already," Verena told him briskly; and, turning to Dolly, said: "Morris and I are going up to Washington this week to get a copyright on these labels and register a patent for the medicine—naming you as the inventor, naturally. Now the point is, Dolly, you must sit down and write out a complete formula for us."

Dolly's face loosened; and the labels scattered on the floor, skimmed. Leaning her hands on the table, she pushed herself upward; slowly her features came together again, she lifted her head and looked blinkingly at

Dr. Ritz, at Verena. "It won't do," she said quietly. She moved to the door, put a hand on its handle. "It won't do: because you haven't any right, Verena. Nor you, sir."

I helped Catherine clear the table: the ruined roses, the uncut cakes, the vegetables no one had touched. Verena and her guest had left the house together; from the kitchen window we watched them as they went toward town nodding and shaking their heads. Then we sliced the devil's-food cake and took it into Dolly's room.

Hush now! hush now! she said when Catherine began lighting into That One. But it was as though the rebellious inner whispering had become a raucous voice, an opponent she must outshout: Hush now! hush now! until Catherine had to put her arms around Dolly and say hush, too.

We got out a deck of Rook cards and spread them on the bed. Naturally, Catherine had to go and remember it was Sunday; she said maybe we could risk another black mark in the Judgment Book, but there were too many beside her name already. After thinking it over, we told fortunes instead. Sometime around dusk Verena came home. We heard her footsteps in the hall; she opened the door without knocking, and Dolly, who was in the middle of my fortune, tightened her hold on my hand. Verena said: "Collin, Catherine, we will excuse you."

Catherine wanted to follow me up the ladder into the attic, except she had on her fine clothes. So I went alone. There was a good knothole that looked straight down into the pink room; but Verena was standing directly under it, and all I could see was her hat, for she was still wearing the hat she'd put on when she left the house. It was a straw skimmer decorated with a cluster of celluloid fruit. "Those are facts," she was saying, and the fruit shivered, shimmered in the blue dimness. "Two thousand for the old factory, Bill Tatum and four carpenters working out there at eighty cents an hour, seven thousand dollars' worth of machinery already ordered, not to mention what a specialist like Morris Ritz is costing. And why? All for you!"

"All for me?" and Dolly sounded sad and failing as the dusk. I saw her shadow as she moved from one part of the room to another. "You are my own flesh, and I love you tenderly; in my heart I love you. I could prove it now by giving you the only thing that has ever been mine: then you would have it all. Please, Verena," she said, faltering, "let this one thing belong to me."

Verena switched on a light. "You speak of giving," and her voice was hard as the sudden bitter glare. "All these years that I've worked like a fieldhand: what haven't I given you? This house, that . . ."

"You've given everything to me," Dolly interrupted softly. "And to

Catherine and to Collin. Except, we've earned our way a bit: we've kept a nice home for you, haven't we?"

"Oh a fine home," said Verena, whipping off her hat. Her face was full of blood. "You and that gurgling fool. Has it not struck you that I never ask anyone into this house? And for a very simple reason: I'm ashamed to. Look what happened today."

I could hear the breath go out of Dolly. "I'm sorry," she said faintly. "I am truly. I'd always thought there was a place for us here, that you needed us somehow. But it's going to be all right now, Verena. We'll go away."

Verena sighed. "Poor Dolly. Poor poor thing. Wherever would you go?"

The answer, a little while in coming, was fragile as the flight of a moth: "I know a place."

Later, I waited in bed for Dolly to come and kiss me good-night. My room, beyond the parlor in a faraway corner of the house, was the room where their father, Mr. Uriah Talbo, had lived. In his mad old age, Verena had brought him here from the farm, and here he'd died, not knowing where he was. Though dead ten, fifteen years, the pee and tobacco old-man smell of him still saturated the mattress, the closet, and on a shelf in the closet was the one possession he'd carried away with him from the farm, a small yellow drum: as a lad my own age, he'd marched in a Dixie regiment rattling this little yellow drum, and singing. Dolly said that when she was a girl she'd liked to wake up winter mornings and hear her father singing as he went about the house building fires; after he was old, after he'd died, she sometimes heard his songs in the field of Indian grass. Wind, Catherine said; and Dolly told her: But the wind is us—it gathers and remembers all our voices, then sends them talking and telling through the leaves and the fields—I've heard Papa clear as day.

On such a night, now that it was September, the autumn winds would be curving through the taut red grass, releasing all the gone voices, and I wondered if he was singing among them, the old man in whose bed I lay falling asleep.

Then I thought Dolly at last had come to kiss me good-night, for I woke up sensing her near me in the room; but it was almost morning, beginning light was like a flowering foliage at the windows, and roosters ranted in distant yards. "Shhh, Collin," Dolly whispered, bending over me. She was wearing a woolen winter suit and a hat with a traveling veil that misted her face. "I only wanted you to know where we are going."

"To the tree house?" I said, and thought I was talking in my sleep.

Dolly nodded. "Just for now. Until we know better what our plans will be." She could see that I was frightened, and put her hand on my forehead.

"You and Catherine: but not me?" and I was jerking with a chill. "You can't leave without me."

The town clock was tolling; she seemed to be waiting for it to finish before making up her mind. It struck five, and by the time the note had died away I had climbed out of bed and rushed into my clothes. There was nothing for Dolly to say except: "Don't forget your comb."

Catherine met us in the yard; she was crooked over with the weight of a brimming oilcloth satchel; her eyes were swollen, she had been crying, and Dolly, oddly calm and certain of what she was doing, said it doesn't matter, Catherine—we can send for your goldfish once we find a place. Verena's closed quiet windows loomed above us; we moved cautiously past them and silently out the gate. A fox terrier barked at us; but there was no one on the street, and no one saw us pass through the town except a sleepless prisoner gazing from the jail. We reached the field of Indian grass at the same moment as the sun. Dolly's veil flared in the morning breeze, and a pair of pheasants, nesting in our path, swept before us, their metal wings swiping the cockscomb-scarlet grass. The China tree was a September bowl of green and greenish gold: Gonna fall, gonna bust our heads, Catherine said, as all around us the leaves shook down their dew.

2

If it hadn't been for Riley Henderson, I doubt anyone would have known, or at least known so soon, that we were in the tree.

Catherine had loaded her oilcloth satchel with the leftovers from Sunday dinner, and we were enjoying a breakfast of cake and chicken when gunfire slapped through the woods. We sat there with cake going dry in our mouths. Below, a sleek bird dog cantered into view, followed by Riley Henderson; he was shouldering a shotgun and around his neck there hung a garland of bleeding squirrels whose tails were tied together. Dolly lowered her veil, as though to camouflage herself among the leaves.

He paused not far away, and his wary, tanned young face tightened; propping his gun into position, he took a roaming aim, as if waiting for a target to present itself. The suspense was too much for Catherine, who shouted: "Riley Henderson, don't you dare shoot us!"

His gun wavered, and he spun around, the squirrels swinging like a loose necklace. Then he saw us in the tree, and after a moment said, "Hello there, Catherine Creek; hello, Miss Talbo. What are you folks doing up there? Wildcat chase you?"

"Just sitting," said Dolly promptly, as though she were afraid for either Catherine or I to answer. "That's a fine mess of squirrels you've got."

"Take a couple," he said, detaching two. "We had some for supper last night and they were real tender. Wait a minute, I'll bring them up to you."

"You don't have to do that; just leave them on the ground." But he said ants would get at them, and hauled himself into the tree. His blue shirt was spotted with squirrel blood, and flecks of blood glittered in his rough leather-colored hair; he smelled of gunpowder, and his homely well-made face was brown as cinnamon. "I'll be damned, it's a tree house," he said, pounding his foot as though to test the strength of the boards. Catherine warned him that maybe it was a tree house now, but it wouldn't be for long if he didn't stop that stamping. He said, "You build it, Collin?" and it was with a happy shock that I realized he'd called my name: I hadn't thought Riley Henderson knew me from dust. But I knew him, all right.

No one in our town ever had themselves so much talked about as Riley Henderson. Older people spoke of him with sighing voices, and those nearer his own age, like myself, were glad to call him mean and hard: that was because he would only let us envy him, would not let us love him, be his friend.

Anyone could have told you the facts.

He was born in China, where his father, a missionary, had been killed in an uprising. His mother was from this town, and her name was Rose; though I never saw her myself, people say she was a beautiful woman until she started wearing glasses; she was rich, too, having received a large inheritance from her grandfather. When she came back from China she brought Riley, then five, and two younger children, both girls; they lived with her unmarried brother, Justice of the Peace Horace Holton, a meaty spinsterish man with skin yellow as quince. In the following years Rose Henderson grew strange in her ways: she threatened to sue Verena for selling her a dress that shrank in the wash; to punish Riley, she made him hop on one leg around the yard reciting the multiplication table; otherwise, she let him run wild, and when the Presbyterian minister spoke to her about it she told him she hated her children and wished they were dead. And she must have meant it, for one Christmas morning she locked the bathroom door and tried to drown her two little girls in the tub: it was said that Riley broke the door down with a hatchet, which seems a tall order for a boy of nine or ten, whatever he was. Afterward, Rose was sent off to a place on the Gulf Coast, an institution, and she may still be living there, at least I've never heard that she died. Now Riley and his uncle Horace Holton couldn't get on. One night he stole Horace's Oldsmobile and drove out to the Dance-N-Dine with Mamie Curtiss: she was fast as lightning, and maybe five years older than Riley, who was not more than fifteen at the time. Well, Horace heard they were at the Dance-N-Dine and got the Sheriff to drive him out there: he said he was going to teach Riley a lesson and have him arrested. But Riley said Sheriff, you're after the wrong party.

Right there in front of a crowd he accused his uncle of stealing money that belonged to Rose and that was meant for him and his sisters. He offered to fight it out on the spot; and when Horace held back, he just walked over and socked him in the eye. The Sheriff put Riley in jail. But Judge Cool, an old friend of Rose's, began to investigate, and sure enough it turned out Horace had been draining Rose's money into his own account. So Horace simply packed his things and took the train to New Orleans, where, a few months later, we heard that, billed as the Minister of Romance, he had a job marrying couples on an excursion steamer that made moonlight cruises up the Mississippi. From then on, Riley was his own boss. With money borrowed against the inheritance he was coming into, he bought a red racy car and went skidding round the countryside with every floozy in town; the only nice girls you ever saw in that car were his sisters—he took them for a drive Sunday afternoons, a slow respectable circling of the square. They were pretty girls, his sisters, but they didn't have much fun, for he kept a strict watch, and boys were afraid to come near them. A reliable colored woman did their housework, otherwise they lived alone. One of his sisters, Elizabeth, was in my class at school, and she got the best grades, straight A's. Riley himself had quit school; but he was not one of the pool-hall loafs, nor did he mix with them; he fished in the daytime, or went hunting; around the old Holton house he made many improvements, as he was a good carpenter; and a good mechanic, too: for instance, he built a special car horn, it wailed like a train-whistle, and in the evening you could hear it howling as he roared down the road on his way to a dance in another town. How I longed for him to be my friend! and it seemed possible, he was just two years older. But I could remember the only time he ever spoke to me. Spruce in a pair of white flannels, he was off to a dance at the clubhouse, and he came into Verena's drugstore, where I sometimes helped out on Saturday nights. What he wanted was a package of Shadows, but I wasn't sure what Shadows were, so he had to come behind the counter and get them out of the drawer himself; and he laughed, not unkindly, though it was worse than if it had been: now he knew I was a fool, we would never be friends.

Dolly said, "Have a piece of cake, Riley," and he asked did we always have picnics this early in the day? then went on to say he considered it a fine idea: "Like swimming at night," he said. "I come down here while it's still dark, and go swimming in the river. Next time you have a picnic, call out so I'll know you're here."

"You are welcome any morning," said Dolly, raising her veil. "I daresay we will be here for some while."

Riley must have thought it a curious invitation, but he did not say so. He produced a package of cigarettes and passed it around; when Catherine took one, Dolly said: "Catherine Creek, you've never touched tobacco in your life." Catherine allowed as to how she may have been missing something: "It must be a comfort, so many folks speak in its favor; and Dolly-heart, when you get to be our age you've got to look for comforts." Dolly bit her lip. "Well, I don't suppose there's any harm," she said, and accepted a cigarette herself.

There are two things that will drive a boy crazy (according to Mr. Hand, who caught me smoking in the lavatory at school) and I'd given up one of them, cigarettes, two years before: not because I thought it would make me crazy, but because I thought it was imperiling my growth. Actually, now that I was a normal size, Riley was no taller than me, though he seemed to be, for he moved with the drawn-out cowboy awkwardness of a lanky man. So I took a cigarette, and Dolly, gushing uninhaled smoke, said she thought we might as well all be sick together; but no one was sick, and Catherine said next time she would like to try a pipe, as they smelled so good. Whereupon Dolly volunteered the surprising fact that Verena smoked a pipe, something I'd never known: "I don't know whether she does anymore, but she used to have a pipe and a can of Prince Albert with half an apple cut up in it. But you mustn't tell that," she added, suddenly aware of Riley, who laughed aloud.

Usually, glimpsed on the street or seen passing in his car, Riley wore a tense, trigger-tempered expression; but there in the China tree he seemed relaxed: frequent smiles enriched his whole face, as though he wanted at least to be friendly, if not friends. Dolly, for her part, appeared to be at ease and enjoying his company. Certainly she was not afraid of him: perhaps it was because we were in the tree house, and the tree house was her own.

"Thank you for the squirrels, sir," she said, as he prepared to leave. "And don't forget to come again."

He swung himself to the ground. "Want a ride? My car's up by the cemetery."

Dolly told him: "That's kind of you; but really, we haven't any place to go."

Grinning, he lifted his gun and aimed it at us; and Catherine yelled: You ought to be whipped, boy; but he laughed and waved and ran, his bird dog barking, booming ahead. Dolly said gaily, "Let's have a cigarette," for the package had been left behind.

By the time Riley reached town the news was roaring in the air like a flight of bees: how we'd run off in the middle of the night. Though neither Catherine nor I knew it, Dolly had left a note, which Verena found when she went for her morning coffee. As I understand it, this note simply said that we were going away and that Verena would not be bothered by us anymore. She at once rang up her friend Morris Ritz at the Lola Hotel, and together they traipsed off to rouse the Sheriff. It was Verena's backing that had put the Sheriff into office; he was a fast-stepping, brassy young fellow with a brutal jaw and the bashful eyes of a cardsharp; his name was Junius Candle (can you believe it? the same Junius Candle who is a Senator today!). A searching party of deputies was gathered; telegrams were hurried off to Sheriffs in other towns. Many years later, when the Talbo estate was being settled, I came across the handwritten original of this telegram —composed, I believe, by Dr. Ritz. *Be on lookout for following persons traveling together. Dolly Augusta Talbo, white, aged 60, yellow grayish hair, thin, height 5 feet 3, green eyes, probably insane but not likely to be dangerous, post description bakeries as she is cake eater. Catherine Creek, Negro, pretends to be Indian, age about 60, toothless, confused speech, short and heavy, strong, likely to be dangerous. Collin Talbo Fenwick, white, age 16, looks younger, height 5 feet 7, blond, gray eyes, thin, bad posture, scar at corner of mouth, surly natured. All three wanted as runaways.* They sure haven't run far, Riley said in the post office; and postmistress Mrs. Peters rushed to the telephone to say Riley Henderson had seen us in the woods below the cemetery.

While this was happening, we were peaceably setting about to make the tree house cozy. From Catherine's satchel we took a rose and gold scrap-quilt, and there was a deck of Rook cards, soap, rolls of toilet paper, oranges and lemons, candles, a frying pan, a bottle of blackberry wine, and two shoeboxes filled with food: Catherine bragged that she'd robbed the pantry of everything, leaving not even a biscuit for That One's breakfast.

Later, we all went to the creek and bathed our feet and faces in the cold water. There are as many creeks in River Woods as there are veins in a leaf: clear, crackling, they crook their way down into the little river that crawls through the woods like a green alligator. Dolly looked a sight, standing in the water with her winter suit-skirt hiked up and her veil pestering her like a cloud of gnats. I asked her, Dolly, why are you wearing that veil? and she said, "But isn't it proper for ladies to wear veils when they go traveling?"

Returning to the tree, we made a delicious jar of orangeade and talked of the future. Our assets were: forty-seven dollars in cash, and several pieces of jewelry, notably a gold fraternity ring Catherine had found in the intestines of a hog while stuffing sausages. According to Catherine, forty-seven dollars would buy us bus tickets anywhere: she knew somebody who had gone all the way to Mexico for fifteen dollars. Both Dolly and I were opposed to Mexico: for one thing, we didn't know the language. Besides, Dolly said, we shouldn't venture outside the state, and wherever we went it ought to be near a forest, otherwise how would we be able to make the dropsy cure? "To tell you the truth, I think we should set up right here in River Woods," she said, gazing about speculatively.

"In this old tree?" said Catherine. "Just put that notion out of your head,

Dollyheart." And then: "You recall how we saw in the paper where a man bought a castle across the ocean and brought it every bit home with him? You recall that? Well, we maybe could put my little house on a wagon and haul it down here." But, as Dolly pointed out, the house belonged to Verena, and was therefore not ours to haul away. Catherine answered: "You wrong, sugar. If you feed a man, and wash his clothes, and born his children, you and that man are married, that man is yours. If you sweep a house, and tend its fires and fill its stove, and there is love in you all the years you are doing this, then you and that house are married, that house is yours. The way I see it, both those houses up there belong to us: in the eyes of God, we could put That One right out."

I had an idea: down on the river below us there was a forsaken houseboat, green with the rust of water, half-sunk; it had been the property of an old man who made his living catching catfish, and who had been run out of town after applying for a certificate to marry a fifteen-year-old colored girl. My idea was, why shouldn't we fix up the old houseboat and live there?

Catherine said that if possible, she hoped to spend the rest of her life on land: "Where the Lord intended us," and she listed more of His intentions, one of these being that trees were meant for monkeys and birds. Presently she went silent and, nudging us, pointed in amazement down to where the woods opened upon the field of grass.

There, stalking toward us, solemnly, stiffly, came a distinguished party: Judge Cool, the Reverend and Mrs. Buster, Mrs. Macy Wheeler; and leading them, Sheriff Junius Candle, who wore high-laced boots and had a pistol flapping on his hip. Sun-motes lilted around them like yellow butterflies, brambles brushed their starched town clothes, and Mrs. Macy Wheeler, frightened by a vine that switched against her leg, jumped back, screeching: I laughed.

And, hearing me, they looked up at us, an expression of perplexed horror collecting on some of their faces: it was as though they were visitors at a zoo who had wandered accidentally into one of the cages. Sheriff Candle slouched forward, his hand cocked on his pistol. He stared at us with puckered eyes, as if he were gazing straight into the sun. "Now look here . . ." he began, and was cut short by Mrs. Buster, who said: "Sheriff, we agreed to leave this to the Reverend." It was a rule of hers that her husband, as God's representative, should have first say in everything. The Reverend Buster cleared his throat, and his hands, as he rubbed them together, were like the dry scraping feelers of an insect. "Dolly Talbo," he said, his voice very fine-sounding for so stringy, stunted a man, "I speak to you on behalf of your sister, that good gracious woman . . ."

"That she is," sang his wife, and Mrs. Macy Wheeler parroted her.

". . . who has this day received a grievous shock."

"That she has," echoed the ladies in their choir-trained voices.

Dolly looked at Catherine, touched my hand, as though asking us to explain what was meant by the group glowering below like dogs gathered around a tree of trapped possums. Inadvertently, and just, I think, to have something in her hands, she picked up one of the cigarettes Riley had left.

"Shame on you," squalled Mrs. Buster, tossing her tiny baldish head: those who called her an old buzzard, and there were several, were not speaking of her character alone: in addition to a small vicious head, she had high hunched shoulders and a vast body. "I say shame on you. How can you have come so far from God as to sit up in a tree like a drunken Indian —sucking cigarettes like a common . . ."

"Floozy," supplied Mrs. Macy Wheeler.

". . . floozy, while your sister lies in misery flat on her back."

Maybe they were right in describing Catherine as dangerous, for she reared up and said: "Preacher lady, don't you go calling Dolly and us floozies; I'll come down there and slap you bowlegged." Fortunately, none of them could understand her; if they had, the Sheriff might have shot her through the head: no exaggeration; and many of the white people in town would have said he did right.

Dolly seemed stunned, at the same time self-possessed. You see, she simply dusted her skirt and said: "Consider a moment, Mrs. Buster, and you will realize that we are nearer God than you—by several yards."

"Good for you, Miss Dolly. I call that a good answer." The man who had spoken was Judge Cool; he clapped his hands together and chuckled appreciatively. "Of course they are nearer God," he said, unfazed by the disapproving, sober faces around him. "They're in a tree, and we're on the ground."

Mrs. Buster whirled on him. "I'd thought you were a Christian, Charlie Cool. My ideas of a Christian do not include laughing at and encouraging a poor mad woman."

"Mind who you name as mad, Thelma," said the Judge. "That isn't especially Christian either."

The Reverend Buster opened fire. "Answer me this, Judge. Why did you come with us if it wasn't to do the Lord's will in a spirit of mercy?"

"The Lord's will?" said the Judge incredulously. "You don't know what that is anymore than I do. Perhaps the Lord told these people to go live in a tree; you'll admit, at least, that He never told you to drag them out —unless, of course, Verena Talbo is the Lord, a theory several of you give credence to, eh, Sheriff? No, sir, I did not come along to do anyone's will but my own: which merely means that I felt like taking a walk—the woods are very handsome at this time of year." He picked some brown violets and put them in his buttonhole.

"To hell with all that," began the Sheriff, and was again interrupted by Mrs. Buster, who said that under no circumstances would she tolerate swearing: Will we, Reverend? and the Reverend, backing her up, said he'd be damned if they would. "I'm in charge here," the Sheriff informed them, thrusting his bully-boy jaw. "This is a matter for the law."

"Whose law, Junius?" inquired Judge Cool quietly. "Remember that I sat in the courthouse twenty-seven years, rather a longer time than you've lived. Take care. We have no legal right whatever to interfere with Miss Dolly."

Undaunted, the Sheriff hoisted himself a little into the tree. "Let's don't have anymore trouble," he said coaxingly, and we could see his curved dog-teeth. "Come on down from there, the pack of you." As we continued to sit like three nesting birds, he showed more of his teeth and, as though he were trying to shake us out, angrily swayed a branch.

"Miss Dolly, you've always been a peaceful person," said Mrs. Macy Wheeler. "Please come on home with us; you don't want to miss your dinner." Dolly replied matter-of-factly that we were not hungry: were they? "There's a drumstick for anybody that would like it."

Sheriff Candle said, "You make it hard on me, ma'am," and pulled himself nearer. A branch, cracking under his weight, sent through the tree a sad cruel thunder.

"If he lays a hand on any one of you, kick him in the head," advised Judge Cool. "Or I will," he said with sudden gallant pugnacity: like an inspired frog he hopped and caught hold to one of the Sheriff's dangling boots. The Sheriff, in turn, grabbed my ankles, and Catherine had to hold me around the middle. We were sliding, that we should all fall seemed inevitable, the strain was immense. Meanwhile, Dolly started pouring what was left of our orangeade down the Sheriff's neck, and abruptly, shouting an obscenity, he let go of me. They crashed to the ground, the Sheriff on top of the Judge and the Reverend Buster crushed beneath them both. Mrs. Macy Wheeler and Mrs. Buster, augmenting the disaster, fell upon them with crowlike cries of distress.

Appalled by what had happened, and the part she herself had played, Dolly became so confused that she dropped the empty orangeade jar: it hit Mrs. Buster on the head with a ripe thud. "Beg pardon," she apologized, though in the furor no one heard her.

When the tangle below unraveled, those concerned stood apart from each other embarrassedly, gingerly feeling of themselves. The Reverend looked rather flattened out, but no broken bones were discovered, and only Mrs. Buster, on whose skimpy-haired head a bump was pyramiding, could have justly complained of injury. She did so forthrightly. "You attacked me, Dolly Talbo, don't deny it, everyone here is a witness, everyone saw you aim that mason jar at my head. Junius, arrest her!"

The Sheriff, however, was involved in settling differences of his own. Hands on hips, swaggering, he bore down on the Judge, who was in the process of replacing the violets in his buttonhole. "If you weren't so old, I'd damn well knock you down."

"I'm not so old, Junius: just old enough to think men ought not to fight in front of ladies," said the Judge. He was a fair-sized man with strong shoulders and a straight body: though not far from seventy, he looked to be in his fifties. He clenched his fists and they were hard and hairy as coconuts. "On the other hand," he said grimly, "I'm ready if you are."

At the moment it looked like a fair enough match. Even the Sheriff seemed not so sure of himself; with diminishing bravado, he spit between his fingers, and said Well, nobody was going to accuse him of hitting an old man. "Or standing up to one," Judge Cool retorted. "Go on, Junius, tuck your shirt in your pants and trot along home."

The Sheriff appealed to us in the tree. "Save yourselves a lot of trouble: get out of there and come along with me now." We did not stir, except that Dolly dropped her veil, as though lowering a curtain on the subject once for all. Mrs. Buster, the lump on her head like a horn, said portentously, "Never mind, Sheriff. They've had their chance," and, eyeing Dolly, then the Judge, added: "You may imagine you are getting away with something. But let me tell you there will be a retribution—not in heaven, right here on earth."

"Right here on earth," harmonized Mrs. Macy Wheeler.

They left along the path, erect, haughty as a wedding procession, and passed into the sunlight, where the red rolling grass swept up, swallowed them. Lingering under the tree, the Judge smiled at us and, with a small courteous bow, said: "Do I remember you offering a drumstick to anybody that would like it?"

He might have been put together from parts of the tree, for his nose was like a wooden peg, his legs were strong as old roots, and his eyebrows were thick, tough as strips of bark. Among the topmost branches were beards of silvery moss the color of his center-parted hair, and the cowhide sycamore leaves, sifting down from a neighboring taller tree, were the color of his cheeks. Despite his canny, tomcat eyes, the general impression his face made was that of someone shy and countrified. Ordinarily he was not the one to make a show of himself, Judge Charlie Cool; there were many who had taken advantage of his modesty to set themselves above him. Yet none of them could have claimed, as he could, to be a graduate of Harvard University or to have twice traveled in Europe. Still, there were those who were resentful and felt that he put on airs: wasn't he supposed to read a page of Greek every morning before breakfast? and what kind of a man was it that would always have flowers in his buttonhole? If he wasn't stuck-up, why, some people asked, had he gone all the way to Kentucky to find a wife instead of marrying one of our own women? I do not remember the Judge's wife; she died before I was old enough to be aware of her, therefore all that I repeat comes second-hand. So: the town never warmed up to Irene Cool, and apparently it was her own fault. Kentucky women are difficult to begin with, keyed-up, hellion-hearted, and Irene Cool, who was born a Todd in Bowling Green (Mary Todd, a second cousin once removed, had married Abraham Lincoln), let everyone around here know she thought them a backward, vulgar lot: she received none of the ladies of the town, but Miss Palmer, who did sewing for her, spread news of how she'd transformed the Judge's house into a place of taste and style with Oriental rugs and antique furnishings. She drove to and from church in a Pierce-Arrow with all the windows rolled up, and in church itself she sat with a cologned handkerchief against her nose: *the smell of God ain't good enough for Irene Cool.* Moreover, she would not permit either of the local doctors to attend her family, this though she herself was a semi-invalid: a small backbone dislocation necessitated her sleeping on a bed of boards. There were crude jokes about the Judge getting full of splinters. Nevertheless, he fathered two sons, Todd and Charles Jr., both born in Kentucky, where their mother had gone in order that they could claim to be natives of the bluegrass state. But those who tried to make out the Judge got the brunt of his wife's irritableness, that he was a miserable man, never had much of a case, and after she died even the hardest of their critics had to admit old Charlie must surely have loved his Irene. For during the last two years of her life, when she was very ill and fretful, he retired as circuit judge, then took her abroad to the places they had been on their honeymoon. She never came back; she is buried in Switzerland. Not so long ago Carrie Wells, a schoolteacher here in town, went on a group tour to Europe; the only thing connecting our town with that continent is graves, the graves of soldier boys and Irene Cool; and Carrie, armed with a camera for snapshots, set out to visit them all: though she stumbled about in a cloud-high cemetery one whole afternoon, she could not find the Judge's wife, and it is funny to think of Irene Cool, serenely there on a mountainside still unwilling to receive. There was not much left for the Judge when he came back; politicians like Meiself Tallsap and his gang had come into power: those boys couldn't afford to have Charlie Cool sitting in the courthouse. It was sad to see the Judge, a fine-looking man dressed in narrow-cut suits with a black silk band sewn around his sleeve and a Cherokee rose in his buttonhole, sad to see him with nothing to do except go to the post office or stop in at the bank. His sons worked in the bank, prissy-mouthed, prudent men who might have been twins, for they both were marshmallow-white, slump-shouldered, watery-eyed. Charles Jr., he was the one who had lost his hair while still in college, was vice-president of the bank, and Todd, the younger son, was chief cashier. In no way did they resemble their father, except that they had married Kentucky women. These daughters-in-law had taken over the Judge's house and divided it into two apartments with separate entrances; there was an arrangement whereby the old man lived with first one son's family, then the other. No wonder he'd felt like taking a walk to the woods.

"Thank you, Miss Dolly," he said, wiping his mouth with the back of his hand. "That's the best drumstick I've had since I was a boy."

"It's the least we can do, a drumstick; you were very brave." There was in Dolly's voice an emotional, feminine tremor that struck me as unsuitable, not dignified; so, too, it must have seemed to Catherine: she gave Dolly a reprimanding glance. "Won't you have something more, a piece of cake?"

"No, ma'am, thank you, I've had a sufficiency." He unloosened from his vest a gold watch and chain, then lassoed the chain to a strong twig above his head; it hung like a Christmas ornament, and its feathery faded ticking might have been the heartbeat of a delicate thing, a firefly, a frog. "If you can hear time passing, it makes the day last longer. I've come to appreciate a long day." He brushed back the fur of the squirrels, which lay curled in a corner as though they were only asleep. "Right through the head: good shooting, son."

Of course I gave the credit to the proper party. "Riley Henderson, was it?" said the Judge, and went on to say it was Riley who had let our whereabouts be known. "Before that, they must have sent off a hundred dollars' worth of telegrams," he told us, tickled at the thought. "I guess it was the idea of all that money that made Verena take to her bed."

Scowling, Dolly said, "It doesn't make a particle of sense, all of them behaving ugly that way. They seemed mad enough to kill us, though I can't see why, or what it has to do with Verena: she knew we were going away to leave her in peace, I told her, I even left a note. But if she's sick—is she, Judge? I've never known her to be."

"Never a day," said Catherine.

"Oh, she's upset all right," the Judge said with a certain contentment. "But Verena's not the woman to come down with anything an aspirin couldn't fix. I remember when she wanted to rearrange the cemetery, put up some kind of mausoleum to house herself and all you Talbos. One of the ladies around here came to me and said Judge, don't you think Verena Talbo is the most morbid person in town, contemplating such a big tomb for herself? and I said No, the only thing morbid was that she was willing to spend the money when not for an instant did she believe she was ever going to die."

"I don't like to hear talk against my sister," said Dolly curtly. "She's worked hard, she deserves to have things as she wants them. It's our fault, someway we failed her, there was no place for us in her house."

Catherine's cotton-wadding squirmed in her jaw like chewing tobacco. "Are you my Dollyheart? or some hypocrite? He's a friend, you ought to tell him the truth, how That One and the little Jew was stealing our medicine. . . ."

The Judge applied for a translation, but Dolly said it was simply nonsense, nothing worth repeating and, diverting him, asked if he knew how to skin a squirrel. Nodding dreamily, he gazed away from us, above us, his acornlike eyes scanning the sky-fringed, breeze-fooled leaves. "It may be that there is no place for any of us. Except we know there is, somewhere; and if we found it, but lived there only a moment, we could count ourselves blessed. This could be your place," he said, shivering as though in the sky spreading wings had cast a cold shade. "And mine."

Subtly as the gold watch spun its sound of time, the afternoon curved toward twilight. Mist from the river, autumn haze, trailed moon-colors among the bronze, the blue trees, and a halo, an image of winter, ringed the paling sun. Still the Judge did not leave us: "Two women and a boy? at the mercy of night? and Junius Candle, those fools up to God knows what? I'm sticking with you." Surely, of the four of us, it was the Judge who had most found his place in the tree. It was a pleasure to watch him, all twinkly as a hare's nose, and feeling himself a man again, more than that, a protector. He skinned the squirrels with a jackknife, while in the dusk I gathered sticks and built under the tree a fire for the frying pan. Dolly opened the bottle of blackberry wine; she justified this by referring to a chill in the air. The squirrels turned out quite well, very tender, and the Judge said proudly that we should taste his fried catfish sometime. We sipped the wine in silence; a smell of leaves and smoke carrying from the cooling fire called up thoughts of other autumns, and we sighed, heard, like sea-roar, singings in the field of grass. A candle flickered in a mason jar, and gypsy moths, balanced, blowing about the flame, seemed to pilot its scarf of yellow among the black branches.

There was, just then, not a footfall, but a nebulous sense of intrusion: it might have been nothing more than the moon coming out. Except there was no moon; nor stars. It was dark as the blackberry wine. "I think there is someone—something down there," said Dolly, expressing what we all felt.

The Judge lifted the candle. Night-crawlers slithered away from its lurching light, a snowy owl flew between the trees. "Who goes there?" he challenged with the conviction of a soldier. "Answer up, who goes there?"

"Me, Riley Henderson." It was indeed. He separated from the shadows, and his upraised, grinning face looked warped, wicked in the candlelight. "Just thought I'd see how you were getting on. Hope you're not sore at me: I wouldn't have told where you were, not if I'd known what it was all about."

"Nobody blames you, son," said the Judge, and I remembered it was he who had championed Riley's cause against his uncle Horace Holton: there was an understanding between them. "We're enjoying a small taste of wine. I'm sure Miss Dolly would be pleased to have you join us."

Catherine complained there was no room; another ounce, and those old boards would give way. Still, we scrunched together to make a place for Riley, who had no sooner squeezed into it than Catherine grabbed a fistful of his hair. "That's for today with you pointing your gun at us like I told you not to; and this," she said, yanking again and speaking distinctively enough to be understood, "pays you back for setting the Sheriff on us."

It seemed to me that Catherine was impertinent, but Riley grunted good-naturedly, and said she might have better cause to be pulling somebody's hair before the night was over. For there was, he told us, excited feelings in the town, crowds like Saturday night; the Reverend and Mrs. Buster especially were brewing trouble: Mrs. Buster was sitting on her front porch showing callers the bump on her head. Sheriff Candle, he said, had persuaded Verena to authorize a warrant for our arrest on the grounds that we had stolen property belonging to her.

"And, Judge," said Riley, his manner grave, perplexed, "they've even got the idea they're going to arrest you. Disturbing the peace and obstructing justice, that's what I heard. Maybe I shouldn't tell you this—but outside the bank I ran into one of your boys, Todd. I asked him what he was going to do about it, about them arresting you, I mean; and he said Nothing, said they'd been expecting something of the kind, that you'd brought it on yourself."

Leaning, the Judge snuffed out the candle; it was as though an expression was occurring in his face which he did not want us to see. In the dark one of us was crying, after a moment we knew that it was Dolly, and the sound of her tears set off silent explosions of love that, running the full circle round, bound us each to the other. Softly, the Judge said: "When they come we must be ready for them. Now, everybody listen to me. . . ."

3

"We must know our position to defend it; that is a primary rule. Therefore: what has brought us together? Trouble. Miss Dolly and her friends, they are in trouble. You, Riley: we both are in trouble. We belong in this tree or we wouldn't be here." Dolly grew silent under the confident sound of the Judge's voice; he said: "Today, when I started out with the Sheriff's party, I was a man convinced that his life will have passed uncommunicated and without trace. I think now that I will not have been so unfortunate. Miss Dolly, how long? fifty, sixty years? it was that far ago that I remember you, a stiff and blushing child riding to town in your father's wagon—never getting down from the wagon because you didn't want us town-children to see you had no shoes."

"They had shoes, Dolly and That One," Catherine muttered. "It was me that didn't have no shoes."

"All the years that I've seen you, never known you, not ever recognized, as I did today, what you are: a spirit, a pagan . . ."

"A pagan?" said Dolly, alarmed but interested.

"At least, then, a spirit, someone not to be calculated by the eye alone. Spirits are accepters of life, they grant its differences—and consequently are always in trouble. Myself, I should never have been a Judge; as such, I was too often on the wrong side: the law doesn't admit differences. Do you remember old Carper, the fisherman who had a houseboat on the river? He was chased out of town—wanted to marry that pretty little colored girl, I think she works for Mrs. Postum now; and you know she loved him. I used to see them when I went fishing, they were very happy together; she was to him what no one has been to me, the one person in the world—from whom nothing is held back. Still, if he had succeeded in marrying her, it would have been the Sheriff's duty to arrest and my duty to sentence him. I sometimes imagine all those whom I've called guilty have passed the real guilt on to me: it's partly that that makes me want once before I die to be right on the right side."

"You on the right side now. That One and the Jew . . ."

"Hush," said Dolly.

"The one person in the world." It was Riley repeating the Judge's phrase; his voice lingered inquiringly.

"I mean," the Judge explained, "a person to whom everything can be said. Am I an idiot to want such a thing? But ah, the energy we spend hiding from one another, afraid as we are of being identified. But here we are, identified: five fools in a tree. A great piece of luck provided we know how to use it: no longer any need to worry about the picture we present —free to find out who we truly are. If we know that no one can dislodge us; it's the uncertainty concerning themselves that makes our friends conspire to deny the differences. By scraps and bits I've in the past surrendered myself to strangers—men who disappeared down the gangplank, got off at the next station: put together, maybe they would've made the one person in the world—but there he is with a dozen different faces moving down a hundred separate streets. This is my chance to find that man—you are him, Miss Dolly, Riley, all of you."

Catherine said, "I'm no man with any dozen faces: the notion," which irritated Dolly, who told her if she couldn't speak respectably, why not just go to sleep. "But, Judge," said Dolly, "I'm not sure I know what it is you have in mind we should tell each other. Secrets?" she finished lamely.

"Secrets, no, no." The Judge scratched a match and relighted the candle; his face sprang upon us with an expression unexpectedly pathetic: we must help him, he was pleading. "Speak of the night, the fact there is no moon. What one says hardly matters, only the trust with which it is said, the sympathy with which it is received. Irene, my wife, a remarkable woman, we might have shared anything, and yet, yet nothing in us combined, we could not touch. She died in my arms, and at the last I said, Are you happy, Irene? have I made you happy? Happy happy happy, those were her last words: equivocal. I have never understood whether she was saying yes, or merely answering with an echo: I should know if I'd ever known her. My sons. I do not enjoy their esteem: I've wanted it, more as a man than as a father. Unfortunately, they feel they know something shameful about me. I'll tell you what it is." His virile eyes, faceted with candle-glow, examined us one by one, as though testing our attention, trust. "Five years ago, nearer six, I sat down in a train-seat where some child had left a child's magazine. I picked it up and was looking through it when I saw on the back cover addresses of children who wanted to correspond with other children. There was a little girl in Alaska, her name appealed to me, Heather Falls. I sent her a picture postcard; Lord, it seemed a harmless and pleasant thing to do. She answered at once, and the letter quite astonished me; it was a very intelligent account of life in Alaska—charming descriptions of her father's sheep ranch, of northern lights. She was thirteen and enclosed a photograph of herself—not pretty, but a wise and kind-looking child. I hunted through some old albums, and found a Kodak made on a fishing trip when I was fifteen—out in the sun and with a trout in my hand: it looked new enough. I wrote her as though I were still that boy, told her of the gun I'd got for Christmas, how the dog had had pups and what we'd named them, described a tent-show that had come to town. To be growing up again and have a sweetheart in Alaska—well, it was fun for an old man sitting alone listening to the noise of a clock. Later on she wrote she'd fallen in love with a fellow she knew, and I felt a real pang of jealousy, the way a youngster would; but we have remained friends: two years ago, when I told her I was getting ready for law school, she sent me a gold nugget—it would bring me luck, she said." He took it from his pocket and held it out for us to see: it made her come so close, Heather Falls, as though the gently bright gift balanced in his palm was part of her heart.

"And that's what they think is shameful?" said Dolly, more piqued than indignant. "Because you've helped keep company a lonely little child in Alaska? It snows there so much."

Judge Cool closed his hand over the nugget. "Not that they've mentioned it to me. But I've heard them talking at night, my sons and their wives: wanting to know what to do about me. Of course they'd spied out the letters. I don't believe in locking drawers—seems strange a man can't live without keys in what was at least once his own house. They think it all a sign of . . ." He tapped his head.

"I had a letter once. Collin, sugar, pour me a taste," said Catherine, indicating the wine. "Sure enough, I had a letter once, still got it somewhere, kept it twenty years wondering who was wrote it. Said Hello Catherine, come on to Miami and marry with me, love Bill."

"Catherine. A man asked you to marry him—and you never told one word of it to me?"

Catherine lifted a shoulder. "Well, Dollyheart, what was the Judge saying? You don't tell anybody everything. Besides, I've known a peck of Bills—wouldn't study marrying any of them. What worries my mind is, which one of the Bills was it wrote that letter? I'd like to know, seeing as it's the only letter I ever got. It could be the Bill that put the roof on my house; course, by the time the roof was up—my goodness, I have got old, been a long day since I've given it two thoughts. There was Bill that came to plow the garden, spring of 1913 it was; that man sure could plow a straight row. And Bill that built the chicken-coop: went away on a Pullman job; might have been him wrote me that letter. Or Bill—uh uh, his name was Fred—Collin, sugar, this wine is mighty good."

"I may have a drop more myself," said Dolly. "I mean, Catherine has given me such a . . ."

"Hmn," said Catherine.

"If you spoke more slowly, or chewed less . . ." The Judge thought Catherine's cotton was tobacco.

Riley had withdrawn a little from us; slumped over, he stared stilly into the inhabited dark: I, I, I, a bird cried, "I—you're wrong, Judge," he said.

"How so, son?"

The caught-up uneasiness that I associated with Riley swamped his face. "I'm not in trouble: I'm nothing—or would you call that my trouble? I lie awake thinking what do I know how to do? hunt, drive a car, fool around; and I get scared when I think maybe that's all it will ever come to. Another thing, I've got no feelings—except for my sisters, which is different. Take for instance, I've been going with this girl from Rock City nearly a year, the longest time I've stayed with one girl. I guess it was a week ago she flared up and said where's your heart? said if I didn't love her, she'd as soon die. So I stopped the car on the railroad track; well, I said, let's just sit here, the Crescent's due in about twenty minutes. We didn't take our eyes off each other, and I thought isn't it mean that I'm looking at you and I don't feel anything except . . ."

"Except vanity?" said the Judge.

Riley did not deny it. "And if my sisters were old enough to take care of themselves, I'd have been willing to wait for the Crescent to come down on us."

It made my stomach hurt to hear him talk like that; I longed to tell him he was all I wanted to be.

"You said before about the one person in the world. Why couldn't I think of her like that? It's what I want, I'm no good by myself. Maybe, if I could care for somebody that way, I'd make plans and carry them out: buy that stretch of land past Parson's Place and build houses on it—I could do it if I got quiet."

Wind surprised, pealed the leaves, parted night clouds; showers of starlight were let loose: our candle, as though intimidated by the incandescence of the opening, star-stabbed sky, toppled, and we could see, unwrapped above us, a late wayaway wintery moon: it was like a slice of snow, near and far creatures called to it, hunched moon-eyed frogs, a claw-voiced wildcat. Catherine hauled out the rose scrapquilt, insisting Dolly wrap it around herself; then she tucked her arms around me and scratched my head until I let it relax on her bosom—You cold? she said, and I wiggled closer: she was good and warm as the old kitchen.

"Son, I'd say you were going at it the wrong end first," said the Judge, turning up his coat collar. "How could you care about one girl? Have you ever cared about one leaf?"

Riley, listening to the wildcat with an itchy hunter's look, snatched at the leaves blowing about us like midnight butterflies; alive, fluttering as though to escape and fly, one stayed trapped between his fingers. The Judge, too: he caught a leaf; and it was worth more in his hand than in Riley's. Pressing it mildly against his cheek, he distantly said, "We are speaking of love. A leaf, a handful of seed—begin with these, learn a little what it is to love. First, a leaf, a fall of rain, then someone to receive what a leaf has taught you, what a fall of rain has ripened. No easy process, understand; it could take a lifetime, it has mine, and still I've never mastered it—I only know how true it is: that love is a chain of love, as nature is a chain of life."

"Then," said Dolly with an intake of breath, "I've been in love all my life." She sank down into the quilt. "Well, no," and her voice fell off, "I guess not. I've never loved a," while she searched for the word wind frolicked her veil, "gentleman. You might say that I've never had the opportunity. Except Papa." She paused, as though she'd said too much. A gauze of starlight wrapped her closely as the quilt; something, the reciting frogs, the string of voices stretching from the field of grass, lured, impelled her: "But I have loved everything else. Like the color pink; when I was a child I had one colored crayon, and it was pink; I drew pink cats, pink trees—for thirty-four years I lived in a pink room. And the box I kept, it's somewhere in the attic now, I must ask Verena please to give it to me, it would be nice to see my first loves again: what is there? a dried honeycomb, an empty hornet's nest, other things, or an orange stuck with cloves and a jaybird's egg—when I loved those, love collected inside me so that it went flying about like a bird in a sunflower field. But it's best not to show such things, it burdens people and makes them, I don't know why, unhappy. Verena scolds at me for what she calls hiding in corners, but I'm afraid of scaring people if I show that I care for them. Like Paul Jimson's wife; after he got sick and couldn't deliver the papers anymore, remember she took over his route? poor thin little thing just dragging herself with that sack of papers. It was one cold afternoon, she came up on the porch her nose running and tears of cold hanging in her eyes—she put down the paper, and I said wait, hold on, and took my handkerchief to wipe her eyes: I wanted to say, if I could, that I was sorry and that I loved her—my hand grazed her face, she turned with the smallest shout and ran down the steps. Then on, she always tossed the papers from the street, and whenever I heard them hit the porch it sounded in my bones."

"Paul Jimson's wife: worrying yourself over trash like that!" said Catherine, rinsing her mouth with the last of the wine. "I've got a bowl of goldfish, just 'cause I like them don't make me love the world. Love a lot of mess, my foot. You can talk what you want, not going to do anything but harm, bringing up what's best forgot. People ought to keep more things to themselves. The deepdown ownself part of you, that's the good part: what's left of a human being that goes around speaking his privates? The Judge, he say we all up here 'cause of trouble some kind. Shoot! We here for very plain reasons. One is, this our tree house, and two, That One and the Jew's trying to steal what belongs to us. Three: you here, every one of you, 'cause you want to be: the deepdown part of you tells you so. This last don't apply to me. I like a roof over my own head. Dollyheart, give the Judge a portion of that quilt: man's shivering like was Halloween."

Shyly Dolly lifted a wing of the quilt and nodded to him; the Judge, not at all shy, slipped under it. The branches of the China tree swayed like immense oars dipping into a sea rolling and chilled by the far far stars. Left alone, Riley sat hunched up in himself like a pitiful orphan. "Snuggle up, hard head: you cold like anybody else," said Catherine, offering him the position on her right that I occupied on her left. He didn't seem to want to; maybe he noticed that she smelled like bitterweed, or maybe he thought it was sissy; but I said come on, Riley, Catherine's good and warm, better than a quilt. After a while Riley moved over to us. It was quiet for so long I thought everyone had gone to sleep. Then I felt Catherine stiffen. "It's just come to me who it was sent my letter: Bill Nobody. That One, that's who. Sure as my name's Catherine Creek she got some nigger in Miami to mail me a letter, thinking I'd scoot off there never to be heard from again." Dolly sleepily said hush now hush, shut your eyes: "Nothing to be afraid of; we've men here to watch out for us." A branch swung back, moonlight ignited the tree: I saw the Judge take Dolly's hand. It was the last thing I saw.

4

Riley was the first to wake, and he wakened me. On the skyline three morning stars swooned in the flush of an arriving sun; dew tinseled the leaves, a jet chain of blackbirds swung out to meet the mounting light. Riley beckoned for me to come with him; we slid silently down through the tree. Catherine, snoring with abandon, did not hear us go; nor did Dolly and the Judge, who, like two children lost in a witch-ruled forest, were asleep with their cheeks together.

We headed toward the river, Riley leading the way. The legs of his canvas trousers whispered against each other. Every little bit he stopped and stretched himself, as though he'd been riding on a train. Somewhere we came to a hill of already about and busy red ants. Riley unbuttoned his fly and began to flood them; I don't know that it was funny, but I laughed to keep him company. Naturally I was insulted when he switched around and peed on my shoe. I thought it meant he had no respect for me. I said to him why would he want to do a thing like that? Don't you know a joke? he said, and threw a hugging arm around my shoulder.

If such events can be dated, this I would say was the moment Riley Henderson and I became friends, the moment, at least, when there began in him an affectionate feeling for me that supported my own for him. Through brown briars under brown trees we walked deep in the woods down to the river.

Leaves like scarlet hands floated on the green slow water. A poking end of a drowned log seemed the peering head of some river-beast. We moved on to the old houseboat, where the water was clearer. The houseboat was slightly tipped over; drifts of waterbay sheddings were like a rich rust on its roof and declining deck. The inside cabin had a mystifying tended-to look. Scattered around were issues of an adventure magazine, there was a kerosene lamp and a line of beer empties ranged on a table; the bunk sported a blanket, a pillow, and the pillow was colored with pink markings of lipstick. In a rush I realized the houseboat was someone's hideout; then, from the grin taking over Riley's homely face, I knew whose it was. "What's more," he said, "you can get in a little fishing on the side. Don't you tell anybody." I crossed an admiring heart.

While we were undressing, I had a kind of dream. I dreamed the houseboat had been launched on the river with the five of us aboard: our laundry flapped like sails, in the pantry a coconut cake was cooking, a geranium bloomed on the windowsill—together we floated over changing rivers past varying views.

The last of summer warmed the climbing sun, but the water, at first plunge, sent me chattering and chicken-skinned back to the deck, where I stood watching Riley unconcernedly propel himself to and fro between the banks. An island of bamboo reeds, standing like the legs of cranes, shivered in a shallow patch, and Riley waded out among them with lowered, hunting eyes. He signaled to me. Though it hurt, I eased down into the cold river and swam to join him. The water bending the bamboo was clear and divided into knee-deep basins—Riley hovered above one: in the thin pool a coal-black catfish lay dozingly trapped. We closed in upon it with fingers tense as forkprongs: thrashing backward, it flung itself straight into my hands. The flailing razory whiskers made a gash across my palm, still I had the sense to hold on—thank goodness, for it's the only fish I ever caught. Most people don't believe it when I tell about catching a catfish barehanded; I say well ask Riley Henderson. We drove a spike of bamboo through its gills and swam back to the houseboat holding it aloft. Riley said it was one of the fattest catfish he'd ever seen: we would take it back to the tree and, since he'd bragged what a great hand he was at frying a catfish, let the Judge fix it for breakfast. As it turned out, that fish never got eaten.

All this time at the tree house there was a terrible situation. During our absence Sheriff Candle had returned backed by deputies and a warrant of arrest. Meanwhile, unaware of what was in store, Riley and I lazed along kicking over toadstools, sometimes stopping to skip rocks on the water.

We still were some distance away when rioting voices reached us; they rang in the trees like axe-blows. I heard Catherine scream: roar, rather. It made such soup of my legs I couldn't keep up with Riley, who grabbed a stick and began to run. I zigged one way, zagged another, then, having made a wrong turn, came out on the grass-field's rim. And there was Catherine.

Her dress was ripped down the front: she was good as naked. Ray Oliver, Jack Mill and Big Eddie Stover, three grown men, cronies of the Sheriff, were dragging and slapping her through the grass. I wanted to kill them; and Catherine was trying to: but she didn't stand a chance—though she butted them with her head, bounced them with her elbows. Big Eddie Stover was legally born a bastard; the other two made the grade on their own. It was Big Eddie that went for me, and I slammed my catfish flat in his face. Catherine said, "You leave my baby be, he's an orphan"; and, when she saw that he had me around the waist: "In the booboos, Collin, kick his old booboos." So I did. Big Eddie's face curdled like clabber. Jack Mill (he's the one who a year later got locked in the ice-plant and froze to death: served him right) snatched at me, but I bolted across the field and crouched down in the tallest grass. I don't think they bothered to look for me, they had their hands so full with Catherine; she fought them the whole way, and I watched her, sick with knowing there was no help to give, until they passed out of sight over the ridge into the cemetery.

Overhead two squawking crows crossed, recrossed, as though making an evil sign. I crept toward the woods—near me, then, I heard boots cutting through the grass. It was the Sheriff; with him was a man called Will Harris. Tall as a door, buffalo-shouldered, Will Harris had once had his throat eaten out by a mad dog; the scars were bad enough, but his damaged voice was worse: it sounded giddy and babyfied, like a midget's. They passed so close I could have untied Will's shoes. His tiny voice, shrilling at the Sheriff, jumped with Morris Ritz's name and Verena's: I couldn't make out exactly, except something had happened about Morris Ritz and Verena had sent Will to bring back the Sheriff. The Sheriff said: "What in hell does the woman want, an army?" When they were gone I sprang up and ran into the woods.

In sight of the China tree I hid behind a fan of fern: I thought one of the Sheriff's men might still be hanging around. But there was nothing, simply a lonely singing bird. And no one in the tree house: smoky as ghosts, streamers of sunlight illuminated its emptiness. Numbly I moved into view and leaned my head against the tree's trunk; at this, the vision of the houseboat returned: our laundry flapped, the geranium bloomed, the carrying river carried us out to sea into the world.

"Collin." My name fell out of the sky. "Is that you I hear? are you crying?"

It was Dolly, calling from somewhere I could not see—until, climbing to the tree's heart, I saw in the above distance Dolly's dangling childish shoe. "Careful, boy," said the Judge, who was beside her, "you'll shake us out of here." Indeed, like gulls resting on a ship's mast, they were sitting in the absolute tower of the tree; afterward, Dolly was to remark that the view afforded was so enthralling she regretted not having visited there before. The Judge, it developed, had seen the approach of the Sheriff and his men in time for them to take refuge in those heights. "Wait, we're coming," she said; and, with one arm steadied by the Judge, she descended like a fine lady sweeping down a flight of stairs.

We kissed each other; she continued to hold me. "She went to look for you—Catherine; we didn't know where you were, and I was so afraid, I . . ." Her fear tingled my hands: she felt like a shaking small animal, a rabbit just taken from the trap. The Judge looked on with humbled eyes, fumbling hands; he seemed to feel in the way, perhaps because he thought he'd failed us in not preventing what had happened to Catherine. But then, what could he have done? Had he gone to her aid, he would only have got himself caught: they weren't fooling, the Sheriff, Big Eddie Stover and the others. I was the one to feel guilty. If Catherine hadn't gone to look for me, they probably never would have caught her. I told of what had taken place in the field of grass.

But Dolly really wanted not to hear. As though scattering a dream, she brushed back her veil. "I want to believe Catherine is gone: and I can't. If I could, I would run to find her. I want to believe Verena has done this: and I can't. Collin, what do you think: is it that after all the world is a bad place? Last night I saw it so differently."

The Judge focused his eyes on mine: he was trying, I think, to tell me how to answer. But I knew myself. No matter what passions compose them, all private worlds are good, they are never vulgar places: Dolly had been made too civilized by her own, the one she shared with Catherine and me, to feel the winds of wickedness that circulate elsewhere: No, Dolly, the world is not a bad place. She passed a hand across her forehead: "If you are right, then in a moment Catherine will be walking under the tree—she won't have found you or Riley, but she will have come back."

"By the way," said the Judge, "where *is* Riley?"

He'd run ahead of me, that was the last I'd seen of him; with an anxiety that struck us simultaneously, the Judge and I stood up and started yelling his name. Our voices, curving slowly around the woods, again, again swung back on silence. I knew what had happened: he'd fallen into an old Indian well—many's the case I could tell you of. I was about to suggest this when abruptly the Judge put a finger to his lips. The man must have had ears like a dog: I couldn't hear a sound. But he was right, there was someone on the path. It turned out to be Maude Riordan and Riley's older sister, the smart one, Elizabeth. They were very dear friends and wore white matching sweaters. Elizabeth was carrying a violin case.

"Look here, Elizabeth," said the Judge, startling the girls, for as yet they had not discovered us. "Look here, child, have you seen your brother?"

Maude recovered first, and it was she who answered. "We sure have," she said emphatically. "I was walking Elizabeth home from her lesson when Riley came along doing ninety miles an hour; nearly ran us over. You should speak to him, Elizabeth. Anyway, he asked us to come down here and tell you not to worry, said he'd explain everything later. Whatever that means."

Both Maude and Elizabeth had been in my class at school; they'd jumped a grade and graduated the previous June. I knew Maude especially well because for a summer I'd taken piano lessons from her mother; her father taught violin, and Elizabeth Henderson was one of his pupils. Maude herself played the violin beautifully; just a week before, I'd read in the town paper where she'd been invited to play on a radio program in Birmingham: I was glad to hear it. The Riordans were nice people, considerate and cheerful. It was not because I wanted to learn piano that I took lessons with

Mrs. Riordan—rather, I liked her blond largeness, the sympathetic, educated talk that went on while we sat before the splendid upright that smelled of polish and attention; and what I particularly liked was afterward, when Maude would ask me to have a lemonade on the cool back porch. She was snub-nosed and elfin-eared, a skinny excitable girl who from her father had inherited Irish black eyes and from her mother platinum hair pale as morning—not the least like her best friend, the soulful and shadowy Elizabeth. I don't know what those two talked about, books and music maybe. But with me Maude's subjects were boys, dates, drugstore slander: didn't I think it was terrible, the awful girls Riley Henderson chased around with? she felt so sorry for Elizabeth, and thought it wonderful how, despite all, Elizabeth held up her head. It didn't take a genius to see that Maude was heartset on Riley; nevertheless, I imagined for a while that I was in love with her. At home I kept mentioning her until finally Catherine said Oh Maude Riordan, she's too scrawny—nothing on her to pinch, a man's crazy to give her the time of day. Once I showed Maude a big evening, made for her with my own hands a sweet-pea corsage, then took her to Phil's Café, where we had Kansas City steaks; afterward, there was a dance at the Lola Hotel. Still she behaved as though she hadn't expected to be kissed good-night. "I don't think that's necessary, Collin—though it was cute of you to take me out." I was let down, you can see why; but as I didn't allow myself to brood over it, our friendship went on little changed. One day, at the end of a lesson, Mrs. Riordan omitted the usual new piece for home practice; instead, she kindly informed me that she preferred not to continue with my lessons: "We're very fond of you, Collin, I don't have to say that you're welcome in this house at any time. But, dear, the truth is you have no ability for music; it happens that way occasionally, and I don't think it's fair on either of us to pretend otherwise." She was right, all the same my pride was hurt, I couldn't help feeling pushed-out, it made me miserable to think of the Riordans, and gradually, in about the time it took to forget my few hard-learned tunes, I drew a curtain on them. At first Maude used to stop me after school and ask me over to her house; one way or another I always got out of it; furthermore, it was winter then and I liked to stay in the kitchen with Dolly and Catherine. Catherine wanted to know: How come you don't talk anymore about Maude Riordan? I said because I don't, that's all. But while I didn't talk, I must have been thinking; at least, seeing her there under the tree, old feelings squeezed my chest. For the first time I considered the circumstances self-consciously: did we, Dolly, the Judge and I, strike Maude and Elizabeth as a ludicrous sight? I could be judged by them, they were my own age. But from their manner we might just have met on the street or at the drugstore.

The Judge said, "Maude, how's your daddy? Heard he hasn't been feeling too good."

"He can't complain. You know how men are, always looking for an ailment. And yourself, sir?"

"That's a pity," said the Judge, his mind wandering. "You give your daddy my regards, and tell him I hope he feels better."

Maude submitted agreeably: "I will, sir, thank you. I know he'll appreciate your concern." Draping her skirt, she dropped on the moss and settled beside her an unwilling Elizabeth. For Elizabeth no one used a nickname; you might begin by calling her Betty, but in a week it would be Elizabeth again: that was her effect. Languid, banana-boned, she had dour black hair and an apathetic, at moments saintly face—in an enamel locket worn around her lily-stalk neck she preserved a miniature of her missionary father. "Look, Elizabeth, isn't that a becoming hat Miss Dolly has on? Velvet, with a veil."

Dolly roused herself; she patted her head. "I don't generally wear hats —we intended to travel."

"We heard you'd left home," said Maude; and, proceeding more frankly: "In fact that's all anyone talks about, isn't it, Elizabeth?" Elizabeth nodded without enthusiasm. "Gracious, there are some peculiar stories going around. I mean, on the way here we met Gus Ham and he said that colored woman Catherine Crook (is that her name?) had been arrested for hitting Mrs. Buster with a mason jar."

In sloping tones, Dolly said, "Catherine—had nothing to do with it."

"I guess someone did," said Maude. "We saw Mrs. Buster in the post office this morning; she was showing everybody a bump on her head, quite large. It looked genuine to us, didn't it, Elizabeth?" Elizabeth yawned. "To be sure, I don't care who hit her, I think they ought to get a medal."

"No," sighed Dolly, "it isn't proper, it shouldn't have happened. We all will have a lot to be sorry for."

At last Maude took account of me. "I've been wanting to see you, Collin," she said, hurrying as though to hide an embarrassment: mine, not hers. "Elizabeth and I are planning a Halloween party, a real scary one, and we thought it would be grand to dress you in a skeleton suit and sit you in a dark room to tell people's fortunes: because you're so good at . . ."

"Fibbing," said Elizabeth disinterestedly.

"Which is what fortune-telling is," Maude elaborated.

I don't know what gave them the idea I was such a storyteller, unless it was at school I'd shown a superior talent for alibis. I said it sounded fine, the party. "But you better not count on me. We might be in jail by then."

"Oh well, in that case," said Maude, as if accepting one of my old and usual excuses for not coming to her house.

"Say, Maude," said the Judge, helping us out of the silence that had fallen, "you're getting to be a celebrity: I saw in the paper where you're going to play on the radio."

As though dreaming aloud, she explained the broadcast was the finals of a state competition; if she won, the prize was a musical scholarship at the University: even second prize meant a half-scholarship. "I'm going to play a piece of Daddy's, a serenade: he wrote it for me the day I was born. But it's a surprise, I don't want him to know."

"Make her play it for you," said Elizabeth, unclasping her violin case.

Maude was generous, she did not have to be begged. The wine-colored violin, coddled under her chin, trilled as she tuned it; a brazen butterfly, lighting on the bow, was spiraled away as the bow swept across the strings singing a music that seemed a blizzard of butterflies flying, a sky-rocket of spring sweet to hear in the gnarled fall woods. It slowed, saddened, her silver hair drooped across the violin. We applauded; after we'd stopped there went on sounding a mysterious extra pair of hands. Riley stepped from behind a bank of fern, and when she saw him Maude's cheeks pinked. I don't think she would have played so well if she'd known he was listening.

Riley sent the girls home; they seemed reluctant to go, but Elizabeth was not used to disobeying her brother. "Lock the doors," he told her, "and, Maude, I'd appreciate it if you'd spend the night at our place: anybody comes by asking for me, say you don't know where I am."

I had to help him into the tree, for he'd brought back his gun and a knapsack heavy with provisions—a bottle of rose-and-raisin wine, oranges, sardines, wieners, rolls from the Katydid Bakery, a jumbo box of animal crackers: each item appearing stepped up our spirits, and Dolly, overcome by the animal crackers, said Riley ought to have a kiss.

But it was with grave face that we listened to his report.

When we'd separated in the woods it was toward the sound of Catherine that he'd run. This had brought him to the grass: he'd been watching when I had my encounter with Big Eddie Stover. I said well why didn't you help me? "You were doing all right: I don't figure Big Eddie's liable to forget you too soon: poor fellow limped along doubled over." Besides, it occurred to him that no one knew he was one of us, that he'd joined us in the tree: he was right to have stayed hidden, it made it possible for him to follow Catherine and the deputies into town. They'd stuffed her into the rumble-seat of Big Eddie's old coupé and driven straight to jail: Riley trailed them in his car. "By the time we reached the jail she seemed to have got quieted down; there was a little crowd hanging around, kids, some old farmers—you would have been proud of Catherine, she walked through them holding her dress together and her head like this." He tilted his head at a royal angle. How often I'd seen Catherine do that, especially when anyone criticized her (for hiding puzzle pieces, spreading misinformation, not having her teeth fixed); and Dolly, recognizing it too, had to blow her nose. "But," said Riley, "as soon as she was inside the jail she kicked up another fuss." In the jail there are only four cells, two for colored and two for white. Catherine had objected to being put in a colored people's cell.

The Judge stroked his chin, waved his head. "You didn't get a chance to speak to her? She ought to have had the comfort of knowing one of us was there."

"I stood around hoping she'd come to the window. But then I heard the other news."

Thinking back, I don't see how Riley could have waited so long to tell us. Because, my God: our friend from Chicago, that hateful Dr. Morris Ritz, had skipped town after rifling Verena's safe of twelve thousand dollars in negotiable bonds and more than seven hundred dollars in cash: that, as we later learned, was not half his loot. But wouldn't you know? I realized this was what baby-voiced Will Harris had been recounting to the Sheriff: no wonder Verena had sent a hurry call: her troubles with us must have become quite a side issue. Riley had a few details: he knew that Verena, upon discovering the safe door swung open (this happened in the office she kept above her drygoods store), had whirled around the corner to the Lola Hotel, there to find that Morris Ritz had checked out the previous evening: she fainted: when they revived her she fainted all over again.

Dolly's soft face hollowed; an urge to go to Verena was rising, at the same moment some sense of self, a deeper will, held her. Regretfully she gazed at me. "It's better you know it now, Collin; you shouldn't have to wait until you're as old as I am: the world is a bad place."

A change, like a shift of wind, overcame the Judge: he looked at once his age, autumnal, bare, as though he believed that Dolly, by accepting wickedness, had forsaken him. But I knew she had not: he'd called her a spirit, she was really a woman. Uncorking the rose-and-raisin wine, Riley spilled its topaz color into four glasses; after a moment he filled a fifth, Catherine's. The Judge, raising the wine to his lips, proposed a toast: "To Catherine, give her trust." We lifted our glasses, and "Oh, Collin," said Dolly, a sudden stark thought widening her eyes, "you and I, we're the only ones that can understand a word she says!"

5

The following day, which was the first of October, a Wednesday, is one day I won't forget.

First off, Riley woke me by stepping on my fingers. Dolly, already awake, insisted I apologize for cursing him. Courtesy, she said, is more important in the morning than at any other time: particularly when one is living in such close quarters. The Judge's watch, still bending the twig like a heavy gold apple, gave the time as six after six. I don't know whose idea it was, but we breakfasted on oranges and animal crackers and cold hotdogs. The Judge grouched that a body didn't feel human till he'd had a pot of hot coffee. We agreed that coffee was what we all most missed. Riley volunteered to drive into town and get some; also, he would have a chance to scout around, find out what was going on. He suggested I come with him: "Nobody's going to see him, not if he stays down in the seat." Although the Judge objected, saying he thought it foolhardy, Dolly could tell I wanted to go: I'd yearned so much for a ride in Riley's car that now the opportunity presented itself nothing, even the prospect that no one might see me, could have thinned my excitement. Dolly said, "I can't see there's any harm. But you ought to have a clean shirt: I could plant turnips in the collar of that one."

The field of grass was without voice, no pheasant rustle, furtive flurry; the pointed leaves were sharp and blood-red as the aftermath arrows of a massacre; their brittleness broke beneath our feet as we waded up the hill into the cemetery. The view from there is very fine: the limitless trembling surface of River Woods, fifty unfolding miles of plowed, windmilled farmland, far-off the spired courthouse tower, smoking chimneys of town. I stopped by the graves of my mother and father. I had not often visited them, it depressed me, the tomb-cold stone—so unlike what I remembered of them, their aliveness, how she'd cried when he went away to sell his frigidaires, how he'd run naked into the street. I wanted flowers for the terra-cotta jars sitting empty on the streaked and muddied marble. Riley helped me; he tore beginning buds off a japonica tree, and watching me arrange them, said: "I'm glad your ma was nice. Bitches, by and large." I wondered if he meant his own mother, poor Rose Henderson, who used to make him hop around the yard reciting the multiplication table. It did seem to me, though, that he'd made up for those hard days. After all, he had a car that was supposed to have cost three thousand dollars. Second-hand, mind you. It was a foreign car, an Alfa-Romeo roadster (Romeo's Alfa, the joke was) he'd bought in New Orleans from a politician bound for the penitentiary.

As we purred along the unpaved road toward town I kept hoping for a witness: there were certain persons it would have done my heart good to have seen me sailing by in Riley Henderson's car. But it was too early for anyone much to be about; breakfast was still on the stove, and smoke soared out the chimneys of passing houses. We turned the corner by the church, drove around the square and parked in the dirt lane that runs between Cooper's Livery and the Katydid Bakery. There Riley left me with orders to stay put: he wouldn't be more than an hour. So, stretching out on the seat, I listened to the chicanery of thieving sparrows in the livery stable's haystacks, breathed the fresh bread, tart as currant odors escaping from the bakery. The couple who owned this bakery, County was their name, Mr. and Mrs. C. C. County, had to begin their day at three in the morning to be ready by opening time, eight o'clock. It was a clean prosperous place. Mrs. County could afford the most expensive clothes at Verena's dry goods store. While I lay there smelling the good things, the back door of the bakery opened and Mr. County, broom in hand, swept flour dust into the lane. I guess he was surprised to see Riley's car, and surprised to find me in it.

"What you up to, Collin?"

"Up to nothing, Mr. County," I said, and asked myself if he knew about our trouble.

"Sure am happy October's here," he said, rubbing the air with his fingers as though the chill woven into it was a material he could feel. "We have a terrible time in the summer: ovens and all make it too hot to live. See here, son, there's a gingerbread man waiting for you—come on in and run him down."

Now, he was not the kind of man to get me in there and then call the Sheriff.

His wife welcomed me into the spiced heat of the oven room as though she could think of nothing pleasanter than my being there. Most anyone would have liked Mrs. County. A chunky woman with no fuss about her, she had elephant ankles, developed arms, a muscular face permanently fire-flushed; her eyes were like blue cake-icing, her hair looked as if she'd mopped it around in a flour barrel, and she wore an apron that trailed to the tips of her toes. Her husband also wore one; sometimes, with the oversized apron still tied around him, I'd seen him crossing the street to have a time-off beer with the men that lean around the corner at Phil's Café: he seemed a painted clown, flopping, powdered, elegantly angular.

Clearing a place on her work table, Mrs. County set me down to a cup of coffee and a warm tray of cinnamon rolls, the kind Dolly relished. Mr. County suggested I might prefer something else: "I promised him, what did I promise? a gingerbread man." His wife socked a lump of dough: "Those are for kids. He's a grown man; or nearly. Collin, just how old are you?"

"Sixteen."

"Same as Samuel," she said, meaning her son, whom we all called Mule: inasmuch as he was not much brighter than one. I asked what was their news of him? because the previous autumn, after having been left back in the eighth grade three years running, Mule had gone to Pensacola and joined the Navy. "He's in Panama, last we heard," she said, flattening the dough into a piecrust. "We don't hear often. I wrote him once, I said Samuel you do better about writing home or I'm going to write the

President exactly how old you are. Because you know he joined up under false pretenses. I was darned mad at the time—blamed Mr. Hand up at the schoolhouse: that's why Samuel did it, he just couldn't tolerate always being left behind in the eighth grade, him getting so tall and the other children so little. But now I can see Mr. Hand was right: it wouldn't be fair to the rest of you boys if they promoted Samuel when he didn't do his work proper. So maybe it turned out for the best. C.C., show Collin the picture."

Photographed against a background of palms and real sea, four smirking sailors stood with their arms linked together; underneath was written, God Bless Mom and Pop, Samuel. It rankled me. Mule, off seeing the world, while I, well, maybe I deserved a gingerbread man. As I returned the picture, Mr. County said: "I'm all for a boy serving his country. But the bad part of it is, Samuel was just getting where he could give us a hand around here. I sure hate to depend on nigger help. Lying and stealing, never know where you are."

"It beats me why C.C. carries on like that," said his wife, knotting her lips. "He knows it irks me. Colored people are no worse than white people: in some cases, better. I've had occasion to say so to other people in this town. Like this business about old Catherine Creek. Makes me sick. Cranky she may be, and peculiar, but there's as good a woman as you'll find. Which reminds me, I mean to send her a dinner-tray up to the jail, for I'll wager the Sheriff doesn't set much of a table."

So little, once it has changed, changes back: the world knew us: we would never be warm again: I let go, saw winter coming toward a cold tree, cried, cried, came apart like a rain-rotted rag. I'd wanted to since we left the house. Mrs. County begged pardon if she'd said anything to upset me; with her kitchen-slopped apron she wiped my face, and we laughed, had to, at the mess it made, the paste of flour and tears, and I felt, as they say, a lot better, kind of lighthearted. For manly reasons I understood, but which made me feel no shame, Mr. County had been mortified by the outburst: he retired to the front of the shop.

Mrs. County poured coffee for herself and sat down. "I don't pretend to follow what's going on," she said. "The way I hear it, Miss Dolly broke up housekeeping because of some disagreement with Verena?" I wanted to say the situation was more complicated than that, but wondered, as I tried to array events, if really it was. "Now," she continued thoughtfully, "it may sound as though I'm talking against Dolly: I'm not. But this is what I feel—you people should go home, Dolly ought to make her peace with Verena: that's what she's always done, and you can't turn around at her time of life. Also, it sets a poor example for the town, two sisters quarreling, one of them sitting in a tree; and Judge Charlie Cool, for the first time in my life I feel sorry for those sons of his. Leading citizens have to behave themselves; otherwise the entire place goes to pieces. For instance, have you seen that wagon in the square? Well then, you better go have a look. Family of cowboys, they are. Evangelists, C.C. says—all I know is there's been a great racket over them and something to do with Dolly." Angrily she puffed up a paper sack. "I want you to tell her what I said: go home. And here, Collin, take along some cinnamon rolls. I know how Dolly dotes on them."

As I left the bakery the bells of the courthouse clock were ringing eight, which meant that it was seven-thirty. This clock has always run a half-hour fast. Once an expert was imported to repair it; at the end of almost a week's tinkering he recommended, as the only remedy, a stick of dynamite; the town council voted he be paid in full, for there was a general feeling of pride that the clock had proved so incorrigible. Around the square a few storekeepers were preparing to open; broom-sweepings fogged doorways, rolled trashbarrels berated the cool cat-quiet streets. At the Early Bird, a better grocery store than Verena's Jitney Jungle, two colored boys were fancying the window with cans of Hawaiian pineapple. On the south side of the square, beyond the cane benches where in all seasons sit the peaceful, perishing old men, I saw the wagon Mrs. County had spoken of—in reality an old truck contrived with tarpaulin covering to resemble the Western wagons of history. It looked forlorn and foolish standing alone in the empty square. A homemade sign, perhaps four feet high, crested the cab like a shark's fin. Let Little Homer Honey Lasso Your Soul For The Lord. Painted on the other side there was a blistered greenish grinning head topped by a ten-gallon hat. I would not have thought it a portrait of anything human, but, according to a notice, this was: Child Wonder Little Homer Honey. With nothing more to see, for there was no one around the truck, I took myself toward the jail, which is a box-shaped brick building next door to the Ford Motor Company. I'd been inside it once. Big Eddie Stover had taken me there, along with a dozen other boys and men; he'd walked into the drugstore and said come over to the jail if you want to see something. The attraction was a thin handsome gypsy boy they'd taken off a freight train; Big Eddie gave him a quarter and told him to let down his pants; nobody could believe the size of it, and one of the men said, "Boy, how come they keep you locked up when you got a crowbar like that?" For weeks you could tell girls who had heard that joke: they giggled every time they passed the jail.

There is an unusual emblem decorating a side wall of the jail. I asked Dolly, and she said that in her youth she remembers it as a candy advertisement. If so, the lettering has vanished; what remains is a chalky tapestry: two flamingo-pink trumpeting angels swinging, swooping above a huge horn filled with fruit like a Christmas stocking; embroidered on the brick, it seems a faded mural, a faint tattoo, and sunshine flutters the imprisoned angels as though they were the spirits of thieves. I knew the risk I was taking, parading around in plain sight; but I walked past the jail, then back, and whistled, later whispered Catherine, Catherine, hoping this would bring her to the window. I realized which was her window: on the sill, reflecting beyond the bars, I saw a bowl of goldfish, the one thing, as subsequently we learned, she'd asked to have brought her. Orange flickerings of the fish fanned around the coral castle, and I thought of the morning I'd helped Dolly find it, the castle, the pearl pebbles. It had been the beginning and, chilled suddenly by a thought of what the end could be, Catherine coldly shadowed and peering downward, I prayed she would not come to the window: she would have seen no one, for I turned and ran.

Riley kept me waiting in the car more than two hours. By the time he showed up he was himself in such a temper I didn't dare show any of my own. It seems he'd gone home and found his sisters, Anne and Elizabeth, and Maude Riordan, who had spent the night, still lolling abed: not just that, but Coca-Cola bottles and cigarette butts all over the parlor. Maude took the blame: she confessed to having invited some boys over to listen to the radio and dance; but it was the sisters who got punished. He'd dragged them out of bed and whipped them. I asked what did he mean, whipped them? Turned them over my knee, he said, and whipped them with a tennis shoe. I couldn't picture this; it conflicted with my sense of Elizabeth's dignity. You're too hard on those girls, I said, adding vindictively: Maude, now there's the bad one. He took me seriously, said yes he'd intended to whip her if only because she'd called him the kind of names he wouldn't take off anybody; but before he could catch her she'd bolted out the back door. I thought to myself maybe at last Maude's had her bait of you.

Riley's ragged hair was glued down with brilliantine; he smelled of lilac water and talcum. He didn't have to tell me he'd been to the barber's; or why.

Though he has since retired, there was in those days an exceptional fellow running the barbershop. Amos Legrand. Men like the Sheriff, for that matter Riley Henderson, oh everybody come to think of it, said: that old sis. But they didn't mean any harm; most people enjoyed Amos and really wished him well. A little monkeyman who had to stand on a box to cut your hair, he was agitated and chattery as a pair of castanets. All his steady customers he called honey, men and women alike, it made no difference to him. "Honey," he'd say, "it's about time you got this hair cut: was about to buy you a package of bobby-pins." Amos had one tremendous gift: he could tattle along on matters of true interest to businessmen and girls of ten—everything from what price Ben Jones got for his peanut crop to who would be invited to Mary Simpson's birthday party.

It was natural that Riley should have gone to him to get the news. Of course he repeated it straightforwardly; but I could imagine Amos, hear his hummingbird whirr: "There you are, honey, that's how it turns out when you leave money lying around. And of all people, Verena Talbo: here we thought she trotted to the bank with every dime came her way. Twelve thousand seven hundred dollars. But don't think it stops there. Seems Verena and this Dr. Ritz were going into business together, that's why she bought the old canning factory. Well get this: she gave Ritz over ten thousand to buy machinery, mercy knows what, and now it turns out he never bought one blessed penny's worth. Pocketed the whole thing. As for him, they've located not hide nor hair; South America, that's where they'll find him when and if. I never was somebody to insinuate any monkeyshines went on between him and her; I said Verena Talbo's too particular: honey, that Jew had the worst case of dandruff I've ever seen on a human head. But a smart woman like her, maybe she *was* stuck on him. Then all this to-do with her sister, the uproar over that. I don't wonder Doc Carter's giving her shots. But Charlie Cool's the one kills me: what do you make of him out there catching his death?"

We cleared town on two wheels; pop, pulp, insects spit against the windshield. The dry, starched blue day whistled round us, there was not a cloud. And yet I swear storms foretell themselves in my bones. This is a nuisance common to old people, but fairly rare with anyone young. It's as though a damp rumble of thunder had sounded in your joints. The way I hurt, I felt nothing less than a hurricane could be headed our way, and said so to Riley, who said go on, you're crazy, look at the sky. We were making a bet about it when, rounding that bad curve so convenient to the cemetery, Riley winced and froze his brakes; we skidded long enough for a detailed review of our lives.

It was not Riley's fault: square in the road and struggling along like a lame cow was the Little Homer Honey wagon. With a clatter of collapsing machinery it came to a dead halt. In a moment the driver climbed out, a woman.

She was not young, but there was a merriness in the seesaw of her hips, and her breasts rubbed and nudged against her peach-colored blouse in such a coaxing way. She wore a fringed chamois skirt and knee-high cowboy boots, which was a mistake, for you felt that her legs, if fully exposed, would have been the best part. She leaned on the car door. Her eyelids drooped as though the lashes weighed intolerably; with the tip of her tongue she wettened her very red lips. "Good morning, fellows," she said, and it was a dragging slow-fuse voice. "I'd appreciate a few directions."

"What the hell's wrong with you?" said Riley, asserting himself. "You nearly made us turn over."

"I'm surprised you mention it," said the woman, amiably tossing her large head; her hair, an invented apricot color, was meticulously curled, and the curls, shaken out, were like bells with no music in them. "You were speeding, dear," she reproved him complacently. "I imagine there's a law against it; there are laws against everything, especially here."

Riley said, "There should be a law against that truck. A broken-down pile like that, it oughtn't to be allowed."

"I know, dear," the woman laughed. "Trade with you. Though I'm afraid we couldn't all fit into this car; we're even a bit squeezed in the wagon. Could you help me with a cigarette? That's a doll, thanks." As she lighted the cigarette I noticed how gaunt her hands were, rough; the nails were unpainted and one of them was black as though she'd crushed it in a door. "I was told that out this way we'd find a Miss Talbo. Dolly Talbo. She seems to be living in a tree. I wish you'd kindly show us where . . ."

Back of her there appeared to be an entire orphanage emptying out of the truck. Babies barely able to toddle on their rickety bowlegs, towheads dribbling ropes of snot, girls old enough to wear brassieres, and a ladder of boys, man-sized some of them. I counted up to ten, this including a set of cross-eyed twins and a diapered baby being lugged by a child not more than five. Still, like a magician's rabbits, they kept coming, multiplied until the road was thickly populated.

"These all yours?" I said, really anxious; in another count I'd made a total of fifteen. One boy, he was about twelve and had tiny steel-rimmed glasses, flopped around in a ten-gallon hat like a walking mushroom. Most of them wore a few cowboy items, boots, at least a rodeo scarf. But they were a discouraged-looking lot, and sickly too, as though they'd lived years off boiled potatoes and onions. They pressed around the car, ghostly quiet except for the youngest, who thumped the headlights and bounced on the fenders.

"Sure enough, dear: all mine," she answered, swatting at a mite of a girl playing maypole on her leg. "Sometimes I figure we've picked up one or two that don't belong," she added with a shrug, and several of the children smiled. They seemed to adore her. "Some of their daddies are dead; I guess the rest are living—one way and another: either case it's no concern of ours. I take it you weren't at our meeting last night. I'm Sister Ida, Little Homer Honey's mother." I wanted to know which one was Little Homer. She blinked around and singled out the spectacled boy, who, wobbling up under his hat, saluted us: "Praise Jesus. Want a whistle?" and, swelling his cheeks, blasted a tin whistle.

"With one of those," explained his mother, tucking up her back hairs, "you can give the devil a scare. They have a number of practical uses as well."

"Two bits," the child bargained. He had a worried little face white as cold cream. The hat came down to his eyebrows.

I would have bought one if I'd had the money. You could see they were hungry. Riley felt the same, at any rate he produced fifty cents and took two of the whistles. "Bless you," said Little Homer, slipping the coin between his teeth and biting hard. "There's so much counterfeit going around these days," his mother confided apologetically. "In our branch of endeavor you wouldn't expect that kind of trouble," she said, sighing. "But if you kindly would show us—we can't go on much more, just haven't got the gas."

Riley told her she was wasting her time. "Nobody there anymore," he said, racing the motor. Another driver, blockaded behind us, was honking his horn.

"Not in the tree?" Her voice was plaintive above the motor's impatient roar. "But where will we find her then?" Her hands were trying to hold back the car. "We've important business, we . . ."

Riley jumped the car forward. Looking back, I saw them watching after us in the raised and drifting road dust. I said to Riley, and was sullen about it, that we ought to have found out what they wanted.

And he said: "Maybe I know."

He did know a great deal, Amos Legrand having informed him thoroughly on the subject of Sister Ida. Although she'd not previously been to our town, Amos, who does a little traveling now and then, claimed to have seen her once at a fair in Bottle, which is a county town not far from here. Nor, apparently, was she a stranger to the Reverend Buster, who, the instant she arrived, had hunted out the Sheriff and demanded an injunction to prevent the Little Homer Honey troupe from holding any meetings. Racketeers, he called them; and argued that the so-called Sister Ida was known throughout six states as an infamous trollop: think of it, fifteen children and no sign of a husband! Amos, too, was pretty sure she'd never been married; but in his opinion a woman so industrious was entitled to respect. The Sheriff said didn't he have enough problems? and said: Maybe those fools have the right idea, sit in a tree and mind your own business—for five cents he'd go out there and join them. Old Buster told him in that case he wasn't fit to be Sheriff and ought to hand in his badge. Meanwhile, Sister Ida had, without legal interference, called an evening of prayers and shenanigans under the oak trees in the square. Revivalists are popular in this town; it's the music, the chance to sing and congregate in the open air. Sister Ida and her family made a particular hit; even Amos, usually so critical, told Riley he'd missed something: those kids really could shout, and that Little Homer Honey, he was cute as a button, dancing and twirling a rope. Everybody had a grand time except the Reverend and Mrs. Buster, who had come to start a fuss. What got their goat was when the children started hauling in God's Washline, a rope with clothespins to which you could attach a contribution. People who never dropped a dime in Buster's collection plate were hanging up dollar bills. It was more than he could stand. So he'd skipped off to the house on Talbo Lane and had a small shrewd talk with Verena, whose support, he realized, was necessary if he were going to get action. According to Amos, he'd incited Verena by telling her some hussy of a revivalist was describing Dolly as an infidel, an enemy of Jesus, and that Verena owed it to the Talbo name to see this woman was run out of town. It was unlikely that at the time Sister Ida had ever heard the name Talbo. But sick as she was, Verena went right to work; she rang up the Sheriff and said now look here Junius, I want these tramps run clear across the county line. Those were orders; and old Buster made it his duty to see they were carried out. He accompanied the Sheriff to the square, where Sister Ida and her brood were cleaning up after the meeting. It had ended in a real scuffle, mainly because Buster, charging illegal gain, had insisted on confiscating the money gathered off God's Washline. He got it, too—along with a few scratches. It made no difference that many bystanders had taken Sister Ida's side: the Sheriff told them they'd better be out of town by noon the next day. Now after I'd heard all this I said to Riley why, when these people had been wrongly treated, hadn't he wanted to be more helpful? You'd never guess the answer he gave me. In dead earnest he said a loose woman like that was no one to associate with Dolly.

A twig fire fizzed under the tree; Riley collected leaves for it, while the Judge, his eyes smarting with smoke, set about the business of our midday meal. We were the indolent ones, Dolly and I. "I'm afraid," she said, dealing a game of Rook, "really afraid Verena's seen the last of that money. And you know, Collin, I doubt if it's losing the money that hurts her most. For whatever reason, she trusted him: Dr. Ritz, I mean. I keep remembering Maudie Laura Murphy. The girl who worked in the post office. She and Verena were very close. Lord, it was a great blow when Maudie Laura took up with that whiskey salesman, married him. I couldn't criticize her; 'twas only fitting if she loved the man. Just the same, Maudie Laura and Dr. Ritz, maybe those are the only two Verena ever trusted, and both of them—well, it could take the heart out of anyone." She thumbed the Rook cards with wandering attention. "You said something before—about Catherine."

"About her goldfish. I saw them in the window."

"But not Catherine?"

"No, the goldfish, that's all. Mrs. County was awfully nice: she said she was going to send some dinner around to the jail."

She broke one of Mrs. County's cinnamon rolls and picked out the raisins. "Collin, suppose we let them have their way, gave up, that is: they'd have to let Catherine go, wouldn't they?" Her eyes tilted toward the heights of the tree, searching, it seemed, a passage through the braided leaves. "Should I—let myself lose?"

"Mrs. County thinks so: that we should go home."

"Did she say why?"

"Because—she did run on. Because you always have. Always made your peace, she said."

Dolly smiled, smoothed her long skirt; sifting rays placed rings of sun upon her fingers. "Was there ever a choice? It's what I want, a choice. To know I could've had another life, all made of my own decisions. That would be making my peace, and truly." She rested her eyes on the scene below, Riley cracking twigs, the Judge hunched over a steaming pot. "And the Judge, Charlie, if we gave up, it would let him down so badly. Yes," she tangled her fingers with mine, "he is very dear to me," and an immeasurable pause lengthened the moment, my heart reeled, the tree closed inward like a folding umbrella.

"This morning, while you were away, he asked me to marry him."

As if he'd heard her, the Judge straightened up, a schoolboy grin reviving the youthfulness of his countrified face. He waved: and it was difficult to disregard the charm of Dolly's expression as she waved back. It was as though a familiar portrait had been cleaned and, turning to it, one discovered a fleshy luster, clearer, till then unknown colors: whatever else, she could never again be a shadow in the corner.

"And now—don't be unhappy, Collin," she said, scolding me, I thought, for what she must have recognized as my resentment.

"But are you . . .?"

"I've never earned the privilege of making up my own mind; when I do, God willing, I'll know what is right. Who else," she said, putting me off further, "did you see in town?"

I would have invented someone, a story to retrieve her, for she seemed to be moving forward into the future, while I, unable to follow, was left with my sameness. But as I described Sister Ida, the wagon, the children, told the wherefores of their run-in with the Sheriff and how we'd met them on the road inquiring after the lady in the tree, we flowed together again like a stream that for an instant an island had separated. Though it would have been too bad if Riley had heard me betraying him, I went so far as to repeat what he'd said about a woman of Sister Ida's sort not being fit company for Dolly. She had a proper laugh over this; then, with sudden soberness: "But it's wicked—taking the bread out of children's mouths and using my name to do it. Shame on them!" She straightened her hat determinedly. "Collin, lift yourself; you and I are going for a little walk. I'll bet those people are right where you left them. Leastways, we'll see."

The Judge tried to prevent us, or at any rate maintained that if Dolly wanted a stroll he would have to accompany us. It went a long way toward mollifying my jealous rancor when Dolly told him he'd best tend to his chores: with Collin along she'd be safe enough—it was just to stretch our legs a bit.

As usual, Dolly could not be hurried. It was her habit, even when it rained, to loiter along an ordinary path as though she were dallying in a garden, her eyes primed for the sight of precious medicine flavorings, a sprig of penny-royal, sweet mary and mint, useful herbs whose odor scented her clothes. She saw everything first, and it was her one real vanity to prefer that she, rather than you, point out certain discoveries: a birdtrack bracelet, an eave of icicles—she was always calling come see the cat-shaped cloud, the ship in the stars, the face of frost. In this slow manner we crossed the grass, Dolly amassing a pocketful of withered dandelions, a pheasant's quill: I thought it would be sundown before we reached the road.

Fortunately we had not that far to go: entering the cemetery, we found Sister Ida and all her family encamped among the graves. It was like a lugubrious playground. The cross-eyed twins were having their hair cut by older sisters, and Little Homer was shining his boots with spit and leaves; a nearly grown boy, sprawled with his back against a tombstone, picked melancholy notes on a guitar. Sister Ida was suckling the baby; it lay curled against her breasts like a pink ear. She did not rise when she realized our presence, and Dolly said, "I do believe you're sitting on my father."

For a fact it was Mr. Talbo's grave, and Sister Ida, addressing the headstone (Uriah Fenwick Talbo, 1844–1922, Good Soldier, Dear Husband, Loving Father) said, "Sorry, soldier." Buttoning her blouse, which made the baby wail, she started to her feet.

"Please don't; I only meant—to introduce myself."

Sister Ida shrugged, "He was beginning to hurt me anyway," and rubbed herself appropriately. "You again," she said, eyeing me with amusement. "Where's your friend?"

"I understand . . ." Dolly stopped, disconcerted by the maze of children drawing in around her; "Did you," she went on, attempting to ignore a boy no bigger than a jackrabbit who, having raised her skirt, was sternly examining her shanks, "wish to see me? I'm Dolly Talbo."

Shifting the baby, Sister Ida threw an arm around Dolly's waist, embraced her, actually, and said, as though they were the oldest friends, "I knew I could count on you, Dolly. Kids," she lifted the baby like a baton, "tell Dolly we never said a word against her!"

The children shook their heads, mumbled, and Dolly seemed touched. "We can't leave town, I kept telling them," said Sister Ida, and launched into the tale of her predicament. I wished that I could have a picture of them together, Dolly, formal, as out of fashion as her old face-veil, and Sister Ida with her fruity lips, fun-loving figure. "It's a matter of cash; they took it all. I ought to have them arrested, that puke-faced Buster and what's-his-name, the Sheriff: thinks he's King Kong." She caught her breath; her cheeks were like a raspberry patch. "The plain truth is, we're stranded. Even if we'd ever heard of you, it's not our policy to speak ill of anyone. Oh I know that was just the excuse; but I figured you could straighten it out and . . ."

"I'm hardly the person—dear me," said Dolly.

"But what would you do? with a half gallon of gas, maybe not that, fifteen mouths and a dollar ten? We'd be better off in jail."

Then, "I have a friend," Dolly announced proudly, "a brilliant man, he'll know an answer," and I could tell by the pleased conviction of her voice that she believed this one hundred percent. "Collin, you scoot ahead and let the Judge know to expect company for dinner."

Licketysplit across the field with the grass whipping my legs: couldn't wait to see the Judge's face. It was not a disappointment. "Lordylaw!" he said, raring back, rocking forward; "Sixteen people," and, observing the meager stew simmering on the fire, struck his head. For Riley's benefit I tried to make out it was none of my doing, Dolly's meeting Sister Ida; but he just stood there skinning me with his eyes: it could have led to bitter words if the Judge hadn't sent us scurrying. He fanned up his fire, Riley fetched more water, and into the stew we tossed sardines, hotdogs, green bay-leaves, in fact whatever lay at hand, including an entire box of Saltines, which the Judge claimed would help thicken it: a few stuffs got mixed in by mistake—coffee grounds, for instance. Having reached that over-wrought hilarious state achieved by cooks at family reunions, we had the gall to stand back and congratulate ourselves: Riley gave me a forgiving, comradely punch, and as the first of the children appeared the Judge scared them with the vigor of his welcome.

None of them would advance until the whole herd had assembled. Whereupon Dolly, apprehensive as a woman exhibiting the results of an afternoon at an auction, brought them forward to be introduced. The children made a rollcall of their names: Beth, Laurel, Sam, Lillie, Ida, Cleo, Kate, Homer, Harry—here the melody broke because one small girl refused to give her name. She said it was a secret. Sister Ida agreed that if she thought it a secret, then so it should remain.

"They're all so fretful," she said, favorably affecting the Judge with her smoky voice and grasslike eyelashes. He prolonged their handshake and overdid his smile, which struck me as peculiar conduct in a man who, not three hours before, had asked a woman to marry him, and I hoped that if Dolly noticed, it would give her pause. But she was saying, "Why certain they're fretful: hungry as they can be," and the Judge, with a hearty clap and a boastful nod toward the stew, promised he'd fix that soon enough. In the meantime, he thought it would be a good idea if the children went to the creek and washed their hands. Sister Ida vowed they'd wash more than that. They needed to, I'll tell you.

There was trouble with the little girl who wanted her name a secret; she wouldn't go, not unless her papa rode her piggy-back. "You are too my papa," she told Riley, who did not contradict her. He lifted her onto his shoulders, and she was tickled to death. All the way to the creek she acted the cut-up, and when, with her hands thrust over his eyes, Riley stumbled blindly into a bullis vine, she ripped the air with in-heaven shrieks. He said he'd had enough of that and down you go. "Please: I'll whisper you my name." Later on I remembered to ask him what the name had been. It was Texaco Gasoline; because those were such pretty words.

The creek is nowhere more than knee-deep; glossy beds of moss green the banks, and in the spring snowy dew-drops and dwarf violets flourish there like floral crumbs for the new bees whose hives hang in the water-bays. Sister Ida chose a place on the bank from which she could supervise the bathing. "No cheating now—I want to see a lot of commotion." We did. Suddenly girls old enough to be married were trotting around and not a stitch on; boys, too, big and little all in there together naked as jaybirds. It was as well that Dolly had stayed behind with the Judge; and I wished Riley had not come either, for he was embarrassing in his embarrassment. Seriously, though, it's only now, seeing the kind of man he turned out to be, that I understand the paradox of his primness: he wanted so to be respectable that the defections of others somehow seemed to him backsliding on his own part.

Those famous landscapes of youth and woodland water—in after years how often, trailing through the cold rooms of museums, I stopped before such a picture, stood long haunted moments having it recall that gone scene, not as it was, a band of goosefleshed children dabbling in an autumn creek, but as the painting presented it, husky youths and wading water-diamonded girls; and I've wondered then, wonder now, how they fared, where they went in this world, that extraordinary family.

"Beth, give your hair a douse. Stop splashing Laurel, I mean you, Buck, you quit that. All you kids get behind your ears, mercy knows when you'll have the chance again." But presently Sister Ida relaxed and left the children at liberty. "On such a day as this . . ." she sank against the moss; with the full light of her eyes she looked at Riley, "There is something: the mouth, the same jug ears—cigarette, dear?" she said, impervious to his distaste for her. A smoothing expression suggested for a moment the girl she had been. "On such a day as this . . .

". . . but in a sorrier place, no trees to speak of, a house in a wheatfield and all alone like a scarecrow. I'm not complaining: there was mama and papa and my sister Geraldine, and we were sufficient, had plenty of pets and a piano and good voices every one of us. Not that it was easy, what with all the heavy work and only the one man to do it. Papa was a sickly man besides. Hired hands were hard to come by, nobody liked it way out there for long: one old fellow we thought a heap of, but then he got drunk and tried to burn down the house. Geraldine was going on sixteen, a year older than me, and nice to look at, both of us were that, when she got it into her head to marry a man who'd run the place with papa. But where we were there wasn't much to choose from. Mama gave us our schooling, what of it we had, and the closest town was ten miles. That was the town of Youfry, called after a family; the slogan was You Won't Fry In Youfry: because it was up a mountain and well-to-do people went there in the summer. So the summer I'm thinking of, Geraldine got waitress work at the Lookout Hotel in Youfry. I used to hitch a ride in on Saturdays and stay the night with her. This was the first either of us had ever been away from home. Geraldine didn't care about it particular, town life, but as for me, I looked toward those Saturdays like each of them was Christmas and my birthday rolled into one. There was a dancing pavilion, it didn't cost a cent, the music was free and the colored lights. I'd help Geraldine with her work so we could go there all the sooner; we'd run hand in hand down the street, and I used to start dancing before I got my breath—never had to wait for a partner, there were five boys to every girl, and we were the prettiest girls anyway. I wasn't boy-crazy especially, it was the dancing— sometimes everyone would stand still to watch me waltz, and I never got more than a glimpse of my partners, they changed so fast. Boys would follow us to the hotel, then call under our window Come out! Come out! and sing, so silly they were—Geraldine almost lost her job. Well we'd lie awake considering the night in a practical way. She was not romantic, my sister; what concerned her was which of our beaux was surest to make things easier out home. It was Dan Rainey she decided on. He was older than the others, twenty-five, a man, not handsome in the face, he had jug ears and freckles and not much chin, but Dan Rainey, oh he was smart in his own steady way and strong enough to lift a keg of nails. End of summer he came out home and helped bring in the wheat. Papa liked him from the first, and though mama said Geraldine was too young, she didn't make any ruckus about it. I cried at the wedding, and thought it was because the nights at the dancing pavilion were over, and because Geraldine and I would never lie cozy in the same bed again. But as soon as Dan Rainey took over, everything seemed to go right; he brought out the best in the land and maybe the best in us. Except when winter came on, and we'd be sitting round the fire, sometimes the heat, something made me feel just faint. I'd go stand in the yard with only my dress on, it was like I couldn't feel the cold because I'd become a piece of it, and I'd close my eyes, waltz round and round, and one night, I didn't hear him sneaking up, Dan Rainey caught me in his arms and danced me for a joke. Only it wasn't such a joke. He had feelings for me; way back in my head I'd known it from the start. But he didn't say it, and I never asked him to; and it wouldn't have come to anything provided Geraldine hadn't lost her baby. That was in the spring. She was mortally afraid of snakes, Geraldine, and it was seeing one that did it; she was collecting eggs, it was only a chicken snake, but it scared her so bad she dropped her baby four months too soon. I don't know what happened to her—got cross and mean, got where she'd fly out about anything. Dan Rainey took the worst of it; he kept out of her way as much as he could; used to roll himself in a blanket and sleep down in the wheatfield. I knew if I stayed there— So I went to Youfry and got Geraldine's old job at the hotel. The dancing pavilion, it was the same as the summer before, and I was even prettier: one boy nearly killed another over who was going to buy me an orangeade. I can't say I didn't enjoy myself, but my mind wasn't on it; at the hotel they asked where was my mind—always filling the sugar bowl with salt, giving people spoons to cut their meat. I never went home the whole summer. When the time came —it was such a day as this, a fall day blue as eternity—I didn't let them know I was coming, just got out of the coach and walked three miles through the wheat stacks till I found Dan Rainey. He didn't speak a word, only plopped down and cried like a baby. I was that sorry for him, and loved him more than tongue can tell."

Her cigarette had gone out. She seemed to have lost track of the story; or worse, thought better of finishing it. I wanted to stamp and whistle, the way rowdies do at the picture-show when the screen goes unexpectedly blank; and Riley, though less bald about it, was impatient too. He struck a match for her cigarette: starting at the sound, she remembered her voice again, but it was as if, in the interval, she'd traveled far ahead.

"So papa swore he'd shoot him. A hundred times Geraldine said tell us who it was and Dan here'll take a gun after him. I laughed till I cried; sometimes the other way round. I said well I had no idea; there were five or six boys in Youfry could be the one, and how was I to know? Mama slapped my face when I said that. But they believed it; even after a while I think Dan Rainey believed it—wanted to anyway, poor unhappy fellow. All those months not stirring out of the house; and in the middle of it papa died. They wouldn't let me go to the funeral, they were so ashamed for anyone to see. It happened this day, with them off at the burial and me alone in the house and a sandy wind blowing rough as an elephant, that I got in touch with God. I didn't by any means deserve to be Chosen: up till then, mama'd had to coax me to learn my Bible verses; afterward, I memorized over a thousand in less than three months. Well I was practicing a tune on the piano, and suddenly a window broke, the whole room turned topsy-turvy, then fell together again, and someone was with me, papa's spirit I thought; but the wind died down peaceful as spring—He was there, and standing as He made me, straight, I opened my arms to welcome Him. That was twenty-six years ago last February the third; I was sixteen, I'm forty-two now, and I've never wavered. When I had my baby I didn't call Geraldine or Dan Rainey or anybody, only lay there whispering my verses one after the other and not a soul knew Danny was born till they heard him holler. It was Geraldine named him that. He was hers, everyone thought so, and people round the countryside rode over to see her new baby, brought presents, some of them, and the men hit Dan Rainey on the back and told him what a fine son he had. Soon as I was able I moved thirty miles away to Stoneville, that's a town double the size of Youfry and where they have a big mining camp. Another girl and I, we started a laundry, and did a good business on account of in a mining town there's mostly bachelors. About twice a month I went home to see Danny; I was seven years going back and forth; it was the only pleasure I had, and a strange one, considering how it tore me up every time: such a beautiful boy, there's no describing. But Geraldine died for me to touch him: if I kissed him, she'd come near to jumping out of her skin; Dan Rainey wasn't much different, he was so scared I wouldn't leave well enough alone. The last time I ever was home I asked him would he meet me in Youfry. Because for a crazy long while I'd had an idea, which was: if I could live it again, if I could bear a child that would be a twin to Danny. But I was wrong to think it could have the same father. It would've been a dead child, born dead: I looked at Dan Rainey (it was the coldest day, we sat by the empty dancing pavilion, I remember he never took his hands out of his pockets) and sent him away without saying why it was I'd asked him to come. Then years spent hunting the likeness of him. One of the miners in Stoneville, he had the same freckles, yellow eyes; a goodhearted boy, he obliged me with Sam, my oldest. As best I recall, Beth's father was a dead ringer for Dan Rainey; but being a girl, Beth didn't favor Danny. I forget to tell you that I'd sold my share of the laundry and gone to Texas—had restaurant work in Amarillo and Dallas. But it wasn't until I met Mr. Honey that I saw why the Lord had chosen me and what my task was to be. Mr. Honey possessed the True Word; after I heard him preach that first time I went round to see him: we hadn't talked twenty minutes than he said I'm going to marry you provided you're not married a'ready. I said no I'm not married, but I've got some family; fact is, there was five by then. Didn't faze him a bit. We got married a week later on Valentine's Day. He wasn't a young man, and he didn't look a particle like Dan Rainey; stripped of his boots he couldn't make it to my shoulder; but when the Lord brought us together He knew certain what He was doing: we had Roy, then Pearl and Kate and Cleo and Little Homer—most of them born in that wagon you saw up there. We traveled all over the country carrying His Word to folks who'd never heard it before, not the way my man could tell it. Now I must mention a sad circumstance, which is: I lost Mr. Honey. One morning, this was in a queer part of Louisiana, Cajun parts, he walked off down the road to buy some groceries: you know, we never saw him again. He disappeared right into thin air. I don't give a hoot what the police say; he wasn't the kind to run out on his family; no sir it was foul play."

"Or amnesia," I said. "You forget everything, even your own name."

"A man with the whole Bible on the tip of his tongue—would you say he was liable to forget something like his name? One of them Cajuns murdered him for his amethyst ring. Naturally I've known men since then; but not love. Lillie Ida, Laurel, the other kids, they happened like. Seems somehow I can't get on without another life kicking under my heart: feel so sluggish otherwise."

When the children were dressed, some with their clothes inside out, we returned to the tree where the older girls, bending over the fire, dried and combed their hair. In our absence Dolly had cared for the baby; she seemed now not to want to give it back: "I wish one of us had had a baby, my sister or Catherine," and Sister Ida said yes, it was entertaining and a satisfaction too. We sat finally in a circle around the fire. The stew was too hot to taste, which perhaps accounted for its thorough success, and the Judge, who had to serve it in rotation, for there were only three cups, was full of gay stunts and nonsense that exhilarated the children: Texaco Gasoline decided she'd made a mistake—the Judge, not Riley, was her papa, and the Judge rewarded her with a trip to the moon, swung her, that is, high over his head: *Some flocked south, Some flocked west, You go flying after the rest, Away! Awhee!* Sister Ida said say you're pretty strong. Of course he lapped it up, all but asked her to feel his muscles. Every quarter-minute he peeked to see if Dolly was admiring him. She was.

The croonings of a ringdove wavered among the long last lances of sunlight. Chill green, blues filtered through the air as though a rainbow had dissolved around us. Dolly shivered: "There's a storm nearby. I've had the notion all day." I looked at Riley triumphantly: hadn't I told him?

"And it's getting late," said Sister Ida. "Buck, Homer—you boys chase up to the wagon. Gracious knows who's come along and helped themselves. Not," she added, watching her sons vanish on the darkening path, "that there's a whole lot to take, nothing much except my sewing machine. So, Dolly? Have you . . ."

"We've discussed it," said Dolly, turning to the Judge for confirmation.

"You'd win your case in court, no question of it," he said, very professional. "For once, the law would be on the right side. As matters stand, however . . ."

Dolly said, "As matters stand," and pressed into Sister Ida's hand the forty-seven dollars which constituted our cash assets; in addition, she gave her the Judge's big gold watch. Contemplating these gifts, Sister Ida shook her head as though she should refuse them. "It's wrong. But I thank you."

A light thunder rolled through the woods, and in the perilous quiet of its wake Buck and Little Homer burst upon the path like charging cavalry. "They're coming! They're coming!" both got out at once, and Little Homer, pushing back his hat, gasped: "We ran all the way."

"Make sense, boy: who?"

Little Homer swallowed. "Those fellows. The Sheriff one, and I don't know how many more. Coming down through the grass. With guns, too."

Thunder rumbled again; tricks of wind rustled our fire.

"All right now," said the Judge, assuming command. "Everybody keep their heads." It was as though he'd planned for this moment, and he rose to it, I do concede, gloriously. "The women, you little kids, get up in the tree house. Riley, see that the rest of you scatter out, shinny up those other trees and take a load of rocks." When we'd followed these directions, he alone remained on the ground; firm-jawed, he stayed there guarding the tense twilighted silence like a captain who will not abandon his drowning ship.

6

Five of us roosted in the sycamore tree that overhung the path. Little Homer was there, and his brother Buck, a scowling boy with rocks in either hand. Across the way, straddling the limbs of a second sycamore, we could see Riley surrounded by the older girls: in the deepening burnished light their white faces glimmered like candle-lanterns. I thought I felt a raindrop: it was a bead of sweat slipping along my cheek; still, and though the thunder lulled, a smell of rain intensified the odor of leaves and wood-smoke. The overloaded tree house gave an evil creak; from my vantage point, its tenants seemed a single creature, a many-legged, many-eyed spider upon whose head Dolly's hat sat perched like a velvet crown.

In our tree everybody pulled out the kind of tin whistles Riley had bought from Little Homer: good to give the devil a scare, Sister Ida had said. Then Little Homer took off his huge hat and, removing from its vast interior what was perhaps God's Washline, a thick long rope, at any rate, proceeded to make a sliding noose. As he tested its efficiency, stretched and tightened the knot, his steely miniature spectacles cast such a menacing sparkle that, edging away, I put the distance of another branch between us. The Judge, patrolling below, hissed to stop moving around up there; it was his last order before the invasion began.

The invaders themselves made no pretense at stealth. Swinging their rifles against the undergrowth like canecutters, they swaggered up the path, nine, twelve, twenty strong. First, Junius Candle, his Sheriff's star winking in the dusk; and after him, Big Eddie Stover, whose squint-eyed search of our hiding places reminded me of those newspaper picture puzzles; find five boys and an owl in this drawing of a tree. It requires someone cleverer than Big Eddie Stover. He looked straight at me, and through me. Not many of that gang would have troubled you with their braininess: good for nothing but a lick of salt and swallow of beer most of them. Except I recognized Mr. Hand, the principal at school, a decent enough fellow taken all around, no one, you would have thought, to involve himself in such shabby company on so shameful an errand. Curiosity explained the attendance of Amos Legrand; he was there, and silent for once: no wonder: as though he were a walking-stick, Verena was leaning a hand on his head, which came not quite to her hip. A grim Reverend Buster ceremoniously supported her other arm. When I saw Verena I felt a numbed reliving of the terror I'd known when, after my mother's death, she'd come to our house to claim me. Despite what seemed a lameness, she moved with her customary tall authority and, accompanied by her escorts, stopped under our sycamore.

The Judge didn't give an inch; toe to toe with the Sheriff, he stood his ground as if there were a drawn line he dared the other to cross.

It was at this crucial moment that I noticed Little Homer. He gradually was lowering his lasso. It crawled, dangled like a snake, the wide noose open as a pair of jaws, then fell, with an expert snap, around the neck of the Reverend Buster, whose strangling outcry Little Homer stifled by giving the rope a mighty tug.

His friends hadn't long to consider old Buster's predicament, his blood-gorged face and flailing arms; for Little Homer's success inspired an all-out attack: rocks flew, whistles shrilled like the shriekings of savage birds, and the men, pummeling each other in the general rout, took refuge where they could, principally under the bodies of comrades already fallen. Verena had to box Amos Legrand's ears: he tried to sneak up under her skirt. She alone, you might say, behaved like a real man: shook her fists at the trees and cursed us blue.

At the height of the din, a shot slammed like an iron door. It quelled us all, the serious endless echo of it; but in the hush that followed we heard a weight come crashing through the opposite sycamore.

It was Riley, falling; and falling: slowly, relaxed as a killed cat. Covering their eyes, the girls screamed as he struck a branch and splintered it, hovered, like the torn leaves, then in a bleeding heap hit the ground. No one moved toward him.

Until at last the Judge said, "Boy, my boy," and in a trance sank to his knees; he caressed Riley's limp hands. "Have mercy. Have mercy, son: answer." Other men, sheepish and frightened, closed round; some offered advice, which the Judge seemed unable to comprehend. One by one we dropped down from the trees, and the children's gathering whisper is he dead? is he dead? was like the moan, the delicate roar of a sea trumpet. Doffing their hats respectfully, the men made an aisle for Dolly; she was too stunned to take account of them, or of Verena, whom she passed without seeing.

"I want to know," said Verena, in tones that summoned attention, ". . . which of you fools fired that gun?"

The men guardedly looked each other over: too many of them fixed on Big Eddie Stover. His jowls trembled, he licked his lips: "Hell, I never meant to shoot nobody; was doing my duty, that's all."

"Not all," Verena severely replied. "I hold you responsible, Mr. Stover."

At this Dolly turned round; her eyes, vague beyond the veiling, seemed to frame Verena in a gaze that excluded everyone else. "Responsible? No one is that; except ourselves."

Sister Ida had replaced the Judge at Riley's side; she completely stripped off his shirt. "Thank your stars, it's his shoulder," she said, and the relieved sighs, Big Eddie's alone, would have floated a kite. "He's fairly knocked out, though. Some of you fellows better get him to a doctor." She stopped Riley's bleeding with a bandage torn off his shirt. The Sheriff and three of his men locked arms, making a litter on which to carry him. He was not the only one who had to be carried; the Reverend Buster had also come to considerable grief: loose-limbed as a puppet, and too weak to know the noose still hung around his neck, he needed several assistants to get up the path. Little Homer chased after him: "Hey, hand me back my rope!"

Amos Legrand waited to accompany Verena; she told him to go without her, as she had no intention of leaving unless Dolly— Hesitating, she looked at the rest of us, Sister Ida in particular: "I would like to speak with my sister alone."

With a wave of her hand that quite dismissed Verena, Sister Ida said, "Never mind, lady. We're on our way." She hugged Dolly. "Bless us, we love you. Don't we, kids?" Little Homer said, "Come with us, Dolly. We'll have such good times. I'll give you my sparkle belt." And Texaco Gasoline threw herself upon the Judge, pleading for him to go with them, too. Nobody seemed to want me.

"I'll always remember that you asked me," said Dolly, her eyes hurrying as though to memorize the children's faces. "Good luck. Good-bye. Run now," she raised her voice above new and nearer thunder, "run, it's raining."

It was a tickling feathery rain fine as a gauze curtain, and as they faded into the folds of it, Sister Ida and her family, Verena said: "Do I understand you've been conniving with that—woman? After she made a mockery of our name?"

"I don't think you can accuse me of conniving with anyone," Dolly answered serenely. "Especially not with bullies who," she a little lost control, "steal from children and drag old women into jail. I can't set much store by a name that endorses such methods. It ought to be a mockery."

Verena received this without flinching. "You're not yourself," she said, as if it were a clinical opinion.

"You'd best look again: I am myself." Dolly seemed to pose for inspection. She was as tall as Verena, as assured; nothing about her was incomplete or blurred. "I've taken your advice: stopped hanging my head, I mean. You told me it made you dizzy. And not many days ago," she continued, "you told me that you were ashamed of me. Of Catherine. So much of our lives had been lived for you; it was painful to realize the waste that had been. Can you know what it is, such a feeling of waste?"

Scarcely audible, Verena said, "I do know," and it was as if her eyes crossed, peered inward upon a stony vista. It was the expression I'd seen when, spying from the attic, I'd watched her late at night brooding over the Kodak pictures of Maudie Laura Murphy, Maudie Laura's husband and children. She swayed, she put a hand on my shoulder; except for that, I think she might have fallen.

"I imagined I would go to my dying day with the hurt of it. I won't. But it's no satisfaction, Verena, to say that I'm ashamed of you, too."

It was night now; frogs, sawing insects celebrated the slow-falling rain. We dimmed as though the wetness had snuffed the light of our faces. Verena sagged against me. "I'm not well," she said in a skeleton voice. "I'm a sick woman, I am, Dolly."

Somewhat unconvinced, Dolly approached Verena, presently touched her, as though her fingers could sense the truth. "Collin," she said, "Judge, please help me with her into the tree." Verena protested that she couldn't go climbing trees; but once she got used to the idea she went up easily enough. The raftlike tree house seemed to be floating over shrouded vaporish waters; it was dry there, however, for the mild rain had not penetrated the parasol of leaves. We drifted in a current of silence until Verena said, "I have something to say, Dolly. I could say it more easily if we were alone."

The Judge crossed his arms. "I'm afraid you'll have to put up with me, Miss Verena." He was emphatic, though not belligerent. "I have an interest in the outcome of what you might have to say."

"I doubt that: how so?" she said, recovering to a degree her exalted manner.

He lighted a stub of candle, and our sudden shadows stooped over us like four eavesdroppers. "I don't like talking in the dark," he said. There was a purpose in the proud erectness of his posture: it was, I thought, to let Verena know she was dealing with a man, a fact too few men in her experience had enough believed to assert. She found it unforgivable. "You don't remember, do you, Charlie Cool? Fifty years ago, more maybe. Some of you boys came blackberry stealing out at our place. My father caught your cousin Seth, and I caught you. It was quite a licking you got that day."

The Judge did remember; he blushed, smiled, said: "You didn't fight fair, Verena."

"I fought fair," she told him drily. "But you're right—since neither of us like it, let's not talk in the dark. Frankly, Charlie, you're not a welcome sight to me. My sister couldn't have gone through such tommyrot if you hadn't been goading her on. So I'll thank you to leave us; it can be no further affair of yours."

"But it is," said Dolly. "Because Judge Cool, Charlie . . ." she dwindled, appeared for the first time to question her boldness.

"Dolly means that I have asked her to marry me."

"That," Verena managed after some suspenseful seconds, "is," she said, regarding her gloved hands, "remarkable. Very. I wouldn't have credited either of you with so much imagination. Or is it that I am imagining? Quite likely I'm dreaming of myself in a wet tree on a thundery night. Except I never have dreams, or perhaps I only forget them. This one I suggest we all forget."

"I'll own up: I think it is a dream, Miss Verena. But a man who doesn't dream is like a man who doesn't sweat: he stores up a lot of poison."

She ignored him; her attention was with Dolly, Dolly's with her: they might have been alone together, two persons at far ends of a bleak room, mutes communicating in an eccentric sign language, subtle shifting of the eye; and it was as though, then, Dolly gave an answer, one that sapped all color from Verena's face. "I see. You've accepted him, have you?"

The rain had thickened, fish could have swum through the air; like a deepening scale of piano notes, it struck its blackest chord, and drummed into a downpour that, though it threatened, did not at once reach us: drippings leaked through the leaves, but the tree house stayed a dry seed in a soaking plant. The Judge put a protective hand over the candle; he waited as anxiously as Verena for Dolly's reply. My impatience equaled theirs, yet I felt exiled from the scene, again a spy peering from the attic, and my sympathies, curiously, were nowhere; or rather, everywhere: a tenderness for all three ran together like raindrops, I could not separate them, they expanded into a human oneness.

Dolly, too. She could not separate the Judge from Verena. At last, excruciatingly, "I can't," she cried, implying failures beyond calculation. "I said I would know what was right. But it hasn't happened; I don't know:

do other people? A choice, I thought: to have had a life made of my own decisions . . ."

"But we have had our lives," said Verena. "Yours has been nothing to despise, I don't think you've required more than you've had; I've envied you always. Come home, Dolly. Leave decisions to me: that, you see, has been my life."

"Is it true, Charlie?" Dolly asked, as a child might ask where do falling stars fall? and: "Have we had our lives?"

"We're not dead," he told her; but it was as if, to the questioning child, he'd said stars fall into space: an irrefutable, still unsatisfactory answer. Dolly could not accept it: "You don't have to be dead. At home, in the kitchen, there is a geranium that blooms over and over. Some plants, though, they bloom just the once, if at all, and nothing more happens to them. They live, but they've had their life."

"Not you," he said, and brought his face nearer hers, as though he meant their lips to touch, yet wavered, not daring it. Rain had tunneled through the branches, it fell full weight; rivulets of it streamed off Dolly's hat, the veiling clung to her cheeks; with a flutter the candle failed. "Not me."

Successive strokes of lightning throbbed like veins of fire, and Verena, illuminated in that sustained glare, was not anyone I knew; but some woman woebegone, wasted—with eyes once more drawn toward each other, their stare settled on an inner territory, a withered country; as the lightning lessened, as the hum of rain sealed us in its multiple sounds, she spoke, and her voice came so weakly from so very far, not expecting, it seemed, to be heard at all. "Envied you, Dolly. Your pink room. I've only knocked at the doors of such rooms, not often—enough to know that now there is no one but you to let me in. Because little Morris, little Morris—help me, I loved him, I did. Not in a womanly way; it was, oh I admit it, that we were kindred spirits. We looked each other in the eye, we saw the same devil, we weren't afraid; it was—merry. But he outsmarted me; I'd known he could, and hoped he wouldn't, and he did, and now: it's too long to be alone, a lifetime. I walk through the house, nothing is mine: your pink room, your kitchen, the house is yours, and Catherine's too, I think. Only don't leave me, let me live with you. I'm feeling old, I want my sister."

The rain, adding its voice to Verena's, was between them, Dolly and the Judge, a transparent wall through which he could watch her losing substance, recede before him as earlier she had seemed to recede before me. More than that, it was as if the tree house were dissolving. Lunging wind cast overboard the soggy wreckage of our Rook cards, our wrapping papers; animal crackers crumbled, the rain-filled mason jars spilled over like fountains; and Catherine's beautiful scrapquilt was ruined, a puddle. It was going: like the doomed houses rivers in flood float away; and it was as though the Judge were trapped there—waving to us as we, the survivors, stood ashore. For Dolly had said, "Forgive me; I want my sister, too," and the Judge could not reach her, not with his arms, not with his heart: Verena's claim was too final.

Somewhere near midnight the rain slackened, halted; wind barreled about wringing out the trees. Singly, like delayed guests arriving at a dance, appearing stars pierced the sky. It was time to leave. We took nothing with us: left the quilt to rot, spoons to rust; and the tree house, the woods we left to winter.

7

For quite a while it was Catherine's custom to date events as having occurred before or after her incarceration. "Prior," she would begin, "to the time That One made a jailbird of me." As for the rest of us, we could have divided history along similar lines; that is, in terms of before and after the tree house. Those few autumn days were a monument and a signpost.

Except to collect his belongings, the Judge never again entered the house he'd shared with his sons and their wives, a circumstance that must have suited them, at least they made no protest when he took a room at Miss Bell's boardinghouse. This was a brown solemn establishment which lately has been turned into a funeral home by an undertaker who saw that to effect the correct atmosphere a minimum of renovation would be necessary. I disliked going past it, for Miss Bell's guests, ladies thorny as the blighted rosebushes littering the yard, occupied the porch in a dawn-to-dark marathon of vigilance. One of them, the twice-widowed Mamie Canfield, specialized in spotting pregnancies (some legendary fellow is supposed to have told his wife Why waste money on a doctor? just trot yourself past Miss Bell's: Mamie Canfield, she'll let the world know soon enough whether you is or ain't). Until the Judge moved there, Amos Legrand was the only man in residence at Miss Bell's. He was a godsend to the other tenants: the moments most sacred to them were when, after supper, Amos swung in the seat-swing with his little legs not touching the floor and his tongue trilling like an alarm clock. They vied with each other in knitting him socks and sweaters, tending to his diet: at table all the best things were saved for his plate—Miss Bell had trouble keeping a cook because the ladies were forever poking around in the kitchen wanting to make a delicacy that would tempt their pet. Probably they would have done the same for the Judge, but he had no use for them, never, so they complained, stopped to pass the time of day.

The last drenching night in the tree house had left me with a bad cold, Verena with a worse one; and we had a sneezing nurse, Dolly. Catherine wouldn't help: "Dollyheart, you can do like you please—tote That One's slopjar till you drop in your tracks. Only don't count on me to lift a finger. I've put down the load."

Rising at all hours of the night, Dolly brought the syrups that eased our throats, stoked the fires that kept us warm. Verena did not, as in other days, accept such attention simply as her due. "In the spring," she promised Dolly, "we'll make a trip together. We might go to the Grand Canyon and call on Maudie Laura. Or Florida: you've never seen the ocean." But Dolly was where she wanted to be, she had no wish to travel: "I wouldn't enjoy it, seeing the things I've known shamed by nobler sights."

Doctor Carter called regularly to see us, and one morning Dolly asked would he mind taking her temperature; she felt so flushed and weak in the legs. He put her straight to bed, and she thought it was very humorous when he told her she had walking pneumonia. "Walking pneumonia," she said to the Judge, who had come to visit her, "it must be something new, I've never heard of it. But I do feel as though I were skylarking along on a pair of stilts. Lovely," she said and fell asleep.

For three, nearly four days she never really woke up. Catherine stayed with her, dozing upright in a wicker chair and growling low whenever Verena or I tiptoed into the room. She persisted in fanning Dolly with a picture of Jesus, as though it were summertime; and it was a disgrace how she ignored Doctor Carter's instructions: "I wouldn't feed that to a hog," she'd declare, pointing to some medicine he'd sent around. Finally Doctor Carter said he wouldn't be responsible unless the patient were removed to a hospital. The nearest hospital was in Brewton, sixty miles away. Verena sent over there for an ambulance. She could have saved herself the expense, because Catherine locked Dolly's door from the inside and said the first one to rattle the knob would need an ambulance themselves. Dolly did not know where they wanted to take her; wherever it was, she begged not to go: "Don't wake me," she said, "I don't want to see the ocean."

Toward the end of the week she could sit up in bed; a few days later she was strong enough to resume correspondence with her dropsy-cure customers. She was worried by the unfilled orders that had piled up; but Catherine, who took the credit for Dolly's improvement, said, "Shoot, it's no time we'll be out there boiling a brew."

Every afternoon, promptly at four, the Judge presented himself at the garden gate and whistled for me to let him in; by using the garden gate, rather than the front door, he lessened the chance of encountering Verena —not that she objected to his coming: indeed, she wisely supplied for his visits a bottle of sherry and a box of cigars. Usually he brought Dolly a gift, cakes from the Katydid Bakery or flowers, bronze balloonlike chrysanthemums which Catherine swiftly confiscated on the theory that they ate up all the nourishment in the air. Catherine never learned he had proposed to Dolly; still, intuiting a situation not quite to her liking, she sharply chaperoned the Judge's visits and, while swigging at the sherry that had been put out for him, did most of the talking as well. But I suspect that neither he nor Dolly had much to say of a private nature; they accepted each other without excitement, as people do who are settled in their affections. If in other ways he was a disappointed man, it was not because of Dolly, for I believe she became what he'd wanted, the one person in the world—to whom, as he'd described it, everything can be said. But when everything can be said perhaps there is nothing more to say. He sat beside her bed, content to be there and not expecting to be entertained. Often, drowsy with fever, she went to sleep, and if, while she slept, she whimpered or frowned, he wakened her, welcoming her back with a daylight smile.

In the past Verena had not allowed us to have a radio; cheap melodies, she contended, disordered the mind; moreover, there was the expense to consider. It was Doctor Carter who persuaded her that Dolly should have a radio; he thought it would help reconcile her to what he foresaw as a long convalescence. Verena bought one, and paid a good price, I don't doubt; but it was an ugly hood-shaped box crudely varnished. I took it out in the yard and painted it pink. Even so, Dolly wasn't certain she wanted it in her room; later on, you couldn't have pried it away from her. That radio was always hot enough to hatch a chicken, she and Catherine played it so much. They favored broadcasts of football games. "Please don't," Dolly admonished the Judge when he attempted to explain the rules of this game. "I like a mystery. Everybody shouting, having such a fine time: it might not sound so large and happy if I knew why." Primarily the Judge was peeved because he couldn't get Dolly to root for any one team. She thought both sides should win: "They're all nice boys, I'm sure."

Because of the radio Catherine and I had words one afternoon. It was the afternoon Maude Riordan was playing in a broadcast of the state musical competition. Naturally I wanted to hear her, Catherine knew that, but she was tuned in on a Tulane–Georgia Tech game and wouldn't let me near the radio. I said, "What's come over you, Catherine? Selfish, dissatisfied, always got to have your own way, why you're worse than Verena ever was." It was as though, in lieu of prestige lost through her encounter with the law, she'd had to double her power in the Talbo house: we at least would have to respect her Indian blood, accept her tyranny. Dolly was willing; in the matter of Maude Riordan, however, she sided with me: "Let Collin find his station. It wouldn't be Christian not to listen to Maude. She's a friend of ours."

Everyone who heard Maude agreed that she should've won first prize. She placed second, which pleased her family, for it meant a half-scholarship in music at the University. Still it wasn't fair, because she performed beautifully, much better than the boy who won the larger prize. She played her father's serenade, and it seemed to me as pretty as it had that day in the woods. Since that day I'd wasted hours scribbling her name, describing in my head her charms, her hair the color of vanilla ice cream. The Judge arrived in time to hear the broadcast, and I know Dolly was glad because it was as if we were reunited again in the leaves with music like butterflies flying.

Some days afterward I met Elizabeth Henderson on the street. She'd been at the beauty parlor, for her hair was finger-waved, her nails tinted, she did look grown-up and I complimented her. "It's for the party. I hope your costume is ready." Then I remembered: the Halloween party to which she and Maude had asked me to contribute my services as a fortune-teller. "You can't have forgotten? Oh, Collin," she said, "we've worked like dogs! Mrs. Riordan is making a *wine* punch. I shouldn't be surprised if there's drunkenness and everything. And after all it's a celebration for Maude, because she won the prize, and because," Elizabeth glanced along the street, a glum perspective of silent houses and telephone poles, "she'll be going away—to the University, you know." A loneliness fell around us, we did not want to go our separate ways: I offered to walk her home.

On our way we stopped by the Katydid, where Elizabeth placed an order for a Halloween cake, and Mrs. C. C. County, her apron glittering with sugar crystals, appeared from the oven room to inquire after Dolly's condition. "Doing well as can be expected I suppose," she lamented. "Imagine it, walking pneumonia. My sister, now she had the ordinary lying-down kind. Well, we can be thankful Dolly's in her own bed; it eases my mind to know you people are home again. Ha ha, guess we can laugh about all that foolishness now. Look here, I've just pulled out a pan of doughnuts; you take them to Dolly with my blessings." Elizabeth and I ate most of those doughnuts before we reached her house. She invited me in to have a glass of milk and finish them off.

Today there is a filling station where the Henderson house used to be. It was some fifteen draughty rooms casually nailed together, a place stray animals would have claimed if Riley had not been a gifted carpenter. He had an outdoor shed, a combination of workshop and sanctuary, where he spent his mornings sawing lumber, shaving shingles. Its wall-shelves sagged with the relics of outgrown hobbies: snakes, bees, spiders preserved in alcohol, a bat decaying in a bottle; ship models. A boyhood enthusiasm for taxidermy had resulted in a pitiful zoo of nasty-odored beasts: an eyeless rabbit with maggot-green fur and ears that drooped like a bloodhound's— objects better off buried. I'd been lately to see Riley several times; Big Eddie Stover's bullet had shattered his shoulder, and the curse of it was he had to wear an itching plaster cast which weighed, he said, a hundred pounds. Since he couldn't drive his car, or hammer a proper nail, there wasn't much for him to do except loaf around and brood.

"If you want to see Riley," said Elizabeth, "you'll find him out in the shed. I expect Maude's with him."

"Maude Riordan?" I had reason to be surprised, because on the occasions I'd visited Riley he'd made a point of our sitting in the shed; the girls wouldn't bother us there, for it was, he'd boasted, one threshold no female was permitted to cross.

"Reading to him. Poetry, plays. Maude's been absolutely adorable. And it's not as though my brother had ever treated her with common human decency. But she's let bygones be bygones. I guess coming so near to being killed the way he was, I guess that would change a person—make them more receptive to the finer things. He lets her read to him by the hour."

The shed, shaded by fig trees, was in the backyard. Matronly Plymouth hens waddled about its doorstep picking at the seeds of last summer's fallen sunflowers. On the door a childhood word in faded whitewash feebly warned Beware! It aroused a shyness in me. Beyond the door I could hear Maude's voice—her poetry voice, a swooning chant certain louts in school had dearly loved to mimic. Anyone who'd been told Riley Henderson had come to this, they'd have said that fall from the sycamore had affected his head. Stealing over to the shed's window, I got a look at him: he was absorbed in sorting the insides of a clock and, to judge from his face, might have been listening to nothing more uplifting than the hum of a fly; he jiggled a finger in his ear, as though to relieve an irritation. Then, at the moment I'd decided to startle them by rapping on the window, he put aside his clockworks and, coming around behind Maude, reached down and shut the book from which she was reading. With a grin he gathered in his hand twists of her hair—she rose like a kitten lifted by the nape of its neck. It was as though they were edged with light; some brilliance that smarted my eyes. You could see it wasn't the first time they'd kissed.

Not one week before, because of his experience in such matters, I'd taken Riley into my confidence, confessed to him my feelings for Maude: please look. I wished I were a giant so that I could grab hold of that shed and shake it to a splinter; knock down the door and denounce them both. Yet—of what could I accuse Maude? Regardless of how bad she'd talked about him I'd always known she was heartset on Riley. It wasn't as if there had ever been an understanding between the two of us; at the most we'd been good friends: for the last few years, not even that. As I walked back through the yard the pompous Plymouth hens cackled after me tauntingly.

Elizabeth said, "You didn't stay long. Or weren't they there?"

I told her it hadn't seemed right to interrupt. "They were getting on so well with the finer things."

But sarcasm never touched Elizabeth: she was, despite the subtleties her soulful appearance promised, too literal a person. "Wonderful, isn't it?"

"Wonderful."

"Collin—for heaven's sake: what are you sniveling about?"

"Nothing. I mean, I've got a cold."

"Well I hope it doesn't keep you away from the party. Only you must have a costume. Riley's coming as the devil."

"That's appropriate."

"Of course we want you in a skeleton suit. I know there's only a day left. . . ."

I had no intention of going to the party. As soon as I got home I sat down to write Riley a letter. Dear Riley . . . Dear Henderson. I crossed out the dear; plain Henderson would do. Henderson, your treachery has not gone unobserved. Pages were filled with recording the origins of our friendship, its honorable history; and gradually a feeling grew that there must be a mistake: such a splendid friend would not have wronged me. Until, toward the end, I found myself deliriously telling him he was my best friend, my brother. So I threw these ravings in a fireplace and five minutes later was in Dolly's room asking what were the chances of my having a skeleton suit made by the following night.

Dolly was not much of a seamstress, she had her difficulties lifting a hemline. This was also true of Catherine; it was in Catherine's make-up, however, to pretend professional status in all fields, particularly those in which she was least competent. She sent me to Verena's drygoods store for seven yards of their choicest black satin. "With seven yards there ought to be some bits left over: me and Dolly can trim our petticoats." Then she made a show of tape-measuring my lengths and widths, which was sound procedure except that she had no idea of how to apply such information to scissors and cloth. "This little piece," she said, hacking off a yard, "it'd make somebody lovely bloomers. And this here," snip, snip, ". . . a black satin collar would dress up my old print considerable." You couldn't have covered a midget's shame with the amount of material allotted me.

"Catherine, now dear, we mustn't think of our own needs," Dolly warned her.

They worked without recess through the afternoon. The Judge, during his usual visit, was forced to thread needles, a job Catherine despised: "Makes my flesh crawl, like stuffing worms on a fishhook." At suppertime she called quits and went home to her house among the butterbean stalks.

But a desire to finish had seized Dolly; and a talkative exhilaration. Her needle soared in and out of the satin; like the seams it made, her sentences linked in a wiggling line. "Do you think," she said, "that Verena would let me give a party? Now that I have so many friends? There's Riley, there's Charlie, couldn't we ask Mrs. County, Maude and Elizabeth? In the spring; a garden party—with a few fireworks. My father was a great hand for sewing. A pity I didn't inherit it from him. So many men sewed in the old days; there was one friend of Papa's that won I don't know how many prizes for his scrapquilts. Papa said it relaxed him after the heavy rough work around a farm. Collin. Will you promise me something? I was against your coming here, I've never believed it was right, raising a boy in a houseful of women. Old women and their prejudices. But it was done; and somehow I'm not worried about it now: you'll make your mark, you'll get on. It's this that I want you to promise me: don't be unkind to Catherine, try not to grow too far away from her. Some nights it keeps me wide awake to think of her forsaken. There," she held up my suit, "let's see if it fits."

It pinched in the crotch and in the rear drooped like an old man's B.V.D.'s; the legs were wide as sailor pants, one sleeve stopped above my wrist, the other shot past my fingertips. It wasn't, as Dolly admitted, very stylish. "But when we've painted on the bones . . ." she said. "Silver paint. Verena bought some once to dress up a flagpole—before she took against the government. It should be somewhere in the attic, that little can. Look under the bed and see if you can locate my slippers."

She was forbidden to get up, not even Catherine would permit that. "It won't be any fun if you scold," she said and found the slippers herself. The courthouse clock had chimed eleven, which meant it was ten-thirty, a dark hour in a town where respectable doors are locked at nine; it seemed later still because in the next room Verena had closed her ledgers and gone to bed. We took an oil lamp from the linen closet and by its tottering light tiptoed up the ladder into the attic. It was cold up there; we set the lamp on a barrel and lingered near it as though it were a hearth. Sawdust heads that once had helped sell St. Louis hats watched while we searched; wherever we put our hands it caused a huffy scuttling of fragile feet. Overturned, a carton of mothballs clattered on the floor. "Oh dear, oh dear," cried Dolly, giggling, "if Verena hears that she'll call the Sheriff."

We unearthed numberless brushes; the paint, discovered beneath a welter of dried holiday wreaths, proved not to be silver but gold. "Of course that's better, isn't it? Gold, like a king's ransom. Only do see what else I've found." It was a shoebox secured with twine. "My valuables," she said, opening it under the lamp. A hollowed honeycomb was demonstrated against the light, a hornet's nest and a clove-stuck orange that age had robbed of its aroma. She showed me a blue perfect jaybird's egg cradled in cotton.

"I was too principled. So Catherine stole the egg for me, it was her Christmas present." She smiled; to me her face seemed a moth suspended beside the lamp's chimney, as daring, as destructible. "Charlie said that love is a chain of love. I hope you listened and understood him. Because when you can love one thing," she held the blue egg as preciously as the Judge had held a leaf, "you can love another, and that is owning, that is something to live with. You can forgive everything. Well," she sighed, "we're not getting you painted. I want to amaze Catherine; we'll tell her that while we slept the little people finished your suit. She'll have a fit."

Again the courthouse clock was floating its message, each note like a banner stirring above the chilled and sleeping town. "I know it tickles," she said, drawing a branch of ribs across my chest, "but I'll make a mess if you don't hold still." She dipped the brush and skated it along the sleeves, the trousers, designing golden bones for my arms and legs. "You must remember all the compliments: there should be many," she said as she immodestly observed her work. "Oh dear, oh dear . . ." She hugged herself, her laughter rollicked in the rafters. "Don't you see . . ."

For I was not unlike the man who painted himself into a corner. Freshly gilded front and back, I was trapped inside the suit: a fine fix for which I blamed her with a pointing finger.

"You have to whirl," she teased. "Whirling will dry you." She blissfully extended her arms and turned in slow ungainly circles across the shadows of the attic floor, her plain kimono billowing and her thin feet wobbling in their slippers. It was as though she had collided with another dancer: she stumbled, a hand on her forehead, a hand on her heart.

Far on the horizon of sound a train whistle howled, and it wakened me to the bewilderment puckering her eyes, the contractions shaking her face. With my arms around her, and the paint bleeding its pattern against her, I called Verena; somebody help me!

Dolly whispered, "Hush now, hush."

Houses at night announce catastrophe by their sudden pitiable radiance. Catherine dragged from room to room switching on lights unused for years. Shivering inside my wrecked costume, I sat in the glare of the entrance hall sharing a bench with the Judge. He had come at once, wearing only a raincoat slung over a flannel nightshirt. Whenever Verena approached he brought his naked legs together primly, like a young girl. Neighbors, summoned by our bright windows, came softly inquiring. Verena spoke to them on the porch: her sister, Miss Dolly, she'd suffered a stroke. Doctor Carter would allow none of us in her room, and we accepted this, even Catherine, who, when she'd set ablaze the last light, stood leaning her head against Dolly's door.

There was in the hall a hat tree with many antlers and a mirror. Dolly's velvet hat hung there, and at sunrise, as breezes trickled through the house, the mirror reflected its quivering veil.

Then I knew as good as anything that Dolly had left us. Some moments past she'd gone by unseen; and in my imagination I followed her. She had crossed the square, had come to the church, now she'd reached the hill. The Indian grass gleamed below her, she had that far to go.

It was a journey I made with Judge Cool the next September. During the intervening months we had not often encountered each other—once we met on the square and he said to come see him any time I felt like it. I meant to, yet whenever I passed Miss Bell's boardinghouse I looked the other way.

I've read that past and future are a spiral, one coil containing the next and predicting its theme. Perhaps this is so; but my own life has seemed to me more a series of closed circles, rings that do not evolve with the freedom of a spiral: for me to get from one to the other has meant a leap, not a glide. What weakens me is the lull between, the wait before I know where to jump. After Dolly died I was a long while dangling.

My own idea was to have a good time.

I hung around Phil's Café winning free beers on the pinball machine; it was illegal to serve me beer, but Phil had it on his mind that someday I would inherit Verena's money and maybe set him up in the hotel business. I slicked my hair with brilliantine and chased off to dances in other towns, shined flashlights and threw pebbles at girls' windows late at night. I knew a Negro in the country who sold a brand of gin called Yellow Devil. I courted anyone who owned a car.

Because I didn't want to spend a waking moment in the Talbo house. It was too thick with air that didn't move. Some stranger occupied the kitchen, a pigeon-toed colored girl who sang all day, the wavery singing of a child bolstering its spirit in an ominous place. She was a sorry cook. She let the kitchen's geranium plant perish. I had approved of Verena hiring her. I thought it would bring Catherine back to work.

On the contrary, Catherine showed no interest in routing the new girl. For she'd retired to her house in the vegetable garden. She had taken the radio with her and was very comfortable. "I've put down the load, and it's down to stay. I'm after my leisure," she said. Leisure fattened her, her feet swelled, she had to cut slits in her shoes. She developed exaggerated versions of Dolly's habits, such as a craving for sweet foods; she had her suppers delivered from the drugstore, two quarts of ice cream. Candy wrappers rustled in her lap. Until she became too gross, she contrived to squeeze herself into clothes that had belonged to Dolly; it was as though, in this way, she kept her friend with her.

Our visits together were an ordeal, and I made them grudgingly, resenting it that she depended on me for company. I let a day slip by without seeing her, then three, a whole week once. When I returned after an absence I imagined the silences in which we sat, her offhand manner, were meant reproachfully; I was too conscience-ridden to realize the truth, which was that she didn't care whether or not I came. One afternoon she proved it. Simply, she removed the cotton wads that jacked up her jaws. Without the cotton her speech was as unintelligible to me as it ordinarily was to others. It happened while I was making an excuse to shorten my call. She lifted the lid of a potbellied stove and spit the cotton into the fire;

and her cheeks caved in, she looked starved. I think now this was not a vengeful gesture: ~~it was~~ intended to let me know that I was under no obligation: the future was something she preferred not to share.

Occasionally Riley rode me around—but I couldn't count on him or his car; neither was much available since he'd become a man of affairs. He had a team of tractors clearing ninety acres of land he'd bought on the outskirts of town; he planned to build houses there. Several locally important persons were impressed by another scheme of his: he thought the town should put up a silk-mill in which every citizen would be a stockholder; aside from the possible profits, having an industry would increase our population. There was an enthusiastic editorial in the paper about this proposal; it went on to say that the town should be proud of having produced a man of young Henderson's enterprise. He grew a mustache; he rented an office and his sister Elizabeth worked as his secretary. Maude Riordan was installed at the State University, and almost every weekend he drove his sisters over there; it was supposed to be because the girls were so lonesome for Maude. The engagement of Miss Maude Riordan to Mr. Riley Henderson was announced in the *Courier* on April Fool's Day.

They were married the middle of June in a double-ring ceremony. I acted as an usher, and the Judge was Riley's best man. Except for the Henderson sisters, all the bridesmaids were society girls Maude had known at the University; the *Courier* called them beautiful debutantes, a chivalrous description. The bride carried a bouquet of jasmine and lilac; the groom wore spats and stroked his mustache. They received a sumptuous tableload of gifts. I gave them six cakes of scented soap and an ashtray.

After the wedding I walked home with Verena under the shade of her black umbrella. It was a blistering day, heatwaves jiggled like a soundgraph of the celebrating Baptist bells, and the rest of summer, a vista rigid as the noon street, lengthened before me. Summer, another autumn, winter again: not a spiral, but a circle confined as the umbrella's shadow. If I ever were to make the leap— With a heartskip, I made it: "Verena, I want to go away."

We were at the garden gate; "I know. I do myself," she said, closing her umbrella. "I'd hoped to make a trip with Dolly. I wanted to show her the ocean." Verena had seemed a tall woman because of her authoritative carriage; now she stooped slightly, her head nodded. I wondered that I ever could have been so afraid of her, for she'd grown feminine, fearful, she spoke of prowlers, she burdened the doors with bolts and spiked the roof with lightning rods. It had been her custom the first of every month to stalk around collecting in person the various rents owed her; when she stopped doing this it caused an uneasiness in the town, people felt wrong without their rainy day. The women said she's got no family, she's lost without her sister; their husbands blamed Dr. Morris Ritz: he knocked the gumption out of her, they said; and, much as they had quarreled with Verena, held it against him. Three years ago, when I returned to this town, my first task was to sort the papers of the Talbo estate, and among Verena's private possessions, her keys, her pictures of Maudie Laura Murphy, I found a postcard. It was dated two months after Dolly died, at Christmas, and it was from Paraguay: *As we say down here, Feliz Navidad. Do you miss me? Morris.* And I thought, reading it, of how her eyes had come permanently to have an uneven cast, an inward and agonized gaze, and I remembered how her eyes, watering in the brassy sunshine of Riley's wedding day, had straightened with momentary hope: "It could be a long trip. I've considered selling a few—a few properties. We might take a boat; you've never seen the ocean." I picked a sprig of honeysuckle from the vine flowering on the garden fence, and she watched me shred it as if I were pulling apart her vision, the voyage she saw for us. "Oh," she brushed at the mole that spotted her cheek like a tear, "well," she said in a practical voice, "what are your ambitions?"

So it was not until September that I called upon the Judge, and then it was to tell him good-bye. The suitcases were packed, Amos Legrand had cut my hair ("Honey, don't you come back here baldheaded. What I mean is, they'll try to scalp you up there, cheat you every way they can."); I had a new suit and new shoes, gray fedora ("Aren't you the cat's pajamas, Mr. Collin Fenwick?" Mrs. County exclaimed. "A lawyer you're going to be? And already dressed like one. No, child, I won't kiss you. I'd be mortified to dirty your finery with my bakery mess. You write us, hear?"): that very evening a train would rock me northward, parade me through the land to a city where in my honor pennants flurried.

At Miss Bell's they told me the Judge had gone out. I found him on the square, and it gave me a twinge to see him, a spruce sturdy figure with a Cherokee rose sprouting in his buttonhole, encamped among the old men who talk and spit and wait. He took my arm and led me away from them; and while he amiably advised me of his own days as a law student, we strolled past the church and out along the River Woods road. This road or this tree: I closed my eyes to fix their image, for I did not believe I would return, did not foresee that I would travel the road and dream the tree until they had drawn me back.

It was as though neither of us had known where we were headed. Quietly astonished, we surveyed the view from the cemetery hill, and arm in arm descended to the summer-burned, September-burnished field. A waterfall of color flowed across the dry and strumming leaves; and I wanted then for the Judge to hear what Dolly had told me: that it was a grass harp, gathering, telling, a harp of voices remembering a story. We listened.

Breakfast at Tiffany's

(1958)

I AM ALWAYS DRAWN BACK TO PLACES where I have lived, the houses and their neighborhoods. For instance, there is a brownstone in the East Seventies where, during the early years of the war, I had my first New York apartment. It was one room crowded with attic furniture, a sofa and fat chairs upholstered in that itchy, particular red velvet that one associates with hot days on a train. The walls were stucco, and a color rather like tobacco-spit. Everywhere, in the bathroom too, there were prints of Roman ruins freckled brown with age. The single window looked out on a fire escape. Even so, my spirits heightened whenever I felt in my pocket the key to this apartment; with all its gloom, it still was a place of my own, the first, and my books were there, and jars of pencils to sharpen, everything I needed, so I felt, to become the writer I wanted to be.

It never occurred to me in those days to write about Holly Golightly, and probably it would not now except for a conversation I had with Joe Bell that set the whole memory of her in motion again.

Holly Golightly had been a tenant in the old brownstone; she'd occupied the apartment below mine. As for Joe Bell, he ran a bar around the corner on Lexington Avenue; he still does. Both Holly and I used to go there six, seven times a day, not for a drink, not always, but to make telephone calls: during the war a private telephone was hard to come by. Moreover, Joe Bell was good about taking messages, which in Holly's case was no small favor, for she had a tremendous many.

Of course this was a long time ago, and until last week I hadn't seen Joe Bell in several years. Off and on we'd kept in touch, and occasionally I'd stopped by his bar when passing through the neighborhood; but actually we'd never been strong friends except inasmuch as we were both friends of Holly Golightly. Joe Bell hasn't an easy nature, he admits it himself, he says it's because he's a bachelor and has a sour stomach. Anyone who knows him will tell you he's a hard man to talk to. Impossible if you don't share his fixations, of which Holly is one. Some others are: ice hockey, Weimaraner dogs, *Our Gal Sunday* (a soap serial he has listened to for fifteen years), and Gilbert and Sullivan—he claims to be related to one or the other, I can't remember which.

And so when, late last Tuesday afternoon, the telephone rang and I heard "Joe Bell here," I knew it must be about Holly. He didn't say so, just: "Can you rattle right over here? It's important," and there was a croak of excitement in his froggy voice.

I took a taxi in a downpour of October rain, and on my way I even thought she might be there, that I would see Holly again.

But there was no one on the premises except the proprietor. Joe Bell's is a quiet place compared to most Lexington Avenue bars. It boasts neither neon nor television. Two old mirrors reflect the weather from the streets; and behind the bar, in a niche surrounded by photographs of ice-hockey stars, there is always a large bowl of fresh flowers that Joe Bell himself arranges with matronly care. That is what he was doing when I came in.

"Naturally," he said, rooting a gladiola deep into the bowl, "naturally I wouldn't have got you over here if it wasn't I wanted your opinion. It's peculiar. A very peculiar thing has happened."

"You heard from Holly?"

He fingered a leaf, as though uncertain of how to answer. A small man with a fine head of coarse white hair, he has a bony, sloping face better suited to someone far taller; his complexion seems permanently sunburned: now it grew even redder. "I can't say exactly heard from her. I mean, I don't know. That's why I want your opinion. Let me build you a drink. Something new. They call it a White Angel," he said, mixing one-half vodka, one-half gin, no vermouth. While I drank the result, Joe Bell stood sucking on a Tums and turning over in his mind what he had to tell me. Then: "You recall a certain Mr. I. Y. Yunioshi? A gentleman from Japan."

"From California," I said, recalling Mr. Yunioshi perfectly. He's a photographer on one of the picture magazines, and when I knew him he lived in the studio apartment on the top floor of the brownstone.

"Don't go mixing me up. All I'm asking, you know who I mean? Okay. So last night who comes waltzing in here but this selfsame Mr. I. Y. Yunioshi. I haven't seen him, I guess it's over two years. And where do you think he's been those two years?"

"Africa."

Joe Bell stopped crunching on his Tums, his eyes narrowed. "So how did you know?"

"Read it in Winchell." Which I had, as a matter of fact.

He rang open his cash register, and produced a manila envelope. "Well, see did you read this in Winchell."

In the envelope were three photographs, more or less the same, though taken from different angles: a tall delicate Negro man wearing a calico skirt and with a shy, yet vain smile, displaying in his hands an odd wood sculpture, an elongated carving of a head, a girl's, her hair sleek and short as a young man's, her smooth wood eyes too large and tilted in the tapering face, her mouth wide, overdrawn, not unlike clown-lips. On a glance it resembled most primitive carving; and then it didn't, for here was the spit-image of Holly Golightly, at least as much of a likeness as a dark still thing could be.

"Now what do you make of that?" said Joe Bell, satisfied with my puzzlement.

"It looks like her."

"Listen, boy," and he slapped his hand on the bar, "it *is* her. Sure as I'm a man fit to wear britches. The little Jap knew it was her the minute he saw her."

"He saw her? In Africa?"

"Well. Just the statue there. But it comes to the same thing. Read the facts for yourself," he said, turning over one of the photographs. On the reverse was written: Wood Carving, S Tribe, Tococul, East Anglia, Christmas Day, 1956.

He said, "Here's what the Jap says," and the story was this: On Christmas Day, Mr. Yunioshi had passed with his camera through Tococul, a village in the tangles of nowhere and of no interest, merely a congregation of mud huts with monkeys in the yards and buzzards on the roofs. He'd decided to move on when he saw suddenly a Negro squatting in a doorway carving monkeys on a walking stick. Mr. Yunioshi was impressed and asked to see more of his work. Whereupon he was shown the carving of the girl's head: and felt, so he told Joe Bell, as if he were falling in a dream. But when he offered to buy it the Negro cupped his private parts in his hand (apparently a tender gesture, comparable to tapping one's heart) and said no. A pound of salt and ten dollars, a wristwatch and two pounds of salt and twenty dollars, nothing swayed him. Mr. Yunioshi was in all events determined to learn how the carving came to be made. It cost him his salt and his watch, and the incident was conveyed in African and pig-English and finger-talk. But it would seem that in the spring of that year a party of three white persons had appeared out of the brush riding horseback. A young woman and two men. The men, both red-eyed with fever, were forced for several weeks to stay shut and shivering in an isolated hut, while the young woman, having presently taken a fancy to the wood-carver, shared the woodcarver's mat.

"I don't credit that part," Joe Bell said squeamishly. "I know she had her ways, but I don't think she'd be up to anything as much as that."

"And then?"

"Then nothing," he shrugged. "By and by she went like she come, rode away on a horse."

"Alone, or with the two men?"

Joe Bell blinked. "With the two men, I guess. Now the Jap, he asked about her up and down the country. But nobody else had ever seen her." Then it was as if he could feel my own sense of letdown transmitting itself to him, and he wanted no part of it. "One thing you got to admit, it's the only *definite* news in I don't know how many"—he counted on his fingers: there weren't enough—"years. All I hope, I hope she's rich. She must be rich. You got to be rich to go mucking around in Africa."

"She's probably never set foot in Africa," I said, believing it; yet I could see her there, it was somewhere she would have gone. And the carved head: I looked at the photographs again.

"You know so much, where is she?"

"Dead. Or in a crazy house. Or married. I think she's married and quieted down and maybe right in this very city."

He considered a moment. "No," he said, and shook his head. "I'll tell you why. If she was in this city, I'd have seen her. You take a man that likes to walk, a man like me, a man's been walking in the streets going on ten or twelve years, and all those years he's got his eye out for one person, and nobody's ever her, don't it stand to reason she's not there? I see pieces of her all the time, a flat little bottom, any skinny girl that walks fast and straight—" He paused, as though too aware of how intently I was looking at him. "You think I'm round the bend?"

"It's just that I didn't know you'd been in love with her. Not like that."

I was sorry I'd said it; it disconcerted him. He scooped up the photographs and put them back in their envelope. I looked at my watch. I hadn't any place to go, but I thought it was better to leave.

"Hold on," he said, gripping my wrist. "Sure I loved her. But it wasn't that I wanted to touch her." And he added, without smiling: "Not that I don't think about that side of things. Even at my age, and I'll be sixty-seven January ten. It's a peculiar fact—but, the older I grow, that side of things seems to be on my mind more and more. I don't remember thinking about it so much even when I was a youngster and it's every other minute. Maybe the older you grow and the less easy it is to put thought into action, maybe that's why it gets all locked up in your head and becomes a burden. Whenever I read in the paper about an old man disgracing himself, I know it's because of this burden. But"—he poured himself a jigger of whiskey and swallowed it neat—"I'll never disgrace myself. And I swear, it never crossed my mind about Holly. You can love somebody without it being like that. You keep them a stranger, a stranger who's a friend."

Two men came into the bar, and it seemed the moment to leave. Joe Bell followed me to the door. He caught my wrist again. "Do you believe it?"

"That you didn't want to touch her?"

"I mean about Africa."

At that moment I couldn't seem to remember the story, only the image of her riding away on a horse. "Anyway, she's gone."

"Yeah," he said, opening the door. "Just gone."

Outside, the rain had stopped, there was only a mist of it in the air, so I turned the corner and walked along the street where the brownstone stands. It is a street with trees that in the summer make cool patterns on the pavement; but now the leaves were yellowed and mostly down, and the rain had made them slippery, they skidded underfoot. The brownstone is midway in the block, next to a church where a blue tower-clock tolls the hours. It has been sleeked up since my day; a smart black door has replaced the old frosted glass, and gray elegant shutters frame the windows. No one I remember still lives there except Madame Sapphia Spanella, a husky coloratura who every afternoon went roller-skating in Central Park. I know she's still there because I went up the steps and looked at the mailboxes. It was one of these mailboxes that had first made me aware of Holly Golightly.

I'd been living in the house about a week when I noticed that the mailbox belonging to Apt. 2 had a name-slot fitted with a curious card. Printed, rather Cartier-formal, it read: *Miss Holiday Golightly;* and, underneath, in the corner, *Traveling.* It nagged me like a tune: *Miss Holiday Golightly, Traveling.*

One night, it was long past twelve, I woke up at the sound of Mr. Yunioshi calling down the stairs. Since he lived on the top floor, his voice fell through the whole house, exasperated and stern. "Miss Golightly! I must protest!"

The voice that came back, welling up from the bottom of the stairs, was silly-young and self-amused. "Oh, darling, I *am* sorry. I lost the goddamn key."

"You cannot go on ringing my bell. You must please, please have yourself a key made."

"But I lose them all."

"I work, I have to sleep," Mr. Yunioshi shouted. "But always you are ringing my bell . . ."

"Oh, *don't* be angry, you *dear* little man: I *won't* do it again. And if you promise not to be angry"—her voice was coming nearer, she was climbing the stairs—"I might let you take those pictures we mentioned."

By now I'd left my bed and opened the door an inch. I could hear Mr. Yunioshi's silence: hear, because it was accompanied by an audible change of breath.

"When?" he said.

The girl laughed. "Sometime," she answered, slurring the word.

"Any time," he said, and closed his door.

I went out into the hall and leaned over the banister, just enough to see without being seen. She was still on the stairs, now she reached the landing, and the ragbag colors of her boy's hair, tawny streaks, strands of albino-blond and yellow, caught the hall light. It was a warm evening, nearly summer, and she wore a slim cool black dress, black sandals, a pearl choker. For all her chic thinness, she had an almost breakfast-cereal air of health, a soap and lemon cleanness, a rough pink darkening in the cheeks. Her mouth was large, her nose upturned. A pair of dark glasses blotted out her eyes. It was a face beyond childhood, yet this side of belonging to a woman. I thought her anywhere between sixteen and thirty; as it turned out, she was shy two months of her nineteenth birthday.

She was not alone. There was a man following behind her. The way his plump hand clutched at her hip seemed somehow improper; not morally, aesthetically. He was short and vast, sun-lamped and pomaded, a man in a buttressed pin-stripe suit with a red carnation withering in the lapel. When they reached her door she rummaged in her purse in search of a key, and took no notice of the fact that his thick lips were nuzzling the nape of her neck. At last, though, finding the key and opening her door, she turned to him cordially: "Bless you, darling—you were sweet to see me home."

"Hey, baby!" he said, for the door was closing in his face.

"Yes, Harry?"

"Harry was the other guy. I'm Sid. Sid Arbuck. You like me."

"I worship you, Mr. Arbuck. But good night, Mr. Arbuck."

Mr. Arbuck stared with disbelief as the door shut firmly. "Hey, baby, let me in, baby. You like me, baby. I'm a liked guy. Didn't I pick up the check, five people, *your* friends, I never seen them before? Don't that give me the right you should like me? You like me, baby."

He tapped on the door gently, then louder; finally he took several steps back, his body hunched and lowering, as though he meant to charge it, crash it down. Instead, he plunged down the stairs, slamming a fist against the wall. Just as he reached the bottom, the door of the girl's apartment opened and she poked out her head.

"Oh, Mr. Arbuck . . ."

He turned back, a smile of relief oiling his face: she'd only been teasing.

"The next time a girl wants a little powder-room change," she called, not teasing at all, "take my advice, darling: *don't* give her twenty cents!"

She kept her promise to Mr. Yunioshi; or I assume she did not ring his bell again, for in the next days she started ringing mine, sometimes at two in the morning, three and four: she had no qualms at what hour she got me out of bed to push the buzzer that released the downstairs door. As I had few friends, and no one who would come around so late, I always knew that it was her. But on the first occasions of its happening, I went to my door, half-expecting bad news, a telegram; and Miss Golightly would call up: "Sorry, darling—I forgot my key."

Of course we'd never met. Though actually, on the stairs, in the street, we often came face-to-face; but she seemed not quite to see me. She was never without dark glasses, she was always well groomed, there was a consequential good taste in the plainness of her clothes, the blues and grays and lack of luster that made her, herself, shine so. One might have thought her a photographer's model, perhaps a young actress, except that it was obvious, judging from her hours, she hadn't time to be either.

Now and then I ran across her outside our neighborhood. Once a visiting relative took me to "21," and there, at a superior table, surrounded by four men, none of them Mr. Arbuck, yet all of them interchangeable with him, was Miss Golightly, idly, publicly combing her hair; and her expression, an unrealized yawn, put, by example, a dampener on the excitement I felt over dining at so swanky a place. Another night, deep in the summer, the heat of my room sent me out into the streets. I walked down Third Avenue to Fifty-first Street, where there was an antique store with an object in its window I admired: a palace of a birdcage, a mosque of minarets and bamboo rooms yearning to be filled with talkative parrots. But the price was three hundred and fifty dollars. On the way home I noticed a cab-driver crowd gathered in front of P. J. Clarke's saloon, apparently attracted there by a happy group of whiskey-eyed Australian army officers baritoning "Waltzing Matilda." As they sang they took turns spin-dancing a girl over the cobbles under the El; and the girl, Miss Golightly, to be sure, floated round in their arms light as a scarf.

But if Miss Golightly remained unconscious of my existence, except as a doorbell convenience, I became, through the summer, rather an authority on hers. I discovered, from observing the trash-basket outside her door, that her regular reading consisted of tabloids and travel folders and astrological charts; that she smoked an esoteric cigarette called Picayunes; survived on cottage cheese and melba toast; that her vari-colored hair was somewhat self-induced. The same source made it evident that she received V-letters by the bale. They were always torn into strips like bookmarks. I used

occasionally to pluck myself a bookmark in passing. *Re* ...
and *rain* and *please write* and *damn* and *goddamn* were ...
recurred most often on these slips; those, and *lonesome* and ...

Also, she had a cat and she played the guitar. On days when the ...
strong, she would wash her hair, and together with the cat, a red ...
striped tom, sit out on the fire escape thumbing a guitar while her hai ...
dried. Whenever I heard the music, I would go stand quietly by my
window. She played very well, and sometimes sang too. Sang in the hoarse,
breaking tones of a boy's adolescent voice. She knew all the show hits, Cole
Porter and Kurt Weill; especially she liked the songs from *Oklahoma!*,
which were new that summer and everywhere. But there were moments
when she played songs that made you wonder where she learned them,
where indeed she came from. Harsh-tender wandering tunes with words
that smacked of pineywoods or prairie. One went: *Don't wanna sleep, Don't
wanna die, Just wanna go a-travelin' through the pastures of the sky;* and this
one seemed to gratify her the most, for often she continued it long after
her hair had dried, after the sun had gone and there were lighted windows
in the dusk.

But our acquaintance did not make headway until September, an evening with the first ripple-chills of autumn running through it. I'd been to
a movie, come home and gone to bed with a bourbon nightcap and the
newest Simenon: so much my idea of comfort that I couldn't understand
a sense of unease that multiplied until I could hear my heart beating. It was
a feeling I'd read about, written about, but never before experienced. The
feeling of being watched. Of someone in the room. Then: an abrupt
rapping at the window, a glimpse of ghostly gray: I spilled the bourbon.
It was some little while before I could bring myself to open the window,
and ask Miss Golightly what she wanted.

"I've got the most terrifying man downstairs," she said, stepping off the
fire escape into the room. "I mean he's sweet when he isn't drunk, but let
him start lapping up the vino, and oh God quel beast! If there's one thing
I loathe, it's men who bite." She loosened a gray flannel robe off her
shoulder to show me evidence of what happens if a man bites. The robe
was all she was wearing. "I'm sorry if I frightened you. But when the beast
got so tiresome I just went out the window. I think he thinks I'm in the
bathroom, not that I give a damn what he thinks, the hell with him, he'll
get tired, he'll go to sleep, my God he should, eight martinis before dinner
and enough wine to wash an elephant. Listen, you can throw me out if you
want to. I've got a gall barging in on you like this. But that fire escape was
damned icy. And you looked so cozy. Like my brother Fred. We used to
sleep four in a bed, and he was the only one that ever let me hug him on
a cold night. By the way, do you mind if I call you Fred?" She'd come
completely into the room now, and she paused there, staring at me. I'd

never seen her before not wearing dark glasses, and it was obvious now that they were prescription lenses, for without them her eyes had an assessing squint, like a jeweler's. They were large eyes, a little blue, a little green, dotted with bits of brown: vari-colored, like her hair; and, like her hair, they gave out a lively warm light. "I suppose you think I'm very brazen. Or *très fou*. Or something."

"Not at all."

She seemed disappointed. "Yes, you do. Everybody does. I don't mind. It's useful."

She sat down on one of the rickety red-velvet chairs, curved her legs underneath her, and glanced round the room, her eyes puckering more pronouncedly. "How can you bear it? It's a chamber of horrors."

"Oh, you get used to anything," I said, annoyed with myself, for actually I was proud of the place.

"I don't. I'll never get used to anything. Anybody that does, they might as well be dead." Her dispraising eyes surveyed the room again. "What do you *do* here all day?"

I motioned toward a table tall with books and paper. "Write things."

"I thought writers were quite old. Of course Saroyan isn't old. I met him at a party, and really he isn't old at all. In fact," she mused, "if he'd give himself a closer shave . . . By the way, is Hemingway old?"

"In his forties, I should think."

"That's not bad. I can't get excited by a man until he's forty-two. I know this idiot girl who keeps telling me I ought to go to a head-shrinker; she says I have a father complex. Which is so much *merde*. I simply *trained* myself to like older men, and it was the smartest thing I ever did. How old is W. Somerset Maugham?"

"I'm not sure. Sixty-something."

"That's not bad. I've never been to bed with a writer. No, wait: do you know Benny Shacklett?" She frowned when I shook my head. "That's funny. He's written an awful lot of radio stuff. But quel rat. Tell me, are you a real writer?"

"It depends on what you mean by real."

"Well, darling, does anyone *buy* what you write?"

"Not yet."

"I'm going to help you," she said. "I can, too. Think of all the people I know who know people. I'm going to help you because you look like my brother Fred. Only smaller. I haven't seen him since I was fourteen, that's when I left home, and he was already six-feet-two. My other brothers were more your size, runts. It was the peanut butter that made Fred so tall. Everybody thought it was dotty, the way he gorged himself on peanut butter; he didn't care about anything in this world except horses and peanut butter. But he wasn't dotty, just sweet and vague and terribly slow;

he'd been in the eighth grade three years when I ran away. Poor Fred. I wonder if the Army's generous with their peanut butter. Which reminds me, I'm starving."

I pointed to a bowl of apples, at the same time asked her how and why she'd left home so young. She looked at me blankly, and rubbed her nose, as though it tickled: a gesture, seeing often repeated, I came to recognize as a signal that one was trespassing. Like many people with a bold fondness for volunteering intimate information, anything that suggested a direct question, a pinning-down, put her on guard. She took a bite of apple, and said: "Tell me something you've written. The story part."

"That's one of the troubles. They're not the kind of stories you *can* tell."

"Too dirty?"

"Maybe I'll let you read one sometime."

"Whiskey and apples go together. Fix me a drink, darling. Then you can read me a story yourself."

Very few authors, especially the unpublished, can resist an invitation to read aloud. I made us both a drink and, settling in a chair opposite, began to read to her, my voice a little shaky with a combination of stage fright and enthusiasm: it was a new story, I'd finished it the day before, and that inevitable sense of shortcoming had not had time to develop. It was about two women who share a house, schoolteachers, one of whom, when the other becomes engaged, spreads with anonymous notes a scandal that prevents the marriage. As I read, each glimpse I stole of Holly made my heart contract. She fidgeted. She picked apart the butts in an ashtray, she mooned over her fingernails, as though longing for a file; worse, when I did seem to have her interest, there was actually a telltale frost over her eyes, as if she were wondering whether to buy a pair of shoes she'd seen in some window.

"Is that the *end?*" she asked, waking up. She floundered for something more to say. "Of course I like dykes themselves. They don't scare me a bit. But stories about dykes bore the bejesus out of me. I just can't put myself in their shoes. Well really, darling," she said, because I was clearly puzzled, "if it's not about a couple of old bull-dykes, what the hell *is* it about?"

But I was in no mood to compound the mistake of having read the story with the further embarrassment of explaining it. The same vanity that had led to such exposure, now forced me to mark her down as an insensitive, mindless show-off.

"Incidentally," she said, "do you happen to *know* any nice lesbians? I'm looking for a roommate. Well, don't laugh. I'm so disorganized, I simply can't afford a maid; and really, dykes are wonderful homemakers, they love to do all the work, you never have to bother about brooms and defrosting and sending out the laundry. I had a roommate in Hollywood, she played in Westerns, they called her the Lone Ranger; but I'll say this for her, she was better than a man around the house. Of course people couldn't help but think I must be a bit of a dyke myself. And of course I am. Everyone is: a bit. So what? That never discouraged a man yet, in fact it seems to goad them on. Look at the Lone Ranger, married twice. Usually dykes only get married once, just for the name. It seems to carry such cachet later on to be called Mrs. Something Another. That's not true!" She was staring at an alarm clock on the table. "It can't be four-thirty!"

The window was turning blue. A sunrise breeze bandied the curtains.

"What is today?"

"Thursday."

"*Thursday.*" She stood up. "My God." she said, and sat down again with a moan. "It's too gruesome."

I was tired enough not to be curious. I lay down on the bed and closed my eyes. Still it was irresistible: "What's gruesome about Thursday?"

"Nothing. Except that I can never remember when it's coming. You see, on Thursdays I have to catch the eight forty-five. They're so particular about visiting hours, so if you're there by ten, that gives you an hour before the poor men eat lunch. Think of it, lunch at eleven. You *can* go at two, and I'd so much rather, but he likes me to come in the morning, he says it sets him up for the rest of the day. I've *got* to stay awake," she said, pinching her cheeks until the roses came, "there isn't time to sleep, I'd look consumptive, I'd sag like a tenement, and that wouldn't be fair: a girl can't go to Sing Sing with a green face."

"I suppose not." The anger I felt at her over my story was ebbing; she absorbed me again.

"All the visitors *do* make an effort to look their best, and it's very tender, it's sweet as hell, the way the women wear their prettiest everything, I mean the old ones and the really poor ones too, they make the dearest effort to look nice and smell nice too, and I love them for it. I love the kids too, especially the colored ones. I mean the kids the wives bring. It should be sad, seeing the kids there, but it isn't, they have ribbons in their hair and lots of shine on their shoes, you'd think there was going to be ice cream; and sometimes that's what it's like in the visitors' room, a party. Anyway it's not like the movies: you know, grim whisperings through a grille. There isn't any grille, just a counter between you and them, and the kids can stand on it to be hugged; all you have to do to kiss somebody is lean across. What I like most, they're so happy to see each other, they've saved up so much to talk about, it isn't possible to be dull, they keep laughing and holding hands. It's different afterwards," she said. "I see them on the train. They sit so quiet watching the river go by." She stretched a strand of hair to the corner of her mouth and nibbled it thoughtfully. "I'm keeping you awake. Go to sleep."

"Please. I'm interested."

"I know you are. That's why I want you to go to sleep. Because if I keep on, I'll tell you about Sally. I'm not sure that would be quite cricket." She chewed her hair silently. "They never *told* me not to tell anyone. In so many words. And it *is* funny. Maybe you could put it in a story with different names and whatnot. Listen, Fred," she said, reaching for another apple, "you've got to cross your heart and kiss your elbow—"

Perhaps contortionists can kiss their elbow; she had to accept an approximation.

"Well," she said, with a mouthful of apple, "you may have read about him in the papers. His name is Sally Tomato, and I speak Yiddish better than he speaks English; but he's a darling old man, terribly pious. He'd look like a monk if it weren't for the gold teeth; he says he prays for me every night. Of course he was never my lover; as far as that goes, I never knew him until he was already in jail. But I adore him now, after all I've been going to see him every Thursday for seven months, and I think I'd go even if he didn't pay me. This one's mushy," she said, and aimed the rest of the apple out the window. "By the way, I *did* know Sally by sight. He used to come to Joe Bell's bar, the one around the corner: never talked to anybody, just stand there, like the kind of man who lives in hotel rooms. But it's funny to remember back and realize how closely he must have been watching me, because right after they sent him up (Joe Bell showed me his picture in the paper. Blackhand. Mafia. All that mumbo jumbo: but they gave him five years) along came this telegram from a lawyer. It said to contact him immediately for information to my advantage."

"You thought somebody had left you a million?"

"Not at all. I figured Bergdorf was trying to collect. But I took the gamble and went to see this lawyer (if he *is* a lawyer, which I doubt, since he doesn't seem to have an office, just an answering service, and he always wants to meet you in Hamburg Heaven: that's because he's fat, he can eat ten hamburgers and two bowls of relish and a whole lemon meringue pie). He asked me how I'd like to cheer up a lonely old man, at the same time pick up a hundred a week. I told him look, darling, you've got the wrong Miss Golightly, I'm not a nurse that does tricks on the side. I wasn't impressed by the honorarium either; you can do as well as that on trips to the powder room: any gent with the slightest chic will give you fifty for the girl's john, and I always ask for cab fare too, that's another fifty. But then he told me his client was Sally Tomato. He said dear old Sally had long admired me *à la distance*, so wouldn't it be a good deed if I went to visit him once a week. Well, I couldn't say no: it was too romantic."

"I don't know. It doesn't sound right."

She smiled. "You think I'm lying?"

"For one thing, they can't simply let *any*one visit a prisoner."

"Oh, they don't. In fact they make quite a boring fuss. I'm supposed to be his niece."

"And it's as simple as that? For an hour's conversation he gives you a hundred dollars?"

"He doesn't, the lawyer does. Mr. O'Shaughnessy mails it to me in cash as soon as I leave the weather report."

"I think you could get into a lot of trouble," I said, and switched off a lamp; there was no need of it now, morning was in the room and pigeons were gargling on the fire escape.

"How?" she said seriously.

"There must be something in the law books about false identity. After all, you're *not* his niece. And what about this weather report?"

She patted a yawn. "But it's nothing. Just messages I leave with the answering service so Mr. O'Shaughnessy will know for sure that I've been up there. Sally tells me what to say, things like, oh, 'there's a hurricane in Cuba' and 'it's snowing in Palermo.' Don't worry, darling," she said, moving to the bed, "I've taken care of myself a long time." The morning light seemed refracted through her: as she pulled the bed covers up to my chin she gleamed like a transparent child; then she lay down beside me. "Do you mind? I only want to rest a moment. So let's don't say another word. Go to sleep."

I pretended to, I made my breathing heavy and regular. Bells in the tower of the next-door church rang the half-hour, the hour. It was six when she put her hand on my arm, a fragile touch careful not to waken. "Poor Fred," she whispered, and it seemed she was speaking to me, but she was not. "Where are you, Fred? Because it's cold. There's snow in the wind." Her cheek came to rest against my shoulder, a warm damp weight.

"Why are you crying?"

She sprang back, sat up. "Oh, for God's sake," she said, starting for the window and the fire escape, "I *hate* snoops."

The next day, Friday, I came home to find outside my door a grand-luxe Charles & Co. basket with her card: *Miss Holiday Golightly, Traveling:* and scribbled on the back in a freakishly awkward, kindergarten hand: *Bless you darling Fred. Please forgive the other night. You were an angel about the whole thing. Mille tendresse—Holly. P.S. I won't bother you again.* I replied, *Please do*, and left this note at her door with what I could afford, a bunch of street-vendor violets. But apparently she'd meant what she said; I neither saw nor heard from her, and I gathered she'd gone so far as to obtain a downstairs key. At any rate she no longer rang my bell. I missed that; and as the days merged I began to feel toward her certain far-fetched resentments, as if I were being neglected by my closest friend. A disquieting loneliness came into my life, but it induced no hunger for friends of longer acquaintance: they seemed now like a salt-free, sugarless diet. By Wednesday thoughts of Holly, of Sing Sing and Sally Tomato, of worlds where men forked over fifty dollars for the powder room, were so constant that I couldn't work. That night I left a message in her mailbox: *Tomorrow is Thursday.* The next morning rewarded me with a second note in the play-pen script: *Bless you for reminding me. Can you stop for a drink tonight 6-ish?*

I waited until ten past six, then made myself delay five minutes more.

A creature answered the door. He smelled of cigars and Knize cologne. His shoes sported elevated heels; without these added inches, one might have taken him for a Little Person. His bald freckled head was dwarf-big: attached to it were a pair of pointed, truly elfin ears. He had Pekingese eyes, unpitying and slightly bulged. Tufts of hair sprouted from his ears, from his nose; his jowls were gray with afternoon beard, and his handshake almost furry.

"Kid's in the shower," he said, motioning a cigar toward a sound of water hissing in another room. The room in which we stood (we were standing because there was nothing to sit on) seemed as though it were being just moved into; you expected to smell wet paint. Suitcases and unpacked crates were the only furniture. The crates served as tables. One supported the mixings of a martini; another a lamp, a Libertyphone, Holly's red cat and a bowl of yellow roses. Bookcases, covering one wall, boasted a half-shelf of literature. I warmed to the room at once, I liked its fly-by-night look.

The man cleared his throat. "You expected?"

He found my nod uncertain. His cold eyes operated on me, made neat, exploratory incisions. "A lot of characters come here, they're not expected. You know the kid long?"

"Not very."

"So you don't know the kid long?"

"I live upstairs."

The answer seemed to explain enough to relax him. "You got the same layout?"

"Much smaller."

He tapped ash on the floor. "This is a dump. This is unbelievable. But the kid don't know how to live even when she's got the dough." His speech had a jerky metallic rhythm, like a teletype. "So," he said, "what do you think: is she or ain't she?"

"Ain't she what?"

"A phony."

"I wouldn't have thought so."

"You're wrong. She is a phony. But on the other hand you're right. She isn't a phony because she's a *real* phony. She believes all this crap she believes. You can't talk her out of it. I've tried with tears running down my cheeks. Benny Polan, respected everywhere, Benny Polan tried. Benny had it on his mind to marry her, she don't go for it, Benny spent maybe thousands sending her to head-shrinkers. Even the famous one, the one can only speak German, boy, did he throw in the towel. You can't talk her out of these"—he made a fist, as though to crush an intangible—"ideas. Try it sometime. Get her to tell you some of the stuff she believes. Mind you," he said, "I like the kid. Everybody does, but there's lots that don't. I do. I sincerely like the kid. I'm sensitive, that's why. You've got to be sensitive to appreciate her: a streak of the poet. But I'll tell you the truth. You can beat your brains out for her, and she'll hand you horseshit on a platter. To give an example—who is she like you see her today? She's strictly a girl you'll read where she ends up at the bottom of a bottle of Seconals. I've seen it happen more times than you've got toes: and those kids, they weren't even nuts. She's nuts."

"But young. And with a great deal of youth ahead of her."

"If you mean future, you're wrong again. Now a couple of years back, out on the Coast, there was a time it could've been different. She had something working for her, she had them interested, she could've really rolled. But when you walk out on a thing like that, you don't walk back. Ask Luise Rainer. And Rainer was a star. Sure, Holly was no star; she never got out of the still department. But that was before *The Story of Dr. Wassell*. Then she could've really rolled. I know, see, 'cause I'm the guy was giving her the push." He pointed his cigar at himself. "O. J. Berman."

He expected recognition, and I didn't mind obliging him, it was all right by me, except I'd never heard of O. J. Berman. It developed that he was a Hollywood actor's agent.

"I'm the first one saw her. Out at Santa Anita. She's hanging around the track every day. I'm interested: professionally. I find out she's some jock's regular, she's living with the shrimp. I get the jock told Drop It if he don't want conversation with the vice boys: see, the kid's fifteen. But stylish: she's okay, she comes across. Even when she's wearing glasses *this* thick; even when she opens her mouth and you don't know if she's a hillbilly or an Okie or what. I still don't. My guess, nobody'll ever know where she came from. She's such a goddamn liar, maybe she don't know herself any more. But it took us a year to smooth out that accent. How we did it finally, we gave her French lessons: after she could imitate French, it wasn't so long she could imitate English. We modeled her along the Margaret Sullavan type, but she could pitch some curves of her own, people were interested, big ones, and to top it all, Benny Polan, a respected guy, Benny wants to marry her. An agent could ask for more? Then wham! *The Story of Dr. Wassell*. You see that picture? Cecil B. De Mille. Gary Cooper. Jesus.

I kill myself, it's all set: they're going to test her for the part of Dr. Wassell's nurse. One of his nurses, anyway. Then wham! The phone rings." He picked a telephone out of the air and held it to his ear. "She says, this is Holly, I say honey, you sound far away, she says I'm in New York, I say what the hell are you doing in New York when it's Sunday and you got the test tomorrow? She says I'm in New York 'cause I've never been to New York. I say get your ass on a plane and get back here, she says I don't want it. I say what's your angle, doll? She says you got to want it to be good and I don't want it, I say well, what the hell do you want, and she says when I find out you'll be the first to know. See what I mean: horseshit on a platter."

The red cat jumped off its crate and rubbed against his leg. He lifted the cat on the toe of his shoe and gave him a toss, which was hateful of him except he seemed not aware of the cat but merely his own irritableness.

"*This* is what she wants?" he said, flinging out his arms. "A lot of characters they aren't expected? Living off tips. Running around with bums. So maybe she could marry Rusty Trawler? You should pin a medal on her for that?"

He waited, glaring.

"Sorry, I don't know him."

"You don't know Rusty Trawler, you can't know much about the kid. Bad deal," he said, his tongue clucking in his huge head. "I was hoping you maybe had influence. Could level with the kid before it's too late."

"But according to you, it already is."

He blew a smoke ring, let it fade before he smiled; the smile altered his face, made something gentle happen. "I could get it rolling again. Like I told you," he said, and now it sounded true, "I sincerely like the kid."

"What scandals are you spreading, O.J.?" Holly splashed into the room, a towel more or less wrapped round her and her wet feet dripping footmarks on the floor.

"Just the usual. That you're nuts."

"Fred knows that already."

"But you don't."

"Light me a cigarette, darling," she said, snatching off a bathing cap and shaking her hair. "I don't mean you, O.J. You're such a slob. You always nigger-lip."

She scooped up the cat and swung him onto her shoulder. He perched there with the balance of a bird, his paws tangled in her hair as if it were knitting yarn; and yet, despite these amiable antics, it was a grim cat with a pirate's cutthroat face; one eye was gluey-blind, the other sparkled with dark deeds.

"O.J. is a slob," she told me, taking the cigarette I'd lighted. "But he does know a terrific lot of phone numbers. What's David O. Selznick's number, O.J.?"

"Lay off."

"It's not a joke, darling. I want you to call him up and tell him what a genius Fred is. He's written barrels of the most marvelous stories. Well, don't blush, Fred: you didn't say you were a genius, I did. Come on, O.J. What are you going to do to make Fred rich?"

"Suppose you let me settle that with Fred."

"Remember," she said, leaving us, "I'm his agent. Another thing: if I holler, come zipper me up. And if anybody knocks, let them in."

A multitude did. Within the next quarter-hour a stag party had taken over the apartment, several of them in uniform. I counted two Naval officers and an Air Force colonel; but they were outnumbered by graying arrivals beyond draft status. Except for a lack of youth, the guests had no common theme, they seemed strangers among strangers; indeed, each face, on entering, had struggled to conceal dismay at seeing others there. It was as if the hostess had distributed her invitations while zigzagging through various bars; which was probably the case. After the initial frowns, however, they mixed without grumbling, especially O. J. Berman, who avidly exploited the new company to avoid discussing my Hollywood future. I was left abandoned by the bookshelves; of the books there, more than half were about horses, the rest baseball. Pretending an interest in *Horseflesh and How to Tell It* gave me sufficiently private opportunity for sizing Holly's friends.

Presently one of these became prominent. He was a middle-aged child that had never shed its baby fat, though some gifted tailor had almost succeeded in camouflaging his plump and spankable bottom. There wasn't a suspicion of bone in his body; his face, a zero filled in with pretty miniature features, had an unused, a virginal quality: it was as if he'd been born, then expanded, his skin remaining unlined as a blown-up balloon, and his mouth, though ready for squalls and tantrums, a spoiled sweet puckering. But it was not appearance that singled him out; preserved infants aren't all that rare. It was, rather, his conduct; for he was behaving as though the party were his: like an energetic octopus, he was shaking martinis, making introductions, manipulating the phonograph. In fairness, most of his activities were dictated by the hostess herself: *Rusty, would you mind; Rusty, would you please.* If he was in love with her, then clearly he had his jealousy in check. A jealous man might have lost control, watching her as she skimmed around the room, carrying her cat in one hand but leaving the other free to straighten a tie or remove lapel lint; the Air Force colonel wore a medal that came in for quite a polish.

The man's name was Rutherfurd ("Rusty") Trawler. In 1908 he'd lost both his parents, his father the victim of an anarchist and his mother of shock, which double misfortune had made Rusty an orphan, a millionaire and a celebrity, all at the age of five. He'd been a stand-by of the Sunday supplements ever since, a consequence that had gathered hurricane momentum when, still a schoolboy, he had caused his godfather-custodian to be arrested on charges of sodomy. After that, marriage and divorce sustained his place in the tabloid-sun. His first wife had taken herself, and her alimony, to a rival of Father's Divine's. The second wife seems unaccounted for, but the third had sued him in New York State with a full satchel of the kind of testimony that entails. He himself divorced the last Mrs. Trawler, his principal complaint stating that she'd started a mutiny aboard his yacht, said mutiny resulting in his being deposited on the Dry Tortugas. Though he'd been a bachelor since, apparently before the war he'd proposed to Unity Mitford, at least he was supposed to have sent her a cable offering to marry her if Hitler didn't. This was said to be the reason Winchell always referred to him as a Nazi; that, and the fact that he attended rallies in Yorkville.

I was not told these things. I read them in *The Baseball Guide,* another selection off Holly's shelf which she seemed to use for a scrapbook. Tucked between the pages were Sunday features, together with scissored snippings from gossip columns. *Rusty Trawler and Holly Golightly two-on-the-aisle at "One Touch of Venus" preem.* Holly came up from behind, and caught me reading: *Miss Holiday Golightly, of the Boston Golightlys, making every day a holiday for the 24-karat Rusty Trawler.*

"Admiring my publicity, or are you just a baseball fan?" she said, adjusting her dark glasses as she glanced over my shoulder.

I said, "What was this week's weather report?"

She winked at me, but it was humorless: a wink of warning. "I'm all for horses, but I loathe baseball," she said, and the sub-message in her voice was saying she wished me to forget she'd ever mentioned Sally Tomato. "I hate the sound of it on a radio, but I have to listen, it's part of my research. There're so few things men can talk about. If a man doesn't like baseball, then he must like horses, and if he doesn't like either of them, well, I'm in trouble anyway: he don't like girls. And how are you making out with O.J.?"

"We've separated by mutual agreement."

"He's an opportunity, believe me."

"I do believe you. But what have I to offer that would strike him as an opportunity?"

She persisted. "Go over there and make him think he isn't funny-looking. He really can help you, Fred."

"I understand you weren't too appreciative." She seemed puzzled until I said: *"The Story of Doctor Wassell."*

"He's still harping?" she said, and cast across the room an affectionate look at Berman. "But he's got a point, I *should* feel guilty. Not because they would have given me the part or because I would have been good: they wouldn't and I wouldn't. If I do feel guilty, I guess it's because I let him go on dreaming when I wasn't dreaming a bit. I was just vamping for time to make a few self-improvements: I knew damn well I'd never be a movie star. It's too hard; and if you're intelligent, it's too embarrassing. My complexes aren't inferior enough: being a movie star and having a big fat ego are supposed to go hand-in-hand; actually, it's essential not to have any ego at all. I don't mean I'd mind being rich and famous. That's very much on my schedule, and someday I'll try to get around it; but if it happens, I'd like to have my ego tagging along. I want to still be me when I wake up one fine morning and have breakfast at Tiffany's. You need a glass," she said, noticing my empty hands. "Rusty! Will you bring my friend a drink?"

She was still hugging the cat. "Poor slob," she said, tickling his head, "poor slob without a name. It's a little inconvenient, his not having a name. But I haven't any right to give him one: he'll have to wait until he *belongs* to somebody. We just sort of took up by the river one day, we don't belong to each other: he's an independent, and so am I. I don't want to own anything until I know I've found the place where me and things belong together. I'm not quite sure where that is just yet. But I know what it's like." She smiled, and let the cat drop to the floor. "It's like Tiffany's," she said. "Not that I give a hoot about jewelry. Diamonds, yes. But it's tacky to wear diamonds before you're forty; and even that's risky. They only look right on the really old girls. Maria Ouspenskaya. Wrinkles and bones, white hair and diamonds: I can't wait. But that's not why I'm mad about Tiffany's. Listen. You know those days when you've got the mean reds?"

"Same as the blues?"

"No," she said slowly. "No, the blues are because you're getting fat or maybe it's been raining too long. You're sad, that's all. But the mean reds are horrible. You're afraid and you sweat like hell, but you don't know what you're afraid of. Except something bad is going to happen, only you don't know what it is. You've had that feeling?"

"Quite often. Some people call it *angst.* "

"All right. *Angst.* But what do you do about it?"

"Well, a drink helps."

"I've tried that. I've tried aspirin, too. Rusty thinks I should smoke marijuana, and I did for a while, but it only makes me giggle. What I've found does the most good is just to get into a taxi and go to Tiffany's. It calms me down right away, the quietness and the proud look of it; nothing very bad could happen to you there, not with those kind men in their nice suits, and that lovely smell of silver and alligator wallets. If I could find a real-life place that made me feel like Tiffany's, then I'd buy some furniture

and give the cat a name. I've thought maybe after the war, Fred and I—"
She pushed up her dark glasses, and her eyes, the differing colors of them,
the grays and wisps of blue and green, had taken on a far-seeing sharpness.
"I went to Mexico once. It's wonderful country for raising horses. I saw
one place near the sea. Fred's good with horses."

Rusty Trawler came carrying a martini; he handed it over without
looking at me. "I'm hungry," he announced, and his voice, retarded as the
rest of him, produced an unnerving brat-whine that seemed to blame
Holly. "It's seven-thirty, and I'm hungry. You know what the doctor
said."

"Yes, Rusty. I know what the doctor said."

"Well, then break it up. Let's go."

"I want you to behave, Rusty." She spoke softly, but there was a governess threat of punishment in her tone that caused an odd flush of pleasure,
of gratitude, to pink his face.

"You don't love me," he complained, as though they were alone.

"Nobody loves naughtiness."

Obviously she'd said what he wanted to hear; it appeared to both excite
and relax him. Still he continued, as though it were a ritual: "Do you love
me?"

She patted him. "Tend to your chores, Rusty. And when I'm ready,
we'll go eat wherever you want."

"Chinatown?"

"But that doesn't mean sweet and sour spareribs. You know what the
doctor said."

As he returned to his duties with a satisfied waddle, I couldn't resist
reminding her that she hadn't answered his question. "*Do* you love him?"

"I told you: you can make yourself love anybody. Besides, he had a
stinking childhood."

"If it was so stinking, why does he cling to it?"

"Use your head. Can't you see it's just that Rusty feels safer in diapers
than he would in a skirt? Which is really the choice, only he's awfully
touchy about it. He tried to stab me with a butter knife because I told him
to grow up and face the issue, settle down and play house with a nice
fatherly truck driver. Meantime, I've got him on my hands; which is okay,
he's harmless, he thinks girls are dolls literally."

"Thank God."

"Well, if it were true of most men, I'd hardly be thanking God."

"I meant thank God you're not going to marry Mr. Trawler."

She lifted an eyebrow. "By the way, I'm not pretending I don't know
he's rich. Even land in Mexico costs something. Now," she said, motioning
me forward, "let's get hold of O.J."

I held back while my mind worked to win a postponement. Then I remembered: "Why *Traveling?*"

"On my card?" she said, disconcerted. "You think it's funny?"

"Not funny. Just provocative."

She shrugged. "After all, how do I know where I'll be living tomorrow? So I told them to put *Traveling*. Anyway, it was a waste of money, ordering those cards. Except I felt I owed it to them to buy some little *some* thing. They're from Tiffany's." She reached for my martini, I hadn't touched it; she drained it in two swallows, and took my hand. "Quit stalling. You're going to make friends with O.J."

An occurrence at the door intervened. It was a young woman, and she entered like a wind-rush, a squall of scarves and jangling gold. "H-H-Holly," she said, wagging a finger as she advanced, "you miserable h-h-hoarder. Hogging all these simply r-r-riveting m-m-men!"

She was well over six feet, taller than most men there. They straightened their spines, sucked in their stomachs; there was a general contest to match her swaying height.

Holly said, "What are you doing here?" and her lips were taut as drawn string.

"Why, n-n-nothing, sugar. I've been upstairs working with Yunioshi. Christmas stuff for the *Ba-ba-zaar*. But you sound vexed, sugar?" She scattered a roundabout smile. "You b-b-boys not vexed at me for butting in on your p-p-party?"

Rusty Trawler tittered. He squeezed her arm, as though to admire her muscle, and asked her if she could use a drink.

"I surely could," she said. "Make mine bourbon."

Holly told her, "There *isn't* any." Whereupon the Air Force colonel suggested he run out for a bottle.

"Oh, I declare, don't let's have a f-f-fuss. I'm happy with ammonia. Holly, honey," she said, slightly shoving her, "don't you bother about me. I can introduce myself." She stooped toward O. J. Berman, who, like many short men in the presence of tall women, had an aspiring mist in his eye. "I'm Mag W-w-wildwood, from Wild-w-w-wood, Arkansas. That's hill country."

It seemed a dance, Berman performing some fancy footwork to prevent his rivals cutting in. He lost her to a quadrille of partners who gobbled up her stammered jokes like popcorn tossed to pigeons. It was a comprehensible success. She was a triumph over ugliness, so often more beguiling than real beauty, if only because it contains paradox. In this case, as opposed to the scrupulous method of plain good taste and scientific grooming, the trick had been worked by exaggerating defects; she'd made them ornamental by admitting them boldly. Heels that emphasized her height, so steep her ankles trembled; a flat tight bodice that indicated she could go to a beach in bathing trunks; hair that was pulled straight back, accentuating the spareness, the starvation of her fashion-model face. Even the stutter, certainly genuine but still a bit laid on, had been turned to advantage. It was the master stroke, that stutter; for it contrived to make her banalities sound somehow original, and secondly, despite her tallness, her assurance, it served to inspire in male listeners a protective feeling. To illustrate: Berman had to be pounded on the back because she said, "Who can tell me w-w-where is the j-j-john?"; then, completing the cycle, he offered an arm to guide her himself.

"That," said Holly, "won't be necessary. She's been here before. She knows where it is." She was emptying ashtrays, and after Mag Wildwood had left the room, she emptied another, then said, sighed rather: "It's really very sad." She paused long enough to calculate the number of inquiring expressions; it was sufficient. "And so mysterious. You'd think it would show more. But heaven knows, she *looks* healthy. So, well, *clean.* That's the extraordinary part. Wouldn't you," she asked with concern, but of no one in particular, "wouldn't you say she *looked* clean?"

Someone coughed, several swallowed. A Naval officer, who had been holding Mag Wildwood's drink, put it down.

"But then," said Holly, "I hear so many of these Southern girls have the same trouble." She shuddered delicately, and went to the kitchen for more ice.

Mag Wildwood couldn't understand it, the abrupt absence of warmth on her return; the conversations she began behaved like green logs, they fumed but would not fire. More unforgivably, people were leaving without taking her telephone number. The Air Force colonel decamped while her back was turned, and this was the straw too much: he'd asked her to dinner. Suddenly she was blind. And since gin to artifice bears the same relation as tears to mascara, her attractions at once dissembled. She took it out on everyone. She called her hostess a Hollywood degenerate. She invited a man in his fifties to fight. She told Berman, Hitler was right. She exhilarated Rusty Trawler by stiff-arming him into a corner. "You know what's going to happen to you?" she said, with no hint of a stutter. "I'm going to march you over to the zoo and feed you to the yak." He looked altogether willing, but she disappointed him by sliding to the floor, where she sat humming.

"You're a bore. Get up from there," Holly said, stretching on a pair of gloves. The remnants of the party were waiting at the door, and when the bore didn't budge Holly cast me an apologetic glance. "Be an angel, would you, Fred? Put her in a taxi. She lives at the Winslow."

"Don't. Live Barbizon. Regent 4-5700. Ask for Mag Wildwood."

"You *are* an angel, Fred."

They were gone. The prospect of steering an Amazon into a taxi obliterated whatever resentment I felt. But she solved the problem herself. Rising on her own steam, she stared down at me with a lurching loftiness. She said, "Let's go Stork. Catch lucky balloon," and fell full-length like an axed oak. My first thought was to run for a doctor. But examination proved her pulse fine and her breathing regular. She was simply asleep. After finding a pillow for her head, I left her to enjoy it.

The following afternoon I collided with Holly on the stairs. "*You,*" she said, hurrying past with a package from the druggist. "There she is, on the verge of pneumonia. A hang-over out to here. And the mean reds on top of it." I gathered from this that Mag Wildwood was still in the apartment, but she gave me no chance to explore her surprising sympathy. Over the weekend, mystery deepened. First, there was the Latin who came to my door: mistakenly, for he was inquiring after Miss Wildwood. It took a while to correct his error, our accents seemed mutually incoherent, but by the time we had I was charmed. He'd been put together with care, his brown head and bullfighter's figure had an exactness, a perfection, like an apple, an orange, something nature has made just right. Added to this, as decoration, were an English suit and a brisk cologne and, what is still more un-Latin, a bashful manner. The second event of the day involved him again. It was toward evening, and I saw him on my way out to dinner. He was arriving in a taxi; the driver helped him totter into the house with a load of suitcases. That gave me something to chew on: by Sunday my jaws were quite tired.

Then the picture became both darker and clearer.

Sunday was an Indian summer day, the sun was strong, my window was open, and I heard voices on the fire escape. Holly and Mag were sprawled there on a blanket, the cat between them. Their hair, newly washed, hung lankly. They were busy, Holly varnishing her toenails, Mag knitting on a sweater. Mag was speaking.

"If you ask me, I think you're l-l-lucky. At least there's one thing you can say for Rusty. He's an American."

"Bully for him."

"*Sugar.* There's a war on."

"And when it's over, you've seen the last of me, boy."

"I don't feel that way. I'm p-p-proud of my country. The men in my family were great soldiers. There's a statue of Papadaddy Wildwood smack in the center of Wildwood."

"Fred's a soldier," said Holly. "But I doubt if he'll ever be a statue. Could be. They say the more stupid you are the braver. He's pretty stupid."

"Fred's that boy upstairs? I didn't realize he was a soldier. But he *does* look stupid."

"Yearning. Not stupid. He wants awfully to be on the inside staring out: anybody with their nose pressed against a glass is liable to look stupid. Anyhow, he's a different Fred. Fred's my brother."

"You call your own f-f-flesh and b-b-blood stupid?"

"If he is, he is."

"Well, it's poor taste to say so. A boy that's fighting for you and me and all of us."

"What is this: a bond rally?"

"I just want you to know where I stand. I appreciate a joke, but underneath I'm a s-s-serious person. Proud to be an American. That's why I'm sorry about José." She put down her knitting needles. "You *do* think he's terribly good-looking, don't you?" Holly said Hmn, and swiped the cat's whiskers with her lacquer brush. "If only I could get used to the idea of m-m-marrying a Brazilian. And *being* a B-b-brazilian myself. It's such a canyon to cross. Six thousand miles, and not knowing the language—"

"Go to Berlitz."

"Why on earth would they be teaching P-p-portuguese? It isn't as though anyone spoke it. No, my only chance is to try and make José forget politics and become an American. It's such a useless thing for a man to want to be: the p-p-president of *Brazil*." She sighed and picked up her knitting. "I must be madly in love. You saw us together. Do you think I'm madly in love?"

"Well. Does he bite?"

Mag dropped a stitch. "Bite?"

"You. In bed."

"Why, no. *Should* he?" Then she added, censoriously: "But he does laugh."

"Good. That's the right spirit. I like a man who sees the humor; most of them, they're all pant and puff."

Mag withdrew her complaint; she accepted the comment as flattery reflecting on herself. "Yes. I suppose."

"Okay. He doesn't bite. He laughs. What else?"

Mag counted up her dropped stitch and began again, knit, purl, purl. "I said—"

"I heard you. And it isn't that I don't want to tell you. But it's so difficult to remember. I don't d-d-dwell on these things. The way you seem to. They go out of my head like a dream. I'm sure that's the n-n-normal attitude."

"It may be normal, darling; but I'd rather be natural." Holly paused in the process of reddening the rest of the cat's whiskers. "Listen. If you can't remember, try leaving the lights on."

"Please understand me, Holly. I'm a very-very-very *conventional* person."

"Oh, balls. What's wrong with a decent look at a guy you like? Men are beautiful, a lot of them are, José is, and if you don't even want to *look* at him, well, I'd say he's getting a pretty cold plate of macaroni."

"L-l-lower your voice."

"You can't possibly be in love with him. Now. Does that answer your question?"

"No. Because I'm not a cold plate of m-m-macaroni. I'm a warm-hearted person. It's the basis of my character."

"Okay. You've got a warm heart. But if I were a man on my way to bed, I'd rather take along a hot-water bottle. It's more tangible."

"You won't hear any squawks out of José," she said complacently, her needles flashing in the sunlight. "What's more, I *am* in love with him. Do you realize I've knitted ten pairs of Argyles in less than three months? And this is the second sweater." She stretched the sweater and tossed it aside. "What's the point, though? Sweaters in Brazil. I ought to be making s-s-sun helmets."

Holly lay back and yawned. "It must be winter sometime."

"It *rains,* that I know. Heat. Rain. J-j-jungles."

"Heat. Jungles. Actually, I'd like that."

"Better you than me."

"Yes," said Holly, with a sleepiness that was not sleepy. "Better me than you."

On Monday, when I went down for the morning mail, the card on Holly's box had been altered, a name added: Miss Golightly and Miss Wildwood were now traveling together. This might have held my interest longer except for a letter in my own mailbox. It was from a small university review to whom I'd sent a story. They liked it; and, though I must understand they could not afford to pay, they intended to publish. Publish: that meant *print*. Dizzy with excitement is no mere phrase. I had to tell someone: and, taking the stairs two at a time, I pounded on Holly's door.

I didn't trust my voice to tell the news; as soon as she came to the door, her eyes squinty with sleep, I thrust the letter at her. It seemed as though she'd had time to read sixty pages before she handed it back. "I wouldn't let them do it, not if they don't pay you," she said, yawning. Perhaps my face explained she'd misconstrued, that I'd not wanted advice but congratulations: her mouth shifted from a yawn into a smile. "Oh, I see. It's wonderful. Well, come in," she said. "We'll make a pot of coffee and celebrate. No. I'll get dressed and take you to lunch."

Her bedroom was consistent with her parlor: it perpetuated the same camping-out atmosphere; crates and suitcases, everything packed and ready to go, like the belongings of a criminal who feels the law not far behind. In the parlor there was no conventional furniture, but the bedroom had the bed itself, a double one at that, and quite flashy: blond wood, tufted satin.

She left the door of the bathroom open, and conversed from there; between the flushing and the brushing, most of what she said was unintelligible, but the gist of it was: she *supposed* I knew Mag Wildwood had moved in, and wasn't that *convenient?* because if you're going to *have* a roommate, and she *isn't* a dyke, then the next best thing is a *perfect* fool, which Mag *was*, because then you can dump the lease on them *and* send them out for the laundry.

One could see that Holly had a laundry problem; the room was strewn, like a girl's gymnasium.

"—and you know, she's quite a successful model: isn't that *fan*tastic? But a good thing," she said, hobbling out of the bathroom as she adjusted a garter. "It ought to keep her out of my hair most of the day. And there shouldn't be too much trouble on the man front. She's engaged. Nice guy, too. Though there's a tiny difference in height: I'd say a foot, her favor. Where the hell—" She was on her knees poking under the bed. After she'd found what she was looking for, a pair of lizard shoes, she had to search for a blouse, a belt, and it was a subject to ponder, how, from such wreckage, she evolved the eventual effect: pampered, calmly immaculate, as though she'd been attended by Cleopatra's maids. She said, "Listen," and cupped her hand under my chin, "I'm glad about the story. Really I am."

That Monday in October, 1943. A beautiful day with the buoyancy of a bird. To start, we had Manhattans at Joe Bell's; and, when he heard of my good luck, champagne cocktails on the house. Later, we wandered toward Fifth Avenue, where there was a parade. The flags in the wind, the thump of military bands and military feet, seemed to have nothing to do with war, but to be, rather, a fanfare arranged in my personal honor.

We ate lunch at the cafeteria in the park. Afterwards, avoiding the zoo (Holly said she couldn't bear to see anything in a cage), we giggled, ran, sang along the paths toward the old wooden boathouse, now gone. Leaves floated on the lake; on the shore, a park-man was fanning a bonfire of them, and the smoke, rising like Indian signals, was the only smudge on the quivering air. Aprils have never meant much to me, autumns seem that season of beginning, spring; which is how I felt sitting with Holly on the railings of the boathouse porch. I thought of the future, and spoke of the past. Because Holly wanted to know about my childhood. She talked of her own, too; but it was elusive, nameless, placeless, an impressionistic recital, though the impression received was contrary to what one expected, for she gave an almost voluptuous account of swimming and summer,

Christmas trees, pretty cousins and parties: in short, happy in a way that she was not, and never, certainly, the background of a child who had run away.

Or, I asked, wasn't it true that she'd been out on her own since she was fourteen? She rubbed her nose. "That's true. The other isn't. But really, darling, you made such a tragedy out of *your* childhood I didn't feel I should compete."

She hopped off the railing. "Anyway, it reminds me: I ought to send Fred some peanut butter." The rest of the afternoon we were east and west worming out of reluctant grocers cans of peanut butter, a wartime scarcity; dark came before we'd rounded up a half-dozen jars, the last at a delicatessen on Third Avenue. It was near the antique shop with the palace of a birdcage in its window, so I took her there to see it, and she enjoyed the point, its fantasy: "But still, it's a cage."

Passing a Woolworth's, she gripped my arm: "Let's steal something," she said, pulling me into the store, where at once there seemed a pressure of eyes, as though we were already under suspicion. "Come on. Don't be chicken." She scouted a counter piled with paper pumpkins and Halloween masks. The saleslady was occupied with a group of nuns who were trying on masks. Holly picked up a mask and slipped it over her face; she chose another and put it on mine; then she took my hand and we walked away. It was as simple as that. Outside, we ran a few blocks, I think to make it more dramatic; but also because, as I'd discovered, successful theft exhilarates. I wondered if she'd often stolen. "I used to," she said. "I mean I had to. If I wanted anything. But I still do it every now and then, sort of to keep my hand in."

We wore the masks all the way home.

I have a memory of spending many hither and yonning days with Holly; and it's true, we did at odd moments see a great deal of each other; but on the whole, the memory is false. Because toward the end of the month I found a job: what is there to add? The less the better, except to say it was necessary and lasted from nine to five. Which made our hours, Holly's and mine, extremely different.

Unless it was Thursday, her Sing Sing day, or unless she'd gone horseback riding in the park, as she did occasionally, Holly was hardly up when I came home. Sometimes, stopping there, I shared her wake-up coffee while she dressed for the evening. She was forever on her way out, not always with Rusty Trawler, but usually, and usually, too, they were joined by Mag Wildwood and the handsome Brazilian, whose name was José Ybarra-Jaegar: his mother was German. As a quartet, they struck an unmusical note, primarily the fault of Ybarra-Jaegar, who seemed as out of place in their company as a violin in a jazz band. He was intelligent, he was presentable, he appeared to have a serious link with his work, which was obscurely governmental, vaguely important, and took him to Washington several days a week. How, then, could he survive night after night in La Rue, El Morocco, listening to the Wildwood ch-ch-chatter and staring into Rusty's raw baby-buttocks face? Perhaps, like most of us in a foreign country, he was incapable of placing people, selecting a frame for their picture, as he would at home; therefore all Americans had to be judged in a pretty equal light, and on this basis his companions appeared to be tolerable examples of local color and national character. That would explain much; Holly's determination explains the rest.

Late one afternoon, while waiting for a Fifth Avenue bus, I noticed a taxi stop across the street to let out a girl who ran up the steps of the Forty-second Street public library. She was through the doors before I recognized her, which was pardonable, for Holly and libraries were not an easy association to make. I let curiosity guide me between the lions, debating on the way whether I should admit following her or pretend coincidence. In the end I did neither, but concealed myself some tables away from her in the general reading room, where she sat behind her dark glasses and a fortress of literature she'd gathered at the desk. She sped from one book to the next, intermittently lingering on a page, always with a frown, as if it were printed upside down. She had a pencil poised above paper—nothing seemed to catch her fancy, still now and then, as though for the hell of it, she made laborious scribblings. Watching her, I remembered a girl I'd known in school, a grind, Mildred Grossman. Mildred: with her moist hair and greasy spectacles, her stained fingers that dissected frogs and carried coffee to picket lines, her flat eyes that only turned toward the stars to estimate their chemical tonnage. Earth and air could not be more opposite than Mildred and Holly, yet in my head they acquired a Siamese twinship, and the thread of thought that had sewn them together ran like this: the average personality reshapes frequently, every few years even our bodies undergo a complete overhaul—desirable or not, it is a natural thing that we should change. All right, here were two people who never would. That is what Mildred Grossman had in common with Holly Golightly. They would never change because they'd been given their character too soon; which, like sudden riches, leads to a lack of proportion: the one had splurged herself into a top-heavy realist, the other a lopsided romantic. I imagined them in a restaurant of the future, Mildred still studying the menu for its nutritional values, Holly still gluttonous for everything on it. It would never be different. They would walk through life and out of it with the same determined step that took small notice of those cliffs at the left. Such profound observations made me forget where I was; I came to, startled to find myself in the gloom of the library, and surprised all over again to see Holly there. It was after seven, she was freshening her lipstick and perking up her appearance from what she deemed correct for a library to what, by adding a bit of scarf, some earrings, she considered suitable for the Colony. When she'd left, I wandered over to the table where her books remained; they were what I had wanted to see. *South by Thunderbird. Byways of Brazil. The Political Mind of Latin America.* And so forth.

On Christmas Eve she and Mag gave a party. Holly asked me to come early and help trim the tree. I'm still not sure how they maneuvered that tree into the apartment. The top branches were crushed against the ceiling, the lower ones spread wall-to-wall; altogether it was not unlike the yuletide giant we see in Rockefeller Plaza. Moreover, it would have taken a Rockefeller to decorate it, for it soaked up baubles and tinsel like melting snow. Holly suggested she run out to Woolworth's and steal some balloons; she did: and they turned the tree into a fairly good show. We made a toast to our work, and Holly said: "Look in the bedroom. There's a present for you."

I had one for her, too: a small package in my pocket that felt even smaller when I saw, square on the bed and wrapped with a red ribbon, the beautiful birdcage.

"But, Holly! It's dreadful!"

"I couldn't agree more; but I thought you wanted it."

"The money! Three hundred and fifty dollars!"

She shrugged. "A few extra trips to the powder room. Promise me, though. Promise you'll never put a living thing in it."

I started to kiss her, but she held out her hand. "Gimme," she said, tapping the bulge in my pocket.

"I'm afraid it isn't much," and it wasn't: a St. Christopher's medal. But at least it came from Tiffany's.

Holly was not a girl who could keep anything, and surely by now she has lost that medal, left it in a suitcase or some hotel drawer. But the birdcage is still mine. I've lugged it to New Orleans, Nantucket, all over Europe, Morocco, the West Indies. Yet I seldom remember that it was Holly who gave it to me, because at one point I chose to forget: we had a big falling-out, and among the objects rotating in the eye of our hurricane were the birdcage and O. J. Berman and my story, a copy of which I'd given Holly when it appeared in the university review.

Sometime in February, Holly had gone on a winter trip with Rusty, Mag and José Ybarra-Jaegar. Our altercation happened soon after she returned. She was brown as iodine, her hair was sun-bleached to a ghost-color, she'd had a wonderful time: "Well, first of all we were in Key West, and Rusty got mad at some sailors, or vice versa, *any*way he'll have to wear a spine

256

brace the rest of his life. Dearest Mag ended up in the hospital, too. First-degree sunburn. Disgusting: all blisters and citronella. We couldn't stand the smell of her. So José and I left them in the hospital and went to Havana. He says wait till I see Rio; but as far as I'm concerned Havana can take my money right now. We had an irresistible guide, most of him Negro and the rest of him Chinese, and while I don't go much for one or the other, the combination was fairly riveting: so I let him play kneesie under the table, because frankly I didn't find him at all banal; but then one night he took us to a blue movie, and what do you suppose? There *he* was *on* the screen. Of course when we got back to Key West, Mag was positive I'd spent the whole time sleeping with José. So was Rusty: but he doesn't care about that, he simply wants to hear the details. Actually, things were pretty tense until I had a heart-to-heart with Mag."

We were in the front room, where, though it was now nearly March, the enormous Christmas tree, turned brown and scentless, its balloons shriveled as an old cow's dugs, still occupied most of the space. A recognizable piece of furniture had been added to the room: an army cot; and Holly, trying to preserve her tropic look, was sprawled on it under a sun lamp.

"And you convinced her?"

"That I hadn't slept with José? God, yes. I simply told—but you know: made it sound like an *ago*nized confession—simply told her I was a dyke."

"She couldn't have believed that."

"The hell she didn't. Why do you think she went out and bought this army cot? Leave it to me: I'm always top banana in the shock department. Be a darling, darling, rub some oil on my back." While I was performing this service, she said: "O. J. Berman's in town, and listen, I gave him your story in the magazine. He was quite impressed. He thinks maybe you're worth helping. But he says you're on the wrong track. Negroes and children: who cares?"

"Not Mr. Berman, I gather."

"Well, I agree with him. I read that story twice. Brats and niggers. Trembling leaves. *Description*. It doesn't *mean* anything."

My hand, smoothing oil on her skin, seemed to have a temper of its own: it yearned to raise itself and come down on her buttocks. "Give me an example," I said quietly. "Of something that means something. In your opinion."

"*Wuthering Heights*," she said, without hesitation.

The urge in my hand was growing beyond control. "But that's unreasonable. You're talking about a work of genius."

"It was, wasn't it? *My wild sweet Cathy*. God, I cried buckets. I saw it ten times."

I said, "Oh" with recognizable relief, "oh" with a shameful, rising inflection, "the *movie*."

Her muscles hardened, the touch of her was like stone warmed by the sun. "Everybody has to feel superior to somebody," she said. "But it's customary to present a little proof before you take the privilege."

"I don't compare myself to you. Or Berman. Therefore I can't feel superior. We want different things."

"Don't you want to make money?"

"I haven't planned that far."

"That's how your stories sound. As though you'd written them without knowing the end. Well, I'll tell you: you'd better make money. You have an expensive imagination. Not many people are going to buy you bird-cages."

"Sorry."

"You will be if you hit me. You wanted to a minute ago: I could feel it in your hand; and you want to now."

I did, terribly; my hand, my heart was shaking as I recapped the bottle of oil. "Oh no, I wouldn't regret that. I'm only sorry you wasted your money on me: Rusty Trawler is too hard a way of earning it."

She sat up on the army cot, her face, her naked breasts coldly blue in the sun-lamp light. "It should take you about four seconds to walk from here to the door. I'll give you two."

I went straight upstairs, got the birdcage, took it down and left it in front of her door. That settled that. Or so I imagined until the next morning when, as I was leaving for work, I saw the cage perched on a sidewalk ashcan waiting for the garbage collector. Rather sheepishly, I rescued it and carried it back to my room, a capitulation that did not lessen my resolve to put Holly Golightly absolutely out of my life. She was, I decided, "a crude exhibitionist," "a time waster," "an utter fake": someone never to be spoken to again.

And I didn't. Not for a long while. We passed each other on the stairs with lowered eyes. If she walked into Joe Bell's, I walked out. At one point, Madame Sapphia Spanella, the coloratura and roller-skating enthusiast who lived on the first floor, circulated a petition among the brownstone's other tenants asking them to join her in having Miss Golightly evicted: she was, said Madame Spanella, "morally objectionable" and the "perpetrator of all-night gatherings that endanger the safety and sanity of her neighbors." Though I refused to sign, secretly I felt Madame Spanella had cause to complain. But her petition failed, and as April approached May, the open-windowed, warm spring nights were lurid with the party sounds, the loud-playing phonograph and martini laughter that emanated from Apt. 2.

It was no novelty to encounter suspicious specimens among Holly's callers, quite the contrary; but one day late that spring, while passing through the brownstone's vestibule, I noticed a *very* provocative man examining her mailbox. A person in his early fifties with a hard, weathered face, gray forlorn eyes. He wore an old sweat-stained gray hat, and his cheap summer suit, a pale blue, hung too loosely on his lanky frame; his shoes were brown and brand-new. He seemed to have no intention of ringing Holly's bell. Slowly, as though he were reading Braille, he kept rubbing a finger across the embossed lettering of her name.

That evening, on my way to supper, I saw the man again. He was standing across the street, leaning against a tree and staring up at Holly's windows. Sinister speculations rushed through my head. Was he a detective? Or some underworld agent connected with her Sing Sing friend, Sally Tomato? The situation revived my tenderer feelings for Holly; it was only fair to interrupt our feud long enough to warn her that she was being watched. As I walked to the corner, heading east toward the Hamburg Heaven at Seventy-ninth and Madison, I could feel the man's attention focused on me. Presently, without turning my head, I knew that he was following me. Because I could hear him whistling. Not any ordinary tune, but the plaintive, prairie melody Holly sometimes played on her guitar: *Don't wanna sleep, Don't wanna die, Just wanna go a-travelin' through the pastures of the sky.* The whistling continued across Park Avenue and up Madison. Once, while waiting for a traffic light to change, I watched him out of the corner of my eye as he stooped to pet a sleazy Pomeranian. "That's a fine animal you got there," he told the owner in a hoarse, countrified drawl.

Hamburg Heaven was empty. Nevertheless, he took a seat right beside me at the long counter. He smelled of tobacco and sweat. He ordered a cup of coffee, but when it came he didn't touch it. Instead, he chewed on a toothpick and studied me in the wall mirror facing us.

"Excuse me," I said, speaking to him via the mirror, "but what do you want?"

The question didn't embarrass him; he seemed relieved to have had it asked. "Son," he said, "I need a friend."

He brought out a wallet. It was as worn as his leathery hands, almost falling to pieces; and so was the brittle, cracked, blurred snapshot he handed me. There were seven people in the picture, all grouped together on the sagging porch of a stark wooden house, and all children, except for the man himself, who had his arm around the waist of a plump blond little girl with a hand shading her eyes against the sun.

"That's me," he said, pointing at himself. "That's her . . ." he tapped the plump girl. "And this one over here," he added, indicating a tow-headed bean-pole, "that's her brother, Fred."

I looked at "her" again: and yes, now I could see it, an embryonic resemblance to Holly in the squinting, fat-cheeked child. At the same moment, I realized who the man must be.

"You're Holly's *father.*"

He blinked, he frowned. "Her name's not Holly. She was a Lulamae Barnes. Was," he said, shifting the toothpick in his mouth, "till she married me. I'm her husband. Doc Golightly. I'm a horse doctor, animal man. Do some farming, too. Near Tulip, Texas. Son, why are you laughin'?"

It wasn't real laughter: it was nerves. I took a swallow of water and choked; he pounded me on the back. "This here's no humorous matter, son. I'm a tired man. I've been five years lookin' for my woman. Soon as I got that letter from Fred, saying where she was, I bought myself a ticket on the Greyhound. Lulamae belongs home with her husband and her churren."

"Children?"

"*Them's* her churren," he said, almost shouted. He meant the four other young faces in the picture, two barefooted girls and a pair of overalled boys. Well, of course: the man was deranged. "But Holly can't be the mother of those children. They're older than she is. Bigger."

"Now, son," he said in a reasoning voice, "I didn't claim they was her natural-born churren. Their own precious mother, precious woman, Jesus rest her soul, she passed away July 4th, Independence Day, 1936. The year of the drought. When I married Lulamae, that was in December, 1938, she was going on fourteen. Maybe an ordinary person, being only fourteen, wouldn't know their right mind. But you take Lulamae, she was an exceptional woman. She knew good-and-well what she was doing when she promised to be my wife and the mother of my churren. She plain broke our hearts when she ran off like she done." He sipped his cold coffee, and glanced at me with a searching earnestness. "Now, son, do you doubt me? Do you believe what I'm saying is so?"

I did. It was too implausible not to be fact; moreover, it dovetailed with O. J. Berman's description of the Holly he'd first encountered in California: "You don't know if she's a hillbilly or an Okie or what." Berman couldn't be blamed for not guessing that she was a child-wife from Tulip, Texas.

"Plain broke our hearts when she ran off like she done," the horse doctor repeated. "She had no cause. All the housework was done by her daughters. Lulamae could just take it easy: fuss in front of mirrors and wash her hair. Our own cows, our own garden, chickens, pigs: son, that woman got positively fat. While her brother growed into a giant. Which is a sight different from how they come to us. 'Twas Nellie, my oldest girl, 'twas Nellie brought 'em into the house. She come to me one morning, and said: 'Papa, I got two wild younguns locked in the kitchen. I caught 'em outside stealing milk and turkey eggs.' That was Lulamae and Fred. Well, you never saw a more pitiful something. Ribs sticking out everywhere, legs so puny they can't hardly stand, teeth wobbling so bad they can't chew mush. Story was: their mother died of the TB, and their papa done the same—and all the churren, a whole raft of 'em, they been sent off to live with different mean people. Now Lulamae and her brother, them two been living with some mean, no-count people a hundred miles east of Tulip. She had good cause to run off from that house. She didn't have none to leave mine. 'Twas her home." He leaned his elbows on the counter and, pressing his closed eyes with his fingertips, sighed. "She plumped out to be a real pretty woman. Lively, too. Talky as a jaybird. With something smart to say on every subject: better than the radio. First thing you know, I'm out picking flowers. I tamed her a crow and taught it to say her name. I showed her how to play the guitar. Just to look at her made the tears spring to my eyes. The night I proposed, I cried like a baby. She said: 'What you want to cry for, Doc? 'Course we'll be married. I've never been married before.' Well, I had to laugh, hug and squeeze her: *never been married before!*" He chuckled, chewed on his toothpick a moment. "Don't tell me that woman wasn't happy!" he said, challengingly. "We all doted on her. She didn't have to lift a finger, 'cept to eat a piece of pie. 'Cept to comb her hair and send away for all the magazines. We must've had a hunnerd dollars' worth of magazines come into that house. Ask me, that's what done it. Looking at show-off pictures. Reading dreams. That's what started her walking down the road. Every day she'd walk a little further: a mile, and come home. Two miles, and come home. One day she just kept on." He put his hands over his eyes again; his breathing made a ragged noise. "The crow I give her went wild and flew away. All summer you could hear him. In the yard. In the garden. In the woods. All summer that damned bird was calling: Lulamae, Lulamae."

He stayed hunched over and silent, as though listening to the long-ago summer sound. I carried our checks to the cashier. While I was paying, he joined me. We left together and walked over to Park Avenue. It was a cool, blowy evening; swanky awnings flapped in the breeze. The quietness between us continued until I said: "But what about her brother? He didn't leave?"

"No, sir," he said, clearing his throat. "Fred was with us right till they took him in the Army. A fine boy. Fine with horses. He didn't know what got into Lulamae, how come she left her brother and husband and churren. After he was in the Army, though, Fred started hearing from her. The other day he wrote me her address. So I come to get her. I know she's sorry for what she done. I know she wants to go home." He seemed to be asking me to agree with him. I told him that I thought he'd find Holly, or Lulamae, somewhat changed. "Listen, son," he said, as we reached the steps of the brownstone, "I advised you I need a friend. Because I don't want to surprise her. Scare her none. That's why I've held off. Be my friend: let her know I'm here."

The notion of introducing Mrs. Golightly to her husband had its satisfying aspects; and, glancing up at her lighted windows, I hoped her friends were there, for the prospect of watching the Texan shake hands with Mag and Rusty and José was more satisfying still. But Doc Golightly's proud earnest eyes and sweat-stained hat made me ashamed of such anticipations. He followed me into the house and prepared to wait at the bottom of the stairs. "Do I look nice?" he whispered, brushing his sleeves, tightening the knot of his tie.

Holly was alone. She answered the door at once; in fact, she was on her way out—white satin dancing pumps and quantities of perfume announced gala intentions. "Well, idiot," she said, and playfully slapped me with her purse. "I'm in too much of a hurry to make up now. We'll smoke the pipe tomorrow, okay?"

"Sure, Lulamae. If you're still around tomorrow."

She took off her dark glasses and squinted at me. It was as though her eyes were shattered prisms, the dots of blue and gray and green like broken bits of sparkle. "*He* told you that," she said in a small, shivering voice. "Oh, please. *Where* is he?" She ran past me into the hall. "Fred!" she called down the stairs. "Fred! Where are you, darling?"

I could hear Doc Golightly's footsteps climbing the stairs. His head appeared above the banister, and Holly backed away from him, not as though she were frightened, but as though she were retreating into a shell of disappointment. Then he was standing in front of her, hangdog and shy. "Gosh, Lulamae," he began, and hesitated, for Holly was gazing at him vacantly, as though she couldn't place him. "Gee, honey," he said, "don't they feed you up here? You're so skinny. Like when I first saw you. All wild around the eye."

Holly touched his face; her fingers tested the reality of his chin, his beard stubble. "Hello, Doc," she said gently, and kissed him on the cheek. "Hello, Doc," she repeated happily, as he lifted her off her feet in a rib-crushing grip. Whoops óf relieved laughter shook him. "Gosh, Lulamae. Kingdom come."

Neither of them noticed me when I squeezed past them and went up to my room. Nor did they seem aware of Madame Sapphia Spanella, who opened her door and yelled: "Shut up! It's a disgrace. Do your whoring elsewhere."

"*Divorce* him? Of course I never divorced him. I was only fourteen, for God's sake. It couldn't have been *legal.*" Holly tapped an empty martini glass. "Two more, my darling Mr. Bell."

Joe Bell, in whose bar we were sitting, accepted the order reluctantly. "You're rockin' the boat kinda early," he complained, crunching on a Tums. It was not yet noon, according to the black mahogany clock behind the bar, and he'd already served us three rounds.

"But it's Sunday, Mr. Bell. Clocks are slow on Sundays. Besides, I haven't been to bed yet," she told him, and confided to me: "Not to sleep." She blushed, and glanced away guiltily. For the first time since I'd known her, she seemed to feel a need to justify herself: "Well, I had to. Doc really loves me, you know. And I love him. He may have looked old and tacky to *you*. But you don't know the sweetness of him, the confidence he can give to birds and brats and fragile things like that. Anyone who ever gave you confidence, you owe them a lot. I've always remembered Doc in my prayers. Please stop smirking!" she demanded, stabbing out a cigarette. "I *do* say my prayers."

"I'm not smirking. I'm smiling. You're the most amazing person."

"I suppose I am," she said, and her face, wan, rather bruised-looking in the morning light, brightened; she smoothed her tousled hair, and the colors of it glimmered like a shampoo advertisement. "I must look fierce. But who wouldn't? We spent the rest of the night roaming around in a bus station. Right up till the last minute Doc thought I was going to go with him. Even though I kept telling him: But, Doc, I'm not fourteen any more, and I'm not Lulamae. But the terrible part is (and I realized it while we were standing there) I am. I'm still stealing turkey eggs and running through a brier patch. Only now I call it having the mean reds."

Joe Bell disdainfully settled the fresh martinis in front of us.

"Never love a wild thing, Mr. Bell," Holly advised him. "That was Doc's mistake. He was always lugging home wild things. A hawk with a hurt wing. One time it was a full-grown bobcat with a broken leg. But you can't give your heart to a wild thing: the more you do, the stronger they get. Until they're strong enough to run into the woods. Or fly into a tree. Then a taller tree. Then the sky. That's how you'll end up, Mr. Bell. If you let yourself love a wild thing. You'll end up looking at the sky."

"She's drunk," Joe Bell informed me.

"Moderately," Holly confessed. "But Doc knew what I meant. I explained it to him very carefully, and it was something he could understand. We shook hands and held on to each other and he wished me luck." She glanced at the clock. "He must be in the Blue Mountains by now."

"What's she talkin' about?" Joe Bell asked me.

Holly lifted her martini. "Let's wish the Doc luck, too," she said, touching her glass against mine. "Good luck: and believe me, dearest Doc—it's better to look at the sky than live there. Such an empty place; so vague. Just a country where the thunder goes and things disappear."

TRAWLER MARRIES FOURTH. I was on a subway somewhere in Brooklyn when I saw that headline. The paper that bannered it belonged to another passenger. The only part of the text that I could see read: *Rutherfurd "Rusty" Trawler, the millionaire playboy often accused of pro-Nazi sympathies, eloped to Greenwich yesterday with a beautiful*—Not that I wanted to read any more. Holly had married him: well, well. I wished I were under the wheels of the train. But I'd been wishing that before I spotted the headline. For a headful of reasons. I hadn't seen Holly, not really, since our drunken Sunday at Joe Bell's bar. The intervening weeks had given me my own case of the mean reds. First off, I'd been fired from my job: deservedly, and for an amusing misdemeanor too complicated to recount here. Also, my draft board was displaying an uncomfortable interest; and, having so recently escaped the regimentation of a small town, the idea of entering another form of disciplined life made me desperate. Between the uncertainty of my draft status and a lack of specific experience, I couldn't seem to find another job. That was what I was doing on a subway in Brooklyn: returning from a discouraging interview with an editor of the now-defunct newspaper *PM*. All this, combined with the city heat of the summer, had reduced me to a state of nervous inertia. So I more than half meant it when I wished I were under the wheels of the train. The headline made the desire quite positive. If Holly could marry that "absurd foetus," then the army of wrongness rampant in the world might as well march over me. Or, and the question is apparent, was my outrage a little the result of being in love with Holly myself? A little. For I *was* in love with her. Just as I'd once been in love with my mother's elderly colored cook and a postman who let me follow him on his rounds and a whole family named McKendrick. That category of love generates jealousy, too.

When I reached my station I bought a paper; and, reading the tail-end of that sentence, discovered that Rusty's bride was: *a beautiful cover girl from the Arkansas hills, Miss Margaret Thatcher Fitzhue Wildwood.* Mag! My legs went so limp with relief I took a taxi the rest of the way home.

Madame Sapphia Spanella met me in the hall, wild-eyed and wringing her hands. "Run," she said. "Bring the police. She is killing somebody! Somebody is killing her!"

It sounded like it. As though tigers were loose in Holly's apartment. A riot of crashing glass, of rippings and fallings and overturned furniture. But there were no quarreling voices inside the uproar, which made it seem unnatural. "Run," shrieked Madame Spanella, pushing me. "Tell the police murder!"

I ran; but only upstairs to Holly's door. Pounding on it had one result: the racket subsided. Stopped altogether. But pleadings to let me in went unanswered, and my efforts to break down the door merely culminated in a bruised shoulder. Then below I heard Madame Spanella commanding some newcomer to go for the police. "Shut up," she was told, "and get out of my way."

It was José Ybarra-Jaegar. Looking not at all the smart Brazilian diplomat; but sweaty and frightened. He ordered me out of his way, too. And, using his own key, opened the door. "In here, Dr. Goldman," he said, beckoning to a man accompanying him.

Since no one prevented me, I followed them into the apartment, which was tremendously wrecked. At last the Christmas tree had been dismantled, very literally: its brown dry branches sprawled in a welter of torn-up books, broken lamps and phonograph records. Even the icebox had been emptied, its contents tossed around the room: raw eggs were sliding down the walls, and in the midst of the debris Holly's no-name cat was calmly licking a puddle of milk.

In the bedroom, the smell of smashed perfume bottles made me gag. I stepped on Holly's dark glasses; they were lying on the floor, the lenses already shattered, the frames cracked in half.

Perhaps that is why Holly, a rigid figure on the bed, stared at José so blindly, seemed not to see the doctor, who, testing her pulse, crooned: "You're a tired young lady. Very tired. You want to go to sleep, don't you? Sleep."

Holly rubbed her forehead, leaving a smear of blood from a cut finger. "Sleep," she said, and whimpered like an exhausted, fretful child. "He's the only one would ever let me. Let me hug him on cold nights. I saw a place in Mexico. With horses. By the sea."

"With horses by the sea," lullabied the doctor, selecting from his black case a hypodermic.

José averted his face, queasy at the sight of a needle. "Her sickness is only grief?" he asked, his difficult English lending the question an unintended irony. "She is grieving only?"

"Didn't hurt a bit, now did it?" inquired the doctor, smugly dabbing Holly's arm with a scrap of cotton.

She came to sufficiently to focus the doctor. "*Everything* hurts. Where are my glasses?" But she didn't need them. Her eyes were closing of their own accord.

"She is only grieving?" insisted José.

"Please, sir," the doctor was quite short with him, "if you will leave me alone with the patient."

José withdrew to the front room, where he released his temper on the snooping, tiptoeing presence of Madame Spanella. "Don't touch me! I'll call the police," she threatened as he whipped her to the door with Portuguese oaths.

He considered throwing me out, too; or so I surmised from his expression. Instead, he invited me to have a drink. The only unbroken bottle we could find contained dry vermouth. "I have a worry," he confided. "I have a worry that this should cause scandal. Her crashing everything. Conducting like a crazy. I must have no public scandal. It is too delicate: my name, my work."

He seemed cheered to learn that I saw no reason for a "scandal"; demolishing one's own possessions was, presumably, a private affair.

"It is only a question of grieving," he firmly declared. "When the sadness came, first she throws the drink she is drinking. The bottle. Those books. A lamp. Then I am scared. I hurry to bring a doctor."

"But why?" I wanted to know. "Why should she have a fit over Rusty? If I were her, I'd celebrate."

"Rusty?"

I was still carrying my newspaper, and showed him the headline.

"Oh, that." He grinned rather scornfully. "They do us a grand favor, Rusty and Mag. We laugh over it: how they think they break our hearts when all the time we *want* them to run away. I assure you, we were laughing when the sadness came." His eyes searched the litter on the floor; he picked up a ball of yellow paper. "This," he said.

It was a telegram from Tulip, Texas: *Received notice young Fred killed in action overseas stop your husband and children join in the sorrow of our mutual loss stop letter follows love Doc.*

Holly never mentioned her brother again: except once. Moreover, she stopped calling me Fred. June, July, all through the warm months she hibernated like a winter animal who did not know spring had come and gone. Her hair darkened, she put on weight. She became rather careless about her clothes: used to rush round to the delicatessen wearing a rainslicker and nothing underneath. José moved into the apartment, his name replacing Mag Wildwood's on the mailbox. Still, Holly was a good deal alone, for José stayed in Washington three days a week. During his absences she entertained no one and seldom left the apartment—except on Thursdays, when she made her weekly trip to Ossining.

Which is not to imply that she had lost interest in life; far from it, she seemed more content, altogether happier than I'd ever seen her. A keen sudden un-Holly-like enthusiasm for homemaking resulted in several un-Holly-like purchases: at a Parke-Bernet auction she acquired a stag-at-bay hunting tapestry and, from the William Randolph Hearst estate, a gloomy pair of Gothic "easy" chairs; she bought the complete Modern Library, shelves of classical records, innumerable Metropolitan Museum reproductions (including a statue of a Chinese cat that her own cat hated and hissed at and ultimately broke), a Waring mixer and a pressure cooker and a library of cook books. She spent whole hausfrau afternoons slopping about in the sweatbox of her midget kitchen: "José says I'm better than the Colony. Really, who would have dreamed I had such a great natural talent? A month ago I couldn't scramble eggs." And still couldn't, for that matter. Simple dishes, steak, a proper salad, were beyond her. Instead, she fed José, and occasionally myself, *outré* soups (brandied black terrapin poured into avocado shells), Nero-ish novelties (roasted pheasant stuffed with pomegranates and persimmons) and other dubious innovations (chicken and saffron rice served with a chocolate sauce: "An East Indian classic, *my* dear"). Wartime sugar and cream rationing restricted her imagination when it came to sweets—nevertheless, she once managed something called Tobacco Tapioca: best not describe it.

Nor describe her attempts to master Portuguese, an ordeal as tedious to me as it was to her, for whenever I visited her an album of Linguaphone records never ceased rotating on the phonograph. Now, too, she rarely spoke a sentence that did not begin, "After we're married—" or "When we move to Rio—" Yet José had never suggested marriage. She admitted it. "But, after all, he *knows* I'm preggers. Well, I am, darling. Six weeks gone. I don't see why *that* should surprise you. It didn't me. Not *un peu* bit. I'm delighted. I want to have at least nine. I'm sure some of them will be rather dark—José has a touch of *le nègre*, I suppose you guessed that? Which is fine by me: what could be prettier than a quite coony baby with bright green beautiful eyes? I wish, please don't laugh—but I wish I'd been a virgin for him, for José. Not that I've warmed the multitudes some people say: I don't blame the bastards for *saying* it, I've always thrown out such a jazzy line. Really, though, I toted up the other night, and I've only had eleven lovers—not counting anything that happened before I was thirteen because, after all, that just *doesn't* count. Eleven. Does that make me a whore? Look at Mag Wildwood. Or Honey Tucker. Or Rose Ellen Ward. They've had the old clap-yo'-hands so many times it amounts to applause. Of course I haven't anything *against* whores. Except this: some of them may have an honest tongue but they all have dishonest hearts. I mean, you can't bang the guy and cash his checks and at least not *try* to believe you love him. I never have. Even Benny Shacklett and all those rodents. I sort of hypnotized myself into thinking their sheer rattiness had a certain allure. Actually, except for Doc, if you want to count Doc, José is my first non-rat romance. Oh, he's not my idea of the absolute finito. He tells little lies and he worries what people *think* and he takes about fifty baths a day: men ought to smell *some*what. He's too prim, too cautious to be my guy ideal; he always turns his back to get undressed and he makes too much noise when he eats and I don't like to see him run because there's something funny-looking about him when he runs. If I were free to choose from everybody alive, just snap my fingers and say come here you, I wouldn't pick José. Nehru, he's nearer the mark. Wendell Willkie. I'd settle for Garbo any day. Why not? A person ought to be able to marry men or women or— Listen, if you came to me and said you wanted to hitch up with Man o' War, I'd respect your feeling. No, I'm serious. Love should be allowed. I'm all for it. Now that I've got a pretty good idea what it is. Because I *do* love José—I'd stop smoking if he asked me to. He's *friendly*, he can laugh me out of the mean reds, only I don't have them much any more, except sometimes, and even then they're not so hideola that I gulp Seconal or have to haul myself to Tiffany's: I take his suit to the cleaner, or stuff some mushrooms, and I feel fine, just great. Another thing, I've thrown away my horoscopes. I must have spent a dollar on every goddamn star in the goddamn planetarium. It's a bore, but the answer is good things only happen to you if you're good. Good? Honest is more what I mean. Not law-type honest—I'd rob a grave, I'd steal two-bits off a dead man's eyes if I thought it would contribute to the day's enjoyment—but unto-thyself-type honest. Be anything but a coward, a pretender, an emotional crook, a whore: I'd rather have cancer than a dishonest heart. Which isn't being pious. Just practical. Cancer *may* cool you, but the other's sure to. Oh, screw it, cookie—hand me my guitar and I'll sing you a *fada* in *the* most perfect Portuguese."

Those final weeks, spanning end of summer and the beginning of another autumn, are blurred in memory, perhaps because our understanding of each other had reached that sweet depth where two people communicate more often in silence than in words: an affectionate quietness replaces the tensions, the unrelaxed chatter and chasing about that produce a friendship's more showy, more, in the surface sense, dramatic moments. Frequently, when *he* was out of town (I'd developed hostile attitudes toward *him*, and seldom used his name) we spent entire evenings together during which we exchanged less than a hundred words; once, we walked all the way to Chinatown, ate a chow-mein supper, bought some paper lanterns and stole a box of joss sticks, then moseyed across the Brooklyn Bridge, and on the bridge, as we watched seaward-moving ships pass between the cliffs of burning skyline, she said: "Years from now, years and years, one of those ships will bring me back, me and my nine Brazilian brats. Because yes, they *must* see this, these lights, the river—I love New York, even though it isn't mine, the way something has to be, a tree or a street or a house, something, anyway, that belongs to me because I belong to it." And I said: "Do shut up," for I felt infuriatingly left out—a tugboat in dry-dock while she, glittery voyager of secure destination, steamed down the harbor with whistles whistling and confetti in the air.

So the days, the last days, blow about in memory, hazy, autumnal, all alike as leaves: until a day unlike any other I've lived.

. . .

It happened to fall on the 30th of September, my birthday, a fact which had no effect on events, except that, expecting some form of monetary remembrance from my family, I was eager for the postman's morning visit. Indeed, I went downstairs and waited for him. If I had not been loitering in the vestibule, then Holly would not have asked me to go horseback riding; and would not, consequently, have had the opportunity to save my life.

"Come on," she said, when she found me awaiting the postman. "Let's walk a couple of horses around the park." She was wearing a windbreaker and a pair of blue jeans and tennis shoes; she slapped her stomach, drawing attention to its flatness: "Don't think I'm out to lose the heir. But there's a horse, my darling old Mabel Minerva—I can't go without saying goodbye to Mabel Minerva."

"Good-bye?"

"A week from Saturday. José bought the tickets." In rather a trance, I let her lead me down to the street. "We change planes in Miami. Then over the sea. Over the Andes. Taxi!"

Over the Andes. As we rode in a cab across Central Park it seemed to me as though I, too, were flying, desolately floating over snow-peaked and perilous territory.

"But you can't. After all, what about. Well, what about. Well, you can't *really* run off and leave everybody."

"I don't think anyone will miss me. I have no friends."

"I will. Miss you. So will Joe Bell. And oh—millions. Like Sally. Poor Mr. Tomato."

"I loved old Sally," she said, and sighed. "You know, I haven't been to see him in a month? When I told him I was going away, he was an angel. *Actually*"—she frowned—"he seemed *delighted* that I was leaving the country. He said it was all for the best. Because sooner or later there might be trouble. If they found out I wasn't his real niece. That fat lawyer, O'Shaughnessy, O'Shaughnessy sent me five hundred dollars. In cash. A wedding present from Sally."

I wanted to be unkind. "You can expect a present from me, too. When, and if, the wedding happens."

She laughed. "He'll marry me, all right. In church. And with his family there. That's why we're waiting till we get to Rio."

"Does he know you're married already?"

"What's the matter with you? Are you trying to ruin the day? It's a beautiful day: leave it alone!"

"But it's perfectly possible—"

"It *isn't* possible. I've told you, that wasn't legal. It *couldn't* be." She rubbed her nose, and glanced at me sideways. "Mention that to a living soul, darling. I'll hang you by your toes and dress you for a hog."

The stables—I believe they have been replaced by television studios— were on West Sixty-sixth street. Holly selected for me an old sway-back black and white mare: "Don't worry, she's safer than a cradle." Which, in my case, was a necessary guarantee, for ten-cent pony rides at childhood carnivals were the limit of my equestrian experience. Holly helped hoist me into the saddle, then mounted her own horse, a silvery animal that took the lead as we jogged across the traffic of Central Park West and entered a riding path dappled with leaves denuding breezes danced about.

"See?" she shouted. "It's great!"

And suddenly it was. Suddenly, watching the tangled colors of Holly's hair flash in the red-yellow leaf light, I loved her enough to forget myself, my self-pitying despairs, and be content that something she thought happy was going to happen. Very gently the horses began to trot, waves of wind splashed us, spanked our faces, we plunged in and out of sun and shadow pools, and joy, a glad-to-be-alive exhilaration, jolted through me like a jigger of nitrogen. That was one minute; the next introduced farce in grim disguise.

For all at once, like savage members of a jungle ambush, a band of Negro boys leapt out of the shrubbery along the path. Hooting, cursing, they launched rocks and thrashed at the horse's rumps with switches.

Mine, the black and white mare, rose on her hind legs, whinnied, tee-tered like a tightrope artist, then blue-streaked down the path, bouncing my feet out of the stirrups and leaving me scarcely attached. Her hooves made the gravel stones spit sparks. The sky careened. Trees, a lake with little-boy sailboats, statues went by licketysplit. Nursemaids rushed to rescue their charges from our awesome approach; men, bums and others, yelled: "Pull in the reins!" and "Whoa, boy, whoa!" and "Jump!" It was only later that I remembered these voices; at the time I was simply con-scious of Holly, the cowboy-sound of her racing behind me, never quite catching up, and over and over calling encouragements. Onward: across the park and out into Fifth Avenue: stampeding against the noonday traffic, taxis, buses that screechingly swerved. Past the Duke mansion, the Frick Museum, past the Pierre and the Plaza. But Holly gained ground; more-over, a mounted policeman had joined the chase: flanking my runaway mare, one on either side, their horses performed a pincer movement that brought her to a steamy halt. It was then, at last, that I fell off her back. Fell off and picked myself up and stood there, not altogether certain where I was. A crowd gathered. The policeman huffed and wrote in a book: presently he was most sympathetic, grinned and said he would arrange for our horses to be returned to their stable.

Holly put us in a taxi. "Darling. How do you feel?"

"Fine."

"But you haven't *any* pulse," she said, feeling my wrist.

"Then I must be dead."

"No, idiot. This is serious. Look at me."

The trouble was, I couldn't see her; rather, I saw several Holly's, a trio of sweaty faces so white with concern that I was both touched and embarrassed. "Honestly. I don't feel anything. Except ashamed."

"Please. Are you sure? Tell me the truth. You might have been killed."

"But I wasn't. And thank you. For saving my life. You're wonderful. Unique. I love you."

"Damn fool." She kissed me on the cheek. Then there were four of her, and I fainted dead away.

That evening, photographs of Holly were front-paged by the late edition of the *Journal-American* and by the early editions of both the *Daily News* and the *Daily Mirror*. The publicity had nothing to do with runaway horses. It concerned quite another matter, as the headlines revealed: PLAYGIRL ARRESTED IN NARCOTICS SCANDAL (*Journal-American*), ARREST DOPE-SMUGGLING ACTRESS (*Daily News*), DRUG RING EXPOSED, GLAMOUR GIRL HELD (*Daily Mirror*). Of the lot, the *News* printed the most striking picture: Holly, entering police headquarters, wedged between two muscular detectives, one male, one female. In this squalid context even her clothes (she was still wearing her riding costume, windbreaker and blue jeans) suggested a gang-moll hooligan: an impression dark glasses, disarrayed coiffure and a Picayune cigarette dangling from sullen lips did not diminish. The caption read: *Twenty-year-old Holly Golightly, beautiful movie starlet and café society celebrity D.A. alleges to be key figure in international drug-smuggling racket linked to racketeer Salvatore "Sally" Tomato. Dets. Patrick Connor and Sheilah Fezzonetti (L. and R.) are shown escorting her into 67th St. Precinct. See story on Pg. 3.* The story, featuring a photograph of a man identified as Oliver "Father" O'Shaughnessy (shielding his face with a fedora), ran three full columns. Here, somewhat condensed, are the pertinent paragraphs: *Members of café society were stunned today by the arrest of gorgeous Holly Golightly, twenty-year-old Hollywood starlet and highly publicized girl-about-New York. At the same time, 2 P.M., police nabbed Oliver O'Shaughnessy, 52, of the Hotel Seabord, W. 49th St., as he exited from a Hamburg Heaven on Madison Ave. Both are alleged by District Attorney Frank L. Donovan to be important figures in an international drug ring dominated by the notorious Mafia-führer Salvatore "Sally" Tomato, currently in Sing Sing serving a five-year rap for political bribery. . . . O'Shaughnessy, a defrocked priest variously known in crimeland circles as "Father" and "The Padre," has a history of arrests dating back to 1934, when he served two years for operating a phony Rhode Island mental institution, The Monastery. Miss Golightly, who has no previous criminal record, was arrested in her luxurious apartment at a swank East Side address. . . . Although the D.A.'s office has issued no formal statement, responsible sources insist the blond and beautiful actress, not long ago the constant companion of multimillionaire Rutherfurd Trawler, has been acting as "liaison" between the imprisoned Tomato and his chief-lieutenant, O'Shaughnessy. . . . Posing as a relative of Tomato's, Miss Golightly is said to have paid weekly visits to Sing Sing, and on these occasions Tomato supplied her with verbally coded messages which she then transmitted to O'Shaughnessy. Via this link, Tomato, believed to have been born in Cefalu, Sicily, in 1874, was able to keep first-hand control of a world-wide narcotics syndicate with outposts in Mexico, Cuba, Sicily, Tangier, Tehran and Dakar. But the D.A.'s office refused to offer any detail on these allegations or even verify them. . . . Tipped off, a large number of reporters were on hand at the E. 67th St. Precinct station when the accused pair arrived for booking. O'Shaughnessy, a burly red-haired man, refused comment and kicked one cameraman in the groin. But Miss Golightly, a fragile eyeful, even though attired like a tomboy in slacks and leather jacket, appeared relatively unconcerned. "Don't ask me what the hell this is about," she told reporters. "Parce-que je ne sais pas, mes chères. (Because I do not know, my dears). Yes—I have visited Sally Tomato. I used to go to see him every week. What's wrong with that? He believes in God, and so do I.". . . Then, under* the subheading ADMITS OWN DRUG ADDICTION: *Miss Golightly smiled when a reporter asked whether or not she herself is a narcotics user. "I've had a little go at marijuana. It's not half so destructive as brandy. Cheaper, too. Unfortunately, I prefer brandy. No, Mr. Tomato never mentioned drugs to me. It makes me furious, the way these wretched people keep persecuting him. He's a sensitive, a religious person. A darling old man."*

There is one especially gross error in this report: she was not arrested in her "luxurious apartment." It took place in my own bathroom. I was soaking away my horse-ride pains in a tub of scalding water laced with Epsom salts; Holly, an attentive nurse, was sitting on the edge of the tub waiting to rub me with Sloan's liniment and tuck me into bed. There was a knock at the front door. As the door was unlocked, Holly called Come in. In came Madame Sapphia Spanella, trailed by a pair of civilian-clothed detectives, one of them a lady with thick yellow braids roped around her head.

"*Here* she is: the wanted woman!" boomed Madame Spanella, invading the bathroom and leveling a finger, first at Holly's, then my nakedness. "Look. What a whore she is." The male detective seemed embarrassed: by Madame Spanella and by the situation; but a harsh enjoyment tensed the face of his companion—she plumped a hand on Holly's shoulder and, in a surprising baby-child voice, said: "Come along, sister. You're going places." Whereupon Holly coolly told her: "Get them cotton-pickin' hands off of me, you dreary, driveling old bull-dyke." Which rather enraged the lady: she slapped Holly damned hard. So hard, her head twisted on her neck, and the bottle of liniment, flung from her hand, smithereened on the tile floor—where I, scampering out of the tub to enrich the fray, stepped on it and all but severed both big toes. Nude and bleeding a path of bloody footprints, I followed the action as far as the hall. "Don't forget," Holly managed to instruct me as the detectives propelled her down the stairs, "please feed the cat."

Of course I believed Madame Spanella to blame: she'd several times called the authorities to complain about Holly. It didn't occur to me the affair could have dire dimensions until that evening when Joe Bell showed up flourishing the newspapers. He was too agitated to speak sensibly; he caroused the room hitting his fists together while I read the accounts.

Then he said: "You think it's so? She was mixed up in this lousy business?"

"Well, yes."

He popped a Tums in his mouth and, glaring at me, chewed it as though he were crunching my bones. "Boy, that's rotten. And you meant to be her friend. What a bastard!"

"Just a minute. I didn't say she was involved *knowingly*. She wasn't. But there, she did do it. Carry messages and whatnot—"

He said: "Take it pretty calm, don't you? Jesus, she could get ten years. More." He yanked the papers away from me. "You know her friends. These rich fellows. Come down to the bar, we'll start phoning. Our girl's going to need fancier shysters than I can afford."

I was too sore and shaky to dress myself; Joe Bell had to help. Back at his bar he propped me in the telephone booth with a triple martini and a brandy tumbler full of coins. But I couldn't think whom to contact. José was in Washington, and I had no notion where to reach him there. Rusty Trawler? Not that bastard! Only: what other friends of hers did I know? Perhaps she'd been right when she'd said she had none, not really.

I put through a call to Crestview 5-6958 in Beverly Hills, the number long-distance information gave me for O. J. Berman. The person who answered said Mr. Berman was having a massage and couldn't be disturbed: sorry, try later. Joe Bell was incensed—told me I should have said it was a life and death matter; and he insisted on my trying Rusty. First, I spoke to Mr. Trawler's butler—Mr. and Mrs. Trawler, he announced, were at dinner and might he take a message? Joe Bell shouted into the receiver: "This is urgent, mister. Life and death." The outcome was that I found myself talking—listening, rather—to the former Mag Wildwood: "Are you starkers?" she demanded. "My husband and I will positively *sue* anyone who attempts to connect our names with that ro-ro-*rovol*ting and de-de-de*gen*erate girl. I always *knew* she was a hop-hop-head with no more morals than a hound-bitch in heat. Prison is where she belongs. And my husband agrees one thousand percent. We will positively *sue* anyone who—" Hanging up, I remembered old Doc down in Tulip, Texas; but no, Holly wouldn't like it if I called him, she'd kill me good.

I rang California again; the circuits were busy, stayed busy, and by the time O. J. Berman was on the line I'd emptied so many martinis he had to tell me why I was phoning him: "About the kid, is it? I know already. I spoke already to Iggy Fitelstein. Iggy's the best shingle in New York. I said Iggy you take care of it, send me the bill, only keep my name anonymous, see. Well, I owe the kid something. Not that I owe her *any*thing, you want to come down to it. She's crazy. A phony. But a *real* phony, you know? Anyway, they only got her in ten thousand bail. Don't worry, Iggy'll spring her tonight—it wouldn't surprise me she's home already."

But she wasn't; nor had she returned the next morning when I went down to feed her cat. Having no key to the apartment, I used the fire escape and gained entrance through a window. The cat was in the bedroom, and he was not alone: a man was there, crouching over a suitcase. The two of us, each thinking the other a burglar, exchanged uncomfortable stares as I stepped through the window. He had a pretty face, lacquered hair, he resembled José; moreover, the suitcase he'd been packing contained the wardrobe José kept at Holly's, the shoes and suits she fussed over, was always carting to menders and cleaners. And I said, certain it was so: "Did Mr. Ybarra-Jaegar send you?"

"I am the cousin," he said with a wary grin and just-penetrable accent. "Where is José?"

He repeated the question, as though translating it into another language. "Ah, *where* she is! She is waiting," he said and, seeming to dismiss me, resumed his valet activities.

So: the diplomat was planning a powder. Well, I wasn't amazed; or in the slightest sorry. Still, what a heartbreaking stunt: "He ought to be horsewhipped."

The cousin giggled, I'm sure he understood me. He shut the suitcase and produced a letter. "My cousin, she ask me leave that for his chum. You will oblige?"

On the envelope was scribbled: *For Miss H. Golightly—Courtesy Bearer.*

I sat down on Holly's bed, and hugged Holly's cat to me, and felt as badly for Holly, every iota, as she could feel for herself.

"Yes, I will oblige."

And I did: without the least wanting to. But I hadn't the courage to destroy the letter; or the will power to keep it in my pocket when Holly very tentatively inquired if, if by any chance, I'd had news of José. It was two mornings later; I was sitting by her bedside in a room that reeked of iodine and bedpans, a hospital room. She had been there since the night of her arrest. "Well, darling," she'd greeted me, as I tiptoed toward her carrying a carton of Picayune cigarettes and a wheel of new-autumn violets, "I lost the heir." She looked not quite twelve years: her pale vanilla hair brushed back, her eyes, for once minus their dark glasses, clear as rain water—one couldn't believe how ill she'd been.

Yet it was true: "Christ, I nearly cooled. No fooling, the fat woman almost had me. She was yakking up a storm. I guess I couldn't have told you about the fat woman. Since I didn't know about her myself until my brother died. Right away I was wondering where he'd gone, what it meant, Fred's dying; and then I saw her, she was there in the room with me, and she had Fred cradled in her arms, a fat mean red bitch rocking in a rocking chair with Fred on her lap and laughing like a brass band. The mockery of it! But it's all that's ahead for us, my friend: this comedienne waiting to give you the old razz. Now do you see why I went crazy and broke everything?"

Except for the lawyer O. J. Berman had hired, I was the only visitor she had been allowed. Her room was shared by other patients, a trio of triplet-like ladies who, examining me with an interest not unkind but total, speculated in whispered Italian. Holly explained that: "They think you're my downfall, darling. The fellow what done me wrong"; and, to a suggestion that she set them straight, replied: "I can't. They don't speak English. Anyway, I wouldn't dream of spoiling their fun." It was then that she asked about José.

The instant she saw the letter she squinted her eyes and bent her lips in a tough tiny smile that advanced her age immeasurably. "Darling," she instructed me, "would you reach in the drawer there and give me my purse. A girl doesn't read this sort of thing without her lipstick."

Guided by a compact mirror, she powdered, painted every vestige of twelve-year-old out of her face. She shaped her lips with one tube, colored her cheeks from another. She penciled the rims of her eyes, blued the lids, sprinkled her neck with 4711; attached pearls to her ears and donned her dark glasses; thus armored, and after a displeased appraisal of her manicure's shabby condition, she ripped open the letter and let her eyes race through it while her stony small smile grew smaller and harder. Eventually she asked for a Picayune. Took a puff: "Tastes bum. But divine," she said and, tossing me the letter: "Maybe this will come in handy—if you ever write a rat-romance. Don't be hoggy: read it aloud. I'd like to hear it myself."

It began:" 'My dearest little girl—' "

Holly at once interrupted. She wanted to know what I thought of the handwriting. I thought nothing: a tight, highly legible, uneccentric script. "It's him to a T. Buttoned up and constipated," she declared. "Go on."

" 'My dearest little girl, I have loved you knowing you were not as others. But conceive of my despair upon discovering in such a brutal and public style how very different you are from the manner of woman a man of my faith and career could hope to make his wife. Verily I grief for the disgrace of your present circumstance, and do not find it in my heart to add my condemn to the condemn that surrounds you. So I hope you will find it in your heart not to condemn me. I have my family to protect, and my name, and I am a coward where those institutions enter. Forget me, beautiful child. I am no longer here. I am gone home. But may God always be with you and your child. May God be not the same as—José.' "

"Well?"

"In a way it seems quite honest. And even touching."

"*Touching?* That square-ball jazz!"

"But after all, he *says* he's a coward; and from his point of view, you must see—"

Holly, however, did not want to admit that she saw; yet her face, despite its cosmetic disguise, confessed it. "All right, he's not a rat without reason. A super-sized, King Kong-type rat like Rusty. Benny Shacklett. But oh gee, golly goddamn," she said, jamming a fist into her mouth like a bawling baby, "I *did* love him. The rat."

The Italian trio imagined a lover's *crise* and, placing the blame for Holly's groanings where they felt it belonged, tut-tutted their tongues at me. I was flattered: proud that anyone should think Holly cared for me. She quieted when I offered her another cigarette. She swallowed and said: "Bless you, Buster. And bless you for being such a bad jockey. If I hadn't had to play Calamity Jane, I'd still be looking forward to the grub in an unwed mama's home. Strenuous exercise, that's what did the trick. But I've scared *la merde* out of the whole badge-department by saying it was because Miss Dykeroo slapped me. Yessir, I can sue them on several counts, including false arrest."

Until then, we'd skirted mention of her more sinister tribulations, and this jesting reference to them seemed appalling, pathetic, so definitely did it reveal how incapable she was of recognizing the bleak realities before her. "Now, Holly," I said, thinking: be strong, mature, an uncle. "Now, Holly. We can't treat it as a joke. We have to make plans."

"You're too young to be stuffy. Too small. By the way, what business is it of yours?"

"None. Except you're my friend, and I'm worried. I mean to know what you intend doing."

She rubbed her nose, and concentrated on the ceiling. "Today's Wednesday, isn't it? So I suppose I'll sleep until Saturday, really get a good *schlafen*. Saturday morning I'll skip out to the bank. Then I'll stop by the apartment and pick up a nightgown or two and my Mainbocher. Following which, I'll report to Idlewild. Where, as you damn well know, I have a perfectly fine reservation on a perfectly fine plane. And since you're such a friend, I'll let you wave me off. *Please* stop shaking your head."

"Holly. Holly. You can't do that."

"*Et pourquoi pas?* I'm not hot-footing after José, if that's what you suppose. According to my census, he's strictly a citizen of Limboville. It's only: why should I waste a perfectly fine ticket? Already paid for? Besides, I've never been to Brazil."

"Just what kind of pills have they been feeding you here? Can't you realize, you're under a criminal indictment. If they catch you jumping bail, they'll throw away the key. Even if you get away with it, you'll never be able to come home."

"Well, so, tough titty. Anyway, home is where you feel at home. I'm still looking."

"No, Holly, it's stupid. You're innocent. You've got to stick it out."

She said, "Rah, team, rah," and blew smoke in my face. She was impressed, however; her eyes were dilated by unhappy visions, as were mine: iron rooms, steel corridors of gradually closing doors. "Oh, screw it," she said, and stabbed out her cigarette. "I have a fair chance they *won't* catch me. Provided *you* keep your *bouche fermez*. Look. Don't despise me, darling." She put her hand over mine and pressed it with sudden immense sincerity. "I haven't much choice. I talked it over with the lawyer: oh, I didn't tell *him* anything *re* Rio—he'd tip the badgers himself, rather than lose his fee, to say nothing of the nickels O.J. put up for bail. Bless O.J.'s heart; but once on the Coast I helped him win more than ten thou in a single poker hand: we're square. No, here's the real shake: all the badgers want from me is a couple of free grabs and my services as a state's witness against Sally—nobody has any intention of prosecuting me, they haven't a ghost of a case. Well, I may be rotten to the core, Maude, *but:* testify against a friend I will not. Not if they can prove he doped Sister Kenny. My yardstick is how somebody treats me, and old Sally, all right he wasn't absolutely white with me, say he took a slight advantage, just the same Sally's an okay shooter, and I'd let the fat woman snatch me sooner than help the law-boys pin him down." Tilting her compact mirror above her face, smoothing her lipstick with a crooked pinkie, she said: "And to be honest, that isn't all. Certain shades of limelight wreck a girl's complexion.

Even if a jury gave me the Purple Heart, this neighborhood holds no future: they'd still have up every rope from La Rue to Perona's Bar and Grill—take my word, I'd be about as welcome as Mr. Frank E. Campbell. And if you lived off my particular talents, Cookie, you'd understand the kind of bankruptcy I'm describing. Uh, uh, I don't just fancy a fade-out that finds me belly-bumping around Roseland with a pack of West Side hillbillies. While the excellent Madame Trawler sashays her twat in and out of Tiffany's. I couldn't take it. Give me the fat woman any day."

A nurse, soft-shoeing into the room, advised that visiting hours were over. Holly started to complain, and was curtailed by having a thermometer popped in her mouth. But as I took leave, she unstoppered herself to say: "Do me a favor, darling. Call up the *Times,* or whatever you call, and get a list of the fifty richest men in Brazil. I'm *not* kidding. The fifty richest: regardless of race or color. Another favor—poke around my apartment till you find that medal you gave me. The St. Christopher. I'll need it for the trip."

The sky was red Friday night, it thundered, and Saturday, departing day, the city swayed in a squall-like downpour. Sharks might have swum through the air, though it seemed improbable a plane could penetrate it.

But Holly, ignoring my cheerful conviction that her flight would not go, continued her preparations—placing, I must say, the chief burden of them on me. For she had decided it would be unwise of her to come near the brownstone. Quite rightly, too: it was under surveillance, whether by police or reporters or other interested parties one couldn't tell—simply a man, sometimes men, who hung around the stoop. So she'd gone from the hospital to a bank and straight then to Joe Bell's bar. "She don't figure she was followed," Joe Bell told me when he came with a message that Holly wanted me to meet her there as soon as possible, a half-hour at most, bringing: "Her jewelry. Her guitar. Toothbrushes and stuff. And a bottle of hundred-year-old brandy: she says you'll find it hid down in the bottom of the dirty-clothes basket. Yeah, oh, and the cat. She wants the cat. But hell," he said, "I don't know we should help her at all. She ought to be protected against herself. Me, I feel like telling the cops. Maybe if I go back and build her some drinks, maybe I can get her drunk enough to call it off."

Stumbling, skidding up and down the fire escape between Holly's apartment and mine, wind-blown and winded and wet to the bone (clawed to the bone as well, for the cat had not looked favorably upon evacuation, especially in such inclement weather) I managed a fast, first-rate job of assembling her going-away belongings. I even found the St. Christopher's medal. Everything was piled on the floor of my room, a poignant pyramid of brassières and dancing slippers and pretty things I packed in Holly's only suitcase. There was a mass left over that I had to put in paper grocery bags. I couldn't think how to carry the cat; until I thought of stuffing him in a pillowcase.

Never mind why, but once I walked from New Orleans to Nancy's Landing, Mississippi, just under five hundred miles. It was a light-hearted lark compared to the journey to Joe Bell's bar. The guitar filled with rain, rain softened the paper sacks, the sacks split and perfume spilled on the pavement, pearls rolled in the gutter: while the wind pushed and the cat scratched, the cat screamed—but worse, I was frightened, a coward to equal José: those storming streets seemed aswarm with unseen presences waiting to trap, imprison me for aiding an outlaw.

The outlaw said: "You're late, Buster. Did you bring the brandy?"

And the cat, released, leaped and perched on her shoulder: his tail swung like a baton conducting rhapsodic music. Holly, too, seemed inhabited by melody, some bouncy *bon voyage* oompahpah. Uncorking the brandy, she said: "This was meant to be part of my hope chest. The idea was, every anniversary we'd have a swig. Thank Jesus I never bought the chest. Mr. Bell, sir, three glasses."

"You'll only need two," he told her. "I won't drink to your foolishness."

The more she cajoled him ("Ah, Mr. Bell. The lady doesn't vanish every day. Won't you toast her?"), the gruffer he was: "I'll have no part of it. If you're going to hell, you'll go on your own. With no further help from me." An inaccurate statement: because seconds after he'd made it a chauffeured limousine drew up outside the bar, and Holly, the first to notice it, put down her brandy, arched her eyebrows, as though she expected to see the District Attorney himself alight. So did I. And when I saw Joe Bell blush, I had to think: by God, he *did* call the police. But then, with burning ears, he announced: "It's nothing. One of them Carey Cadillacs. I hired it. To take you to the airport."

He turned his back on us to fiddle with one of his flower arrangements. Holly said: "Kind, dear Mr. Bell. Look at me, sir."

He wouldn't. He wrenched the flowers from the vase and thrust them at her; they missed their mark, scattered on the floor. "Good-bye," he said; and, as though he were going to vomit, scurried to the men's room. We heard the door lock.

The Carey chauffeur was a worldly specimen who accepted our slapdash luggage most civilly and remained rock-faced when, as the limousine swished uptown through a lessening rain, Holly stripped off her clothes, the riding costume she'd never had a chance to substitute, and struggled into a slim black dress. We didn't talk: talk could have only led to argument; and also, Holly seemed too preoccupied for conversation. She hummed to herself, swigged brandy, she leaned constantly forward to peer out the windows, as if she were hunting an address—or, I decided, taking a last impression of a scene she wanted to remember. It was neither of these. But this: "Stop here," she ordered the driver, and we pulled to the curb of a street in Spanish Harlem. A savage, a garish, a moody neighborhood garlanded with poster-portraits of movie stars and Madonnas. Sidewalk litterings of fruit-rind and rotted newspaper were hurled about by the wind, for the wind still boomed, though the rain had hushed and there were bursts of blue in the sky.

Holly stepped out of the car; she took the cat with her. Cradling him, she scratched his head and asked: "What do you think? This ought to be the right kind of place for a tough guy like you. Garbage cans. Rats galore. Plenty of cat-bums to gang around with. So scram," she said, dropping him; and when he did not move away, instead raised his thug-face and questioned her with yellowish pirate-eyes, she stamped her foot: "I said beat it!" He rubbed against her leg. "I said fuck off!" she shouted, then jumped back in the car, slammed the door, and: "Go," she told the driver. "Go. Go."

I was stunned. "Well, you *are*. You *are* a bitch."

We'd traveled a block before she replied. "I told you. We just met by the river one day: that's all. Independents, both of us. We never made each other any promises. We never—" she said, and her voice collapsed, a tic, an invalid whiteness seized her face. The car had paused for a traffic light. Then she had the door open, she was running down the street; and I ran after her.

But the cat was not at the corner where he'd been left. There was no one, nothing on the street except a urinating drunk and two Negro nuns herding a file of sweet-singing children. Other children emerged from doorways and ladies leaned over their window sills to watch as Holly darted up and down the block, ran back and forth chanting: "You. Cat. Where are you? Here, cat." She kept it up until a bumpy-skinned boy came forward dangling an old tom by the scruff of its neck: "You wants a nice kitty, miss? Gimme a dollar."

The limousine had followed us. Now Holly let me steer her toward it. At the door, she hesitated; she looked past me, past the boy still offering his cat ("Halfa dollar. Two-bits, maybe? Two-bits, it ain't much"), and she shuddered, she had to grip my arm to stand up: "Oh, Jesus God. We did belong to each other. He was mine."

Then I made her a promise, I said I'd come back and find her cat: "I'll take care of him, too. I promise."

She smiled: that cheerless new pinch of a smile. "But what about me?" she said, whispered, and shivered again. "I'm very scared, Buster. Yes, at last. Because it could go on forever. Not knowing what's yours until you've thrown it away. The mean reds, they're nothing. The fat woman, she's nothing. This, though: my mouth's so dry, if my life depended on it I couldn't spit." She stepped in the car, sank in the seat. "Sorry, driver. Let's go."

TOMATO'S TOMATO MISSING. And: DRUG-CASE ACTRESS BELIEVED GANGLAND VICTIM. In due time, however, the press reported: FLEEING PLAYGIRL TRACED TO RIO. Apparently no attempt was made by American authorities to recover her, and soon the matter diminished to an occasional gossip-column mention; as a news story, it was revived only once: on Christmas Day, when Sally Tomato died of a heart attack at Sing Sing. Months went by, a winter of them, and not a word from Holly. The owner of the brownstone sold her abandoned possessions, the white-satin bed, the tapestry, her precious Gothic chair; a new tenant acquired the apartment, his name was Quaintance Smith, and he entertained as many gentlemen callers of a noisy nature as Holly ever had—though in this instance Madame Spanella did not object, indeed she doted on the young man and supplied filet mignon whenever he had a black eye. But in the spring a postcard came: it was scribbled in pencil, and signed with a lipstick kiss: *Brazil was beastly but Buenos Aires the best. Not Tiffany's, but almost. Am joined at the hip with dubvine $enor. Love? Think so. Anyboo am looking for somewhere to live ($enor has wife, 7 brats) and will let you know address when I know it myself. Mille tendresse.* But the address, if it ever existed, never was sent, which made me sad, there was so much I wanted to write her: that I'd *sold* two stories, had read where the Trawlers were countersuing for divorce, was moving out of the brownstone because it was haunted. But mostly, I wanted to tell about her cat. I had kept my promise; I had found him. It took weeks of after-work roaming through those Spanish Harlem streets, and there were many false alarms—flashes of tiger-striped fur that, upon inspection, were not him. But one day, one cold sunshiny Sunday winter afternoon, it was. Flanked by potted plants and framed by clean lace curtains, he was seated in the window of a warm-looking room: I wondered what his name was, for I was certain he had one now, certain he'd arrived somewhere he belonged. African hut or whatever, I hope Holly has, too.

TRAVEL
SKETCHES

New Orleans

(1946)

IN THE COURTYARD THERE WAS AN angel of black stone, and its angel head rose above giant elephant leaves; the stark glass angel eyes, bright as the bleached blue of sailor eyes, stared upward. One observed the angel from an intricate green balcony—mine, this balcony, for I lived beyond in three old white rooms, rooms with elaborate wedding-cake ceilings, wide sliding doors, tall French windows. On warm evenings, with these windows open, conversation was pleasant there, tuneful, for wind rustled the interior like fan-breeze made by ancient ladies. And on such warm evenings the town is quiet. Only voices: family talk weaving on an ivy-curtained porch; a barefoot woman humming as she rocks a sidewalk chair, lulling to sleep a baby she nurses quite publicly; the complaining foreign tongue of an irritated lady who, sitting on her balcony, plucks a fryer, the loosened feathers floating from her hands, slipping into air, sliding lazily downward.

One morning—it was December, I think, a cold Sunday with a sad gray sun—I went up through the Quarter to the old market, where at that time of year there are exquisite winter fruits, sweet satsumas, twenty cents a dozen, and winter flowers, Christmas poinsettia and snow japonica. New Orleans streets have long, lonesome perspectives; in empty hours their atmosphere is like Chirico, and things innocent, ordinarily (a face behind the slanted light of shutters, nuns moving in the distance, a fat dark arm lolling lopsidedly out some window, a lonely black boy squatting in an alley, blowing soap bubbles and watching sadly as they rise to burst), acquire qualities of violence. Now, on that morning, I stopped still in the middle of a block, for I'd caught out of the corner of my eye a tunnel-passage, an overgrown courtyard. A crazy-looking white hound stood stiffly in the green fern light shining at the tunnel's end, and compulsively I went toward it. Inside there was a fountain; water spilled delicately from a monkey-statue's bronze mouth and made on pool pebbles desolate bell-like sounds. He was hanging from a willow, a bandit-faced man with kinky platinum hair; he hung so limply, like the willow itself. There was terror in that silent suffocated garden. Closed windows looked on blindly; snail tracks glittered silver on elephant ears, nothing moved except his shadow. It swung a little, back and forth, yet there was no wind. A rhinestone ring he wore winked in the sun, and on his arm was tattooed a name, "Francy." The hound lowered its head to drink in the fountain, and I ran. Francy —was it for her he'd killed himself? I do not know. N.O. is a secret place.

My rock angel's glass eyes were like sundials, for they told, by the amount of light focused on them, time: white at noon, they grew gradually dimmer, dark at dusk, black—nightfall eyes in a nightfall head.

The torn lips of golden-haired girls leer luridly on faded leaning house fronts: Drink Dr. Nutt, Dr. Pepper, NEHI, Grapeade, 7-Up, Koke, Coca-Cola. N.O., like every Southern town, is a city of soft-drink signs; the streets of forlorn neighborhoods are paved with Coca-Cola caps, and after rain, they glint in the dust like lost dimes. Posters peel away, lie mangled until storm wind blows them along the street, like desert sage—and there are those who think them beautiful; there are those who paper their walls with Dr. Nutt and Dr. Pepper, with Coca-Cola beauties who, smiling above tenement beds, are night guardians and saints of the morning. Signs everywhere, chalked, printed, painted: Madame Ortega—Readings, Love-potions, Magic Literature, C Me; If You Haven't Anything To Do . . . Don't Do It Here; Are You Ready To Meet Your Maker?; B Ware, Bad Dog; Pity The Poor Little Orphans; I Am A Deaf & Dumb Widow With 2 Mouths To Feed; Attention; Blue Wing Singers At Our Church Tonight (signed) The Reverend.

There was once this notice on a door in the Irish Channel district, "Come In And See Where Jesus Stood."

"And so?" said a woman who answered when I rang the bell. "I'd like to see where Jesus stood," I told her, and for a moment she looked blank; her face, cut in razorlike lines, was marshmallow-white; she had no eye-brows, no lashes, and she wore a calico kimono. "You too little, honey," she said, a jerky laugh bouncing her breasts, "you too damn little for to see where Jesus stood."

In my neighborhood there was a certain café no fun whatever, for it was the emptiest café around N.O., a regular funeral place. The proprietress,

Mrs. Morris Otto Kunze, did not, however, seem to mind; she sat all day behind her bar, cooling herself with a palmetto fan, and seldom stirred except to swat flies. Now glued over an old cracked mirror backing the bar were seven little signs all alike: Don't Worry About Life . . . You'll Never Get Out Of It Alive.

July 3. An "at home" card last week from Miss Y., so I made a call this afternoon. She is delightful in her archaic way, amusing, too, though not by intent. The first time we met, I thought: Edna May Oliver; and there is a resemblance most certainly. Miss Y. speaks in premediated tones but what she says is haphazard, and her sherry-colored eyes are forever searching the surroundings. Her posture is military, and she carries a man's Malacca cane, one of her legs being shorter than the other, a condition which gives her walk a penguinlike lilt. "It made me unhappy when I was your age; yes, I must say it did, for Papa had to squire me to all the balls, and there we sat on such pretty little gold chairs, and there we sat. None of the gentlemen ever asked Miss Y. to dance, indeed no, though a young man from Baltimore, a Mr. Jones, came here one winter, and gracious!— poor Mr. Jones—fell off a ladder, you know—broke his neck—died instantly."

My interest in Miss Y. is rather clinical, and I am not, I embarrassedly confess, quite the friend she believes, for one cannot feel close to Miss Y.: she is too much a fairy tale, someone real—and improbable. She is like the piano in her parlor—elegant, but a little out of tune. Her house, old even for N.O., is guarded by a black broken iron fence; it is a poor neighborhood she lives in, one sprayed with room-for-rent signs, gasoline stations, jukebox cafés. And yet, in the days when her family first lived here—that, of course, was long ago—there was in all N.O. no finer place. The house, smothered by slanting trees, has a graying exterior; but inside, the fantasy of Miss Y.'s heritage is everywhere visible: the tapping of her cane as she descends birdwing stairs trembles crystal; her face, a heart of wrinkled silk, reflects fumelike on ceiling-high mirrors; she lowers herself (notice, as this happens, how carefully she preserves the comfort of her bones) into father's father's father's chair, a wickedly severe receptacle with lion-head handrests. She is beautiful here in the cool dark of her house, and safe. These are the walls, the fence, the furniture of her childhood. "Some people are born to be old; I, for instance, was an atrocious child lacking any quality whatever. But I like being old. It makes me feel somehow more"—she paused, indicated with a gesture the dim parlor—"more suitable."

Miss Y. does not believe in the world beyond N.O.; at times her insularity results, as it did today, in rather chilling remarks. I had mentioned a recent trip to New York, whereupon she, arching an eyebrow, replied gently, "Oh? And how *are* things in the country?"

. . . .

1. Why is it, I wonder, that all N.O. cabdrivers sound as though they were imported from Brooklyn?

2. One hears so much about food here, and it is probably true that such restaurants as Arnaud's and Kolb's are the best in America. There is an attractive, lazy atmosphere about these restaurants: the slow-wheeling fans, the enormous tables and lack of crowding, the silence, the casual but expert waiters who all look as though they were sons of the management. A friend of mine, discussing N.O. and New York, once pointed out that comparable meals in the East, aside from being considerably more expensive, would arrive elaborate with some chef's mannerisms, with all kinds of froufrou and false accessories. Like most good things, the quality of N.O. cookery derived, he thought, from its essential simplicity.

3. I am more or less disgusted by that persistent phrase "old charm." You will find it, I suppose, in the architecture here, and in the antique shops (where it rightly belongs), or in the minglings of dialect one hears around the French Market. But N.O. is no more charming than any other Southern city—less so, in fact, for it is the largest. The main portion of this city is made up of spiritual bottomland, streets and sections rather outside the tourist belt.

(From a letter to R.R.) There are new people in the apartment below, the third tenants in the last year; a transient place, this Quarter, hello and good-bye. A real bona-fide scoundrel lived there when I first came. He was unscrupulous, unclean and crooked—a kind of dissipated satyr. Mr. Buddy, the one-man band. More than likely you have seen him—not here of course, but in some other city, for he keeps on the move, he and his old banjo, drum, harmonica. I used to come across him banging away on various street corners, a gang of loafers gathered round. Realizing he was my neighbor, these meetings always gave me rather a turn. Now, to tell the truth, he was not a bad musician—an extraordinary one, in fact, when, late of an afternoon, and for his own pleasure, he sang to his guitar, sang ghostly ballads in a grieving whiskey voice: how terrible it was for those in love.

"Hey, boy, you! You up there . . ." I was *you*, for he never knew my name, and never showed much interest in finding it out. "Come on down and help me kill a couple."

His balcony, smaller than mine, was screened with sweet-smelling wisteria; as there was no furniture to speak of, we would sit on the floor in the green shade, drinking a brand of gin close kin to rubbing alcohol, and he would finger his guitar, its steady plaintive whine emphasizing the deep roll of his voice. "Been all over, been in and out, all around; sixty-five, and any woman takes up with me ain't got no use for nobody else; yessir, had myself a lota wives and a lota kids, but christamighty if I know what come of any of 'em—and don't give a hoot in hell—'cept maybe about Rhonda Kay. There was a woman, man, sweet as swamp honey, and was she hot on me! On fire all the time, and her married to a Baptist preacher, too, and her got four kids—five, countin' mine. Always kinda wondered what it was —boy or girl—boy, I spec. I always give 'em boys . . . Now that's all a long time ago, and it happened in Memphis, Tennessee. Yessir, been everywhere, been to the penitentiary, been in big fine houses like the Rockefellers' houses, been in and out, been all around."

And he could carry on this way until moonrise, his voice growing froggy, his words locking together to make a chant.

His face, stained and wrinkled, had a certain deceptive kindness, a childish twinkle, but his eyes slanted in an Oriental manner, and he kept his fingernails long, knife-sharp and polished as a Chinaman's. "Good for scratching, and handy in a fight, too."

He always wore a kind of costume: black trousers, engine-red socks, tennis shoes with the toes slit for comfort, a morning coat, a gray velvet waistcoat which, he said, had belonged to his ancestor Benjamin Franklin, and a beret studded with Vote for Roosevelt buttons. And there is no getting around it—he *did* have a good many lady friends—a different one each week, to be sure, but there was hardly ever a time when some woman wasn't cooking his meals; and on those occasions when I came to visit he would invariably, and in a most courtly fashion, say, "Meet Mrs. Buddy."

Late one night I woke with the feeling I was not alone; sure enough, there was someone in the room, and I could see him in the moonlight on my mirror. It was he, Mr. Buddy, furtively opening, closing bureau drawers, and suddenly my box of pennies splattered on the floor, rolled riotously in all directions. There was no use pretending then, so I turned on a lamp, and Mr. Buddy looked at me squarely, scarcely fazed, and grinned. "Listen," he said, and he was the most sober I'd ever seen him. "Listen, I've got to get out of here in a hurry."

I did not know what to say, and he looked down at the floor, his face turning slightly red. "Come on, be a good guy, have you got any money?"

I could only point to the spilt pennies; without another word he got down on his knees, gathered them and, walking very erectly, went out the door.

He was gone the next morning. Three women have come around asking for him, but I do not know his whereabouts. Maybe he is in Mobile. If you see him around there, R., won't you drop me a card, please?

. . .

I want a big fat mama, yes yes! Shotgun's fingers, long as bananas, thick as dill pickles, pound the keys, and his foot, pounding the floor, shakes the café. Shotgun! The biggest show in town! Can't sing worth a damn, but man, can he rattle that piano—listen: *She's cool in the summer and warm in the fall, she's a four-season mama and that ain't all . . .* There he goes, his fat mouth yawning like a crocodile's, his wicked red tongue tasting the tune, loving it, making love to it; jelly, Shotgun, jelly-jelly-jelly. Look at him laugh, that black, crazy face all scarred with bullet-shot, all glistening with sweat. Is there any human vice he doesn't know about? A shame, though . . . Hardly any white folks ever see Shotgun, for this is a Negro café. Last year's dusty Christmas decorations color the peeling arsenic walls; orange-green-purple strips of fluted paper, dangling from naked light bulbs, flutter in the wind of a tired fan; the proprietor, a handsome quadroon with hooded milk-blue eyes, leans over the bar, squalling, "Look here, what you think this is, some kinda charity? Get up that two-bits, nigger, and mighty quick."

And tonight is Saturday. The room floats in cigarette smoke and Saturday-night perfume. All the little greasy wood tables have double rings of chairs, and everyone knows everyone, and for a moment the world is this room, this dark, jazzy, terrible room; our heartbeat is Shotgun's stamping foot, every joyous element of our lives is focused in the shine of his malicious eyes. *I want a big fat mama, yes yes!* He rocks forward on his stool, and as he lifts his face to look straight at us, a great riding holler goes up in the night: *I want a big fat mama with the meat shakin' on her, yes!*

New York

(1946)

I T IS A MYTH, THE CITY, THE ROOMS
and windows, the steam-spitting streets;
for anyone, everyone, a different myth, an idol-head with traffic-light eyes
winking a tender green, a cynical red. This island, floating in river water
like a diamond iceberg, call it New York, name it whatever you like; the
name hardly matters because, entering from the greater reality of elsewhere, one is only in search of a city, a place to hide, to lose or discover
oneself, to make a dream wherein you prove that perhaps after all you are
not an ugly duckling, but wonderful, and worthy of love, as you thought
sitting on the stoop where the Fords went by; as you thought planning
your search for a city.

Have seen Garbo twice in the last week, once at the theater, where she sat
in the next seat, and again at a Third Avenue antique shop. When I was
twelve I had a tiresome series of mishaps, and so stayed a good deal in bed,
spending most of my time in the writing of a play that was to star the most
beautiful woman in the world, which is how I described Miss Garbo in the
letter accompanying my script. But neither play nor letter was ever acknowledged, and for a long time I bore a desperate grudge, one which was
indeed not dispelled until the other night when, with an absolute turn
over of the heart, I identified the woman in the adjoining seat

surprising to find her so small, and so vividly colored: as Loren MacIver pointed out, along with those lines one scarcely expects color, too.

Someone asked, "Do you suppose she is at all intelligent?," which seems to me an outrageous question; really, who cares whether or not she is intelligent? Surely it is enough that such a face could even exist, though Garbo herself must have come to regret the rather tragic responsibility of owning it. Nor is it any joke about her wanting to be alone; of course she does. I imagine it is the only time she does not feel alone: if you walk a singular path, you carry always a certain grief, and one does not mourn in public.

Yesterday, at the antique store, she roamed around, quite intent about everything, not really interested in anything, and for one mad moment I thought I might speak to her, just to hear her voice, you know; the moment passed, thank heaven, and presently she was out the door. I went to the window and watched her hurrying along the blue dusk street with that long, loping step. At the corner she hesitated, as if uncertain which direction she wanted. The street lights went on, and a trick of glare created suddenly on the avenue a blank white wall: wind lashing her coat, and alone, Garbo, still the most beautiful woman in the world, Garbo, a symbol, walked directly toward it.

Lunch today with M. Whatever is one to do about her? She says the money is gone finally, and unless she goes home, her family refuse absolutely to help. Cruel, I suppose, but I told her I did not see the alternative. On one level, to be sure, I do not think going home possible for her. She belongs to that sect most swiftly, irrevocably trapped by New York, the talented untalented; too acute to accept a more provincial climate, yet not quite acute enough to breathe freely within the one so desired, they go along neurotically feeding upon the fringes of the New York scene.

Only success, and that at a perilous peak, can give relief, but for artists without an art, it is always tension without release, irritation with no resulting pearl. Possibly there would be if the pressure to succeed were not so tremendous. They feel compelled to prove something, because middle-class America, from which they mostly spring, has withering words for its men of feeling, for its young of experimental intelligence, who do not show immedi̶ ̶ ̶ ̶hat these endeavors pay off on a cash basis. But if a civilization f̶ ̶ ̶ ̶ ̶ ̶ ̶ ̶he inheritors find among the ruins? Or is it a statue, a poem,

̶ ̶ ̶o say that the world owes M., or anyone, a living; alas, ̶ ̶ ̶with her, she most likely could not make a poem, a good ̶ ̶ ̶is important, her values are balanced by more than the ̶ ̶ ̶th, she deserves a finer destiny than to pass from

belated adolescence to premature middle age, with no intervening period, and nothing to show.

Down the street there is a radio-repair shop run by an elderly Italian, Joe Vitale. Early in the summer there appeared across the front of his store a strange sign: *The Black Wido*. And in smaller lettering: WATCH THIS WINDOW FOR NEWS OF THE BLACK WIDO. So our neighborhood wondered, waited. A few days later two yellowed photographs were added to the display; these, taken some twenty years before, showed Mr. Vitale as a husky man dressed in a black knee-length bathing suit, a black swimming cap and a mask. Typed captions below the pictures explained that Joe Vitale, whom we'd all known only as a stoop-shouldered, sad-eyed radio-repair man, had once been, in a more supreme incarnation, a champion swimmer and a lifeguard at Rockaway Beach.

We were warned to continue watching the windows; our reward came the following week: in a bold streamer, Mr. Vitale announced that The Black Wido was about to resume his career. There was a poem in the window, and the poem was called "The Dream of Joe Vitale"; it told of how he'd dreamed of again breasting the waves, conquering the sea.

On the next day appeared a final notice; it was an invitation, really, one which said we were all welcome to come to Rockaway on August 20, for this day he planned to swim from that beach to Jones Beach, a far piece. Through the intervening summer days, Mr. Vitale sat outside his store on a camp stool, observing the reactions of passers-by to his various declarations, sat there, dreamy and detached, nodding, smiling politely when neighbors stopped to wish him luck. A smart-aleck kid asked him why he'd left out the last letter of Wido, and he answered very gently that widow with a *w* is for ladies.

For a while nothing more happened. Then one morning the world woke up and laughed at the dream of Joe Vitale. His story was in every paper; the tabloids put his picture on the front pages. And sorry pictures they were, too, for here he was, in a moment not of triumph, but agony, here he was standing on the beach at Rockaway with policemen on either side. And in their accounts this is the attitude most of the papers took: once upon a time there was a mad silly old man who rubbed himself with grease and trotted down to the sea, but when the lifeguards saw him out swimming so far, they put to their boats and brought him to shore; such a shy one, this comical old man, for the instant their backs were turned, he was off again, and so out the lifeguards rowed once more, and The Black Wido, forced upon the beach like a half-dead shark, returned to hear not the mermaids singing, but curses, catcalls, police whistles.

The proper thing to do would be to go and tell Joe Vitale how sorry you are, how brave you think him, and say, well, whatever you can; the death of a dream is no less sad than death, and, indeed, demands of those who have lost as deep a mourning. But his radio store is closed; it has been for a long time; there is no sign of him anywhere, and his poem has slipped from place, has fallen beyond view.

Hilary said to come and have tea before the other guests arrived. Even though he had an extravagant cold, he insisted on going ahead with the party; naturally, why not? Playing host is his cure-all. No matter whose house you may be in, if Hilary is there, it is his house, you are his guest. Some think this a too high-handed attitude, but the real hosts are always pleased, for Hilary, with his large, spectacular appearance and roaring, giggling monologues, gives even the dreariest occasions a bubbling glamour. Hilary so wants everyone to be glamorous, to be a story-book creature; somehow he persuades himself that the grayest folk are coated with legend-making glitter; what is more, he persuades them, too, and that in part accounts for the tenderness with which a usually not soft-hearted public refers to him.

Another appealing point is that Hilary is always the same; always making you laugh when you damn well want to cry; and there is this curious feeling that after you have gone, he does your crying for you. Hilary with a velvet lap robe spread over his knees, a telephone in one hand, a book in the other, a radio, a music box, another telephone and a phonograph all sounding in surrounding rooms.

When I arrived for tea, Hilary was propped up in bed, from which he intended to conduct his party. The walls of this room are papered with photographs, almost everyone he has ever known: maiden ladies, debutantes, somebody's secretary, film stars, college professors, chorus girls, circus freaks, Westchester couples, businessmen: they may part with him, but he cannot bear to lose anyone; or anything. Books are piled in the corners, are sagging on shelves, among them his old school texts, and ancient theater programs, mounds of sea shells, broken records, dead flowers, amusement-park souvenirs turn the apartment into a wonderland attic.

A time may come when there is no Hilary; it would be easy to destroy him—it may be that someone will. Could it be that the transition from innocence to wisdom happens in that moment when we discover not all the world loves us? Most of us learn this too early. But Hilary does not know it yet. I hope he never does, for I should hate it if suddenly he saw he was playing in a playground all alone, and spending love upon an audience that had never been there.

. . .

August. Although the morning papers said simply fair and warm, it was apparent by noon that something exceptional was happening, and office workers, drifting back from lunch with the dazed, desperate expression of children being bullied, began to dial Weather. Toward midafternoon, as the heat closed in like a hand over a murder victim's mouth, the city thrashed and twisted, but with its outcry muffled, its hurry hampered, its ambitions hindered, it was like a dry fountain, some useless monument, and so sank into a coma. The steaming willow-limp stretches of Central Park were like a battlefield where many have fallen: rows of exhausted casualties lay crumpled in the dead-still shade, while newspaper photographers, documenting the disaster, moved sepulchrally among them. At night, hot weather opens the skull of a city, exposing its white brain and its central nerves, which sizzle like the inside of an electric-light bulb.

I should probably get a good deal more work done if I left New York. However, more than likely that is not true either. Until one is a certain age, the country seems a bore; and anyway, I like nature not in general, but in particular. Nevertheless, unless one is in love, or satisfied, or ambition-driven, or without curiosity, or reconciled (which appears to be the modern synonym for happiness), the city is like a monumental machine restlessly devised for wasting time, devouring illusions. After a little, the search, the exploration, can become sinisterly hurried, sweatingly anxious, a race over hurdles of Benzedrine and Nembutal. Where is what you were looking for? And by the way, what *are* you looking for? It is misery to refuse an invitation; one is always declining them, only to put in a surprise appearance; after all, it is difficult to stay away when whispers eerily persist to suggest that in keeping to yourself, you've let love fly out the window, denied your answer, forever lost what you were looking for: oh to think! all this awaits a mere ten blocks away: hurry, put on your hat, don't bother with the bus, grab a taxi, there now, hurry, ring the doorbell: hello, sucker, April fool.

Today is my birthday and, as always, Selma remembered: her customary offering, a dime carefully wadded in a sheet of john paper, arrived with the morning mail. In both time and age, Selma is my oldest friend; for eighty-three years she has lived in the same small Alabama town; a hooked little woman with parched cinder-dark skin and spicy, hooded eyes, she was for forty-seven years a cook in the house of my three aunts; but now that they are dead, she has moved to her daughter's farm, just, as she says, to sit quiet and take her ease. But accompanying her gift there was a sort of note, and in it she said to make ready, for any day now she was going to take a Greyhound bus for that "grandus city." It does not mean anything; she will never come; but she has been threatening to for as long as memory. The summer before I first saw New York, and that was fourteen years ago, we used to sit talking in the kitchen, our voices strumming away the whole lazy day; and what we talked about mostly was the city where I was soon to go. It was her understanding that there were no trees there, nor flowers, and she'd heard it said that most of the people lived underground or, if not underground, in the sky. Furthermore, there were "no nourishin' vittles," no good butterbeans, black-eyes, okra, yams, sausage—like we had at home. And it's cold, she said, yessireebobtail, go on up in that cold country, time we see you again your nose will have freeze and fall off.

But then Mrs. Bobby Lee Kettle brought over some picture slides of New York, and after that Selma began telling her friends that when I went North she was going with me. The town seemed to her suddenly shriveled and mean. And so my aunts bought her a round-trip ticket, the idea being that she should ride up with me, turn around and go back. Everything was fine until we reached the depot; and there Selma began to cry, and say that she couldn't go, that she would die so far from home.

It was a sad winter, inside and out. For a child the city is a joyless place. Later on, when one is older and in love, it is the double vision of sharing with your beloved which gives experience texture, shape, significance. To travel alone is to journey through a wasteland. But if you love enough, sometimes you can see for yourself, and for another, too. That is the way it was with Selma. I saw twice over everything: the first snow, and skaters skimming in the park, the fine fur coats of the funny cold country children, the Chute-the-Chute at Coney, subway chewing-gum machines, the magical Automat, the islands in the river and the glitter upon the twilight bridge, the blue upward floating of a Paramount band, the men who came in the courtyard day after day and sang the same ragged, hoarse songs, the magnificent fairy tale of a ten-cent store where one went after school to steal things; I watched, listened, storing up for the quiet kitchen-hours when Selma would say, as she did, "Tell stories about that place, true stories now, none of them lies." But mostly they were lies I told; it wasn't my fault, I couldn't remember, because it was as though I'd been to one of those supernatural castles visited by characters in legends: once away, you do not remember, all that is left is the ghostly echo of haunting wonder.

Brooklyn

(1946)

AN ABANDONED CHURCH, A FOR RENT sign defacing its baroque façade, towers black and broken at the corner of this lost square; sparrows nest among the stone flowers carved above its chalked-up door (Kilroy Was Here, Seymour Loves Betty, You Stink!); inside, where sunlight falls on shattered pews, all manner of stray beasts have found a home: one sees misty cats watching from its windows, hears queer animal cries, and neighborhood children, who dare each other to enter there, come forth toting bones they claim as human (yeah, they is so! I'm tellin' yuh; the guy was kilt). Definitive in its ugliness, the church for me symbolizes some elements of Brooklyn: if a similar structure were destroyed, I have the uneasy premonition that another, equally old and monstrous, would swiftly be erected, for Brooklyn, or the chain of cities so-called, has, unlike Manhattan, no interest in architectural change. Nor is it lenient toward the individual: in despair one views the quite endless stretches of look-alike bungalows, gingerbread and brownstones, the inevitable empty, ashy lot where the sad, sweet, violent children, gathering leaves and tenement-wood, make October bonfires, the sad, sweet children chasing down these glassy August streets to Kill the Kike! Kill the Wop! Kill the Dinge!—a custom of this country where the mental architecture, like the houses, is changeless.

Manhattan friends, unwilling to cope with the elaborately dismal subway trip (Oh, B., do come, I swear to you it takes only forty minutes, and honest, you don't have to change trains but three times), say so-sorry to any invitation. For this reason I've often daydreamed of leasing and renovating the church: who could resist visiting so curious a residence? As matters stand I have two rooms in a brownstone duplicated by twenty others on the square; the interior of the house is a grimy jungle of Victoriana: lily-pale, plump-faced ladies garbed in rotting Grecian veils prance tribally on wallpaper; in the hall an empty, tarnished bowl for calling cards and a hat tree gnarled like a spruce glimpsed on the coast of Brittany are elegant mementos from Brooklyn's less blighted days; the parlor bulges with dusty fringed furniture, a family history in daguerreotype parades across an old untuned piano, everywhere antimacassars are like little crocheted flags declaring a state of Respectability, and when a draught goes through this room beaded lamps tinkle Oriental tunes.

However, there are telephones: two upstairs, three down, and 125 in the basement; for it is in the basement that my landladies are more or less locked to a switchboard: Mrs. Q., a waddling, stunted woman with a red bulldog face, knobby lavender eyes and bright orange, unbelievable hair which, like her daughter Miss Q., she wears wild and waist-length, is a suspicious person, and her suspicion is the sort that goes with those who, despising everything, are looking for a reason. Poor Miss Q. is simply tired; soft and honeyed, she labors under what is essentially a birth-to-death fatigue, and at times I wonder whether she is really Miss Q. or Zasu Pitts. Nevertheless, there is established between us an agreeable rapport. It is based principally on the fact that we are both harassed by hair-raising headaches. Almost every day she sneaks upstairs, and giggling at her naughty daring, begs an aspirin; her mother, a devotee of Bernarr MacFadden, forbids aspirin and all medicine as "stew from the devil's stove." Their story is an old story: Mr. Q., "a very decidedly prominent mortician," just "passed away with no word of warning while reading the *New York Sun,*" leaving his wife and spinster daughter to "go on living with no visible means of doing so," because "a crook got Papa to invest all his money in a factory to make artificial funeral wreathes." So she and her mother set up a telephone-answering service in the basement. Day and night for ten years they'd alternated intercepting calls for persons out-of-town or not at home. "Oh, it's a misery," says Miss Q. with counterfeit despondency, for this career-woman role is the realest illusion of her illusioned life. "I tell you God's truth, I couldn't count the years since I've had a straight hour's rest. Mama's right there on the job, too, bless her soul, but Mama's got a good many complaints, you know, and I just have to practically tie her in the bed. Sometimes when it's late at night and my head starts to hurt— why, I look at the switchboard, and suddenly it's like all those long wires were arms and fingers squeezing me to death." Upon occasion Mrs. Q. has been known to visit a Turkish bath near Borough Hall, but her tired daughter's isolation is absolute; if one is to believe her, she has left the basement only once in eight years, and on this holiday she went with her mother to watch Mr. MacFadden do calisthenics on the stage of Carnegie Hall.

In dread I some nights listen as Mrs. Q. comes heaving up the stairs, presently to present herself at my door; standing there, shrouded in a sleazy sateen kimono, her sunset-colored hair falling Viking-fashion, she regards me with a baleful glitter. "Two more," she says, her hairy baritone voice suggesting fire and brimstone. "We saw them from the window, two whole families riding by in moving vans."

When she has squeezed dry the lemon of her sourness, I ask, "Families of what, Mrs. Q.?"

"Africans," she announces with a righteous owl-like blink, "the whole neighborhood's turning into a black nightmare; first Jews, now this; robbers and thieves, all of them—makes my blood run cold."

Though I suspect Mrs. Q. herself does not realize it, this is not a performance, she is seriously frightened: what is going on outside corresponds with nothing she has known; the husband whose mind she fed upon is gone, and she herself, having possessed merely borrowed attitudes, has never owned an idea. She has had fixed on every door an abnormal number of catches and locks, a few of the windows are barred, there is a mongrel with an ear-splitting bark: someone without, some shapeless someone, desires to be within. Each step remarks her weight as she descends the stairs; below, an image, her own, is groping on the mirror: not recognizing Mrs. Q., she pauses, her breath coming heavy as she wonders who is waiting there: a chill starts in her bones: two more today, more tomorrow, a flood is rising, her Brooklyn is the lost Atlantis, even her reflection on the mirror (a wedding present, remember? forty years: oh, what has happened, tell me, God?), even it is someone, something. "Good night," she calls. The locks go clink-clunk, the gates are closed; 125 telephones are singing in the dark, the Grecian ladies dance in shadow, the house sighs, settles. Outside, wind brings the sweet cookie smell of a bakery blocks away; sailors, bound for Sands Street, cross the lamplit square, and look up at the skeleton church to meet the yellow knowledge of cold cat-eyes. "Good night, Mrs. Q."

I heard a cock crow. Strange at first, it seemed less so remembering the secret unseen city, the continent of backyard lots, nowhere more flourishing than here: ribbon-clerk and shoe-salesman, tillers of the soil: "Our own radishes, you know." Recently a Flatbush woman was arrested for keeping hogs in her backyard. Envy doubtless drove her neighbors to complain. In the evening, arriving from Manhattan, it is somewhat unnerving to see a sky where real stars are really shining, to mosey down leaf-strewn streets where the smoky autumn smells drift undiluted, and the voices of children, roller-skating in the twilight, bring on the silence homecoming messages:

"Look, Myrtle, it's a moon—like a Halloween pumpkin!" Underneath, the subway seethes; above, neon cuts the night, yes, still I heard a cock crow.

As a group, Brooklynites form a persecuted minority; the uninventive persistence of not very urbane clowns has made any mention of their homeland a signal for compulsory guffaws; their dialect, appearance and manners have become, by way of such side-splitting propaganda, synonymous with the crudest, most vulgar aspects of contemporary life. All this, which perhaps began good-naturedly enough, has turned the razory road toward malice: an address in Brooklyn is now not altogether respectable. A peculiar irony, to be sure, for in this unfortunate region the average man, being on the edge of an outcast order, guards averageness with morbid intensity; he does, in fact, make of respectability a religion; still, insecurity makes for hypocrisy, and so he greets The Big Joke with the loudest hee-haw of all: "Yaaah, ain't Brooklyn a kick—talk about funny!" Terribly funny, yes, but Brooklyn is also sad brutal provincial lonesome human silent sprawling raucous lost passionate subtle bitter immature innocent perverse tender mysterious, a place where Crane and Whitman found poems, a mythical dominion against whose shores the Coney Island sea laps a wintry lament. Here, scarcely anyone can give directions; nobody knows where anything is, even the oldest taxi driver seems uncertain; luckily, I've earned my degree in subway travel, though learning to ride these rails, which, buried in the stone, are like the veins found on fossilized fern, requires fiercer application, I'm sure, than working toward a master's. Rocking through the sunless, starless tunnels is an outward-bound feeling: the train, hurtling below unlikely land, seems destined for fog and mist, only the flash-by of familiar stations revealing our identities. Once, thundering under the river, I saw a girl, she was sixteen or so and being initiated into some sorority, I suspect, who carried a basket filled with little hearts cut from scarlet paper. "Buy a lonely heart," she wailed, passing through the car. "Buy a lonely heart." But the pale, expressionless passengers, none of whom needed one, merely flipped the pages of their *Daily News*.

Several nights a week I have dinner at the Cherokee Hotel. It is an apartment hotel, and exceedingly antique, both in décor and clientele: the youngest Cherokee, as they call themselves, is sixty-six, and the oldest, ninety-eight; females, of course, predominate, but there is a skin-and-bone assortment of widowers, too. Now and then war breaks out between the sexes, and it is easy to deduce when this has happened, for the general sitting room will be deserted; there is a men's parlor and a ladies' parlor, and to these respective sanctuaries the embattled retire, the ladies in a pouting huff, the men, as always, silent, grim. Both parlors, along with a lot of depressing statuary, sport radios, and when a war is on, the ladies, who ordinarily are not in the least interested, turn the volume of theirs as loud as it will go, trying, as it were, to drown out the men's after-dinner news. You can hear the boom three blocks away, and Mr. Littlelow, the proprietor, a nervous young man to begin with, scampers back and forth threatening to abolish the radios altogether, or, worse still, call in his guests' relatives. From time to time he has to resort to this last-mentioned measure; for instance, take the case of Mr. Gilbert Crocker, who sins so constantly poor Littlelow had at last to send for his grandson, and together they reprimanded the old man publicly. "A perpetual center of dissension," accused Littlelow, a finger lifted toward the culprit, "he spreads vicious rumors about the management, says we read his mail, says we have a percentage deal with the Cascades Funeral Home, told Miss Brockton the seventh floor is closed because we've rented it to a fugitive from the law (an ax murderess, he said) when everybody knows the water pipes have burst. Scared Miss Brockton out of her wits; her heart-flutter is ever so much worse. We were willing to overlook all this, but when he started dropping light bulbs from the windows, we thought: well really, the time has come!"

"Why did you drop light bulbs, Grandfather?" said the grandson, glancing anxiously at his watch and obviously wishing the old man had met his Maker.

"Not light bulbs, son," corrected Mr. Crocker patiently. "They were bombs."

"Yes, certainly, Grandfather. And why did you drop the bombs?"

Mr. Crocker surveyed the assemblage of fellow Cherokees; then, with a saturnine smile, bobbed his head in the direction of Miss Brockton. "Her—" he said, "I wanted to blow her up. She's a stinking pig; she and Cook have it fixed up between them never to give me any chocolate sauce so she can gobble it all her big fat self."

Promptly the ladies gathered around his intended victim, whose heart-flutter seemed suddenly on the verge of flying her to the ceiling; above their outraged clucking, Mrs. Allen T. Bonaparte's *non sequiturs* carried clearest: "Murder dear Miss Brockton, imagine, did you ever visit the waxworks in London? You know the ones I mean: look alike, don't they?" And it was understood the radios that night would set every window trembling.

Now, among the tenants there is one so formidable she gives pause even to Littlelow. Very grand is Mrs. T. T. Huett-Smith, and when she appears in the dining room, twinkling with yellowed musty diamonds, her entrance lacks only musical fanfare: with stuttering steps she advances toward her table (the one with a rose, the only one with a rose: paper, at that), accepting, in passage, the homage of the socially ambitious: she is the last souvenir they have of those faraway days when Brooklyn, too, supported an altitudinous society. But like most things which have lingered beyond their valid bloom, Mrs. T. T. has turned decadent, has become a tragicomic exaggeration: lipstick and rouge, of which she uses an inordinate quantity, look rancid on her narrow, shriveled face, and her pleasures are perverse: she enjoys nothing so much as making some sadistic revelations. When Mrs. Bonaparte first moved into the hotel, Mrs. T. T., seeing her enter the dining room, announced vociferously, "I remember that creature when her mother was a scrub-woman in the *lowest* bath in Coney Island." The shy and silent Webster sisters are another target: "Damned old maids, my husband always called them."

I know a secret about Mrs. T. T. She is a thief. For years she has been slipping the Cherokee's dime-store silverware into her embroidered handbag, and one day, during what was doubtless a mental blackout, she appeared at the desk asking to have her collection locked safely in the hotel safe. "But my dear Mrs. Huett-Smith," said Littlelow, rising above his astonishment, "this can hardly belong to you; after all, it isn't your pattern." Mrs. T. T. examined the knives and forks with a puzzled frown: "Of course not," she said, "no, of course not: we always had the best."

Weeks have gone by since I was last at the Cherokee. I had a dream. I dreamt one of Mr. Crocker's bombs blew them all away; to tell the truth, I'm rather afraid to go and see.

December 28. A blue crystal day, too exquisite for the stuffy precincts of Mrs. Q.'s, and so with a friend I went for a walk on Brooklyn Heights; Boston's Beacon Hill and Charleston, these alone of places I have known, can project a comparable sense of the past (the *vieux carré* of New Orleans is exempt because its quality is too directly foreign); and of the three, Brooklyn Heights seems the less contrived, and certainly the least exploited. It is condemned, of course; even now a tunnel is coming through, a highway is planned; steel-teethed machines are eating at its palisades, many of the old mansions wait in derelict darkness for the demolition crew; the red newness of *Danger! Men Working* signs glitters in the sober shade of dwarfed Dickensian streets: Cranberry, Pineapple, Willow, Middagh. The dust of dynamited stone hangs its sentence in the air. As it was getting dusk we bought a pecan pie; we sat down on a bench and watched the honeycomb of lights go on in the towers across the river. Wind whipped whitecaps on the cold water, sang through the harplike bridge, swept crying gulls in looping patterns. Eating my portion of the pie, I sat looking at Manhattan and wondering what sort of ruins it would make: as for Brooklyn, archaeologists of another civilization, like taxi drivers of our own, will never decipher the secret of its streets, their destination, their meaning.

Hollywood

(1947)

Approaching Los Angeles, at least by air, is like, I should imagine, crossing the surface of the moon: prehistoric shapes, looming in stone ripples and corroded, leer upward, and paleozoic fish swim in the shadowy pools between desert mountains: burned and frozen, there is no living thing, only rock that was once a bird, bones that are sand, ferns turned to fiery stone. At last a welcoming fleet of clouds: we have crept between a sorcerer's passage, snow is on the mountains, yet flowers color the land, a summer sun juxtaposes December's winter sea, down, down, the plane splits through plumed, gold, incredible air. Oh, moaned Thelma, I can't stand it, she said, and poured a cascade of Chiclets into her mouth. Thelma had boarded the plane in Chicago; she was a young Negro girl, rather pretty, beautifully dressed, and it was the most wonderful thing that would ever happen to her, this trip to California. "I know it, it's going just to be grand. Three years I've been ushering at the Lola Theater on State Street just to save the fare. My auntie tells the cards, and she said—Thelma, honey, head for Hollywood 'cause there's a job as private secretary to a movie actress just waiting for you. She didn't say what actress, though. I hope it's not Esther Williams. I don't like swimming much."

Later on she asked if I was trying for film work, and because the idea seemed to please her, I said yes. On the whole she was very encouraging, and assured me that as soon as she was established as a private secretary, thereby having access to the ears of the great, she would not forget me, would indeed give me every assistance.

At the airport I helped with her luggage, and eventually we shared a taxi. It came about then that she had no place specific to go, she simply wanted the driver to let her off in the "middle" of Hollywood. It was a long drive, and she sat all the way on the edge of the seat, unbearably watchful. But there was not so much to see as she'd imagined. "It don't look correct," she said finally, quite as if we'd been played a wretched trick, for here again, though in disguise, was the surface of the moon, the noplace of everywhere; but how very correct, after all, that here at continent's end we should find only a dumping ground for all that is most exploitedly American: oil pumps pounding like the heartbeat of demons, avenues of used-car lots, supermarkets, motels, the gee dad I never knew a Chevrolet gee dad gee mom gee whiz wham of publicity, the biggest, broadest, best, sprawled and helplessly etherized by immaculate sunshine and sound of sea and unearthly sweetness of flowers blooming in December.

During the drive the sky had grown ash-colored, and as we turned into the laundered sparkle of Wilshire Boulevard, Thelma, giving her delicate feathered hat a protective touch, grumbled at the possibility of rain. Not a chance, said the driver, just wind blowing in dust from the desert. These words were not out of his mouth before the palm trees shivered under a violent downpour. But Thelma had no place to go, except into the street, so we left her standing there, rain pulling her costume apart. When a traffic light stopped us at the corner, she ran up and stuck her head in the window. "Look here, honey, remember what I say, you get hungry or anything you just find where I'm at." Then, with a lovely smile, "And listen, honey, lotsa luck!"

December 3. Today, through the efforts of a mutual friend, Nora Parker, I was asked to lunch by the fabled Miss C. There is a fortress wall surrounding her place, and at the entrance gate we were more or less frisked by a guard who then telephoned ahead to announce our arrival. All this was very satisfying; it was nice to know that at least someone was living the way a famous actress should. At the door we were met by a red-faced, overly nourished child with a gooey pink ribbon trailing from her hair. "Mummy thinks I should entertain you till she comes down," she said apathetically, then led us into a large and, now that I think about it, preposterous room: it looked as though some rich old rascal had personally decorated himself a lavish hideaway: sly, low-slung couches, piles of lecherous velvet pillows and lamps with sinuous, undulating shapes. "Would you like to see Mummy's things?" said the little girl.

Her first exhibit was an illuminated bibelot cabinet. "This," she said, pointing to a bit of Chinese porcelain, "is Mummy's ancient vase she paid Gump's three thousand dollars for. And that's her gold cocktail shaker and gold cups. I forget how much they cost, an awful lot, maybe five thousand dollars. And you see that old teapot? You wouldn't believe what it's worth . . ."

It was a monstrous recital, and toward the end of it, Nora, looking dazedly round the room for a change of topic, said, "Such lovely flowers. Are they from your own garden?"

"Heavens, no," replied the little girl disdainfully. "Mummy orders them every day from the most expensive florist in Beverly Hills."

"Oh?" said Nora, wincing. "And what is your favorite flower?"

"Orchids."

"Now really. I don't believe orchids could be your favorite flower. A little girl like you."

She thought a moment. "Well, as a matter of fact, they aren't. But Mummy says they are the most expensive."

Just then there was a rustling at the door; Miss C. skipped like a school-girl across the room: her famous face was without make-up; hairpins dangled loosely. She was wearing a very ordinary flannel housecoat. "Nora, darling," she called, her arms outstretched, "do forgive my being so long. I've been upstairs making the beds."

Yesterday, feeling greedy, I remembered ravishing displays of fruit outside a large emporium I'd driven admiringly past a number of times. Mammoth oranges, grapes big as ping-pong balls, apples piled in rosy pyramids. There is a sleight of hand about distances here, nothing is so near as you supposed, and it is not unusual to travel ten miles for a package of cigarettes. It was a two-mile walk before I even caught sight of the fruit store. The long counters were tilted so that from quite far away you could see the splendid wares, apples, pears. I reached for one of these extraordinary apples, but it seemed to be glued into its case. A salesgirl giggled. "Plaster," she said, and I laughed too, a little feverishly perhaps, then wearily followed her into the deeper regions of the store, where I bought six small, rather mealy apples, and six small, rather mealy pears.

It is Christmas week. And it is evening now a long time. Below the window a lake of light bulbs electrifies the valley. From the haunting impermanence of their hilltop homes impermanent eyes are watching them, almost as if suddenly they might go out, like candles at last consumed.

Earlier today I took a bus all the way from Beverly Hills into downtown Los Angeles. The streets are strung with garlands, we passed a motorized sleigh that was spinning along spilling a wake of white cornflakes, at corners sweating woolly men rustle bells under the shade of prefabricated trees; carols, hurled from lamppost loudspeakers, pour their syrup on the air, and tinsel, twinkling in twenty-four-karat sunshine, hangs everywhere like swamp moss. It could not be more Christmas, or less so. I once knew a woman who imported a pink villa stone by stone from Italy and had it reconstructed on a demure Connecticut meadow: Christmas is as out of place in Hollywood as the villa was in Connecticut. And what is Christmas without children, on whom so much of the point depends? Last week I met a man who concluded a set of observations by saying, "And of course you know this is the childless city."

For five days I have been testing his remark, casually at first, now with morbid alarm; preposterous, I know, but since commencing this mysterious campaign I have seen less than half a dozen children. But first, a relevant point: a primary complaint here is overpopulation; old-guard natives tell me the terrain is bulging with "undesirable" elements, hordes of ex-soldiers, workers who moved here during the war, and those spiritual Okies, the young and footloose; yet walking around I sometimes have the feeling of one who awakened some eerie morning into a hushed, deserted world where overnight, like sailors aboard the *Marie Celeste*, all souls had disappeared. There is an air of Sunday vacancy; here where no one walks cars glide in a constant shiny silent stream, my shadow, moving down the stark white street, is like the one living element of a Chirico. It is not the comfortable silence felt in small American towns, though the physical atmosphere of stoops and yards and hedges is very often the same; the difference is that in real towns you can be pretty sure what sorts of people there are hiding beyond those numbered doors, but here, where all seems transient, ephemeral, there is no general pattern to the population, and nothing is intended—this street, that house, mushrooms of accident, and a crack in the wall, which might somewhere else have charm, only strikes an ugly note prophesying doom.

1. A teacher here recently gave a vocabulary test in which she asked her students to provide the antonym of *youth*. Over half the class answered *death*.

2. No stylish Hollywood home is thought quite sanitary without a brace of modern masters to brighten up the walls. One producer has what amounts to a small gallery; he refers to paintings merely as good investments. His wife is less modest: "Sure we know about art. We've been to Greece, haven't we? California is just like Greece. Exactly. You'd be surprised. Go over there and talk to my husband about Picasso; he can give you the real low-down."

The day I saw their famous collection I had a picture that I was taking to a framer, a small colored Klee lithograph. "Pleasant," said the producer's wife cautiously. "Paint it yourself?"

Waiting for a bus, I ran into P., of whom I am rather admiring. She has the sort of wit that excludes malice, and, what is more uncommon, she has managed thirty years of Hollywood with humor and dignity. Naturally, she is not very rich. At the moment she is living above a garage. It is interesting, because by local standards she is a failure, which along with age, is unforgivable; even so, success pays her homage, and her Sunday coffee sessions are quite luminously attended, for above that garage she contrives a momentary sense of security, and for all a feeling of having roots. She is an inexhaustible scrapbook, too, the time sequence of her conversation shifting, sliding, until, as she fixes you with her cornflower eyes, Valentino passes lightly brushing your arm, the young Garbo hovers at the window, John Gilbert appears on the lawn, stands there like a twilight statue, the senior Fairbanks roars up the driveway, two mastiffs baying in the rumble seat.

P. offered to drive me home. We went by way of Santa Monica, in order that she could drop off a present for A., that sad, jittery lady who once, after the departure of her third husband, threw an Oscar into the ocean.

The thing about A. which most intrigued me was the way she applied make-up—such a brutally objective performance; cold-eyed, calculating, she wields her paints and powders altogether as if the face belongs to someone else, managing, in the process, to smooth away whatever time has given her.

As we were leaving, the maid came out to say that A.'s father would like to see us. We found him in a garden facing the ocean; a knotty, phlegmatic old man with blue-white hair and skin browner than iodine, he was slumped in a patch of sunshine, his eyes closed, no sound to disturb him but the slumbering slap of waves, the dozy singing of bees. Old people love California; they close their eyes, and the wind through the winter flowers says sleep, the sea says sleep: it is a preview of heaven. From daybreak to dark A.'s father follows the sun around his garden, and on rainy days he whiles away the time by making bracelets of beer-bottle caps. He gave each of us one of these bracelets, and in a voice that hardly carried through the honeyed, blowing air, said, "A merry Christmas, children."

Haiti

(1948)

TO LOOK AT, HYPPOLITE IS PERHAPS an ugly man: monkey-thin, gaunt-faced, quite dark, he looks (through silver schoolmarm spectacles), listens with the steadiest, most gracious precision, his eyes echoing a subtle and basic understanding. One feels with him a certain safety; there is created between you that too uncommon circumstance, no sense of isolation.

This morning I heard that during the night his daughter died, a daughter eight months old; there are other children, he has been married many times, five or six; even so, how hard it must be, for he is not young. No one has told me, I wonder if there is a wake. In Haiti they are extravagant, these wakes, and excessively stylized: the mourners, strangers in large part, claw air, drum their heads on the ground, in unison moan a low doglike grief. Heard at night, or seen suddenly on a country road, it seems so alien the heart shivers, and then one realizes that in essence these are mimes.

Because he is the most popular of Haiti's primitive painters, Hyppolite could afford a running-water house, real beds, electricity; as it is, he lives by lamp, by candle, and all the neighbors, old withered coconut-headed ladies and handsome sailor boys and hunched sandal makers, can see into his affairs as he can see into theirs. Once, some while back, a friend took it upon himself to rent Hyppolite another house, a sturdy sort of place with concrete floors and walls behind which one could hide, but of course he was not happy there, he has no need for secrecy or comfort. It is for this reason that I find Hyppolite admirable, for there is nothing in his art that has been slyly transposed, he is using what lives within himself, and that is his country's spiritual history, its singings and worships.

Displayed prominently in the room where he paints is an enormous trumpet-shaped shell; pink and elaborately curled, it is like some ocean flower, an underwater rose, and if you blow through it, there comes forth a howl hoarse and lonesome, a windlike sound: it is for sailors a magic horn that calls the wind, and Hyppolite, who plans an around-the-world voyage aboard his own red-sailed ship, practices upon it regularly. Most of his energy and all his money go into the building of this ship; there is about his dedication the quality frequently seen in those who supervise the plotting of their own funerals, the building of their own tombs. Once he sets sail and is out of land's sight, I wonder if again anyone will ever see him.

From the terrace where in the mornings I sit reading or writing, I can see the mountains sliding blue and bluer down to the harbor bay. Below there is the whole of Port-au-Prince, a town whose colors are paled into peeling historical pastels by centuries of sun: sky-gray cathedral, hyacinth fountain, green-rust fence. To the left, and like a city within this other, there is a great chalk garden of baroque stone; here is the cemetery, this is where, amid flat metal light and monuments like birdcages, they will bring his daughter: they will bring her up the hill, a dozen of them dressed in straw hats and black, sweet peas heavy on the air.

1. Tell me, why are there so many dogs? to whom do they belong, and for what purpose? Mangy, hurt-eyed, they pad along the streets in little herds like persecuted Christians, all innocuous enough by day, but come night how their vanity and their voices exaggerate! First one, another, then all, through the hours you can hear their enraged, embittered, moon-imploring tirades. S. says it is like a reversed alarm clock, for as soon as the dogs commence, and that indeed is early, it is time to go to bed. You might as well; the town has drawn shutters by ten, except, that is, on rahrah weekends, when drums and drunks drown out the dogs. But I like hearing a morning multitude of cock-crows; they set blowing a windfall of reverberations. On the other hand, what is more irritating than the racket of car horns? Haitians who own cars seem so to adore honking their horns; one begins to suspect this activity of political and/or sexual significance.

2. If it were possible, I should like to make a film here; except for incidental music it would be soundless, nothing but a camera brilliantly framing architecture, objects. There is a flying kite, on the kite there is a crayon eye, now the eye is loose and blowing in the wind, it snags on a fence and we, the eye, the camera, see a house (like M. Rigaud's). This is a tall, brittle, somewhat absurd structure representing no particular period,

but seeming rather to be of an infinitely bastard lineage: the French influence, and England in somber Victorian garb; there is an Oriental quality, too, touches that suggest a lantern of frilled paper. It is a carved house, its turrets, towers, porticoes are laced with angel heads, snowflake shapes, valentine hearts: as the camera traces each of these we hear a tantalizing sub-musical tap-rap of bamboo rods. A window, very sudden; a sugar-white meringue of curtains, and a lumplike eye, and then a face, a woman like an old pressed flower, jet at her throat and jet combs in her hair; we pass through her, and into the room, two green chameleons race over the chifforobe mirror where her image shines. Like dissonant piano notes, the camera shifts with swift sharp jabs, and we are aware of the happenings our eyes never notice: a rose leaf falling, a picture tilting crooked. Now we have begun.

3. Comparatively few tourists come to Haiti, and a fair number of those who do, especially the average American couple, sit around in their hotels in a superior sulk. It is unfortunate, for of all the West Indies, Haiti is quite the most interesting; still, when one considers the objectives of these vacationers their attitude is not without reason: the nearest beach is a three-hour drive, night life is unimpressive, there is no restaurant whose menu is very distinguished. Aside from the hotels, there are only a few public places where late of an evening one can go for a rum soda; among the pleasanter of these are the whorehouses set back among the foliage along the Bizonton Road. All the houses have names, rather egotistical ones: the Paradise, for example. And they are uncompromisingly respectable, perfect parlor decorum is observed: the girls, most of whom are from the Dominican Republic, sit on the front porch rocking in rocking chairs, fanning themselves with cardboard pictures of Jesus and conversing in a gentle, gossipy, laughing way; it is like any American summer scene. Beer, not whiskey or even champagne, is considered *de rigueur,* and if one wants to make an impression, it is the drink to order. One girl I know can down thirty bottles; she is older than the others, wears lavender lipstick, is rumba-hipped and viper-tongued, all of which makes her a popular lady indeed, though she herself says she will never feel like a success until she can afford to have every tooth in her head converted into solid gold.

4. The Estimé government has passed a law which forbids promenading in the streets sans shoes: this is a hard, uneconomical ruling, and an uncomfortable one as well, especially for those peasants who must bring their produce to market afoot. But the government, now anxious to make the country more of a tourist attraction, feels that shoeless Haitians might depress this potential trade, that the poorness of the people should not be overt. By and large, however, Haitians *are* poor, but about this poverty there is none of that vicious, mean atmosphere which surrounds the poverty that demands a keeping-up of appearances. It always makes me rather

wretched when some popular platitude proves true; still, it is a fact, I suppose, that the most generous of us are those that have the least to be generous with. Almost any Haitian who comes to call will conclude his visit by presenting you with a small, usually odd gift: a can of sardines, a spool of thread; but these gifts are given with such dignity and tenderness that, ah! the sardines have swallowed pearls, the thread is purest silver.

5. This is R.'s story. A few days ago he went out into the country to sketch; suddenly, coming to the bottom of a hill, he saw a tall, slant-eyed, ragged girl. She was tied to the trunk of a tree, wire and rope binding her there. At first, because she laughed at him, he thought it was a joke, but when he tried to let her loose several children appeared and began to poke at him with sticks; he asked them why the girl was tied to the tree, but they giggled and shouted and would not give an answer. Presently an old man joined them; he was carrying a gourd filled with water. When R. asked again about the girl, the old man, tears misting his eyes, said, "She is bad, monsieur, there is no use she is so bad," and shook his head. R. started back up the hill; then, turning, he saw the man was letting her drink from the gourd, and as she took a last swallow she spat into his face; with a gentle patience the old man wiped himself and walked away.

6. I like Estelle, and I must say I have come to care less for S. because he doesn't: there is no brand of intolerance so tiresome as that which results in condemning characteristics you yourself possess: in the opinion of S., Estelle is lusty, vulgar, a fraud; S., to be sure, and except for the first mentioned, is not without these qualities himself. In any event, it shows a finer nature to be unconsciously vulgar than to be consciously virtuous. But of couse S. is very much "in" with the American colony here, and their views, with a few isolated exceptions, are often gray and always severe. Estelle isn't cherished by any group. "Who gives a damn?" says she. "Listen, egghead, there's nothing wrong with me but the fact that I'm so almighty good-looking, and when a girl's as good-looking as me and she won't let a lot of crumbs crawl all over, well, thumbs down, get it?"

Estelle is one of the tallest girls I've ever seen, an easy six feet; her face is strong and bony, in the Swedish manner, her hair rosy, her eyes cat-green: somehow there is always an aura about her which suggests that she has just been tossed about in a hurricane. She is several Estelles, actually. One of them is the heroine of a not-too-good novel: here today—gone tomorrow, hello, you heartache of a world, that school of antics. Another Estelle is a big puppy of a girl dizzy for love: she is always quite sure the most improbable people have the most honorable intentions. A third Estelle is not so much shady as she is shadowy: who is Estelle? what is she doing here? how long does she intend to stay? what is it that makes her get up in the morning? Now and then this third element of the multiple Miss E. will refer to her "work." But the nature of her work is never labeled. Most of the time she sits in a café on the Champ de Mars and, at a cost of ten cents a round, drinks rum punches. The bartender is always asleep, and whenever she wants anything she swaggers over and thumps his head as though it were a ripe watermelon. There is a crazy little lop-eared dog that follows her everywhere, and usually she has some human crony with her, too. Her favorite is a pale, prim man who might be a Bible salesman; as it happens, he is a traveling entertainer who hops from island to island with a suitcase full of puppets and a head full of nonsense. On clear evenings Estelle sets up headquarters at a table on the sidewalk outside the café; many of the young native girls bring their love problems here to this table: about other people's love she is serious and sad. Once she herself was married, when or to whom I do not know, she is so altogether vague, but, and even though she is only twenty-five, it must have been a very long time ago. Last night I passed by the café, and as usual she was sitting at her sidewalk table. But there was a difference. She was wearing make-up, which she seldom does, and a neat, conventional dress; there were two pink carnations burning in her hair, the sort of decoration of which I'd thought her incapable. Also, I'd never seen her really drunk before. "Egghead, hello, is it you? Yesyesyes," she said, tapping me on the chest, "listen, kid, I'm going to give you proof positive, I'm going to show you it's a fact, it's a fact that when you love somebody that somebody can make you eat *any* goddamn thing. Look now"—and she yanked a carnation from her hair—"he's nuts about me," she said, thrusting the flower at the little dog crouched at her feet, "he'll eat it just because I say to, damn if he won't."

But the dog merely sniffed.

The last few weekends here have been devoted to the rahrahs preceding carnival, and carnival, which began yesterday, continues for three days. Rahrahs are miniature previews of carnival itself; Saturday, sometime past noon, the drums commence, separately at first, one high in the hills, another nearer town, back and forth these signals run, insinuating, insistent, until there is established a pervasive vibration which shimmers the surface of silence, ripples like heat waves, and here where I am, alone in this arsenic-colored room, all action seems to stem from their sound: doom die doom, over there, look: light quivers in the water jar, a crystal bubble, set in motion, rolls across a table, shatters on the floor, wind, catching curtains, curling Bible leaves, tells doom die doom. By dusk the island takes the expanding shape of a sound of drums. Small bands carouse the streets; these are made of family groups, or secret societies, all singing different songs which sound the same; the leader of each band wears feathers in his hair, a spangled crazy-quilt suit, and each has a pair of cheap dark glasses; while the others sing and stamp their feet he spins around, grinds his hips, cocks his head from side to side like an evil parrot: everybody laughs, and some couples join together, dancing with their heads thrown back, their lips ajar, doom die doom, the rhythm rotates their haunches, their eyes are rich moons, doom die doom.

Last night R. took me into the midst of the carnival. We were going to see the ceremony of a young *boungan,* that is to say, Voodou priest, this one an extraordinary boy whose name I never heard. It was held at a distance from the city, and so we had to take an autobus, a small wagon which can inconveniently carry ten passengers; but there were almost double that number, some of them in costume, including a dwarf wearing a cap of bells and an old man with a mask like raven wings; R. sat next to the old man, who at one point said, "Do you understand the sky? Yes, I thought you would, but it was I who made it."

To which R. answered, "I suppose you made the moon, too?"

The man nodded. "And the stars, they are my grandchildren."

A rowdy woman clapped her hands and announced that the old man was crazy. "But, dear lady," he replied, "if I am crazy, then how could I have done these beautiful things?"

It was a slow trip; the autobus stalled, crowds surged around, faces concealed behind masks dangled in the dark, archaic light of candle torches showering them like some eccentric yellow rain.

When we reached the *boungan's,* which is above the town, a quiet place shrill only with the night noises of insects, the ceremony had already begun, although the *boungan* himself had not yet appeared. Surrounding the temple, a long thatch-roofed shed with altar rooms at either end (the doors to these rooms were closed, for beyond one the *boungan* awaited his entrance), were perhaps a hundred silent, solemn Haitians. In the open clearing between the rooms seven or eight barefoot girls, all dressed in white with white bandannas wrapped around their heads, moved in a snaking circle, smacking their sides and singing a chant that two drummers echoed. A kerosene lamp cast smoky, horizontal shadows of the dancers, and the drummers, both intent, both froglike, wavered on the walls. Suddenly the drums stopped, the girls made an aisle leading to an altar door. It was so quiet one could almost identify the various species of serenading insects. R. asked for a cigarette, but I would not give it to him: who smokes in church? and Voodou after all is a real, very complex religion, one which is nevertheless frowned on by the Haitian bourgeoisie, who, when they are anything, are Catholics, and that is why, as a compromise you might think, so much Catholicism has seeped into Voodou: a picture of the Virgin Mary, for example, and an image of the Infant Jesus, who is represented sometimes by a homemade doll, will be found adorning the altar of almost any *boungan.* And the primary functions of Voodou do not seem to me basically different from those of other religions: appeals to certain gods, symbols, appease the pressures of evil, man is weak but God protects him, there is magic abroad, the gods own it, they can provide a man's wife with child or allow the sun to burn his crops, steal the breath from his body but reward him with a soul. In Voodou, however, there is no boundary between the countries of the living and the dead; the dead rise and walk among the living.

Now again the drums began, the voices of the girls spacing every slow, dramatic beat, and then the door to the altar opened: three boys came out, each carrying a plate filled with a different substance—ashes, cornmeal, black powder—and candles, like those for a birthday cake, burned in the center of these materials; balancing the plates on a rounded stone, the boys knelt facing the door. The drums grew softer, there began a nervous rhythmical rattling, this made by a gourd encasing snake vertebrae, and swiftly, like a spirit that has unexpectedly solidified, the *boungan* glided airy as a bird through the column of girls and around the room, his feet, the ankles tinkling with silver bracelets, seeming not at all to touch the floor, and his loose silk scarlet robes rustling winglike. There was a caul of red velvet draped around his head, a pearl gleamed in his ear. Here and there he paused, like a hummingbird, and clasped the hands of a worshiper: he took mine, and I looked into his face, an amazing, androgynous face, beautiful, really, a troubling combination of blue-black skin and Caucasian features; he could not have been more than twenty, still, there was something about him unaccountably old, asleep, transfixed.

At last, taking a handful of cornmeal and ashes, he started drawing on the ground a *verver;* there are in Voodou hundreds of *ververs,* which are intricate, somewhat surrealist designs whose every detail has implications, and to execute them demands not only the sort of academic memory required of a pianist who would, say, play an entire program of Bach, but also unusually deft technique, artistry. While the drums grew explosively fast he stooped about, deep in his art, like a red spider that, instead of silk, spills forth an ashy, ferocious web of crowns, crisscrosses, snakes, phallic shapes, eyes, fishtails. Then, the *verver* completed, he went back to the altar room, and reappeared wearing green, in his hands a great iron ball; as he stood there the ball caught fire, holy blue wrapping it like the atmospheres of earth; still carrying it, he fell to his knees, crawled, chants and shouts applauding him, and when the flames cooled he arose, stretching his unburned palms upward. A tremor swept his body, as if an unknown wind passed through him, his eyes rolled into his skull, the spirit (god and demon) opened like a seed and flowered in his flesh: unsexed, unidentifiable, he gathered in his arms man and woman. Whoever his partner, they whirled over the snakes and eyes of the *verver,* mysteriously never quite disturbing them, and when he changed to another, the castoff partner flung himself, as it were, into infinity, tore his breast, screamed. And the young *boungan*, shining with sweat, his pearl earring loosened, ran smash into the farthest, unopened door: singing, crying, he beat his hands upon it until they left blood prints. It was as if he were a moth, the door the bright enormity of an electric bulb, for beyond this obstacle, immediately beyond it, there was magic: truth's secret, pure peace. And if the door had opened, as it never will, would he have found it, this unobtainable? That he believed so is all that matters.

To
Europe

(1948)

STANDING VERY STILL YOU COULD hear a harp. We climbed the wall, and there, among the burning rain-drenched flowers of the castle's garden, sat four mysterious figures, a young man who thumbed a hand harp and three rusted old men who were dressed in patched-together black: how stark they were against the storm-green air. And they were eating figs, those Italian figs so fat the juice ran out of their mouths. At the garden's edge lay the marble shore of Lago di Garda, its waters swarming in the wind, and I knew then I would be always afraid to swim there, for, like distortions beyond the beauty of ivy-glass, Gothic creatures must move in the depths of water so ominously clear. One of the old men tossed too far a fig peel, and a trio of swans, thus disturbed, rustled the reeds of the waterway.

D. jumped off the wall and gestured for me to join him; but I couldn't, not quite then: because suddenly it was true and I wanted the trueness of it to last a moment longer—I could never feel it so absolutely again, even the movement of a leaf and it would be lost, precisely as a cough would forever ruin Tourel's high note. And what was this truth? Only the truth of justification: a castle, swans and a boy with a harp, for all the world out of a childhood storybook—before the prince has entered or the witch has cast her spell.

It was right that I had gone to Europe, if only because I could look again with wonder. Past certain ages or certain wisdoms it is very difficult to look with wonder; it is best done when one is a child; after that, and if you are lucky, you will find a bridge of childhood and walk across it. Going to Europe was like that. It was a bridge of childhood, one that led over the seas and through the forests straight into my imagination's earliest landscapes. One way or another I had gone to a good many places, from Mexico to Maine—and then to think I had to go all the way to Europe to go back to my hometown, my fire and room where stories and legends seemed always to live beyond the limits of our town. And that is where the legends were: in the harp, the castle, the rustling of the swans.

A rather mad bus ride that day had brought us from Venice to Sirmione, an enchanted, infinitesimal village on the tip of a peninsula jutting into Lago di Garda, bluest, saddest, most silent, most beautiful of Italian lakes. Had it not been for the gruesome circumstance of Lucia, I doubt that we should have left Venice. I was perfectly happy there, except of course that it is incredibly noisy: not ordinary city noise, but ceaseless argument of human voices, scudding oars, running feet. It was once suggested that Oscar Wilde retire there from the world. "And become a monument for tourists?" he asked.

It was an excellent advice, however, and others than Oscar have taken it: in the palazzos along the Grand Canal there are colonies of persons who haven't shown themselves publicly in a number of decades. Most intriguing of these was a Swedish countess whose servants fetched fruit for her in a black gondola trimmed with silver bells; their tinkling made a music atmospheric but eerie. Still, Lucia so persecuted us we were forced to flee. A muscular girl, exceptionally tall for an Italian and smelling always of wretched condiment oils, she was the leader of a band of juvenile gangsters, displaced roaming youths who had flocked north for the Venetian season. They could be delightful, some of them, even though they sold cigarettes that contained more hay than tobacco, even though they would short-circuit you on a currency exchange. The business with Lucia began one day in the Piazza San Marco.

She came up and asked us for a cigarette; whereupon D., whose heart doesn't know that we are off the gold standard, gave her a whole package of Chesterfields. Never were two people more completely adopted. Which at first was quite pleasant; Lucia shadowed us wherever we went, abundantly giving us the benefits of her wisdom and protection. But there were frequent embarrassments; for one thing, we were always being turned out of the more elegant shops because of her overwrought haggling with the proprietors; then, too, she was so excessively jealous that it was impossible for us to have any contact with anyone else whatever: we chanced once to meet in the piazza a harmless and respectable young woman who had been with us in the carriage from Milan. "Attention!" said Lucia in that hoarse voice of hers. "Attention!" and proceeded almost to persuade us that this was a lady of infamous past and shameless future. On another occasion D. gave one of her cohorts a dollar watch which he had much admired. Lucia was furious; the next time we saw her she had the watch suspended on a cord around her neck, and it was said the young man had left overnight for Trieste.

Lucia had a habit of appearing in our hotel at any hour that pleased her (she lived no place that we could divine); scarcely sixteen, she would sit herself down, drain a whole bottle of Strega, smoke all the cigarettes she could lay hold of, then fall into an exhausted sleep; only when she slept did her face resemble a child's. But then one dreadful day the hotel manager stopped her in the lobby and told her that she could no longer visit our rooms. It was, he said, an insupportable scandal. So Lucia, rounding up a dozen of her more brutish companions, laid such siege to the hotel that it was necessary to bring down iron shutters over the doors and call the carabinieri. After that we did our best to avoid her.

But to avoid anyone in Venice is much the same as playing hide-and-seek in a one-room apartment, for there was never a city more compactly composed. It is like a museum with carnivalesque overtones, a vast palace that seems to have no doors, all things connected, one leading into another. Over and over in a day the same faces repeat like prepositions in a long sentence: turn a corner, and there was Lucia, the dollar watch dangling between her breasts. She was so in love with D. But presently she turned on us with that intensity of the wounded; perhaps we deserved it, but it was unendurable: like clouds of gnats her gang would trail us across the piazza spitting invective; if we sat down for a drink, they would gather in the dark beyond the table and shout outrageous jokes. Half the time we didn't know what they were saying, though it was apparent that everyone else did. Lucia herself did not overtly contribute to this persecution; she remained aloof, directing her operations at a distance. So at last we decided to leave Venice. Lucia knew this. Her spies were everywhere. The morning we left it was raining; just as our gondola slipped into the water, a little crazy-eyed boy appeared and threw at us a bundle wrapped in newspaper. D. pulled the paper apart. Inside there was a dead yellow cat, and around its throat there was tied the dollar watch. It gave you a feeling of endless falling. And then suddenly we saw her, Lucia; she was standing alone on one of the little canal bridges, and she was so far hunched over the railing it looked as if she were going to fall. "*Perdonami*," she cried, "*ma t'amo*" (forgive me, but I love you).

. . .

In London a young artist said to me, "How wonderful it must be for an American traveling in Europe the first time; you can never be a part of it, so none of the pain is yours, you will never have to endure it—yes, for you there is only the beauty."

Not understanding what he meant, I resented this; but later, after some months in France and Italy, I saw that he was right: I was not a part of Europe, I never would be. Safe, I could leave when I wanted to, and for me there was only the honeyed, hallowed air of beauty. But it was not so wonderful as the young man had imagined; it was desperate to feel that one could never be a part of moments so moving, that always one would be isolated from this landscape and these people; and then gradually I realized I did not have to be a part of it: rather, it could be a part of me. The sudden garden, opera night, wild children snatching flowers and running up a darkening street, a wreath for the dead and nuns in noon light, music from the piazza, a Paris pianola and fireworks on La Grande Nuit, the heart-shaking surprise of mountain visions and water views (lakes like green wine in the chalice of volcanoes, the Mediterranean flickering at the bottoms of cliffs), forsaken far-off towers falling in twilight and candles igniting the jeweled corpse of St. Zeno of Verona—all a part of me, elements for the making of my own perspective.

When we left Sirmione, D. returned to Rome and I went back to Paris. Mine was a curious journey. First off, I'd engaged through a dizzy Italian ticket agent a *wagonlit* aboard the Orient Express, but when I reached Milan, I discovered the arrangement had been entirely spurious and that there were no such accommodations for me; in fact, if I hadn't stepped on a few toes, I doubt that I should have got on the train at all, for everything was holiday-jammed. As it was, I managed to squeeze myself into an airless, August-hot compartment along with six other people. The name of the Orient Express evoked for me the most spine-tingling expectations: think of the extraordinary things that have occurred on that train, at least if one is to believe Miss Agatha Christie or Mr. Graham Greene. But I was not at all prepared for what happened actually.

In the compartment there were a pair of dreary Swiss businessmen, a somewhat more exotic businessman traveling from Istanbul, an American teacher and two elegant snow-headed Italian ladies with haughty eyes and features as delicate as fishbones. They were dressed like twins, these ladies; flowing black and wisps of lace caught at the throat with pearl-studded amethysts. They sat with their gloved hands clasped together and never spoke except when exchanging a box of expensive chocolates. Their only luggage appeared to be a huge birdcage; inside this cage, though it was partially covered by a silk shawl, you could see scuttling around a moldy green parrot. Now and then the parrot would let forth a burst of demented laughter; whenever this happened the two ladies would smile at each other. The American teacher asked them if the parrot could speak, and one of the ladies, with the slightest nod, replied yes, but that the parrot's grammar was very poor. As we neared the Italian-Swiss frontier, customs and passport officials began their tiresome little duties. We thought they were finished with our compartment, but presently they returned, several of them, and stood outside the glass door looking in at the aristocratic ladies. It seemed they were having quite a discussion about them. Everyone in the compartment grew quite still, except the parrot, who laughed in an unearthly way. The old ladies paid no attention whatever. Other men in uniform joined those already in the corridor. Then one of the ladies, plucking at her amethyst brooch, turned to the rest of us and, first in Italian, then German, then English, said, "We have done nothing wrong."

But at that moment the door slid open and two of the officials entered. They did not look at the old ladies but went straight to the birdcage and stripped away its covering shawl. "*Basta, basta,*" screamed the parrot.

With a lurch the train came to a halt in the mountain darkness. The abruptness of this toppled the cage, and the parrot, suddenly free, flew laughingly from wall to wall of the compartment while the ladies, flurried and flying themselves, grasped for it. The customs men went on taking the cage apart; in the feed tray were a hundred or so papers of heroin wrapped like headache powders, and in the brass ball atop the cage there were still more. The discovery did not seem to irritate the ladies at all; it was the loss of their parrot that upset them. For all at once it had flown out the lowered window, and the desperate ladies stood calling after it, "Tokyo, you will freeze, little Tokyo, come back! Come back!"

He was laughing somewhere in the dark. There was a cold northern moon, and for an instant we saw him flying flat and dark against its brilliance. They turned then and faced the door; it was crowded now with onlookers. Poised, disdainful, the ladies stepped forward to meet faces they seemed not to see, and voices they certainly never heard.

Ischia

(1949)

I FORGET WHY WE CAME HERE: ISCHIA.
It was being very much talked about,
though few people seemed actually to have seen it—except, perhaps, as a
jagged blue shadow glimpsed across the water from the heights of its
celebrated neighbor, Capri. Some people advised against Ischia and, as I
remember, they gave rather spooky reasons: You realize that there is an
active volcano? And do you know about the plane? A plane, flying a
regular flight between Cairo and Rome, crashed on top an Ischian mountain; there were three survivors, but no one ever saw them alive, for they
were stoned to death by goatherds intent on looting the wreckage.

Consequently, we watched the chalky façade of Naples fade with mixed
anticipation. It was a classic day, a little cold for southern Italy in March,
but crisp and lofty as a kite, and the *Princepessa* spanked across the bay like
a sassy dolphin. It is a small civilized boat with a tiny bar and a somewhat
outré clientele: convicts on their way to the prison island of Procida or, at
the opposite extreme, young men about to enter the monastery on Ischia.
Of course, there are less dramatic passengers: islanders who have been
shopping in Naples; here and there a foreigner—extraordinarily few, however: Capri is the tourist catch-all.

Islands are like ships at permanent anchor. To set foot on one is like
starting up a gangplank: one is seized by the same feeling of charmed
suspension—it seems nothing unkind or vulgar can happen to you; and as

the *Princepessa* eased into the covelike harbor of Porto d'Ischia it seemed, seeing the pale, peeling ice-cream colors of the waterfront, as intimate and satisfying as one's own heartbeat. In the wrangle of disembarking, I dropped and broke my watch—an outrageous bit of symbolism, too pointed: at a glance it was plain that Ischia was no place for the rush of hours, islands never are.

I suppose you might say that Porto is the capital of Ischia; at any rate, it is the largest town and even rather fashionable. Most people who visit the island seldom stray from there, for there are several superior hotels, excellent beaches and, perched in the offing like a giant hawk, the Renaissance castle of Vittoria Colonna. The three other fair-sized towns are more rugged. These are: Lacco Ameno, Cassamiciola and, at the farthest end of the island, Forio. It was in Forio that we planned to settle.

We drove there through a green twilight and under a sky of early stars. The road passed high above the sea, where fishing boats, lighted with torches, crawled below like brilliant water-spiders. Furry little bats skimmed in the dusk; *buena séra, buena séra,* dim evening voices called along the way, and herds of goats, jogging up the hills, bleated like rusty flutes; the carriage spun through a village square—there was no electricity, and in the cafés the tricky light of candles and kerosene lamps smoked the faces of masculine company. Two children chased after us into the darkness beyond the village. They clung panting to the carriage as we began a steep careening climb, and our horse, nearing the crest, breathed back on the chilled air a stream of mist. The driver flicked his whip, the horse swayed, the children pointed: look. It was there, Forio, distant, moon-white, the sea simmering at its edges, a faint sound of vesper bells rising off it like a whirl of birds. *Multo bella?* said the driver. *Multo bella?* said the children.

When one rereads a journal it is usually the less ambitious jottings, the haphazard, accidental notations that, seen again, plow a furrow through your memory. For example: "Today Gioconda left in the room assorted slips of colored paper. Are they presents? Because I gave her the bottle of cologne? They will make delightful bookmarks." This reverberates. First, Gioconda. She is a beautiful girl, though her beauty depends upon her mood: when she is feeling glum, and this seems too often the case, she looks like a bowl of cold oatmeal; you are likely to forget the richness of her hair and the mildness of her Mediterranean eyes. Heaven knows, she is overworked: here at the *pensione,* where she is both chambermaid and waitress, she gets up before dawn and is kept on the run sometimes until midnight. To be truthful, she is lucky to have the job, for employment is the island's major problem; most girls here would like nothing better than to supplant her. Considering that there is no running water (with all that that implies), Gioconda makes us remarkably comfortable. It is the pleasantest *pensione* in Forio, an interesting bargain, too: we have two huge rooms with great expanses of tiled floor and tall shutter-doors which lead onto little iron balconies overlooking the sea; the food is good, and there is rather too much of it—five courses with wine at lunch and dinner. All included, this costs each of us about one hundred dollars a month. Gioconda speaks no English, and my Italian is—well, never mind. Nevertheless, we are confidantes. With pantomime and extravagant use of a bilingual dictionary we manage to convey an astonishing lot—which is why the cakes are always a flop: on gloomy days when there is nothing else to do we sit in the patio-kitchen experimenting with recipes for American pastries ("Toll House, what is?"), but these are never a success because we are too busy thumbing through the dictionary to give our baking much attention. Gioconda: "Last year, in the room where you are, there was a man from Rome. Is Rome like he said, so wonderful? He said I should come and visit him in Rome, and that it would be all right because he was a veteran of three wars. First World War, Second, and Ethiopia. You can see how old he was. No, I have never seen Rome. I have friends who have been there, and who have sent me postcards. You know the woman who works at the *posta?* Of course you believe in the evil eye? She has one. It is known, yes. That is why my letter never comes from Argentina."

Not receiving this Argentine letter is the real cause of Gioconda's misery. A faithless lover? I have no idea; she refuses to discuss it. So many young Italians have migrated to South America looking for work; there are wives here who have waited five years for their husbands to send them passage. Each day, when I come bringing the mail, Gioconda rushes to meet me.

Collecting the mail is a self-appointed chore. It is the first time during the day that I see the other Americans living here: there are four at the moment and we meet at Maria's café in the piazza (from the journal: "We all know that Maria waters her drinks. But does she water them with water? God, I feel awful!"). With the sun warming you, and Maria's bamboo curtains tinkling in the breeze, there is no nicer place to wait for the postman. Maria is a sawed-off woman with a gypsy face and a shrugging, cynical nature; if there is anything you want around here, from a house to a package of American cigarettes, she can arrange it; some people claim she is the richest person in Forio. There are never any women in her café; I doubt that she would allow it. As noon heightens, the village converges in the piazza: like blackbirds schoolchildren in capes and wooden sandals flock and sing in the alleys, and squadrons of unemployed men lounge under the trees laughing roughly—women passing them lower their eyes. When the mailman comes he gives me the letters for our *pensione;* then I must go down the hill to face Gioconda. Sometimes she looks at me as though it were my fault that the letter never comes, as though the evil eye were mine. One day she warned me not to come home empty-handed; and so I brought her a bottle of cologne.

But the slips of gaudy paper that I found in my room were not, as I had supposed, a present in return. It was intended that we should shower these upon a statue of the Virgin which, newly arrived on the island, was being toured through most of the villages. The day the Virgin was to visit here every balcony was draped with fine laces, finer linens—an old bedspread if the family had nothing better; woven flowers garlanded the cramped streets, old ladies brought out their longest shawls, men combed their mustaches, someone put the town idiot into a clean shirt, and the children, dressed all in white, had angel-wings of golden cardboard strapped to their shoulders. The procession was supposed to enter town and pass below our balcony at about four o'clock. Alerted by Gioconda, we were at our station on time, ready to throw the pretty papers and shout, as instructed, *"Viva La Vergenie Immocalata."* A drizzling dull rain began; at six it was getting dark, but like the street-tightening crowd that waited below, we remained steadfast. A priest, scowling with annoyance, and his black skirts flapping, roared off on a motorcycle—he'd been sent to hurry along the procession. It was night, then, and a flare-path of kerosene was spilled along the route the procession was to follow. Suddenly, incongruously, the stirring *ratata* of a military band sounded and, with a scary crackle, the flare-path leapt alive as if to salute the arriving Virgin: swaying on a flower-filled litter, her face shrouded in a black veil, and followed by half the island, she was laden with gold and silver watches, and as she passed, a hush surrounding her immediate presence, there was only the enchanting, surrealistic noise of these offerings, the watches: *tickticktick.* Later, Gioconda was very put out to discover us still clutching the bits of bright paper which in our excitement we'd forgotten to throw.

"April 5. A long, perilous walk. We discovered a new beach." Ischia is stony, a stark island that suggests Greece or the coast of Africa. There are orange trees, lemon trees and, terracing the mountains, silvery-green grape arbors: the wine of Ischia is highly considered, and it is here that they make Lachrimae Christi. When you walk beyond the town you soon come upon the branching paths that climb through the grape fields where bees are like a blizzard and lizards burn greenly on the budding leaves. The peasants are brown and thick as earthenware, and they are horizon-eyed, like sailors. For the sea is always with them. The path by the sea runs along straight-dropping volcanic cliffs; there are junctures when it is best just to close your eyes: it would make a long fall, and the rocks below are like sleeping dinosaurs. One day, walking on the cliffs, we found a poppy, then another; they were growing singly among the somber stones, like Chinese bells strung on a stretching string. Presently the trail of poppies led us down a path to a strange and hidden beach. It was enclosed by the cliffs, and the water was so clear you could observe sea-flowers and the dagger movements of fish; not far from shore, flat, exposed rocks were like swimming rafts, and we paddled from one to another: hauling ourselves into the sun, we could look back above the cliffs and see the green grape terraces and a cloudy mountain. Into one rock the sea had carved a chair, and it was the greatest pleasure to sit there and let the waves rush up and over you.

But it is not hard to find a private beach on Ischia. I know of at least three that no one ever goes to. The town beach in Forio is strewn with fishing nets and overturned boats. It was on this beach that I first encountered the Mussolini family. The late dictator's widow and three of their children live here in what I presume to be a quiet self-imposed exile. Something about them is sad and sympathetic. The daughter is young, blond, lame and apparently witty: the local boys who talk with her on the beach seem always to be laughing. Like any of the island's plain women, Signora Mussolini is often to be seen dressed in shabby black and trudging up a hill with the weight of a shopping bag lopsiding her figure. She is quite expressionless, but once I saw her smile. There was a man passing through town with a parrot who plucked printed fortunes out of a glass jar, and Signora Mussolini, pausing to consult him, read her future with a shadowy, Da Vincian curling of her lips.

"June 5. The afternoon is a white midnight." Now that hot weather is here the afternoons are like white midnights; shutters are drawn, sleep stalks the streets. At five the shops will open again, a crowd will gather in the harbor to welcome the *Princepessa*, and later everyone will promenade in the piazza, where someone will be playing a banjo, a harmonica, a guitar. But now it is siesta, and there is only the blue unbroken sky, the crowing of a cock. There are two idiots in the town, and they are friends. One is always carrying a bouquet of flowers which, when he meets his friend, he divides into equal parts. In the silent shadowless afternoons they alone are seen in the streets. Hand in hand, and holding their flowers, they stroll across the beach and out along the stone wall that juts far into the water. From my balcony I can see them there, sitting among the fishnets and the slowly rocking boats, their shaved heads glinting in the sun, their eyes pale as space. The white midnight is meant for them; it is then that the island is theirs.

We have followed spring. In the four months since we came here the nights have warmed, the sea has grown softer, the green, still wintry water of March has turned in June to blue, and the grape vines, once gray and barren on their twisting stalks, are fat with their first green bunches. There is a hatching of butterflies, and on the mountain there are many sweet things for the bees; in the garden, after a rainfall, you can faintly, yes, hear the breaking of new blooms. And we are waking earlier, a sign of summer, and stay lingering out late in the evening, which is a sign, too. But it is hard to bring yourself indoors these nights: the moon is drawing nearer, it winks on the water with a frightful brightness; and on the parapet of the fishermen's church, which points to sea like the prow of a ship, the young whispering people wander back and forth and through the piazza and into some secret dark. Gioconda says it has been the longest spring she can remember: the longest is the loveliest.

Tangier

(1950)

T ANGIER? IT IS TWO DAYS BY BOAT
from Marseille, a charming trip that
takes you along the coast of Spain, and if you are someone escaping from
the police, or merely someone escaping, then by all means come here:
hemmed with hills, confronted by the sea, and looking like a white cape
draped on the shores of Africa, it is an international city with an excellent
climate eight months of the year, roughly March to November. There are
magnificent beaches, really extraordinary stretches of sugar-soft sand and
surf; and if you have a mind for that sort of thing, the nightlife, though
neither particularly innocent nor especially varied, is dark to dawn, which,
when you consider that most people nap all afternoon, and that very few
dine before ten or eleven, is not too unusual. Almost everything else in
Tangier is unusual, however, and before coming here you should do three
things: be inoculated for typhoid, withdraw your savings from the bank,
say good-bye to your friends—heaven knows you may never see them
again. This advice is quite serious, for it is alarming, the number of travelers
who have landed here on a brief holiday, then settled down and let the
years go by. Because Tangier is a basin that holds you, a timeless place; the
days slide by less noticed than foam in a waterfall; this, I imagine, is
the way time passes in a monastery, unobtrusive and on slippered feet; for
that matter, these two institutions, a monastery and Tangier, have another
common denominator: self-containment. The average Arab, for example,

thinks Europe and America are the same thing and in the same place, wherever that may be—in any event, he doesn't care; and frequently Europeans, hypnotized by the tinkling of an oud and the swarming drama around them, come to agree.

One spends a great lot of time sitting in the Petit Soko, a café-cluttered square at the foot of the Casbah. Offhand, it seems to be a miniature version of the Galleria in Naples, but on closer acquaintance it assumes a character so grotesquely individual you cannot fairly compare it with any other place in the world. At no hour of the day or night is the Petit Soko not crowded; Broadway, Piccadilly, all these places have their off moments, but the little Soko booms around the clock. Twenty steps away, and you are swallowed in the mists of the Casbah; the apparitions drifting out of these mists into the hurdy-gurdy clamor of the Soko make a lively show: it is a display ground for prostitutes, a depot for drug-peddlers, a spy center; it is also the place where some simpler folk drink their evening *apéritif*.

The Soko has its own celebrities, but it is a precarious honor, one is so likely at any second to be cut down and cast away, for the Soko audience, having seen just about everything, is excessively fickle. Currently, however, they are starring Estelle, a beautiful girl who walks like a rope unwinding. She is half-Chinese and half-Negro, and she works in a bordello called the Black Cat. Rumor has it that she once was a Paris model, and that she arrived here on a private yacht, planning, of course, to leave by the same means; but it appears that the gentleman to whom the yacht belonged sailed away one fine morning, leaving Estelle stranded. For a while there Maumi was giving her rather a race; the Soko appreciated Maumi's talents, both as a *flamenco* dancer and as a conversationalist: wherever he sat, there were always loud bursts of laughter. Alas, poor Maumi, an exotic young man given to cooling his face with a lacy fan, was stabbed in a bar the other night, and is now out of the running. Less heralded, but to me more intriguing, are Lady Warbanks and her two hangers-on, a curious trio that arrive each morning and have their breakfast at one of the sidewalk tables: this breakfast is unvarying—a bowl of fried octopus and a bottle of Pernod. Someone who ought really to know says that at one time the now very *déclassé* Lady Warbanks was considered the greatest beauty in London; probably it is true, her features are finely made and she has, despite the tight sailor suits she lumps herself into, a peculiar innate style. But her morals are not all they might be, and the same may be said of her companions. About these two: one is a sassy-faced, busy youth whose tongue is like a ladle stirring in a cauldron of scandal—he knows everything; and the other friend is a tough Spanish girl with brief, slippery hair and leather-colored eyes. She is called Sunny, and I am told that financed by Lady Warbanks, she is on her way to becoming the only female in Morocco with an organized gang of smugglers: smuggling is a high-powered profession here, employing hundreds, and Sunny, it appears, has a boat and crew that nightly runs the Straits to Spain. The precise relation of these three to each other is not altogether printable; suffice to say that between them they combine every known vice. But this does not interest the Soko, for the Soko is concerned by quite another angle: how soon will Lady Warbanks be murdered, and which of the two will do it, the young man or Sunny? She is very rich, the Englishwoman, and if it is greed, as so obviously it is, that holds her companions, then clearly violence is indicated. Everyone is waiting. Meanwhile, Lady Warbanks sits innocently nibbling octopus and sipping her morning Pernod.

The Soko is also something of a fashion center, a proving ground for the latest fads. One innovation that has got off to a popular start among the flashier types are shoes with ribbon laces that wind right up to the knee. They are unbecoming, but not nearly so regrettable as the passion for dark glasses that has developed among Arab women, whose eyes, peering just above their veiling, have been always so provocative. Now all one sees are these great black lenses imbedded like coal-hunks in a snowball of cloth.

Of an evening at seven the Soko reaches its height. It is the crowded *apéritif* hour, some twenty nationalities are rubbing elbows in the tiny square, and the hum of their voices is like the singing of giant mosquitoes. Once, when we were sitting there, a sudden silence fell: an Arab orchestra, trumpeting in a gay style, moved along up the street past the bright cafés —it was the only cheerful Moorish music I've ever heard, all the rest sounds like a sad and fragmentary wailing. But death, it would seem, is not an unhappy event among Arabs, for this orchestra proved to be the vanguard of a funeral procession that then came joyfully winding through the throng. Presently the corpse, a half-naked man carried on an open litter, wobbled past, and a rhinestone lady, leaning from her table, sentimentally saluted him with a glass of Tio Pepe: a moment later she was laughing gold-toothed laughter, plotting, planning. And so was the little Soko.

"If you are going to write something about Tangier," said a person to whom I applied for certain information, "please leave out the riffraff; we have a lot of nice people here, and it's hard on us that the town has such a bad reputation."

Well, and though I'm not at all sure our definitions coincide, there are at least three people I think eminently nice. Jonny Winner, for instance. A sweet, funny girl, Jonny Winner. She is very young, very American, and you would never believe, looking at her clouded, wistful face, that she is able to take care of herself: to tell the truth, I don't think she is. Nevertheless, she has lived here two years, been across Morocco and to the Sahara alone. Why Jonny Winner wants to spend the rest of her life in Tangier is of course her own business; obviously she is in love: "But don't you love it, too? to wake up and know that you're here, and know that you can always be yourself, never be anyone that isn't you? And always to have flowers, and to look out your window and see the hills getting dark and the lights in the harbor? Don't you love it, too?" On the other hand, she and the town are always at war; whenever you meet her she is undergoing a new *crise:* "Have you heard? the most awful mess: some fool in the Casbah painted his house yellow, and now everybody's doing it—I'm just on my way to see if I can't put a stop to the whole thing."

The Casbah, traditionally blue and white, like snow at twilight, would be hideous painted yellow, and I hope Jonny gets her way—though certainly she has had no success in her campaign to keep them from clearing the Grand Soko, a heartrending business that has reduced her to prowling the streets, in tears. The Grand Soko is the great Arab market square: Berbers, down from the mountains with their goatskins and baskets, squat in circles under the trees listening to storytellers, flute players, magicians; cornucopia stalls spill over with flowers and fruit; hashish fume and the minty scent of *thé Arabe* cling to the air; vivid spices burn in the sun. All this is to be moved elsewhere, presumably to make way for a park, and Jonny is wringing her hands: "Why shouldn't I be upset? I feel as though Tangier were my house, and how would you like it if somebody came into your house and started moving the furniture around?"

So she has been out saving the Soko in four languages, French, Spanish, English and Arabic; though she speaks all of these exceedingly well, the closest she has come to official sympathy is the doorman at the Dutch consulate, and her only real emotional support has been an Arab taxi driver, who thinks her not the least mad and drives her around free of charge. One late afternoon a few days ago we saw Jonny dragging along through her beloved, dissolving Grand Soko; she looked absolutely done in, and she was carrying a mangy, sore-covered kitten. Jonny has a way of launching right into what she wants to say, and she said, "I was feeling just as though I couldn't go on living, and then I found Monroe. This is Monroe"—she patted the kitten—"and he's made me ashamed: he's so interested in living, and if he can be, why shouldn't I?"

Looking at them, Jonny and the kitten, both so bedraggled and bruised, you knew that somehow something would see them through: if not common sense, then their interest in life.

Ferida Green has plenty of common sense. When Jonny spoke to her about the situation in the Grand Soko, Miss Green said, "Oh, my dear, you mustn't worry. They are always tearing down the Soko, but it never really happens; I remember in 1906 they wanted to make it into a whaling center: imagine the odor!"

Miss Ferida is one of the three great Green ladies of Tangier, which includes her cousin, Miss Jessie, and her sister-in-law, Mrs. Ada Green; between them they manage more often than not to have the last say here. All three are past seventy: Mrs. Ada Green is famous for her chic, Miss Jessie for her wit, and Miss Ferida, the oldest, for her wisdom. She has not visited her native England in over fifty years; even so, observing the straw skimmer skewered to her hair and the black ribbon trailing from her pince-nez, one knows she goes out in the noonday sun and has never given up tea at five. Every Friday in her life there is a ritual known as Flour Morning. Seated at a table at the foot of her garden, and judging each case as it is presented, she rations flour to Arab applicants, usually old women who otherwise would starve: from the flour they make a paste which must last them until the next Friday. There is much joking and laughter, for the Arabs adore Miss Ferida, and for her, all these old women, such anonymous bundles of laundry to the rest of us, are friends whose personalities she comments on in a large ledger. "Fathma has a bad temper but is not bad," she writes of one, and of another: "Halima is a good girl. One can take her at face value."

And that, I suppose, is what you would have to say about Miss Ferida.

Anyone in Tangier longer than overnight is bound to hear about Nysa: how at the edge of twelve she was taken off the streets by an Australian who, in true Pygmalion fashion, created out of this raggedy Arab child an accomplished, extremely elegant personage. Nysa is, as far as I know, the only example in Tangier of a Europeanized Arab woman, a fact which, strangely, no one quite forgives her, neither the Europeans, nor the Arabs, who are avowedly bitter and who, because she lives in the Casbah, have constant opportunity to vent their malice: women send their children to scrawl obscenities on her door, men do not hesitate to spit at her on the street—for in their eyes she has committed the gravest sin possible: become a Christian. Such a situation must make for terrible resentment, but Nysa, at least as far as surface appearances go, never seems aware that there is anything to resent. She is a charming, calm girl of twenty-three; it is in itself an entertainment just to sit quietly and marvel over her beauty, the tilted eyes and the flowerlike hands. She does not see many people; like the princess in a storybook, she stays behind the walls and in the shade of her patio, reading, playing with her cats and a large white cockatoo who mimics whatever she does: sometimes the cockatoo flares forward and kisses her on the lips. The Australian lives with her; since he found her as a child she has never for a moment been separated from him; if something should happen to him, there really would be no way for Nysa to turn: she could not ever be an Arab again, and it isn't likely that she could pass completely into a European world. But the Australian is an old man now.

One day I rang Nysa's bell; no one came to answer. There is a grillwork at the top of the door; peering, I saw her through a veil of vine and leaves standing in the shadows of her patio. When I rang again she remained dark and still as a statute. Later I heard that during the night the Australian had had a stroke.

At the end of June, and with the start of a new moon, *Ramadan* begins. For the Arabs, *Ramadan* is a month of abstinence. As dark comes on, a colored string is stretched in the air, and when the string grows invisible, conch horns signal the Arabs to the food and drink that during the day they cannot touch. These dark-night feasts emanate a festive spirit that lasts until dawn. From distant towers oboe players serenade before prayers; drums, hidden but heard, tom-tom behind closed doors, and the voices of men, singsonging the Koran, carry out of the mosques into the narrow, moon-bright streets. Even high on the mountain above Tangier you can hear the oboe player wailing in the far-off dark, a solemn thread of melody winding across Africa from here to Mecca and back.

Sidi Kacem is a limitless, Sahara-like beach bordered by olive groves; at the end of *Ramadan*, Arabs from all over Morocco arrive at Sidi Kacem in trucks, astride donkeys, on foot: for three days a city appears there, a fragile dream city of colored lights and cafés under lantern-lighted trees. We drove out there around midnight; the first glimpse of the city was like seeing a birthday cake blazing in a darkened room, and it filled you with the same exciting awe: you knew you could not blow out all the candles. Right away we got separated from the people we'd come with, but in the surge and sway it was impossible to stay together, and after the first few frightened moments we never bothered looking for them; the night caught us in its hand and there was nothing to do but become another of the masked, ecstatic faces flashing in the torch-flare. Everywhere little orchestras played. Voices, sweet and sultry as *kif* smoke, chanted over drums, and somewhere, stumbling through the silver, floating trees, we got smothered in a crowd of dancers: a circle of old bearded men beat the rhythm, and the dancers, so concentrated you could put a pin in them, rippled as though wind were moving them around. According to the Arab calendar this is the year 1370; seeing a shadow through the silk of a tent, watching a family fry honeycakes on a flat twig fire, moving among the dancers and hearing the trill of a lonely flute on the beach, it was simple to believe that one was living in 1370 and that time would never move forward.

Occasionally we had to rest; there were straw mats under the olive trees, and if you sat on one of these, a man would bring you a glass of hot mint tea. It was while we were drinking tea that we saw a curious line of men file past. They wore beautiful robes, and the man in front, old like a piece of ivory, carried a bowl of rose water which, to the accompaniment of bagpipes, he sprinkled from side to side. We got up to follow them, and they took us out of the grove onto the beach. The sand was as cold as the moon; humped dunes of it drifted toward the water, and flickers of light burst in the dark like fallen stars. At last the priest and his followers went into a temple which it was forbidden us to enter, and so we wandered down across the beach. J. said, "Look, a shooting star"; and then we counted the shooting stars, there were so many. Wind whispered on the sand like the sound of the seas; cutthroat figures outlined themselves against the kneeling orange moon, and the beach was as cold as a snowfield, but J. said, "Oh, I can't keep my eyes open any longer."

We woke up in a blue, almost dawn light. We were high on a dune, and there below us, spread along the shore, were all the celebrants, their brilliant clothes fluttering in the morning breeze. Just as the sun touched the horizon a great roar went up, and two horsemen, riding bareback, splashed through the surf and swept down the beach. Like a lifting curtain sunrise crept toward us across the sand, and we shuddered at its coming, knowing that when it reached us we would be back in our own century.

A Ride
Through Spain

(1950)

C ERTAINLY THE TRAIN WAS OLD. THE
seats sagged like the jowls of a bulldog,
windows were out and strips of adhesive held together those that were left;
in the corridor a prowling cat appeared to be hunting mice, and it was not
unreasonable to assume his search would be rewarded.

Slowly, as though the engine were harnessed to elderly coolies, we crept
out of Granada. The southern sky was white and burning as a desert;
there was one cloud, and it drifted like a traveling oasis.

We were going to Algeciras, a Spanish seaport facing the coast of Africa.
In our compartment there was a middle-aged Australian wearing a soiled
linen suit; he had tobacco-colored teeth and his fingernails were unsanitary.
Presently he informed us that he was a ship's doctor. It seemed curious,
there on the dry, dour plains of Spain, to meet someone connected with
the sea. Seated next to him there were two women, a mother and daughter.
The mother was an overstuffed, dusty woman with sluggish, disapproving
eyes and a faint mustache. The focus for her disapproval fluctuated; first,
she eyed me rather strongly because as the sunlight fanned brighter, waves
of heat blew through the broken windows and I had removed my jacket
—which she considered, perhaps rightly, discourteous. Later on, she took
a dislike to the young soldier who also occupied our compartment. The
soldier, and the woman's not very discreet daughter, a buxom girl with the
scrappy features of a prizefighter, seemed to have agreed to flirt. Whenever

334

the wandering cat appeared at our door, the daughter pretended to be frightened, and the soldier would gallantly shoo the cat into the corridor: this by-play gave them frequent opportunity to touch each other.

The young soldier was one of many on the train. With their tasseled caps set at snappy angles, they hung about in the corridors smoking sweet black cigarettes and laughing confidentially. They seemed to be enjoying themselves, which apparently was wrong of them, for whenever an officer appeared the soldiers would stare fixedly out the windows, as though enraptured by the landslides of red rock, the olive fields and stern stone mountains. Their officers were dressed for a parade, many ribbons, much brass; and some wore gleaming, improbable swords strapped to their sides. They did not mix with the soldiers, but sat together in a first-class compartment, looking bored and rather like unemployed actors. It was a blessing, I suppose, that something finally happened to give them a chance at rattling their swords.

The compartment directly ahead was taken over by one family: a delicate, attenuated, exceptionally elegant man with a mourning ribbon sewn around his sleeve, and traveling with him, six thin, summery girls, presumably his daughters. They were beautiful, the father and his children, all of them, and in the same way: hair that had a dark shine, lips the color of pimientos, eyes like sherry. The soldiers would glance into their compartment, then look away. It was as if they had seen straight into the sun.

Whenever the train stopped, the man's two youngest daughters would descend from the carriage and stroll under the shade of parasols. They enjoyed many lengthy promenades, for the train spent the greatest part of our journey standing still. No one appeared to be exasperated by this except myself. Several passengers seemed to have friends at every station with whom they could sit around a fountain and gossip long and lazily. One old woman was met by different little groups in a dozen-odd towns —between these encounters she wept with such abandon that the Australian doctor became alarmed: why no, she said, there was nothing he could do, it was just that seeing all her relatives made her so happy.

At each stop cyclones of barefooted women and somewhat naked children ran beside the train sloshing earthen jars of water and furrily squalling *Agua! Agua!* For two pesetas you could buy a whole basket of dark runny figs, and there were trays of curious white-coated candy doughnuts that looked as though they should be eaten by young girls wearing Communion dresses. Toward noon, having collected a bottle of wine, a loaf of bread, a sausage and a cheese, we were prepared for lunch. Our companions in the compartment were hungry, too. Packages were produced, wine uncorked, and for a while there was a pleasant, almost graceful festiveness. The soldier shared a pomegranate with the girl, the Australian told an amusing story, the witch-eyed mother pulled a paper-wrapped fish from between her bosoms and ate it with a glum relish.

Afterward everyone was sleepy; the doctor went so solidly to sleep that a fly meandered undisturbed over his open-mouthed face. Stillness etherized the whole train; in the next compartment the lovely girls leaned loosely, like six exhausted geraniums; even the cat had ceased to prowl, and lay dreaming in the corridor. We had climbed higher, the train moseyed across a plateau of rough yellow wheat, then between the granite walls of deep ravines where wind, moving down from the mountains, quivered in strange, thorny trees. Once, at a parting in the trees, there was something I'd wanted to see, a castle on a hill, and it sat there like a crown.

It was a landscape for bandits. Earlier in the summer, a young Englishman I know (rather, know of) had been motoring through this part of Spain when, on the lonely side of a mountain, his car was surrounded by swarthy scoundrels. They robbed him, then tied him to a tree and tickled his throat with the blade of a knife. I was thinking of this when without preface a spatter of bullet fire strafed the dozy silence.

It was a machine gun. Bullets rained in the trees like the rattle of castanets, and the train, with a wounded creak, slowed to a halt. For a moment there was no sound except the machine gun's cough. Then, "Bandits!" I said in a loud, dreadful voice.

"*Bandidos!*" screamed the daughter.

"*Bandidos!*" echoed her mother, and the terrible word swept through the train like something drummed on a tom-tom. The result was slapstick in a grim key. We collapsed on the floor, one cringing heap of arms and legs. Only the mother seemed to keep her head; standing up, she began systematically to stash away her treasures. She stuck a ring into the buns of her hair and without shame hiked up her skirts and dropped a pearl-studded comb into her bloomers. Like the cryings of birds at twilight, airy twitterings of distress came from the charming girls in the next compartment. In the corridor the officers bumped about yapping orders and knocking into each other.

Suddenly, silence. Outside, there was the murmur of wind in leaves, of voices. Just as the weight of the doctor's body was becoming too much for me, the outer door of our compartment swung open, and a young man stood there. He did not look clever enough to be a bandit.

"*Hay un médico en el tren?*" he said, smiling.

The Australian, removing the pressure of his elbow from my stomach, climbed to his feet. "I'm a doctor," he admitted, dusting himself. "Has someone been wounded?"

"*Si, Señor.* An old man. He is hurt in the head," said the Spaniard, who was not a bandit: alas, merely another passenger. Settling back in our seats, we listened, expressionless with embarrassment, to what had happened. It seemed that for the last several hours an old man had been stealing a ride by clinging to the rear of the train. Just now he'd lost his hold, and a soldier, seeing him fall, had started firing a machine gun as a signal for the engineer to stop the train.

My only hope was that no one remembered who had first mentioned bandits. They did not seem to. After acquiring a clean shirt of mine which he intended to use as a bandage, the doctor went off to his patient, and the mother, turning her back with sour prudery, reclaimed her pearl comb. Her daughter and the soldier followed after us as we got out of the carriage and strolled under the trees, where many passengers had gathered to discuss the incident.

Two soldiers appeared carrying the old man. My shirt was wrapped around his head. They propped him under a tree and all the women clustered about vying with each other to lend him their rosary; someone brought a bottle of wine, which pleased him more. He seemed quite happy, and moaned a great deal. The children who had been on the train circled around him, giggling.

We were in a small wood that smelled of oranges. There was a path, and it led to a shaded promontory; from here, one looked across a valley where sweeping stretches of scorched golden grass shivered as though the earth were trembling. Admiring the valley, and the shadowy changes of light on the hills beyond, the six sisters, escorted by their elegant father, sat with their parasols raised above them like guests at a *fête champêtre.* The soldiers moved around them in a vague, ambitious manner; they did not quite dare to approach, though one brash, sassy fellow went to the edge of the promontory and called, "*Yo te quiero mucho.*" The words returned with the hollow sub-music of a perfect echo, and the sisters, blushing, looked more deeply into the valley.

A cloud, somber as the rocky hills, had massed in the sky, and the grass below stirred like the sea before a storm. Someone said he thought it would rain. But no one wanted to go: not the injured man, who was well on his way through a second bottle of wine, nor the children, who, having discovered the echo, stood happily caroling into the valley. It was like a party, and we all drifted back to the train as though each of us wished to be the last to leave. The old man, with my shirt like a grand turban on his head, was put into a first-class carriage and several eager ladies were left to attend him.

In our compartment, the dark, dusty mother sat just as we had left her. She had not seen fit to join the party. She gave me a long, glittering look. "*Bandidos,*" she said with a surly, unnecessary vigor.

The train moved away so slowly butterflies blew in and out the windows.

Fontana
Vecchia

(1951)

ONTANA VECCHIA, OLD FOUNTAIN. SO
the house is called. *Pace*, peace: this
word is carved into the stone doorstep. There is no fountain; there has
been, I think, something rather like peace. It is a rose-colored house domi-
nating a valley of almond and olive trees that sinks into the sea. Across the
water there is a view on clear days of Italy's tip end, the peninsula of
Calabria. Back of us, a stony, wavering path, traveled mostly by farming
peasants, their donkeys and goats, leads along the side of the mountain into
the town of Taormina. It is very like living in an airplane, or a ship
trembling on the peak of a tidal wave: there is a momentous feeling each
time one looks from the windows, steps onto the terrace, a feeling of being
suspended, like the white reeling doves, between the mountains and above
the sea. This vastness reduces to an intimate size particulars of the landscape—the cypress trees are small as green pen quills; each passing ship
could be held in the palm of your hand.

Before dawn, when drooping stars drift at the bedroom window fat as
owls, a racket begins along the steep, at moments perilous, path that descends from the mountains. It is the farm families on their way to the
marketplace in Taormina. Loose rocks scatter under the stumbling hoofs
of overloaded donkeys; there are swells of laughter, a sway of lanterns: it
is as though the lanterns were signaling to the far-below night fishermen,
who just then are hauling in their nets. Later, in the market, the farmers

338

and the fishermen meet: a small people, not unlike the Japanese, but brawny; indeed there is something almost lush about their lean walnut-hardness. If you question the freshness of a fish, the ripeness of a fig, they are great showmen. *Si, buono:* your head is pushed down to smell the fish; you are told, with an ecstatic and threatening roll of eyes, how delicious it is. I am always intimidated; not so the villagers, who poke stonily among the tiny jewel tomatoes and never hesitate to sniff a fish or bruise a melon. Shopping, and the arranging of meals, is universally a problem, I know; but after a few months in Sicily even the most skilled householder might consider the noose—no, I exaggerate: the fruit, at least when first it comes into season, is more than excellent; the fish is always good, the *pasta*, too. I'm told you can find edible meat; I've never been so fortunate. Also, there is not much choice of vegetables; in winter, eggs are rare. But of course the real trouble is we can't cook; neither, I'm afraid, can our cook. She is a spirited girl, very charming, a little superstitious: our gas bill, for instance, is sometimes astronomical, as she is fond of melting immense pots of lead on the stove, then twisting the lead into carven images. As long as she keeps to simple Sicilian dishes, really simple and really Sicilian, they are, well, something to eat.

But let me tell about the chicken. Not long ago Cecil Beaton, in Sicily on a holiday, came to stay with us. After a few days he was beginning to look a bit peaked: we saw that a more proper effort toward feeding him would have to be made. We sent for a chicken; it appeared, quite alive, and accompanied by the cagey peasant woman who lives slightly higher on the mountain. It was a great black bird—I said it must be very old. No, said the woman, not old, just large. Its neck was wrung and G., the cook, put it to boil. Around twelve she came to say the chicken was still *troppo duro* —in other words, hard as nails. We advised her to keep trying, and settling on the terrace with glasses of wine, prepared to wait. Several hours, several wine liters later, I went out to the kitchen to find G. in a critical condition: after boiling the chicken, she had roasted it, then fried it, and now, in desperation, was giving it another boil. Though there was nothing else to eat, it should never have been brought to the table, for when it was set before us we had to avert our eyes: crowning this steaming heap was the poor bird's severed head, its withered eyes gazing at us, its blackened cockscomb still attached. That evening Cecil, who previously had been staying with other friends on the island, informed us, quite suddenly, that he must return to them.

When first we leased Fontana Vecchia—this was in the spring, April— the valley was high with wheat green as the lizards racing among its stalks. It begins in January, the Sicilian spring, and accumulates into a kingly bouquet, a wizard's garden where all things have bloomed: the creek sprouts mint; dead trees are wreathed in wild clamber roses; even the brutal cactus shoots tender blossoms. April, Eliot writes, is the cruelest month: not here. It is bright as the snows on Etna's summit. Children climb along the mountainside filling sacks of petals in preparation for a Saint's Day, and fishermen, passing with their baskets of pearl-colored *pesce*, have geraniums tucked behind their ears. May, and the spring is in its twilight: the sun enlarges; you remember that Africa is only eighty miles away; like a bronze shadow autumn color falls across the land. By June the wheat was ready to harvest. We listened with a certain melancholy to the scythes swinging in the golden field. When the work was over, our landlord, to whom the crop belonged, gave a party for the harvesters. There were only two women—a young girl who sat nursing a baby, and an old woman, the girl's grandmother. The old woman loved to dance; barefooted, she whirled with all the men—no one could make her take a rest, she would spring up in the middle of a tune to grab herself a partner. The men, who took turns playing the accordion, all danced together, which is a rural custom in Sicily. It was the best kind of party: too much dancing, far too much wine. Later, as I went exhaustedly to bed, I thought of the old woman. After working all day in the field and dancing all evening, she had now to start on a five-mile upward climb to her house in the mountains.

It is a walk to the beach, or beaches; there are several, all of them pebbly, and only one of them, Mazzaro, especially inhabited. The most attractive, Isola Bella, a guarded cove with water clear as barrel rain, is a mile and a half straight down; getting up again is the trick. A few times we have walked into Taormina and taken the bus, or a taxi. But mostly we go on foot. You can swim from March until Christmas (so the hearty souls say), but I confess I was not too enthusiastic until we bought the water mask. The mask had a round glass viewing plate, and a breathing tube that closes when you dive. Swimming silently among the rocks, it is as though one had discovered a new visual dimension: in the underwater dusk a red phosphorescent fish looms at alarming proximity; your shadow drifts over a field of ermine-colored grass; blue, silver bubbles rise from some long-legged sleeping thing lying in a field of blowing sea flowers, and it is as if a wind of music were moving them; the sea flowers, the Javanese tendrils of purple jelly. Coming to shore, how static, gross, the upper world seems.

If we do not go to the beach, then there is only one other reason for leaving the house: to shop in Taormina, and have an *apéritif* in the piazza. Taormina, really an extension of Naxos, the earliest Greek city in Sicily, has had a continuous existence since 396 B.C. Goethe explored here in 1787; he describes it thus: "Now sitting at the spot where formerly sat the uppermost spectators, you confess at once that never did any audience, in any theater, have before it such a spectacle as you there behold. On the right, and on high rocks at the side, castles tower in the air; farther on, the city lies below you, and although all of its buildings are of a modern date, still similar ones, no doubt, stood of old on the same site. After this the eye falls on the whole of the long range of Aetna, then on the left it catches a view of the seashore as far as Catania, and even Syracuse, and then the wide and extensive view is closed by the immense smoking volcano, but not horribly, for the atmosphere, with its softening effect, makes it look more distant and milder than it really is." Goethe's vantage point was, I gather, the Greek theater, a superb cliff-top ruin where even today plays and concerts are occasionally given.

Taormina is as scenically extravagant as Goethe claims; but it is a curious town. During the war it was the headquarters of Kesselring, the German general; consequently, it came in for a share of Allied bombing. The damage was slight. Nevertheless, the war has been the town's undoing. Up until 1940 it was, with the exception of Capri, the most successful Mediterranean resort south of the French Riviera. Though Americans have never come here, at least in any quantity, it had considerable reputation among English and Germans. (A guidebook to Sicily, written by an Englishman, and published in 1905, remarks: "Taormina is flooded with Germans. At some hotels they have separate tables for them, because the other nations do not like sitting with Germans.") Now, of course, the Germans are in no position to travel; due to currency restrictions, neither are the English. Last year the San Domenico, an old convent that late in the nineteenth century was converted into a most luxurious hotel, was never more than a quarter filled; before the war it was necessary to have your reservations a year in advance. This winter, as perhaps a frantic last measure, the town, in the hope that it will attract the international audience, is opening a gambling casino. I wish them luck: it is imperative that someone come along and buy all those hand-woven hats, handbags, that junk in the shops along the Corso. For myself, Taormina suits me the way it is; it has the comforts of a tourist center (running water, a shop with foreign newspapers, a bar where you can buy a good martini) without the tourists.

The town, not large, is contained between two gates; near the first of these, the Porto Messina, there is a small tree-shaded square with a fountain and a stone wall along which village idlers are arranged like birds on a telephone wire. Taking one of my first walks through Taormina, I was startled to see perched upon this wall an old man wearing velvet trousers and wrapped in a black cape; his hat, an olive fedora, had been dented into a peaked tricorne crown, and the brim threw a shadow over his broad, yellowed, somewhat Mongolian face. It was a surprisingly theatrical appearance, merely that, until looking closely I realized it was André Gide. Through the spring and early summer I often saw him there, either sitting unnoticed on the wall, apparently only another of the old men, or browsing about the fountain, where, with his cape drawn about him in a Shakespearean manner, he seemed to be observing in the water his own reflection: *si jeunesse savait, si vieillesse pouvait.*

Beneath the excess trappings Taormina is an ordinary town, and its people have ordinary ambitions, occupations. However, many of them, the young men in particular, possess what I think of as the mentality of hotel-children, children who have spent their lives in hotels, and who know that all things are transient, that the heart must never be involved, for friendship is a matter of days. These young men live, as it were, "outside" the town; they are interested in foreigners, not so much for gainful reasons as the distinction they believe it bestows upon them to have English and American acquaintances, and as most of them have a primitive way with several languages, they spend their days at piazza cafés courteously, artificially, chattering with travelers.

It is a beautiful piazza centering around a promontory with a view of Etna and the sea. Toy Sardinian donkeys, attached to delicately carved carts, go prancing past, their bells jangling, their carts filled with bananas and oranges. On Sunday afternoons, while the town band plays an eccentric but catchy concert, there is a grand promenade, and if I am there, I always look out for the butcher's daughter, a stout, beefy girl who all week swings a meat ax with the ferocity of any two men; but on Sunday, coiffed and scented, careening on two-inch heels, and accompanied by her fiancé, a slender boy rising not quite to her shoulder, there is about her a romance, an atmosphere of triumph that stalls the satiric tongue: hers is the haughtiness, the belief in oneself, that should be the spirit of a promenade. Occasionally traveling entertainers appear in the piazza: goatlike mountain boys who play on hair-covered bagpipes haunting, yodelerlike tunes; or, as in the spring, a singer, a child whose family supported themselves by each year touring him around the island: his stage was the limb of a tree, and there, his head thrown back and his throat trembling with heart-bursts of soprano song, he sang until his voice tired to the saddest whisper.

When shopping, the *tabacchi* is my last stop before starting out into the country. In Sicily all tobacconists are irritable fellows. Their places are usually crowded, but few of the customers buy more than three or four loose cigarettes: with a pinched solemnity the weathered men put down their ragged lire, then minutely examine the cigarettes, the poky cigars that have been doled out to them—it seems the most important moment of their day, this visit to the *tabacchi;* perhaps that is why they are so reluctant to give up their place in line. There are possibly twenty different Sicilian newspapers; great garlands of them are strung in front of the tobacconist shop. One afternoon as I walked into town it started to rain. It was not a serious rainfall; still, the streets were deserted, not a soul about until I came alongside the *tabacchi*—a crowd was gathered where the newspapers, shriekingly headlined, fluttered in the rain. Young boys, bareheaded, unmindful, stood with their heads leaning together, while an older boy, his finger pointing to an enormous photograph of a man stretched in a pool of blood, read aloud to them: Giuliano, dead, shot in Castelvetrano. *Triste, triste,* a shame, a pity, the older people said; the young ones said nothing, but two girls went into the shop and came out with copies of *La Sicilia,* a paper whose front page was taken up by a giant portrait of the slain bandit; protecting their papers against the rain, the girls ran hand in hand skidding along the shining street.

Then it was August; we felt the sun before it had risen. Strangely, here on the open mountain, the days were cooler than the nights, for more often than not a booming breeze blew off the water; at sunset the wind turned, plowed seaward, south, toward Greece, Africa. It was a month of silent leaves, shooting stars, red moons, a season of gorgeous moths, sleeping lizards. Figs split, plums swelled, the almonds hardened. One morning I woke to hear in the almond trees the rattle of bamboo canes. In the valley, off on the hills, hundreds of peasants, working in family groups, were knocking down the almonds, then gathering them off the ground; and they sang to each other, one voice leading the rest, Moorish, flamencolike voices whose songs began nowhere, ended nowhere, and yet contained the marrow of work, heat, a harvest. They were a week bringing in the almonds, and each day the singing reached a not quite sane intensity. I could not think for it; there was in me such an overriding sense of extra-life. At the end, during the mad last days, the fierce fine voices seemed to rise from the sea, the almond roots; it was as if one were lost in a cave of echoes, and when darkness came, and stillness, even so I could hear, at the edge of sleep, the sound of singing, and it seemed, though one tried to push it back, about to tell a pitiful, painful story, about to impart some terrible knowledge.

We do not have many visitors at Fontana Vecchia; it is too far a walk for casual callers, and days go by when no one knocks at the door except the ice boy. Blond, witty, the ice boy is a scholarly-looking child of eleven. He has a beautiful young aunt, surely one of the most attractive girls I've ever known, and I often talk to him about her. Why, I wanted to know, does A., the aunt, have no beau? Why is she always alone, never at the dances or the Sunday promenade? The ice boy says it is because his aunt has no use for the local men, that she is very unhappy and longs only to go to America. Perhaps. But it is my own theory that the men in her family are so jealous of her that no one dares come too near. Sicilian males have quite a lot to say about what their women do or don't; heaven knows, the women seem to like it. For instance our cook, G., who is nineteen, has a somewhat older brother. One morning she appeared with a split lip, blackened eyes, a knife gash in her arm, and bruised yellow-green top to toe. It was astonishing; she should have been in a hospital. Smiling lopsidedly, G. said, Well, her brother had beat her up; they'd quarreled because he felt she went too often to the beach. Of course, we thought that an odd objection; when did she go to the beach—at night? I told her to pay no attention to her brother, that he was *brute*, ugly. Her reply, in effect, was that I should mind my own business; she said her brother was a fine man. "He is good-looking and has many friends—only to me is he *brute*." Nevertheless, I went to our landlord and complained that G.'s brother must be warned that we would not tolerate his sister's coming to work in this kind of condition. He seemed mystified: why should I blame the brother? After all, a brother is entitled to reprimand his sister. When I spoke of it to the ice boy he agreed with the landlord, and stated firmly that if he had a sister who didn't do what he said, he would beat her up too. One evening in August, when the moons were so preposterous, the ice boy and I had a small but chilling exchange. He asked, What do you think of the werewolf? Are you afraid to go out after dark? As it happened, I'd just that day heard of the werewolf scare: a boy walking home late at night claimed to have been set upon by a howling animal, a human on all fours. But I laughed. You don't believe in werewolves, do you? Oh yes. "There used to be many werewolves in Taormina," he said, his gray eyes regarding me steadily; then, with a disdainful shrug, "Now there are only two or three."

And so autumn came, is here at this moment, a tambourine wind, a ghost of smoke moving between the yellow trees. It has been a good year for grapes; sweet in the air is the smell of fallen grapes in the mold of leaves, new wine. The stars are out at six; still, it is not too chilly to have a cocktail on the terrace and watch, in the bright starlight, the sheep with their Buster Keaton faces coming down from pasture, and the goats, whose herd-movement makes a sound like the dragging of dry branches. Yesterday men brought us a wagonload of wood. So I am not afraid of winter's coming: what better prospect than to sit by a fire and wait for spring?

Extreme
Magic

(1967)

AUGUST, 1966! ABOARD THE *TRI-tona*. Others aboard: Gianni and Marella Agnelli (hosts), Stash and Lee Radziwill, Luciana Pignatelli, Eric Nielsen, Sandro Durso, Adolfo Caracciolo, his daughter Allegra and his nephew Carlo. Seven Italians, one Dane, one Pole, and two of *us* (Lee *et moi*). Hmm.

Point of departure: Brindisi, a rather sexy seaport on the Italian Adriatic. Destination: the islands and coast of Yugoslavia, a twenty-day cruise ending in Venice.

It is now eleven P.M., and we had hoped to sail at midnight, but the captain, a no-nonsense gentleman from Germany, complains of a rising wind and thinks it unsafe to risk the sea before sunrise. Never mind!—the quay alongside the yacht is awash with café lights and piano sounds and Negro and Norwegian sailors browsing among brigades of pretty little purse-swinging tarts (one a really speedy baby with pimiento-colored hair).

Groan. Moan. Oh oh oh hold on to the wall. And crawl, Jesus, please. Please, Jesus. Slowly, slowly, one at a time: Yes, I am crawling up the stairs from my cabin (where green waves are smashing against the portholes), *crawling* toward the presumed safety of the salon.

345

The *Tritona* is a luxurious craft constructed on a wide-bottomed principle of a Grecian caïque. The property of Conte Theo Rossi, who lent it to the Agnellis for their cruise, it is furnished throughout like the apartment of an elegantly humorous art collector: The salon is a greenhouse of flowering plants—a huge Rubens dominates the wall above an arrangement of brown velvet couches.

But on this particular morning, the first day of the voyage, as we crossed the swelling seas between Italy and Yugoslavia, the salon, when at last I've crawled my way to it, is a rocking wreck. A television set is overturned. Bottles from the bar are rolling on the floor. Bodies are strewn all over like the aftermath of an Indian massacre. One of the choicest belongs to Lee (Radziwill). As I crawl past her, she opens a seasick eye and, in a hospital whisper, says: "Oh, it's *you*. What time is it?"

"Nine. Thereabouts."

Moan. "Only *nine?* And this is going to last the *whole* day. Oh I wish I'd listened to Stash. He said we shouldn't have come. How do you feel?"

"Maybe I'll live."

"You look incredible. Yellow. Have you taken a pill? They help. A *little.*"

Eric Nielsen, lying face-down and somewhat askew, as though he'd been felled from behind by an ax murderer, says: "Shut up. I'm worse off than either of you."

"The trouble," says Lee, "the trouble with the pills is they make you so thirsty. And then you're dying for water. But if you drink water, that only makes you sicker."

How true—as I learned after swallowing two pills. Thirst is not the word; it was as if one had been a prisoner in the Sahara half a year or more.

A steward had arranged a buffet breakfast, but no one has gone near it —until presently Luciana (Pignatelli) appears. Luciana, looking impossibly serene and lovely—her slacks immaculate, every strand of golden hair just so, and her face, the eyes particularly, a triumph of precise maquillage.

"Oh, *Luciana*," says Lee in a grieving, drowning tone, "how ever did you do it?"

And Luciana, buttering a slice of toast and spreading it with apricot jam, says: "Do what, darling?"

"Put on your face. I'm trembling so—I can't hold a lipstick. If I'd tried to do what you've done to your eyes—all those *Egyptian* lines—I would have blinded myself."

"Trembling?" says Luciana, crunching her toast. "Oh I *see*. You are troubled by the motion of the boat. But really it is not so bad, no?"

Eric says: "Shut up, girl. I've been on hundreds of boats, and I've never been seasick before."

Luciana shrugs. "As you like." Then she calls for the steward, who arrives careening to and fro. "May I have an egg, please?"

Lee says: "Oh, Luciana. How *can* you?"

At dusk this day the sea calmed as the *Tritona* approached the stony Montenegro coast. Everyone, feeling vastly better, is on deck staring down at the green-crystal depths skidding below. Suddenly a trio of sailors, standing in the ship's prow, start to shout and gesture: An immense porpoise is racing along beside us.

The porpoise leaps, arcs, gleefully descends out of sight, leaps like laughter materialized, plunges again, and this time disappears. Then the sailors, leaning over the rail, begin to whistle a curious intense whistle-chant, and the whistling is some Ondine melody the seamen know will lure the creature back. Back it comes!—soaring heavenward wreathed in water-spark.

The porpoise guides us along the coast as far as a cave, then turns and seeks the deeper, now darkening outer sea.

Village lamps light the distance; but only Gianni (Agnelli), ever the questing spirit, wants to go ashore. The rest of us have more sense. And anyway, it's my policy to leave heavy sightseeing to others—I've never cared to burden myself with churches and such relics. I like people, cafés and the stuff in shop windows. Unfortunately Yugoslavia, much as it happily differs from most socialist states, nonetheless is afflicted by that same *tristesse*, that same atmosphere of empty vistas, of nowhere to go and nothing to do when you get there, that starts just the other side of the Berlin Wall.

As usual in these countries, the store shelves are crammed with merchandise, but none of it is anything you would care to buy, not even as a gift for a cruel stepmother. Occasionally one encounters a street peddler selling pretty-enough native rugs; and if you like liqueurs, the best Maraschino in the world, a masterpiece of the distilling art, is a Yugoslavian creation. Otherwise zero, a shopper's hell.

Nor can we praise the restaurants; as in Russia, the service is very Stepin Fetchit, every meal an endurance test. Dinner at the best restaurant in Dubrovnik is an only so-so affair. And the queer thing is, the quality of produce available in the marketplace is excellent. In the larger coastal cities, say Split, the markets sprawl like immense crazy quilts, a pattern composed of tomatoes and peaches and roses and soap and pickles and pigs' feet and severed carcasses strung upside down. And over it all, over everything, hovers a buzzy, prickly cloud of wasps. These wasps are like a political emblem, a subtly evoked threat—they seldom sting, but one cannot escape them, for they are a constant factor in the Yugoslavian landscape: a part of the air, unavoidable even aboard the *Tritona*, where, when we lunch on deck, the wasps dance in a yellow haze above the wines and melon.

Some quite unusual melons were served at lunch yesterday—cantaloupe-colored, yet spongy and sweet as honeydews. Marella said: "Absolutely *divino!* I wonder where the melons come from." And pretty Princess Pignatelli, who has spent much of the voyage raptly reading a book called *The Big Spenders* (by Lucius Beebe), snaps to attention: "The Mellons?" says she. "The Mellons? They come from Pittsburgh."

"A week is enough. Ten days is the absolute maximum," so remarked Stash (Radziwill), referring to the amount of time he considered it possible to spend within the confines of a yacht cruise; and apparently most people in a position to judge second his opinion—that ten days is the limit, regardless of the charm of the company or the fascination of the scenery. But I do not agree with this. To my mind, the longer a cruise lasts the more intoxicating it becomes—a strange drifting awake-dream, a drug compounded of sun and motion and floating-by views that both lifts and lowers the spirit into a condition of alert slumber.

Also, I like boat routine. *Tritona* mornings are spent ashore in city-ports or island-villages; around noon the cast, separated in twos and threes, wanders back aboard, then departs again by various speedboats to isolated coves and beaches for an hour's swim. When everyone has once more reassembled, we gather on the sun-exposed upper deck for drinks and, for the athletes, a session of exercises conducted by Luciana ("my figure has improved seventy percent since I started weight-lifting").

Then lunch (Italian chef, lots of great pasta concoctions, am gaining about a half-pound a day, oh what the hell). And as we start lunch, the yacht sets sail; we cruise all afternoon to our next destination, usually arriving at sunset.

Yesterday, abandoning the languors of a Norwegian-like fjord, we went all together in two speedboats to explore the beautiful waters surrounding a rocky little island. That was where we encountered the unpleasant fisherman.

He was a husky, handsome man, brown and naked except for denim trousers rolled up to his knees; not young—but a youthful fifty. His sturdy little boat was anchored in the cove where we had stopped to swim. He and his crew, three men much smaller than their captain, were ashore building a fire under a big iron kettle. The captain, a cleaver in his hand, was chopping up great hunks of fish and tossing them into the pot.

It was Eric who said why not buy fish from them, so we all swam to the beach, and Eric and I went over to discuss the matter with the fishermen. None of them acknowledged our approach. They just, in a rather eerie way, pretended we weren't there. Finally Eric, speaking Italian, which most Yugoslavian seamen speak or understand, complimented them on their fine haul and, pointing out a particular *loup*, asked its price. The sullen captain, with a mirthless grunt, replied: "Three hundred dollars." And he said it in English!

At this juncture Marella arrived, and she said to us: "He thinks we are all Americans. That's why he is being so rude." Then, turning to the captain, still unconcernedly preparing his stew, she announced: "*I* am an Italian."

And in Italian the captain said: "Italians are no good either. Why," he shouted, pointing at the delicious-looking mess simmering in his kettle, "why do you people come here and stare at our food? Do *we* stare at your food?" He gestured toward the yacht riding at a distance on the ultra-clear sea. "Do we go aboard your fine ship and watch you while you eat your food?"

"Well," said Marella, as we walked away, "the old boy has a point, you know."

"Personally," said Eric, "I think he ought to be reported to the Tourist Bureau."

What new can one say about Dubrovnik anyway? It is like some section of Venice drained of its canals and stripped of color: gray, medieval, Italian without Italian brio. In autumn and winter it must, in its emptiness, be most impressive; but in summer it is so crowded with excursion-fare vacationers, one can scarcely keep the pavement. And for those holiday-makers the government has arranged a quite startling night life, altogether unlike any this diarist has seen in other so-called Communist countries (which, excepting Albania and China, includes the lot).

Above the city, nightclubs with sea-panorama vistas throb through the night; one in particular, an al fresco affair attached to a full-scale gambling casino, puts on a floor show reminiscent of those erotic hoedowns in pre-Castro Havana. And in fact the star of the show turned out to be that old-time Cuban legend: Superman!

All those who remember Superman from Havana will be interested to hear that his act, which formerly consisted of vigorous sexual intercourse on a brightly lighted stage, has changed: He is now the male section of a dance team. He and his partner writhe around to the banging of bongo drums, gradually removing one another's attire until such nakedness appears that Superman seems ready to go into the routine that once made him so famous—but there it stops. The whole thing is fairly humorous, though

God knows the audience doesn't think so: Their response is a kind of stupor, the dazed attention of pimply boys at an Ann Corio exhibit.

Now, leaving the warm moist southern climate, we steam steadily northward into spheres where the air, though it is only late August, trembles already with a beyond-September chill. It is as if a cold crystal ball had descended, enclosing and stilling the green sea, sky, the growing-greener coast bobbing by: gone is the harsh and stony Montenegrin grayness, the subtropic pallor, for now each northward-going day the scene is more fruitful, there are trees and fields of wild flowers and grape vineyards and shepherds munching close to the Adriatic's edge.

I feel touched by some extreme magic, an expectant happiness—as I always do when that sense of autumn arrives, for autumn never seems to me an end but a start, the true beginning of all our new years.

And so our voyage stopped in the mists of a Venetian evening. With sea mists blurring the lights of San Marco, and sea buoys mournfully tolling watery warnings, the *Tritona* entered the saddest and loveliest of cities and anchored *alla* Salute.

The mood aboard is not all sad; the sailors, many of them Venetians, whistle and amiably shout as they swing ropes and lower launches. In the salon, Eric and Allegra are dancing to the phonograph. And I, huddled in the dark, on the upper deck, am very pleased myself—pleased with the air's promising chill, and the oily flickering lights, and the thought of an imminent visit to Harry's Bar.

I've starved myself all day because . . . Oh, what joy to step out of the night into the chattering warmth of Harry's Bar and wash down those little shrimp sandwiches with an icy martini or three!

Greek
Paragraphs

(1968)

A FEW SUMMERS AGO ITALIAN FRIENDS invited me on a cruise through the Greek Islands aboard an especially graceful sailing yacht. We were to depart from Piraeus on a morning in July. The sea was calm, the ship sparkled, the captain and his crew awaited us in uniforms as white as the churches of Mykonos; and I was there, oh yes. Unfortunately, a sudden tragedy, a death in the family, had detained my hosts; but, though unable to meet me, they insisted I should proceed with the cruise. Just imagine! —a whole yacht at the disposal of one passenger. Only the nuttiest, richest, most selfish person could deliberately conceive such an adventure. However, as it had happened by accident, I felt neither guilt nor hesitation. *Avanti.*

Herewith, some notes from the voyage.

PEACHES

I dislike Greek wines; however, there is one unresinated white wine that is as dry and light as the best Italian soaves. It's called King Minos, and just now, sitting under the starlight on the afterdeck, I drank a half bottle of it while eating two enormous peaches. Peaches the size of cantaloupes and the color of cantaloupe meat. Peaches of a deliciously yielding texture and a juicy liqueurlike sweetness. And to think they are the product of a Greek island, these mountainous bits of sea-surrounded desert. One would not have thought they could grow such peaches in the greenest Persian garden, much less here on these sun-seared rocks. Yet it is true, for the cook bought them at Santorin, where we are harbored for the night.

The crew have gone ashore: up Up UP to Santorin village. Quite a climb, a matter of several thousand steps and dizzying views. I made it there this afternoon astride one of these fragile and courageous little fly-pestered donkeys, bless its put-upon heart. Felt very ashamed of myself, also was rump-sore, so returned afoot.

The sky, a bonfire of stars—as ablaze as the skies above the Sahara. The sway of caiques. The sway of moored caiques. Music from a harbor café. An ouzo-scented old man dancing in front of the café. The cool King Minos warming my veins, the taste of peaches lingering, the perfume of peach skins saturating the soft, salt-tart air.

MELTEMI

That cursed wind, the meltemi. Yesterday we were caught in one, an inevitable event on the summer seas of Greece, for the damn thing blasts about the whole of July and August. Some years ago I spent a summer in the Cyclades on the island of Paros, which is surely the meltemi's favored haunt: indeed, it seldom departs, but hurls around the island howling like the spectral voices of drowned sailors, centuries of sailors smashed against its shores.

It *is* an evil wind, scratchy, nerve-twisting. And look what it does to the economy, the diet of the islanders: when fishermen can't fish, as they can't when the meltemi roars, an islander's already sufficiently meager menu is reduced by half.

April is the finest month to visit here: fields of wild flowers, wild anemones, white violets, and the water, green as spring buds, is just warm enough for a brisk swim. April . . . or late September, when the water is still warm enough (if you don't object to sharing it with migrating geese who abruptly plunge from the heavens and swim along beside you), and the meltemi has stopped prowling.

But until yesterday I had never experienced one at sea. I was below when it arrived; even so, I could hear it approaching across the water—a dark rippling feathery noise. The ship lurched, spun, fish peered into the portholes; it seemed the mast must crack: how close we all come to joining that complaining choir of drowned mariners! At dusk it died and we hurried to hide in a cove.

A TERRIBLE TALE

There are Yugoslavs in the crew, Greeks, mostly Italians. The captain is Italian. He doesn't much like the yacht because he doesn't like sailing yachts, not even that black pearl of the Aegean, Niarchos's *Creole*. He says they are romantic but too much work for the crew. He speaks English, speaks it well, and is a rather youngish man with dramatic eyes and a dark-toned voice; he might easily have been an actor, and all actors are liars, I've never met one that wasn't. But perhaps the captain is not a liar. Anyway, this morning we passed Delos, not stopping because I'd been there twice before, and a glimpse of the marble ruins drifting by in a shimmering lavender haze reminded him of a story. At lunch he told it to me. He swore it was true.

"This happened when I was a boy of seventeen, and in the crew of a yacht owned by an Englishman, Lord Sickle. Now, Lord Sickle often chartered his yacht, and in August of that year he chartered it to a beautiful Englishwoman: a widow, I would say forty, very tall, a tiny waist, so elegant. She had a son, a lad sixteen or so and also very beautiful and elegant. Crippled, however: a withered leg in a brace, and he walked with two canes. But a genius, this boy. A scholar. It was for his sake that the mother undertook a Greek cruise; he wanted to see the places he knew so well from his studies.

"They came aboard accompanied by a maid and a manservant; otherwise they were alone, and I've often thought what a pity that was. Perhaps it wouldn't have happened if they had had friends with them.

"There was a strange island the boy wanted to visit. North of Delos. Yes, north. I can't remember precisely. It was an island of only a few acres and all but unknown; still, he knew of it and spoke of a well-preserved temple there.

"We arrived *après midi*, and because of the shallows, had to anchor more than a mile offshore. The boy was very excited. He had made up his mind to pack a supper and spend the night alone with his mother on the island; he wanted to see the temple by moonlight and sleep on the shore. The mother loved him very much. Too much. She laughed and ordered a picnic.

"It was I who rowed them there, set them ashore; and it was I who returned at dawn to collect them. The boy was dead, stripped to a skeleton; and the mother, whom I found wading in the water, was unrecognizable —fearfully mutilated, half mad.

"Only months later, months spent in an Athens hospital, was she able to tell a court of inquiry what had happened. She said, 'At first it was very peaceful and lovely. We wandered around the temple until twilight, then spread our supper on a flight of steps; my son Eric said oh, look, it's going to be a full moon. We could see the lights of the yacht riding far out—I wished we had kept the sailor with us. Because, as the moon thickened, brightened, somehow I mistrusted the landscape. And gradually I became aware of a sound. Claws. An icy scuttling. And a huge brown rat, another and another, leapt with tearing teeth into our picnic. A horde of rats pouring out of the temple, hundreds flailing in the moonlight. Eric screamed; he tried to run and fell, and I had to drag him by the arms, but the rats were at us, all over us, they even swam after us into the water, pulled Eric back onto the beach, and no one heard me the whole night I bled and screamed and cried there in the sea.' "

The captain lit a cigar. "This woman is still alive. She lives in Nice. I've seen her—sitting in a chaise on the promenade. She wears a full veil. I'm told she never speaks to anyone."

OBSERVATIONS

(1) Numerous educated Greek men share a snobbish affectation—obsessed by their fingernails, they pamper them ceaselessly, letting the nails on either little finger grow to Dragon Lady length. This is to let the lesser folk know that they work with their heads, not their hands. (2) Greek businessmen also share an eccentric hobby: playing with ropes of amber or ivory beads, their nervous fingers twitching from bead to bead, rubbing, counting. This conduct is said to relieve the pressure of affairs and prevent ulcers. (3) And what most Greeks, male or female, have in common are medical superstitions. The humblest village has a vendor who sells small replicas, stamped from sheets of polished tin, of hands, hearts, feet, ears, eyes. If, say, you are recovering from a coronary, why, you simply acquire a tin heart, carry it on your person, and presently the actual ailing organ will have magically healed itself. The True Believers are not limited to peasants and middle-class housewives, but include many intellectuals. Once, when I was living on Paros, I mentioned to a Professor Calliope, a linguist of great renown, that my father was virtually blind and that I myself had a considerable fear of failing eyesight. He bought me a pair of tin eyes, and insisted we walk, through curtains of quivering August heat, to a nunnery in the mountains where there resided a remarkable abbess endowed with witch-powers: once she had blessed my medals, my worries were over. At the monastery I was made to feel like a missionary captive in some perilous Hottentot village: the nuns, very unused to visitors, gathered around me, all giggling and poking and pinching—really pinching, as if to judge how

juicy I'd be when put to boil. But soon the professor had them calmed down and we were served cool water and a crystal candy that smelled of roses and contained inside each piece a roseleaf. As for the abbess—we were too late: she had died the week before.

A BLUE COVE

The only scenery that bores me is any that I can't imagine purchasing a part of: usually, if a place provides the slightest uplift, I instantly consider buying or building a house. The hundreds of properties I've constructed mentally! But now something serious has occurred. For the past few days we've been cruising around Rhodes, lingering a lot at the perfect little bay of Lindos. An American acquaintance who has a house above Lindos took me to see something he thinks I should own. I think so too. It is a small stone farmhouse situated inside a horseshoe-shaped cove; the beach is a sandy confection, and the water, being entirely protected, tranquil as a sapphire winking in a jeweler's window. It could be mine for three thousand dollars: an investment of another five or six would put the house in delicious order. It is a prospect that sizzles the imagination.

At night I think, Yes I will, but in the morning I recall—politics, old mortality, inconvenient emotional commitments, the impossibilities of the Greek tongue, a trillion difficulties. Still, I ought to have the courage; I'll never again find anything quite as ideal as that.

AT A CAFÉ

I left the yacht at Rhodes, and this morning flew to Athens. Now at not quite midnight am sitting alone in an outdoor café on Constitution Square. There are not many patrons, though I recognize one of them as someone I'd seen years ago in Tangier, where she was quite the Queen of the Casbah (Southern Belle Version): Eugenia Bankhead, Tallulah's even more voluble sister. She is arguing with a Negro companion.

Come to consider, many of the world-trampers who used to hang around Tangier now frequent Athens. Across the street from where I sit I see every conceivable breed of hustler, from muscled dockhands to plump Egyptian lovelies wearing wavy platinum wigs.

It is very hot, and the ubiquitous white dust of Athens mists the air, coats the street and my tabletop like the pale rough crust on a bilious tongue. I am remembering the stone house in the blue cove. But that is all I will ever do. Remember it.

Music for
Chameleons

(1979)

S HE IS TALL AND SLENDER, PERHAPS
seventy, silver-haired, soigné, neither
black nor white, a pale golden rum color. She is a Martinique aristocrat
who lives in Fort de France but also has an apartment in Paris. We are
sitting on the terrace of her house, an airy, elegant house that looks as if
it were made of wooden lace: it reminds me of certain old New Orleans
houses. We are drinking iced mint tea slightly flavored with absinthe.

Three green chameleons race one another across the terrace; one pauses
at Madame's feet, flicking its forked tongue, and she comments: "Chameleons. Such exceptional creatures. The way they change color. Red. Yellow.
Lime. Pink. Lavender. And did you know they are very fond of music?"
She regards me with her fine black eyes. "You don't believe me?"

During the course of the afternoon she had told me many curious things.
How at night her garden was filled with mammoth night-flying moths.
That her chauffeur, a dignified figure who had driven me to her house in
a dark green Mercedes, was a wife-poisoner who had escaped from Devil's
Island. And she had described a village high in the northern mountains that
is entirely inhabited by albinos: "Little pink-eyed people white as chalk.
Occasionally one sees a few on the streets of Fort de France."

"Yes, of course I believe you."

She tilts her silver head. "No, you don't. But I shall prove it."

So saying, she drifts into her cool Caribbean salon, a shadowy room with gradually turning ceiling fans, and poses herself at a well-tuned piano. I am still sitting on the terrace, but I can observe her, this chic, elderly woman, the product of varied bloods. She begins to perform a Mozart sonata.

Eventually the chameleons accumulated: a dozen, a dozen more, most of them green, some scarlet, lavender. They skittered across the terrace and scampered into the salon, a sensitive, absorbed audience for the music played. And then not played, for suddenly my hostess stood and stamped her foot, and the chameleons scattered like sparks from an exploding star.

Now she regards me. "*Et maintenant? C'est vrai?*"

"Indeed. But it seems so strange."

She smiles. "*Alors.* The whole island floats in strangeness. This very house is haunted. Many ghosts dwell here. And not in darkness. Some appear in the bright light of noon, saucy as you please. Impertinent."

"That's common in Haiti, too. The ghosts there often stroll about in daylight. I once saw a horde of ghosts working in a field near Petionville. They were picking bugs off coffee plants."

She accepts this as fact, and continues: "*Oui. Oui.* The Haitians work their dead. They are well known for that. Ours we leave to their sorrows. And their frolics. So coarse, the Haitians. So Creole. And one can't bathe there, the sharks are so intimidating. And their mosquitoes: the size, the audacity! Here in Martinique we have no mosquitoes. None."

"I've noticed that; I wondered about it."

"So do we. Martinique is the only island in the Caribbean not cursed with mosquitoes, and no one can explain it."

"Perhaps the night-flying moths devour them all."

She laughs. "Or the ghosts."

"No. I think ghosts would prefer moths."

"Yes, moths are perhaps more ghostly fodder. If I was a hungry ghost, I'd rather eat anything than mosquitoes. Will you have more ice in your glass? Absinthe?"

"Absinthe. That's something we can't get at home. Not even in New Orleans."

"My paternal grandmother was from New Orleans."

"Mine, too."

As she pours absinthe from a dazzling emerald decanter: "Then perhaps we are related. Her maiden name was Dufont. Alouette Dufont."

"Alouette? Really? Very pretty. I'm aware of two Dufont families in New Orleans, but I'm not related to either of them."

"Pity. It would have been amusing to call you cousin. *Alors.* Claudine Paulot tells me this is your first visit to Martinique."

"Claudine Paulot?"

"Claudine and Jacques Paulot. You met them at the Governor's dinner the other night."

I remember: he was a tall, handsome man, the First President of the Court of Appeals for Martinique and French Guiana, which includes Devil's Island. "The Paulots. Yes. They have eight children. He very much favors capital punishment."

"Since you seem to be a traveler, why have you not visited here sooner?"

"Martinique? Well, I felt a certain reluctance. A good friend was murdered here."

Madame's lovely eyes are a fraction less friendly than before. She makes a slow pronouncement: "Murder is a rare occurrence here. We are not a violent people. Serious, but not violent."

"Serious. Yes. The people in restaurants, on the streets, even on the beaches have such severe expressions. They seem so preoccupied. Like Russians."

"One must keep in mind that slavery did not end here until 1848."

I fail to make the connection, but do not inquire, for already she is saying: "Moreover, Martinique is *très cher*. A bar of soap bought in Paris for five francs costs twice that here. The price of everything is double what it should be because everything has to be imported. If these troublemakers got their way, and Martinique became independent of France, then that would be the close of it. Martinique could not exist without subsidy from France. We would simply perish. *Alors*, some of us have serious expressions. Generally speaking, though, do you find the population attractive?"

"The women. I've seen some amazingly beautiful women. Supple, suave, such beautifully haughty postures; bone structure as fine as cats. Also, they have a certain alluring aggressiveness."

"That's the Senegalese blood. We have much Senegalese here. But the men—you do not find them so appealing?"

"No."

"I agree. The men are not appealing. Compared to our women, they seem irrelevant, without character: *vin ordinaire*. Martinique, you understand, is a matriarchal society. When that is the case, as it is in India, for example, then the men never amount to much. I see you are looking at my black mirror."

I am. My eyes distractedly consult it—are drawn to it against my will, as they sometimes are by the senseless flickerings of an unregulated television set. It has that kind of frivolous power. Therefore, I shall overly describe it—in the manner of those "avant-garde" French novelists who, having chosen to discard narrative, character and structure, restrict themselves to page-length paragraphs detailing the contours of a single object, the mechanics of an isolated movement: a wall, a white wall with a fly meandering across it. So: the object in Madame's drawing room is a black mirror. It is seven inches tall and six inches wide. It is framed within a worn black leather case that is shaped like a book. Indeed, the case is lying open on a table, just as though it were a deluxe edition meant to be picked up and browsed through; but there is nothing there to be read or seen—except the mystery of one's own image projected by the black mirror's surface before it recedes into its endless depths, its corridors of darkness.

"It belonged," she is explaining, "to Gauguin. You know, of course, that he lived and painted here before he settled among the Polynesians. That was his black mirror. They were a quite common artifact among artists of the last century. Van Gogh used one. As did Renoir."

"I don't quite understand. What did they use them for?"

"To refresh their vision. Renew their reaction to color, the tonal variations. After a spell of work, their eyes fatigued, they rested themselves by gazing into these dark mirrors. Just as gourmets at a banquet, between elaborate courses, reawaken their palates with a *sorbet de citron.*" She lifts the small volume containing the mirror off the table and passes it to me. "I often use it when my eyes have been stricken by too much sun. It's soothing."

Soothing, and also disquieting. The blackness, the longer one gazes into it, ceases to be black, but becomes a queer silver-blue, the threshold to secret visions; like Alice, I feel on the edge of a voyage through a looking-glass, one I'm hesitant to take.

From a distance I hear her voice—smoky, serene, cultivated: "And so you had a friend who was murdered here?"

"Yes."

"An American?"

"Yes. He was a very gifted man. A musician. A composer."

"Oh, I remember—the man who wrote operas! Jewish. He had a mustache."

"His name was Marc Blitzstein."

"But that was long ago. At least fifteen years. Or more. I understand you are staying at the new hotel. La Bataille. How do you find it?"

"Very pleasant. In a bit of a turmoil because they are in the process of opening a casino. The man in charge of the casino is called Shelley Keats. I thought it was a joke at first, but that really happens to be his name."

"Marcel Proust works at Le Foulard, that fine little seafood restaurant in Schoelcher, the fishing village. Marcel is a waiter. Have you been disappointed in our restaurants?"

"Yes and no. They're better than anywhere else in the Caribbean, but too expensive."

"*Alors.* As I remarked, everything is imported. We don't even grow our own vegetables. The natives are too lackadaisical." A hummingbird penetrates the terrace and casually balances on the air. "But our sea-fare is exceptional."

"Yes and no. I've never seen such enormous lobsters. Absolute whales; prehistoric creatures. I ordered one, but it was tasteless as chalk, and so tough to chew that I lost a filling. Like California fruit: splendid to look at, but without flavor."

She smiles, not happily: "Well, I apologize"—and I regret my criticism, and realize I'm not being very gracious.

"I had lunch at your hotel last week. On the terrace overlooking the pool. I was shocked."

"How so?"

"By the bathers. The foreign ladies gathered around the pool wearing nothing above and very little below. Do they permit that in your country? Virtually naked women parading themselves?"

"Not in so public a place as a hotel pool."

"Exactly. And I don't think it should be condoned here. But of course we can't afford to annoy the tourists. Have you bothered with any of our tourist attractions?"

"We went yesterday to see the house where Empress Josephine was born."

"I never advise anyone to visit there. That old man, the curator, what a chatterbox! And I can't say which is worse—his French or his English or his German. Such a bore. As though the journey getting there weren't tiring enough."

Our hummingbird departs. Far off we hear steel-drum bands, tambourines, drunken choirs ("*Ce soir, ce soir nous danserons sans chemise, sans pantalons*": Tonight, tonight we dance without shirts, without pants), sounds reminding us that it is Carnival week in Martinique.

"Usually," she announces, "I leave the island during Carnival. It's impossible. The racket, the stench."

When planning for this Martinique experience, which included traveling with three companions, I had not known our visit would coincide with Carnival; as a New Orleans native, I've had my fill of such affairs. However, the Martinique variation proved surprisingly vital, spontaneous and vivid as a bomb explosion in a fireworks factory. "We're enjoying it, my friends and I. Last night there was one marvelous marching group: fifty men carrying black umbrellas and wearing silk tophats and with their torsos painted with phosphorescent skeleton bones. I love the old ladies with gold-tinsel wigs and sequins pasted all over their faces. And all those men wearing their wives' white wedding gowns! And the millions of children holding candles, glowing like fireflies. Actually, we did have one near-disaster. We borrowed a car from the hotel, and just as we arrived in Fort de France, and were creeping through the midst of the crowds, one of our tires blew out, and immediately we were surrounded by red devils with pitchforks—"

Madame is amused: "*Oui. Oui.* The little boys who dress as red devils. That goes back centuries."

"Yes, but they were dancing all over the car. Doing terrific damage. The roof was a positive samba floor. But we couldn't abandon it, for fear they'd wreck it altogether. So the calmest of my friends, Bob MacBride, volunteered to change the tire then and there. The problem was that he had on a new white linen suit and didn't want to ruin it."

"Therefore, he disrobed. Very sensible."

"At least it was funny. To watch MacBride, who's quite a solemn sort of fellow, stripped to his briefs and trying to change a tire with Mardi Gras madness swirling around him and red devils jabbing at him with pitchforks. Paper pitchforks, luckily."

"But Mr. MacBride succeeded."

"If he hadn't, I doubt that I'd be here abusing your hospitality."

"Nothing would have happened. We are not a violent people."

"Please. I'm not suggesting we were in any danger. It was just—well, part of the fun."

"Absinthe? *Un peu?*"

"A mite. Thank you."

The hummingbird returns.

"Your friend, the composer?"

"Marc Blitzstein."

"I've been thinking. He came here once to dinner. Madame Derain brought him. And Lord Snowdon was here that evening. With his uncle, the Englishman who built all those houses on Mustique—"

"Oliver Messel."

"*Oui. Oui.* It was while my husband was still alive. My husband had a fine ear for music. He asked your friend to play the piano. He played some German songs." She is standing now, moving to and fro, and I am aware of how exquisite her figure is, how ethereal it seems silhouetted inside a frail green lace Parisian dress. "I remember that, yet I can't recall how he died. Who killed him?"

All the while the black mirror has been lying in my lap, and once more my eyes seek its depths. Strange where our passions carry us, floggingly pursue us, forcing upon us unwanted dreams, unwelcome destinies.

"Two sailors."

"From here? Martinique?"

"No. Two Portuguese sailors off a ship that was in harbor. He met them in a bar. He was here working on an opera, and he'd rented a house. He took them home with him—"

361

"I *do* remember. They robbed him and beat him to death. It was dreadful. An appalling tragedy."

"A tragic accident." The black mirror mocks me: Why did you say that? It wasn't an accident.

"But our police caught those sailors. They were tried and sentenced and sent to prison in Guiana. I wonder if they are still there. I might ask Paulot. He would know. After all, he is the First President of the Court of Appeals."

"It really doesn't matter."

"Not matter! Those wretches ought to have been guillotined."

"No. But I wouldn't mind seeing them at work in the fields in Haiti, picking bugs off coffee plants."

Raising my eyes from the mirror's demonic shine, I notice my hostess has momentarily retreated from the terrace into her shadowy salon. A piano chord echoes, and another. Madame is toying with the same tune. Soon the music lovers assemble, chameleons scarlet, green, lavender, an audience that, lined out on the floor of the terra-cotta terrace, resembles a written arrangement of musical notes. A Mozartean mosaic.

REPORTAGE

The Muses
Are Heard

(1956)

PART I

ON SATURDAY, THE SEVENTEENTH OF December, 1955, a foggy wet day in West Berlin, the cast of the American production of *Porgy and Bess* and others associated with the company, a total of ninety-four persons, were asked to assemble at the company's rehearsal hall for a "briefing" to be conducted by Mr. Walter N. Walmsley, Jr., and Mr. Roye L. Lowry, respectively Counsel and Second Secretary of the American Embassy in Moscow. Mr. Walmsley and Mr. Lowry had traveled from Moscow expressly to advise and answer any questions members of the production might have concerning their forthcoming appearance in Leningrad and Moscow.

This trip to Russia, the first of its kind ever attempted by an American theatrical group, was to be the culmination of a four-year world tour for *Porgy and Bess*. It had come about after many months of complicated, in some areas still beclouded, negotiation between the U.S.S.R. and the producers of the Gershwin opera, Robert Breen and Blevins Davis, who operate under the name Everyman Opera, Incorporated.

Although the Russians had not yet delivered their actual visas, the enormous troupe, consisting of fifty-eight actors, seven backstage personnel, two conductors, assorted wives and office workers, six children and their schoolteacher, three journalists, two dogs and one psychiatrist, were all set to depart within the next forty-eight hours, traveling by train from East Berlin via Warsaw and Moscow to Leningrad, a distance of some eleven hundred miles, yet requiring, apparently, three days and nights.

On my way to the diplomatic briefing, I shared a taxi with Mrs. Ira Gershwin and a square-cut, muscular man called Jerry Laws, who was formerly a boxer and is presently a singer. Mrs. Gershwin is of course the wife of the lyricist, who, aside from being the brother of its composer, is himself co-author of *Porgy and Bess*. Periodically, for the past four years, she has left her husband at home in Beverly Hills to accompany the opera on its around-the-world wanderings: "Ira's such a stick-in-the-mud. He hates to go from one room to the next. But I'm a gypsy, darling. I love wheels." Known to her friends as Lee, an abbreviation of Lenore, she is a small and fragile woman devoted to diamonds, and wears them, quite a few, at both breakfast and dinner. She has sun-streaked hair and a heart-shaped face. The flighty fragments of her conversation, delivered in a girlish voice that rushes along in an unsecretive whisper, are pasted together with terms of endearment.

"Oh, love," she said, as we rode through the dark drizzle along the Kurfurstendam, "have you heard about the Christmas tree? The Russians are giving us a Christmas tree. In Leningrad. I think that's so sweet of them. Since they don't *believe* in Christmas. They don't—do they, darling? Anyway, their Christmas comes much later. Because they have a different calendar. Darling, do you think it's true?"

"About whether they believe in Christmas?" said Jerry Laws.

"*No*, love," said Mrs. Gershwin impatiently. "About the microphones. And the photographs."

For several days there had been speculation among the company on the subject of personal privacy in Russia. It was based on the rumor that their letters would be censored, their hotel rooms wired and the walls encrusted with concealed cameras.

After a thoughtful moment, Laws said, "I believe it."

"Oh, darling, you don't!" Mrs. Gershwin protested. "It can't be true! After all, *where* are we going to gossip? Unless we simply stand in the bathroom and keep flushing. As for the cameras—"

"I believe that, too," said Laws.

Mrs. Gershwin settled into a musing silence until we reached the street where the rehearsal hall was located. Then, rather wistfully, she said, "I *still* think it's nice about the Christmas tree."

We were five minutes late, and had difficulty in finding seats among the folding chairs that had been set up at one end of the mirrored rehearsal hall.

It was crowded and the room was well heated; nevertheless many of those present, as though they could feel already the cold winds of the steppes, sat bundled in the paraphernalia, the scarves and woolly coats, they'd specially acquired for their Russian journey. A competitive spirit had pervaded the purchasing of these outfits, of which more than several had a certain Eskimo-look.

The meeting was called to order by Robert Breen. In addition to being the co-producer of *Porgy and Bess,* he is also its director. After he'd introduced the representatives from the Moscow Embassy, Mr. Walmsley and Mr. Lowry, who were seated behind a table facing us, Mr. Walmsley, a stocky middle-aged man with a Mencken-style haircut and a dry, drawling manner, began by speaking of the "unique opportunity" the proposed tour offered and congratulating the company in advance on the "great success" he was sure they would have behind the iron curtain.

"Since nothing happens in the Soviet Union that isn't planned, and since it is *planned* that you should have a success there, I feel perfectly safe in congratulating you now."

As though sensing a faultiness in his colleague's presumed compliment, Mr. Lowry, a youngish man with the straitlaced façade of a schoolmaster, interposed to suggest that while what Mr. Walmsley had said was perfectly correct, it was also true that there was "a genuine excitement in Russia about your coming there. They know the Gershwin music. In fact, a Russian acquaintance of mine told me he was at a party the other night where three friends of his sang 'Bess, You Is My Woman Now' all the way through."

The cast smiled appreciatively, and Mr. Walmsley resumed. "Yes, there are some nice Russians. Very nice people. But they have a bad government," he said, in slow spelling-it-out tones. "You must always bear in mind that their system of government is basically hostile to our own. It is a system, with rules and regulations, such as you have never experienced before. Certainly in my experience, which is a long one, I've never encountered anything like it."

A member of the cast, John McCurry, raised his hand to ask a question. McCurry plays the villainous part of Crown, and is, in his own appearance, high and heavy and somewhat forbidding, as befits the role. He wanted to know, "Suppose some of these people invite us into their home? See, most places we go, people do that. Now, is it all right for us to go?"

The two diplomats exchanged an amused glance. "As you may well imagine," said Mr. Walmsley, "we at the Embassy have never been bothered with that problem. We're never invited *any*where. Except officially. I can't say *you* won't be. And if so, by all means take advantage of the opportunity. From what I understand," he continued, "your hosts plan an extensive program of entertainment. Something every minute. Enough to wear you out."

Some of the youngsters smacked their lips at this prospect, but one of them complained, "I don't touch a drop of nothing. So when they're making all these toasts we've heard about, how do I get out of it gracefully?"

Mr. Walmsley shrugged. "You don't have to drink if you don't want to."

"Sure, man," the worried one was advised by a friend, "nobody's got to drink what they don't want to. And what you don't want, you hand to me."

Now the questions came quickly. The parents, for instance, were concerned about their children. Would there be pasteurized milk? Yes. Still, Mr. Lowry thought it advisable to take a supply of Starlac, which is what he fed his own two children. And the water, was it fit to drink? Perfectly safe. Mr. Walmsley often drank it from the tap. How does one address a Soviet citizen? "Well," said Mr. Walmsley, "I *wouldn't* call them Comrade. Mr. and Mrs. will do." What about shopping, was it expensive? "Outrageously," but it hardly mattered, since there was nothing much to buy anyway. How cold did it get? Oh, it *could* occasionally go to thirty-two below zero. In that case, would their hotel room be warm? Yes, indeed. Overheated, actually.

When these fundamentals had been gone through, a voice from the back raised itself to say, "There's been so much myth talk around here. We heard we're going to be trailed all the time."

"Trailed?" Mr. Walmsley smiled. "Perhaps. Though not in the manner you're thinking of. If they assign anyone to follow you, it will be for your own protection. You must, you see, expect to attract extraordinary attention, crowds wherever you go. It won't be like walking down a street in Berlin. For that reason you may be followed, yes."

"After all," said Mr. Lowry, "the Ministry of Culture has been so anxious to have you come there that you will probably receive very generous treatment, free of the niggling-naggling that a stray foreign visitor might expect."

The voice from the back persisted, somewhat in a key of disappointment, "We heard they were going to trail us. And open our letters."

"Ah," said Mr. Walmsley, "*that* is another matter. Something you take for granted. I always assume my letters have been opened."

His audience shifted in their chairs, their eyes swerving with I-told-you-so's. Robert Breen's secretary, Nancy Ryan, stood up. Miss Ryan (Radcliffe '52) had been with the company three months, having taken the job because of an interest in the theater. A New Yorker, she is blond, very blue-eyed, tall, just under six feet in fact, and bears considerable resemblance to her mother, an often-photographed and celebrated beauty, Mrs.

William Rhinelander Stewart. She wanted to make a suggestion. "Mr. Walmsley, if it's true our letters will be censored, then wouldn't it be better to do all our correspondence on postcards? I mean, if they didn't have to open it to read it, wouldn't that cause less of a delay in outgoing mail?"

Mr. Walmsley seemed not to think Miss Ryan's plan had much merit, as either a time-saving or trouble-saving device. Meanwhile, Mrs. Gershwin had been urging Jerry Laws into action. "Go on, darling. Ask him about the microphones."

Laws caught the diplomat's attention. "A lot of us," he said, "we've been worried about the possibility of wire-tapping in our rooms."

Mr. Walmsley nodded. "I should say it's more than a possibility. Again, it's the sort of thing you should assume. Of course, no one really *knows.*"

There was a silent pause, during which Mrs. Gershwin, plucking at a diamond brooch, seemed to wait for Jerry Laws to bring up the matter of concealed cameras, but he hadn't the chance before McCurry regained the floor.

McCurry leaned forward, hunching his burly shoulders. He said he thought it was about time they stopped beating around the bush and came to grips with "the big problem. The big problem is, now what do we say when they ask us political stuff? I'm speaking of the Negro situation."

McCurry's deep voice made the question ride across the room like a wave, collecting as it went the complete interest of the audience. Mr. Walmsley hesitated, as though uncertain whether to ride over it or swim under; at all events, he seemed not prepared to meet it head-on.

"You don't have to answer political questions, any more than they would answer questions of that nature put to them by you." Walmsley cleared his throat, and added, "It's all dangerous ground. Treading on eggs."

Mutterings in the audience indicated that they felt the diplomat's advice was inadequate. Lowry whispered in Walmsley's ear, and McCurry consulted his wife, a melancholy woman who was sitting beside him with their three-year-old daughter on her lap. Then McCurry said, "But they're bound to ask us about the Negro situation. They always do. Last year we were in Yugoslavia, and all the time we were there—"

"Yes, I know," said Walmsley peremptorily. "That's what this whole thing is about. That's the point, isn't it?"

Walmsley's statement, or possibly the manner in which it was made, seemed to rub several people the wrong way; and Jerry Laws, a legend in the company for his fighting quick temper, jumped to his feet, his body stiff with tension. "Then how do we handle it? Should we answer it the way it is? Tell the truth? Or do you want us to gloss it over?"

Walmsley blinked. He took off a pair of horn-rimmed glasses and polished them with a handkerchief. "Why, tell the truth," he said. "Believe me, sir, the Russians know as much about the Negro situation as you do.

And they don't give a damn one way or another. Except for statements, propaganda, anything they can turn to their own interests. I think you ought to keep in mind that any interviews you give will be picked up by the American press and reprinted in your hometown newspapers."

A woman, the first who had spoken, rose from her seat in the front row. "We all know there's discrimination back home," she said in a shy voice to which everyone listened respectfully. "But in the last eight years Negroes have made a lot of progress. We've come a long way and that's the truth. We can point with pride to our scientists, artists. If we did that [in Russia], it might do a lot of good."

Others agreed, and addressed the group in a similar vein. Willem Van Loon, a Russian-speaking son of the late historian, and one of the persons handling publicity for Everyman Opera, announced that he was "very, very glad this matter is being gone into so thoroughly. The other day I had a couple of the cast taping an interview for the American Service stations here in Germany, and touching on this point, this racial question, I knew we had to be very, very careful, because of being so near to East Berlin and the possibility of our being monitored—"

"Of course," said Walmsley, quietly interrupting. "I suppose you realize that we're being monitored right now."

Clearly Van Loon had not, nor had anyone else, to judge from the general consternation and gazing-round to see who could be the cause of Walmsley's remark. But any evidence, at least in the shape of mysterious strangers, was not apparent. Van Loon, however, didn't finish what he'd intended saying. His voice trailed away, as did the meeting itself, which shortly came to a meandering conclusion. Both of the diplomats blushed when the company thanked them with applause.

"Thank you," said Walmsley. "It's been a great pleasure to talk to you. Mr. Lowry and I don't often get into contact with the atmosphere of greasepaint."

The director, Robert Breen, then called his cast to rehearsal, but before it began, there was much milling about and swapping of opinions on the "briefing." Jerry Laws restricted himself to one word, "Uninformative." Mrs. Gershwin, on the contrary, seemed to have found it too informative. "I'm stunned, darling. Think of living like that! Always assuming. Never *knowing*. Seriously, darling, where are we going to gossip?"

Downstairs, I was offered a return ride to the hotel by Warner Watson, production assistant to Mr. Breen. He introduced me to Dr. Fabian Schupper, who also shared the taxi. Dr. Schupper is an American student at the German Psychoanalytic Institute. I was told he'd been invited on the Russian tour to counteract any "stresses" members of the company might experience. At the last moment, much to his disappointment, Dr. Schupper did not actually go, the management having decided that a psychiatrist was perhaps, after all, not necessary; though the fact that psychoanalysis and its practitioners are not welcome in the Soviet Union may well have been a contributing cause. But at the moment, in the taxi, he was advising Warner Watson to "relax."

Watson, lighting a cigarette with hands that trembled noticeably, said, "Relaxed people do *not* get productions like this played on the samovar circuit."

Watson is in his late thirties. He has a graying crew-cut, and timid, resigned brown eyes. There is about his face, and his manner too, a blurred gentleness, a beyond-his-years fatigue. At one time an actor, he has been associated with Everyman Opera since its inception in 1952. In his job, he is primarily concerned with what he calls "fencing things in." During the past two weeks in Berlin, he'd very nearly taken up residence at the Soviet Embassy, attempting to get a few things fenced in. Despite these efforts, there remained a multiplicity of matters that had escaped corralling. Among them, there was the situation over the company's passports, which, at this late date, were still lurking in Russian hands waiting to be visaed. Then, too, Watson was encountering trouble on the subject of the train by which the troupe was to travel to Leningrad. The production had requested four sleeping cars. The Russians had replied, quite flatly, that they could supply only three second-class cars with "soft-bed" (the Russian term for sleeping berth) accommodations. These, together with a baggage car and a car for the show's scenery, would be attached to The Blue Express, a regularly scheduled Soviet train running between East Berlin and Moscow. Watson's difficulty was that he could not obtain from the Russians a plan of the "soft-bed" cars, and so was unable to chart out sleeping arrangements. He therefore imagined on the train a slapstick *Walpurgisnacht:* "More bodies than berths." He'd also not been able to learn at what hotels in either Leningrad or Moscow the troupe would be staying, and other details of that nature. "They'll never tell you the whole thing about anything. Not all at once. If they tell you A, they *might* tell you B, but between the two there's a long, long wait."

Apparently, though, the Russians themselves did not practice the same patience they required of others. Some hours earlier a cable had arrived from Moscow that Watson counted among the causes for his trembling hands. UNLESS ORCHESTRATIONS DELIVERED EMBASSY BERLIN TONIGHT WILL POSTPONE LENINGRAD OPENING REDUCE FEE. The Soviets had for weeks been demanding the orchestrations because they wanted their musicians to rehearse in advance of the company's arrival. Breen, fearing the orchestrations, his only copy, might be lost in transit, had refused to comply. But this ultimatum cable, with its two dire last words, seemed to have changed his mind, and now Watson was on his way to deliver the orchestrations to the Soviet Embassy.

"Don't worry," said Watson, wiping beads of moisture from his upper lip. "*I'm* not worried. We're going to get all this fenced in."

"Relax," said Dr. Schupper.

Back at my hotel, the Kempenski, where many of the company were staying, I stopped by Breen's suite to see his wife, Wilva. She'd just returned from an overnight flight to Brussels, where she'd gone to consult a doctor. For some while twinges of appendicitis had been troubling her, and when, the day before, she'd flown to Brussels, it was with the knowledge that she might have to undergo an immediate operation, thereby canceling her part in the trip to Russia. The previous October she'd spent ten days in Moscow discussing arrangements for the tour with the Ministry of Culture, a "fascinating" experience that had made her anxious to return.

"It's all right, the doctor says I can go. I didn't know how much I wanted to until I thought I couldn't," she said, smiling the smile that seems less an expression than a circumstance of her eager, her anxious-to-please personality. Mrs. Breen has dimples and large brown eyes. Her hair, a maple color, is worn upswept and held in place by huge pins that could serve as weapons. At the moment, she was wearing a dress of purple wool, the color that dominates her wardrobe: "Robert's mad for purple." She and Breen met at the University of Minnesota, where both were graduate students in the drama department. They have been married eighteen years. Though Mrs. Breen has played professionally on the stage, once as Shakespeare's Juliet, her real devotions, in the words of one of their associates, are to "Robert and Robert's career." If she could find enough paper, she'd wrap up the world and hand it to him.

On the surface of it, a shortage of paper would not appear to be one of Mrs. Breen's problems, for she lives with a traveling mountain of letters and clippings and files. The international correspondence for Everyman Opera is among her principal responsibilities; that, and seeing that the company is "kept happy." In the latter role, she'd brought back from Brussels a parcel of toys to be distributed among the children of the cast at Christmastime in Leningrad. "*If* I can get them away from Robert long enough to pack them again," she said, pointing to a bathroom where an armada of mechanical boats floated in a filled tub. "Robert's mad for toys. Really," she sighed, "it's dreadful to think of getting all *this* into suitcases." Several of the objects on view, in the bedroom and in the living room which doubled as an office, presented obvious packing difficulties, especially a large seesawlike apparatus known as a Relaxer Board. "I don't see why I can't take it to Russia. I've taken it everywhere else. It does me a world of good."

Mrs. Breen asked if I were looking forward to boarding The Blue

Express, and was exaggeratedly pleased to hear that I was. "Oh, Robert and I wouldn't miss this train ride for the world! Everybody in the cast is so darling. I know it's going to be the kind of fun you'll never stop talking about. But," she said, with a sudden sorrow in her voice that sounded not altogether sincere, "Robert and I have decided to go by plane. Of course we'll see you off at the station here—and be right there on the platform when you pull into Leningrad. At least I *hope* we will. Only I can't believe it. That it's really going to happen." She paused; for an instant a frown marred her immaculate enthusiasm. "Someday I'll tell you the real story behind it all. The people who didn't want this to happen! Oh, we've had such blows." She struck her breast. "Real body blows. And they're still coming. Right up to the last minute," she said, glancing at a sheaf of cables on a desk.

A few of the Breens' tribulations were already common knowledge. For instance, it seemed an accepted fact, in the rumor and publicity surrounding the Soviet venture, that the Russians had, on their own initiative, and out of a Geneva-spirit impulse, invited *Porgy and Bess* to tour their country. The truth of the matter is, Everyman Opera had invited itself. Breen, having long considered a trip to Russia the logical extension of his company's "good will" travels, sat down and wrote a letter to the Soviet Premier, Marshal Bulganin, saying, in effect, that *Porgy and Bess* would be pleased to undertake the journey if the U.S.S.R. was willing to have them. The appeal must have impressed Bulganin favorably, for he forwarded the letter to the Ministry of Culture, the government monopoly which, under the direction of Nikolai Mikhailov, controls every facet of artistic life inside the Soviet Union. Theater, music, films, publishing, painting, each of these activities comes under the specific, not always lenient, supervision of the Ministry of Culture, whose headquarters are in Moscow. Therefore, with the implied blessings of Bulganin, the Ministry began negotiations with Everyman Opera, though to do so could not have been a casual decision. Casual, say, as the decisions might have been in the case of the Comédie Française, whose company had appeared in Moscow a year earlier, or a British production of *Hamlet*, which had been given a Moscow première in the autumn of 1955. Both of these troupes had enjoyed wholehearted success. But from any point of view, whether that of the visiting artists or their hosts, the risks involved were merely aesthetic. Molière and Shakespeare do not lend themselves to the intentions of modern political propaganda.

The same cannot be said of *Porgy and Bess*. Here, either side of the curtain, American or Soviet, had much to concern them, for the Gershwin opera, when slipped under the dialectical microscope, proves a test tube brimming with the kind of bacteria to which the present Russian regime is most allergic. It is extremely erotic, a serious cause for dismay in a nation with laws so prim, persons can be arrested for kissing in public. It is God-fearing; over and again it stresses the necessity of faith in a world above the stars rather than below, demonstrates in song and dialogue the comforts to be derived from religious belief ("the opium of the people"). Furthermore, it discourses, in an uncritical vein, on the subject of superstition, i.e., "The Buzzard Song." As if this weren't anathema enough, it also sings out loud that people can be happy with plenty of nothin', an unwelcome message indeed.

Certainly the Ministry of Culture must have taken these drawbacks into account, and then reflected that, though the pill was definitely there, at least it was sugar-coated. After all, and despite its accent on folkish fun, the situation of the American Negro as depicted in *Porgy and Bess,* an exploited race at the mercy of ruthless Southern whites, poverty-pinched and segregated in the ghetto of Catfish Row, could not be more agreeably imagined if the Ministry of Culture had assigned one of their own writers to the job. And so, midsummer of 1955, the Ministry informed Everyman Opera they were prepared to roll out the red carpet.

Assured of a welcome in Russia, Breen then faced the problem of getting there, and that required money, an estimated $150,000. The first newspaper announcements of the Russian "invitation" to *Porgy and Bess* more or less suggested that the American State Department would not only be the spiritual heart of this "unprecedented project," as Breen occasionally called it, but would also provide its financial backbone. Breen believed so, and with good reason. Over the last several years the State Department had received universal praise for its moral and financial sponsoring of *Porgy and Bess,* which *The New York Times,* among others, frequently summarized as the "best ambassador" the State Department had ever sent abroad. But Breen soon discovered, after a series of pleading trips to Washington, that he could no longer rely on the patronage of his Potomac friends. Apparently they thought his project too unprecedented, or, in their own phrase, "politically premature." In other words, not one cent.

In New York, theatrical circles theorized that the State Department had withdrawn its support because they feared the opera too vulnerable to the purposes of Soviet propaganda. Defenders of the enterprise considered this attitude nonsensical. In their opinion, the fact that such social-critical aspects as the opera contained could be freely presented in the American theater counteracted the possibilities of effective propaganda on that score. A further argument was that in Russia the very presence of the Negro cast, their affluent appearance, their so obviously unoppressed outspokenness, their educated, even worldly manner ("Why," said Mrs. Breen, "some of our cast speak three and four languages. Perfectly") would impress on the Russian people a different image of the American Negro from the stereotype that continues to make Harriet Beecher Stowe one of the Soviet's best-selling authors.

Variety, the theatrical trade paper, reported as rumor a more straightforward explanation for the State Department's reversal. According to them, the International Exchange Program, a branch of the American National Theater and Academy (ANTA), whose advice on theatrical matters carries great weight in Washington, had registered opposition on the grounds that the State Department had already spent enough money on *Porgy and Bess,* and that the funds at their disposal should be more evenly spread to allow a larger catalogue of events in cultural exchange.

Nonetheless, ANTA and the State Department wished Everyman Opera the best of luck. They were not disowning, simply disinheriting. But well-wishers added little to Breen's bank account, and as he pondered the possibilities of raising the needed amount of private subscription, there was an unexpected development. The Russians stepped forward and offered to pick up the tab themselves. While the feeblest linguist could translate the meaning of this gesture, designed, as it was, to embarrass the State Department, American partisans of Breen's venture welcomed it for the very reason it was offered. They felt it would shame Washington into taking a less miserly position. They were mistaken.

Consequently, with time growing short, Breen had the choice of abandoning his plan or permitting the Soviet to capitalize it. A contract, dated December 3, 1955, was drawn up in Moscow between the Ministry of Culture of the U.S.S.R. ("designated hereinafter under the name of the 'Ministry') and Everyman Opera, Inc. ("hereinafter under the name of the 'Company'). The contract consists of three and a half closely typed pages, and contains several quaint items—the Ministry agrees to supply a Russian member of the cast, namely, "one domesticated she-goat." But the burden of it is set forth in Article 5. When the writhings of language in this long clause are disentangled, it emerges that during their stay in the Soviet Union, the company would receive weekly payments of $16,000, a figure quite below their customary fee, especially so since the payments were to be made half "in U. S. Dollars in a bank check in New York, the remainder in cash Rubles at the official rate." (As everyone knows, the official rate is an arbitrary four rubles to the dollar. Opinion wavers on what a fair exchange would be, but on the Moscow black market it is possible to get ten to one, and if a person were willing to take a chance on transporting currency out of the country, thereby risking Siberian detention, he could obtain in Switzerland only one dollar for every fifteen rubles.) In addition to these monetary agreements, Article 5 also promised that the Ministry would supply the Company with: "Free lodging and food in first-class hotels or, when traveling, with sleeper accommodations and food in a dining car. Furthermore, it is understood and agreed that the Ministry pay all expenses for traveling of all members of the Company and the transportation of its scenic equipment to and through the Soviet Union and back to a European border of the Soviet Union."

All told, the Russians were investing approximately $150,000. This should not be construed as cultural philanthropy. Actually, for them it was a sound business proposition. If every performance sold out, as was almost certain to happen, the Ministry would double its investment, that is, have a total box-office gross the equivalent of $300,000. Whereas, on the basis of the Ministry-Company contract, and by applying the laws of income versus operating cost, it could be calculated that Everyman Opera would lose around $4,000 a week. Presumably Breen had devised a formula for sustaining such a loss. "But don't ask *me* what it is, darling," said Mrs. Gershwin. "It's an absolute mystery."

While Mrs. Breen was still on the theme of "body blows," her husband returned from the studio where he'd been rehearsing the cast after the diplomatic briefing. She asked him if he'd like a drink. He said he would, very much. Straight brandy, please.

Breen is around forty-five, a man of medium height. He has an excellent figure, and one is kept aware of it by the fit of his clothes, for he is partial to trim Eisenhower jackets and those close-cut, narrow-legged trousers known as frontier pants. He wears custom-made shirts, preferably in the colors black and purple. He has thinning blond hair and is seldom indoors or out without a black beret. Depending on the expression, whether solemn or smiling, his face, pale and with a smoothly gaunt bone structure, suggests altogether opposite personalities. In the solemn moments, which can last hours, his face presents a mask of brooding aloofness, as though he were posing for a photographer who had warned him not to move a muscle. Inevitably, one is reminded that Breen, like his wife, has acted Shakespeare—and that the part was Hamlet, which he played in a production that, soon after the war, toured Europe and was even staged at Elsinore itself. But when Breen relaxes, or when something succeeds in catching his interest, he has a complete physical altering in the direction of extreme liveliness and boyish grinning good humor. A shyness, a vulnerable, gullible look replaces the remote and seeming self-assurance. The dual nature of Breen's appearance may explain why an Everyman Opera employee could complain in one breath, "You never know where you stand with Mr. Breen," and say in the next, "Anybody can take advantage of him. He's just too kind."

Breen took a swallow of brandy and beckoned me into the bathroom, where he wanted to demonstrate how one of the toy boats operated. It was a tin canoe with a windup Indian that paddled. "Isn't that wonderful?" he said, as the Indian paddled back and forth across the tub. "Did you ever see anything like that?" He has an actor's trained voice, "placed" in a register so very deep that it makes for automatic pomposity, and as he speaks his manicured hands move with his words, not in an excitable, Latin style, but in a gracefully slow ritualistic manner, rather as though he were saying Mass. Indeed, Breen's earliest ambitions *were* ecclesiastical. Before his interest turned toward the stage, he spent a year training to become a priest.

I asked him how the rehearsal had gone. "Well, it's a good cast," he said. "But they're a little spoiled, they take it too much for granted. Curtain calls and ovations. Rave reviews. I keep telling them I want them to understand going to Russia isn't just another engagement. We've got to be the best we've ever been."

If Breen expected the wish contained in this last sentence to come true, then, in the estimation of some observers, he had his work cut out for him. In 1952, when Breen and his co-producer, Blevins Davis, revived the Gershwin opera, which had been a box-office and somewhat of a critical failure in its original (1935) Theater Guild presentation, the program listed William Warfield as Porgy, Leontyne Price as Bess, and Cab Calloway in the role of Sportin' Life. Since then, these stars had been replaced, and even their replacements replaced, not always with artists of comparable quality. It is difficult to maintain a high level in performance of any long-run production, especially if the show is on tour. The strain of overnight hops, the dreamlike flow of rooms and restaurants, the electric emotional climate surrounding groups who continuously live and work together are factors which create an accumulative fatigue that the show often reflects. Horst Kuegler, a Berlin theater critic who, when he'd reviewed *Porgy and Bess* three years earlier (it was then appearing in Germany as part of the Berlin Music Festival), had been so enthusiastic he'd gone to see it five times, now felt, seeing it again, that it was "still full of energy and charm, though the production has deteriorated greatly." For the past week, Breen had rehearsed his cast to the limit Actors Equity permits; but whether or not the show could be whipped into prime shape, Breen had no qualms about its reception at the Leningrad première. It was going to be a "bombshell"! The Russians would be "stunned"! And, what was an unarguable prediction, "They'll never have seen anything like it!"

As Breen was finishing his brandy, his wife called from the next room, "You'd better get ready, Robert. They'll be here at six, and I've reserved a private dining room."

"Four Russians from the Embassy," Breen explained, showing me to the door. "They're coming over for dinner. You know, get friendly. It's friendship that counts."

When I arrived back in my own room in the Kempenski, I found waiting on my bed a large package wrapped in plain brown paper. My name was on it, the name of the hotel and the number of my room, but nothing to identify the sender. Inside, there were half a dozen thick anti-Communist pamphlets, and a handwritten card, without signature, which said, *Dear Sir —You can be saved.* Saved, one presumed, from the fates described in the accompanying literature, most of which purported to be the case histories of individuals, primarily Germans, who had gone behind the iron curtain, either voluntarily or as the result of force, and had not been heard from again. It was absorbing, as only case histories can be, and I would have read through the lot uninterrupted if the telephone hadn't rung.

The caller was Breen's secretary, Nancy Ryan. "Listen," she said, "how would you like to sleep with me? On the train, I mean. The way it works out, there are going to be four in a compartment, so I'm afraid we'll have to do as the Russians do. They always put boys and girls together. *Anyway,* I'm helping assign the berths, and what with all the affections and frictions and those who want to be together and those who definitely do *not,* well, really, it's *frightening.* So it would simplify the situation if you and I shared a compartment with the lovebirds."

The so-called "lovebirds" were Earl Bruce Jackson, one of three alternates in the role of Sportin' Life, and Helen Thigpen, a soprano who plays the part of Serena. Jackson and Miss Thigpen had been engaged for many months. According to Everyman Opera's publicity releases, they planned to be married in Moscow.

I told Miss Ryan the arrangement sounded satisfactory. "That's brilliant," she said. "Well, see you on the train. If our visas ever come through . . ."

On Monday, the nineteenth of December, passports and visas were still in abeyance. Regardless, around three o'clock that afternoon a trio of chartered buses began circling through Berlin to collect, from the hotels and pensions where they were staying, the personnel of Everyman Opera and transport them to the railway station in East Berlin where the Soviet train, The Blue Express, was scheduled to depart at four or six or midnight, no one seemed to know for certain.

A small group, spoken of by Warner Watson as "our distinguished guests," waited together in the lobby of the Hotel Kempenski. The distinguished guests were persons who had no direct connection with *Porgy and Bess,* but had, nevertheless, been invited by the management to travel with the troupe into Russia. They amounted to: Herman Sartorius, a New York financier and close friend of Breen's; a newspaper columnist, Leonard Lyons, who was described to the Soviets in Everyman Opera's official dossier as "Company Historian," neglecting to mention that he would be mailing his history to the *New York Post;* another journalist, a Pulitzer Prize winner, Ira Wolfert, accompanied by his wife, Helen. Mr. Wolfert is on the staff of the *Reader's Digest,* and the Breens, who keep extensive scrapbooks, hoped he would do an article on their Russian adventures for that publication. Mrs. Wolfert is also an author, a poet. "A *modern* poet," she emphasized.

Mr. Lyons paced the lobby, impatient for the bus to arrive. "I'm excited. I can't sleep. Just before I left New York, Abe Burrows called me up. We live in the same building. He said you know how cold it is in Moscow? He heard on the radio it was forty below. That was day before yesterday. You got on your long underwear?" He hiked up his trouser leg to flash a stretch of red wool. Ordinarily a trim-looking man of average size, Lyon had so well prepared himself for the cold that, resplendent in a fur hat and fur-lined coat and gloves and shoes, he seemed to bulge like a shoplifter. "My wife, Sylvia, bought me three pairs of these. From Saks. They don't itch."

The financier, Herman Sartorius, attired in a conservative topcoat and business suit, as though he were setting off for Wall Street, said that no, he was not wearing long underwear. "I didn't have time to buy anything. Except a map. Did you ever try to buy a road map in Russia? Well, it's the damnedest thing. Had to turn New York upside down before I found one. Good to have on the train. Know where we are."

Lyons agreed. "But," he said, lowering his voice, and with his alert black eyes snapping from side to side, "better keep it out of sight. They might not like it. A map."

"Hmm," said Sartorius, as though he could not quite follow the drift of Lyons's thought. "Yes, well, I'll keep that in mind." Sartorius has gray hair, a height, a weight, a gentlemanly reserve that inspire the kind of confidence desirable in a financier.

"I had a letter from a friend," continued Lyons. "President Truman. He wrote me I'd better be careful in Russia because he was no longer in any position to bail me out. Russia! What a dateline!" he said, glancing around as if hunting some evidence that his elation was shared by others.

Mrs. Wolfert said, "I'm hungry."

Her husband patted her on the shoulder. The Wolferts, who are the parents of grown children, resemble each other in that both have pink cheeks and silvering hair, a long-married, settled-down calm. "That's all right, Helen," he said, between puffs on a pipe. "Soon as we get on the train, we'll go right to the dining car."

"Sure," said Lyons. "Caviar and vodka."

Nancy Ryan came racing through the lobby, her blond hair flying, her coat flapping. "Don't stop me! There's a crisis!" She stopped, of course; and, rather as though she enjoyed imparting the bad news, said, "*Now* they tell us! Ten minutes before we leave! That there *isn't* a dining car on the train. And there *won't* be, not until we reach the Russian border. Thirty hours!"

"I'm hungry," said Mrs. Wolfert plaintively.

Miss Ryan hurried onward. "We're doing the best we can." By which she meant the management of Everyman Opera were out scouring the delicatessens of Berlin.

It was turning dark, a rain-mist was sifting through the streets when the bus arrived, and with a joking, shouting full load of passengers, rumbled off through West Berlin toward the Brandenburg Gate, where the Communist world begins.

In the bus I sat behind a couple, a young pretty member of the cast and an emaciated youth who was supposed to be a West German journalist. They had met in a Berlin jazz cellar, presumably he had fallen in love, at any rate he was now seeing her off, amid whispers and tears and soft laughter. As we neared the Brandenburg Gate, he protested that he must get off the bus. "It would be dangerous for me to go into East Berlin." Which, in retrospect, was an interesting remark. Because several weeks later who should turn up in Russia, grinning and swaggering and with no plausible explanation of how he'd got there, but this selfsame young man, still claiming to be a West German and a journalist and in love.

Beyond the Brandenburg Gate, we rode for forty minutes through the blackened acres of bombed-out East Berlin. The two additional buses, with the rest of the company, had arrived at the station before us. We joined the others on the platform where The Blue Express waited. Mrs. Gershwin was there, supervising the loading of her luggage onto the train. She was wearing a nutria coat and, over her arm, carried a mink coat zippered into a plastic bag. "Oh, the mink's for Russia, darling. Darling," she said, "why do they call it The Blue Express? When it's not blue at all?"

It was green, a sleek collection of dark green cars hitched to a diesel engine. The letters CCCP were painted in yellow on the side of each car, and below them, in different languages, the train's cities of destination: Berlin-Warsaw-Moscow. Soviet train officers, elegantly turned out in black Persian lamb hats and flaring princess-cut coats, were stationed at the entrances to every car. Sleeping-car attendants, more humbly dressed, stood beside them. Both the officers and the attendants were smoking cigarettes in long vamp-style holders. As they watched the confusion around them, the excited milling about of the troupe, they managed to preserve a stony uninterest despite the bold attentions of those Americans who approached and stared at them as though amazed, and rather peeved, to discover Russians had two eyes correctly located.

A man from the cast walked over to one of the officers. "Tell me something, kid," he said, indicating the lettering on the side of the train, "what's that mean, CCCP?"

The Russian pointed his cigarette holder at the man. Frowning, he said, *"Sie sind Deutsch?"*

The actor laughed. "I'd make a kind of funny-looking German. Seems to me I would."

A second Russian, a car attendant, spoke up. *"Sind sie nicht Deutsch?"*

"Man," said the actor, "let's us settle this misery." He glanced down the platform and beckoned to Robin Joachim, a young Russian-speaking New Yorker whom Everyman Opera had hired to go along on the trip as a translator.

The two Russians smiled with pleasure when Joachim began to talk to them in their own language; pleasure gave way to astonishment as he explained that the passengers boarding their train were not Germans, but "Amerikansky" on their way to perform an opera in Leningrad and Moscow.

"Isn't that peculiar?" said Joachim, turning to a group of listeners that included Leonard Lyons. "Nobody told them a thing about us being on the train. They never heard of *Porgy and Bess.*"

Lyons, the first of the Americans to recover from the shock of this news, whipped out a notebook and pencil. "Well, what do they think? What's their reaction?"

"Oh," said Joachim, "they couldn't be happier. They're delirious with joy."

It was true that the Russians were nodding and laughing. The officer gave the attendant a hearty slap on the back and shouted an order.

"What did he say?" asked Lyons, pencil poised.

Joachim said, "He told him to go put some tea on the samovar."

A station clock said six-five. There were signs of departure, whistle sounds, a clanging of doors. In the corridors of the train a radio began blaring martial music, and the company, now all aboard, were hanging out the windows waving at dispirited German luggage porters, none of whom had received the "capitalist insult," as we'd been warned the People's Democracies consider it, of a tip. Suddenly, at every window, a cheer went up. It was for the Breens, Robert and Wilva, who were plunging along the platform, followed by a wagonload of food supplies, cardboard cases of beer and wine, frankfurters, rolls and sweet buns, cold cuts, apples and oranges. There was only time to carry the cases onto the train before the radio's military fanfare reached a crescendo, and the Breens, watching with brave parental smiles, saw their "unprecedented project" slide away from them into the night.

The space to which I'd been assigned was in Car 2, Compartment 6. It seemed larger than an ordinary *wagon-lit* compartment, and had a certain prettiness about it, despite the presence of a radio loudspeaker that could not be completely turned off, and a blue light bulb, burning in a blue ceiling, that could never be extinguished. The walls were blue, the window was framed with blue plush curtains which matched the seat upholstery. There was a small table between the seats, and on it a lamp with a rosy silk shade.

Miss Ryan introduced me to our companions in Compartment 6, Earl Bruce Jackson and his fiancée, Helen Thigpen, whom I'd not met before.

Jackson is tall and lean, a live-wire with slanting eyes and a saturnine face. He affects a chin goatee, and his hands are radiant with rings, diamonds and sapphires and rubies. We shook hands. "Peace, brother, peace. That's the word," he said, and resumed peeling an orange, letting the hulls drop on the floor.

"No, Earl," said Miss Ryan, "that's *not* the word. The word is, keep things tidy. Put your orange hulls in the ashtray. After all," she said, looking out the window where the lonely last lights of East Berlin were fading, "this is going to be our home for a hell-uva long time."

"That's right, Earl. Our home," said Miss Thigpen.

"Peace, brother, peace. That's the word. Tell the boys back in New York," said Jackson, and spit out some seed.

Miss Ryan began to distribute part of the last-minute picnic the Breens had provided. With a sigh, Miss Thigpen refused a bottle of beer and a salami sandwich. "I don't know what I'll eat. There's nothing goes with my diet. Since I met Earl, I went on a diet and lost fifty-six pounds. Five tablespoons of caviar add up to one hundred calories."

"*This* isn't caviar. For God's sake," said Miss Ryan, her mouth full of salami sandwich.

"I'm thinking of the future," said Miss Thigpen glumly. She yawned. "Anybody object if I slip into my negligee? Might as well make ourselves comfortable."

Miss Thigpen, a concert artist before she joined *Porgy and Bess* four years ago, is a small, plump woman, lavishly powdered. She wears the highest heels, the tallest hats, and generous sprinklings of Joy ("The World's Costliest Perfume").

"Hi there, good-lookin'," said Jackson, admiring his fiancée's efforts to make herself comfortable. "The number to play is seven seven three, and peace is the word. Ooble-ee-do!"

Miss Thigpen ignored these compliments. "Earl," she said, "it *was* São Paulo, honey?"

"Was what?"

"Was where we got engaged."

"Yeah. São Paulo. Brazil."

Miss Thigpen seemed relieved. "That's what I told Mr. Lyons. He wanted to know. He's the one writes for the paper. You met him?"

"Yeah," said Jackson. "I rubbed palms with that cat."

"Maybe you heard?" said Miss Thigpen, looking at me. "About us being married in Moscow. 'Twas Earl's idea. I didn't even know we were engaged. I lost fifty-six pounds, but I didn't know we were engaged until Earl had this idea about us being married in Moscow."

"Bound to be a big story," said Jackson, and though he snapped his glittering fingers, his tone was serious, slow, as though thinking long thoughts. "The first couple of Negro Americans married in Moscow. That's front page. That's TV." He turned to Miss Thigpen. "And I don't want you to go telling that cat Lyons anything about it. Not till we're sure the magnetic vibrations are right. With a big thing like this, you got to feel the right vibrations."

Miss Thigpen said, "You ought to see Earl's wedding suit. He had it made in Munich."

"Crazy, man, crazy," said Jackson. "Brown tails with champagne satin lapels. Shoes to match, natch. And on top of that, I've got a brand-new overcoat with a—how d'ya call it—Persian lamb collar. But man, nobody's going to see *none* of it, not till The Day."

I asked when that would be, and Jackson admitted that no exact date had been set. "Mr. Breen's handling all the arrangements. He's talking to the Russians. It'll be a big thing for them, too."

"Sure," said Miss Ryan, retrieving orange hulls off the floor. "Put Russia on the map."

Miss Thigpen stretched out in her negligee and prepared to study a musical score; but she seemed troubled, unable to concentrate. "What bothers me, it won't be legal. Back home, in several states, they don't consider it legal, people married in Russia."

"*What* states?" said Jackson, as though resuming with her a tedious argument.

Miss Thigpen thought. "Several," she said finally.

"It's legal in Washington, D.C.," he told her. "And that's your hometown. So if it's legal in your hometown, what have you got to worry about?"

"Earl," said Miss Thigpen wearily, "why don't you go find your friends and have a game of Tonk?"

Tonk, popular with some elements among the cast, is a five-card variation of ordinary rummy. Jackson complained that it was useless for him to try getting up a game. "There's nowhere for us to play. All the sharps [gamblers] are bunked in with a lot of squares [nongamblers]."

The door of our compartment was open, and Ducky James, a boyish, blond Englishman who is prop man for the production, passed by, announcing, in his Cockney accent, "Anybody wants a drink, we've set up a bar in our place. Martinis . . . Manhattans . . . Scotch . . ."

"That Ducky!" said Miss Thigpen. "If *he's* not the lucky one! I don't wonder he's handing out drinks. You know what happened to him? Just before we got on the train along comes this telegram. His aunt died. Leaving him ninety thousand pounds."

Jackson whistled. "How much is that in real money?"

"Two hundred and seventy thousand dollars, thereabouts," said Miss Thigpen. Then, as her future husband stood up to leave the compartment, "Where you going, Earl?"

"Just thought I'd find out if Ducky plays Tonk."

Presently we had a visit from Twerp, an all-white boxer puppy who gaily trotted into the compartment and promptly proved herself unhousebroken. She belonged to the company's wardrobe mistress, a young woman from Brooklyn named Marilyn Putnam. Miss Putnam appeared, calling, "Twerp! Twerp! Oh, *there* you are, you little bitch. Isn't she a little bitch?"

"Yes," said Miss Ryan, down on her hands and knees scrubbing at the carpet with wadded newspaper. "We have to live in here. For God's sake."

"The Russians don't mind," said Miss Putnam defensively. She scooped up her puppy and kissed its forehead. "Twerp's been being naughty up and down the corridor—haven't you, angel? The Russians just smile. *They* understand she's only a baby." She turned to leave and almost collided at the door with a girl who stood there crying. "Why, Delirious," she said to the girl, "darling, what's the matter—are you sick?"

The girl shook her head. Her chin trembled, her large eyes quivered with fresh tears.

"Delirious, honey, don't take on so," said Miss Thigpen. "Sit down. Say what's wrong."

The girl sat down. Her name was Dolores Swann; but like many of the cast, she had acquired a nickname, in this case the descriptive Delirious. A singer in the chorus, she has red poodle-cut hair. Her pale gold face is as round as her eyes, and has the same quality of show-girl innocence. She swallowed and wailed, "I lost both my coats. Both of them. My fur coat and the blue one, too. I left them back there in the station. Not insured or anything."

Miss Thigpen clucked her tongue. "Only *you* could do a thing like that, Delirious."

"But it wasn't my fault," said Miss Swann. "I was so scared. You see, I got left behind. I missed the bus. And it was terrible, running around trying to find a taxi to take me to the station. Because none of them wanted to go to *East* Berlin. Well, finally this man spoke English and he felt sorry for me and he said he would. Well, it was terrible. Because police kept stopping us and asking questions and wanting to see papers and, oh—I was sure I was going to be left there in the pitch-black with police and Communists and what-all. I was sure I'd never see any of you again."

The reliving of her ordeal brought on more tears. Miss Ryan poured her a brandy, and Miss Thigpen squeezed her hand, saying, "It's all right, honey."

"But you can imagine how I felt, how relieved I was when I got to the station—and there everybody was. You hadn't left without me. I wanted to hug everybody. I put down my coats to hug Ducky. I hugged Ducky and forgot about my coats. Until just now."

"Think of it like this, Delirious," said Miss Thigpen, as though searching for a comforting phrase, "just remember, you're the only person who ever went to Russia without a coat."

"I know a more unique claim that we can *all* make," said Miss Ryan. "Not only unique, but nuts. I mean, here we are—rattling off to Russia without our passports. No passports, no visa, no nothin'."

Half an hour later Miss Ryan's claim became less valid, for when the train stopped at Frankfurt a. d. Oder, which marks the German-Polish border, a delegation of officials boarded the train and, quite literally, dumped the company's long-absent passports into Warner Watson's lap.

"I don't understand it," said Watson, parading through the train delivering the passports to their individual owners. "This very morning the Russian Embassy told me the passports had gone to Moscow. Now they suddenly turn up at the Polish border."

Miss Ryan quickly riffled through her passport and found blankness on those pages where the Russian visa should have been stamped. "For God's sake, Warner. There's nothing here."

"They've issued a collective visa. They have, or they're going to, don't ask me which," said Watson, his timid, tired voice skidding to a hoarse whisper. His skin was gray, and under his eyes purple bruises of fatigue were prominent as paint.

"But, Warner . . ."

Watson held up a protesting hand. "I'm not human," he said. "I've got to go to bed. I'm going to go to bed and stay there until we get to Leningrad."

"Well, it's a pity," said Miss Ryan as Watson fled, "a damned shame we can't have a stamp in our passports. I like souvenirs."

The train was scheduled to stay at the border forty minutes. I decided to get off and look around. At the end of the car, I found the exit door open and started down the small iron steps leading onto the tracks. Far ahead I could see the lights of a station, and a misty red lantern swinging back and forth. But it was dark where I was, except for the yellow squares cast by the train's windows. I walked along the tracks, liking the fresh feel of the cold and wondering whether I was in Germany or Poland. Suddenly

I noticed figures running toward me, a set of shadows that, drawing nearer, turned into three soldiers, pale flat-faced men with awkward ankle-length coats and bayoneted rifles strapped to their shoulders. They stared at me in silence. Then one of them pointed to the train; he grunted and motioned for me to get back on it. We marched along together, the four of us, and I said in English that I was sorry, I hadn't realized passengers were not allowed off the train. There was no response, merely another grunt and an urging forward. I climbed the train steps and turned to wave at them. They didn't wave back.

"Darling, you haven't been *out*," said Mrs. Gershwin, whose compartment I passed in returning. "Well, you shouldn't. It isn't safe." Mrs. Gershwin was one of the two people occupying compartments to themselves. (The other was Leonard Lyons, who had obtained privacy by threatening to leave the train unless his erstwhile roommates, Herman Sartorius and Warner Watson, were removed. "It's nothing personal," he said, "but I'm a working man. I've got to turn out a thousand words a day. I can't write with a lot of characters sitting around." Sartorius and Watson had therefore been forced to move in with the Ira Wolferts. As for Mrs. Gershwin, she'd been allotted her solo status because, in the view of the management, "She deserves it. She's a Gershwin.") Without discarding her diamonds, Mrs. Gershwin had changed into slacks and a sweater; she'd tied ribbons in her hair and slippered her feet in bits of fluff. "It must have been freezing out there. I see snow on the ground. You ought to have some hot tea. Mmmmm, it's lovely," she said, sipping dark, almost black tea from a tall glass set in a silver holder with a silver handle. "That darling little man is brewing it on his samovar."

I went to look for the tea-maker, who was the attendant for Car 2; but when I found him, at the end of the corridor, he was contending with more than a blazing samovar. Twerp, the boxer puppy, was yapping between his legs and snapping at his trousers. Moreover, he was undergoing an intense interview, Lyons asking the questions and Robin Joachim acting as translator. Small and haggard, the Russian had a pushed-in, Pekingese face creased with wrinkles that seemed to indicate nutritional defects rather than age. His mouth was studded with steel teeth, and his eyelids drooped, as though he were on the verge of sleep. Between dispensing tea and fending off Twerp, he answered Lyons's quick-fire queries like a wilted housewife talking to the censor. He said he was from Smolensk. He said his feet hurt him, his back hurt him, that he always had a headache from overwork. He said he only made two hundred rubles a month ($50, but much less in actual buying power) and considered himself underpaid. He said yes, he'd very much appreciate a tip.

Lyons paused in his note-taking and said, "I didn't know they were allowed to complain like this. The way it sounds, I get the impression this guy is a discontent."

The attendant gave me my tea, and at the same time offered me, from a crumpled pack, one of his own cigarettes. It was two-thirds filter and one-third tobacco, good for seven or eight harsh puffs, though I didn't enjoy that many, for as I started back to my compartment the train lurched forward with an abruptness that sent both tea and cigarette flying.

Marilyn Putnam poked her head into the corridor. "Holy mackerel," she said, surveying the wreckage, "did *Twerp* do that?"

In Compartment 6 the berths had been made for the night, indeed for the whole journey, since they were never remade. Clean coarse linen, a crunchy pillow that smelled of hay, a single thin blanket. Miss Ryan and Miss Thigpen had gone to bed to read, having first turned the radio as low as it would go and opened the window a finger's width.

Miss Thigpen yawned, and asked me, "Did you see Earl, honey?"

I told her that I had. "He's teaching Ducky to play Tonk."

"Oh," said Miss Thigpen, giggling sleepily, "that means Earl won't be home till dawn."

I kicked off my shoes, and lay down in my berth, thinking in a moment I'd finish undressing. Overhead, in the berth above mine, I could hear Miss Ryan muttering to herself, as though she were reading aloud. It developed that she was studying Russian, using for the purpose an old English-Russian phrase book the U.S. Army had issued during the war for the benefit of American soldiers who might come in contact with Russians.

"Nancy," said Miss Thigpen, like a child asking for a bedtime story, "Nancy, say us something in Russian."

"The only thing I've learned is *Awr-ga-nib-ya raneen* . . ." Miss Ryan faltered. She took a deep breath ". . . *V-pa-lavih-yee.* Wow! I only wanted to learn the alphabet. So I can read street signs."

"But that was nice, Nancy. What does it mean?"

"It means, 'I have been wounded in the privates.' "

"Really, Nancy," said Miss Thigpen, bewildered, "why on earth would you care to memorize something like that?"

"Go to sleep," said Miss Ryan, turning off her reading light.

Miss Thigpen yawned again. She pulled the covers up to her chin. "I'm about ready to."

Soon, lying there, I had a sense of stillness traveling through the train, seeping through the cars like the wintry color of the blue light bulb. Frost was spreading at the corners of the window; it seemed like a web-weaving in reverse. On the muted radio an orchestra of balalaikas made shivery music; like an odd and lonely counterpoint, someone somewhere nearby was playing a harmonica.

"Listen," whispered Miss Thigpen, calling attention to the harmonica. "That's Junior," she said, meaning Junior Mignatt, a member of the cast still in his teens. "Don't you know that boy is lonesome? He's from Panama. He's never seen snow before."

"Go to sleep," said Miss Ryan. The northern roar of wind at the window seemed to echo her command. The train shrieked into a tunnel. For me, fallen asleep fully clothed, the tunnel lasted all night long.

Coldness woke me. Snow was blowing through the window's opening. Enough had settled at the foot of my berth to scoop into a snowball. I got up, glad I'd gone to bed with my clothes on, and closed the window. It was blurred with ice. I rubbed a part of it until I could peer out. There were hints of sunrise on the rim of the sky, yet it was still dark, and the traces of morning color were like goldfish swimming in ink. We were on the outskirts of a city. Rural lamplighted houses gave way to cement blocks of forlorn, look-alike apartment dwellings. The train rumbled over a bridge that spanned a street; below, a frail streetcar, jammed with people on their way to work, careened round a curve like a rickety bobsled. Moments later we pulled into a station, which by now I realized must be Warsaw. On a dim, snow-deep platform gangs of men stood clustered together stamping their feet and slapping their ears. I noticed our car attendant, the tea-maker, join one of the groups. He gestured toward the train and said something that made them laugh. An explosion of breath-smoke filled the air. Still laughing, several of the men approached the train. I slipped back into bed, for it was obvious that they intended to peek in the windows. One after another, distorted faces mashed themselves against the glass. Presently I heard a short scream. It came from a compartment farther ahead and sounded like Dolores Swann. Screams were understandable if she'd wakened to see, looming at the window, one of these frosty masks. Though it roused none of my own companions, I waited, expecting a commotion in the car, but quietness resumed, except for Twerp, who started barking with a regular rhythm that sent me off to sleep again.

At ten, when I opened my eyes, we were in a wild, crystal world of frozen rivers and snowfields. Here and there, like printing on paper, stretches of fir trees interrupted the whiteness. Flights of crows seemed to skate on a sky hard and shiny as ice.

"Man," said Earl Bruce Jackson, just awake and sleepily scratching himself as he stared out the window. "I'm telling you. They don't grow oranges here."

The washroom in Car 2 was a bleak, unheated chamber. There was a rusty washbasin with the customary two faucets, hot and cold. Unfortunately, they both leaked a frigid trickle. That first morning a long queue of men waited at the washroom door, toothbrushes in one hand, shaving tackle in the other. Ducky James had the notion of asking the attendant, who was busily stoking the little coal fire under his samovar, to part with some of his tea water and "give us blokes a chance at a decent shave." Everyone thought this a splendid idea except the Russian, for when the request was translated to him, he looked at his samovar as though it were bubbling with melted diamonds. Then he did a curious thing.

He stepped up to each man and brushed his fingertips against their cheeks, examining their beard stubble. There was a tenderness in the action that made it memorable. "Boy," said Ducky James, "he sure is affectionate."

But the attendant concluded his researches with a headshake. Absolute no, *nyet*, he would not give away his hot water. The condition of the gentlemen's beards did not justify such a sacrifice, and besides, when traveling, the "realistic" man should expect to go unshaven. "My water is for tea," he said. "Hot and sweet and good for the spirit."

A steaming glass of it went with me into the washroom. I used it for brushing my teeth, and then, combining it with soap, transformed it into a shaving cream. Rather sticky, but not bad at all.

Afterward, feeling spruce, I commenced a round of visits. The occupant of Compartment 1, Leonard Lyons, was having a professional tête-à-tête with Earl Bruce Jackson. Clearly Jackson had overcome his fear that Lyons might not possess the "right vibrations," for he was describing to him the details of his forthcoming Moscow marriage.

"That's great. Just great, Earl," said Lyons, scribbling away. "Brown tails. Champagne satin lapels. Now—who's going to be your best man?"

Jackson told him he'd invited Warner Watson to serve in that capacity. Lyons seemed reluctant to approve the choice. "Listen," he said, tapping Jackson on the knee, "did you ever think of asking somebody, well, important?"

"Like you, you mean?"

"Like *Khrushchev*," said Lyons. "Like *Bulganin.*"

Jackson's eyes narrowed, as though he couldn't decide whether Lyons's suggestion was serious or a leg pull. "But I already asked Warner. But maybe, under that kind of circumstance . . ."

"Sure," said Lyons, "Warner would understand."

Still, Jackson had one last vestige of doubt. "You think Mr. Breen can arrange it, to get me one of those cats?"

"He could try," said Lyons. "And just trying, see, that could land you on the front page."

"*C'est* ooble-ee-do," said Jackson, gazing at Lyons with perfect admiration. "Really crazy, man. Gone."

Farther along the corridor, I called on the Wolferts, who were sharing their compartment with Herman Sartorius and Warner Watson, the pair Lyons had evicted, the latter in more ways than one. But Watson was still asleep, unaware of his impending dismissal as Jackson's best man. Sartorius and Ira Wolfert were sitting with an immense map spread across their collective lap, and Mrs. Wolfert, bundled in a fur coat, was hunched over a manuscript. I asked if she were keeping a journal.

"I *do*. Only this is a poem. I've been working on it since last January. I thought I might finish it on the train. But the way I feel . . ." she said dismally. "I didn't sleep a wink last night. My hands are cold. My head's whirling with impressions. I don't know where I am."

Sartorius placed a fastidious finger on his map. "I'll tell you where we are. We've passed Lidice. Now we've got about five more hours of Poland before Brest Litovsk."

Brest Litovsk was to be the first stop in Russia. A good deal was scheduled to happen there. The wheels of the train would be changed to fit Russia's wide-gauge tracks; a dining car would be attached, and, most importantly, representatives from the Ministry of Culture were to meet the company and travel on with them to Leningrad.

"Know what this reminds me of," said Ira Wolfert, pointing a pipe at the severe landscape. "Parts of America. The West."

Sartorius nodded. "Wyoming in the winter."

Returning to the corridor, I encountered Miss Ryan, still wearing her bed costume, a red flannel nightshirt. She was hopping on one foot, her other foot having made contact with a sample of Twerp's misbehavior.

I said, "Good morning."

She said, *"Don't speak to me,"* and hopped away toward the washroom.

Next, I went to Car 3, where the family groups, children and their parents, were installed. School had just let out; that is, the children had finished their morning lessons and were consequently in sportive spirit. Paper planes sailed through the air. Caricatures were being finger-drawn on the frosted windows. The Russian attendant, who looked even more mournful and harassed than his colleague in Car 2, was kept at such a hop protecting

Soviet property that he hadn't noticed what was happening to his samovar. Two little boys had taken it over and were roasting hot dogs. One of them, Davy Bey, offered me a bite. "Good, huh?" I told him it was indeed. Well, he said, if I liked it that much, then I could have the rest of it; he'd already eaten fifteen.

"You see the wolves?" he asked.

An older friend, Gail Barnes, told him, "Stop making stories, Davy. They weren't wolves. They were plain dogs."

"Was wolves," said Davy, who has a snub nose and a wicked tilt to his eyes. "Everybody saw them. Out the window. They *looked* like dogs. Police dogs, only littler. And what they were up to, they were chasing each other round and round in the snow. Like they were having a grand time. I coulda killed one dead. Wooooooolves," he howled, and poked me in the stomach with a cowboy pistol.

Gail said that she hoped I understood. "Davy's only a child." Gail, whose father, Irving Barnes, alternates in the role of Porgy, is eleven, the oldest of the company's six children, most of whom play minor parts in the show. Because of her seniority, she has developed a sense of big-sister responsibility toward all the children, and handles them with mature good nature, a firm politeness that could set any governess an example. "Excuse me," she said, glancing down the corridor where several of her charges, by managing to open a window, were letting in blasts of Arctic wind. "I'm afraid I'll have to put a stop to that."

But before she had completed her mission, Gail herself was swept away into being a child again. "Oh, look," she cried, hanging out the very window she'd gone to close. "Look, kids . . . *People!*"

The people were two small children ice-skating on a long ribbon of pond at the edge of a white wood. They skated fast as they could, trying to keep up with the train, and as it sped beyond them they stretched out their arms, as though to catch the shouted greetings, the blown kisses of Gail and her friends.

Meanwhile, the Russian attendant had discovered smoke billowing from his samovar. He snatched charred hot dogs off the fire, and tossed them on the floor. Then, sucking blistered fingers and employing a vocabulary that must have been, to judge from its tone, on the blistery side itself, he rushed to pry the children away from the window and slam it shut.

"Aw, don't be a sorehead," Davy told him. "We're just having a grand time."

The remnants of a cheese and fruit lunch were scattered on the table (and the carpet) of Compartment 6. Midafternoon sunlight sparkled in a glass of Chianti Miss Ryan was revolving in her hand. "I adore wine," she said fervently. "I began drinking it when I was twelve. Heavily. It's a wonder I'm not a wino." She sipped and sighed with a contentment that reflected the general mood. Miss Thigpen and her fiancé, who'd had their share of Chianti, were nestled together in a corner of their seat, her head resting on his shoulder. The drowsy, dreaming spell was broken by a knock at the door, and someone saying, "This is it. Russia."

"Places, please," said Miss Ryan. "Curtain going up."

The first signs of an approaching frontier came into view: stark wooden guard towers, not unsimilar to those that encircle Southern convict farms. Spread at wide intervals, they marched across the wastes like giant telephone poles. In the nearest of them I could see a man watching the train through binoculars. The train slowed round a curve and slackened to a stop. We were in a switch yard, surrounded by a maze of tracks and halted freight cars. It was the Soviet border, forty minutes from Brest Litovsk.

Along the tracks, herds of women with shawl-wrapped heads, like a woolly version of purdah, were swinging picks, shoveling snow, pausing only to blow their noses into naked, raw-red hands. The few who even glanced at The Blue Express risked sharp looks from various militiamen lounging about with their hands stuffed in their coat pockets.

"If that's not a *shame,*" said Miss Thigpen. "Ladies doing all the work, while the men just stand around. How disgraceful!"

"That's what it is here, honey," said Jackson, puffing on one of his ruby rings, and polishing it against his lapel. "Every man a Sportin' Life."

"I'd like to see somebody treat *me* that way," replied Miss Thigpen, warningly.

"But I must say," said Miss Ryan, "the men are pretty divine." Her interest was fixed on a pair of officers pacing below the window, tall-strong-silent types with thin lips and rugged, windburned faces. One of them looked up and, catching sight of Miss Ryan's blue eyes and long golden hair, lost step with his partner. Miss Ryan whimpered, "Oh, wouldn't it be awful!"

"Awful what, honey?" said Miss Thigpen.

"If I fell in love with a Russian," said Miss Ryan. "Wouldn't that be the absolute *fin?* Actually, my mother's afraid that I might. She said if I fell in love with any Russians, I needn't bother coming home. But," she added, her gaze again drifting toward the officer, "if they're all like *that* . . ."

Quite suddenly Miss Ryan's admirer had no time for flirtation. He became part of a small Russian army chasing round the yard after Robin Joachim. Joachim, an overly avid photographer, had broken the rules by getting off the train, then compounded that error by attempting to take pictures. Now he was racing zigzag across the tracks, narrowly avoiding the wrathful swipe of a woman worker's shovel, barely eluding the grasp of a guard.

"I hope they catch him," said Miss Ryan coldly. "Him and his goddamn cameras. I knew he'd get us into trouble."

Joachim, however, turned out to be a resourceful young man. Slipping past his pursuers, he hurled himself onto the train, rushed into a compartment, threw his coat, his camera and cap under the seat, and to further alter his appearance, whipped off his horn-rimmed glasses. Seconds later, when the angry Soviets came aboard, he calmly assumed his role of company translator and helped them hunt the culprit, a search that included every compartment. Warner Watson, roused from his slumbers, was the person least amused by the situation. He promised Joachim a good talking-to. "This," he said, "is *not* the way to begin a cultural exchange."

The incident caused the train to be delayed forty-five minutes and had other repercussions as well, one of them involving Twerp, for the Russians, in the course of their search, had been appalled by certain conditions in Car 2 attributable to the puppy. Twerp's owner, Marilyn Putnam, said later, "I put it to them straight. I said, since we're never allowed off the train, what the hell do you expect? That shut 'em up."

We reached Brest Litovsk in a luminous twilight. Statues of political heroes, painted cheap-silver like those souvenir figures sold at Woolworth's, saluted us along the last mile of track leading to the station. The station was on high ground that afforded a partial view of the city dim and blue and dominated, far-off, by an Orthodox cathedral, whose onion-domes and mosaic towers still projected, despite the failing light, their Oriental colors.

Among the company it had been rumored that we would be allowed off the train here, and perhaps, while the wheels were changed and the dining car added, permitted to tour the city. Leonard Lyons was most anxious that this should happen. "I can't write a thousand words a day just sitting on a train. I need action." Lyons had gone so far as to discuss with the cast the kind of action he would like. He wanted them to traipse around Brest Litovsk singing spirituals. "It's a good story and it's good showmanship. I'm surprised Breen didn't think of it." When the train stopped, the doors opened all right, but were immediately closed again, after admitting a five-man delegation from Moscow's Ministry of Culture.

One of these emissaries was a middle-aged woman with straying dishwater hair and, except for her eyes, what seemed a kind, motherly face. The eyes, dull gray and flecked with dots of milky white, had an embalmed glaze that did not blend with the cheerful contours of her expression. She wore a black cloth coat and a rusty black dress that sagged at the breasts from the weight of an ivory rose. In introducing herself and her colleagues, she ran the names together so that it sounded like a patter song. "You

will please to meet SaschaMenashaTiomkenKerinskyIvorsIvanovich-
NikolaiSavchenkoPlesitskyaGrutchenkoRickiSomanenko . . ."

In due time, the Americans were to sort and simplify these names until
their owners became familiar as Miss Lydia, Henry, Sascha and Igor; the
latter, young underlings from the Ministry who, like the middle-aged Miss
Lydia, had been assigned to the company as translators. But the fifth
member of the quintet, Nikolai Savchenko, was not the man you call Nick.
An important official in the Ministry, Savchenko was in charge of the
Porgy and Bess tour.

The victim of a slightly receding chin, mildly bulging eyes and a tendency toward fat, he was nevertheless a formidable figure—well over six
feet, with a stern, no-nonsense attitude and a handshake like a nutcracker.
Beside him, his young assistants looked like sickly children, though two of
them, Sascha and Igor, were strapping boys whose shoulders were too
broad for their fur-collared coats; and Henry, a spidery mite with huge ears
so red they were purple, made up by personal vividness what he lacked in
stature.

It seemed natural that Miss Lydia and the young men should react
awkwardly to this, their first encounter with Westerners; understandable
that they should hesitate to test their English, so tediously learned at
Moscow's Institute of Foreign Languages but never before practiced on
bona fide foreigners; forgivable that they should, instead, stare as though
the Americans represented pawns in a chess problem. But Savchenko also
gave an impression of being ill at ease, of preferring, in fact, a stretch in
Lubyanka to his present chores. Which was excusable, too; though rather
odd when you consider that for two years during the war he served as
Counsel at the Soviet Embassy in Washington. Even so, he seemed to find
Americans such a tongue-tying novelty that for the moment he affected not
to speak English. He delivered a small speech of welcome in gruff Russian,
then had it translated by Miss Lydia. "We hope each and all have had a
pleasant journey. Too bad you see us in the winter. It is not the good time
of year. But we have the saying, Better now than never. Your visit is a step
forward in the march toward peace. When the cannons are heard, the
muses are silent; when the cannons are silent, the muses are heard."

The muse-cannon metaphor, which was to prove a Savchenko favorite,
the starring sentence of all future speeches, was an instant hit with his
listeners ("A beautiful thing." "Just great, Mr. Savchenko." "That's cool
cookin', man."), and Savchenko, warmed by success and beginning to
relax, decided there was perhaps no reason to keep the company cooped
up in the train. Why not step out on the platform and watch the changing
of the wheels?

Outside, Lyons canvassed the group, trying to work up a song fest. But
the temperature, ten below zero, was not conducive to a musical mood.

Moreover, a large percentage of those who had been grateful to escape The Blue Express were, after the briefest exposure, shoving each other to get back in. The hearties who remained watched in the nightfall as workers of both sexes uncoupled the cars and jacked them to the height of a man. The old wheels, spraying sparks, were then rolled from under the train, while from the opposite direction the new wide-gauge wheels came gliding into place. Ira Wolfert called the operation "very efficient"; Herman Sartorius considered it "most impressive"; but Miss Ryan thought it was a "damned bore" and said that if I'd follow her into the station, she would buy me a vodka.

No one stopped us. We crossed a hundred yards of track, walked down a dirt lane between warehouses, and arrived at what appeared to be a combination of a parking lot and a marketplace. Brightly lighted kiosks circled it like candles burning on a cake. It was puzzling to discover that each of the kiosks sold the same products: cans of Red Star salmon, Red Star sardines, dusty bottles of Kremlin perfume, dusty boxes of Kremlin candy, pickled tomatoes, hairy slabs of raw bacon slapped between thick slices of grime-colored bread, weird liqueurs, cross buns (without the cross) that one somehow felt had been baked last July. And though the kiosks were attracting a brisk trade, the most sought-after item was not on sale at any of them. It was in the private hands of a peddler, an elderly Chinese who carried a tray of apples. The apples were as shriveled and miniature as himself, but his waiting line of customers appeared disconsolate when the last of them evaporated. At the far end of the area a flight of steps led to the main entrance of the station, and the Chinese, folding his empty tray, wandered over to them and sat down next to a friend. The friend was a beggar bundled in an old army coat and with a pair of crutches sprawled beside him like the wings of a wounded bird. Every third or fourth person going by dropped a coin into his hand. The Chinese gave him something, too. An apple. He'd saved one for the beggar, and one for himself. The two friends gnawed their apples and leaned against each other in the cutting cold.

The constant wailing of a train whistle seemed to fuse the apple-eaters and the kiosks and the batlike passings of fur-shrouded faces into a smoky, single image of its woeful sound. "I've never been homesick. Never in my life," Miss Ryan informed me. "But sometimes, for God's sake. Sometimes," she said, running up the steps and pushing open the doors of the station, "you do feel a long *way* from home."

Since Brest Litovsk is one of Russia's most strategic railroad centers, its station is among the country's largest. Looking for somewhere to buy a drink, we explored lofty corridors and a series of waiting rooms, the principal one furnished with handsome oak benches occupied by many passengers with very few suitcases. Children and paper bundles filled their laps. The stone floors, soggy with black slush, made slippery walking, and there was an odor in the air, a saturation so heavy it seemed less a smell than a pressure. Travelers to Venice often remark on the vivid scents of that city. The public places of Russia, terminals and department stores, restaurants and theaters, also have a reek instantly recognizable. And Miss Ryan, taking her first sniff of it, said, "Boy, I wouldn't want a bottle of this. Old socks and a million yawns."

In the search for a bar, we began opening doors at random. Miss Ryan sailed through one and out again. It was a men's room. Then, spotting a pair of dead-drunks as they emerged from behind a small red door, she decided, "That's the place we're looking for." The red door led into an extraordinary restaurant. The size of a gymnasium, it looked as if it had been done over for a school prom by a decorating committee with Victorian tastes. Plush crimson draperies were looped along the walls. Other-era chandeliers distributed a tropic glare that beat down on a jungle of borscht-stained tablecloths and withering rubber plants. The maître d'hôtel seemed appropriate to this atmosphere of grandeur gone to seed. He was at least eighty years old, a white-bearded patriarch with ferocious eyes that peered at us, through a sailor's-dive haze of cigarette smoke, as though questioning our right to be there.

Miss Ryan smiled at him and said, "Vodka, *pjolista.*" The old man stared at her with more hostility then comprehension. She tried varying pronunciations, "Woedka . . . Wadka . . . Woodka," and even performed a bottoms-up pantomime. "The poor thing's deaf," she said, and shouted, "*Vodka.* For God's sake."

Although his expression remained unenlightened, the old man beckoned us forward and, following the Russian custom of seating strangers together, put us at a table with two men. They both were drinking beer, and the old man pointed at it, as if asking if this was what we wanted. Miss Ryan, resigning herself, nodded.

Our companions at the table were two very different specimens. One, a beefy boy with a shaved head and wearing some sort of faded uniform, was well on his way to being drunk, a condition shared by a surprising lot of the restaurant's clientele, most of whom were male, many of them either boisterous or slumped across their tables mumbling to themselves. The second man was an enigma. In appearance he might have been a Wall Street partner of Herman Sartorius, the kind of person better imagined dining at the Pavillon than sipping beer in Brest Litovsk. His suit was pressed, and one could see that he hadn't sewn it himself. There were gold cuff links in his shirt, and he was the only man in the room sporting a tie.

After a moment the shaven-headed soldier spoke to Miss Ryan. "I'm afraid I don't speak Russian," she told him. "We're Americans. *Amerikansky.*" Her declaration had a somewhat sobering effect. His reddened eyes slowly came into semifocus. He turned to the well-dressed man and made a long statement, at the end of which the man answered him with several chiseled, cold-sounding sentences. There followed between them a sharp repartee, then the soldier took his beer and stalked to another table, where he sat glowering. "Well," said Miss Ryan, glowering back, "not *all* the men are attractive, that's for sure." However, she considered our apparent defender, the well-dressed man: "Very attractive. Sort of Otto Kruger. Funny, I've always liked older men. Stop staring. He'll know we're talking about him. Listen," she said, after calling attention to his shirt, his cuff links, his clean fingernails, "do you suppose there's such a thing as a Russian millionaire?"

The beer arrived. A quart bottle and two glasses. The maître d'hôtel poured an inch of beer into my glass, then waited expectantly. Miss Ryan saw the point before I did. "He wants you to *taste* it, like wine." Lifting the glass, I wondered if beer-tasting was a Soviet commonplace, or if it was a ceremony, some confused champagne-memory of Czarist elegance that the old man had revived to impress us. I sipped, nodded, and the old man proudly filled our glasses with a warm and foamless brew. But Miss Ryan said suddenly, "Don't touch it. It's dreadful!" I told her I didn't think it was that bad. "I mean, we're in dreadful trouble," she said. "I mean, my God, we can't pay for this. I completely forgot. We haven't any rubles."

"Please, won't you be my guests?" inquired a soft voice in beautifully accented English. It was the well-dressed man who had spoken, and though his face was perfectly straight, his eyes, a bright Nordic blue, wrinkled with an amusement that took full measure of our discomfort. "I am not a Russian millionaire. They *do* exist—I know quite a few—but it would give me pleasure to pay for your drink. No, please, there is no cause to apologize," he said, in response to Miss Ryan's stammered efforts, and openly smiling, "It's been the keenest enjoyment. Very unusual. Very unusual to run across Americans in this part of the world. Are you Communists?"

After disabusing him of that notion, Miss Ryan told him where we were going, and why. "You are fortunate that you go to Leningrad first. A lovely city," he said, "very quiet, really European, the one place in Russia I could imagine living, not that I do, but still . . . Yes, I like Leningrad. It's not the least like Moscow. I'm on my way to Warsaw, but I've just been two weeks in Moscow. That's equal to two months anywhere else." He told us that he was Norwegian, and that his business, lumber, had required him to visit the Soviet Union several weeks of every year, except for a gap during the war, since 1931. "I speak the language quite well, and among my friends I don't mind passing as a Russian authority. But to be honest, I can't say I understand much more about it now than I did in 1931. Whenever I go to your country—I've been there, oh, I guess a half-dozen times—it always strikes me that Americans are the only people who remind me of Russians. You don't object to my saying that? Americans are so generous. Energetic. And underneath all that brag they have such a wishing to be loved, they want to be petted, like dogs and children, and told that they are just as good and even better than the rest of us. Well, Europeans are inclined to agree with them. But they simply won't believe it. They go right on feeling inferior and far away. Alone. Like Russians. Precisely."

Miss Ryan wanted to know the substance of his dialogue with the soldier who had left the table. "Oh, silly rot," he said. "Alcoholic bravado. For some foozled reason he thought you had insulted him. I told him he was being *nye kulturni*. Remember that: *nye kulturni*. You'll find it extremely useful, because when these chaps are rude and you feel obliged to tick them off, it means not a whit to call them a bastard, a son of a dog, but to tell him he's *uncultured*, that really strikes home."

Miss Ryan was growing anxious about the time. We shook hands with the gentleman and thanked him for the beer. "You've been very *kulturni*," she said. "And by the way, I think you're *more* attractive than Otto Kruger."

"I shall certainly tell my wife," he said, grinning. "*Dazvedanya*. Good luck."

An hour out of Brest Litovsk, the first call to the dining car was announced. It was an event the company had looked forward to with appetites excited by both genuine hunger and the conviction that the Soviet hosts were bound to make this, the company's first Russian meal, a "real spread"; or, as another of the cast forthrightly phrased it, "a bust-gut."

Miss Thigpen's desires were the most modest. "Five spoons of caviar and a piece of dry toast. That's one hundred and thirty calories." Calories were Mrs. Gershwin's last concern. "Don't think I'm not going to tear into the cavy, darling. It cost thirty-five dollars a pound in Beverly Hills." The dreams of Leonard Lyons centered around hot borscht and sour cream. Earl Bruce Jackson planned to "stone" himself with vodka and "slay" himself with shashlik. Marilyn Putnam hoped that everyone would save little tidbits for Twerp.

The first sitting, fifty strong, marched into the dining car and took their places at linen-covered tables, each seating four, that ran down either side of the aisle. The tables were set with white crockery and smoothly worn silver. The diner itself seemed as old as the silver, and the smell of cooking, a half-century's worth, hung in the air like a visible steam. Savchenko was absent, but Miss Lydia and the three young men from the Ministry played host at different tables. The young men kept gazing round, as though silently calling to each other from separate islands of exile and misery.

Miss Lydia shared a table with Lyons, Miss Ryan and myself. One sensed that for this middle-aged woman, who said that her ordinary life was translating articles and living in a room in Moscow, the unique experience, the one that brought such a flush to her cheeks, was not that she was talking to foreigners, but that she was sitting in a dining car riding on a train. Something about the silver and the clean cloth and a little basket of puckered apples, like those the Chinese man had sold, made her fuss with her ivory rose and tuck up the straying ends of her hair. "Ah, we eat!" she said, her eyes shifting toward a quartet of chunky waitresses who came waddling down the aisle with trayloads of the first course.

Those whose palates had been anticipating iced caviar and chilled carafes of vodka were a bit chagrined to see, set before them, yogurt accompanied by bottles of raspberry soda. Miss Thigpen, seated behind me, was the sole voice expressing enthusiasm: "I just could kiss them! More proteins than a steak and only half the calories." But across the aisle, Mrs. Gershwin warned Miss Putnam not to ruin her appetite by eating it. "Don't, darling, I'm sure the cavy will come along next." The next course, however, consisted of stiff noodles lying like sunken logs in a watery broth. The entree that followed featured breaded veal cutlets, boiled potatoes, and peas that rattled on the plate like gunshot; to wash this down, there were further provisions of raspberry soda. Miss Putnam said to Mrs. Gershwin, "It's not *my* stomach I'm worried about. It's Twerp's," and Mrs. Gershwin, sawing at her cutlet, said, "Do you suppose they could be saving the cavy for dessert? You know, with little pancakes?"

Miss Lydia's cheeks bulged, her eyes popped, her jaws pumped like pistons, a trickle of sweat ran down her neck. "Eat, eat," she urged, "it's good, yes?" Miss Ryan told her it was wonderful, and Miss Lydia, swabbing her plate with a quarter loaf of black bread, nodded vehemently: "You will not obtain better in Moscow itself."

During the lull between entree and dessert, she went to work on the basket of apples; as the cores piled up, she paused occasionally to answer questions. Lyons was anxious to learn at what hotel the company would be staying in Leningrad. Miss Lydia was startled that he didn't know. "The Astoria. For weeks the rooms have been reserved," she said, and went on to describe the Astoria as "very old-fashion but exquisite." "Well," said Lyons, "what about the night life in Leningrad, any action there?" Miss Lydia replied by saying that perhaps her English was not all it should be, and proceeded, from her Muscovite point of view, to discuss Leningrad rather as a New Yorker might Philadelphia; it was "old-fashion," it was "provincial," it was "not the same like Moscow." At the end of this recital, Lyons said glumly, "Sounds like a two-day town to me." Miss Ryan thought to ask when was the last time Miss Lydia had visited Leningrad. Miss Lydia blinked. "The last time? Never. I have never been there. It will be interesting to see, yes?"

Presently she had a question of her own. "I would appreciate you to explain to me. Why is Paul Robeson not in with the players? *He* is a colored person, yes?"

"Yes," said Miss Ryan; and so, she added, were sixteen million other Americans. Surely Miss Lydia didn't expect *Porgy and Bess* to employ them all?

Miss Lydia leaned back in her chair with a cunning, I'm-no-fool expression. "It is because *you,* " she said, smiling at Miss Ryan, "*you* do not permit him his passport."

The dessert arrived. It was vanilla ice cream, and it was excellent. Behind me, Miss Thigpen said to her fiancé, "Earl, honey, I wouldn't touch it. Maybe it's not pasteurized." Across the aisle, Mrs. Gershwin observed to Miss Putnam, "It's my theory they send it all to California. It cost thirty-five dollars a pound in Beverly Hills."

Coffee followed, and with it an altercation. Jackson and several of his friends had taken over a table and were dealing out a game of Tonk. The two huskiest of the Ministry's young men, Sascha and Igor, converged on the card players and informed them, their voices struggling to sound firm, that "gambling" was illegal in the Soviet Union. "Man," said one of the players, "nobody's gambling here. We got to do *something*. We don't have a friendly game, we blow our stacks." Sascha insisted, "It's illegal. Not allowed." The men threw down their cards, and Jackson, tucking them into a case, said, "Old Squareville. Home for dead cats. The number to play is zero. Tell the boys back in New York."

"They are unhappy. We regret," said Miss Lydia. "But we must remember our restaurant workers." Her stubby-fingered hand motioned elegantly toward the waitresses, whose blear-eyed, solid faces glistened with perspiration as they shambled down the aisle balancing a hundred pounds of dirty dishes. "You understand. It would not look well for them to see the laws disenforced." She gathered the last few apples, and stuffed them into a cloth handbag. "Now," she said cheerfully, "we go to dream. We unravel the sleeve of care."

On the morning of December 21, The Blue Express was twenty-four hours from Leningrad, another day and night, though the difference between the two seemed, as the train crawled deeper into Russia, tenuous indeed, so little did the sun, a gray ghost rising at ten and returned to its grave by three, help to divide them. The fragile span of daylight continued to reveal winter at its uncrackable hardest: birches, their branches broken from the weight of snow; a log-cabin village, not a soul in sight and the roofs hung with icicles heavy as elephant tusks. Once, a village cemetery, poor plain wooden crosses, wind-bent and all but buried. But here and there haystacks, standing in deserted fields, were evidence that even this harsh ground could, in distant spring, grow green again.

Aboard, among the passengers, the emotional pendulum had settled at that nirvana point between the strains of departure and the tensions of arrival. An on and on timeless nowhere that one accepted as perhaps lasting forever, like the wind that swept white cauldrons of snow-spray against the train. At last, even Warner Watson relaxed. "Well," he said, lighting a cigarette with hands that scarcely trembled, "I guess maybe I've got my nerves fenced in." Twerp snoozed in the corridor, pink stomach upturned, paws awry. In Compartment 6, by now a welter of unmade berths, orange peelings, spilled face powder and cigarette butts floating in cold tea, Jackson practiced card-shuffling while his fiancée buffed her nails, and Miss Ryan, pursuing her Russian studies, memorized a new phrase out of the old army textbook: "SLOO-*sha eess-ya ee-lee ya* BOO-*doo streel-* YAHT! Obey or I'll fire!" Lyons alone stayed faithful to the pressures of a workaday world. "Nobody gets in my tax bracket looking at scenery," he said, sternly typing the heading for a new column: *"Showtrain to Leningrad."*

At seven that evening, when the others had gone off to the day's third round of yogurt and raspberry soda, I stayed in the compartment and dined on a Hershey chocolate bar. I thought Twerp and I had the car to ourselves until I noticed one of the Ministry's interpreters, Henry, the child-sized young man with the large ears, pass my door, then pass again, each time giving me a glance that quivered with curiosity. It was as though he wanted to speak, but caution and timidity prevented him. When finally, after another reconnoiter, he did come into the compartment, the approach he'd designed was official.

"Give me your passport," he said, with that bluntness shy people often assume.

He sat on Miss Thigpen's berth, and studied the passport through a pair of spectacles that kept sliding to the tip of his nose; like everything he wore, from his shiny black suit with its bell-bottom trousers to his brown worn-down shoes, they were much too big for him. I said if he would tell me what he was looking for, possibly I could help him. "It is necessary," he mumbled, his red ears burning like hot coals. The train must have traveled several miles while he fingered through the passport like a boy poring over a stamp album; and though he carefully examined the mementos left on its pages by immigration authorities, his attention lingered longest on the data that states one's occupation, height and color, date of birth.

"Here is correct?" he said, pointing to my birth date. I told him it was. "We are three years apart," he said. "I am youngest—*younger?*—I am

younger, thank you. But you have seen much. So. I have seen Moscow."
I asked him if he would like to travel. His anger began as a physical action,
a queer sequence of shrugs and flutterings, shrinking inside his fat man's
suit that seemed to mean yes and no, perhaps. He pushed up his spectacles,
and said, "I have not the time. I am a worker like him and him. Three years,
it could also happen my passport has many imprimaturs. But I am content
with the scenic—no, *scenery*—scenery of the mind. The world is the same,
but here," he tapped his forehead, struck it really, "*here,*" he spread a hand
over his heart, "are changefuls. Which is correct; chang*ings* or change-
fuls?" I said either one; as used, they both made sense.

The effort of shaping these sentences, and an excess of feeling behind
them, had left him breathless. He leaned on his elbow and rested a spell
before suddenly observing, "You resemble Shostakovich. That is correct?"
I told him I wouldn't have thought so, not from the photographs of
Shostakovich that I'd seen. "We have discuss it. Mr. Savchenko has also
the opinion," he said, as though this were final, for who were we, either
of us, to challenge Savchenko? Shostakovich's name led to mention of
David Oistrakh, the great Soviet violinist who had recently played concerts
in New York and Philadelphia. He listened to my report of Oistrakh's
American triumphs as if I were praising him, Henry; his hunched shoulders straightened, all at once he seemed to fill out his flapping suit, and the
heels of his shoes, dangling over the side of the berth, swung together and
clicked, clicked and swung, as though he were dancing a jig. I asked him
if he thought *Porgy and Bess* would have a success in Russia comparable
to Oistrakh's American reception. "It is not my ability to say. But we at
the Ministry hope more than you hope. A real man's job for us, that
Porgy-Bess." He told me that although he'd worked at the Ministry for five
years, this was the only time his job had taken him outside Moscow.
Usually, he said, he spent six days a week at a desk in the Ministry ("I have
my own telephone"), and on Sundays he stayed home reading ("Among
your writers, the powerful one is A. J. Cronin. But Sholikov is more
powerful, yes?"). Home was an apartment on the outskirts of Moscow,
where he lived with his family and, as he was unmarried ("My stipend is
not yet equal to the aspiration"), shared a bedroom with his brother.

The conversation moved with an increasing ease; he ate a piece of
Hershey, he laughed, his heels clicked; and then I offered him some books.
They were stacked on the table, and his eyes continually strayed toward
them, a gaudy collection of twenty-five-cent thrillers mixed in with Edmund Wilson's *To the Finland Station,* a history of the rise of Socialism,
and Nancy Mitford's biography, *Madame de Pompadour.* I told him he
could have them, if he liked.

At first, he was pleased. Then, as he reached for the books, his hands
hesitated, withdrew, and his personal tic started; more shrugs, shrinkings,

until he was swallowed again in the looseness of his clothes. "I have not the time," he said regretfully. Afterward there seemed nothing left to say. He informed me that my passport was in order, and left.

Between midnight and two in the morning, The Blue Express stood still in a railroad siding near Moscow. The exterior coldness had stolen into the cars, forming lenses of ice on the inside surface of the windowpanes; looking out, one saw merely spectral diffusions, as if your vision were deformed by cataracts. As soon as the train left Moscow, a restless mood rippled through the compartments; those who had been asleep wakened, began to flutter about like chickens tricked by a false dawn. The stay-ups poured another drink and breathed a second wind. Already the pendulum was swinging toward the tensions of arrival.

Miss Thigpen woke up, calling, "Earl! Earl!" as though she'd had a bad dream.

"Gone," said Miss Ryan, who was curled in her berth nursing a brandy and reading Mickey Spillane. "He's out defying the law. Somebody's running a bootleg Tonk in the next car."

"That's no way to do. Earl ought to be getting his rest," said Miss Thigpen grouchily.

"Give him hell," Miss Ryan advised her. "He's *got* to marry you."

"Nancy, *quelle heure est-il?*"

"Twenty to four." At four Miss Thigpen again inquired the time; and again at ten past. "For God's sake, Helen. Either get a watch or take an *Oblivon.*"

Miss Thigpen kicked back her covers. "No sense trying. I'm better off dressed." It took her an hour and twenty-five minutes to select her costume and apply the right proportions of cosmetics and perfume. At five thirty-five she put on a feathered hat with a veil and sat down on her berth, completely clothed except for stockings and shoes. "I'm worried sick what to wear on my legs. I don't want to be poisoned," she said. Her fear was founded on a memo the Russians had issued to the ladies of the company on the subject of nylon hosiery. In conditions of severe cold, nylon, they announced, had a tendency to disintegrate, which might cause nylon poisoning. Miss Thigpen rubbed her naked legs and groaned. "What kind of place *is* this we're going? Where a lady's stockings fall to pieces on the street and maybe kill her?"

"Forget it," said Miss Ryan.

"But the Russians . . ."

"How the hell would they know? They don't have any nylons. That's why they say it."

It was eight in the morning before Jackson returned from his Tonk game. "Earl," said Miss Thigpen, "is this how you're going to do after we're married?"

"Sweet-girl," he said, wearily climbing into his berth, "the cat has howled his last. He's zero point zero. Ooble-ee-dood out."

Miss Thigpen was unsympathetic. "Earl, don't you dare go to sleep now. We're almost there. Go to sleep for such a little bit and you'll wake up an ugly mess."

Jackson muttered and drew a blanket over his head.

"Earl," said Miss Ryan softly, "I suppose you know they're going to make newsreels at the station?"

Very shortly afterward, Jackson had shaved, changed shirts and arrayed himself in a caramel-colored fur coat. He owned a hat of the same fur that he'd had "custom-made" fedora-style. While working his hands into a pair of gloves with holes along the fingers to reveal his rings, he gave his fiancée instructions on how to handle the expected cameras: "See, honey, we don't want to get stuck with a lot of still-men. That's a waste of time when they're busting out the flicker stuff." He scratched at the window with his jeweled fist, and squinted out; it was nine-five and still pitch-black, not the ideal color for photography. But half an hour later the darkness had turned to steel-gray mist and one could see the blueness of lightly falling snow.

One of the Ministry's representatives, Sascha, passed through the car, knocking at compartment doors. "Ladies and gentlemen, in twenty minutes we are arriving Leningrad."

I finished dressing and squeezed my way into the crowded corridor, where an excitement was moment by moment accelerating like the wheels of the train. Even Twerp, shawl-wrapped and hugged in Miss Putnam's arms, was prepared to disembark. Mrs. Gershwin was more prepared than Twerp. She bristled with mink, was frosted with diamonds, and her curls peeked charmingly from under a rich soft sable hat. "The hat, darling? I bought it in California. I've been saving it for a surprise. You do, love? How sweet of you, darling. *Darling* . . ." she said, an abrupt silence adding volume to her voice, "we're *there!*"

A stunned instant of disbelief, then a collective pushing toward the vestibule. The sad-eyed car attendant, stationed there to receive his tips, found himself not only ignored but also crushed against the wall. Alert as horses at the starting gate, Jackson and John McCurry jockeyed by the exit for position. McCurry is the heftier of the two, and when the door opened, he was the first man out.

He stepped straight into a gray throng, and a flash bulb's pop. "Bless you," said McCurry, as women vied to thrust bouquets into his hand. "Bless your little pointed heads."

.   .   .

"As we arrived, there were many birds flying about—black and white," wrote Warner Watson, as he later recorded the scene in his diary. "The white ones are *sakaros.* I write it down for my bird-watching friends. We were greeted by many friendly Russians. The women and men (of the company) were given bouquets of flowers. I wonder where they got them this time of year. Pathetic little bouquets like those made by a child."

Miss Ryan, also the keeper of a diary, wrote: "Official welcoming party of giant men and shabby ladies dressed more to meet a coffin than a theatrical company (black clothes, gray faces) but perhaps that's what they *were* doing. My useless plastic galoshes kept falling off, making it impossible to elbow efficiently through the press of microphones, cameras, and those battling to get at them. The Breens were on hand, Robert still half asleep but Wilva smile-smiling. At the head of the quay, dull brass letters spelled out LENINGRAD—and then I knew it was true."

The poet, Helen Wolfert, composed for her journal a lengthy description. Here is an excerpt: "As we advanced along the platform to the exit, two columns of people stood on either side applauding. When we reached the street a press of spectators closed in on us. Policemen pushed them away to let us pass but the people in return pushed them with equal vigor. The actors responded to the warmth and bustle and welcome with grace, graciousness, expansiveness and flair. If the Russian people fell in love with them, they weren't alone. I fell in love with them myself."

Perhaps a few footnotes should be added to these entries. The persons Miss Ryan refers to as "giant men and shabby ladies" were a hundred or more of Leningrad's leading theatrical artists who had been organized to meet the train. Remarkably, none of them had known in advance that *Porgy and Bess* had a Negro cast, and before the committee could rearrange their bewildered faces into expressions of positive welcome, the company were halfway out of the station. The "press of spectators" noted by Mrs. Wolfert consisted of ordinary citizens whose presence was the result of an item printed in the local edition of the previous day's *Izvestia.* "A touring American opera company will arrive by train tomorrow morning in Leningrad. It is expected they will perform here." These two lines were, by the way, the first publicity the Soviet press had given Breen's venture; but despite its meager detail, the announcement had proved sufficiently intriguing to attract the at least one thousand Leningraders who lined the length of the station, cascaded down a flight of stairs, and spilled into the street. I was less aware of the "warmth and bustle" that impressed Mrs. Wolfert. Except for light sprinklings of applause, the crowd, so it seemed to me, watched the exiting cast with immense silence, an almost catatonic demeanor that provided few clues as to what they thought of the American parade—Mrs. Gershwin, loaded with more bouquets than a bride; small Davy Bey, dancing an impromptu Suzy-Q; Jackson, dispensing royal waves; and John McCurry, walking with his hands clenched above his head like a prize fighter.

While the Russian reaction may have been inscrutable, the official Company Historian, Leonard Lyons, had a very definite opinion of his own. Taking professional note of the scene, he shook his head. "It hasn't been handled right. No showmanship. Why, if Breen knew his business," he said, passing through the door of the station, "we would've come out singing!"

PART 2

The Leningrad première of *Porgy and Bess*, an event expected to reap international publicity, was planned for the evening of Monday, December 26, which gave the company five days to prepare and rehearse, a sufficient time considering that the show had been touring the world nearly four years. But Robert Breen, the production's director, was determined that the audience at the Leningrad première would see the finest possible rendering of the Negro opera. Breen and his energetic partner-wife, Wilva, and their chief assistant, the gentle, yet highly strung Warner Watson, were confident that the Russians would be "stunned" by the musical folk tale, that they would "never have seen anything like it." Several observers, though sympathetic, were not as sure. However looked at, by the Americans or by their Russian sponsors, the opening night promised to be one of the most suspenseful in theatrical annals. But that event was, on the morning of arrival, over a hundred hours away; and after the company had been driven in chartered buses from the Leningrad terminal to the Hotel Astoria, their feelings of suspense were centered around room accommodations.

The Astoria, situated on the impressive expanse of St. Isaac's Square, is an Intourist hotel, which means that it is run by the Soviet agency in control of all hotels where foreigners are permitted to stay. The Astoria justifiably claims to be the best hotel in Leningrad. Some think it the Ritz of all Russia. But it contains few concessions to Western ideas of a deluxe establishment. Of these, one is a room off the lobby that advertises itself as an *Institut De Beauté*, where guests may obtain *Pedicure*, and *Coiffeur pour Madame*. The *Institut*, with its mottled whiteness, its painful appurtenances, resembles a charity clinic supervised by not too sanitary nurses, and the coiffure that Madame receives there is liable to leave her hair with a texture excellent for scouring pans. There is also on the lobby floor a trio of restaurants, each leading into the other, cavernous affairs cheerful as airplane hangars. The center one is Leningrad's smartest restaurant, and in the evenings, from eight till midnight, an orchestra plays Russian jazz for a local *haut monde* who seldom dance but sit morosely counting the bubbles in syrupy glasses of Georgian champagne. The hotel's Intourist office is located behind a low counter in the main lobby; its dozen desks are so arranged that the employees have a broad view, which simplifies their task of keeping tabs on the comings and goings of the guests. It is a job they have made still simpler, or foolproof, by stationing dormitory matrons on each of the residential floors, vigilantes who are on duty from dawn to dawn, never allowing anyone to leave his room without giving her the key, and constantly, like human punch-clocks, recording ins and outs in a bulky ledger. Perhaps Houdini could've eluded them, but it is hard to see how, since they sit at desks that face both the staircase and the elevator, an ancient birdcage that creaks on its cables.

Actually, there is a rear, unguarded staircase connecting the upper floors with a remote side-lobby; and for the clandestine visitor, or the resident wishing to depart unnoticed, this would make the ideal route. Would, except that it is barricaded top to bottom with wooden fences reinforced by old settees and armoires. It might be that the management can find nowhere else to stash these pieces of furniture. Certainly there is no more room in the rooms. For the average Astoria abode is like the annex in a Victorian attic where some poor relation lives buried among the family discards: a miasma of romantic marble statuary, weak-bulbed lamps with tulle shades like ballerina skirts, tables, several of them, covered with Oriental carpeting, chairs galore, plush settees, armoires that could store steamer trunks, flower-papered walls kaleidoscopic with gilt-framed paintings of fruit and country idylls, beds concealed in cavelike alcoves behind dank velvet curtains: all this crammed into a tomb-dark, unventilated area (you can't open the windows in winter, and wouldn't want to if you could) quadruple the size of a train compartment. The hotel has grander quarters, of course, suites with five and six rooms, but the effect of the décor is the same, merely more abundantly so.

Nevertheless, the majority of the *Porgy and Bess* company were most approving of the Astoria, many because they had anticipated "something so much *worse*" and, instead, found their rooms "cozy," "kind of atmospheric" or, as the production's sophisticated publicist, Willem Van Loon, put it, "Full of art-nouveau charms. Really me!" But when the troupe first entered the lobby of the hotel, already milling with Chinese dignitaries and high-booted Cossacks, actual occupancy of these rooms was, in some instances, distant and debatable.

The Astoria's assigning of the rooms and, particularly, the suites seemed to be governed by a protocol, or lack of one, that embittered rather a few. Nancy Ryan volunteered a theory that the Russians had arrived at their system of room distribution by consulting Everyman Opera's payroll:

"The less you get the more they give you." Whatever the reason, several of the leading players and prominent personalities, who were traveling as guests of the company, thought it "grotesque" and "crazy, man, crazy" that stagehands and wardrobe mistresses, carpenters and electricians were being led straight-away to the V.I.P. apartments, while they, the "real people," were supposed to content themselves with the hotel's backwater leftovers. "Are they kidding?" said Leonard Lyons. Another company guest, the New York financier Herman Sartorius, had valid cause to complain; he'd been assigned no room at all. Nor had Mrs. Gershwin, who sat on her luggage in the lobby being soothed by Wilva Breen and Warner Watson.

"Don't you worry, baby," said Mrs. Breen, who had arrived the night before by plane and was ensconced with her husband in six rooms of Astorian splendor. "The Russians may be slow, they may get things a little mixed up, but everything comes out straight in the end. Look what happened when I went to Moscow," she added, referring to a visit she had made to Moscow the previous October in connection with the present tour. "It took me nine days to do two hours' work. But everything came out fine in the end."

"Sure, Lee," said Warner Watson, brushing down his graying crew-cut with an agitated hand. "Sure, honey, we'll get this room business fenced in."

"Darling, I'm perfectly happy, darling," Mrs. Gershwin assured them. "I just think it's so wonderful *being* here."

"To think we really made it," said Mrs. Breen, beaming round her. "And what sweet, kind, adorable people. Wasn't that adorable when the train arrived?"

"Adorable," said Mrs. Gershwin, glancing at the mass of wilting bouquets that had been given her at the station.

"And the hotel's simply beautiful, isn't it?"

"Yes, Wilva," said Mrs. Gershwin blankly, as though her friend's enthusiasm was beginning to tire her.

"You'll have a beautiful room, Lee," said Mrs. Breen, and Warner Watson added, "If you don't like it, you can change it. Anything you want, Lee, we'll get it fenced in."

"Darling, please. It's not important, not the tiniest bit. If they'll just put me *some*where, I wouldn't dream of moving," said Mrs. Gershwin, who was destined, in the course of the next few days, to insist on changing her accommodations three times.

The Ministry of Culture's delegation, headed by Nikolai Savchenko, the businesslike, formidable six-footer, were now in a whirl of pacifying, rectifying, promising everyone they would get the rooms they deserved. "Patience," pleaded one of them, the middle-aged Russian interpreter called

Miss Lydia. "Do not contribute to the misery. We have plenty rooms. No one will stride the streets." Nancy Ryan said she wouldn't mind striding the streets, and suggested to me that we escape the confusion in the lobby by taking a walk.

St. Isaac's Square is hemmed on one side by a canal stemming from the Neva, a river that in winter threads through the city like a frozen Seine, and on the other by St. Isaac's Cathedral, which is now an antireligious museum. We walked toward the canal. The sky was sunless gray, and there was snow in the air, buoyant motes, playthings that seethed and floated like the toy flakes inside a crystal. It was noon, but there was no modern traffic on the square except for a car or two and a bus with its headlights burning. Now and then, though, horse-drawn sleds slithered across the snowy pavement. Along the embankments of the Neva, men on skis silently passed, and mothers aired their babies, dragging them in small sleds. Everywhere, like darting blackbirds, black-furred schoolchildren ice-skated on the sidewalks. Two of these children stopped to inspect us. They were twins, girls of nine or ten, and they wore gray rabbit coats and blue velvet bonnets. They had divided a pair of skates between them, but by holding hands and pushing together, they managed very well on one skate apiece. They looked at us with pretty brown puzzled eyes, as though wondering what made us different: Our clothes? Miss Ryan's lipstick? The soft waves in her loose blond hair? Most foreigners in Russia soon become accustomed to this: the slight frown of the passer-by who is disturbed by something about you that he can't at once put his finger on, and who stops, stares, keeps glancing back, even quite often feels compelled to follow you. The twins followed us onto a footbridge that crossed the Neva, and watched while we paused to look at the view.

The canal, no more than a snow ditch, was a sporting ground for children whose laughing shrillness combined with a ringing of bells, both sounds carrying on the strong, shivery winds that blow from the Bay of Finland. Skeleton trees, sheathed in ice, glittered against the austere fronts of palaces that lined the embankments and stretched to the distant Nevsky Prospekt. Leningrad, currently a city of four million, the Soviet Union's second largest and northernmost metropolis, was built to the taste of the Czars, and Czarist taste ran to French and Italian architecture, which accounts not only for the style but also for the coloring of the palaces along the Neva and in other old quarters. Parisian blacks and grays predominate, but suddenly, here and there, the hot Italian palette intervenes: a palace of bitter green, of brilliant ocher, pale blue, orange. A few of the palaces have been converted into apartments, most are used for offices. Peter the Great, who is given high marks by the current regime because he introduced the sciences to Russia, would probably approve the myriad television aerials that have settled like a swarm of metal insects on the roofs of his once imperial city.

We crossed the bridge and wandered through opened iron gates into the deserted courtyard of a blue palace. It was the beginning of a labyrinth, an arctic Casbah where one courtyard led into another via arcades and tunnels and across narrow streets snow-hushed and silent except for sleigh horses stamping their hooves, a drifting sound of bells, an occasional giggle from the twins, still trailing behind us.

The cold was like an anesthetic; gradually I felt numb enough to undergo major surgery. But Miss Ryan refused to turn back. She said, "This is St. Petersburg, for God's sake. We're not just walking anywhere. I want to see as much as I can. And I'd better. From now on, you know where *I'll* be? Locked in a room typing a lot of nonsense for the Breens." But I saw that she couldn't last much longer, her face was drunkard-red, a frostbite spot whitened the tip of her nose. Minutes later, feeling its first sting, she was ready to seek the Astoria.

The trouble was, we were lost. It amused the twins greatly to see us rotating round the same streets and courtyards. They screeched and hugged each other with laughter when we came on an old man chopping wood and begged him for directions by swinging our arms like compass needles and shouting, *Astoria! Astoria!* The woodchopper didn't understand; he put down his ax and accompanied us to a street corner, where we were required to repeat our pantomime for three swarthy friends of his, none of whom got the point, but nevertheless beckoned us up another street. On the way, out of curiosity, we were joined by a gangly boy carrying a violin case, and a woman who must have been a butcher, for over her coat she was wearing an apron splattered with blood. The Russians babbled and argued; we decided they were taking us to a police station, and neither of us cared, as long as it was heated. By now the moisture in my nose had frozen, my eyes were unfocused with cold. Still, I could see well enough to know that abruptly we were back at the Neva Canal footbridge. I wanted to grab Miss Ryan's hand and run. But she felt our entourage had been so faithful they deserved to see the mystery solved. From woodchopper to violinist, the procession, led by the twins, who skated ahead like pied pipers, convoyed us across the square and straight to the Astoria's entrance. While they surrounded one of the Intourist limousines that stay parked in front of the hotel, and began to question its chauffeur about us, we rushed inside, collapsed on a bench and sucked the warm air like divers who have been too long underwater.

Leonard Lyons walked by. "Looks like you've been out," he said. Miss Ryan nodded, and Lyons, lowering his voice, asked, "Anybody follow you?"

"Yes," said Miss Ryan, *"crowds."*

. . .

A company bulletin board had been installed in the lobby. Attached to it were announcements concerning the company's rehearsal schedule, and a list of entertainments their Soviet hosts had planned for them, which included, in the days before the première, ballet and opera performances, a ride on the new Leningrad subway, a visit to the Hermitage Museum, and a Christmas party. Under the heading PROMPTLY, the dining hours had also been posted, and these, influenced by the fact that in the Russian theater matinées start at noon and evening performances at eight, were listed as: Breakfast 9:30 A.M., Lunch 11:00 A.M., Dinner 5 P.M., Evening snack 11:30 P.M.

But at five on that first evening, I was enjoying a hot tub too much to bother about dinner. The bathroom, which belonged to the third-floor room assigned to me, had peeling sulphur walls, a cold radiator and a broken toilet that rumbled like a mountain brook. The tub itself, circa 1900, was splotched with rust stains, and the water that poured from its taps was brown as iodine; but it was warm, it made a wonderful steam, and I basked in it, idly wondering if downstairs in the bleak dining room the company were at last being treated to caviar and vodka, shashlik, blinis and sour cream. (Ironically, as I learned later, they were receiving the same menu that had been served at every meal on the train: yogurt and raspberry soda, broth, breaded veal cutlets, carrots and peas.) My water-logged drowsing was interrupted when the telephone rang in the outer room. I let it go awhile, the way you might if you were sitting in a bath at home. Then I realized I wasn't home, remembered that, looking at the telephone earlier, I'd thought what a dead object it was to me in Russia, as useless as if the wires were cut. Naked and dripping, I picked up the receiver to hear the interpreter, Miss Lydia, telling me I had a call from Moscow. The telephone was on a desk next to the window. In the street below, a regiment of soldiers marched by singing a military song, and when Moscow came through I could hardly hear for the robust boom of their voices. The caller was someone I'd never met, Henry Shapiro, a United Press correspondent. He said, "What's going on there? Anything'd make a story?" He told me he'd been intending to travel to Leningrad for "the big story," the *Porgy and Bess* première, but now he couldn't because he had to cover "another opening," the Supreme Soviet, which was happening in Moscow the same night. He would therefore appreciate it if he could call again on Monday after the première and have me report to him "how it went, what really happened." I said all right, I'd try.

The call, and the shock of standing unclothed in a cold room, had brought me back to life. The company were expected to attend a ballet, and I started to get dressed for it. There was a problem here. The Breens had decreed that the men should wear black-tie, and the ladies short evening dresses. "It's more respectful," said Mrs. Breen, "and besides, Robert and I like everything to be gala." There was an opposing clique who felt that the Breens' pronouncement would, if obeyed, make them look "ridiculous" in a country where no one dressed formally for any occasion whatever. I compromised by putting on a gray flannel suit *and* a black tie. While dressing, I moved around the room straightening some of the fruit and flower paintings that clotted the walls. They were rather atilt, owing to an inspective visit from Leonard Lyons, who was convinced the Astoria's rooms were wired for sound. Lyons's theories were shared by most of the company, which was not remarkable, considering that the two American diplomats from the Moscow Embassy had told them at a briefing in Berlin that during their Russian visit, they should "assume" their rooms would be wired and their letters opened. Even Breen, who called the diplomatic advice "a lot of blah," had unwittingly encouraged the company's suspicions by declaring that regardless of what anyone might individually feel, he hoped in correspondence they simply would write how "interesting" Russia was and what a "good time" they were having; this, some pointed out, was a contradiction, for why would Breen make such a request if he, too, didn't believe they were living in an atmosphere of microphones and steam kettles?

On my way out, I stopped at the floor desk and handed my key to the guardian, a plump pale woman with a Kewpie-doll smile who wrote in her ledger *224–1900*: the number of my room and hour of departure.

Downstairs, there was a row in progress. The company, dressed and ready to leave for the ballet, stood around the lobby like mortified figures in a tableau, while one of the cast, John McCurry, a husky bull-like man, stomped about yelling, "Goddamn if I will. I'm not gonna pay any goddamn crooked somebody seven bucks fifty to baby-sit anybody." McCurry was complaining of the price a Russian baby-sitter was charging to stay with his four-year-old daughter while he and his wife went to the ballet. At a cost of thirty rubles per sitter, Intourist had supplied a batch to all the parents of the troupe's six children; they had even arranged one for Twerp, the boxer puppy belonging to the production's wardrobe mistress. Thirty rubles, at the exchange of four to one, amounts to $7.50, a stiff tariff; but actually, to the Russians, thirty rubles has a buying power equivalent to $1.70, and the Russians, who had only this modest fee in mind, couldn't fathom why McCurry was causing such a scene. Savchenko, head man from the Ministry of Culture, was rosy with indignation, Miss Lydia white. Breen spoke sharply to McCurry, and McCurry's wife, a shy woman whose eyes are usually downcast, told him if he would please be quiet, she would remain home with the child. Warner Watson and Miss Ryan hustled everyone out of the lobby and onto the two buses that had been chartered for the duration of their Leningrad stay.

Later, Breen apologized to Savchenko for the "conduct" of a few members of the company. The apology was intended to cover more than the McCurry incident. Free liquor was not included in the contract that had been drawn up between the Ministry of Culture and Everyman Opera, Inc. Savchenko was distressed because several persons had ordered drinks brought to their rooms and refused to pay for them, fought and insulted the waiters. Further, it had come to Savchenko's attention that many of the Americans were referring to him and his staff as "spies." Breen, too, felt that this was "unwarranted and outrageous," and Savchenko, in accepting his apologies, said, "Well, of course, in a company this size, we must expect some who will fall below the mark."

The ballet was at the Mariinsky theater, which has been renamed, though no one calls it that, the Kirov, after the old revolutionary and friend of Stalin's whose assassination in 1934 is said to have initiated the first of the Moscow trials. Galina Ulanova, the Bolshoi's prima ballerina, made her debut in this theater, and the Leningrad Opera and Ballet Company, which is now installed there on a repertorial basis, is considered first-class by Soviet critics. Except for the Fenice in Venice, a theater it somewhat resembles in its eighteenth-century size and style and heating system, I think it the most beautiful theater I've seen. Unfortunately, the old seats have been replaced by wooden ones, rather like those in a school auditorium, and their harsh, natural color makes too raw a contrast against the subtle grays and silvers of the Mariinsky's simplified rococo interior.

Despite the chilliness of the theater, all of us, ladies included, were required to leave our coats at the cloakroom; even Mrs. Gershwin was forced to part with her mink, for in Russia it is thought uncultured, *nye kulturni* at its extremest, to enter a theater, restaurant, museum, any such place, wearing a coat or wrap. At the moment, the principal sufferer from the ruling was Miss Ryan. A tall, striking blonde, Miss Ryan was wearing a low strapless dress that hugged her curves cleverly; and as she swayed down the aisle, masculine eyes swerved in her direction like flowers turning toward the sun. For that matter, the entrance of the entire company was creating a mass stir in the crowded audience. People were standing up to get a better view of the Americans and their black ties, silks and sparkles. Much of the attention was centered on Earl Bruce Jackson and his fiancée, Helen Thigpen. They were sitting in the Royal Box, where a hammer-and-sickle blotted out the Imperial crest. Jackson, lolling his hand over the edge of the box so that his jewelry, a ring on every finger, could be seen to advantage, was slowly inclining his head right and left, like Queen Victoria.

"I'd be freezing, if I weren't so embarrassed," said Miss Ryan, as an usher seated her. "Just look, they think I'm *indecent*." One couldn't deny that there was a touch of criticism in the glances Miss Ryan's bare shoulders were receiving from surrounding Russian women. Mrs. Gershwin, who was wearing a becoming green cocktail dress, said, "I *told* Wilva Breen we shouldn't get all dressed up. I knew we'd look ridiculous. Well, darling, never again. But really, what *should* we wear?" she asked, looking about as if hunting fashion hints among the audience's melancholy, shapeless attire. "I didn't bring anything that wasn't pretty."

Sitting in the row ahead, there was one girl whose hair was neither plaited nor a sour bundle of string; she had an urchin-cut, which suited her curious, wild-faun face. She was wearing a black cardigan and a pearl necklace. I pointed her out to Miss Ryan.

"But I *know* her," said Miss Ryan excitedly. "She's from Long Island, we went to Radcliffe together! *Priscilla* Johnson," she called, and the girl, squinting near-sighted eyes, turned around. "For God's sake, Priscilla. What are you doing here?"

"Gosh. Gee whiz, Nancy," said the girl, rubbing back her tomboy bangs. "What are *you* doing here?"

Miss Ryan told her, and the girl, who said that she too was staying at the Astoria, explained that she had been granted a lengthy visa to live in the Soviet Union and study Russian law, a subject that had interested her since Radcliffe, where she'd also learned the Russian language.

"But, darling," said Mrs. Gershwin, "how can anyone study Russian law? When it changes so often?"

"Gosh. Ha ha," said Miss Johnson. "Well, that's not the *only* thing I'm doing. I'm making a kind of Kinsey report. It's great fun, gosh."

"I should think," said Miss Ryan. "The research."

"Oh, that's easy," Miss Johnson assured her. "I just keep steering the conversation toward sex; and gee whiz, you'd be surprised what Russians think about it. Gosh, Nancy, the number of men who have mistresses! Or wished they did. I'm sending articles to *Vogue* and *Harper's Bazaar*. I thought they might be interested."

"Priscilla's a sort of genius," Miss Ryan whispered to me, as chandeliers dimmed and the orchestra conductor raised his baton.

The ballet, in three acts with two intermissions, was called *Corsair*. The average Soviet ballet is far less concerned with dancing than with stupendous production, and *Corsair*, though a minor work in their repertory, involves as much change of scenery as the extravagant vaudevilles at Radio City Music Hall or the Folies Bergère, two theaters where *Corsair* would feel quite at home, except that the choreography and its execution are not up to the standards of the former, and the latter would never tolerate a scene of dancing slave girls swathed to the neck. The theme of *Corsair* is very similar to *The Fountains of Bahchisarai*, a poem of Pushkin's that the

Bolshoi ballet has taken and swollen into one of its prize exhibits. In *Fountains,* an aristocratic girl is kidnaped by a barbaric Tartar chieftain and hauled off to his harem, where, for three hours of playing time, many vile adventures befall her. In *Corsair,* this girl's twin sister undergoes somewhat the same ordeal; here she is the victim of a shipwreck (brilliantly simulated onstage with thunder, lightning, torrents of water crashing against the stricken vessel) who is captured by pirates, after which, for three hours, ditto. Both these tales, and countless like them, reflect a tendency in the contemporary Soviet theater to rely on fantasy and legend; it would seem that the modern author who wishes to roam beyond the propagandist garden finds that the only safe path is the one that leads him into the forest of fairy stories. But even fantasy needs realistic underpinning, reminders of the recognizable, the human; without them, the power of life is not there, nor is art, a dual absence that occurs too often in the Soviet theater, whose practitioners appear to believe that trick effects and technical wizardry can be made to supplant them. The Ministry of Culture frequently boasts that Russia is the sole country to have produced an art-culture *en rapport* with its population. The reaction of the audience to *Corsair* was nothing to disprove the claim; every set, every solo brought chandelier-shaking rounds of applause.

The Americans were enthusiastic too. "Magnificent, a dream," Mrs. Breen told Mrs. Gershwin during an intermission spent in the Mariinsky's café-salon. The opinion was seconded by her husband. Yet while praising the ballet, Breen, a dapper man whose facial expressions alternate between boyish beamings and Buster Keaton calm, had a troubled flickering in his eyes, as though perhaps he was comparing the physical elaborateness of *Corsair* with *Porgy and Bess*'s three simple changes of scenery; if lavish effects were the criterion, then Soviet audiences were certain to be disappointed with his production.

"Well, *I* don't like it," said Mrs. Gershwin rebelliously, as the Breens moved on to another group. "I can hardly keep awake. And I'm not going to say I like it if I don't. They [the Breens] would put the words in your mouth if they could." That, of course, was the difficulty of the Breens' position. Like parents who have taken their children on a visit to the neighbors, they lived in dreadful anticipation of *gaffes*, of breakage and misconduct.

Refreshments were on sale in the Mariinsky's café-salon: beer, liqueurs, raspberry soda, sandwiches, candy and ice cream. Earl Bruce Jackson said he was starving: "But, man, that ice cream costs a dollar a lick. And guess what they want for a little bitty piece of chocolate not big as your toe? Five-fifty." Ice cream, advertised by the Soviets to be a delicacy of their own contriving, started to become a national passion in the U.S.S.R. in 1939, when American machinery was imported for its making. Most of the customers jammed into the salon stood spooning it out of paper cups while watching the Americans pose for photographs, informal ones, balancing beer bottles on their foreheads, demonstrating the shimmy, doing imitations of Louis Armstrong.

At the second interval I looked for Miss Ryan and found her backed into a corner, haughtily smoking a cigarette in a long holder and trying to pretend she was not the cynosure of puffy girls and leaden-faced women gathered to giggle and comment on her clinging gown and naked shoulders. Leonard Lyons, standing with her, said, "See, now you know how Marilyn Monroe feels. Would she be a wow here! She ought to get a visa. I'm going to tell her."

"Ohhhh," moaned Miss Ryan, "if *only* I could get my coat."

A man in his late thirties, clean-shaven, dignified, an athletic figure with a scholar's face, stepped up to Miss Ryan. "I should like to shake your hand," he said respectfully. "I want you to know how much my friends and I are looking forward to *Porgy and Bess*. It will be a powerful event for us, I can assure you. Some of us have obtained tickets for the first night. I," he said, smiling, "am among the fortunate." Miss Ryan said she was pleased to hear that, and remarked on the excellence of his English, which he explained by saying that he'd spent several of the war years in Washington as part of a Russian Purchasing Commission. "But can you really understand me? It's been so long since I've had the opportunity of speaking —it makes my heart pound." One sensed, in the admiring intensity of his attitude toward Miss Ryan, that the pounding of his heart was not altogether due to the English language. His smile slackened as a fluttering light signaled the end of intermission; and urgently, as though spurred by an impulse he couldn't resist, he said, "Please let me see you again. I'd like to show you Leningrad." The invitation was directed to Miss Ryan, but by polite necessity included Lyons and myself. Miss Ryan told him to call us at the Astoria, and he jotted our names on a program, then wrote out his own and handed it to Miss Ryan.

"Stefan Orlov," Miss Ryan read, as we returned for the last act. "He's quite sweet."

"Yeah," said Lyons. "But he won't call. He'll think it over and get cold feet."

Arrangements had been made for the company to go backstage and meet the ballet artists. The final scene of *Corsair* is partly played on the deck of a ship hung with rope nets, and at the end of the performance, when the Americans came behind the curtain, there was such a congestion onstage that half the dancers had to stand on the ship's deck or climb the rope nets to get a glimpse of the Western colleagues whose entrance they cheered and applauded a full four minutes before enough quiet could be summoned for Breen to make a speech, which began, "It is *we* who should applaud *you.* Your thrilling artistry has produced an evening none of us will ever forget, and we only hope on Monday evening we can a little repay you for the pleasure you have given us." While Breen finished his speech, and the director of the Mariinsky made another, the little ballerinas, sweat seeping through their make-up, crept close to the American performers, and their painted eyes rolled, their lips ohd-ahd as they gazed at the visitors' shoes, shyly, then boldly, touched the dresses, rubbed bits of silk and taffeta between their fingers. One of them reached out and put her arm around a member of the company named Georgia Burke. "Why, precious-child," said Miss Burke, a warm, happy-natured woman, "hug me all you like. It's good to know somebody loves you."

It was nearer one than midnight when the company started the bus ride back to the Astoria. The buses, rolling refrigerators, had the same seating plan as those that operate on Madison Avenue. I sat on the long back seat between Miss Ryan and the interpreter, Miss Lydia. Street lamps, yellowing the snows of empty streets, flashed at the windows like wintry fireflies, and Miss Ryan, looking out, said, "The palaces are so beautiful in the lamplight."

"Yes," said Miss Lydia, stifling a sleepy yawn, "the private homes are beautiful." Then, as though suddenly awake, she added, "The *former* private homes."

The next morning I went shopping on the Nevsky Prospekt with Lyons and Mrs. Gershwin. Leningrad's principal street, the Nevsky is not a third the length of Fifth Avenue, but it is twice as wide; to get across its skidding aisles of traffic is a perilous chore and a rather pointless one, for the stores on either side of the street are all government-owned emporiums selling, in their different classifications, the same stock at the same prices. Bargain hunters, buyers on the lookout for "something a little different" would find shopping on the Nevsky a discouraging experience.

Lyons had set out with starry hopes of picking up "a nice piece of Fabergé" to take home to his wife. After the revolution, the Bolsheviks sold to French and English collectors almost all the jeweled eggs and boxes that Fabergé had created for the royal amusement; the few known examples of his work left in Russia are on display in Leningrad's Hermitage Museum and in the Armory at the Kremlin. Today, on the international market, the beginning price of a small Fabergé box is over two thousand dollars. None of this information impressed Lyons, who felt he was going to locate his Fabergé quickly and quite cheaply at a Commission Shop. Which was right thinking as far as it went, for if such an item existed, then a Commission Shop, a state-controlled pawn brokerage where a comrade can turn the last of his hidden heirlooms into spot cash, is probably the only place you would discover it. We visited several, drafty establishments with the going-gone sadness of auction halls.

In one, the largest, a glass cabinet ran the length of the room, and the spectacle its contents presented, the conglomeration of spookily diverse objects, seemed a dadaist experiment. Rows of secondhand shoes, so worn the spectral shape of the previous owner's foot could be pathetically discerned, were neatly set forth under glass like treasures, which indeed they were at $50 to $175 a pair; a selection of headgear flanked the shoes, flapper cloches and velvet cartwheels; after the hats, the surrealistic variety and value of the cabinet's contents spiraled: a shattered fan ($30), a soiled powder puff ($7), an amber comb with broken teeth ($45), tarnished mesh handbags ($100 and up), a silver umbrella handle ($340), an unexceptional ivory chess set with five pawns missing ($1,450), a celluloid elephant ($25), a pink plaster doll cracked and flaked as though it had been left in the rain ($25). All these articles, and yards more, were placed and numbered with a care that suggested an exhibition of mementos, the possessions of some dead beloved figure, and it was this, the reverence of the display, that made it poignant. Lyons said, "Who do you s'pose *buys* this stuff?" But he had only to look around him to see that there were those who, in lieu of anything else, found the moth-nibbled fan and the silver umbrella handle still fetching, still desirable, quite worth their quoted costs. According to the Russian calendar, Christmas was two weeks off, but Russians prefer to give gifts at New Year's and the Commission Shops, like all the stores along the Nevsky, were packed with spenders. Though Lyons failed to flush any Fabergé, one pawnbroker came up with a unique nineteenth-century snuffbox, an immense topaz, hollowed and split in half. But the price, $80,000, was more than the customer had in mind.

Mrs. Gershwin, who intended giving a "really good" Christmas present to every member of the *Porgy and Bess* cast ("After all, darling, it's the company's fourth Christmas together, and I do want to show the darlings my appreciation"), still had a few odds and ends to finish off, though she'd carted a trunkload of gifts from Berlin. And so, struggling through the Nevsky crowds ("You can't deny there's a lot of vitality around here," said Lyons), we visited a furrier where the cheapest sable was a short jacket selling, or rather not selling, for $11,000. Then we stopped at an antique shop declared by Intourist to be Leningrad's most "elegant." The antiques turned out to be used television sets, an icebox, an old American electric fan, some battered pieces of Biedermeier and a colossal number of oil paintings depicting scenes of historical event if not value. "What did you expect, darling?" said Mrs. Gershwin. "There's no such thing as Russian antiques. If there are, they're French." Inquiring for caviar, we went to two fancy-food stores, the local Vendômes; there were pineapples from Africa, oranges from Israel, fresh lichee nuts from China; but no caviar. "Where,

where did I get the idea it was the butter on the workingman's bread?" lamented Mrs. Gershwin, who said she'd settle for a cup of tea, a desire that shortly drove us into a Soviet version of Schrafft's. It was in a cellar, a dungeon where waitresses, wearing knee boots and tiaras made of doily paper, waded across slush-flooded floors carrying trays of ice cream and improbable pastry to gloomy groups of middle-aged women. But Mrs. Gershwin had to do without her tea, for there were no tables available, nor even space to stand.

So far, no one had made a single purchase. Mrs. Gershwin decided to try a department store. On the way, Lyons, who had a camera, paused often to take photographs, of match women and cherry-cheeked girls dragging Christmas trees, of street-corner flower stalls that in winter sell artificial roses, paper tulips stuck in flowerpots, as though they were real. Each of his photographic forays caused pedestrian traffic jams, a gallery of silent spectators who smiled, and sometimes scowled, when he took their pictures, too. Presently I noticed that there was one man who continuously showed up among the onlookers, yet did not seem part of them. He always stood at the rear, a chunky man with a crooked nose. He was bundled in a black coat and astrakhan cap and half his face was hidden behind the kind of windshield dark glasses skiers wear. I lost track of him before we reached the department store.

The store was reminiscent of a carnival alley, consisting, as it did, of counters and alcoves whose shelves seemed mostly stocked with shooting gallery prizes, the cheap familiar dolls, ugly urns, plaster animals, the toilette set bedded in a crumpling of white casket silk. Mrs. Gershwin, overcome by an odor of rancid glue, felt swift necessity to leave the "leather-goods" department, a swifter one to flee the perfume counter.

A crowd began trailing us through the store, and when, in an alcove devoted to hats, I started trying on caps of ersatz Persian lamb, a good thirty grinning, jostling Russians ganged around demanding I buy this one, that one, themselves whisking models on and off my head and ordering the clerk to bring more, more, until hats were toppling off the counter. Someone bent to retrieve one from the floor; it was the man wearing ski glasses. The hat I bought, chosen at desperate random, proved later not to fit. A fake astrakhan, it cost $45; and because of the complicated payment system that operates in all Soviet stores, from the humblest grocery to GUM's in Moscow, it required another forty minutes to complete the transaction. First, the clerk gives you a sales slip, which you carry to a cashier's booth, where you cool your heels while the cashier does her computations on an abacus, an efficient method no doubt, still, some clever Soviet should invent the cash register; when the money has been paid, the cashier stamps the sales slip, and this you take back to the clerk, who by now is attending five other people; eventually, though, the clerk will accept the slip, go to check it with the cashier, come back, hand over your purchase, and direct you to a wrapping department, where you join another queue. At the end of this process, I was given my hat in a green box. "Please, darling," Mrs. Gershwin begged Lyons, who was tempted to buy a hat himself. "*Don't* make us go through all that again."

Ski-glasses was nowhere in sight when we left the store. He turned up soon enough, however, at the edge of a group watching Lyons photograph peddlers selling Christmas trees in a snowy courtyard. It was there in the courtyard that I left the hatbox; I must have put it down to slap my numbed hands together. I didn't realize it was missing until many blocks later. Lyons and Mrs. Gershwin were game to go back and look for it. But that wasn't necessary. For as we turned around, we saw Ski-glasses coming toward us, and dangling in his hand was the green hatbox. He gave it to me with a smile that twitched his crooked nose. Before I could think to say thank you, he'd tipped his cap and walked away.

"Well, ho ho—call that a coincidence?" crowed Lyons, a joyous shine livening his shrewd eyes. "Oh, I've had *him* spotted!"

"So have I," admitted Mrs. Gershwin. "But I think it's darling. Adorable. Simply adorable of them to take such good care of us. It makes you feel so protected. Well, darling," she said, as though determined Lyons should be persuaded to adopt her view, "*isn't* it a comfort to know you can't *lose* anything in Russia?"

At the Astoria, after lunch, I rode up in the elevator with Ira Wolfert, the former war correspondent who supposedly intended writing an article on Everyman Opera's tour for the *Reader's Digest*. "But I'm still looking for a story. What it seems to me is, is repetitious," Wolfert told me. "And you can't talk to anybody around here. Russians, I mean. It's giving me claustrophobia, every time I get into a political talk I keep getting the same old line. I was talking to Savchenko, he's supposed to be an intelligent guy, and I said to him, since this is a private talk, do you *honestly* believe all these things you're saying about America? You know, he was saying how Wall Street runs the country. But you can't talk to them. There's no realism in this social realism. Yesterday I was talking to a Russian—I won't define him, one of the guys we've met around here—and he slips me a note. This note asking me to call his sister in New York. He has a sister living there. Later on I see this guy on the street. I pull him down a side street and say, 'What the hell goes on here?' And he says, 'Everything's fine. Only it's better to be careful.' Everything's fine, but the guy's slipping me notes!" Wolfert bit hard on his pipe, and shook his head. "There's no realism. I'm getting claustrophobia."

Upstairs, I could hear the telephone ringing inside my room as I unlocked the door. It was the man I'd met during an intermission at the ballet, Miss Ryan's admirer, Stefan Orlov. He said he'd been calling Miss Ryan but there was no answer. I suggested he try the Breens' suite, one room of which Miss Ryan was using as an office. "No," he said, sounding nervously apologetic. "I must not call again. So soon. But when may I see Nancy? *And* you?" he added, tactfully. I asked him if he would like to come by the hotel for a drink. There was a pause that lasted until I thought we'd been disconnected. Finally he said, "That would not be convenient. But could you meet me, say, in an hour?" I said yes, where? He told me, "Walk around the cathedral. St. Isaac's. Keep walking. I will see you." He rang off without saying good-bye.

I went down to the Breens' suite to tell Miss Ryan of the invitation. She was delighted, "I knew he'd call," but crestfallen, "I'm stuck with six copies of a rush item," she said, inserting layers of paper and carbon into a portable typewriter. The rush item was a two-page letter written by Robert Breen and addressed to Charles E. Bohlen, the American Ambassador to Russia. It began by expressing gratitude over the fact that Ambassador and Mrs. Bohlen were coming to Leningrad for the *Porgy and Bess* première; but the bulk of the letter was in a tone of grieving complaint. Although the production's Soviet tour had the blessings of the U.S. State Department, it was not, contrary to the popular impression, under their official sponsorship. Indeed, the trip had been made financially possible by Russia's own Ministry of Culture. Nevertheless, Breen felt it was "a crying shame" no member of Ambassador Bohlen's staff had been permanently assigned to the company to observe "the day-to-day and minute-to-minute happenings, the individual contacts, and the spontaneous, warm incidents" that Breen considered necessary if the Embassy intended to "prepare properly the sort of full and valid report which rightfully should be expected on this unprecedented project." Breen wrote, "The need for such documentation concerns not only this goodwill tour, important as it is, but also possible future cultural exchanges. No one can imagine the extreme lengths to which we have gone to provide smooth running—or the infinite amount of details which have to be foreseen and arranged if this type of exchange is to bear the fruit of its promise. The documentation should record not only our successes, but also those facets of public relations which might be improved, and the possible failures."

"Give my love to Stefan," Miss Ryan instructed, as I left to keep the appointment. "And if it turns out to be a spontaneous, warm incident, be sure and tell me so I can put it in the *Porgy and Bess* log," she said, referring to an official journal of that title maintained by her employers.

It's a stone's throw from the Astoria to the semi-Gothic mass of St. Isaac's Cathedral. I left the hotel at exactly three-thirty, the time Orlov had said he would meet me. But on stepping out the door, I found myself confronting a pair of ski glasses. There was an Intourist Ziv parked at the curb, and the man was sitting in the front seat talking to a chauffeur. For a moment I thought of returning to the hotel; it seemed the sensible course if Orlov was concerned that his rendezvous be off the record. But I decided to stroll past the car and see what happened; as I went by, nerves and an unreliable sense of etiquette prompted me to nod at the man. He yawned and averted his face. I didn't look back until I'd crossed the square and was in the shadows of St. Isaac's. By then, the car was gone. I walked slowly around the cathedral, pretending to admire the architecture, though there was no reason to pretend anything, for the sidewalks were deserted. Still, I felt conspicuous, and not quite lawful. Night swept the sky like the black crows that wheeled and cawed overhead. On the third lap around, I began to suspect Orlov had changed his mind. I tried to forget the cold by counting my steps, and had ticked off two hundred and sixteen when, turning a corner, I came on a scene that made the flow of numbers stop like the hands of a dropped watch.

It was this: four men in black had a fifth man backed against the cathedral wall. They were pounding him with their fists, pushing him forward and hitting him with the full weight of their bodies, like football players practicing on a dummy. A woman, respectably dressed and carrying a pocketbook tucked under her arm, stood on the sidelines as though she were casually waiting while some men friends finished a business conversation. Except for the cawing of crows, it was like an episode from a silent film; no one made a sound, and as the four attackers relinquished the man, leaving him spread-eagled on the snow, they glanced at me indifferently, joined the woman and walked off without a word between them. I went over to the man. He was fat, too heavy for me to lift, and the drink on his breath would have killed scorpions. He was not bleeding and he was not unconscious, but he wanted to speak and couldn't; he gazed up at me like a deaf-mute attempting to communicate with his eyes.

A headlighted car pulled alongside the curb. The strip of black and white checks bordering its frame identified it as a taxi. The rear door opened, and Stefan Orlov called my name. Leaning in the door, I tried to explain what had happened and ask him to help the man, but he was impatient, he didn't want to listen, he kept saying, "Get in," and, "Will you *please* get in"; and at last, with a fury that shocked me, "You're an idiot!" he said, yanking me onto the seat. As the taxi swung in a U-turn, its headlights exposed the man sprawled on the sidewalk, his lifted hands plowing the air, like the claws of an insect cruelly tumbled on its back.

"I'm sorry," said Orlov, regaining a civil voice that also managed to sound sincerely remorseful. "But other people's quarrels. They are not so much interesting, you understand. Now, enjoy yourself. We are going to the Eastern." He commented on Miss Ryan's absence and regretted "deeply" that she'd been unable to accept his invitation. "The Eastern is where you want to take a girl like Nancy. Very good food. Music. A bit of Oriental atmosphere." After the clandestine nature of our meeting, it struck me as curious that we were now proceeding anywhere as gay and public as he described; and I said so. He was hurt. "I have no fears, but I'm not an idiot either. The Astoria is a sensitive place. You understand? It's a nuisance to go there. Why shouldn't I see you if I like?" he said, asking himself the question. "You are a singer, I'm interested in music." He was under the impression that both Miss Ryan and myself were singers in the cast of *Porgy and Bess*. When I corrected him, and told him I was a writer, he seemed upset. He had lighted a cigarette, and his lips, pursed to blow out the match, tautened. "Are you a correspondent?" he asked, letting the flame burn. I said no, not what he meant by a correspondent. He blew on the match. "Because I hate correspondents," he said, rather warningly, as though I'd best not be lying to him. "They're filthy. And Americans, it's too bad to say, are the worst. The filthiest." Now that he knew I was a writer, I thought perhaps he saw the situation in a different, less harmless perspective, and so suggested that if the taxi would take me within walking distance of the Astoria, we could amicably part company then and there. He interpreted this as a protest to his opinion of American correspondents. "Please, you misunderstand. I admire so much the American *people,*" he said, and told me that the years he'd spent in Washington "were of a happiness I never forget. The Russians who lived in New York were always very snobbish about the Russians who had to live in Washington; they said, 'Oh, my dear, Washington is so *boring* and provincial.'" He laughed at his grande-dame imitation. "But for me, I liked it there. The hot streets in the summer. Bourbon whiskey. I liked so much my flat. I open my windows and pour myself a bourbon," he said, as though reliving these actions. "I sit in my underwear and drink the bourbon and play the Vic loudly as I like. There is a girl I know. Two girls. One of them always comes by."

The so-called Eastern is a restaurant attached to the Hotel Europa, just off the Nevsky Prospekt. Unless a few desiccated potted palms connote the Orient, I am at a loss to explain Orlov's contention that the place had a slant-eyed atmosphere. The atmosphere, if any, was a discouraging one of yellow-walled drabness and sparsely occupied tables. Orlov was self-conscious; he picked at his tie and smoothed his dark hair. While we crossed an empty dance floor, an ensemble, four musicians as spidery as the palms they stood among, were scratching out a waltz. We climbed a flight of stairs that led to a balcony where there were discreet dining booths. "I'm sure you think the Astoria is more elegant," he said, as we were seated. "But that is for foreigners and large snobs. Here is for smaller snobs. I am *very* small snob."

It worried me that he probably couldn't afford the Eastern at all. His overcoat featured a luxurious sable collar and he had a hat of gleaming sealskin. Still, his suit was a poor, thin plaid and the laundered freshness of his white shirt somehow made more apparent its frayed cuffs and collar. But he gave sumptuous instructions to the waiter, who brought us a 400-gram carafe of vodka and a huge helping of caviar heaped in silver ice-cream dishes, toast and slices of lemon on the side. With a passing thought for Mrs. Gershwin, I dispatched every soft, unsalted, gray, pearly bead of it, and Orlov, marveling at the speed of my accomplishment, asked if I would like another serving. I said no, I couldn't possibly, but he saw that I could, and sent the waiter for more.

Meanwhile, he proposed toasts in honor of Miss Ryan. "To Nancy," he said, draining his glass, then, with a refill, "To Nancy. She is a beautiful girl"; and, again pouring, "That beautiful Nancy. Beautiful girl. Beautiful."

The succession of fast-gulped vodka flushed his pale, almost handsome face. He told me he could drink "a fool's fill" and not get drunk, but a gradual dimming of intelligence in his fine blue eyes belied the boast. He wanted to know if I thought Miss Ryan was partial to him. "Because," he said, leaning forward in an attitude of excessive confidence, "she is a beautiful girl, and I like her." I said yes, I gathered he considered her highly. "But you think I'm an idiot? Because I'm nearly forty and I'm married five years?" He spread his hand on the table to show me a plain gold wedding ring. "I would never do harm to my marriage," he said piously. "We have two babies, little girls." He described his wife as "not beautiful, but my principal friend," and told me that aside from the children, the mutual interests they shared made the marriage "a serious composition." Among professional classes in Russia, it can be observed that persons seldom make alliances with anyone outside their own field of work. Doctors marry doctors; lawyers, lawyers. The Orlovs, it seemed, were both mathematicians who taught at the same Leningrad school. Music and the theater formed their main pleasures; they had taken turns, he said, waiting in line to buy tickets for the *Porgy and Bess* first-night, but in the end they had been allowed just one ticket. "Now my wife pretends she doesn't want to go. That is so I can go." The previous year they had bought a television set as a New Year's present to each other, but now they regretted having spent the money on something "so boring and childish." He expressed himself with equal harshness on the subject of Soviet films. His wife, however, was fond of going to the *kino*, but he himself would only be enthusiastic if ever again they showed American pictures. ("I should like to know. What has happened to that beautiful girl, Joan Bennett? And the other one, Ingrid Bergman? And George Raft? What a wonderful actor! Is he still alive?") Apart from this disagreement on the merits of movie going, his wife's tastes coincided with his at every point; they even, he said, enjoyed the same sport, "boating," and for several years had been saving to buy a small sailboat, which they intended docking at a fishing village near Leningrad where each summer they spent two months' vacation. "That is what I live for—guiding a boat through the poetry of our white nights. You must come back when the white nights are here. They are a true reward for nine months' dark."

The vodka was exhausted, and Orlov, after calling for a replenishment, grumbled that I wasn't keeping pace with him. He said it "disgusted" him to watch me "just tasting," and demanded that I "drink like a decent fellow or leave the table." I was surprised how easy it was to empty a glass in one swallow, how pleasant, and it appeared not to affect me except for a tickling warmth and a feeling that my critical faculties were receding. I began to think that after all Orlov was right, the restaurant did have an Oriental atmosphere, a Moorish coziness, and the music of the orchestra, scraping like cicadas among the palms, seemed to acquire a beguiling, nostalgic lilt.

Orlov, at the stage of repeating himself, said, "I'm a good man and I have a good wife," three times before he could reach the next sentence, which was, "But I have strong muscles." He flexed his arms. "I'm passionate. A lusty dancer. On hot nights, with the window open, and the Vic playing loud as we like . . . and the Vic playing loud as we like. One of them always comes by. And we dance like that. With the window open on hot nights. That's all I want. To dance with Nancy. Beautiful. A beautiful girl. You understand? Just to dance. Just to . . . Where is she?" His hand swept the table. Silverware clattered on the floor. "Why isn't Nancy here? Why won't she sing for us?" With his head tilted back he sang, "Missouri woman on the Mississippi with her apron strings Missouri woman drags her diamond rings by her apron strings down the bad Missouri on the Mississippi blues . . ." His voice grew louder, he lapsed into Russian, a hollering still obscurely associated with the tune of "St. Louis Blues."

I looked at my watch. To my astonishment it was nine o'clock. We'd been sitting in the Eastern almost five hours, which meant I couldn't be as sober as I reckoned. The realization and the proof of it struck simultaneously, like a pair of assassins who had been lying in wait. The tables seemed to slide, the lights swing, as though the restaurant were a ship riding a rough sea. At my request, insistence, Orlov asked for the check, but he went on singing while he counted out his rubles, sang his way down the stairs and waltzed by himself across the dance floor, ignoring the orchestra for his own accompaniment, "Missouri woman you're a bad Missouri woman on the Mississippi blues . . ."

In front of the Eastern there was a vendor selling rubber animals. Orlov bought a rabbit and handed it to me. "Tell Nancy from Stefan." Then he pulled me along a street that led away from the Nevsky Prospekt. As mud lanes replaced pavement it became clear that our destination was not the Astoria. For this was no neighborhood of palaces. Instead it was as though I were walking again through the slums of New Orleans, a district of dirt streets and broken fences, sagging wooden houses. We passed an abandoned church where wind wailed round the domes like a widow at the grave. Not far from the church, sidewalks resumed, and, with them, the city's imperial façade. Orlov headed toward the lighted windows of a café. The cold walk had quietened, somewhat sobered him. At the door, he said, "Here it is better. A workingman's place."

It was as if one had fallen into a bear pit. The body heat and beery breath and damp-fur smell of a hundred growling, quarreling, pawing customers filled the bright-lighted café. Ten and twelve men huddled around each of the room's half-dozen tables.

The only women present were three look-alike waitresses, brawny girls, wide as they were tall, and with faces round and flat as plates. In addition to waiting, they did duty as bouncers. Calmly, expertly, with an odd absence of rancor and less effort than it takes to yawn, they could throw a punch that knocked the stuffings out of men double their size. Lord help the man who fought back. Then all three girls would converge on him, beat him to his knees, literally wipe the floor with him as they dragged his carcass to the door and pitched it into the night. Some men, would-be customers decidedly persona non grata, never got into the café, for as soon as any of these undesirables appeared at the door the ladies of the establishment formed a flying, flailing wedge to drive him out again. Yet they could be courteous. At least they smiled at Orlov, impressed, I think, by his sable collar and expensive hat. One of them showed us to a table where she told two men, young jut-jawed bruisers wearing leather coats, to get up and give us their chairs. One was willing, the other argued. She settled his objections by snatching his hair and twisting his ear.

For the most part, only upper-strata restaurants are licensed to sell vodka, and since the café was not in that category, Orlov ordered Russian cognac, a brackish liquid that came in large tea glasses overflowing their brim. With the blitheness of a man blowing foam off a beer, he emptied a third of his glass and asked if the café "pleased" me, or did I think it "rough." I answered yes, and yes. "Rough, but not hooligan," he differentiated. "On the waterfront, yes, that is hooligan. But here is just ordinary. A workingman's place. No snobs." We had eight companions at the table and they took an interest in me, picked at me like magpies, plucked a cigarette lighter out of my hand, a scarf from around my neck, objects they passed from one to the next, glaring at them, grinning over them, and showing, even the youngest, rows of rotted teeth, wrinkles for which age could not account. The man nearest was jealous and wanted all my attention. It was impossible to guess how old he was, anywhere from forty to seventy. He had an eye missing, and this circumstance enabled him to do a trick which he kept forcing me to watch. It was meant to be a parody of Christ on the Cross. Taking a swallow of beer he would stretch his arms and droop his head. In a moment a trickle of beer came crying out the gaping redness of his hollow eye socket. His friends at the table thought it was an uproarious stunt.

Another favorite of the café was a boy who roamed around with a guitar. If you bought him a drink, he'd sing you a song. He played one for Orlov, who translated it to me, saying it was the kind of song "we" like. It was the lament of a sailor longing for the village of his youth and a lost love called Nina. "The green of the sea is the green of her eyes." The boy sang well, with plaintive flamenco waverings in his voice. I sensed, though, that he was not concentrating on the lyrics. His thoughts and his gaze too were directed toward me. His white face had a sadness that seemed to be painted on, like a clown's. But it was his eyes that bothered me. Then I knew why. It was because they reminded me of the expression, the deaf-mute pleadings, in the eyes of the man left lying on the cathedral sidewalk. When he stopped playing, Orlov told him to sing another song. Instead the boy tried to speak to me.

"I . . . you . . . mother . . . man." He knew about ten words of English and he struggled to pronounce them. I asked Orlov to interpret, and as they talked together in Russian it was as though the boy were singing again. While his voice wove some sorrowful prose melody, his fingers tinkered with the strings of the guitar. Tears sprang to his eyes, and he rubbed them away with the flat of his palm, leaving grimy smudges like a child. I asked Orlov what he was saying. "It's not so much interesting. I'm not interested in politics." It seemed inconceivable the boy was talking politics, and when I persisted, Orlov was annoyed. "It's nothing. A nuisance. He wants you to help him."

Help was a word the boy understood. "Help," he said, nodding vigorously. "Help."

"Isn't he a nuisance?" said Orlov. "He says his father was English and his mother Polish, and because of this he says he's very badly treated in our country. He wants you to write the British Ambassador. Something like that. He wants to go to England."

"English man," said the boy, pointing at himself proudly. "Help." I didn't see how I could, and as he looked at me, despair began to shade the hopeful shine of his wet eyes. "Help," he repeated reproachfully. "Help. Help."

Orlov gave him a coin and told him the name of a song he wanted to hear. It was a comedy song with unending choruses, and though the boy drudged through it listlessly, even the waitresses laughed and roared out the key lines, which everybody seemed to know. The one-eyed man, angry that there should be such laughter for anything except his trick, climbed on his chair and stood like a scarecrow Jesus, beer oozing from the empty socket and dribbling down his cheek. At five minutes to midnight, closing time, the waitresses began to switch the lights on and off, warningly. But the customers kept the song going, clung to these last minutes, as though they loathed to trade the café's camaraderie for cold streets, the fierce lonely journeys homeward. Orlov said he'd walk me to St. Isaac's Square. But first, a final toast. He proposed, "To a long life and a merry one. Is that what they say?" Yes, I told him, that's what they say.

The boy with the guitar blocked our path to the door. Exiting customers were still warbling his song; you could hear their voices echoing down the street. And in the café the waitresses were shooing out the last die-hards, darkening the lights in earnest. "Help," said the boy, gently catching hold of my sleeve. "Help," he said, his eyes full on me, as a waitress, at Orlov's request, pushed him aside to let us by. "Help, help," he called after me, a door between us now, and the words a muted sound fading into nothing like the night-falling snow.

"I think he's a crazy person," said Orlov.

"New York could've been bombed, for all we know," said Leonard Lyons to the financier Herman Sartorius, who was sitting next to him in a bus that was taking the company on a morning visit to the Hermitage Museum. "I've never been in a place I couldn't read a newspaper, find out what's going on in the world. A prisoner, that's how I feel." Sartorius, a tall, graying, solemnly courteous man, confessed that he too missed Western newspapers and wondered aloud if it would seem "not quite the correct thing" if he inquired at a Leningrad bank for the current New York Stock Exchange quotations.

As it happened, there was a passenger seated behind them who could have supplied any information they wanted. It was his business to know what went on beyond the iron curtain, especially in America. A Russian, his name was Josef ("Call me Joe") Adamov, and he was in Leningrad to tape-record interviews with the *Porgy and Bess* cast for Radio Moscow, the station that beams broadcasts to countries outside the Soviet orbit. Adamov's talents are devoted to programs intended for American, or English-speaking, consumption. The programs consist of news reports, music, and soap operas sudsy with propaganda. Listening to one of these plays is a startling experience, not for the content, which is crude, but for the acting, which isn't. The voices pretending to be "average" Americans seem precisely that: one has absolute belief in the man who says he's a Midwest farmer, a Texas cowhand, a Detroit factory worker. Even the voices of "children" sound familiar as the crunch of Wheaties, the crack of a baseball.

Adamov bragged that none of these actors had ever left Russia, their accents were manufactured right in Moscow. Himself a frequent actor in the plays, Adamov has so perfected a certain American accent that he fooled a native of the region, Lyons, who said, "Gee, I'm dumfounded, I keep wondering what's he doing so far from Lindy's." Adamov indeed seems to belong on the corner of Broadway and Fifty-first, a copy of *Variety* jammed under his arm. Although his slang needs dusting off, it is delivered with a bizarrely fluent side-of-the-mouth technique. "Me, I'm no museum-type guy," he said, as we neared the Hermitage. "But if you go in for all that creepy stuff, they tell me this joint's okay, really loaded." Swart, moon-faced, a man in his middle thirties with a jumpy, giggling, coffee-nerves animation, his shifty eyes grow shiftier when, under duress, he admits that his English was learned in New York, where he lived from the ages of eight to twelve with an émigré grandfather. He prefers to skate over this American episode. "I was just a kid," he says, as though he were saying, "I didn't know any better."

A foreign resident in Moscow, who knows Adamov well, described him to me as "no fool. An opportunist with two fingers in every pie." And an Italian correspondent, another old Moscow hand, said, "Ah, *si*. Signor Adamov. The smiler with the knife." In short, Adamov is a successful man, which means, as it does elsewhere, though far more so in Russia, that he enjoys privileges unknown to the ordinary citizen. The one he values most is a two-room bachelor apartment in Moscow's Gorky Street, where he lives, to hear him tell it, the life of a Turk in his seraglio. "Gimme a buzz you come to Moscow, you wanta meet some cute kids." Meanwhile, he thought some members of the *Porgy and Bess* company were "pretty cute kids," particularly the saucer-eyed singer in the chorus named Dolores ("Delirious") Swann. At the museum, when the sightseers were separated into battalions of twelve, Adamov made a point of joining Miss Swann in a group that included, among others, the Wolferts, Mrs. Gershwin, Nancy Ryan, Warner Watson and myself.

The Hermitage is part of the Winter Palace, which in recent years has been repainted the imperial color, a frosty chartreuse-*vert*. Its miles of silvery windows overlook a park and a wide expanse of the Neva River. "The Winter Palace was started working 1764 and took seventy-eight years to finish," said the guide, a mannish girl with a brisk, whip-'em-through attitude. "It consists of four buildings and contains, as you see, the world's greatest museum. This where we are standing is the Ambassadorial Staircase, used by the ambassadors mounting to see the Czar."

In the ectoplasmic wake of those ambassadors our party followed her up marble stairs that curved under a filigree ceiling of white and gold. We passed through a splendid hall of green malachite, like a corridor under the sea, and here there were French windows where a few of us paused to look across the Neva at a misty-hazy view of that celebrated torture chamber, the Peter-Paul fortress. "Come, come," the guide urged. "There is much to see and we will not accomplish our mission if we linger at useless spectacles."

A visit to the treasure vault was the mission's immediate objective. "That's where they keep the ice, the *real* stuff, crown jools, all that crap," Adamov informed Miss Swann. A dragoon of stunted Amazons, several of them in uniform and wearing pistols strapped round their waists, guard the vault's bolted doors. Adamov, jerking a thumb toward the guards, told Warner Watson, "I'll bet you don't have any female cops in America, huh?"

"Sure," said Watson timidly. "We have policewomen, sure."

"But," said Adamov, his moist moon-face going scarlet with laughter, "not as fat as these, huh?"

While the vault's complicated steel doors were being unlocked, the guide announced, "Ladies will please leave their pocketbooks with the custodians." Then, as though to circumvent the obvious implication, "It is a matter of ladies causing damage dropping their pocketbooks. We have had that experience."

The vault is divided into three small, chandelier-lighted rooms, the first two entirely occupied by the museum's most unique display, a sophisticated panorama of Scythian gold, buttons and bracelets, cruel weapons, papery leaves and wreath garlands. "First-century stuff," said Adamov. "B.C. A.D. all that crap." The third room is intellectually duller, and much more dazzling. A dozen glass-enclosed cabinets (bearing the metal marker of their maker, Holland and Sons, 23 Mount Street, Grosvenor Square, London) afire with aristocratic souvenirs. Onyx and ivory walking sticks, musical birds that sing with emerald tongues, a lily bouquet made of pearls, another of ruby roses, rings and boxes that give off a trembling glare like heat waves.

Miss Swann sang, "But dee-*imonds* are a girl's best friend," and someone who shouted, "Where's that Earl Jackson?" was told, "Oh, Earl—you know that cat wouldn't be up this hour of the day. But he's sure going to be sorry he missed this. Him feeling the way he does about sparkles."

Adamov planted himself in front of the cabinet containing one of the collection's few examples of Fabergé, a miniature version of the Czar's symbols of power: crown, scepter and orb. "It's gorgeous," sighed Miss Swann. "Don't you think it's gorgeous, Mr. Adamov?" Adamov smiled indulgently. "If *you* say so, kid. Personally, I think it's junk. What good does it do anybody?"

Ira Wolfert, chewing on an unlit pipe, was rather of Adamov's opinion. At least, "I hate jewelry," he said, glowering at a tray of blazing froufrou. "I don't know the difference between a zircon and a diamond. Except I like zircons better. They're shinier." He put an arm around his wife, Helen. "I'm glad I married a woman who doesn't like jewelry."

"Oh, I like *jewelry*, Ira," said Mrs. Wolfert, a comfortable-looking woman prone to expressing decisive notions in a tentative tone. "I like *creations*. But *this*, this is all trickery and show-off. It makes me ill."

"It makes me ill, too," said Miss Ryan. "But in quite a different way. I'd give anything for that ring—the tiger's eye."

"It makes me ill," Mrs. Wolfert repeated. "I don't call these things creations. This," she said, indicating a brooch of her own, a straightforward design in Mexican silver, "is what *I* call a creation."

Mrs. Gershwin was also making comparisons. "I wish I'd *never* come here," she said, forlornly fingering her diamonds. "I feel so dissatisfied, I'd like to go home and crack my husband on the head." Miss Ryan asked her, "If you could have any of this you wanted, what would you take?"

"All of it, darling," replied Mrs. Gershwin.

Miss Ryan agreed. "And when I got it home, I'd spread it on the floor and rip off my clothes and just *roll.*"

Wolfert desired nothing, he simply wanted to "get the hell out of here and see something interesting," a wish he conveyed to the guide, who acquiesced by herding everyone to the door and counting them as they left. Some six kilometers later, the group, its ranks thinned by fatigue cases, stumbled into the last exhibit hall, weak-legged after two hours of inspecting Egyptian mummies and Italian Madonnas, craning their necks at excellent old masters excruciatingly hung, poking about the sarcophagus of Alexander Nevsky, and marveling over a pair of Peter the Great's Goliath-large boots. "Made," said the guide, "by this progressive man with his *own* hands." Now, in the last hall, the guide commanded us to "go to the window and view the hanging garden."

"But where," bleated Miss Swann, "where *is* the garden?"

"Under the snow," said the guide. "And over here," she said, directing attention to the final item on the agenda, "is our famous The Peacock."

The Peacock, an exotic mechanical folly constructed by the eighteenth-century clockmaker James Cox, was brought to Russia as a gift for Catherine II. It is housed in a glass cage the size of a garden gazebo. The focus of the piece is a peacock perched among the gilded leaves of a bronze tree. Balanced on other branches are an owl, a cock rooster, a squirrel nibbling a nut. At the base of the tree there is a scattering of mushrooms, one of which forms the face of a clock. "When the hour strikes, we have here a forceful happening," said the guide. "The peacock spreads her tail, and the rooster cackles. The owl blinks her eyes, and the squirrel has a good munch."

Adamov grunted. "I don't care what it does. It's dopey." Miss Ryan took him to task. She wanted to know why he should feel that way about an object of such "imaginative craftsmanship." He shrugged. "What's imaginative about it? A lot of jerks going blind so milady can watch a peacock fan her tail. Look at those leaves. Think of the work went into that. All for nothing. A nonutilitarian nothing. What'cha up to, kid?" he said, for Miss Ryan had started scribbling in a notebook. "What'cha doing? Putting down all the dumb things I say?" Actually, as Miss Ryan was surprised into explaining, she was writing a description of the clock. "Uh-huh," he said, his voice not as genial as his smile, "you think I'm pretty dumb, don't you? Well, put this down. I'll tell you a good reason I don't like it. Because that peacock's gonna go on fanning her tail when I'm dust. A man works all his life, he ends up dust. That's what museums are, reminders of death. Death," he repeated, with a nervous titter that expanded into mirthless guffaws.

A gang of soldiers, part of another tour, approached The Peacock just as the hour chimed, and the soldiers, country boys with their heads shaved bald, their drab uniforms sagging in the seat like diapers, had the double enchantment of gaping at foreigners and watching the golden-eyed winkings of an owl, a peacock flash its bronze feathers in the wan light of the Winter Palace. The Americans and the soldiers crowded close to hear the rooster crow. Man and art, for a moment alive together, immune to old mortality.

It was Christmas Eve. The translators from the Ministry of Culture, under the supervision of their chief, Savchenko, had personally set up a skinny fir tree in the center of an Astoria dining room and decorated it with hand-colored paper cards, wisps of tinsel. The members of the company, sentimental over their fourth Christmas together, had gone on spending sprees: a razzledazzle of cellophane and ribbon spread in a knee-deep, twenty-foot circle round the tree. The presents were to be opened at midnight. Long past that hour, Miss Ryan was still in her room wrapping packages and rummaging through suitcases selecting from her possessions trinkets to take the place of gifts she'd neglected to buy. "Maybe I could give the bunny to one of the kids," she said, meaning the rubber rabbit sent her by Stefan Orlov. The rabbit nestled among her bed pillows. She'd inked whiskers on its face and on its side printed STEFAN—THE BUNNY. "I guess not," she decided. "If I gave him away, no one would ever believe I'd snagged a Russian beau. *Almost* did." Orlov had not telephoned again.

I helped Miss Ryan carry her presents down to the dining room, where she was just in time for the end of the gift-distributing. The children had been allowed to stay up for the party, and now, hugging new dolls and squirting water pistols filled with raspberry soda, they cycloned through the gaudy wrapping-paper debris. The grown-ups danced to the music of the Russian jazz band, which could be heard playing in the connecting main restaurant. Mrs. Breen whirled by, a bit of holiday ribbon floating round her neck. "Isn't it bliss?" she said. "Aren't you happy? After all, we don't spend *every* Christmas in Leningrad!" The waitresses, young English-language students who had volunteered to tend table for the American troupe, demurely refused invitations to dance. "Oh, come on, honey," one waitress was urged, "let's you and me melt that curtain together." Vodka, abetting the spirit of the occasion, had already melted the reserve of the Ministry of Culture representatives. They each had received presents from the company, and Miss Lydia, who had been given a compact, wanted to kiss everyone in sight. "It is too kind, so kind," she said, tirelessly examining her pudgy face in the compact's mirror.

Even the aloof Savchenko, a dour, glacial Santa Claus, or Father Frost, as the fellow is known in Russia, seemed after a while willing to forget his dignity, at any rate was unprotesting when a girl in the cast plumped herself on his lap, threw her arms around him and, between kisses, told him, "How come you want to look like a grumpy old bear when you're just a doll? A living doll, that's what you are, Mr. Savchenko." Breen, too, had affectionate words for the Ministry of Culture executive. "Let's all drink to the man we can thank for this wonderful party," he said, hoisting a tumbler of vodka, "one of the best friends we have in the world, Nikolai Savchenko." Savchenko, wiping away lipstick, responded by proposing another toast. "To the free exchange of culture between the artists of our countries. When the cannons are heard, the muses are silent," he continued, quoting his favorite maxim. "When the cannons are silent, the muses are heard."

The radio man from Moscow, "Joe" Adamov, was busily tape-recording aspects of the party on a portable machine. Eight-year-old Davy Bey, solicited for a comment, said into Adamov's microphone, "Hello, everybody, happy Christmas. Daddy wants me to go to bed, but we're all having a grand time, so I'm not going. Well, I got a gun and a boat, only what I wanted was an airplane and not so many clothes. Any kids would like it, why don't they come over and play with us. We got bubble gum, and I know some good places to hide." Adamov also recorded "Silent Night, Holy Night," which the cast, gathered round the tree, sang with a volume that drowned the next-room thumping of the dance band. Ira Wolfert and his wife added their voices to the choir. The Wolferts, parents of adult children, had booked a telephone call to America. "All our children will be together tonight; tomorrow they go different ways," said Mrs. Wolfert when the caroling ended. "Oh, Ira," she squeezed her husband's hand, "that's the only present I want. For our call to come through." It never did. They waited till two, then went to bed.

After two, the Christmas party infiltrated the adjoining room, the As-

toria's "night club," which is permitted to operate later than twelve on
Saturdays, the only night of the week when patrons outnumber personnel.
The Soviet habit of seating strangers together does not encourage uninhibited conversation, and the cavernous restaurant, occupied to near capacity
by Leningrad's elite, was unreasonably subdued, the merest few, mostly
young army and naval officers with their sweethearts, taking advantage of
the orchestra's respectable rhythms. The rest, artists and theatrical personalities, groups of military Chinese, jowly commissars accompanied by
their uncorseted, gold-toothed wives, sat around bored and uncaring as
castaways on a Pacific atoll.

Earl Bruce Jackson took one look, and said, "What-cha say, cats, let's
get the snakes crawlin', put some hotcha in the pot, skin the beast and
sprinkle pepper in his eyes." Whereupon five members of the company
commandeered the bandstand. The hotel musicians had not the least objection to being ousted. They all were fans of American jazz, and one of them,
a devotee of Dizzy Gillespie, had accumulated a large record collection by
listening to foreign broadcasts and recording the music on discs made from
old X-ray plates. Junior Mignatt spit into a trumpet, banana-fingered
Lorenzo Fuller struck piano chords. Moses Lamar, a powerhouse with
sandpaper lungs, stomped his foot, opened his mouth wide as an alligator.
"Grab yo' hat 'n grab yo' coat, leave yo' worry on de do'step . . ." It was
as though the castaways had sighted rescue on the horizon. Smiles broke
out like an unfurling of flags, tables emptied onto the dance floor. ". . . just
direct yo' feet . . ." A Chinese cadet tapped his foot, Russians packed close
to the bandstand, riveted by Lamar's scratchy voice, the drumbeat riding
behind it. ". . . to de sunny *sunny* SUNNY . . ." Couples rocked, swayed
in each other's arms. ". . . side ah de streeeet!"

"Look at them zombies go!" said Jackson, and shouted to Lamar,
"They're skinned, man, skinned. Throw on the gasoline and burn 'em
alive. Ooble-ee-do."

Mrs. Breen, a smiling shepherd gazing at her flock, turned to Leonard
Lyons. "You see. We've broken through. Robert's done what the diplo-
mats couldn't." A skeptical Lyons replied, "All I say is fiddles play while
Rome burns."

At one of the tables I noticed Priscilla Johnson, the college friend of Miss
Ryan's who was studying Russian law, and writing, so she said, articles on
Soviet love life. She was sitting with three Russians, one of whom, a
gnarled unshaven gnome with frothy black hair, splashed champagne into
a glass and thrust it at me. "He wants you to sit down, and, gosh, you'd
better," Miss Johnson advised. "He's a wild man, sort of. But fascinating."
He was a Georgian sculptor, responsible for the heroic statuary in the new
Leningrad subway, and his "wild man" quality came out in sudden rash
assertions. "You see that one with the green tie?" he asked in English,

pointing at a man across the room. "He's a rotten coward. An MVD. He wants to make me trouble." Or, "I like the West. I have been to Berlin, and met Marlene Dietrich. She was in love with me."

The other couple at the table, a man and wife, were silent until Miss Johnson and the sculptor left to dance. Then the woman, a death-pale brunette with Mongolian cheekbones and green almond eyes, said to me, "What an appalling little man. So dirty. A *Georgian*, of course. These people from the South!" She spoke English with the spurious elegance, the strained exactness of Liza Doolittle. "I am Madame Nervitsky. You of course know my husband, the crooner," she said, introducing me to the gentleman, who was twice her age, somewhere in his sixties, a vain, once-handsome man with an inflated stomach and a collapsing chin line. He wore make-up—powder, pencil, a touch of rouge. He knew no English, but told me in French, "*Je suis* Nervitsky. Le Bing Crosby de Russie." His wife was startled that I'd never heard of him. "No? *Nervitsky?* The famous *crooner?*"

Her surprise was justified. In the Soviet Union, Nervitsky is a considerable celebrity, the idol of young girls who swoon over his interpretations of popular ballads. During the twenties and thirties he lived in Paris, enjoying a minor vogue as a cabaret artist. When that faltered, he went on a honkytonk tour of the Far East. Though of Russian parentage, his wife was born in Shanghai, and it was there that she met and married Nervitsky. In 1943 they moved to Moscow, where she launched a not too prosperous career as a film actress. "I am a painter really. But I can't be bothered ingratiating all the right people. That is necessary if you want your pictures shown. And painting is so difficult when one travels." Nervitsky spends most of the year making personal appearances throughout Russia. He was currently engaged for a series of concerts in Leningrad. "Nervitsky is more sold out than the Negroes," his wife informed me. "We are going to the Negro première," she said, and added that she was sure it would be a "delightful" evening because "the Negroes are so amusing and there is so little amusing here. Nothing but work, work. We're all too tired to be amusing. Don't you find Leningrad absolutely dead? A beautiful corpse? And Moscow. Moscow is not quite as dead, but so ugly." She wrinkled her nose and shuddered. "I suppose, coming from New York, you find us very shabby? Speak the truth. You think *me* shabby?" I didn't think that, no. She wore a simple black dress, some good jewelry, there was a mink stole slung over her shoulders. In fact, she was the best-dressed, best-looking woman I'd seen in Russia. "Ah, you're embarrassed to say. But I know. When I look at your friends, these American girls, I *feel* shabby. There are no nice things next to my skin. It isn't that I'm poor. I have money . . ." She hesitated. Miss Johnson and the sculptor were returning to the table. "Please," she said, "I would like to say something to you privately. Do you dance?"

The band was smooching its way through "Somebody Loves Me," and the crowd on the floor listened to Lamar rasp out the lyrics with transfixed, transfigured faces. ". . . who can it be oh *may*-be *ba*-by *may*-be it's you!" Madame Nervitsky danced well, but her body was tense, her hands icy. "*J'adore le musique des Negres.* It's so wicked. So vile," she said, and then, in the same breath, began to whisper rapidly in my ear, "You and your friends must find Russia very expensive. Take my advice, don't change your dollars. Sell your clothes. That is the way to get rubles. Sell. Anyone will buy. If it can be done discreetly. I am here in the hotel, Room 520. Tell your friends to bring me shoes, stockings, things for close to the skin. Anything," she said, digging her nails into my sleeve, "tell them I will buy *anything*. Really," she sighed, resuming a normal voice and raising it above the shriek of Mignatt's trumpet, "the Negroes are so delightful."

Somewhat set back from the Nevsky Prospekt, there is an arcaded building bearing a marked resemblance to St. Peter's. This is the Kazin Cathedral, Leningrad's largest antireligious museum. Inside, in an atmosphere of stained-glass gloom, the management has produced a Grand Guignol indictment against the teachings of the church. Statues and sinister portraits of the Popes follow each other down the galleries like a procession of witches. Everywhere ecclesiastics leer and grimace, make, in captioned cartoons, satyr suggestions to nunlike women, revel in orgies, snub the poor to cavort with the decadent rich. Ad infinitum the museum demonstrates its favorite thesis: that the church, the Roman Catholic in particular, exists solely as a protection to capitalism. One caricature, an enormous oil, depicts Rockefeller, Krupp, Hetty Green, Morgan and Ford plunging ferocious hands into a mountainous welter of coins and blood-soaked war helmets.

The Kazin Cathedral is popular with children. Understandably so, since the exhibition is liberally sprinkled with horror-comic scenes of brutality and torture. The schoolteachers who herd daily swarms of pupils through the place have difficulty dragging them away from such attractions as The Chamber of the Inquisitors. The Chamber is a real room peopled with the life-sized wax figures of four Inquisitors relishing the agonies of a heretic. The naked victim, chained to a table, is being branded with hot coals by a pair of masked torturers. The coals are electrically lighted. Children, even when pulled away, keep sneaking back for a second look.

Outside the cathedral, on the many columns supporting its arcades, there is another kind of display. Coarse chalk drawings, the usual men's room graffiti, scarcely worth mentioning, except that it seems on first thought an odd place to find it; and on second it doesn't. In a way it belongs.

Antireligious museums were not among the sightseeing projects their hosts had lined up for the *Porgy and Bess* cast. Quite the contrary, on Sunday, Christmas Day, the Soviets provided the choice of attending a Catholic Mass or a Baptist service. Eleven members of the company, including Rhoda Boggs, a soprano playing the part of the Strawberry Woman, went to the Baptist Evangelical Church, whose Leningrad parishioners number two thousand. Afterward I saw Miss Boggs sitting alone in the Astoria dining room. She is a round, honey-colored, jolly-faced woman, always carefully groomed, but now her little Sunday best hat was slightly askew, the handkerchief she kept dabbing at her eyes was wet as a washcloth.

"I'm tore to pieces," she told me, her breasts heaving. "I've been going to church since I can walk, but I never felt Jesus like I felt Jesus today. Oh, child, He was *there*. He was out in the open. He was plainly written on every face. He was singing with us, and you never heard such beautiful singing. It was old people mostly, and old people can't sing like that without Jesus is helping them along. The pastor, there was a sweet old man, he asked us colored people would we render a spiritual, and they listened so quiet, all those rows and rows and rows of old faces just looking at us, like we were telling them nobody's alone when Jesus is everywhere on this earth, which is a fact they know already, but it seemed to me like they were glad to hear it. Anybody doubts the presence of Our Savior, he should've been there. Well, it came time to go. To say good-bye. And you know what happened? They stood up, the whole congregation. They took out white handkerchiefs and waved them in the air. And they sang, 'God Be With You Till We Meet Again.' The tears were just pouring down our faces, them and ours. Oh, child, it churned me up. I can't keep nothing on my stomach."

That evening, with the première less than twenty-four hours away, the windows of the Astoria stayed lighted late. All night footsteps hurried along the corridors, doors slammed and telephones rang, as though a calamity were happening.

In Suite 415, Ambassador Bohlen and his wife entertained a small group of aides and friends who had just arrived with them by train from Leningrad. The gathering, which included Roye L. Lowry, Second Secretary at the Embassy and one of the two diplomats who had "briefed" the company in Berlin, was exceptionally quiet, since the Bohlens didn't want their presence in the hotel known until the last possible moment. They concealed themselves so successfully that the next morning Warner Watson, believing the diplomatic contingent were coming by plane, set out for the Leningrad airport with a bouquet for Mrs. Bohlen. Directly below the ambassadorial apartment, in Suite 315, Mrs. Breen was seesawing on a

Relaxer Board, while her husband polished the precurtain speech he planned to deliver. It had been suggested to him that he might circumvent the Communist propaganda potential in *Porgy and Bess* by pointing out that its picture of American Negroes concerned the long ago, not today, and so he added the line, "*Porgy and Bess* is set in the past. It no more reflects the present than if it were about life under the Czars in Russia." In Room 223, Leonard Lyons was at his typewriter outlining the opening-night column he intended cabling his newspaper, the *New York Post*. "On stage were the flags of both nations, the U.S.S.R. and the U.S.A." he wrote, previewing the event. "The last time an American flag was displayed here was when there were only forty-five states in the union. A representative of the Ministry of Culture phoned to inquire how many states are united now. Yesterday a wardrobe mistress sewed three more stars on the old flag." The item finished a page. Lyons inserted a new sheet with fresh carbons. Instead of throwing the old carbon in a wastebasket, he took it to the bathroom and flushed it into oblivion. It was safer, he felt, to destroy used carbons, otherwise the Soviets, or perhaps rival correspondents, might ferret them out and decipher what he was writing. And indeed, the hotel was seething with journalistic competitors. *The Saturday Evening Post* was there in the person of Charles R. Thayer, Ambassador Bohlen's brother-in-law. Thayer, and C. L. Sulzberger of *The New York Times*, had arrived with the Bohlen party. The *Saturday Review* was sending Horace Sutton, *Time* and *Life* already had a photographer-reporting team on hand, and Mrs. Richard O'Malley, of AP's Moscow bureau, was speeding toward Leningrad aboard the crack Red Arrow Express, the same train which had, the night before, brought CBS correspondent Dan Schorr.

Now, on the second floor, in Room 111, Schorr, a heavyset bachelor in his middle thirties, was simultaneously trying to correct a manuscript, keep a pipe lighted and dictate on the telephone to a stenographer in Moscow. "Okay. Here's the story. You put in the slugs. Let's go," he barked, and began to read from typed pages. "*The Porgy and Bess Company comma believed to be the first American theatrical troupe ever to appear in Russia comma will open its Soviet engagement tomorrow night before a selected audience of two thousand two hundred I* repeat two two oh oh *at Leningrad's Palace of Culture comma but off-stage the Negro actors and singers have already scored a smash hit period The sixty members of the cast comma just by being themselves comma have had a tremendous impact on this comma the second largest city in the Soviet Union* . . . that's right, isn't it? It is the second largest?" For twenty minutes more Schorr droned out anecdotes and fact. Long lines of Leningraders had waited all night in the snow to buy tickets at a top-scale of sixty rubles ($15), a price doubled and tripled on the black market. "Hey, what's a synonym for black market that we can get past the censors? Okay, make it curb price." Toward the end, he was saying, "*They*

*have given Leningrad a Christmas probably unlike any in history period Until
four o'clock this morning they gathered around a Christmas tree dash provided
by a solicitous Soviet government dash and sang carols and spirituals period.*
Yeah, I know I'm overfiling this story. But I got excited. Real excited. You
can see it. The impact of one culture on another culture. And by the way,
listen, I'm having a helluva time. They're a great bunch, these *Porgy and
Bess* people. Like living with a circus."

On Monday morning, the day of the première, the cast met at Leningrad's
Palace of Culture for a final dress rehearsal with full orchestra. Originally
the Soviets had intended housing the production in the attractive Mariinsky theater, but the demand for tickets convinced them they could
double their profit by transferring the opera to the huge Palace of Culture.
The Palace, a pile of muddy-orange concrete, was slapped together in the
thirties. From the outside it is not unlike one of those decaying examples
of supermarket architecture along Hollywood and Vine. Several things
about the interior suggest a skating rink. Its temperature, for one. But Davy
Bey, and the other children in the company, thought it was "a grand
place," especially the vast backstage with its black recesses for hiding, its
fly ropes to swing on, and where the tough backstage crew, strong men
and stronger women, caressed them, gave them candy sticks and called
them *"Aluchka,"* a term of affection.

I rode over to the rehearsal in a car shared by two of the Ministry's
interpreters, Miss Lydia and the tall, personable youth named Sascha. Miss
Lydia, a woman who enjoys her food, was in a fine state of excitement, as
though she were about to sit down to a delicious meal. "We will see it, no?
Now we will *see* this *Porgy-Bess,*" she said, wiggling on the seat. And then
it occurred to me that yes, of course, at last Miss Lydia and her Ministry
colleagues would be able to judge for themselves "this *Porgy-Bess,*" the
myth that had for so long consumed their hours and energy. Even Savchenko would be having his first glimpse. Here and there along the route,
Miss Lydia happily pointed at street placards advertising the show. Breen's
name, repeated often, was in bigger, bolder type than Gershwin's, and the
name of his absent co-producer, Blevins Davis, was omitted altogether.
The day before, Mrs. Gershwin had observed to Warner Watson that in
Russia the name Gershwin seemed to be "riding in the rumble seat"; to
which Watson had replied, "Look, Lee, it's got to be Robert's show this
time. He wants it that way. He's just got to have it."

"How do you sit that still?" Miss Lydia inquired of Sascha. "Now we
see it. Before the ordinary people." Sascha *was* still. He had a seasick,
stricken look, and not without reason. That morning Savchenko had
thrown Breen into a tailspin by telling him that the production's theater

programs were still at the printer and would not be obtainable for another few days. It was an authentic crisis because the programs contained a synopsis of the opera's plot, and Breen was afraid that without this guide the audience would have difficulty following the action. Savchenko offered a solution. Why not have one of the Ministry's translators come before the curtain and, prior to each act, outline the plot? Sascha had been chosen for the task. "How will I handle my feet?" he said, his eyes hypnotized with stage fright. "How will I speak when there is no water in my mouth?" Miss Lydia tried to soothe him. "Think only what an honor! Many important people will be present. You will be noticed. If you were *my* son, Sascha, I would be very proud."

Inside the Palace of Culture's darkened auditorium, Sascha and Miss Lydia found seats in the fourth row. I sat down behind them, between Savchenko and "Joe" Adamov, both of whom were exploring their mouths with toothpicks. Other Russians, some thirty-odd who had finagled invitations to watch the run-through, were scattered around in the first several rows. Among them were Moscow journalists and photographers who had come to cover the première. The orchestra in the pit, an importation from Moscow's Stanislavski theater, was winging through the overture with confident ease. The conductor, Alexander Smallens, a Russian-born American who has made rather a life's work of *Porgy and Bess,* having maestroed its every incarnation, including the original 1935 production, said the Stanislavski was the sixty-first orchestra under his command and the best of the lot. "Superb musicians, and a joy to work with. They love the score, and they have the tempo, the rhythm. All they need now is a little more the *mood.* "

On stage, Breen, wearing a beret, a windbreaker, and a pair of close-fitting frontier pants, motioned the cast into place for the first scene. Flat overhead rehearsal lights shadowed the actors' faces, drained the color from the scenery and accentuated its wrinkled wornness. The set, a simple functional job, depicts a corner of Catfish Row with its balconied houses and shuttered windows. Presently, responding to a signal from Breen, a soprano leaned over a balcony and began to sing the opening song, "Summertime." Miss Lydia recognized the melody. She swayed her head and hummed with the music until Savchenko tapped her on the shoulder and growled an admonition that made her shrink in her seat. Midway through the performance, Adamov dug me with his elbow and said, "I speak pretty good English, right? Well *I* can't figure what the hell they're yelling about. All this dialect crap! I think . . ." But I never heard what he thought, for Savchenko turned round with a look that strangled Adamov. Most of the Russians were as silent as Savchenko could have wished. The rows of profiles, silhouetted in the glow from the stage, remained as severely un-marred by expression as coin engravings. At the end, with the last aria sung, there was a quiet drifting off to the cloakrooms. Savchenko and Miss Lydia, Sascha and two other young men from the Ministry, Igor and Henry, waited together while an attendant brought their coats. I walked over and asked Miss Lydia her opinion of what she'd seen. She bit her lower lip, her eyes darted toward Savchenko, who said firmly, "Interesting. Most interesting." Miss Lydia nodded, but neither she nor Sascha, Igor nor Henry, would venture a different adjective. "Yes," they all said, "interesting. Most interesting."

The average playing time of *Porgy and Bess* is approximately two and a half hours, but this final run-through, involving many pauses for corrections, lasted from 10 A.M. until two in the afternoon. The cast, edgy with hunger and anxious to return to the hotel, were annoyed when, after the theater had emptied of Russian spectators, Breen informed them that the rehearsal was not yet over. He wanted to restage the curtain calls.

As matters stood, and though only the two players in the title roles took individual bows, the pattern of calls already established required six minutes to complete. Not many productions can expect an audience to sustain six minutes of applause. Breen now proposed extending these six minutes indefinitely by contriving what amounted to "a separate little show. Just," he said, "an impromptu thing. Sort of like an encore." It consisted of having a drummer beat a bongo while, one at a time, every winking, waving member of the company sashayed across the stage inviting individual applause. Even the stage manager, the wardrobe mistress, the electricians, and naturally the director himself, were set to receive homage from the audience. One had the choice of two conclusions: either Breen was counting on an ovation of volcanic vigor, or he feared the reverse, and so was insuring prolonged applause by staging this "impromptu" extra curtain call. Obviously, under the delicate diplomatic circumstances, no audience would walk out while the performers were still, in a sense, performing.

Private limousines had been put at the disposal of the leading players. Martha Flowers, who alternates with Ethel Ayler in the role of Bess, and who had been assigned to sing the part that evening, offered me a return ride to the Astoria. I asked if she were nervous about the première. "Me? Uh-uh. I've been doing this show two years. The only thing makes me nervous is, maybe I'm ruining my voice for serious work." Miss Flowers, a young Juilliard graduate, is ambitious to make a reputation as a concert recitalist. She is small and perky. Whether smiling or not, her lips are always pursed downward, as though she'd just tasted a green persimmon. "I'm tired, though. I sure am that. This kind of climate's no good for a singer. You've really got to watch your throat," she said, massaging her own. "The other Bess, you know—Ethel, she's in bed with a bad cold. Got a temperature and everything. So I'll have to sing the matinée tomorrow and maybe the evening, too. Well, a person could ruin their voice *forever*, carrying on like that." She described her schedule between now and curtain time. "I ought to eat something. But first I'll take a bath. Can you float in your tub? Mine's so big I can float. I'll take a nap, too. We start for the theater at six. Maybe six-thirty I'll be slipping into my costume and pinning that old red flower in my hair. Then I guess I'll have a long sit."

At six-thirty, the hour when Miss Flowers was presumably in her dressing room pinning on a paper rose, Mrs. Breen and Mrs. Gershwin were in the Bohlens' suite, where they had been asked to have drinks prior to leaving for the Palace of Culture. Breen himself, too busy to accept the Ambassador's hospitality, had already gone to the theater.

The drinks, Scotch and tap water, were being served by Bohlen's aide, Roye L. Lowry, and Mrs. Lowry, a couple harmoniously matched in their conservative, schoolteacherish demeanor. Mrs. Bohlen's close friend, Marina Sulzberger, the quick-witted wife of the *Times* man, was also present to provide the hostess with conversational assistance. Not that Mrs. Bohlen, a serenely efficient woman with a dairymaid complexion and sensible blue eyes, gives an impression of being unable to keep any conversation afloat, however awkward. But there was, if one remembers the exceedingly reproachful letter Breen had dispatched to Bohlen a few days earlier, a certain awkwardness inherent in this meeting between representatives of Everyman Opera and the U.S. State Department. As for the Ambassador, one would not suppose, from his amicable manner, that he'd ever received such a letter. A career diplomat for more than twenty-five years, a large percentage of them spent at the Moscow Embassy, where he first held Lowry's present post, Second Secretary, and where he was ultimately appointed Ambassador in 1952, Bohlen still resembles a photograph taken the year (1927) he graduated from Harvard. Experience has harshened his sportsman's handsomeness, salted his hair and reduced, rather obliterated, a dreaming naïveté around the eyes. But the direct look of youth, of rugged stamina, has stayed with him. He lounged in his chair, sipping Scotch and talking to Mrs. Breen as though they were in a country room with a warm hearth and lazing dogs on the floor.

But Mrs. Breen couldn't relax. She sat on the edge of her seat, like an applicant for a job. "It's so sweet of you to have come. Just dear of you," she told Bohlen in a small-girl voice that was somehow not quite her own. "It means so much to the cast."

"You don't think we would've *missed* it?" said Bohlen, and his wife added, "Not for anything in the world! It's the high point of the winter. We've thought of nothing else, have we, Chip?" she said, using the Ambassador's nickname.

Mrs. Breen modestly lowered her eyes, a touch of color tinged her cheeks. "It means so much to the cast."

"It means so much to *us,* " said Mrs. Bohlen. "Our life isn't so amusing that we could afford to miss something like this. Why, we'd have got here if we'd had to walk the whole way. Crawled on our hands and knees."

Mrs. Breen raised her eyes for an instant and glanced sharply at the Ambassador's wife, as though half suspecting her of satiric intent; then, reassured by Mrs. Bohlen's straight, clear face, she dropped her gaze again. "It's just dear of you," she whispered. "And of course we're all thrilled about the party in Moscow."

"Oh, yes . . . the party," said Mrs. Bohlen, with detectable resignation. In honor of the company's Moscow première, two weeks hence, the Bohlens had promised to give an official reception at their residence, Spaso House.

"Robert and I do hope Mr. Bulganin will be there. We want to thank him personally for all the courtesy we've received. The Ministry of Culture paid Robert a lovely tribute. Seven ivory elephants." Mrs. Breen was referring to a mantelpiece parade of plastic elephants that Savchenko had presented as a gift to Breen.

"How very nice," said Mrs. Bohlen dimly, as though she'd lost the conversational thread. "Well, of course, we can't be quite sure *who's* coming to the party. We're sending out two hundred invitations, more or less, but since Russians never answer an R.S.V.P., we never know who to expect or how many."

"That's right," said the Ambassador. "You don't count on these fellows until they walk in the door. Any of them. And when they give a party themselves they almost never invite you until the last minute. Everyone in the diplomatic corps keeps the evening free when we know there's going to be a big affair at the Kremlin. We just sit around, hoping the phone will ring. Sometimes we're in the middle of dinner before they invite us. Then it's a rush. Fortunately, you never have to dress for these things," he said, reverting to a previous topic, and a painful one for Mrs. Breen, who, earlier in the day, had been chagrined to learn that Bohlen was unwilling to attend the opening in black-tie. Indeed, driven by her determination to "make everything gala," she had gone a step further and envisioned the Ambassador wearing white tie and tails, which is what her husband planned to do. But, "It never occurred to me to bring a dinner jacket," said Bohlen, fingering a button of the dark gray suit he considered proper to the occasion. "No one wears them here. Not even for a première."

Over in a corner, Mrs. Gershwin and Mrs. Sulzberger were elaborating on the same sartorial theme. "Of *course* we shouldn't dress up. That's what I've told Wilva all along. We went to a ballet the other night and looked perfectly ridiculous. Oh, there's too much fuss around here. I don't know what the fuss is all about. After all, it's *only* little old *Porgy.*"

"Actually," said Mrs. Sulzberger, a Greek-born woman whose clever eyes sparkle with Mediterranean mischief, "it might not be a bad thing for the Russians to see people dressed. There's no excuse to go about looking the way they do. When we first came here, I felt sorry for them," she said, and added that she and her husband had been in the Soviet Union two weeks, staying as house guests of the Bohlens. "I thought the way they dressed, the dreariness of it all, I imagined it was because they were terribly poor. But really, you know, that's not true. They look this way because they want to. They do it on purpose."

"Yes," said Mrs. Gershwin, "that's what I think."

"I wonder," mused Mrs. Sulzberger. "I wonder. Do you suppose the Russians are so awful because they've always been beaten? Or have they always been beaten because they're so awful?"

"Yes," said Mrs. Gershwin, "that's what I think."

Lowry caught the Ambassador's eye, and glanced significantly at his watch. Outside the hotel a limousine was purring its engine, preparing to carry the Bohlens to the theater. Other Zivs, a street-long gleam of them, waited for Mrs. Breen and Mrs. Gershwin, for Savchenko and Adamov and the employees of AP, Time-Life, CBS. Soon the cars would start slithering across the square, like a funeral cortège.

Bohlen swallowed his Scotch and accompanied his guests to the door of the suite. "I don't think you have anything to worry about," he told Mrs. Breen. "The Russians are very musical people. You'll have rubles coming out of your ears."

"Adorable man. And she's charming, too," Mrs. Gershwin remarked to Mrs. Breen, as the two ladies descended the stairs.

"Adorable. But," said Mrs. Breen, her shy little-girl voice suddenly maturing, "Robert and I *did* want it to be gala."

"Well, darling, we can't be gala if we're going to be conspicuous," observed Mrs. Gershwin, whose diamonded decorations made her look as though she were moving in a spotlight. "Frankly, myself, I think it would do the Russians a world of good to see people dressed up. There's no excuse for them to go around looking the way they do. When we first came here, I felt sorry for them, but now . . ."

Across town, at the Palace of Culture, snow-sprinkled crowds were massing on the sidewalk to watch the ticket holders arrive, and inside the theater a sizable number, baking in a blaze of newsreel and television arc lights, were already seated. Baskets of flowers, yellow and white, flanked the stage, and crossed flags, an entwining of stars and stripes and hammer and sickle, floated above the proscenium. Backstage, where the tuning orchestra's chirping flutes and moaning oboes echoed like forest sounds,

Martha Flowers, costumed and completely calm, despite the distant, rising audience-roar, was having, as she'd predicted, "a long sit."

And it was very long. The curtain, announced for eight, went up at nine-five and came down at eleven-forty. By midnight I was back at the Astoria waiting for a call from Henry Shapiro, the UP correspondent in Moscow, who'd said he would telephone me after the première to find out "how it went. What really happened." There is no absolute truth in these matters, only opinion, and as I attempted to formulate my own, tried to decide what I was going to tell Shapiro, I stretched on the bed and switched out the light. My eyes smarted from the recent glare of flash bulbs, I seemed still to hear the soft clickety noise of newsreel cameras. And indeed, lying in the dark, it was as though a film were rushing through my head, a disconnected rampage of pictures: Martha Flowers tripping to the foot-lights to throw the audience a kiss, Savchenko striding through the lobby listening for comments, the terror in Sascha's eyes, Miss Ryan covering her face with her hands. I made a conscious effort to slow the film down, let it start at the beginning.

It began with the audience, an army standing at solemn attention while the orchestra played the national anthems of the two countries: Savchenko had courteously insisted that "The Star-Spangled Banner" should be heard first. Then individual faces came into focus: Ambassador and Mrs. Bohlen, the Sulzbergers, the Lowrys, Miss Ryan and Leonard Lyons, all together in a front row. Near them, on a platform extending from the side of the stage, a squadron of photographers waited impatiently until the anthems ended: then the platform resembled a besieged fortress, photographers firing away while assistants reloaded their cameras. Some, like CBS's Dan Schorr, desperately alternated between cameras and tape recorders as they went to work documenting the precurtain ceremonies. There was no need for such haste. The speeches, and their translations, lasted an hour.

The Russians were brief enough. Konstantin Sergeev, the dapper young ballet master of the Leningrad Theater, shook hands with Breen and, speaking into a microphone, said, "Dear Brothers in art, welcome. We in the Soviet Union have always paid attention and tribute to the art of the United States. We know and cherish the works of such fine artists as Mark Twain, Walt Whitman, Harriet Beecher Stowe, Jack London and Paul Robeson. We appreciate the talents of George Gershwin, and that is why this meeting is so joyous." Afterward, apropos of this speech, Mrs. Gershwin said, "I thought I'd faint when I heard the name Gershwin being lumped in with all those Communists."

Breen bowed to Sergeev, and stepped up to the microphone, a preening, impeccable figure in his trim tuxedo and starched shirt. "He just lost his nerve," said Miss Ryan, explaining why at the last minute her employer had abandoned the idea of wearing white tie and tails. But now, watching Breen react to the applause that greeted him, one wouldn't have guessed there was a nerve in his system. His smooth blond face, bleached by the strong lights and exploding flash bulbs, possessed an inward-gazing remoteness, as though he had for so long dreamed the scene before him that it was still a dream; and when he spoke, the measured, sepulchral timbre of his actor's voice strengthened the impression that he thought himself alone on an empty stage addressing an imaginary audience, practicing, as it were, for an ego-satisfying moment that would someday come true. Imaginary audiences are notoriously submissive; but the Palace of Culture assemblage began to grow talkative themselves as Breen rambled on, the Russian translator trailing behind him. With graceful, *grand seigneur* sweepings of the hand, he introduced Ambassador and Mrs. Bohlen, who rose in their seats to acknowledge applause. The Ambassador had been expected to deliver a speech, but much to Bohlen's relief, and Breen's regret, the Soviets, extremely sensitive to protocol, had asked that this part of the program be deleted because they had no one of "comparable eminence" to make, on the Russian behalf, a rejoinder. Mrs. Gershwin was also introduced, and the conductor, Alexander Smallens, who received a sumptuous hand when Breen announced that Smallens was "born right here in Leningrad." The introductions continued as Breen presented members of the cast who were not performing that evening: Ethel Ayler, the alternate Bess, sufficiently recovered from her cold to have climbed out of bed and into a skimpy, strapless blue gown. And Lorenzo Fuller, the alternate Sportin' Life. Fuller had a "few" words to say, among them a Russian phrase he'd memorized, "*Dobro poshlavat, druzya,*" which means "Welcome, friends." The audience roared approval. But as clock hands crept toward nine, even the frenzied photographers paused to consult watches. "Jesus," said one correspondent, "they ought to have a gong around here. Like Major Bowes." It was as though Breen had overheard him, for abruptly the ceremonial group vacated the stage.

The theater grew quieter than a hens' roost at sunset as the audience settled back, confident that now the curtain would rise and reveal what they'd paid their rubles to see, *Porgy and Bess.* Instead, Sascha appeared. He crossed the stage stiff-legged and wobbly, as though he were walking a plank. A sheaf of typewritten pages quivered in his hands, and his face, bloodlessly pallid, was drenched with sweat. The instant the audience caught wind of why he was there, to read them the opera's plot, the hens' roost turned into a hornets' nest. They couldn't tolerate another syllable *about* the show, they simply wanted to see it; and a mutiny that broke out in the balcony, where rude voices started shouting, spread to the orchestra: the patrons clapped, whistled, stamped their feet. "Poor Sascha, oh, poor boy," said Miss Ryan, covering her face with her hands. "It's too terrible. I can't bear to watch." Several rows back of Miss Ryan, Sascha's two friends, Igor and Henry, slumped on their spines, but Miss Lydia, less squeamish, glared round at her neighbors, as though she'd like to crack them with her pocketbook. On stage, Sascha went on reading, mumbling, as if he were whispering a prayer against the deafening tumult; like Breen before him, he seemed locked in a dream, a numbing, naked-in-the-street nightmare. Smallens flicked his baton, and the overture sounded as Sascha retreated into the wings.

It was soon evident that the audience regretted not having paid more attention to Sascha's résumé of the two-act tale the opera tells. In skeleton, the story is this: a crippled beggar, Porgy, falls in love with a Charleston tart, Bess. Alas, this neurotic young woman is under the wicked influence of two other gentlemen. One, a devilish dope peddler, Sportin' Life, has enticed her into drug addiction, while the second, an alluringly muscular criminal named Crown, monopolizes the heroine's libidinous impulses. Porgy dispenses of the latter rival by killing him, and when he is sent to jail for the deed, Bess alleviates her woes by going on a dope binge, during which Sportin' Life persuades her to forget Porgy and traipse off with him to New York: "That's where we belong, sister" he sings as they head for the sugary lights of Harlem. In the last scene, Porgy, acquitted of Crown's murder, sets out for the North in a goat-drawn cart, believing, and leaving the spectator to believe, that he will find Bess and bring her home. Although this narrative line seems straight as a ruler, the intricate vocal-choreographic terms in which it is developed would confuse any audience where the language barrier is present, particularly if the music, the style of dancing, the directorial approach are each and all virgin territory, as they were to the overwhelming majority of those assembled in the Palace of Culture.

"Summertime" ended, and there was no applause. The entrance of Porgy went unheralded. Leslie Scott, playing the part, finished "A Woman Is a Sometimes Thing," and paused for the acclaim the number ordinarily arouses. The fact that none came caused a temporary lapse of stage action. Recovering, the cast launched into a jazzy crap-game sequence: whispering ran through the audience, as though they were asking each other what it meant, these excited men tossing dice? The whispering gathered momentum and turned into gasps, a tremor of shock, when Bess, making her initial appearance, hiked up her skirt to adjust her garter. Miss Ryan observed to Mrs. Lowry, "If they think *that's* so daring, just wait." The words weren't out of her mouth before Sportin' Life's witty, lascivious gyrations ignited fresh firecrackers of audible astonishment. The crap game concludes with

Crown killing one of Porgy's neighbors; a funeral scene follows: while the murdered man's widow sings a lament, "My Man's Gone Now," the mourning inhabitants of Catfish Row sway in a tribal circle around the corpse. At this point, an important Soviet dignitary turned to a correspondent and said in Russian, "Ah, now I see! They are going to *eat* him." The deceased, undevoured, was trundled off to his grave, and the opera progressed to Porgy's optimistic "I've Got Plenty of Nothin'." Scott, a big and solidly constructed baritone, belted it across the footlights with a fervor that should've stopped the show. It didn't.

The audience's persistent silence seemed not altogether attributable to apathy; rather, for the most part, it appeared to be the result of troubled concentration, an anxious desire to understand; and so, fearful of missing the essential phrase, the significant clue that would unmask the mysteries confronting them, they listened and watched with the brooding intentness of students in a lecture hall. But the first act was almost over before the warmth that comes with comprehension wafted through the theater. It was created by "Bess, You Is My Woman Now," a duet sung by the two principals: suddenly it was clear that Porgy and Bess were in love, that their song was a tender rejoicing, and the audience, rejoicing too, deluged the performers with applause that was brief but heavy, like tropic rain. However, the drought set in again as the music segued into the jamboree fanfare of "I Can't Sit Down," the first-act finale. The scene is peppered with folklorish humor; and, occasionally, isolated chuckles, lonely-sounding patches of laughter, indicated there were persons who appreciated it. The curtain descended. Silence. The house lights began to come up; the audience blinked, as though until this instant they hadn't known the act was over. They caught their breath, like passengers at the end of a roller-coaster ride, and began to applaud. The applause lasted thirty-two seconds.

"They're stunned," said Lowry, parroting the words, though somehow transforming the spirit, of Breen's prophecy. "They've never seen anything like it."

If the Russians were stunned, they were not alone. Several of the American journalists huddled together, comparing notes. "It's not going over," a baffled Dan Schorr complained to a bewildered Time-Life photographer. And Mrs. Bohlen, following her husband up the aisle, was poignantly pensive. Later she told me the thought behind the expression: "I was thinking—well, we've laid an egg. Now what are we going to do about it?"

Out in the crowded lobby, Mrs. Breen smilingly expressed sentiments of a sunnier nature; according to her, the performance was going "beautifully." A correspondent interposed to ask why, in that case, the Russians were "sitting on their hands." Mrs. Breen stared at the questioner as though she thought him certifiable. "But they aren't *supposed* to applaud," she said.

"Robert *planned* it that way. So that there wouldn't *be* any applause. It interrupts the mood."

The Wolferts agreed with Mrs. Breen; they felt the première was turning out a triumph. "First time we've seen the show," said Wolfert. "I don't like musicals. Got no use for them. But this one's pretty good."

Another American, the Russian-speaking Priscilla Johnson, spent the intermission eavesdropping on the customers. "They're quite shocked," she reported. "They think it's awfully immoral. But gosh, you can't blame them for not liking it. It's such a second-rate production. That's what makes me sad. If only it were *really* good, then you could blame them. Too bad, too bad," she said, ruffling her bangs, shaking her head. "This whole setup: the Breens, the publicity and all—gosh, it's just not geared for failure."

Like Miss Johnson, Savchenko and Adamov circulated about sampling opinions. "It's a very big success" was all Savchenko would admit; but Adamov, whose slang was growing richer under the company's tutelage, said, "So a lot of squares don't dig it. They don't flip. So is that big news? You got squares in New York, ain'tcha, man?"

Madame Nervitsky and her crooner-husband passed by. "Oh, we're amazed," she told me, flourishing a sword-length cigarette holder. "Nervitsky thinks it *très dépravé*. Not I. I adore the vileness of it all. The rhythm, the sweat. Really, the Negroes are too amusing. And how wonderful their teeth!" Moving closer, she said, "You did tell your friends? Room 520. Don't telephone, come quietly, bring anything. I will pay very well."

Stefan Orlov was standing at a refreshment counter, a glass of mineral water in his hand. "My friend," he said, clapping me on the shoulder. "What a night we had, yes? The next morning, my wife, she had to beat me out of bed. Tie my shoes and knot my tie. Not angry, you understand: laughing at me." He produced a pair of opera glasses, and peered through them. "I saw Nancy. I wondered if I should try to speak to her. But I said to myself no, Nancy is sitting with fashionable people. Will you tell her that I saw her?" I said I would, and asked if he was enjoying *Porgy and Bess*. "I wish I had a ticket for every night. It's an experience. Powerful! Like Jack London. Like Gogol. I will never forget it," he said, pocketing the opera glasses. A frown creased his forehead, he opened his mouth to speak, changed his mind, took a swallow of water instead, then changed his mind again, and decided to tell me. "The question isn't whether I forget. Or what we old ones think. It's the young people who matter. It matters that they have new seeds planted in their hearts. Tonight," he said, looking around the lobby, "all these young people will stay awake. Tomorrow, they'll be whistling the music. A nuisance, humming in the classrooms. And in the summer, that's what you'll hear: young people whistling along the river. They won't forget."

Backstage, a tranquil climate prevailed as the performers readied themselves for the second act. Leslie Scott, not the least unnerved by the reception of the previous stanza, grinned and said, "Sure, they're kinda slow. But most audiences don't warm up until the duet ["Bess, You Is My Woman Now"], and that went over okay. From here on out, we'll sail." Martha Flowers, freshening her make-up in front of a mirror, said, "This audience, that audience, I don't know the difference. You wouldn't either, you been doing this show two years." But Sascha, lacking Miss Flowers' professional *savoir*, was an alarming sight as he waited in the wings to repeat his role of plot narrator: head bowed, and holding to a dancer's practice bar like a fighter on the ropes, he listened dazedly while his seconds, Igor and Henry, whispered encouragement.

To Sascha's surprise, his return bout was victorious. The audience was eager to hear what would happen in the next act, and Sascha, who two weeks later applied to the Moscow Art Theatre for a drama student fellowship, ecstatically recounted Crown's murder and Porgy's imprisonment. He walked off to one of the largest hands of the evening; Miss Lydia was still clapping after the house lights had dimmed.

The element in the opera which seemed most to disturb the Soviets, its sensuality, reaches a peak of Himalayan proportions in the opening twenty minutes of Act Two. A song "I Ain't Got No Shame" ("doin' what I likes to do"), and the shake-that-thing brand of choreography accompanying it, proved too aptly titled, too graphically illustrated, for Russian comfort. But it was the ensuing scene which contained, from a prudish viewpoint, the real affront. The scene, a favorite of the director's and one he'd kept heightening in rehearsal, begins with Crown's attempting to rape Bess—he grips her to him, gropes her buttocks, her breasts; and ends with Bess raping him—she rips off his shirt, wraps her arms around him and writhes, sizzles like bacon in a skillet; blackout. Areas of the audience suffered something of a blackout, too. "Christ," said one correspondent, his voice carrying in the hush, "they wouldn't get away with that on Broadway!" To which another American journalist, a woman, replied, "Don't be silly. It's the best thing in the show."

Leslie Scott had predicted the second act would "sail"; his forecast was almost verified during the opera's remaining forty minutes. The street-cry song of the Strawberry Woman started favorable winds blowing. Again, like the love duet, the melody and the situation, simply a peddler selling strawberries, was one the Russians could grasp, be charmed by. After that, every scene seemed to be accepted; and though the performance did not sail, perhaps because too much water had already been shipped, at least it floated, wallowed along in a current of less frigid temperature.

As the curtain fell, and the calls commenced, cameramen, scooting up and down the aisles, divided their shots between applauding Russians and salaaming actors. "They're stunned," Lowry once more pronounced, and his wife tacked on the inevitable "They've never seen anything like it." The applause, which one experienced witness described as "nothing compared to an opening night at the Bolshoi," sustained a logical number of curtain calls, then swiftly declined. It was now, when people were leaving their seats, that Breen made his bid for a more impressive demonstration by unleashing the extra-added "impromptu" curtain call he'd rehearsed that afternoon. On came the cast, one by one, each of them cavorting to the beat of a bongo drum. "Oh, no," groaned Miss Ryan. "They shouldn't do this. It's just begging." In the endurance test that followed, the audience compromised by substituting a chantlike pattern of clapping for authentic applause. Three minutes passed; four, five, six, seven. At last, when Miss Flowers had blown a final kiss across the footlights, and the electricians, et al., had been acknowledged, Breen, taking the ultimate bow, permitted the curtain to be lowered.

Ambassador and Mrs. Bohlen, and various Soviet officials, were ushered backstage to shake hands with the cast. "I don't know what all the fuss is about," Mrs. Gershwin gaily cried as she squeezed through the backstage pandemonium. "It's *only* little old *Porgy.*" Savchenko pushed toward Mrs. Breen; stiffly offering his hand, he said, "I want to congratulate you on a very big success." Mrs. Breen dabbed at her eyes, as though drying phantom tears. "That ovation. Wasn't it glorious?" she said, turning to gaze at her husband, who was posing for a photograph with Bohlen. "Such a tribute to Robert."

Outside, I had to walk some distance before finding a taxi. A threesome, two young men and a girl, walked ahead of me. I gathered they'd been part of the *Porgy and Bess* audience. Their voices reverberated down the shadowed, snow-silent streets. They were all talking at once, an exhilarated babble now and again mixed with humming: the strawberry street cry, a phrase of "Summertime." Then, as though she had no true understanding of the words but had memorized them phonetically, the girl sang, "There's a boat that's leavin' soon for New York, come with me, that's where we belong, sister . . ." Her friends joined in, whistling. Orlov had said, "And in the summer, that's what you'll hear: young people whistling along the river. They won't forget."

The promise of these young people who wouldn't forget, who'd been stimulated into new visions: surely, I thought, that was enough to justify my telling Henry Shapiro the première was a success. Not the "bombshell" conquest the proprietors of Everyman Opera had expected; but a victory of finer significance, one that would mature and matter. And yet, as I lay in my room thinking it over, qualms seized me when eventually the telephone rang. "How did it go? What really happened?" were questions to be answered on journalism's unsubtle level. Could I, with any honesty, give Shapiro a radiant account of the opera's overall reception? I preferred to; and suspected that it was what he, quite naturally, wanted to hear. But I let the telephone ring while a plethora of *ifs* plunged around in my head: if the Russians had been able to consult a printed program, if the fanfare and ceremonial aspects had been curtailed, if less had been demanded of the audience, if . . . I quit stalling and picked up the receiver. But the person on the line was Miss Lydia, who said she was sorry, someone had called me from Moscow and been disconnected. I had no more calls that evening.

Reviews of the production were published by two of the city's leading papers, *Smena* and *Evening Leningrad*. In Ambassador Bohlen's opinion, the articles were "By and large, really excellent. Very thoughtful. It shows they took it seriously."

The *Evening Leningrad* critic wrote, "*Porgy and Bess* is a work stamped with brilliant talent and unusual mastery . . . warmly received by the audience." A further fifteen hundred words elaborated on that statement. He praised the score ("Gershwin's music is melodic, sincere, intentionally suffused with Negro musical folklore. There are plenty of really expressive and contrasting melodies"), Breen's direction ("The show is directed with great mastery and rivets one's attention with its dynamic sweep"), the conductor ("The musical part of the performance is on a very high level"), and the cast (". . . plays together with a harmony rarely to be seen . . ."). The libretto, however, provoked a gentle reprimand, for the writer noticed in it "some elements of expressionism and melodrama, and abundance of the customary details regarding criminal investigation." Nor did *Evening Leningrad* forget to press the political pedal: "We, Soviet spectators, realize the corrosive effect of the capitalistic system on the consciousness, the mentality and the moral outlook of a people oppressed by poverty. This lifts Heyward's play, as set to music by Gershwin, into the realms of social drama." But such comments seemed a mere pianissimo compared to the loud chords of propaganda that opponents of the *Porgy and Bess* tour had anticipated.

The second critic, U. Kovalyev, writing in *Smena*, mentioned a factor ignored by *Evening Leningrad:* "The astoundingly erotic coloring of some of the dancing scenes is unpleasant. And it is hard to lay the blame on a specific national dance. It is more the taste of the director and perhaps his kind of 'tradition' stemming from Broadway 'burlesques' and 'revues.' But on the whole," continues Kovalyev, "*Porgy and Bess* presents one of the most interesting events of this theatrical season. It is an excellently performed production, colorful, full of movement and music. It testifies to the high talent of the Negro people. Very possibly not all of the music and the staging will be approved by the Soviet audiences and everything will not necessarily be understandable to them. We are not used to the naturalistic details in the dance, to the excessive jazz sound of the symphony orchestra, etc. Nevertheless the performance broadens our concept of the art of contemporary America, and familiarizes us with thus far unknown facets of the musical and theatrical life of the United States."

These reviews did not appear until Thursday, three days after the opening. By then, their publication was rather an anticlimax and the company was inclined to regard them with a yawn. "Sure it's nice they write okay things, but who cares?" said one member of the cast, expressing a prevalent attitude. "It's not what the Russians think. It's the stuff they're hearing about us back home. *That's* what counts."

The company was already aware of what America was hearing, for late Tuesday afternoon, the day following the première, Breen received a cable on the subject from Everyman Opera's New York office. Miss Ryan typed copies of it, and she was about to put one of them on the company's bulletin board when we met in the lobby. "Hi," she said. "Guess what? Stefan the Bunny called. He wants to take me dancing. Do you think it'll be all right? I mean, as long as he just wants to dance? Anyway, I don't care. I'd go dancing with Jack the Ripper, anything to get away from *Porgy and Bess*," she said, and thumbtacked her typewritten version of the cable to the bulletin board.

LT ROBERT BREEN HOTEL ASTORIA LENINGRAD USSR

WONDERFUL ARTICLES HERE ALL DECEMBER 27 PAPERS STOP ALL MENTION TEN MINUTES STANDING OVATION STOP

JOURNALS HEADLINE—"LENINGRAD GOES WILD OVER PORGY AND BESS" STOP

AP FACTUAL RELEASE INCLUDES GREAT TICKET DEMAND AND SIZE AUDIENCE STOP

TRIBUNE STRESSES WARM AUDIENCE RECEPTION STOP

TELEGRAM HEADLINE—"PORGY WINS PRAISE FROM RUSSIA" OVER AP RELEASE STOP

MIRROR EDITORIAL "HEART TO HEART DIPLOMACY—CAST TAKING LENINGRAD BY SONG WE ARE PROUD OF THEM" STOP

AP RELEASE IN SOME PAPERS SAYS MOSCOW RADIO TERMED PREMIERE GREAT SUCCESS STOP

TIMES EDITORIAL TODAY BY SULZBERGER "PORGY BESS OPENING ANOTHER WINDOW TO WEST"

JOURNAL EDITORIAL TODAY—"MADE TREMENDOUS HIT"

NBC CBS NEWSCASTS FABULOUS

CONGRATULATIONS TO EVERY SINGLE SOUL WITH YOU

"Of course," remarked Miss Ryan, perusing the cable, "that's not *exactly* how it arrived. The Breens did a little adding and editing. There was one line: '*Times* says scored moderate success.' You can bet Wilva cut that out! Well," she said with a smile, a sigh, "why not make a good thing better? Wilva just wants everybody to feel wonderful, and I think that's kind of endearing."

All afternoon members of the company, passing through the lobby, stopped to read the message from New York. It made them grin; they walked away with lightened steps. "What'cha say, man?" said Earl Bruce Jackson to Warner Watson as they stood reading the cable. "We're making history!" And Watson, rubbing his hands together, replied, "Yep, uh-huh. I guess we've got *history* fenced in."

Then It All
Came Down

(1979)

Scene: A CELL IN A MAXIMUM-SECUR-
ity cell block at San Quentin prison in
California. The cell is furnished with a single cot, and its permanent
occupant, Robert Beausoleil, and his visitor are required to sit on it in
rather cramped positions. The cell is neat, uncluttered; a well-waxed guitar
stands in one corner. But it is late on a winter afternoon, and in the air
lingers a chill, even a hint of mist, as though fog from San Francisco Bay
had infiltrated the prison itself.

Despite the chill, Beausoleil is shirtless, wearing only a pair of prison-
issue denim trousers, and it is clear that he is satisfied with his appearance,
his body particularly, which is lithe, feline, in well-toned shape considering
that he has been incarcerated more than a decade. His chest and arms are
a panorama of tattooed emblems: feisty dragons, coiled chrysanthemums,
uncoiled serpents. He is thought by some to be exceptionally good-looking; he is, but in a rather hustlerish camp-macho style. Not surprisingly,
he worked as an actor as a child and appeared in several Hollywood films;
later, as a very young man, he was for a while the protégé of Kenneth
Anger, the experimental film-maker *(Scorpio Rising)* and author *(Hollywood Babylon);* indeed, Anger cast him in the title role of *Lucifer Rising,*
an unfinished film.

Robert Beausoleil, who is now thirty-one, is the real mystery figure of
the Charles Manson cult; more to the point—and it's a point that has never

been clearly brought forth in accounts of that tribe—he is the key to the mystery of the homicidal escapades of the so-called Manson family, notably the Sharon Tate–Lo Bianco murders.

It all began with the murder of Gary Hinman, a middle-aged professional musician who had befriended various members of the Manson brethren and who, unfortunately for him, lived alone in a small isolated house in Topanga Canyon, Los Angeles County. Hinman had been tied up and tortured for several days (among other indignities, one of his ears had been severed) before his throat had been mercifully and lastingly slashed. When Hinman's body, bloated and abuzz with August flies, was discovered, police found bloody graffiti on the walls of his modest house ("Death to Pigs!")—graffiti similar to the sort soon to be found in the households of Miss Tate and Mr. and Mrs. Lo Bianco.

However, just a few days prior to the Tate–Lo Bianco slayings, Robert Beausoleil, caught driving a car that had been the property of the victim, was under arrest and in jail, accused of having murdered the helpless Mr. Hinman. It was then that Manson and his chums, in the hopes of freeing Beausoleil, conceived the notion of committing a series of homicides similar to the Hinman affair; if Beausoleil was still incarcerated at the time of these killings, then how could he be guilty of the Hinman atrocity? Or so the Manson brood reasoned. That is to say, it was out of devotion to "Bobby" Beausoleil that Tex Watson and those cutthroat young ladies, Susan Atkins, Patricia Krenwinkel, Leslie Van Hooten, sallied forth on their satanic errands.

RB: Strange. Beausoleil. That's French. My name is French. It means Beautiful Sun. Fuck. Nobody sees much sun inside this resort. Listen to the foghorns. Like train whistles. Moan, moan. And they're worse in the summer. Maybe it must be there's more fog in summer than in winter. Weather. Fuck it, I'm not going anywhere. But just listen. Moan, moan. So what've you been up to today?

TC: Just around. Had a little talk with Sirhan.

RB (laughs): Sirhan *B*. Sirhan. I knew him when they had me up on the Row. He's a sick guy. He don't belong here. He ought to be in Atascadero. Want some gum? Yeah, well, you seem to know your way around here pretty good. I was watching you out on the yard. I was surprised the warden lets you walk around the yard by yourself. Somebody might cut you.

TC: Why?

RB: For the hell of it. But you've been here a lot, huh? Some of the guys were telling me.

TC: Maybe half a dozen times on different research projects.

RB: There's just one thing here I've never seen. But I'd like to see that little apple-green room. When they railroaded me on that Hinman deal and I got the death sentence, well, they had me up on the Row a good spell. Right up to when the court abolished the death penalty. So I used to wonder about the little green room.

TC: Actually, it's more like three rooms.

RB: I thought it was a little round room with a sort of glass-sealed igloo hut set in the center. With windows in the igloo so the witnesses standing outside can see the guys choking to death on that peach perfume.

TC: Yes, that's the gas-chamber room. But when the prisoner is brought down from Death Row he steps from the elevator directly into a "holding" room that adjoins the witness room. There are two cells in this "holding" room, two, in case it's a double execution. They're ordinary cells, just like this one, and the prisoner spends his last night there before his execution in the morning, reading, listening to the radio, playing cards with the guards. But the interesting thing I discovered was that there's a *third* room in this little suite. It's behind a closed door right next to the "holding" cell. I just opened the door and walked in and none of the guards that were with me tried to stop me. And it was the most haunting room I've ever seen. Because you know what's in it? All the leftovers, all the paraphernalia that the different condemned men had had with them in the "holding" cells. Books. Bibles and Western paperbacks and Erle Stanley Gardner, James Bond. Old brown newspapers. Some of them twenty years old. Unfinished crossword puzzles. Unfinished letters. Sweetheart snapshots. Dim, crumbling little Kodak children. Pathetic.

RB: You ever seen a guy gassed?

TC: Once. But he made it look like a lark. He was happy to go, he wanted to get it over with; he sat down in that chair like he was going to the dentist to have his teeth cleaned. But in Kansas, I saw two men hanged.

RB: Perry Smith? And what's his name—Dick Hickock? Well, once they hit the end of the rope, I guess they don't feel anything.

TC: So we're told. But after the drop, they go on living—fifteen, twenty minutes. Struggling. Gasping for breath, the body still battling for life. I couldn't help it, I vomited.

RB: Maybe you're not so cool, huh? You seem cool. So, did Sirhan beef about being kept in Special Security?

TC: Sort of. He's lonesome. He wants to mix with the other prisoners, join the general population.

RB: He don't know what's good for him. Outside, somebody'd snuff him for sure.

TC: Why?

RB: For the same reason he snuffed Kennedy. Recognition. Half the people who snuff people, that's what they want: recognition. Get their picture in the paper.

TC: That's not why you killed Gary Hinman.

RB: (Silence)

TC: That was because you and Manson wanted Hinman to give you money and his car, and when he wouldn't—well . . .

RB: (Silence)

TC: I was thinking. I know Sirhan, and I knew Robert Kennedy. I knew Lee Harvey Oswald, and I knew Jack Kennedy. The odds against that— one person knowing all four of those men—must be astounding.

RB: Oswald? You knew Oswald? Really?

TC: I met him in Moscow just after he defected. One night I was having dinner with a friend, an Italian newspaper correspondent, and when he came by to pick me up, he asked me if I'd mind going with him first to talk to a young American defector, one Lee Harvey Oswald. Oswald was staying at the Metropole, an old Czarist hotel just off Kremlin Square. The Metropole has a big gloomy lobby full of shadows and dead palm trees. And there he was, sitting in the dark under a dead palm tree. Thin and pale, thin-lipped, starved-looking. He was wearing chinos and tennis shoes and a lumberjack shirt. And right away he was angry—he was grinding his teeth, and his eyes were jumping every which way. He was boiling over about everything: the American ambassador; the Russians—he was mad at them because they wouldn't let him stay in Moscow. We talked to him for about half an hour, and my Italian friend didn't think the guy was worth filing a story about. Just another paranoid hysteric; the Moscow woods were rampant with those. I never thought about him again, not until many years later. Not until after the assassination when I saw his picture flashed on television.

RB: Does that make you the only one that knew both of them, Oswald and Kennedy?

TC: No. There was an American girl, Priscilla Johnson. She worked for U.P. in Moscow. She knew Kennedy, and she met Oswald around the same time I did. But I can tell you something else almost as curious. About some of those people your friends murdered.

RB: (Silence)

TC: I knew them. At least, out of the five people killed in the Tate house that night, I knew four of them. I'd met Sharon Tate at the Cannes Film Festival. Jay Sebring cut my hair a couple of times. I'd had lunch once in San Francisco with Abigail Folger and her boyfriend, Frykowski. In other words, I'd known them independently of each other. And yet one night there they were, all gathered together in the same house waiting for your friends to arrive. Quite a coincidence.

RB (lights a cigarette; smiles): Know what I'd say? I'd say you're not such a lucky guy to know. Shit. Listen to that. Moan, moan. I'm cold. You cold?

TC: Why don't you put on your shirt?

RB: (Silence)

TC: It's odd about tattoos. I've talked to several hundred men convicted of homicide—multiple homicide, in most cases. The only common denominator I could find among them was tattoos. A good eighty percent of them were heavily tattooed. Richard Speck. York and Latham. Smith and Hickock.

RB: I'll put on my sweater.

TC: If you weren't here, if you could be anywhere you wanted to be, doing anything you wanted to do, where would you be and what would you be doing?

RB: Tripping. Out on my Honda chugging along the Coast road, the fast curves, the waves and the water, plenty of sun. Out of San Fran, headed Mendocino way, riding through the redwoods. I'd be making love. I'd be on the beach by a bonfire making love. I'd be making music and balling and sucking some great Acapulco weed and watching the sun go down. Throw some driftwood on the fire. Good gash, good hash, just tripping right along.

TC: You can get hash in here.

RB: And everything else. Any kind of dope—for a price. There are dudes in here on everything but roller skates.

TC: Is that what your life was like before you were arrested? Just tripping? Didn't you ever have a job?

RB: Once in a while. I played guitar in a couple of bars.

TC: I understand you were quite a cocksman. The ruler of a virtual seraglio. How many children have you fathered?

RB: (Silence—but shrugs, grins, smokes)

TC: I'm surprised you have a guitar. Some prisons don't allow it because the strings can be detached and used as weapons. A garrote. How long have you been playing?

RB: Oh, since I was a kid. I was one of those Hollywood kids. I was in a couple of movies. But my folks were against it. They're real straight people. Anyway, I never cared about the acting part. I just wanted to write music and play it and sing.

TC: But what about the film you made with Kenneth Anger—*Lucifer Rising?*

RB: Yeah.

TC: How did you get along with Anger?

RB: Okay.

TC: Then why does Kenneth Anger wear a picture locket on a chain around his neck? On one side of the locket there is a picture of you; on the other there is an image of a frog with an inscription: "Bobby Beausoleil changed into a frog by Kenneth Anger." A voodoo amulet, so to say. A curse he put on you because you're supposed to have ripped him off. Left in the middle of the night with his car—and a few other things.

RB (narrowed eyes): Did he tell you that?

TC: No, I've never met him. But I was told it by a number of other people.

RB (reaches for guitar, tunes it, strums it, sings): "This is my song, this is my song, this is my dark song, my dark song . . ." Everybody always wants to know how I got together with Manson. It was through our music. He plays some, too. One night I was driving around with a bunch of my ladies. Well, we came to this old roadhouse, beer place, with a lot of cars outside. So we went inside, and there was Charlie with some of his ladies. We all got to talking, played some together; the next day Charlie came to see me in my van, and we all, his people and my people, ended up camping out together. Brothers and sisters. A family.

TC: Did you see Manson as a leader? Did you feel influenced by him right away?

RB: Hell, no. He had his people, I had mine. If anybody was influenced, it was him. By me.

TC: Yes, he was attracted to you. Infatuated. Or so he says. You seem to have had that effect on a lot of people, men and women.

RB: Whatever happens, happens. It's all good.

TC: Do you consider killing innocent people a good thing?

RB: Who said they were innocent?

TC: Well, we'll return to that. But for now: What is your own sense of morality? How do you differentiate between good and bad?

RB: Good and bad? It's *all* good. If it happens, it's got to be good. Otherwise, it wouldn't be *happening*. It's just the way life flows. Moves together. I move with it. I don't question it.

TC: In other words, you don't question the act of murder. You consider it "good" because it "happens." Justifiable.

RB: I have my own justice. I live by my own law, you know. I don't respect the laws of this society. Because society doesn't respect its own laws. I make my own laws and live by them. I have my own sense of justice.

TC: And what is your sense of justice?

RB: I believe that what goes around comes around. What goes up comes down. That's how life flows, and I flow with it.

TC: You're not making much sense—at least to me. And I don't think you're stupid. Let's try again. In your opinion, it's all right that Manson sent Tex Watson and those girls into that house to slaughter total strangers, innocent people—

RB: I said: Who says they were innocent? They burned people on dope deals. Sharon Tate and that gang. They picked up kids on the Strip and took them home and whipped them. Made movies of it. Ask the cops; they found the movies. Not that they'd tell you the truth.

TC: The truth is, the Lo Biancos and Sharon Tate and her friends were killed to protect you. Their deaths were directly linked to the Gary Hinman murder.

RB: I hear you. I hear where you're coming from.

TC: Those were all imitations of the Hinman murder—to prove that you couldn't have killed Hinman. And thereby get you out of jail.

RB: To get me out of jail. (He nods, smiles, sighs—complimented) None of that came out at any of the trials. The girls got on the stand and tried to really tell how it all came down, but nobody would listen. People couldn't believe anything except what the media said. The media had them programmed to believe it all happened because we were out to start a race war. That it was mean niggers going around hurting all these good white folk. Only—it was like you say. The media, they called us a "family." And it was the only true thing they said. We *were* a family. We were mother, father, brother, sister, daughter, son. If a member of our family was in jeopardy, we didn't abandon that person. And so for the love of a brother, a brother who was in jail on a murder rap, all those killings came down.

TC: And you don't regret that?

RB: No. If my brothers and sisters did it, then it's good. Everything in life is good. It all flows. It's all good. It's all music.

TC: When you were up on Death Row, if you'd been forced to flow down to the gas chamber and whiff the peaches, would you have given that your stamp of approval?

RB: If that's how it came down. Everything that happens is good.

TC: War. Starving children. Pain. Cruelty. Blindness. Prisons. Desperation. Indifference. All good?

RB: What's that look you're giving me?

TC: Nothing. I was noticing how your face changes. One moment, with just the slightest shift of angle, you look so boyish, entirely innocent, a charmer. And then—well, one can see you as a sort of Forty-second Street Lucifer. Have you ever seen *Night Must Fall*? An old movie with Robert Montgomery? No? Well, it's about an impish, innocent-looking delightful young man who travels about the English countryside charming old ladies, then cutting off their heads and carrying the heads around with him in leather hat-boxes.

RB: So what's that got to do with me?

TC: I was thinking—if it was ever remade, if someone Americanized it, turned the Montgomery character into a young drifter with hazel eyes and a smoky voice, you'd be very good in the part.

RB: Are you trying to say I'm a psychopath? I'm not a nut. If I have to use violence, I'll use it, but I don't believe in killing.

TC: Then I must be deaf. Am I mistaken, or didn't you just tell me that it didn't matter what atrocity one person committed against another, it was good, all good?

RB: (Silence)

TC: Tell me, Bobby, how do you view yourself?

RB: As a convict.

TC: But beyond that.

RB: As a man. A *white* man. And everything a white man stands for.

TC: Yes, one of the guards told me you were the ringleader of the Aryan Brotherhood.

RB (hostile): What do *you* know about the Brotherhood?

TC: That it's composed of a bunch of hard-nosed white guys. That it's a somewhat fascist-minded fraternity. That it started in California, and has spread throughout the American prison system, north, south, east and west. That the prison authorities consider it a dangerous, troublemaking cult.

RB: A man has to defend himself. We're outnumbered. You got no idea how rough it is. We're all more scared of each other than we are of the pigs in here. You got to be on your toes every second if you don't want a shiv in your back. The blacks and Chicanos, they got their own gangs. The Indians, too; or I should say the "Native Americans"—that's how these redskins call themselves: what a laugh! Yessir, *rough*. With all the racial tensions, politics, dope, gambling and sex. The blacks really go for the young white kids. They like to shove those big black dicks up those tight white asses.

TC: Have you ever thought what you would do with your life if and when you were paroled out of here?

RB: That's a tunnel I don't see no end to. They'll never let Charlie go.

TC: I hope you're right, and I think you are. But it's very likely that you'll be paroled some day. Perhaps sooner than you imagine. Then what?

RB (strums guitar): I'd like to record some of my music. Get it played on the air.

TC: That was Perry Smith's dream. And Charlie Manson's, too. Maybe you fellows have more in common than mere tattoos.

RB: Just between us, Charlie doesn't have a whole lot of talent. (Strumming chords) "This is my song, my dark song, my dark song." I got my first guitar when I was eleven; I found it in my grandma's attic and taught myself to play it, and I've been nuts about music ever since. My grandma was a sweet woman, and her attic was my favorite place. I liked to lie up there and listen to the rain. Or hide up there when my dad came looking for me with his belt. Shit. You hear that? Moan, moan. It's enough to drive you crazy.

TC: Listen to me, Bobby. And answer carefully. Suppose, when you get out of here, somebody came to you—let's say Charlie—and asked you to commit an act of violence, kill a man, would you do it?

RB (after lighting another cigarette, after smoking it half through): I might. It depends. I never meant to . . . to . . . hurt Gary Hinman. But one thing happened. And another. And then it all came down.

TC: And it was all good.

RB: It was all good.

Handcarved Coffins

A Nonfiction Account of an American Crime

(1979)

M ARCH, 1975.
A town in a small Western state. A
focus for the many large farms and cattle-raising ranches surrounding it,
the town, with a population of less than ten thousand, supports twelve
churches and two restaurants. A movie house, though it has not shown a
movie in ten years, still stands stark and cheerless on Main Street. There
once was a hotel, too; but that also has been closed, and nowadays the only
place a traveler can find shelter is the Prairie Motel.

The motel is clean, the rooms are well heated; that's about all you can
say for it. A man named Jake Pepper has been living there for almost five
years. He is fifty-eight, a widower with four grown sons. He is five-foot-
ten, in top condition, and looks fifteen years younger than his age. He has
a handsome-homely face with periwinkle-blue eyes and a thin mouth that
twitches into quirky shapes that are sometimes smiles and sometimes not.
The secret of his boyish appearance is not his lanky trimness, not his
chunky ripe-apple cheeks, nor his naughty mysterious grins; it's because
of his hair that looks like somebody's kid brother: dark blond, clipped short,

and so afflicted with cowlicks that he cannot really comb it; he sort of wets it down.

Jake Pepper is a detective employed by the State Bureau of Investigation. We had first met each other through a close mutual friend, another detective in a different state. In 1972 he wrote a letter saying he was working on a murder case, something that he thought might interest me. I telephoned him and we talked for three hours. I was very interested in what he had to tell me, but he became alarmed when I suggested that I travel out there and survey the situation myself; he said that would be premature and might endanger his investigation, but he promised to keep me informed. For the next three years we exchanged telephone calls every few months. The case, developing along lines intricate as a rat's maze, seemed to have reached an impasse. Finally I said: Just let me come there and look around.

And so it was that I found myself one cold March night sitting with Jake Pepper in his motel room on the wintry, windblown outskirts of this forlorn little Western town. Actually, the room was pleasant, cozy; after all, off and on, it had been Jake's home for almost five years, and he had built shelves to display pictures of his family, his sons and grandchildren, and to hold hundreds of books, many of them concerning the Civil War and all of them the selections of an intelligent man: he was partial to Dickens, Melville, Trollope, Mark Twain.

Jake sat crosslegged on the floor, a glass of bourbon beside him. He had a chessboard spread before him; absently he shifted the chessmen about.

TC: The amazing thing is, nobody seems to know anything about this case. It's had almost no publicity.

JAKE: There are reasons.

TC: I've never been able to put it into proper sequence. It's like a jigsaw puzzle with half the pieces missing.

JAKE: Where shall we begin?

TC: From the beginning.

JAKE: Go over to the bureau. Look in the bottom drawer. See that little cardboard box? Take a look at what's inside it.

(What I found inside the box was a miniature coffin. It was a beautifully made object, carved from light balsam wood. It was undecorated; but when one opened the hinged lid one discovered the coffin was not empty. It contained a photograph—a casual, candid snapshot of two middle-aged people, a man and a woman, crossing a street. It was not a posed picture; one sensed that the subjects were unaware that they were being photographed.)

That little coffin. I guess that's what you might call the beginning.

TC: And the picture?

JAKE: George Roberts and his wife. George and Amelia Roberts.

TC: Mr. and Mrs. Roberts. Of course. The first victims. He was a lawyer?

JAKE: He was a lawyer, and one morning (to be exact: the tenth of August 1970) he got a present in the mail. That little coffin. With the picture inside it. Roberts was a happy-go-lucky guy; he showed it to some people around the courthouse and acted like it was a joke. One month later George and Amelia were two very dead people.

TC: How soon did you come on the case?

JAKE: Immediately. An hour after they found them I was on my way here with two other agents from the Bureau. When we got here the bodies were still in the car. And so were the snakes. That's something I'll never forget. Never.

TC: Go back. Describe it exactly.

JAKE: The Robertses had no children. Nor enemies, either. Everybody liked them. Amelia worked for her husband; she was his secretary. They had only one car, and they always drove to work together. The morning it happened was hot. A sizzler. So I guess they must have been surprised when they went out to get in their car and found all the windows rolled up. Anyway, they each entered the car through separate doors, and as soon as they were inside—*wham!* A tangle of rattlesnakes hit them like lightning. We found nine big rattlers inside that car. All of them had been injected with amphetamine; they were crazy, they bit the Robertses everywhere: neck, arms, ears, cheeks, hands. Poor people. Their heads were huge and swollen like Halloween pumpkins painted green. They must have died almost instantly. I hope so. That's one hope I really hope.

TC: Rattlesnakes aren't that prevalent in these regions. Not rattlesnakes of that caliber. They must have been brought here.

JAKE: They were. From a snake farm in Nogales, Texas. But now's not the time to tell you how I know that.

> (Outside, crusts of snow laced the ground; spring was a long way off —a hard wind whipping the window announced that winter was still with us. But the sound of the wind was only a murmur in my head underneath the racket of rattling rattlesnakes, hissing tongues. I saw the car dark under a hot sun, the swirling serpents, the human heads growing green, expanding with poison. I listened to the wind, letting it wipe the scene away.)

JAKE: 'Course, we don't know if the Baxters ever got a coffin. I'm sure they did; it wouldn't fit the pattern if they hadn't. But they never mentioned receiving a coffin, and we never found a trace of it.

TC: Perhaps it got lost in the fire. But wasn't there someone with them, another couple?

JAKE: The Hogans. From Tulsa. They were just friends of the Baxters who were passing through. The killer never meant to kill them. It was an accident.

See, what happened was: the Baxters were building a fancy new house, but the only part of it that was really finished was the basement. All the rest was still under construction. Roy Baxter was a well-to-do man; he could've afforded to rent this whole motel while his house was being built. But he chose to live in this underground basement, and the only entrance to it was through a trap door.

It was December—three months after the rattlesnake murders. All we know for certain is: the Baxters invited this couple from Tulsa to spend the night with them in their basement. And sometime just before dawn one humdinger of a fire broke out in that basement, and the four people were incinerated. I mean that literally: burned to ashes.

TC: But couldn't they have escaped through the trap door?

JAKE (twisting his lips, snorting): Hell, no. The arsonist, the murderer, had piled cement blocks on top of it. King Kong couldn't have budged it.

TC: But obviously there had to be some connection between the fire and the rattlesnakes.

JAKE: That's easy to say now. But damned if I could make any connection. We had five guys working this case; we knew more about George and Amelia Roberts, about the Baxters and the Hogans, than they ever knew about themselves. I'll bet George Roberts never knew his wife had had a baby when she was fifteen and had given it away for adoption.

'Course, in a place this size, everybody more or less knows everybody else, at least by sight. But we could find nothing that linked the victims. Or any motivations. There was no reason, none that we could find, why anybody would want to kill any of those people. (He studied his chessboard; he lit a pipe and sipped his bourbon) The victims, all of them were strangers to me. I'd never heard of them till they were dead. But the next fellow was a friend of mine. Clem Anderson. Second-generation Norwegian; he'd inherited a ranch here from his father, a pretty nice spread. We'd gone to college together, though he was a freshman when I was a senior. He married an old girl friend of mine, wonderful girl, the only girl I've ever seen with lavender eyes. Like amethyst. Sometimes, when I'd had a snootful, I used to talk about Amy and her amethyst eyes, and my wife didn't think it was one bit funny. Anyway, Clem and Amy got married and settled out here and had seven children. I had dinner at their house the night before he got killed, and Amy said the only regret she had in life was that she hadn't had more children.

But I'd been seeing a lot of Clem right along. Ever since I came out here on the case. He had a wild streak, he drank too much; but he was shrewd, he taught me a lot about this town.

One night he called me here at the motel. He sounded funny. He said he had to see me right away. So I said come on over. I thought he was drunk, but it wasn't that—he was scared. Know why?

TC: Santa Claus had sent him a present.

JAKE: Uh-huh. But you see, he didn't know what it was. What it meant. The coffin, and its possible connection to the rattlesnake murders, had never been made public. We were keeping that a secret. I had never mentioned the matter to Clem.

So when he arrived in this very room, and showed me a coffin that was an exact replica of the one the Robertses had received, I knew my friend was in great danger. It had been mailed to him in a box wrapped in brown paper; his name and address were printed in an anonymous style. Black ink.

TC: And was there a picture of him?

JAKE: Yes. And I'll describe it carefully because it is very relevant to the manner of Clem's death. Actually, I think the murderer meant it as a little joke, a sly hint as to how Clem was going to die.

In the picture, Clem is seated in a kind of jeep. An eccentric vehicle of his own invention. It had no top and it had no windshield, nothing to protect the driver at all. It was just an engine with four wheels. He said he'd never seen the picture before, and had no idea who had taken it or when.

Now I had a difficult decision. Should I confide in him, admit that the Roberts family had received a similar coffin before their deaths, and that the Baxters probably had as well? In some ways it might be better not to inform him: that way, if we kept close surveillance, he might lead us to the killer, and do it more easily by not being aware of his danger.

TC: But you decided to tell him.

JAKE: I did. Because, with this second coffin in hand, I was certain the murders were connected. And I felt that Clem must know the answer. He *must*.

But after I explained the significance of the coffin, he went into shock. I had to slap his face. And then he was like a child; he lay down on the bed and began to cry: "Somebody's going to kill me. Why? Why?" I told him: "Nobody's going to kill you. I can promise you that. But *think*, Clem! What do you have in common with these people who *did* die? There must be something. Maybe something very trivial." But all he could say was: "I don't know. I don't know." I forced him to drink until he was drunk enough to fall asleep. He spent the night here. In the morning he was calmer. But he still could not think of anything that connected him with the crimes, see how he in any way fitted into a pattern. I told him not to discuss the coffin with anyone, not even his wife; and I told him not to worry—I was importing an extra two agents just to keep an eye on him.

TC: And how long was it before the coffin-maker kept his promise?

JAKE: Oh, I think he must have been enjoying it. He teased it along like a fisherman with a trout trapped in a bowl. The Bureau recalled the extra agents, and finally even Clem seemed to shrug it off. Six months went by. Amy called and invited me out to dinner. A warm summer night. The air was full of fireflies. Some of the children chased about catching them and putting them into jars.

As I was leaving, Clem walked me out to my car. A narrow river ran along the path where it was parked, and Clem said: "About that connection business. The other day I suddenly thought of something. The river." I said what river; and he said that river, the one flowing past us. "It's kind of a complicated story. And probably silly. But I'll tell you the next time I see you."

Of course I never saw him again. At least, not alive.

TC: It's almost as though he must have overheard you.

JAKE: Who?

TC: Santa Claus. I mean, isn't it curious that after all those months Clem Anderson mentions the river, and the very next day, before he can tell you why he suddenly remembered the river, the murderer kept his promise?

JAKE: How's your stomach?

TC: Okay.

JAKE: I'll show you some photographs. But better pour yourself a stiff one. You'll need it.

> (The pictures, three of them, were glossy black-and-whites made at night with a flash camera. The first was of Clem Anderson's home-made jeep on a narrow ranch road, where it had overturned and was lying on its side, headlights still shining. The second photograph was of a headless torso sprawled across the same road: a headless man wearing boots and Levis and a sheepskin jacket. The last picture was of the victim's head. It could not have been more cleanly severed by a guillotine or a master surgeon. It lay alone among some leaves, as though a prankster had tossed it there. Clem Anderson's eyes were open, but they did not look dead, merely serene, and except for a jagged gash along the forehead, his face seemed as calm, as unmarked by violence as his innocent, pale Norwegian eyes. As I examined the photographs, Jake leaned over my shoulder, looking at them with me.)

JAKE: It was around dusk. Amy was expecting Clem home for supper. She sent one of their boys down to the main road to meet him. It was the boy who found him.

First he saw the overturned car. Then, a hundred yards farther on, he found the body. He ran back home, and his mother called me. I cursed myself up one row and down the other. But when we drove out there, it was one of my agents who discovered the head. It was quite a distance from the body. In fact, it was still lying where the wire had hit him.

TC: The wire, yes. I never have understood about the wire. It's so—

JAKE: Clever?

TC: More than clever. Preposterous.

JAKE: Nothing preposterous about it. Our friend had simply figured out a nice neat way to decapitate Clem Anderson. Kill him without any possibility of witnesses.

TC: I suppose it's the mathematical element. I'm always bewildered by anything involving mathematics.

JAKE: Well, the gentleman responsible for this certainly has a mathematical mind. At least he had a lot of very accurate measuring to do.

TC: He strung a wire between two trees?

JAKE: A tree and a telephone pole. A strong steel wire sharpened thin as a razor. Virtually invisible, even in broad daylight. But at dusk, when Clem turned off the highway and was driving in that crazy little wagon along that narrow road, he couldn't possibly have glimpsed it. It caught him exactly where it was supposed to: just under the chin. And, as you can see, sliced off his head as easily as a girl picking petals off a daisy.

TC: So many things could have gone *wrong*.

JAKE: What if they had? What's one failure? He would have tried again. And continued till he succeeded.

TC: *That's* what's so preposterous. He always does succeed.

JAKE: Yes and no. But we'll come back to that later.

(Jake slipped the pictures in a manila envelope. He sucked on his pipe and combed his fingers through his cowlicked hair. I was silent, for I felt a sadness had overtaken him. Finally I asked if he was tired, would he rather I left him? He said no, it was only nine o'clock, he never went to bed before midnight.)

TC: Are you here all alone now?

JAKE: No, Christ, I'd go crazy. I take turns with two other agents. But I'm still the principal guy on the case. And I want it that way. I've got a real investment here. And I'm going to nail our chum if it's the last thing I ever do. He'll make a mistake. In fact, he's already made some. Though I can't say that the manner in which he disposed of Dr. Parsons was one of them.

TC: The coroner?

JAKE: The coroner. The skinny itsy-bitsy hunchbacked little coroner.

TC: Let's see, now. At first you thought that was a suicide?

JAKE: If you'd known Dr. Parsons, you'd have thought it was a suicide, too. There was a man who had every reason to kill himself. Or get himself killed. His wife's a beautiful woman, and he had her hooked on morphine; that's how he got her to marry him. He was a loan shark. An abortionist. At least a dozen dotty old women left him everything in their wills. A true-blue scoundrel, Dr. Parsons.

TC: So you didn't like him?

JAKE: Nobody did. But what I said before was wrong. I said Parsons was a guy who had every reason to kill himself. Actually, he had no reason at all. God was in His heaven, and the sun was shining on Ed Parsons right around the clock. The only thing bothering him was he had ulcers. And a kind of permanent indigestion. He always carried around these big bottles of Maalox. Polished off a couple of those a day.

TC: All the same, everyone was surprised when they heard Dr. Parsons had killed himself?

JAKE: Well, no. Because nobody thought he had killed himself. Not at first.

TC: Sorry, Jake. But I'm getting confused again.

> (Jake's pipe had gone out; he dumped it in an ashtray and unwrapped a cigar, which he did not light; it was an object to chew on, not to smoke. A dog with a bone.)

To begin with, how long was it between funerals? Between Clem Anderson's funeral and Dr. Parsons'?

JAKE: Four months. Just about.

TC: And did Santa send the doctor a gift?

JAKE: Wait. Wait. You're going too fast. The day Parsons died—well, we just thought he had died. Plain and simple. His nurse found him lying on the floor of his office. Alfred Skinner, another doctor here in town, said he'd probably had a heart attack; it would take an autopsy to find out for sure.

That same night I got a call from Parsons' nurse. She said Mrs. Parsons would like to talk to me, and I said fine, I'll drive out there now.

Mrs. Parsons received me in her bedroom, a room I gather she seldom leaves; confined there, I suppose, by the pleasures of morphine. Certainly she isn't an invalid, not in any ordinary sense. She's a lovely woman, and a quite healthy-looking one. Good color in her cheeks, though her skin is smooth and pale as pearls. But her eyes were too bright, the pupils dilated.

She was lying in bed, propped up by a pile of lace-covered pillows. I noticed her fingernails—so long and carefully varnished; and her hands were very elegant, too. But what she was holding in her hands wasn't very elegant.

TC: A gift?

JAKE: Exactly the same as the others.

TC: What did she say?

JAKE: She said "I think my husband was murdered." But she was very calm; she didn't seem upset, under any stress at all.

TC: Morphine.

JAKE: But it was more than that. She's a woman who has already left life. She's looking back through a door—without regret.

TC: Did she realize the significance of the coffin?

JAKE: Not really, no. And neither would her husband. Even though he was the county coroner, and in theory was part of our team, we never confided in him. He knew nothing about the coffins.

TC: Then why did she think her husband had been murdered?

JAKE (chewing his cigar, frowning): *Because* of the coffin. She said her husband had shown it to her a few weeks ago. He hadn't taken it seriously; he thought it was just a spiteful gesture, something sent to him by one of his enemies. But *she* said—she said the moment she saw the coffin and saw the picture of him inside it—she felt "a shadow" had fallen. Strange, but I think she loved him. That beautiful woman. That bristling little hunchback.

When we said goodnight I took the coffin with me and impressed on her the importance of not mentioning it to anyone. After that, all we could do was wait for the autopsy report. Which was: Death by poisoning, probably self-administered.

TC: But *you* knew it was a murder.

JAKE: I knew. And Mrs. Parsons knew. But everybody else thought it was a suicide. Most of them still think so.

TC: And what brand of poison did our friend choose?

JAKE: Liquid nicotine. A very pure poison, fast and powerful, colorless, odorless. We don't know exactly how it was administered, but I suspect it was mixed together with some of the doctor's beloved Maalox. One good gulp, and down you go.

TC: Liquid nicotine. I've never heard of it.

JAKE: Well, it's not exactly a name brand—like arsenic. Speaking of our friend, I came across something the other day, something by Mark Twain, that struck me as very appropriate. (After searching his bookshelves, and finding the volume he wanted, Jake paced the room, reading aloud in a voice unlike his own: a hoarse, angry voice) "Of all the creatures that were made, man is the most *detestable*. Of the entire brood he is the only one, the solitary one, that possesses malice. That is the basest of all instincts, passions, vices—the most hateful. He is the only creature that inflicts pain for sport, knowing it to *be* pain. Also in all the list, he is the only creature that has a nasty mind." (Jake banged the book shut and threw it on the bed) Detestable. Malicious. A nasty mind. Yessir, that describes Mr. Quinn perfectly. Not the whole of him. Mr. Quinn is a man of varied talents.

TC: You never told me his name before.

JAKE: I've only known it myself the last six months. But that's it. Quinn.
(Again and again Jake slammed a hard fist into a cupped hand, like an angry prisoner too long confined, frustrated. Well, he had now been imprisoned by this case for many years; great fury, like great whiskey, requires long fermentation.)

Robert Hawley Quinn, Esquire. A most esteemed gentleman.

TC: But a gentleman who makes mistakes. Otherwise, you wouldn't know his name. Or rather, you wouldn't know he *was* our friend.

JAKE: (Silence; he's not listening)

TC: Was it the snakes? You said they came from a Texas snake farm. If you know that, then you must know who bought them.

JAKE (anger gone; yawning): What?

TC: Incidentally, why were the snakes injected with amphetamine?

JAKE: Why do you think? To stimulate them. Increase their ferocity. It was like throwing a lighted match into a gasoline tank.

TC: I wonder, though. I wonder how he managed to inject the snakes, and install them in that car, all without getting bitten himself.

JAKE: He was taught how to do it.

TC: By whom?

JAKE: By the woman who sold him the snakes.

TC: A *woman*?

JAKE: The snake farm in Nogales, it's owned by a woman. You think that's funny? My oldest boy married a girl who works for the Miami police department; she's a professional deep-sea diver. The best car mechanic I know is a woman—

> (The telephone interrupted; Jake glanced at his wristwatch and smiled, and his smile, so real and relaxed, told me not only that he knew who the caller was, but that it was someone whose voice he'd been happily expecting to hear.)

Hello, Addie. Yeah, he's here. He says it's spring in New York; I said he should've stayed there. Naw, nothin'. Just knocking off some drinks and discussing you-know-what. Is tomorrow Sunday? I thought it was Thursday. Maybe I'm losing my marbles. Sure, we'd love to come to dinner. Addie—don't *worry* about it. He'll like anything you cook. You're the greatest cook either side of the Rockies, east or west. So don't make a big deal out of it. Yeah, well, maybe that raisin pie with the apple crust. Lock your doors. Sleep tight. Yes, I do. You know I do. *Buenas noches.*

> (After he'd hung up, his smile remained, broadened. At last he lit the cigar, puffed on it with pleasure. He pointed at the phone, chuckled.)

That was the mistake Mr. Quinn made. Adelaide Mason. She invited us to dinner tomorrow.

TC: And who is Mrs. Mason?

JAKE: *Miss* Mason. She's a terrific cook.

TC: But other than that?

JAKE: Addie Mason was what I had been waiting for. My big break.

You know, my wife's dad was a Methodist minister. She was very serious about the whole family going to church. I used to get out of it as much as I could, and after she died I never went at all. But about six months ago the Bureau was ready to close shop on this case. We'd spent a lot of time and a lot of money. And we had nothing to show for it; no case at all. Eight murders, and not a single clue that would link the victims together to produce some semblance of a motive. Nothing. Except those three little handcarved coffins.

I said to myself: No! No, it can't be! There's a *mind* behind all this, a reason. I started going to church. There's nothing to do here on Sunday anyway. Not even a golf course. And I prayed: Please, God, don't let this sonofabitch get away with it!

Over on Main Street there's a place called the Okay Café. Everybody knows you can find me there just about any morning between eight and ten. I have my breakfast in the corner booth, and then just hang around reading the papers and talking to the different guys, local businessmen, that stop by for a cup of coffee.

Last Thanksgiving Day, I was having breakfast there as usual. I had the place pretty much to myself, it being a holiday and all; and I was in low spirits anyway—the Bureau was putting the final pressure on me to close this case and clear out. Christ, it wasn't that I didn't want to dust off this damn town! I sure as hell did. But the idea of quitting, of leaving that devil to dance on all those graves, made me sick to my guts. One time, thinking about it, I did vomit. I actually did.

Well, suddenly Adelaide Mason walked into the café. She came straight to my table. I'd met her many times, but I'd never really talked to her. She's a schoolteacher, teaches first grade. She lives here with her sister, Marylee, a widow. Addie Mason said: "Mr. Pepper, surely you're not going to spend Thanksgiving in the Okay Café? If you haven't other plans, why don't you take dinner at our house? It's just my sister and myself." Addie isn't a nervous woman, but despite her smiles and cordiality, she seemed, hmnn, distracted. I thought: Maybe she considers it not quite proper for an unmarried lady to invite an unmarried man, a mere acquaintance, to her home. But before I could say yes or no, she said: "To be truthful, Mr. Pepper, I have a problem. Something I need to discuss with you. This will give us the chance. Shall we say noon?"

I've never eaten better food—and instead of turkey they served squabs with wild rice and a good champagne. All during the meal Addie kept the conversation moving in a very amusing manner. She didn't appear nervous at all, but her sister did.

After dinner we sat down in the living room with coffee and brandy. Addie excused herself from the room, and when she came back she was carrying—

TC: Two guesses?

JAKE: She handed it to me, and said: "This is what I wanted to discuss with you."

(Jake's thin lips manufactured a smoke ring, then another. Until he sighed, the only sound in the room was the meowing wind clawing at the window.)

You've had a long trip. Maybe we ought to call it a night.

TC: You mean you're going to leave me hanging out here?

JAKE (seriously, but with one of his mischievously ambiguous grins): Just until tomorrow. I think you should hear Addie's story from Addie herself. Come along; I'll walk you to your room.

(Oddly, sleep struck me as though I'd been hit by a thief's blackjack; it *had* been a long journey, my sinus was troubling me, I was tired. But within minutes I was awake; or, rather, I entered some sphere between sleep and wakefulness, my mind like a crystal lozenge, a suspended instrument that caught the reflections of spiraling images: a man's head among leaves, the windows of a car streaked with venom, the eyes of serpents sliding through heat-mist, fire flowing from the earth, scorched fists pounding at a cellar door, taut wire gleaming in the twilight, a torso on a roadway, a head among leaves, fire, fire, fire flowing like a river, river, river. Then a telephone rings.)

MAN'S VOICE: How about it? Are you going to sleep all day?

TC (the curtains are drawn, the room is dark, I don't know where I am, who I am): Hello?

MAN'S VOICE: Jake Pepper speaking. Remember him? Mean guy? With mean blue eyes?

TC: Jake! What time is it?

JAKE: A little after eleven. Addie Mason's expecting us in about an hour. So jump under the shower. And wear something warm. It's snowing outside.

(It was a heavy snow, thick flakes too heavy to float; it fell to the ground and covered it. As we drove away from the motel in Jake's car, he turned on his windshield wipers. Main Street was gray and white and empty, lifeless except for a solitary traffic light winking its colors. Everything was closed, even the Okay Café. The somberness, the gloomy snow-silence, infected us; neither of us spoke. But I sensed that Jake was in a good mood, as though he were anticipating pleasant events. His healthy face was shiny, and he smelled, a bit too sharply, of after-shave lotion. Though his hair was rumpled as ever, he was carefully dressed—but not as though he was headed for church. The red tie he wore was appropriate for a more festive occasion. A suitor en route to a rendezvous? The possibility had occurred to me last night when I'd heard him talking to Miss Mason; there was a tone, a timbre, an intimacy.

But the instant I met Adelaide Mason, I crossed the thought right out of my mind. It didn't matter how bored and lonely Jake might be, the woman was simply too plain. That, at least, was my initial impression. She was somewhat younger than her sister, Marylee Connor, who was a woman in her late forties; her face was a nice face, amiable, but too strong, masculine—cosmetics would only have underlined this quality, and very wisely she wore none. Cleanliness was her most attractive physical feature—her brown bobbed hair, her fingernails, her skin: it was as though she bathed in some special spring rain. She and her sister were fourth-generation natives of the town, and she had been teaching school there since she left college; one wondered why —with her intelligence, her character and general sophistication, it was surprising that she hadn't sought a vaster auditorium for her abilities than a schoolroom full of six-year-olds. "No," she told me, "I'm very happy. I'm doing what I enjoy. Teaching first grade. To be there at the beginning, that's what I like. And with first-graders, you see, I get to teach all subjects. That includes manners. Manners are very important. So few of my children ever learn any at home."

The rambling old house that the sisters shared, a family inheritance, reflected, in its warm soothing comfort, its civilized solid colors and atmospheric "touches," the personality of the younger woman, for Mrs. Connor, agreeable as she was, lacked Adelaide Mason's selective eye, imagination.

The living room, mostly blue and white, was filled with flowering plants, and contained an immense Victorian birdcage, the residence of a half-dozen musical canaries. The dining room was yellow and white and green, with pine-plank floors, bare and polished mirror-bright; logs blazed in a big fireplace. Miss Mason's culinary gifts were even greater than Jake had claimed. She served an extraordinary Irish stew, an amazing apple and raisin pie; and there was red wine, white wine, champagne. Mrs. Connor's husband had left her well-off.

It was during dinner that my original impression of our younger hostess began to change. Yes, very definitely an understanding existed between Jake and this lady. They were lovers. And watching her more attentively, seeing her, as it were, through Jake's eyes, I began to appreciate his unmistakable sensual interest. True, her face was flawed, but her figure, displayed in a close-fitting gray jersey dress, was adequate, not bad really; and she *acted* as though it was *sensational*: a rival to the sexiest film star imaginable. The sway of her hips, the loose movements of her fruity breasts, her contralto voice, the fragility of her hand-gestures: all ultra seductive, ultra feminine without being effeminate. Her power resided in her attitude: she behaved as though she believed she was irresistible; and whatever her opportunities may have been, the style of the woman implied an erotic history complete with footnotes.

As dinner ended, Jake looked at her as if he'd like to march her straight into the bedroom: the tension between them was as taut as the steel wire that had severed Clem Anderson's head. However, he un-

wrapped a cigar, which Miss Mason proceeded to light for him. I
laughed.)

JAKE: Eh?

TC: It's like an Edith Wharton novel. *The House of Mirth*—where ladies are
forever lighting gentlemen's cigars.

MRS. CONNOR (defensively): That's quite the custom here. My mother always lighted our father's cigars. Even though she disliked the aroma. Isn't
that so, Addie?

ADDIE: Yes, Marylee. Jake, would you like more coffee?

JAKE: Sit still, Addie. I don't want anything. It was a wonderful dinner,
and it's time for you to quiet down. Addie? How do you feel about the
aroma?

ADDIE (*almost* blushing): I'm very partial to the smell of a good cigar. If I
smoked, I'd smoke cigars myself.

JAKE: Addie, let's go back to last Thanksgiving. When we were sitting
around like we are now.

ADDIE: And I showed you the coffin?

JAKE: I want you to tell my friend your story. Just as you told it to me.

MRS. CONNOR (pushing back her chair): Oh, please! Must we talk about that?
Always! Always! I have nightmares.

ADDIE (rising, placing an arm around her sister's shoulder): That's all right,
Marylee. We won't talk about it. We'll move to the living room, and you
can play the piano for us.

MRS. CONNOR: It's so *vile.* (Then, looking at me) I'm sure you think I'm
a dreadful sissy. No doubt I am. In any event, I've had too much wine.

ADDIE: Darling, what you need is a nap.

MRS. CONNOR: A nap? Addie, how many times have I told you? I have *night-*
mares. (Now, recovering) Of course. A nap. If you'll excuse me.

(As her sister departed, Addie poured herself a glass of red wine, lifted
it, letting the glow from the fireplace enhance its scarlet sparkle. Her
eyes drifted from the fire to the wine to me. Her eyes were brown,
but the various illuminations—firelight, candles on the table—colored
them, made them cat-yellow. In the distance the caged canaries sang,
and snow, fluttering at the windows like torn lace curtains, emphasized the comforts of the room, the warmth of the fire, the redness of
the wine.)

ADDIE: My story. Ho-hum.

I'm forty-four, I've never married, I've been around the world twice, I
try to go to Europe every other summer; but it's fair to say that except for
a drunken sailor who went berserk and tried to rape me on a Swedish
tramp steamer, nothing of a bizarre nature has ever happened to me until
this year—the week before Thanksgiving.

My sister and I have a box at the post office; what they call a "drawer"

—it's not that we have such a lot of correspondence, but we subscribe to so many magazines. Anyway, on my way home from school I stopped to pick up the mail, and in our drawer there was a package, rather large but very light. It was wrapped in old wrinkled brown paper that looked as if it had been used before, and it was tied with old twine. The postmark was local and it was addressed to me. My name was precisely printed in thick black ink. Even before I opened it I thought: What kind of rubbish is this? Of course, you know all about the coffins?

TC: I've seen one, yes.

ADDIE: Well, I knew nothing about them. No one did. That was a secret between Jake and his agents.

(She winked at Jake, and tilting her head back, swallowed all her wine in one swoop; she did this with astonishing grace, an agility that revealed a lovely throat. Jake, winking back, directed a smoke ring toward her, and the empty oval, floating through the air, seemed to carry with it an erotic message.)

Actually, I didn't open the package until quite late that night. Because when I got home I found my sister at the bottom of the stairs; she'd fallen and sprained an ankle. The doctor came. There was so much commotion. I forgot about the package until after I'd gone to bed. I decided: Oh well, it can wait until tomorrow. I wish I'd abided by that decision; at least I wouldn't have lost a night's sleep.

Because. Because it was *shocking*. I once received an anonymous letter, a truly atrocious one—especially upsetting because, just between us, a good deal of what the writer wrote happened to be true. (Laughing, she replenished her glass) It wasn't really the coffin that shocked me. It was the snapshot inside—a quite recent picture of me, taken on the steps outside the post office. It seemed such an intrusion, a theft—having one's picture made when one is unaware of it. I can sympathize with those Africans who run away from cameras, fearing the photographer intends to steal their spirit. I was shocked, but not frightened. It was my sister who was frightened. When I showed her my little gift, she said: "You don't suppose it has anything to do with that other business?" By "other business" she meant what's been happening here the past five years—murders, accidents, suicides, whatever: it depends on whom you're talking to.

I shrugged it off, put it in a category with the anonymous letter; but the more I thought about it—perhaps my sister had stumbled on to something. That package had not been sent to me by some jealous woman, a mere mischief-making ill-wisher. This was the work of a man. A man had whittled that coffin. A man with strong fingers had printed my name on that package. And the whole thing was meant as a threat. But why? I thought: Maybe Mr. Pepper will know.

I'd met Mr. Pepper. Jake. Actually, I had a crush on him.

JAKE: Stick to the story.

ADDIE: I am. I only used the story to lure you into my lair.

JAKE: That's not true.

ADDIE (sadly, her voice in dull counterpoint to the canaries' chirping serenades): No, it isn't true. Because by the time I decided to speak to Jake, I had concluded that someone did indeed intend to kill me; and I had a fair notion who it was, even though the motive was so improbable. Trivial.

JAKE: It's neither improbable nor trivial. Not after you've studied the style of the beast.

ADDIE (ignoring him; and impersonally, as if she were reciting the multiplication table to her students): Everybody knows everybody else. That's what they say about small-town people. But it isn't true. I've never met the parents of some of my pupils. I pass people every day who are virtual strangers. I'm a Baptist, our congregation isn't all that large; but we have some members—well, I couldn't tell you their names if you held a revolver to my head.

The point is: when I began to think about the people who had died, I realized I had known them all. Except the couple from Tulsa who were staying with Ed Baxter and his wife—

JAKE: The Hogans.

ADDIE: Yes. Well, they're not part of this anyway. Bystanders—who got caught in an inferno. Literally.

Not that any of the victims were close friends—except, perhaps, Clem and Amy Anderson. I'd taught all their children in school.

But I knew the others: George and Amelia Roberts, the Baxters, Dr. Parsons. I knew them rather well. And for only one reason. (She gazed into her wine, observed its ruby flickerings, like a gypsy consulting clouded crystal, ghostly glass) The river. (She raised the wineglass to her lips, and again drained it in one long luxuriously effortless gulp) Have you seen the river? Not yet? Well, now is not the time of year. But in the summer it is very nice. By far the prettiest thing around here. We call it Blue River; it is blue—not Caribbean blue, but very clear all the same and with a sandy bottom and deep quiet pools for swimming. It originates in those mountains to the north and flows through the plains and ranches; it's our main source of irrigation, and it has two tributaries—much smaller rivers, one called Big Brother and the other Little Brother.

The trouble started because of these tributaries. Many ranchers, who were dependent on them, felt that a diversion should be created in Blue River to enlarge Big Brother and Little Brother. Naturally, the ranchers whose property was nourished by the main river were against this proposition. None more so than Bob Quinn, owner of the B.Q. Ranch, through which the widest and deepest stretches of Blue River travels.

JAKE (spitting into the fire): Robert Hawley Quinn, Esquire.

ADDIE: It was a quarrel that had been simmering for decades. Everyone knew that strengthening the two tributaries, even at the expense of Blue River (in terms of power and sheer beauty), was the fair and logical thing to do. But the Quinn family, and others among the rich Blue River ranchers, had always, through various tricks, prevented any action from being taken.

Then we had two years of drought, and that brought the situation to a head. The ranchers whose survival depended upon Big Brother and Little Brother were raising holy hell. The drought had hit them hard; they'd lost a lot of cattle, and now they were out full-force demanding their share of Blue River.

Finally the town council voted to appoint a special committee to settle the matter. I have no idea how the members of the committee were chosen. Certainly I had no particular qualification; I remember old Judge Hatfield —he's retired now, living in Arizona—phoned me and asked if I would serve; that's all there was to it. We had our first meeting in the Council Room at the courthouse, January 1970. The other members of the committee were Clem Anderson, George and Amelia Roberts, Dr. Parsons, the Baxters, Tom Henry, and Oliver Jaeger—

JAKE (to me): Jaeger. He's the postmaster. A crazy sonofabitch.

ADDIE: He's not really crazy. You only say that because—

JAKE: Because he's really crazy.

> (Addie was disconcerted. She contemplated her wineglass, moved to refill it, found the bottle empty, and then produced from a small purse, conveniently nestling in her lap, a pretty little silver box filled with blue pills: Valiums; she swallowed one with a sip of water. And Jake had said that Addie was not a nervous woman?)

TC: Who's Tom Henry?

JAKE: Another nut. Nuttier than Oliver Jaeger. He owns a filling station.

ADDIE: Yes, there were nine of us. We met once a week for about two months. Both sides, those for and those against, sent in experts to testify. Many of the ranchers appeared themselves—to talk to us, to present their own case.

But not Mr. Quinn. Not Bob Quinn—we never heard a word from him, even though, as the owner of the B.Q. Ranch, he stood to lose the most if we voted to divert "his" river. I figured: He's too high and mighty to bother with us and our silly little committee; Bob Quinn, he's been busy talking to the governor, the congressmen, the senators; he thinks he's got all those boys in his hip pocket. So whatever we might decide didn't matter. His big-shot buddies would veto it.

But that's not how it turned out. We voted to divert Blue River at exactly the point where it entered Quinn's property; of course, that didn't leave him without a river—he just wouldn't have the hog's share he'd always had before.

The decision would have been unanimous if Tom Henry hadn't gone against us. You're right, Jake. Tom Henry *is* a nut. So the vote stood eight to one. And it proved such a popular decision, a verdict that really harmed no one and benefited many, there wasn't much Quinn's political cronies could do about it, not if they wanted to stay in office.

A few days after the vote I ran into Bob Quinn at the post office. He made a tremendous point of tipping his hat, smiling, asking after my welfare. Not that I expected him to spit on me; still, I'd never met with so much courtesy from him before. One would never have supposed he was resentful. Resentful? Insane!

TC: What does he look like—Mr. Quinn?

JAKE: *Don't tell him!*

ADDIE: Why not?

JAKE: Just because.

> (Standing, he walked over to the fireplace and offered what remained of his cigar to the flames. He stood with his back to the fire, legs slightly apart, arms folded: I'd never thought of Jake as vain, but clearly he was posing a bit—trying, successfully, to look attractive. I laughed.)

Eh?

TC: Now it's a Jane Austen novel. In her novels, sexy gentlemen are always warming their fannies at fireplaces.

ADDIE (laughing): Oh, Jake, it's true! It's true!

JAKE: I never read female literature. Never have. Never will.

ADDIE: Just for that, I'm going to open another bottle of wine, and drink it all myself.

> (Jake returned to the table and sat down next to Addie; he took one of her hands in one of his and entwined their fingers. The effect upon her was embarrassingly visible—her face flushed, splashes of red blotched her neck. As for him, he seemed unaware of her, unaware of what he was doing. Rather, he was looking at me; it was as if we were alone together.)

JAKE: Yes, I know. Having heard what you have, you're thinking: Well, now the case is solved. Mr. Quinn did it.

That's what I thought. Last year, after Addie told me what she told you, I lit out of here like a bear with a bumblebee up his ass. I drove straight to the city. Thanksgiving or no Thanksgiving, that very night we had a meeting of the whole Bureau. I laid it on the line: this is the motive, this is the guy. Nobody said boo!—except the chief, and he said: "Slow down, Pepper. The man you're accusing is no flyweight. And where's your case? This is all speculation. Guesswork." Everybody agreed with him. Said: "Where's the evidence?"

I was so mad I was shouting; I said: "What the hell do you think I'm here for? We've all got to pull together and build the evidence. I know Quinn did it." The chief said: "Well, I'd be careful who you said that to. Christ, you could get us all fired."

ADDIE: That next day, when he came back here, I wish I'd taken Jake's picture. In the line of duty I've had to paddle many boys, but none of them ever looked as sad as you, Jake.

JAKE: I wasn't too happy. That's the fact of that.

The Bureau backed me; we began checking out the life of Robert Hawley Quinn from the year one. But we had to move on tiptoe—the chief was jittery as a killer on Death Row. I wanted a warrant to search the B.Q. Ranch, the houses, the whole property. Denied. He wouldn't even let me question the man—

TC: Did Quinn know you suspected him?

JAKE (snorting): Right off the bat. Someone in the governor's office tipped him off. Probably the governor himself. And guys in our own Bureau—they probably told him, too. I don't trust nobody. Nobody connected with this case.

ADDIE: The whole town knew before you could say Rumpelstiltskin.

JAKE: Thanks to Oliver Jaeger. *And* Tom Henry. That's my fault. Since they had both been on the River Committee, I felt I had to take them into my confidence, discuss Quinn, warn them about the coffins. They both promised me they would keep it confidential. Well, telling them, I might as well have had a town meeting and made a speech.

ADDIE: At school, one of my little boys raised his hand and said: "My daddy told my mama somebody sent you a coffin, like for the graveyard. Said Mr. Quinn done it." And I said: "Oh, Bobby, your daddy was just teasing your mama, telling her fairy tales."

JAKE: One of Oliver Jaeger's fairy tales! That bastard called everybody in Christendom. And you say he isn't crazy?

ADDIE: You think he's crazy because he thinks *you're* crazy. He sincerely believes that you're mistaken. That you're persecuting an innocent man. (Still looking at Jake, but addressing me) Oliver would never win any contest, neither for charm nor brains. But he's a rational man—a gossip, but good-hearted. He's related to the Quinn family; Bob Quinn is his second cousin. That may be relevant to the violence of his opinions. It's Oliver's contention, and one that is shared by most people, that even if some connection exists between the decision of the Blue River Committee and the deaths that have occurred here, why point the finger at Bob Quinn? He's not the only Blue River rancher that might bear a grievance. What about Walter Forbes? Jim Johanssen? The Throby family. The Millers. The Rileys. Why pick on Bob Quinn? What are the special circumstances that single him out?

JAKE: He did it.

ADDIE: Yes, he did. We know that. But you can't even prove he bought the rattlesnakes. And even if you could—

JAKE: I'd like a whiskey.

ADDIE: You shall have it, sir. Anybody else?

JAKE (after Addie left on her errand): She's right. We can't prove he bought the snakes, even though we know he did. See, I always figured those snakes came from a professional source; breeders who breed for the venom—they sell it to medical laboratories. The major suppliers are Florida and Texas, but there are snake farms all across the country. Over the last few years we sent inquiries to most of them—and never received a single reply.

But in my heart I knew those rattlers came from the Lone Star State. It was only logical—why would a man go all the way to Florida when he could find what he wanted more or less next door? Well, as soon as Quinn entered the picture, I decided to zero in on the snake angle—an angle we'd never concentrated on to the degree we should have, mainly because it required personal investigation and traveling expenses. When it comes to getting the chief to spend money—hell, it's easier to crack walnuts with store-bought teeth. But I know this fellow, an old-time investigator with the Texas Bureau; he owed me a favor. So I sent him some material: pictures of Quinn I'd managed to collect, and photographs of the rattlers themselves—nine of them hanging on a washline after we'd killed them.

TC: How did you kill them?

JAKE: Shotguns. Blasted their heads off.

TC: I killed a rattler once. With a garden hoe.

JAKE: I don't think you could've killed these bastards with any hoe. Even put a dent in them. The smallest one was seven feet long.

TC: There were nine snakes. And nine members of the Blue River Committee. Nice quaint coincidence.

JAKE: Bill, my Texas friend, he's a determined guy; he covered Texas from border to border, spent most of his vacation visiting snake farms, talking to the breeders. Now, about a month ago, he called and said he thought he had located my party: a Mrs. Garcia, a Tex-Mex lady who owned a snake farm near Nogales. That's about a ten-hour drive from here. If you're driving a State car and doing ninety miles an hour. Bill promised to meet me there.

Addie went with me. We drove overnight, and had breakfast with Bill at a Holiday Inn. Then we visited Mrs. Garcia. Some of these snake farms are tourist attractions; but her place was nothing like that—it was way off the highway, and quite a small operation. But she sure had some impressive specimens. All the time we were there she kept hauling out these huge rattlers, wrapping them around her neck, her arms: laughing; she had almost solid gold teeth. At first I thought she was a man; she was built like Pancho Villa, and she was wearing cowboy britches with a zipper fly.

She had a cataract in one eye; and the other didn't look too sharp. But she wasn't hesitant about identifying Quinn's picture. She said he had visited her place in either June or July 1970 (the Robertses died 5 September 1970), and that he had been accompanied by a young Mexican; they arrived in a small truck with a Mexican license plate. She said she never spoke to Quinn; according to her, he never said a word—simply listened while she dealt with the Mexican. She said it was not her policy to question a customer as to his reasons for purchasing her merchandise; but, she told us, the Mexican volunteered the information—he wanted a dozen adult rattlers to use in a religious ceremony. That didn't surprise her; she said people often bought snakes for ritualistic usage. But the Mexican wanted her to guarantee that the snakes he bought would attack and kill a bull weighing a thousand pounds. She said yes, that was possible—provided the snakes had been injected with a drug, an amphetamine stimulant, before being put in contact with the bull.

She showed him how to do it, with Quinn observing. She showed us, too. She used a pole, about twice the length of a riding crop and limber as a willow wand; it had a leather loop attached to the end of it. She caught the head of the snake in the loop, dangled him in the air, and jabbed a syringe into the belly. She let the Mexican run a few practice sessions; he did just fine.

TC: Had she ever seen the Mexican before?

JAKE: No. I asked her to describe him, and she described any border-town Mexicali Rose between twenty and thirty. He paid her; she packed the snakes in individual containers, and away they went.

Mrs. Garcia was a very obliging lady. Very cooperative. Until we asked her the important question: would she give us a sworn affidavit that Robert Hawley Quinn was one of two men who had bought a dozen rattlesnakes from her on a certain summer day in 1970? She sure turned sour then. Said she wouldn't sign nothing.

I told her those snakes had been used to murder two people. You should have seen her face then. She walked in the house and locked the doors and pulled down the shades.

TC: An affidavit from her. That wouldn't have carried much legal weight.

JAKE: It would have been something to confront him with: an opening gambit. More than likely, it was the Mexican who put the snakes into Roberts' car; of course, Quinn hired him to do it. Know what? I'll bet that Mexican is dead, buried out there on the lone prairie. Courtesy of Mr. Quinn.

TC: But surely, somewhere in Quinn's history, there must be something to indicate that he was capable of psychotic violence?

(Jake nodded, nodded, nodded.)

JAKE: The gentleman was well acquainted with homicide.

(Addie returned with the whiskey. He thanked her, and kissed her on the cheek. She sat down next to him, and again their hands met, their fingers mingled.)

The Quinns are one of the oldest families here. Bob Quinn is the eldest of three brothers. They all own a share of the B.Q. Ranch, but he's the boss.

ADDIE: No, his wife's the boss. He married his first cousin, Juanita Quinn. Her mother was Spanish, and she has the temper of a hot tamale. Their first child died in childbirth, and she refused to ever have another. It's generally known, though, that Bob Quinn does have children. By another woman in another town.

JAKE: He was a war hero. A colonel in the Marines during the Second World War. He never refers to it himself, but to hear other people tell it, Bob Quinn single-handedly slaughtered more Japanese than the Hiroshima bomb.

But right after the war he did a little killing that wasn't quite so patriotic. Late one night he called the sheriff to come out to the B.Q. Ranch and collect a couple of corpses. He claimed he'd caught two men rustling cattle and had shot them dead. That was his tale, and nobody challenged it, at least not publicly. But the truth is those two guys weren't cattle rustlers; they were gamblers from Denver and Quinn owed them a stack of money. They'd traveled down to B.Q. for a promised payoff. What they got was a load of buckshot.

TC: Have you ever questioned him about that?

JAKE: Questioned who?

TC: Quinn.

JAKE: Strictly speaking, I've never *questioned* him at all.

(His quirky cynical smile bent his mouth; he tinkled the ice in his whiskey, drank some, and chuckled—a deep rough chuckle, like a man trying to bring up phlegm.)

Just lately, I've talked to him plenty. But during the five years I'd been on the case, I'd never met the man. I'd seen him. Knew who he was.

ADDIE: But now they're like two peas in a pod. Real buddies.

JAKE: Addie!

ADDIE: Oh, Jake. I'm only teasing.

JAKE: That's nothing to tease about. It's been pure torture for me.

ADDIE (squeezing his hand): I know. I'm sorry.

(Jake drained his glass, banged it on the table.)

JAKE: Looking at him. Listening to him. Laughing at his dirty jokes. I hate him. He hates me. We both know that.

ADDIE: Let me sweeten you up with another whiskey.

JAKE: Sit still.

ADDIE: Perhaps I ought to peek in on Marylee. See if she's all right.

JAKE: Sit still.

(But Addie wanted to escape the room, for she was uncomfortable with Jake's anger, the numb fury inhabiting his face.)

ADDIE (glancing out the window): It's stopped snowing.

JAKE: The Okay Café is always crowded Monday mornings. After the weekend everybody has to stop by to catch up on the news. Ranchers, businessmen, the sheriff and his gang, people from the courthouse. But on this particular Monday—the Monday after Thanksgiving—the place was packed; guys were squatting on each other's laps, and everybody was yakking like a bunch of sissy old women.

You can guess what they were yakking about. Thanks to Tom Henry and Oliver Jaeger, who'd spent the weekend spreading the word, saying that guy from the Bureau, that Jake Pepper fella, was accusing Bob Quinn of murder. I sat in my booth pretending not to notice. But I couldn't help but notice when Bob Quinn himself walked in; you could hear the whole café hold its breath.

He squeezed into a booth next to the sheriff; the sheriff hugged him, and laughed, and let out a cowboy holler. Most of the crowd mimicked him, yelled wahoo, Bob! hiya, Bob! Yessir, the Okay Café was one hundred percent behind Bob Quinn. I had the feeling—a feeling that even if I could prove dead-certain this man was a murderer many times over, they'd lynch me before I could arrest him.

ADDIE (pressing a hand to her forehead, as though she had a headache): He's right. Bob Quinn has the whole town on his side. That's one reason my sister doesn't like to hear us talk about it. She says Jake's wrong, Mr. Quinn's a fine fellow. It's her theory that Dr. Parsons was responsible for these crimes, and that's why he committed suicide.

TC: But Dr. Parsons was dead long before you received the coffin.

JAKE: Marylee's sweet but not too bright. Sorry, Addie, but that's how it is.

(Addie removed her hand from Jake's: an admonishing gesture, but not a severe one. Anyway, it left Jake free to stand up and pace the floor, which he did. His footsteps echoed on the polished pine planks.)

So back to the Okay Café. As I was leaving, the sheriff reached out and grabbed my arm. He's a fresh Irish bastard. And crooked as the devil's toes. He said: "Hey, Jake. I wantcha to meet Bob Quinn. Bob, this is Jake Pepper. From the Bureau." I shook Quinn's hand. Quinn said: "I heard plenty about you. I hear you're a chess player. I don't find too many games. How about us getting together?" I said sure, and he said: "Tomorrow okay? Come by around five. We'll have a drink and play a couple of games."

That's how I started. I went to the B.Q. Ranch the next afternoon. We played for two hours. He's a better player than I am, but I won often enough to make it interesting. He's garrulous, he'll talk about anything:

politics, women, sex, trout fishing, bowel movements, his trip to Russia, cattle versus wheat, gin versus vodka, Johnny Carson, his safari in Africa, religion, the Bible, Shakespeare, the genius of General MacArthur, bear hunting, Reno whores versus Las Vegas whores, the stock market, venereal diseases, cornflakes versus Shredded Wheat, gold versus diamonds, capital punishment (he's all for it), football, baseball, basketball—*anything*. Anything except why I'm stuck in this town.

TC: You mean he won't discuss the case?

JAKE (halting in his pacing): It's not that he won't discuss the case. He simply behaves as though it doesn't exist. I discuss it, but he never reacts. I showed him the Clem Anderson photographs: I hoped I could shock him into some response. *Some* comment. But he only looked back at the chessboard, made a move, and told me a dirty joke.

So Mr. Quinn and I have been playing our games within a game several afternoons a week for the last few months. In fact, I'm going there later today. And you—(cocking a finger in my direction) are going with me.

TC: Am I welcome?

JAKE: I called him this morning. All he asked was: Does he play chess?

TC: I do. But I'd rather watch.

(A log collapsed, and its crackling drew my attention to the fireplace. I stared into the purring flames, and wondered why he had forbidden Addie to describe Quinn, tell me what he looked like. I tried to imagine him; I couldn't. Rather, I remembered the passage from Mark Twain that Jake had read aloud: "Of all the creatures that were made, man is the most detestable . . . the only one, the solitary one, that possesses malice . . . he is the only creature that has a nasty mind." Addie's voice rescued me from my queasy reverie.)

ADDIE: Oh, dear. It's snowing again. But lightly. Just floating. (Then, as though the resumption of the snow had prompted thoughts of mortality, the evaporation of time) You know, it's been almost five months. That's quite long for him. He usually doesn't wait that long.

JAKE (vexed): Addie, what is it now?

ADDIE: My coffin. It's been almost five months. And as I say, he doesn't usually wait that long.

JAKE: Addie! I'm here. Nothing is going to happen to you.

ADDIE: Of course, Jake. I wonder about Oliver Jaeger. I wonder when he'll receive his coffin. Just think, Oliver is the postmaster. He'll be sorting the mail and— (Her voice was suddenly, startlingly quavery, vulnerable— wistful in a way that accentuated the canaries' carefree songfest) Well, it won't be very soon.

TC: Why not?

ADDIE: Because Quinn will have to fill my coffin first.

. . .

It was after five when we left, the air was still, free of snow, and shimmering with the embers of a sunset and the first pale radiance of a moonrise: a full moon rolling on the horizon like a round white wheel, or a mask, a white featureless menacing mask peering at us through our car windows. At the end of Main Street, just before the town turns into prairie, Jake pointed at a filling station: "That's Tom Henry's place. Tom Henry, Addie, Oliver Jaeger; out of the original River Committee, they're the only three left. I said Tom Henry was a nut. And he is. But he's a lucky nut. He voted against the others. That leaves him in the clear. No coffin for Tom Henry."

TC: *A Coffin for Dimitrios.*

JAKE: What say?

TC: A book by Eric Ambler. A thriller.

JAKE: Fiction? (I nodded; he grimaced) You really read that junk?

TC: Graham Greene was a first-class writer. Until the Vatican grabbed him. After that, he never wrote anything as good as *Brighton Rock*. I like Agatha Christie, love her. And Raymond Chandler is a great stylist, a poet. Even if his plots are a mess.

JAKE: Junk. Those guys are just daydreamers—squat at a typewriter and jerk themselves off, that's all they do.

TC: So no coffin for Tom Henry. How about Oliver Jaeger?

JAKE: He'll get his. One morning he'll be shuffling around the post office, emptying out the incoming mail sacks, and there it will be, a brown box with his very own name printed on it. Forget the cousin stuff; forget that he's been hanging halos over Bob Quinn's head. Saint Bob isn't going to let him off with a few Hail Marys. Not if I know Saint Bob. Chances are, he's already used his whittling knife, made a little something, and popped Oliver Jaeger's picture inside it—

(Jake's voice jolted to a stop, and as though it were a correlated action, his foot hit the brake pedal: the car skidded, swerved, straightened; we drove on. I knew what had happened. He had remembered, as I was remembering, Addie's pathetic complaint: ". . . Quinn will have to fill my coffin first." I tried to hold my tongue; it rebelled.)

TC: But that means—

JAKE: Better turn on my headlights.

TC: That means Addie is going to die.

JAKE: Hell, no! I just knew you were going to say that! (He slapped a flattened palm against the steering wheel) I've built a wall around Addie. I gave her a .38 Detective Special, and taught her how to use it. She can put a bullet between a man's eyes at a hundred yards. She's learned enough karate to split a plank with one hand-chop. Addie's smart; she won't be tricked. And I'm here. I'm watching her. I'm watching Quinn, too. So are other people.

(Strong emotion, fears edging toward terror, can demolish the logic of even so logical a man as Jake Pepper—whose precautions had not saved Clem Anderson. I wasn't prepared to argue the point with him, not in his present irrational humor; but why, since he assumed Oliver Jaeger was doomed, was he so certain Addie was not? That she would be spared? For if Quinn stayed true to his design, then absolutely he would have to dispatch Addie, remove her from the scene before he could start the last step of his task by addressing a package to his second cousin and staunch defender, the local postmaster.)

TC: I know Addie's been around the world. But I think it's time she went again.

JAKE (truculently): She can't leave here. Not now.

TC: Oh? She doesn't strike me as suicidal.

JAKE: Well, for one thing, school. School's not out till June.

TC: Jake! My God! How can you talk about *school*?

(Dim though the light was, I could discern his ashamed expression; at the same time, he jutted his jaw.)

JAKE: We've discussed it. Talked about her and Marylee taking a long cruise. But she doesn't want to go anywhere. She said: "The shark needs bait. If we're going to hook the shark, then the bait has to be available."

TC: So Addie is a stakeout? A goat waiting for the tiger to pounce?

JAKE: Hold on. I'm not sure I like the way you put that.

TC: Then how would you put it?

JAKE: (Silence)

TC: (Silence)

JAKE: Quinn has Addie in his thoughts, he does indeed. He means to keep his promise. And that's when we'll nail him: in the attempt. Catch him when the curtain is up and all the lights are on. There's some risk, sure; but we have to take it. Because—well, to be goddamned honest, it's probably the only damn chance we're gonna get.

(I leaned my head against the window: saw Addie's pretty throat as she threw back her head and drank the dazzling red wine in one delicious swallow. I felt weak, feeble; and disgusted with Jake.)

TC: I like Addie. She's real; and yet there's mystery. I wonder why she never married.

JAKE: Keep this under your hat. Addie's going to marry me.

TC (my mental eye was still elsewhere; still, in fact, watching Addie drink her wine): When?

JAKE: Next summer. When I get my vacation. We haven't told anybody.

488

Except Marylee. So now do you understand? Addie's *safe;* I won't let anything happen to her; I love her; I'm going to marry her.

> (Next summer: a lifetime away. The full moon, higher, whiter now, and celebrated by coyotes, rolled across the snow-gleaming prairies. Clumps of cattle stood in the cold snowy fields, bunched together for warmth. Some stood in pairs. I noticed two spotted calves huddled side by side, lending each other comfort, protection: like Jake, like Addie.)

TC: Well, congratulations. That's wonderful. I know you'll both be very happy.

Soon an impressive barbed-wire fence, like the high fences of a concentration camp, bordered both sides of the highway; it marked the beginnings of the B.Q. Ranch: ten thousand acres, or thereabouts. I lowered the window, and accepted a rush of icy air, sharp with the scent of new snow and old sweet hay. "Here we go," said Jake as we left the highway and drove through wooden swung-open gates. At the entrance, our headlights caught a handsomely lettered sign: *B.Q./Ranch R. H. Quinn/Proprietor.* A pair of crossed tomahawks was painted underneath the proprietor's name; one wondered whether it was the ranch's logo or the family crest. Either way, an ominous set of tomahawks seemed suitable.

The road was narrow, and lined with leafless trees, dark except for a rare glitter of animal-eyes among the silhouetted branches. We crossed a wooden bridge that rumbled under our weight, and I heard the sound of water, deep-toned liquid tumblings, and I knew it must be Blue River, but I couldn't see it, for it was hidden by trees and snowdrifts; as we continued along the road, the sound followed, for the river was running beside us, occasionally eerily quiet, then abruptly bubbling with the broken music of waterfalls, cascades.

The road widened. Sprinklings of electric light pierced the trees. A beautiful boy, a child with bouncing yellow hair and riding a horse bareback, waved at us. We passed a row of bungalows, lamplit and vibrating with the racket of television voices: the homes of ranch hands. Ahead, standing in distinguished isolation, was the main house, Mr. Quinn's house. It was a large white clapboard two-storied structure with a covered veranda running its full length; it seemed abandoned, for all the windows were dark.

Jake honked the car horn. At once, like a fanfare of welcoming trumpets, a blaze of floodlights swept the veranda; lamps boomed in downstairs windows. The front door opened; a man stepped out and waited to greet us.

My first introduction to the owner of the B.Q. Ranch failed to resolve the question of why Jake had not wanted Addie to describe him to me. Although he wasn't a man who would pass unnoticed, his appearance was not excessively unusual; and yet the sight of him startled me: *I knew Mr. Quinn.* I was positive, I would have sworn on my own heartbeat that somehow, and undoubtedly long ago, I had encountered Robert Hawley Quinn, and that together we had, in fact, shared an alarming experience, an adventure so disturbing, memory had kindly submerged it.

He sported expensive high-heel boots, but even without them the man measured over six feet, and if he had stood straight, instead of assuming a stooped, slope-shouldered posture, he would have presented a fine tall figure. He had long simianlike arms; the hands dangled to his knees, and the fingers were long, capable, oddly aristocratic. I recalled a Rachmaninoff concert; Rachmaninoff's hands were like Quinn's. Quinn's face was broad but gaunt, hollow-cheeked, weather-coarsened—the face of a medieval peasant, the man behind the plow with all the woes of the world lashed to his back. But Quinn was no dumb, sadly burdened peasant. He wore thin wire-rimmed glasses, and these professorial spectacles, and the gray eyes looming behind their thick lenses, betrayed him: his eyes were alert, suspicious, intelligent, merry with malice, complacently superior. He had a hospitable, fraudulently genial laugh and voice. But he was not a fraud. He was an idealist, an achiever; he set himself tasks, and his tasks were his cross, his religion, his identity; no, not a fraud—a fanatic; and presently, while we were still gathered on the veranda, my sunken memory surfaced: I remembered where and in what form I had met Mr. Quinn before.

He extended one of his long hands toward Jake; his other hand plowed through a rough white-and-gray mane worn pioneer-style—a length not popular with his fellow ranchers: men who looked as though they visited the barber every Saturday for a close clip and a talcum shampoo. Tufts of gray hair sprouted from his nostrils and his ears. I noticed his belt buckle; it was decorated with two crossed tomahawks made of gold and red enamel.

QUINN: Hey, Jake. I told Juanita, I said honey, that rascal's gonna chicken out. Account of the snow.
JAKE: You call this *snow*?
QUINN: Just pullin' your leg, Jake. (To me) You oughta see the snow we do get! Back in 1952 we had a whole week when the only way I could get out of the house was to climb through the attic window. Lost seven hundred head of cattle, all my Santa Gertrudis. Ha ha! Oh, I tell you that was a time. Well, sir, you play chess?
TC: Rather the way I speak French. *Un peu.*

QUINN (cackling, slapping his thighs with spurious mirth): Yeah, I know. You're the city slicker come to skin us country boys. I'll bet you could play me and Jake at the same time and beat us blindfolded.

(We followed him down a wide high hallway into an immense room, a cathedral stuffed with huge heavy Spanish furniture, armoires and chairs and tables and baroque mirrors commensurate with their spacious surroundings. The floor was covered with brick-red Mexican tiles and dotted with Navajo rugs. An entire wall had been composed from blocks of irregularly cut granite, and this granite cavelike wall housed a fireplace big enough to roast a brace of oxen; in consequence, the dainty fire ensconced there seemed as insignificant as a twig in a forest.

But the person seated near the hearth was not insignificant. Quinn introduced me to her: "My wife, Juanita." She nodded, but was not to be distracted from the television screen confronting her: the set was working with the sound turned off—she was watching the zany dithering of muted images, some visually boisterous game show. The chair in which she sat may well have once decorated the throne room of an Iberian castle; she shared it with a shivering little Chihuahua dog and a yellow guitar, which lay across her lap.

Jake and our host settled themselves at a table furnished with a splendid ebony-and-ivory chess set. I observed the start of a game, listened to their easygoing badinage, and it was strange: Addie was right, they seemed real buddies, two peas in a pod. But eventually I wandered back to the fireplace, determined to further explore the quiet Juanita. I sat near her on the hearth and searched for some topic to start a conversation. The guitar? The quivering Chihuahua, now jealously yapping at me?)

JUANITA QUINN: Pepe! You stupid mosquito!

TC: Don't bother. I like dogs.

(She looked at me. Her hair, center-parted and too black to be true, was slicked to her narrow skull. Her face was like a fist: tiny features tightly bunched together. Her head was too big for her body—she wasn't fat, but she weighed more than she should, and most of the overweight was distributed between her bosom and her belly. But she had slender, nicely shaped legs, and she was wearing a pair of very prettily beaded Indian moccasins. The mosquito yap-yapped, but now she ignored him. The television regained her attention.)

I was just wondering: why do you watch without the sound?

(Her bored onyx eyes returned to me. I repeated the question.)

JUANITA QUINN: Do you drink tequila?

TC: Well, there's a little dump in Palm Springs where they make fantastic Margaritas.

JUANITA QUINN: A man drinks tequila straight. No lime. No salt. Straight. Would you like some?

TC: Sure.

JUANITA QUINN: So would I. Alas, we have none. We can't keep it in the house. If we did, I would drink it; my liver would dry up . . .

> (She snapped her fingers, signifying disaster. Then she touched the yellow guitar, strummed the strings, developed a tune, a tricky, unfamiliar melody that for a moment she happily hummed and played. When she stopped, her face retied itself into a knot.)

I used to drink every night. Every night I drank a bottle of tequila and went to bed and slept like a baby. I was never sick a day; I looked good, I felt good, I slept well. No more. Now I have one cold after the other, headaches, arthritis; and I can't sleep a wink. All because the doctor said I had to stop drinking tequila. But don't jump to conclusions. I'm not a drunk. You can take all the wine and whiskey in the world and dump it down the Grand Canyon. It's only that I like tequila. The dark yellow kind. I like that best. (She pointed at the television set) You asked why I have the sound off. The only time I have the sound on is to hear the weather report. Otherwise, I just watch and imagine what's being said. If I actually listen, it puts me right to sleep. But just imagining keeps me awake. And I have to stay awake—at least till midnight. Otherwise, I'd never get any sleep at all. Where do you live?

TC: New York, mostly.

JUANITA QUINN: We used to go to New York every year or two. The Rainbow Room: now there's a view. But it wouldn't be any fun now. Nothing is. My husband says you're an old friend of Jake Pepper's.

TC: I've known him ten years.

JUANITA QUINN: Why does he suppose my husband has any connection with this thing?

TC: Thing?

JUANITA QUINN (amazed): You *must* have heard about it. Well, why does Jake Pepper think my husband's involved?

TC: *Does* Jake think your husband's involved?

JUANITA QUINN: That's what some people say. My sister told me—

TC: But what do you think?

JUANITA QUINN (lifting her Chihuahua and cuddling him against her bosom): I feel sorry for Jake. He must be lonely. And he's mistaken; there's nothing here. It all ought to be forgotten. He ought to go home. (Eyes closed; utterly weary) Ah well, who knows? *Or* cares? Not I. Not I, said the Spider to the Fly. Not I.

· · ·

Beyond us, there was a commotion at the chess table. Quinn, celebrating a victory over Jake, vociferously congratulated himself: "Sonofagun! Thought you had me trapped there. But the moment you moved your queen—it's hot beer and horse piss for the Great Pepper!" His hoarse baritone rang through the vaulted room with the *brio* of an opera star. "Now you, young man," he shouted at me. "I need a game. A bona fide challenge. Old Pepper here ain't fit to lick my boots." I started to excuse myself, for the prospect of a chess game with Quinn was both intimidating and tiresome; I might have felt differently if I'd thought I could beat him, triumphantly invade that citadel of conceit. I had once won a prep-school chess championship, but that was eons ago; my knowledge of the game had long been stored in a mental attic. However, when Jake beckoned, stood up, and offered me his chair, I acquiesced, and leaving Juanita Quinn to the silent flickerings of her television screen, seated myself opposite her husband; Jake stood behind my chair, an encouraging presence. But Quinn, assessing my faltering manner, the indecision of my first moves, dismissed me as a walkover, and resumed a conversation he'd been having with Jake, apparently concerning cameras and photography.

QUINN: The Krauts are good. I've always used Kraut cameras. Leica. Rolleiflex. But the Japs are whippin' their ass. I bought a new Jap number, no bigger than a deck of cards, that will take five hundred pictures on a single roll of film.

TC: I know that camera. I've worked with a lot of photographers and I've seen some of them use it. Richard Avedon has one. He says it's no good.

QUINN: To tell the truth, I haven't tried mine yet. I hope your friend's wrong. I could've bought a prize bull for what that doodad set me back.

(I suddenly felt Jake's fingers urgently squeezing my shoulder, which I interpreted as a message that he wished me to pursue the subject.)

TC: Is that your hobby—photography?

QUINN: Oh, it comes and goes. Fits and starts. How I started was, I got tired of paying so-called professionals to take pictures of my prize cattle. Pictures I need to send round to different breeders and buyers. I figured I could do just as good, and save myself a nickel to boot.

(Jake's fingers goaded me again.)

TC: Do you make many portraits?

QUINN: Portraits?

TC: Of people.

QUINN (scoffingly): I wouldn't call them *portraits*. Snapshots, maybe. Aside from cattle, mostly I do nature pictures. Landscapes. Thunderstorms. The seasons here on the ranch. The wheat when it's green and then when it's gold. My river—I've got some dandy pictures of my river in full flood.

(The river. I tensed as I heard Jake clear his throat, as though he were about to speak; instead, his fingers prodded me even more firmly. I toyed with a pawn, stalling.)

TC: Then you must shoot a lot of color.

QUINN (nodding): That's why I do my own developing. When you send your stuff off to those laboratories, you never know what the hell you're gonna get back.

TC: Oh, you have a darkroom?

QUINN: If you want to call it that. Nothing fancy.

(Once more Jake's throat rumbled, this time with serious intent.)

JAKE: Bob? You remember the pictures I told you about? The coffin pictures. They were made with a fast-action camera.

QUINN: (Silence)

JAKE: A Leica.

QUINN: Well, it wasn't mine. My old Leica got lost in darkest Africa. Some nigger stole it. (Staring at the chessboard, his face suffused with a look of amused dismay) Why, you little rascal! Damn your hide. Look here, Jake. Your friend almost has me checkmated. *Almost* . . .

It was true; with a skill subconsciously resurrected, I had been marching my ebony army with considerable, though unwitting, competence, and had indeed managed to maneuver Quinn's king into a perilous position. In one sense I regretted my success, for Quinn was using it to divert the angle of Jake's inquiry, to revert from the suddenly sensitive topic of photography back to chess; on the other hand, I was elated—by playing flawlessly, I might now very well win. Quinn scratched his chin, his gray eyes dedicated to the religious task of rescuing his king. But for me the chessboard had blurred; my mind was snared in a time warp, numbed by memories dormant almost half a century.

It was summer, and I was five years old, living with relatives in a small Alabama town. There was a river attached to this town, too; a sluggish muddy river that repelled me, for it was full of water moccasins and whiskered catfish. However, much as I disliked their ferocious snouts, I was fond of captured catfish, fried and dripping with ketchup; we had a cook who served them often. Her name was Lucy Joy, though I've seldom known a less joyous human. She was a hefty black woman, reserved, very serious; she seemed to live from Sunday to Sunday, when she sang in the choir of some pineywoods church. But one day a remarkable change came over Lucy Joy. While I was alone with her in the kitchen she began talking to me about a certain Reverend Bobby Joe Snow, describing him with an excitement that kindled my own imagination: he was a miracle-maker, a famous evangelist, and he was traveling soon to this very town; the Rever-

494

end Snow was due here next week, come to preach, to baptize and save souls! I pleaded with Lucy to take me to see him, and she smiled and promised she would. The fact was, it was necessary that I accompany her. For the Reverend Snow was a white man, his audiences were segregated, and Lucy had figured it out that the only way she would be welcome was if she brought along a little white boy to be baptized. Naturally, Lucy did not let on that such an event was in store for me. The following week, when we set off to attend the Reverend's camp meeting, I only envisioned the drama of watching a holy man sent from heaven to help the blind see and the lame walk. But I began to feel uneasy when I realized we were headed toward the river; when we got there and I saw hundreds of people gathered along the bank, country people, backwoods white trash stomping and hollering, I hesitated. Lucy was furious—she pulled me into the sweltering mob. Jingling bells, cavorting bodies; I could hear one voice above the others, a chanting booming baritone. Lucy chanted, too; moaned, shook. Magically, a stranger hoisted me onto his shoulder and I got a quick view of the man with the dominant voice. He was planted in the river with water up to his white-robed waist; his hair was gray and white, a drenched tangled mass, and his long hands, stretched skyward, implored the humid noon sun. I tried to see his face, for I knew this must be the Reverend Bobby Joe Snow, but before I could, my benefactor dropped me back into the disgusting confusion of ecstatic feet, undulating arms, trembling tambourines. I begged to go home; but Lucy, drunk with glory, held me close. The sun churned; I tasted vomit in my throat. But I didn't throw up; instead, I started to yell and punch and scream: Lucy was pulling me toward the river, and the crowd parted to create a path for us. I struggled until we reached the river's bank; then stopped, silenced by the scene. The white-robed man standing in the river was holding a reclining young girl; he recited biblical scripture before rapidly immersing her underwater, then swooping her up again: shrieking, weeping, she stumbled to shore. Now the Reverend's simian arms reached for me. I bit Lucy's hand, fought free of her grip. But a redneck boy grabbed me and dragged me into the water. I shut my eyes; I smelled the Jesus hair, felt the Reverend's arms carrying me downward into drowning blackness, then hours later lifting me into sunlight. My eyes, opening, looked into his gray, manic eyes. His face, broad but gaunt, moved closer, and he kissed my lips. I heard a loud laugh, an eruption like gunfire: "Checkmate!"

QUINN: Checkmate!
JAKE: Hell, Bob. He was just being polite. He let you win.
  (The kiss dissolved; the Reverend's face, receding, was replaced by a
  face virtually identical. So it was in Alabama, some fifty years earlier,

that I had first seen Mr. Quinn. At any rate, his counterpart: Bobby Joe Snow, evangelist.)

QUINN: How about it, Jake? You ready to lose another dollar?

JAKE: Not tonight. We're driving to Denver in the morning. My friend here has to catch a plane.

QUINN (to me): Shucks. That wasn't much of a visit. Come again soon. Come in the summer and I'll take you trout fishing. Not that it's like what it was. Used to be I could count on landing a six-pound rainbow with the first cast. Back before they ruined my river.

(We departed without saying good-night to Juanita Quinn; she was sound asleep, snoring. Quinn walked with us to the car: "Be careful!" he warned, as he waved and waited until our taillights vanished.)

JAKE: Well, I learned one thing, thanks to you. Now I *know* he developed those pictures himself.

TC: So—why wouldn't you let Addie tell me what he looked like?

JAKE: It might have influenced your first impression. I wanted you to see him with a clear eye, and tell me what you saw.

TC: I saw a man I'd seen before.

JAKE: *Quinn?*

TC: No, not Quinn. But someone like him. His twin.

JAKE: Speak English.

(I described that summer day, my baptism—it was so clear to me, the similarities between Quinn and the Reverend Snow, the linking fibers; but I spoke too emotionally, metaphysically, to communicate what I felt, and I could sense Jake's disappointment: he had expected from me a series of sensible perceptions, pristine, pragmatic insights that would help clarify his own concept of Quinn's character, the man's motivations.

I fell silent, chagrined to have failed Jake. But as we arrived at the highway, and steered toward town, Jake let me know that, garbled, confused as my memoir must have seemed, he had partially deciphered what I had so poorly expressed.)

Well, Bob Quinn *does* think he's the Lord Almighty.

TC: Not think. Knows.

JAKE: Any doubts?

TC: No, no doubts. Quinn's the man who whittles coffins.

JAKE: And some day soon he'll whittle his own. Or my name ain't Jake Pepper.

Over the next few months I called Jake at least once a week, usually on Sundays when he was at Addie's house, which gave me a chance to talk with them both. Jake usually opened our conversations by saying: "Sorry, pardner. Nothing new to report." But one Sunday, Jake told me that he and Addie had settled on a wedding date: August 10. And Addie said: "We hope you can come." I promised I would, though the day conflicted with a planned three-week trip to Europe; well, I'd juggle my dates. However, in the end it was the bride and groom who had to alter schedules, for the Bureau agent who was supposed to replace Jake while he was on his honeymoon ("We're going to Honolulu!") had a hepatitis attack, and the wedding was postponed until the first of September. "That's rotten luck," I told Addie. "But I'll be back by then; I'll be there."

So, early in August, I flew Swissair to Switzerland, and lolled away several weeks in an Alpine village, sunbathing among the eternal snows. I slept, I ate, I reread the whole of Proust, which is rather like plunging into a tidal wave, destination unknown. But my thoughts too often revolved around Mr. Quinn; occasionally, while I slept, he knocked at the door and entered my dreams, sometimes as himself, his gray eyes glittering behind the wire-framed spectacles, but now and then he appeared guised as the white-robed Reverend Snow.

A brief whiff of Alpine air is exhilarating, but extended holidays in the mountains can become claustrophobic, arouse inexplicable depressions. Anyway, one day when one of these black moods descended, I hired a car and drove via the Grand St. Bernard pass into Italy and on to Venice. In Venice one is always in costume and wearing a mask; that is, you are not yourself, and not responsible for your behavior. It wasn't the real me who arrived in Venice at five in the afternoon and before midnight boarded a train bound for Istanbul. It all began in Harry's Bar, as so many Venetian escapades do. I had just ordered a martini when who should slam through the swinging doors but Gianni Paoli, an energetic journalist whom I had known in Moscow when he had been a correspondent for an Italian newspaper: together, aided by vodka, we had enlivened many a morose Russian restaurant. Gianni was in Venice en route to Istanbul; he was catching the Orient Express at midnight. Six martinis later he had talked me into going with him. It was a journey of two days and two nights; the train meandered through Yugoslavia and Bulgaria, but our impressions of those countries were confined to what we glimpsed out the window of our wagon-lit compartment, which we never left except to renew our supply of wine and vodka.

The room spun. Stopped. Spun. I stepped out of bed. My brain, a hunk of shattered glass, painfully clinked inside my head. But I could stand; I could walk; I even remembered where I was: the Hilton Hotel in Istanbul. Gingerly, I made my way toward a balcony overlooking the Bosphorus. Gianni Paoli was basking there in the sunshine, eating breakfast and reading the Paris *Herald Tribune*. Blinking, I glanced at the newspaper's date.

It was the first of September. Now, why should that cause such severe sensations? Nausea; guilt; remorse. Holy smoke, I'd missed the wedding! Gianni couldn't fathom why I was so upset (Italians are always upset; but they never understand why anybody else should be); he poured vodka into his orange juice, offered it to me, and said drink, get drunk: "But first, send them a telegram." I took his advice, all of it. The telegram said: *Unavoidably detained but wish you every happiness on this wonderful day.* Later, when rest and abstinence had steadied my hand, I wrote them a short letter; I didn't lie, I simply didn't explain why I had been "unavoidably detained"; I said I was flying to New York in a few days, and would telephone them as soon as they returned from their honeymoon. I addressed the letter to Mr. and Mrs. Jake Pepper, and when I left it at the desk to be mailed I felt relieved, exonerated; I thought of Addie with a flower in her hair, of Addie and Jake walking at dusk along Waikiki beach, the sea beside them, stars above them; I wondered if Addie was too old to have children.

But I didn't go home; things happened. I encountered an old friend in Istanbul, an archeologist who was working on a dig on the Anatolia coast in southern Turkey; he invited me to join him, he said I would enjoy it, and he was right, I did. I swam every day, learned to dance Turkish folk dances, drank ouzo and danced outdoors all night every night at the local bistro; I stayed two weeks. Afterward I traveled by boat to Athens, and from there took a plane to London, where I had a suit fitted. It was October, almost autumn, before I turned the key that opened the door of my New York apartment.

A friend, who had been visiting the apartment to water the plants, had arranged my mail in orderly stacks on the library table. There were a number of telegrams, and I leafed through those before taking off my coat. I opened one; it was an invitation to a Halloween party. I opened another; it was signed Jake: *Call me urgent.* It was dated August 29, six weeks ago. Hurriedly, not allowing myself to believe what I was thinking, I found Addie's telephone number and dialed it; no answer. Then I placed a person-to-person call to the Prairie Motel: No, Mr. Pepper was not at present registered there; yes, the operator thought he could be contacted through the State Bureau of Investigation. I called it; a man—an ornery bastard—informed me that Detective Pepper was on a leave of absence, and no, he couldn't tell me his whereabouts ("That's against the rules"); and when I gave him my name and told him I was calling from New York he said oh yeah and when I said listen, please, this is very important the sonofabitch hung up.

I needed to take a leak; but the desire, which had been insistent all during the ride from Kennedy airport, subsided, disappeared as I stared at the letters piled on the library table. Intuition attracted me to them. I flipped through the stacks with the professional speed of a mail sorter, seeking a sample of Jake's handwriting. I found it. The envelope was postmarked

September 10; it was on the official stationery of the Investigation Bureau, and had been sent from the state capital. It was a brief letter, but the firm masculine style of the penmanship disguised the author's anguish:

Your letter from Istanbul arrived today. When I read it I was sober. I'm not so sober now. Last August, the day Addie died, I sent a telegram asking you to call me. But I guess you were overseas. But that is what I had to tell you —Addie is gone. I still don't believe it, and I never will, not until I know what really happened. Two days before our wedding she and Marylee were swimming in Blue River. Addie drowned; but Marylee didn't see her drown. I can't write about it. I've got to get away. I don't trust myself. Wherever I go, Marylee Connor will know how to locate me. Sincerely . . .

MARYLEE CONNOR: Why, hello! Why, sure, I recognized your voice right off.

TC: I've been calling you every half-hour all afternoon.

MARYLEE: Where are you?

TC: New York.

MARYLEE: How's the weather?

TC: It's raining.

MARYLEE: Raining here, too. But we can use it. We've had such a dry summer. Can't get the dust out of your hair. You say you've been calling me?

TC: All afternoon.

MARYLEE: Well, I was home. But I'm afraid my hearing's not too good. And I've been down in the cellar and up in the attic. Packing. Now that I'm alone, this house is too much for me. We have a cousin—she's a widow, too—she bought a place in Florida, a condominium, and I'm going to live with her. Well, how are you? Have you spoken to Jake lately?

(I explained that I'd just returned from Europe, and had not been able to contact Jake; she said he was staying with one of his sons in Oregon, and gave me the telephone number.)

Poor Jake. He's taken it all so hard. Somehow he seems to blame himself. Oh? Oh, you didn't *know*?

TC: Jake wrote me, but I didn't get the letter until today. I can't tell you how sorry . . .

MARYLEE (a catch in her voice): You didn't know about Addie?

TC: Not until today . . .

MARYLEE (suspiciously): What did Jake say?

TC: He said she drowned.

MARYLEE (defensively, as though we were arguing): Well, she did. And I don't care what Jake thinks. Bob Quinn was nowhere in sight. He *couldn't* have had anything to do with it.

(I heard her take a deep breath, followed by a long pause—as if, attempting to control her temper, she was counting to ten.)

If anybody's to blame, it's me. It was my idea to drive out to Sandy Cove for a swim. Sandy Cove doesn't even belong to Quinn. It's on the Miller ranch. Addie and I always used to go there; it's shady and you can hide from the sun. It's the safest part of Blue River; it has a natural pool, and it's where we learned to swim when we were little girls. That day we had Sandy Cove all to ourselves; we went into the water together, and Addie remarked how this time next week she'd be swimming in the Pacific Ocean. Addie was a strong swimmer, but I tire easily. So after I'd cooled off, I spread a towel under a tree and started reading through some of the magazines we'd brought along. Addie stayed in the water; I heard her say: "I'm going to swim around the bend and sit on the waterfall." The river flows out of Sandy Cove and sweeps around a bend; beyond the bend a rocky ridge runs across the river, creating a small waterfall—a short drop, not more than two feet. When we were children it was fun to sit on the ridge and feel the water rushing between our legs.

I was reading, not noticing the time until I felt a shiver and saw the sun was slanting toward the mountains; I wasn't worried—I imagined Addie was still enjoying the waterfall. But after a while I walked down to the river and shouted Addie! Addie! I thought: Maybe she's trying to tease me. So I climbed the embankment to the top of Sandy Cove; from there I could see the waterfall and the whole river moving north. There was no one there; no Addie. Then, just below the fall, I saw a white lily pad floating on the water, bobbing. But then I realized it wasn't a lily; it was a hand —with a diamond twinkling: Addie's engagement ring, the little diamond Jake gave her. I slid down the embankment and waded into the river and crawled along the waterfall ridge. The water was very clear and not too deep: I could see Addie's face under the surface and her hair tangled in the twigs of a tree branch, a sunken tree. It was hopeless—I grabbed her hand and pulled and pulled with all my strength but I couldn't budge her. Somehow, we'll never know how, she'd fallen off the ridge and the tree had caught her hair, held her down. *Accidental death by drowning.* That was the coroner's verdict. Hello?

TC: Yes, I'm here.

MARYLEE: My grandmother Mason never used the word "death." When someone died, especially someone she cared about, she always said that they had been "called back." She meant that they had not been buried, lost forever; but, rather, that the person had been "called back" to a happy childhood place, a world of living things. And that's how I feel about my sister. Addie was called back to live among the things she loves. Children. Children and flowers. Birds. The wild plants she found in the mountains.

TC: I'm so very sorry, Mrs. Connor. I . . .

MARYLEE: That's all right, dear.

TC: I wish there was something . . .

MARYLEE: Well, it was good to hear from you. And when you speak to Jake, remember to give him my love.

I showered, set a bottle of brandy beside my bed, climbed under the covers, took the telephone off the night table, nestled it on my stomach, and dialed the Oregon number that I had been given. Jake's son answered; he said his father was out, he wasn't sure where and didn't know when to expect him. I left a message for Jake to call as soon as he came home, no matter the hour. I filled my mouth with all the brandy it could hold, and rinsed it around like a mouthwash, a medicine to stop my teeth from chattering. I let the brandy trickle down my throat. Sleep, in the curving shape of a murmuring river, flowed through my head; in the end, it was always the river; everything returned to it. Quinn may have provided the rattlesnakes, the fire, the nicotine, the steel wire; but the river had inspired those deeds, and now it had claimed Addie, too. Addie: her hair, tangled in watery undergrowths, drifted, in my dream, across her wavering drowned face like a bridal veil.

An earthquake erupted; the earthquake was the telephone, rumbling on my stomach where it had still been resting when I dozed off. I knew it was Jake. I let it ring while I poured myself a guaranteed eye-opener.

TC: Jake?

JAKE: So you finally made it back stateside?

TC: This morning.

JAKE: Well, you didn't miss the wedding, after all.

TC: I got your letter. Jake—

JAKE: No. You don't have to make a speech.

TC: I called Mrs. Connor. Marylee. We had a long talk—

JAKE (alertly): Yeah?

TC: She told me everything that happened—

JAKE: Oh, no she didn't! Damned if she did!

TC (jolted by the harshness of his response): But, Jake, she said—

JAKE: *Yeah*. What did she say?

TC: She said it was an accident.

JAKE: You believed that?

> (The tone of his voice, grimly mocking, suggested Jake's expression: his eyes hard, his thin quirky lips twitching.)

TC: From what she told me, it seems the only explanation.

JAKE: She doesn't know what happened. She wasn't *there*. She was sitting on her butt reading magazines.

TC: Well, if it was Quinn—

JAKE: I'm listening.

TC: Then he must be a magician.

JAKE: Not necessarily. But I can't discuss it just now. Soon, maybe. A little something happened that might hasten matters. Santa Claus came early this year.

TC: Are we talking about Jaeger?

JAKE: Yessir, the postmaster got his package.

TC: When?

JAKE: Yesterday. (He laughed, not with pleasure but excitement, released energy) Bad news for Jaeger but good news for me. My plan was to stay up here till after Thanksgiving. But boy, I was going nuts. All I could hear was slamming doors. All I could think was: Suppose he doesn't go after Jaeger? Suppose he doesn't give me that one last chance? Well, you can call me at the Prairie Motel tomorrow night. Because that's where I'll be.

TC: Jake, wait a minute. It has to have been an accident. Addie, I mean.

JAKE (unctuously patient, as though instructing a retarded aborigine): Now I'll leave you with something to sleep on.

Sandy Cove, where this "accident" occurred, is the property of a man named A. J. Miller. There are two ways to reach it. The shortest way is to take a back road that cuts across Quinn's place and leads straight to Miller's ranch. Which is what the ladies did.

Adios, amigo.

Naturally, the something he had left me to sleep on kept me sleepless until daybreak. Images formed, faded; it was as though I were mentally editing a motion picture.

Addie and her sister are in their car driving along the highway. They turn off the highway and onto a dirt road that is part of the B.Q. Ranch. Quinn is standing on the veranda of his house; or perhaps watching from a window: whenever, however, at some point he spies the trespassing car, recognizes its occupants, and guesses that they are headed for a swim at Sandy Cove. He decides to follow them. By car? or horseback? afoot? Anyway, he approaches the area where the women are bathing by a round-about route. Once there, he conceals himself among the shady trees above Sandy Cove. Marylee is resting on a towel reading magazines. Addie is in the water. He hears Addie tell her sister: "I'm going to swim around the bend and sit on the waterfall." Ideal; now Addie will be unprotected, alone, out of her sister's view. Quinn waits until he is certain she is playfully absorbed at the waterfall. Presently, he slides down the embankment (the same embankment the searching Marylee later used). Addie doesn't hear him; the splashing waterfall covers the sound of his movements. But how can he avoid her eyes? For surely, the instant she sees him, she will acknowledge her danger, protest, scream. No, he obtains her silence with a gun. Addie hears something, looks up, sees Quinn swiftly striding across the ridge, revolver aimed—he shoves her off the waterfall, plunges after her, pulls her under, holds her there: a final baptism.

It was possible.

But daybreak, and the beginning noise of New York traffic, lessened my enthusiasm for fevered fantasizing, briskly dropped me deep into that discouraging abyss—reality. Jake was without choice: like Quinn, he had set himself a passionate task, and his task, his human duty, was to prove that Quinn was responsible for nine indecent deaths, particularly the death of a warm, companionable woman he had wanted to marry. But unless Jake had evolved a theory more convincing than my own imagination had managed, then I preferred to forget it; I was satisfied to fall asleep remembering the coroner's common-sense verdict: *Accidental death by drowning*.

An hour later I was wide awake, a victim of jet lag. Awake but weary, fretful; and hungry, starved. Of course, due to my prolonged absence, the refrigerator contained nothing edible. Soured milk, stale bread, black bananas, rotten eggs, shriveled oranges, withered apples, putrid tomatoes, a chocolate cake iced with fungus. I made a cup of coffee, added brandy to it, and with that to fortify me, examined my accumulated mail. My birthday had fallen on September 30, and a few well-wishers had sent cards. One of them was from Fred Wilson, the retired detective and mutual friend who had first introduced me to Jake Pepper. I knew he was familiar with Jake's case, that Jake often consulted him, but for some reason we had never discussed it, an omission I now rectified by calling him.

TC: Hello? May I speak to Mr. Wilson, please?

FRED WILSON: Speaking.

TC: Fred? You sound like you have a helluva cold.

FRED: You bet. It's a real granddaddy.

TC: Thanks for the birthday card.

FRED: Aw, hell. You didn't have to spend your money just for that.

TC: Well, I wanted to talk to you about Jake Pepper.

FRED: Say, there must be something to this telepathy stuff. I was thinking about Jake when the phone rang. You know, his Bureau has him on leave. They're trying to force him off that case.

TC: He's back on it now.

(After I recounted the conversation I'd had with Jake the previous evening, Fred asked several questions, mostly about Addie Mason's death and Jake's opinions pertaining to it.)

FRED: I'm damned surprised the Bureau would let him go back there. Jake's the fairest-minded man I've ever met. There's nobody in our business I respect more than Pepper. But he's lost all judgment. He's been banging his head against a wall so long he's knocked all the sense out of it. Sure, it was terrible what happened to his girl friend. But it was an accident. She drowned. But Jake can't accept that. He's standing on rooftops shouting murder. Accusing this man Quinn.

TC (resentfully): Jake could be right. It's possible.

FRED: And it's also possible the man is one-hundred-percent innocent. In fact, that seems to be the general consensus. I've talked with guys in Jake's own Bureau, and they say you couldn't swat a fly with the evidence they've got. Said it was downright embarrassing. And Jake's own chief told me, said so far as he knew, Quinn had never killed anybody.

TC: He killed two cattle rustlers.

FRED (chuckles, followed by a coughing fit): Well, sir. We don't exactly call that killin'. Not around these parts.

TC: Except they weren't cattle rustlers. They were two gamblers from Denver; Quinn owed them money. And what's more, I don't think Addie's death was an accident.

(Defiantly, with astounding authority, I related the "murder" as I had imagined it; the surmises I had rejected at dawn now seemed not only plausible but vividly convincing: Quinn *had* trailed the sisters to Sandy Cove, hidden among the trees, slid down the embankment, threatened Addie with a gun, trapped her, drowned her.)

FRED: That's Jake's story.

TC: No.

FRED: It's just something you worked out by yourself?

TC: More or less.

FRED: All the same, that *is* Jake's story. Hang on, I gotta blow my honker.

TC: What do you mean—"that *is* Jake's story"?

FRED: Like I said, there must be something to this telepathy stuff. Give or take a lotta little details, and that *is* Jake's story. He filed a report, and sent me a copy. And in the report that's how he reconstructed events: Quinn saw the car, he followed them . . .

(Fred continued. A hot wave of shame hit me; I felt like a schoolboy caught cheating in an exam. Irrationally, instead of blaming myself, I blamed Jake; I was angry at him for not having produced a solid solution, crestfallen that his conjectures were no better than mine. I trusted Jake, the professional man, and was miserable when I felt that trust seesawing. But it was such a haphazard concoction—Quinn and

Addie and the waterfall. Even so, regardless of Fred Wilson's destructive comments, I knew that the basic faith I had in Jake was justified.)
The Bureau's in a tough spot. They have to take Jake off this case. He's
disqualified himself. Oh, he'll fight them! But it's for the sake of his own
reputation. Safety, too. One night here, it was after he lost his girl friend,
he rang me up around four in the morning. Drunker than a hundred
Indians dancing in a cornfield. The gist of it was: he was gonna challenge
Quinn to a duel. I checked on him the next day. Bastard, he didn't even
remember calling me.

Anxiety, as any expensive psychiatrist will tell you, is caused by depression; but depression, as the same psychiatrist will inform you on a second
visit and for an additional fee, is caused by anxiety. I rotated around in that
humdrum circle all afternoon. By nightfall the two demons had combined;
while anxiety copulated with depression, I sat staring at Mr. Bell's contro-
versial invention, fearing the moment when I would have to dial the Prairie
Motel and hear Jake admit that the Bureau was taking him off the case. Of
course, a good meal might have helped; but I had already abolished my
hunger by eating the chocolate cake with the fungus icing. Or I could have
gone to a movie and smoked some grass. But when you're in that kind of
sweat, the only lasting remedy is to ride with it: accept the anxiety, be
depressed, relax, and let the current carry you where it will.

OPERATOR: Good evening. Prairie Motel. Mr. Pepper? Hey, Ralph, you
seen Jake Pepper? In the bar? Hello, sir—your party's in the bar. I'm
ringing.
TC: Thank you.

(I remembered the Prairie Bar; unlike the motel, it had a certain
comic-strip charm. Cowboy customers, rawhide walls decorated with
girlie posters and Mexican sombreros, a rest room for BULLS, another for BELLES, and a jukebox devoted to the twangs of Country
& Western music. A jukebox blast announced that the bartender had
answered.)

BARTENDER: Jake Pepper! Somebody for you. Hello, mister. He wants to
know who is it?
TC: A friend from New York.
JAKE'S VOICE (distantly; rising in volume as he approaches the phone): Sure
I have friends in New York. Tokyo. Bombay. Hello, my friend from New
York!
TC: You sound jolly.

JAKE: About as jolly as a beggar's monkey.

TC: Can you talk? Or should I call later?

JAKE: This is okay. It's so noisy nobody can hear me.

TC (tentative; wary of opening wounds): So. How's it going?

JAKE: Not so hotsy-totsy.

TC: Is it the Bureau?

JAKE (puzzled): The Bureau?

TC: Well, I thought they might be giving you trouble.

JAKE: They ain't giving *me* no trouble. But I'm giving them plenty. Buncha nitwits. No, it's that knucklehead Jaeger. Our beloved postmaster. He's chicken. He wants to skip the coop. And I don't know how to stop him. But I've got to.

TC: Why?

JAKE: "The shark needs bait."

TC: Have you talked to Jaeger?

JAKE: For hours. He's with me now. Sitting over there in the corner like a little white rabbit ready to jump down a hole.

TC: Well, I can sympathize with that.

JAKE: I can't afford to. I've got to hold on to this old sissy. But how? He's sixty-four; he's got a bundle of dough and a pension coming. He's a bachelor; his closest living relative is Bob Quinn! For Christ's sake. And get this: he still doesn't believe Quinn did it. He says yes, maybe somebody means to harm me, but it can't be Bob Quinn; he's my own flesh and blood. There's just one thing that gives him pause.

TC: Something to do with the package?

JAKE: Uh-huh.

TC: The handwriting? No, it can't be that. It must be the picture.

JAKE: Nice shot. This picture's different. It's not like the others. For one thing, it's about twenty years old. It was made at the State Fair; Jaeger is marching in a Kiwanis parade—he's wearing a Kiwanis hat. *Quinn took the picture.* Jaeger says he saw him take it; the reason he remembers is because he asked Quinn to give him a copy, and Quinn never did.

TC: That ought to make the postmaster think twice. I doubt that it would do much to a jury.

JAKE: Actually, it doesn't do much to the postmaster.

TC: But he's frightened enough to leave town?

JAKE: He's scared, sure. But even if he wasn't, there's nothing to keep him here. He says he always planned to spend the last years of his life traveling. My job is to delay the journey. Indefinitely. Listen, I'd better not leave my little rabbit alone too long. So wish me luck. And keep in touch.

I wished him luck, but he was not lucky; within a week, both the postmaster and the detective had gone their separate ways: the former packed for global wanderings, the latter because the Bureau had removed him from the case.

The following notes are excerpted from my personal journals: 1975 through 1979.

20 October 1975: Spoke to Jake. Very bitter; spewing venom in all directions. He said "for two pins and a Confederate dollar" he'd quit, write in his resignation, go to Oregon and work on his son's farm. "But as long as I'm here with the Bureau, I've still got a whip to crack." Also, if he quit now, he could forfeit his retirement pension, a *beau geste* I'm sure he can't afford.

6 November 1975: Spoke to Jake. He said they were having a cattle-rustling epidemic in the northeast part of the state. Rustlers steal the cattle at night, load them into trucks, and drive them down into the Dakotas. He said that he and some other agents had spent the last few nights out on the open range, hiding among the cattle herds, waiting for rustlers who never showed up: "Man, it's cold out there! I'm too old for this tough-guy stuff." He mentioned that Marylee Connor had moved to Sarasota.

25 November 1975: Thanksgiving. Awoke this morning, and thought of Jake, and remembered it was just a year ago that he had got his "big break": that he had gone to Addie's for dinner and she had told him about Quinn and Blue River. I decided against calling him; it might aggravate, rather than alleviate, the painful ironies attached to this particular anniversary. Did call Fred Wilson and his wife, Alice, to wish them *"bon appétit."* Fred asked about Jake; I said the last I heard he was busy chasing cattle rustlers. Fred said: "Yeah, they're workin' his ass off. Trying to keep his mind off that other deal, what the Bureau guys call 'The Rattlesnake Baby.' They've assigned a young fellow named Nelson to it; but that's just for appearance sake. Legally, the case is open; but for all practical purposes the Bureau has drawn a line through it."

5 December 1975: Spoke to Jake. The first thing he said was: "You'll be pleased to hear the postmaster is safe and sound in Honolulu. He's been mailing postcards to everybody. I'm sure he sent one to Quinn. Well, he got to go to Honolulu, and I didn't. Yessir, life is strange." He said he was still in the "cattle-rustling business. And damned sick of it. I ought to join the rustlers. They make a hundred times the money I do."

20 December 1975: Received a Christmas card from Marylee Connor. She wrote: "Sarasota is lovely! This is my first winter in a warm climate, and I can honestly say I don't miss home. Did you know that Sarasota is famous as a winter quarter for the Ringling Bros. Circus? My cousin and I often drive over to watch the performers practice. It's the best fun! We've

become friendly with a Russian woman who trains acrobats. May God see you through the New Year, and please find enclosed a small gift." The gift was an amateurish family-album snapshot of Addie as a young girl, perhaps sixteen, standing in a flower garden, wearing a white summer dress with a matching hair ribbon, and cradling in her arms, as though it were as fragile as the surrounding foliage, a white kitten; the kitten is yawning. On the back of the picture, Marylee had written: *Adelaide Minerva Mason. Born 14 June 1930. Called Back 29 August 1975.*

1 January 1976: Jake called—"Happy New Year!" He sounded like a gravedigger digging his own grave. He said he'd spent New Year's Eve in bed reading *David Copperfield.* "The Bureau had a big party. But I didn't go. I knew if I did I'd get drunk and knock some heads together. Maybe a lotta heads. Drunk or sober, whenever I'm around the chief it's all I can do not to throw a punch bag into his fat gut." I told him I'd received a card from Marylee at Christmas and described the picture of Addie accompanying it, and he said yes, Marylee had sent him a very similar picture: "But what does it mean? What she wrote—'Called Back'?" When I tried to interpret the phrase as I understood it, he stopped me with a grunt: it was too fanciful for him; and he remarked: "I love Marylee. I've always said she's a sweet woman. But simple. Just a mite simple."

5 February 1976: Last week I bought a frame for Addie's snapshot. I put it on a table in my bedroom. Yesterday I removed it to a drawer. It was too disturbing, alive—especially the kitten's yawn.

14 February 1976: Three valentines—one from an old schoolteacher, Miss Wood; another from my tax accountant; and a third signed Love, Bob Quinn. A joke, of course. Jake's idea of black comedy?

15 February 1976: Called Jake, and he confessed yes, he'd sent the valentine. I said well, you must have been drunk. He said: "I was."

20 April 1976: A short letter from Jake scribbled on Prairie Motel stationery: "Have been here two days collecting gossip, mostly at the Okay Café. The postmaster is still in Honolulu. Juanita Quinn had a pretty bad stroke. I like Juanita, so I was sorry to hear it. But her husband is fit as a fiddle. Which is the way I prefer it. I don't want anything to happen to Quinn until I have a final crack at him. The Bureau may have forgotten this matter, but not me. I'll never give up. Sincerely . . ."

10 July 1976: Called Jake last night, not having heard from him for more than two months. The man I spoke to was a new Jake Pepper; or rather, the old Jake Pepper, vigorous, optimistic—it was as though he had at last emerged from an inebriated slumber, his rested muscles primed to prowl. I quickly learned what had roused him: "I've got a devil by the tail. A humdinger." The humdinger, though it contained one intriguing element, turned out to be a very ordinary murder; or so it struck me. A young man, aged twenty-two, lived alone on a modest farm with an elderly grandfa-

ther. Earlier in the spring the grandson killed the old man in order to inherit his property and steal money the victim had misered away under a mattress. Neighbors noticed the farmer's disappearance and saw that the young man was driving a flashy new car. The police were notified, and they soon discovered that the grandson, who had no explanation for his relative's sudden and complete absence, had bought the new car with old cash. The suspect would neither admit nor deny that he had murdered his grandfather, though the authorities were certain he had. The difficulty was: no corpse. Without a body they couldn't make an arrest. But search as they might, the victim remained invisible. The local constabulary requested aid from the State Bureau of Investigation, and Jake was assigned to the case. "It's fascinating. This kid is smart as hell. Whatever he did to that old man is diabolical. And if we can't find the body, he'll go scot-free. But I'm sure it's somewhere on that farm. Every instinct tells me he chopped Grandpa into mincemeat and buried the parts in different spots. All I need is the head. I'll find it if I have to plow the place up acre by acre. Inch by inch." After we'd hung up, I felt a surge of anger; and jealousy: not just a twinge, but a mean jab, as though I'd recently learned of a lover's betrayal. In truth, I don't want Jake to be interested in any case other than the case that interests me.

20 July 1976: A telegram from Jake. *Have Head One Hand Two Feet Stop Gone Fishing Jake.* I wonder why he sent a telegram instead of calling? Can he imagine that I resent this success? I'm pleased, for I know his pride has been at least partially restored. I only hope that wherever he has "gone fishing," it is somewhere in the neighborhood of Blue River.

22 July 1976: Wrote Jake a congratulatory letter, and told him I was going abroad for three months.

20 December 1976: A Christmas card from Sarasota. "If you ever come this way, please stop by. God bless you. Marylee Connor."

22 February 1977: A note from Marylee: "I still subscribe to the home-town paper, and thought the enclosed clipping might interest you. I've written her husband. He sent me such a lovely letter at the time of Addie's accident." The clipping was Juanita Quinn's obituary; she had died in her sleep. Surprisingly, there was to be no service or burial, for the deceased had requested that she be cremated and her ashes scattered over Blue River.

23 February 1977: Called Jake. He said, rather sheepishly: "Hiya, pardner! You've been quite the stranger." In fact, I'd mailed him a letter from Switzerland, to which he had not replied; and though I'd failed to reach him, had twice phoned during the Christmas holidays. "Oh, yeah, I was in Oregon." Then I came to the point: Juanita Quinn's obituary. Predictably, he said: "I'm suspicious"; and when I asked why, answered: "Crema-tions always make me suspicious." We talked another quarter-hour, but it was a self-conscious conversation, an effort on his part. Perhaps I remind

him of matters that, for all his moral strength, he is beginning to want to forget.

10 July 1977: Jake called, elated. Without preamble, he announced: "Like I told you, cremations always make me suspicious. Bob Quinn's a bride-groom! Well, everybody knew he had another family, a woman with four children fathered by Squire Quinn. He kept them hidden over in Apple-ton, a place about a hundred miles southwest. Last week he married the lady. Brought his bride and brood back to the ranch, proud as a rooster. Juanita would spin in her grave. If she *had* a grave." Stupidly, dazed by the speed of Jake's narrative, I asked: "How old are the children?" He said: "The youngest is ten and the oldest seventeen. All girls. I tell you, the town is in an uproar. Sure, they can handle murder, a couple of homicides don't faze them; but to have their shining knight, their big War Hero, show up with this brazen trollop and her four little bastards is too much for their Presbyterian eyebrows." I said: "I feel sorry for the children. The woman, too." Jake said: "I'll save my sorrow for Juanita. If there was a body to exhume, I'll bet the coroner would find a nice dose of nicotine inside it." I said: "I doubt that. He wouldn't hurt Juanita. She was an alcoholic. He was her savior. He loved her." Quietly, Jake said: "And I gather you don't think he had anything to do with Addie's 'accident'?" I said: "He meant to kill her. He would have, eventually. But then she drowned." Jake said: "Saving him the trouble! Okay. Explain Clem Anderson, the Baxters." I said: "Yes, that was all Quinn's work. He had to do it. He's a messiah with a task." Jake said: "Then why did he let the postmaster glide through his fingers?" I said: "Has he? My guess is that old Mr. Jaeger has an appoint-ment in Samarra. Quinn will cross his path one day. Quinn can't rest until that happens. He's not sane, you know." Jake hung up, but not before acrimoniously asking: "Are you?"

15 December 1977: Saw a black alligator wallet in a pawnshop window. It was in fine condition, and initialed J.P. I bought it, and because our last conversation had ended angrily (he was angry, I wasn't), I sent it to Jake as both a Christmas present and a peace offering.

22 December 1977: A Christmas card from the faithful Mrs. Connor: "I'm working for the circus! No, I'm not an acrobat. I'm a receptionist. It beats shuffleboard! All wishes for the New Year."

17 January 1978: A four-line scrawl from Jake thanking me for the wallet —curtly, inadequately. I'm receptive to hints. I won't write or call again.

20 December 1978: A Christmas card from Marylee Connor, just her signature; nothing from Jake.

12 September 1979: Fred Wilson and his wife were in New York last week, en route to Europe (their first trip), happy as honeymooners. I took them to dinner; all talk was limited to the excitements of their impending tour until, while selecting desserts, Fred said: "I notice you haven't men-

tioned Jake." I pretended surprise, and casually remarked that I hadn't heard from Jake in well over a year. Shrewdly, Fred asked: "You fellows have a falling out?" I shrugged: "Nothing quite so clean-cut. But we haven't always seen eye to eye." Then Fred said: "Jake's had bad health problems lately. Emphysema. He's retiring the end of this month. Now, it's none of my business, but I think it would be a nice gesture if you called him. Just now he needs a pat on the back."

14 September 1979: I shall always be grateful to Fred Wilson; he had made it easy for me to swallow my pride and call Jake. We spoke this morning; it was as if we had talked yesterday, and the day before. One wouldn't believe that there had ever been an interruption in our friendship. He confirmed the news of his retirement: "Just sixteen days to go!"—and said that he planned to live with his son in Oregon. "But before that, I'm going to spend a day or two at the Prairie Motel. I've some unfinished chores in that town. There's some records in the courthouse I want to steal for my files. Hey, listen! Why don't we go together? Have a real reunion. I could meet you at Denver and drive you down." Jake did not have to pressure me; if he hadn't offered the invitation, I would have suggested it myself: I had often dreamed, while awake or asleep, of returning to that melancholy village, for I wanted to see Quinn again—meet and talk with him, just the two of us alone.

It was the second day of October.

Jake, declining an offer to accompany me, had lent me his car, and after lunch I left the Prairie Motel to keep an appointment at the B.Q. Ranch. I remembered the last time I had traveled this territory: the full moon, the fields of snow, the cutting cold, the cattle banded together, gathered in groups, their warm breath smoking the arctic air. Now, in October, the landscape was gloriously different: the macadam highway was like a skinny black sea dividing a golden continent; on either side, the sun-bleached stubble of threshed wheat flamed, rippled with yellow colors, sable shadows under a cloudless sky. Bulls pranced about these pastures; and cows, among them mothers with new calves, grazed, dozed.

At the entrance to the ranch, a young girl was leaning against a sign, the one with the crossed tomahawks. She smiled, and waved for me to stop.

YOUNG GIRL: Afternoon! I'm Nancy Quinn. My dad sent me to meet you.
TC: Well, thanks.
NANCY QUINN (opening the car door, climbing in): He's fishing. I'll have to show you where he is.

(She was a cheerful twelve-year-old snaggle-toothed tomboy. Her tawny hair was chopped short, and she was splashed with freckles from top to bottom. She was wearing only an old bathing suit. One of her knees was wrapped in a dirty bandage.)

TC (referring to the bandage): Hurt yourself?

NANCY QUINN: Naw. Well, I got throwed.

TC: Throwed?

NANCY QUINN: Bad Boy throwed me. He's one mean horse. That's how come they call him Bad Boy. He's throwed every kid on the ranch. Most of the guys, too. I said well, I bet I can ride him. And I did. For 'bout two seconds flat.

You been here before?

TC: Once; years ago. But it was at night. I remember a wooden bridge—

NANCY QUINN: That's it yonder!

(We crossed the bridge: finally I saw Blue River; but it was a glimpse as swift and flurried as a hummingbird's flight, for overhanging trees, leafless when last seen, blazed with obscuring autumn-trimmed foliage.)

You ever been to Appleton?

TC: No.

NANCY QUINN: *Never?* That's funny. I never met nobody that's never been to Appleton.

TC: Have I missed something?

NANCY QUINN: Oh, it's okay. We used to live there. But I like it here better. It's easier to get off by yourself and do the kinda stuff I like. Fish. Shoot coyotes. My dad said he'd give me a dollar for every coyote I shot down; but after he'd give me more'n two hundred dollars, he cut me down to a dime. Well, I don't need money. I'm not like my sisters. Always got their face stuck in a mirror.

I got three sisters, and I'll tell you they're not too happy here. They don't like horses; they hate most everything. Boys. That's all they've got on their mind. When we lived in Appleton, we didn't see so much of my dad. Maybe like once a week. So they put on perfume and lipstick and had plenty of boyfriends. That was okay with my mom. She's a lot like them, someways. She likes to fuss with herself and look pretty. But my dad is real strict. He won't let my sisters have any boyfriends. Or wear lipstick. One time some of their old boyfriends drove over from Appleton, and my dad met them at the door with a shotgun; he told them, said the next time he saw them on his property he'd blow their heads off. Wow, did those guys scoot! The girls cried themselves sick. But the whole thing gives me the biggest laugh.

See that fork in the road? Stop there.

(I stopped the car; we both got out. She pointed to an opening in the trees: a dark, leafy, downward-sloping path.)
Just follow that.
TC (suddenly afraid to be alone): You're not coming with me?
NANCY QUINN: My dad don't like anybody around when he talks business.
TC: Well, thanks again.
NANCY QUINN: My pleasure!

She walked away whistling.

Parts of the path were so overgrown that I had to bend branches, shield my face against brushing leaves. Briars, strange thorns caught at my trousers; high in the trees, crows cawed, screamed. I saw an owl; it's odd to see an owl in daylight; he blinked, but did not stir. Once, I almost stumbled into a beehive—an old hollow tree-stump swarming with wild black bees. Always I could hear the river, a slow soft churning roar; then, at a curve in the path, I saw it; and saw Quinn, too.

He was wearing a rubber suit, and holding aloft, as though it were a conductor's baton, a supple fishing rod. He stood waist-deep, his hatless head in profile; his hair was no longer flecked with gray—it was white as the water-foam circling his hips. I wanted to turn and run, for the scene was so strongly reminiscent of that other day, that long-ago time when Quinn's look-alike, the Reverend Billy Joe Snow, had waited for me in waist-high water. Suddenly I heard my name; Quinn was calling it, and beckoning to me as he waded toward shore.

I thought of the young bulls I had seen parading in the golden pastures; Quinn, glistening in his rubber suit, reminded me of them—vital, powerful, dangerous; except for his whiter hair, he hadn't aged an iota; indeed, he seemed years younger, a man of fifty in perfect health.

Smiling, he squatted on a rock, and motioned for me to join him. He displayed some trout he'd caught. "Kinda puny. But they'll eat good."

I mentioned Nancy. He grinned and said: "Nancy. Oh, yeah. She's a good kid." He left it at that. He didn't refer to his wife's death, or the fact that he had remarried: he assumed I was aware of his recent history.

He said: "I was surprised when you called me."

"Oh?"

"I don't know. Just surprised. Where you staying?"

"At the Prairie Motel. Where else?"

After a silence, and almost shyly, he asked: "Jake Pepper with you?"
I nodded.

"Somebody told me he was leaving the Bureau."

"Yes. He's going to live in Oregon."

"Well, I don't guess I'll ever see the old bastard again. Too bad. We could've been real friends. If he hadn't had all those suspicions. Damn his soul, he even thought I drowned poor Addie Mason!" He laughed; then scowled. "The way I look at it is: it was the hand of God." He raised his own hand, and the river, viewed between his spread fingers, seemed to weave between them like a dark ribbon. "God's work. His will."

PORTRAITS

The Duke in
His Domain

(1956)

MOST JAPANESE GIRLS GIGGLE. THE little maid on the fourth floor of the Miyako Hotel, in Kyoto, was no exception. Hilarity, and attempts to suppress it, pinked her cheeks (unlike the Chinese, the Japanese complexion more often than not has considerable color), shook her plump peony-and-pansy-kimonoed figure. There seemed to be no particular reason for this merriment; the Japanese giggle operates without apparent motivation. I'd merely asked to be directed toward a certain room. "You come see Marron?" she gasped, showing, like so many of her fellow-countrymen, an array of gold teeth. Then, with the tiny, pigeon-toed skating steps that the wearing of a kimono necessitates, she led me through a labyrinth of corridors, promising, "I knock you Marron." The "l" sound does not exist in Japanese, and by "Marron" the maid meant Marlon—Marlon Brando, the American actor, who was at that time in Kyoto doing location work for the Warner Brothers–William Goetz motion-picture version of James Michener's novel *Sayonara*.

My guide tapped at Brando's door, shrieked "Marron!" and fled away along the corridor, her kimono sleeves fluttering like the wings of a parakeet. The door was opened by another doll-delicate Miyako maid, who at once succumbed to her own fit of quaint hysteria. From an inner room, Brando called, "What is it, honey?" But the girl, her eyes squeezed shut with mirth and her fat little hands jammed into her mouth, like a bawling baby's, was incapable of reply. "Hey, honey, what is it?" Brando again inquired, and appeared in the doorway. "Oh, hi," he said when he saw me. "It's seven, huh?" We'd made a seven-o'clock date for dinner; I was nearly twenty minutes late. "Well, take off your shoes and come on in. I'm just finishing up here. And, hey, honey," he told the maid, "bring us some ice." Then, looking after the girl as she scurried off, he cocked his hands on his hips and, grinning, declared, "They kill me. They really kill me. The kids, too. Don't you think they're wonderful, don't you love them—Japanese kids?"

The Miyako, where about half of the *Sayonara* company was staying, is the most prominent of the so-called Western-style hotels in Kyoto; the majority of its rooms are furnished with sturdy, if commonplace and cumbersome, European chairs and tables, beds and couches. But for the convenience of Japanese guests, who prefer their own mode of décor while desiring the prestige of staying at the Miyako, or of those foreign travelers who yearn after authentic atmosphere yet are disinclined to endure the unheated rigors of a real Japanese inn, the Miyako maintains some suites decorated in the traditional manner, and it was in one of these that Brando had chosen to settle himself. His quarters consisted of two rooms, a bath and a glassed-in sun porch. Without the overlying and underlying clutter of Brando's personal belongings, the rooms would have been textbook illustrations of the Japanese penchant for an ostentatious barrenness. The floors were covered with tawny *tatami* matting, with a discreet scattering of raw-silk pillows; a scroll depicting swimming golden carp hung in an alcove, and beneath it, on a stand, sat a vase filled with tall lilies and red leaves, arranged just so. The larger of the two rooms—the inner one— which the occupant was using as a sort of business office where he also dined and slept, contained a long, low lacquer table and a sleeping pallet. In these rooms, the divergent concepts of Japanese and Western decoration —the one seeking to impress by a lack of display, an absence of possession- exhibiting, the other intent on precisely the reverse—could both be ob- served, for Brando seemed unwilling to make use of the apartment's storage space, concealed behind sliding paper doors. All that he owned seemed to be out in the open. Shirts, ready for the laundry; socks, too; shoes and sweaters and jackets and hats and ties, flung around like the costume of a dismantled scarecrow. And cameras, a typewriter, a tape recorder, an electric heater that performed with stifling competence. Here, there, pieces of partly nibbled fruit; a box of the famous Japanese strawberries, each berry the size of an egg. And books, a deep-thought cascade, among which one saw Colin Wilson's *The Outsider* and various works on Buddhist prayer, Zen meditation, Yogi breathing and Hindu mysticism, but no fiction, for Brando reads none. He has never, he professes, opened a novel since April 3, 1924, the day he was born, in Omaha, Nebraska. But while he may not care to read fiction, he does desire to write it, and the long lacquer table was loaded with overfilled ashtrays and piled pages of his most recent creative effort, which happens to be a film script entitled *A Burst of Vermilion*.

In fact, Brando had evidently been working on his story at the moment of my arrival. As I entered the room, a subdued-looking, youngish man, whom I shall call Murray, and who had previously been pointed out to me as "the fellow that's helping Marlon with his writing," was squatted on the matting, fumbling through the manuscript of *A Burst of Vermilion*. Weighing some pages on his hand, he said, "Tell ya, Mar, s'pose I go over this down in my room, and maybe we'll get together again—say, around ten-thirty?"

Brando scowled, as though unsympathetic to the idea of resuming their endeavors later in the evening. Having been slightly ill, as I learned later, he had spent the day in his room, and now seemed restive. "What's this?" he asked, pointing to a couple of oblong packages among the literary remains on the lacquer table.

Murray shrugged. The maid had delivered them; that was all he knew. "People are always sending Mar presents," he told me. "Lots of times we don't know who sent them. True, Mar?"

"Yeah," said Brando, beginning to rip open the gifts, which, like most Japanese packages—even mundane purchases from very ordinary shops—were beautifully wrapped. One contained candy, the other white rice cakes, which proved cement-hard, though they looked like puffs of cloud. There was no card in either package to identify the donor. "Every time you turn around, some Japanese is giving you a present. They're crazy about giving presents," Brando observed. Athletically crunching a rice cake, he passed the boxes to Murray and me.

Murray shook his head, he was intent on obtaining Brando's promise to meet with him again at ten-thirty. "Give me a ring around then," Brando said, finally. "We'll see what's happening."

Murray, as I knew, was only one member of what some of the *Sayonara* company referred to as "Brando's gang." Aside from the literary assistant, the gang consisted of Marlon Brando, Sr., who acts as his son's business manager; a pretty, dark-haired secretary, Miss Levin; and Brando's private make-up man. The travel expenses of this entourage, and all its living expenses while on location, were allowed for in the actor's contract with Warner Brothers. Legend to the contrary, film studios are not usually so lenient financially. A Warner man to whom I talked later explained the tolerance shown Brando by saying, "Ordinarily we wouldn't put up with it. All the demands he makes. Except—well, this picture just *had* to have a big star. Your star—that's the only thing that really counts at the box office."

Among the company were some who felt that the social protection supplied by Brando's inner circle was preventing them from "getting to know the guy" as well as they would have liked. Brando had been in Japan for more than a month, and during that time he had shown himself on the set as a slouchingly dignified, amiable-seeming young man who was always ready to cooperate with, and even encourage, his co-workers—the actors particularly—yet by and large was not socially available, preferring, during the tedious lulls between scenes, to sit alone reading philosophy or scribbling in a schoolboy notebook. After the day's work, instead of accepting his colleagues' invitations to join a group for drinks, a plate of raw fish in a restaurant and a prowl through the old geisha quarter of Kyoto, instead of contributing to the one-big-family, houseparty bonhomie that picture-making on location theoretically generates, he usually returned to his hotel and stayed there. Since the most fervent of movie-star fans are the people who themselves work in the film industry, Brando was a subject of immense interest within the ranks of the *Sayonara* group, and the more so because his attitude of friendly remoteness produced, in the face of such curiosity, such wistful frustrations. Even the film's director, Joshua Logan, was impelled to say, after working with Brando for two weeks, "Marlon's the most exciting person I've met since Garbo. A genius. But I don't know what he's like. I don't know anything about him."

The maid had re-entered the star's room, and Murray, on his way out, almost tripped over the train of her kimono. She put down a bowl of ice, and with a glow, a giggle, an elation that made her little feet, hooflike in their split-toed white socks, lift and lower like a prancing pony's, announced, "Appapie! Tonight on menu appapie."

Brando groaned. "Apple pie. That's all I need." He stretched out on the floor and unbuckled his belt, which dug too deeply into the swell of his stomach. "I'm supposed to be on a diet. But the only things I want to eat are apple pie and stuff like that." Six weeks earlier, in California, Logan had told him he must trim off ten pounds for his role in *Sayonara*, and before arriving in Kyoto, he had managed to get rid of seven. Since reaching Japan, however, abetted not only by American-type apple pie but by the Japanese cuisine, with its delicious emphasis on the sweetened, the starchy, the fried, he'd regained, then doubled this poundage. Now, loosening his belt still more and thoughtfully massaging his midriff, he scanned the menu, which offered, in English, a wide choice of Western-style dishes, and after reminding himself "I've *got* to lose weight," he ordered soup, beefsteak with French-fried potatoes, three supplementary vegetables, a side dish of spaghetti, rolls and butter, a bottle of *sake*, salad, and cheese and crackers.

"And appapie, Marron?"

He sighed. "With ice cream, honey."

Though Brando is not a teetotaler, his appetite is more frugal when it comes to alcohol. While we were awaiting the dinner, which was to be served to us in the room, he supplied me with a large vodka on the rocks and poured himself the merest courtesy sip. Resuming his position on the floor, he lolled his head against a pillow, dropped his eyelids, then shut them. It was as though he'd dozed off into a disturbing dream; his eyelids twitched, and when he spoke, his voice—an unemotional voice, in a way cultivated and genteel, yet surprisingly adolescent, a voice with a probing, asking, boyish quality—seemed to come from sleepy distances.

"The last eight, nine years of my life have been a mess," he said. "Maybe the last two have been a little better. Less rolling in the trough of the wave. Have you ever been analyzed? I was afraid of it at first. Afraid it might destroy the impulses that made me creative, an artist. A sensitive person receives fifty impressions where somebody else may only get seven. Sensitive people are so vulnerable; they're so easily brutalized and hurt just because they *are* sensitive. The more sensitive you are, the more certain you are to be brutalized, develop scabs. Never evolve. Never allow yourself to feel anything, because you always feel too much. Analysis helps. It helped me. But still, the last eight, nine years I've been pretty mixed up, a mess pretty much . . ."

The voice went on, as though speaking to hear itself, an effect Brando's speech often has, for like many persons who are intensely self-absorbed, he is something of a monologuist—a fact that he recognizes and for which he offers his own explanation. "People around me never say anything," he says. "They just seem to want to hear what I have to say. That's why I do all the talking."

Watching him now, with his eyes closed, his unlined face white under an overhead light, I felt as if the moment of my initial encounter with him were being re-created. The year of that meeting was 1947; it was a winter afternoon in New York, when I had occasion to attend a rehearsal of Tennessee Williams's *A Streetcar Named Desire*, in which Brando was to play the role of Stanley Kowalski. It was this role that first brought him general recognition, although among the New York theater's cognoscenti he had already attracted attention, through his student work with the drama coach Stella Adler and a few Broadway appearances—one in a play by Maxwell Anderson, *Truckline Café*, and another as Marchbanks opposite Katharine Cornell's Candida, in which he showed an ability that had been much praised and discussed. Elia Kazan, the director of *A Streetcar Named Desire*, said at that time, and has recently repeated, "Marlon is just the best actor in the world." But ten years ago, on the remembered afternoon, he was still relatively unknown; at least, I hadn't a clue to who he might be when, arriving too early at the *Streetcar* rehearsal, I found the auditorium deserted and a brawny young man stretched out atop a table on the stage under the gloomy glare of work lights, solidly asleep. Because he was wearing a white T-shirt and denim trousers, because of his squat gymnasium physique—the weight-lifter's arms, the Charles Atlas chest (though an opened *Basic Writings of Sigmund Freud* was resting on it)— I took him for a stagehand. Or did until I looked closely at his face. It was as if a stranger's head had been attached to the brawny body, as in certain counterfeit photographs. For this face was so very untough, superimposing, as it did, an almost angelic refinement and gentleness upon hard-jawed good looks: taut skin, a broad, high forehead, wide-apart eyes, an aqualine nose, full lips with a relaxed, sensual expression. Not the least suggestion of Williams's unpoetic Kowalski. It was therefore rather an experience to observe, later that afternoon, with what chameleon ease Brando acquired the character's cruel and gaudy colors, how superbly, like a guileful salamander, he slithered into the part, how his own persona evaporated—just as, in this Kyoto hotel room nine years afterward, my 1947 memory of Brando receded, disappeared into his 1956 self. And the present Brando, the one lounging there on the *tatami* and lazily puffing filtered cigarettes as he talked and talked, was, of course, a different person—bound to be. His body was thicker; his forehead was higher, for his hair was thinner; he was richer (from the producers of *Sayonara* he could expect a salary of three hundred thousand dollars, plus a percentage of the picture's earnings); and he'd become, as one journalist put it, "the Valentino of the bop generation" —turned into such a world celebrity that when he went out in public here in Japan, he deemed it wise to hide his face not only by wearing dark glasses but by donning a surgeon's gauze mask as well. (The latter bit of disguise is not so *outré* in Japan as it may sound, since numerous Asians wear such masks, on the theory that they prevent the spreading of germs.) Those were some of the alterations a decade had made. There were others. His eyes had changed. Although their *caffè-espresso* color was the same, the shyness, any traces of real vulnerability that they had formerly held, had left them; now he looked at people with assurance, and with what can only be called a pitying expression, as though he dwelt in spheres of enlightenment where they, to his regret, did not. (The reactions of the people subjected to this gaze of constant commiseration range from that of a young actress who avowed that "Marlon is really a very *spiritual* person, wise and very sincere; you can see it in his eyes" to that of a Brando acquaintance who said, "The way he looks at you, like he was so damn sorry for you—doesn't it make you want to cut your throat?") Nevertheless, the subtly tender character of his face had been preserved. Or almost. For in the years between he'd had an accident that gave his face a more conventionally masculine aspect. It was just that his nose had been broken.

And maneuvering a word in edgewise, I asked, "How did you break your nose?"

"... by which I don't mean that I'm *always* unhappy. I remember one April I was in Sicily. A hot day, and flowers everywhere. I like flowers, the ones that smell. Gardenias. Anyway, it was April and I was in Sicily, and I went off by myself. Lay down in this field of flowers. Went to sleep. That made me happy. I was happy *then*. What? You say something?"

"I was wondering how you broke your nose."

He rubbed his nose and grinned, as though remembering an experience as happy as the Sicilian nap. "That was a long time ago. I did it boxing. It was when I was in *Streetcar*. We—some of the guys backstage and me —we used to go down to the boiler room in the theater and horse around, mix it up. One night I was mixing it up with this guy and—crack! So I put on my coat and walked around to the nearest hospital—it was off Broadway somewhere. My nose was really busted. They had to give me an anesthetic to set it, and put me to bed. Not that I was sorry. *Streetcar* had been running about a year and I was sick of it. But my nose healed pretty quick, and I guess I would've been back in the show practically right away if I hadn't done what I did to Irene Selznick." His grin broadened as he mentioned Mrs. Selznick, who had been the producer of the Williams play. "There is one shrewd lady, Irene Selznick. When she wants something, she wants it. And she wanted me back in the play. But when I heard she was coming to the hospital, I went to work with bandages and iodine and mercurochrome, and—Christ!—when she walked in the door, I looked like my head had been cut off. At the least. And *sounded* as though I were dying. 'Oh, Marlon,' she said, 'you poor, *poor* boy!' And I said, 'Don't you worry about anything, Irene. I'll be back in the show tonight!' And she said, 'Don't you dare! We can manage without you for—for— well, a *few* days more.' 'No, no,' I said. 'I'm okay. I want to work. Tell them I'll be back tonight.' So she said, 'You're in no condition, you poor darling. I *forbid* you to come to the theater.' So I stayed in the hospital and had myself a ball." (Mrs. Selznick, recalling the incident recently, said, "They didn't set his nose properly at all. Suddenly his face was quite different. Kind of tough. For months afterward I kept telling him, 'But they've *ruined* your face. You must have your nose broken again and reset.' Luckily for him, he didn't listen to me. Because I honestly think that broken nose made his fortune as far as the movies go. It gave him sex appeal. He was too beautiful before.")

Brando made his first trip to the Coast in 1949, when he went out there to play the leading role in *The Men*, a picture dealing with paraplegic war veterans. He was accused, at the time, of uncouth social conduct, and criticized for his black-leather-jacket taste in attire, his choice of motorcycles instead of Jaguars and his preference for obscure secretaries rather than movie starlets; moreover, Hollywood columnists studded their copy with hostile comments concerning his attitude toward the film business, which he himself summed up soon after he entered it by saying, "The only reason I'm here is that I don't yet have the moral courage to turn down the money." In interviews, he repeatedly stated that becoming "simply a movie actor" was the thing furthest from his thoughts. "I may do a picture now and then," he said on one occasion, "but mostly I intend to work on the stage." However, he followed *The Men*, which was more of a *succès d'estime* than a commercial triumph, by re-creating Kowalski in the screen treatment of *A Streetcar Named Desire*, and this role, as it had done on Broadway, established him as a star. (Defined practically, a movie star is any performer who can account for a box-office profit regardless of the quality of the enterprise in which he appears; the breed is so scarce that there are fewer than ten actors today who qualify for the title. Brando is one of them; as a box-office draw, male division, he is perhaps outranked only by William Holden.) In the course of the last five years he has played a Mexican revolutionary *(Viva Zapata!)*, Mark Antony *(Julius Caesar)* and a motorcycle-mad juvenile delinquent *(The Wild One)*; earned an Academy Award in the role of a dockyard thug *(On the Waterfront)*; impersonated Napoleon *(Désirée)*; sung and danced his way through the part of an adult delinquent *(Guys and Dolls)*; and taken the part of the Okinawan interpreter in *The Teahouse of the August Moon*, which, like *Sayonara*, his tenth picture, was partly shot on location in Japan. But he has never, except for a brief period in summer stock, returned to the stage. "Why should I?" he asked with apathy when I remarked on this. "The movies have a greater potential. They can be a factor for good. For moral development. At least some can—the kind of movies I want to do." He paused, seemed to listen, as though his statement had been tape-recorded and he were now playing it back. Possibly the sound of it dissatisfied him; at any rate, his jaw started working, as if he were biting down on an unpleasant mouthful. He looked off into space suddenly and demanded, "What's so hot about New York? What's so hot about working for Cheryl Crawford and Robert Whitehead?" Miss Crawford and Whitehead are two of New York's most prominent theatrical producers, neither of whom has had occasion to employ Brando. "Anyway, what would I be in?" he continued. "There aren't any parts for me."

Stack them, and the playscripts offered him in any given season by hopeful Broadway managements might very well rise to a height exceeding the actor's own. Tennessee Williams wanted him for the male lead in each of his last five plays, and the most recent of these, *Orpheus Descending*, which was pending production at the time of our talk, had been written expressly as a co-starring vehicle for Brando and the Italian actress Anna Magnani. "I can explain very easily why I didn't do *Orpheus*," Brando said. "There are beautiful things in it, some of Tennessee's best writing, and the

Magnani part is great; she stands for something, you can understand her —and she would wipe me off the stage. The character I was supposed to play, this boy, this Val, he never takes a stand. I didn't really know what he was for or against. Well, you can't act a vacuum. And I told Tennessee. So he kept trying. He rewrote it for me, maybe a couple of times. But—" He shrugged. "Well, I had no intention of walking out on any stage with Magnani. Not in that part. They'd have had to mop me up." Brando mused a moment, and added, "I think—in fact, I'm sure—Tennessee has made a fixed association between me and Kowalski. I mean, we're friends and he knows that as a person I am just the opposite of Kowalski, who was everything I'm against—totally insensitive, crude, cruel. But still, Tennessee's image of me is confused with the fact that I played that part. So I don't know if he could write for me in a different color range. The only reason I did *Guys and Dolls* was to work in a lighter color—yellow. Before that, the brightest color I'd played was red. From red down. Brown. Gray. Black." He crumpled an empty cigarette package and bounced it in his hand like a ball. "There aren't any parts for me on the stage. Nobody writes them. Go on. Tell me a part I could do."

In the absence of vehicles by worthy contemporaries, might he not favor the work of older hands? Several responsible persons who appeared with him in the film had admired his reading of Mark Antony in *Julius Caesar*, and thought him equipped, provided the will was there, to essay many of the Mount Everest roles in stage literature—even, possibly, Oedipus.

Brando received reminders of this praise blankly—or, rather, he seemed to be indulging his not-listening habit. But sensing silence again, he dissolved it: "Of course, movies *date* so quickly. I saw *Streetcar* the other day and it was already an old-fashioned picture. Still, movies do have the greatest potential. You can say important things to a lot of people. About discrimination and hatred and prejudice. I want to make pictures that explore the themes current in the world today. In terms of entertainment. That's why I've started my own independent production company." He reached out affectionately to finger *A Burst of Vermilion*, which will be the first script filmed by Pennebaker Productions—the independent company he has formed.

And did *A Burst of Vermilion* satisfy him as a basis for the kind of lofty aims he proposed?

He mumbled something. Then he mumbled something else. Asked to speak more clearly, he said, "It's a Western."

He was unable to restrain a smile, which expanded into laughter. He rolled on the floor and roared. "Christ, the only thing is, will I ever be able to look my friends in the face again?" Sobering somewhat, he said, "Seriously, though, the first picture *has* to make money. Otherwise, there won't be another. I'm nearly broke. No, no kidding. I spent a year and two hundred thousand dollars of my own money trying to get some writer to come up with a decent script. Which used my ideas. The last one, it was so terrible I said I can do better myself. I'm going to direct it, too."

Produced by, directed by, written by, and starring. Charlie Chaplin has managed this, and gone it one better by composing his own scores. But professionals of wide experience—Orson Wells, for one—have caved in under a lesser number of chores than Brando planned to assume. However, he had a ready answer to my suggestion that he might be loading the cart with more than the donkey could haul. "Take producing," he said. "What does a producer do except cast? I know as much about casting as anyone does, and that's all producing is. Casting." In the trade, one would be hard put to it to find anyone who concurred in this opinion. A good producer, in addition to doing the casting—that is, assembling the writer, the director, the actors, the technical crew and the other components of his team—must be a diplomat of the emotions, smoothing and soothing, and above all, must be a skilled mechanic when it comes to dollars-and-cents machinery. "But seriously," said Brando, now excessively sober, "*Burst isn't* just cowboys-and-Indians stuff. It's about this Mexican boy—hatred and discrimination. What happens to a community when those things exist."

Sayonara, too, has moments when it purports to attack race prejudice, telling, as it does, the tale of an American jet pilot who falls in love with a Japanese music-hall dancer, much to the dismay of his Air Force superiors, and also to the dismay of her employers, though the latter's objection is not the racial unsuitability of her beau but simply that she has a beau at all, for she is a member of an all-girl opera company—based on a real-life counterpart, the Takarazuka Company—whose management promotes a legend that offstage its hundreds of girls lead a conventlike existence, unsullied by male presence of any creed or color. Michener's novel concludes with the lovers forlornly bidding each other *sayonara*, a word meaning farewell. In the film version, however, the word, and consequently the title, has lost significance; here the fadeout reveals the twain of East and West so closely met that they are on their way to the matrimonial bureau. At a press conference that Brando conducted upon his Tokyo arrival, he informed some sixty reporters that he had contracted to do this story because "it strikes very precisely at prejudices that serve to limit our progress toward a peaceful world. Underneath the romance, it attacks prejudices that exist on the part of the Japanese as well as on our part," and also he was doing the film because it would give him the "invaluable opportunity" of working under Joshua Logan, who could teach him "what to do and what not to do."

But time had passed. And now Brando said, with a snort, "Oh, *Sayonara*, I love it! This wondrous hearts-and-flowers nonsense that was supposed to be a serious picture about Japan. So what difference does it make? I'm just doing it for the money anyway. Money to put in the kick for my own company." He pulled at his lip reflectively and snorted again. "Back in California, I sat through twenty-two hours of script conferences. Logan said to me, 'We welcome any suggestions you have, Marlon. Any changes you want to make, you just make them. If there's anything you don't like —why, rewrite it, Marlon, write it your own way.' " Brando's friends boast that he can imitate anybody after fifteen minutes' observation; to judge by the eerie excellence with which he mimicked Logan's vaguely Southern voice, his sad-eyed, beaming, aquiver-with-enthusiasm manner, they are hardly exaggerating. "*Rewrite?* Man, I rewrote the whole damn script. And now out of that they're going to use maybe eight lines." Another snort. "I give up. I'm going to walk through the part, and that's that. Sometimes I think nobody knows the difference anyway. For the first few days on the set, I tried to act. But then I made an experiment. In this scene, I tried to do everything wrong I could think of. Grimaced and rolled my eyes, put in all kinds of gestures and expressions that had no relation to the part I'm supposed to be playing. What did Logan say? He just said, 'It's wonderful! Print it!' "

A phrase that often occurs in Brandon's conversation, "I only mean forty percent of what I say," is probably applicable here. Logan, a stage and film director of widely recognized and munificently rewarded accomplishments *(Mister Roberts, South Pacific, Picnic)*, is a man balanced on enthusiasm, as a bird is balanced on air. A creative person's need to believe in the value of what he is creating is axiomatic; Logan's belief in whatever project he is engaged in approaches euphoric faith, protecting him, as it seems designed to do, from the nibbling nuisance of self-doubt. The joy he took in everything connected with *Sayonara*, a film he had been preparing for two years, was so nearly flawless that it did not permit him to conceive that his star's enthusiasm might not equal his own. Far from it. "Marlon," he occasionally announced, "says he's never been as happy with a company as he is with us." And "I've never worked with such an exciting, inventive actor. So pliable. He takes direction beautifully, and yet he always has something to add. He's made up this Southern accent for the part; I never would have thought of it myself, but, well, it's exactly right —it's perfection." Nevertheless, by the night I had dinner in Brando's hotel room Logan had begun to be aware that there was something lacking in his rapport with Brando. He attributed it to the fact that at this juncture, when most of the scenes being filmed concentrated on Japanese background (street crowds, views, spectacles) rather than actors, he had not yet worked with Brando on material that put either of them to much of a test. "That'll come when we get back to California," he said. "The interior stuff, the dramatic scenes. Brando's going to be great—we'll get along fine."

. . . .

There was another reason for Logan's inability, at that point, to give his principal player the kind of attention that might have established closer harmony: he was in serious disharmony with the very Japanese elements that had contributed most to his decision to make the picture. Long infatuated with the Japanese theater, Logan had counted heavily on interlacing *Sayonara* with authentic sequences taken from the classic Kabuki theater, the masked Nō dramas, the Bunraku puppet plays; they were to be, so to say, the highbrow-lights of the film. And to this end Logan, along with William Goetz, the producer, had been in negotiation for over a year with Shochiku, the gigantic film company that controls a major part of Japan's live theatrical activities. The ruler of the Shochiku empire is a small, unsmiling eminence in his eighties, known as Mr. Otani; he has a *prénom*, Takejiro, but there are few men alive on such familiar terms that they would presume to use it. The son of a butcher (and therefore, in Japan's Buddhist society, a member of the outcast group), Otani, together with a brother now dead, founded Shochiku and nurtured it to the point where, for the last four years, its payroll has been the biggest of any single company in Japan. A tycoon to rival Kokichi Mikimoto, the late cultured-pearl potentate, Otani casts a cloaklike shadow over the entire Japanese entertainment industry; in addition to having monopolistic control of the classic theater, he owns the country's most extensive chain of movie houses and music halls, produces many films and has a hand in radio and television. From Otani's vantage point, any transactions with the Messrs. Logan and Goetz must have looked like very small *sake*. However, he was at first in sympathy with their project, largely because he was impressed by the fervor of Logan's veneration for Kabuki, Nō and Bunraku, the three unquestionably genuine gems in the old man's crown, and the ones closest to his heart. (According to some specialists, these ancient arts owe their continued health mainly to his generosity.)

But Otani is not all philanthropist; when Shochiku's negotiations with the *Sayonara* management were supposedly concluded, the former had given the latter, for a handsome price, franchise to photograph scenes in Tokyo's famed Kabuki Theater, and, for a still handsomer honorarium, permission to make free use of the Kabuki troupe, the Nō plays and players and the Bunraku puppeteers. Shochiku had also agreed to the participation of its own all-girl opera company—a necessary factor in the production of the film, since the Takarazuka troupe depicted in the novel had deeply resented Michener's "libel" and refused any cooperation whatever. Logan, leaving for Japan, was so elated he could have flown there under his own power. "Otani's given us carte blanche, and this is going to be it, the real thing," he said. "None of that fake Kabuki, that second-rate stuff, but the real thing—something that's never been put in a picture before." And was not destined to be; for, across the wide Pacific, Logan and his associates had a personal Pearl Harbor awaiting them. Otani is seldom seen; he usually appears in the person of bland assistants, and as Logan and Goetz disembarked from their plane, a group of these informed the film makers that Shochiku had made an error in its financial reckoning; the bill was now much higher than the initial estimate. Producer Goetz objected. Otani, certain that he held the stronger cards (after all, here were these Hollywood people in Japan, accompanied by an expensive cast, an expensive crew and expensive equipment), replied by raising the tab still more. Whereupon Goetz, himself a businessman as tough as tortoise shell, ended the negotiations and told his director they would have to make up their own Kabuki, Nō, Bunraku and all-girl opera company from among unattached, free-lancing artists.

Meanwhile, the Tokyo press was publicizing the contretemps. Several papers, the *Japan Times* among them, implied that Shochiku was to be censured for having "acted in bad faith"; others, taking a pro-Shochiku, or perhaps simply an anti-*Sayonara*, line, expressed themselves as delighted that the Americans would not have the opportunity to "degrade our finest artistic traditions" by representing them in a film version of "a vulgar novel that is in no way a compliment to the Japanese people." The papers antagonistic to the *Sayonara* project especially relished reporting the fact that Logan had cast a Mexican actor, Ricardo Montalban, in the part of a ranking Kabuki performer (Kabuki is traditionally an all-male enterprise; the grander, more difficult roles are those of women, played by female impersonators, and Montalban's assignment was to portray one such) and then had had the "effrontery" to try and hire a genuine Kabuki star to substitute for Montalban in the dance sequences, which, one Japanese writer remarked, was much the same as "asking Ethel Barrymore to be a stand-in."

All in all, the local press was touchily interested in what was taking place down in Kyoto—the city, two hundred and thirty miles south of Tokyo, in which, because of its plethora of historic temples, its photogenic blue hills and misty lakes, and its carefully preserved old-Japan atmosphere, with elegant geisha quarter and paper-lantern-lighted streets, the *Sayonara* staff had decided to take most of their location shots. And, all in all, down in Kyoto the company was encountering as many difficulties as its ill-wishers could have hoped for. In particular, the Americans were finding it a problem to muster nationals willing to appear in their film—an interesting phenomenon, considering how desirous the average Japanese is of having himself photographed. True, the movie makers had rounded up a ragbag-picking of Nō players and puppeteers not under contract to Shochiku, but they were having the devil's own time assembling a presentable all-girl opera company. (These peculiarly Japanese institutions resemble a sort of single-sex, innocent-minded Folies Bergère; oddly, few men attend their performances, the audiences being, on the whole, as all-girl as the cast.) In the hope of bridging this gap, the *Sayonara* management had distributed posters advertising a contest to select "the one hundred most beautiful girls in Japan." The affair, for which they expected a big turnout, was scheduled to take place at two o'clock on a Thursday afternoon in the lobby of the Kyoto Hotel. But there were no winners, because there were no contestants; none showed up.

Producer Goetz, one of the disappointed judges, resorted next, and with some success, to the expedient of luring ladies out of Kyoto's cabarets and bars. Kyoto—or, for that matter, any Japanese city—is a barfly's Valhalla. Proportionately, the number of premises purveying strong liquor is higher than in New York, and the diversity of these saloons—which range from cozy bamboo closets accommodating four customers to many-storied, neon-hued temples of fun featuring, in accordance with the Japanese aptitude for imitation, cha-cha bands and rock 'n' rollers and hillbilly quartets and *chanteuses existentialistes* and Oriental vocalists who sing Cole Porter songs with American Negro accents—is extraordinary. But however low or however deluxe the establishment may be, one thing remains the same: there is always on hand a pride of hostesses to cajole and temper the clientele. Great numbers of these sleekly coifed, smartly costumed, relentlessly festive *jolies jeunes filles* sit sipping Parfaits d'Amour (a syrupy violet-colored cocktail currently fashionable in these surroundings) while performing the duties of a poor man's geisha girl; that is, lightening the spirits, without necessarily corrupting the morals, of weary married men and tense, anxious-to-be-amused bachelors. It is not unusual to see four to a customer. But when the *Sayonara* officials began to try to corral them, they had to contend with the circumstance that nightworkers, such as they were dealing with, have no taste for the early rising that picture-making demands. To acquire their talents, and see that the ladies were on the set at the proper hour, certain of the film's personnel did everything but distribute engagement rings.

Still another annoyance for the makers of *Sayonara* involved the United States Air Force, whose cooperation was vital, but which, though it had previously promised help, now had fits of shilly-shallying, because it gravely objected to one of the basic elements of the plot—that during the Korean War some American Air Force men who married Japanese were shipped home. This, the Air Force complained, may have been the *practice*, but it was not official Pentagon policy. Given the choice of cutting out the offending premise, and thereby removing a sizable section of the script's entrails, or permitting it to remain, and thereby forfeiting Air Force aid, Logan selected surgery.

Then, there was the problem of Miss Miiko Taka, who had been cast as the Takarazuka dancer capable of arousing Air Force Officer Brando's passion. Having first tried to obtain Audrey Hepburn for the part, and found that Miss Hepburn thought not, Logan had started looking for an "unknown," and had come up with Miss Taka, poised, pleasant, an unassuming, quietly attractive nisei, innocent of acting experience, who stepped out of a clerking job with a Los Angeles travel bureau into what she called "this Cinderella fantasy." Although her acting abilities—as well as those of another *Sayonara* principal, Red Buttons, an ex-burlesque, ex-television jokester, who, like Miss Taka, had had meager dramatic training—were apparently causing her director some concern, Logan, admirably undaunted, cheerful despite all, was heard to say, "We'll get away with it. As much as possible, I'll just keep their faces straight and their mouths shut. Anyway, Brando, he's going to be so great *he'll* give us what we need." But as for giving, "I give up," Brando repeated. "I'm going to give up. I'm going to sit back. Enjoy Japan."

At that moment, in the Miyako, Brando was presented with something Japanese to enjoy: an emissary of the hotel management, who, bowing and beaming and soaping his hands, came into the room saying "Ah, Missa Marron Brando—" and was silent, tongue-tied by the awkwardness of his errand. He'd come to reclaim the "gift" packages of candy and rice cakes that Brando had already opened and avidly sampled. "Ah, Missa Marron Brando, it is a missake. They were meant for derivery in another room. Aporogies! Aporogies!" Laughing, Brando handed the boxes over. The eyes of the emissary, observing the plundered contents, grew grave, though his smile lingered—indeed, became fixed. Here was a predicament to challenge the rightly renowned Japanese politeness. "Ah," he breathed, a solution limbering his smile, "since you rike them very much, you muss keep one box." He handed the rice cakes back. "And they"—apparently the rightful owner—"can have the other. So, now everyone is preased."

It was just as well that he left the rice cakes, for dinner was taking a long while to simmer in the kitchen. When it arrived, I was replying to some inquiries Brando had made about an acquaintance of mine, a young American disciple of Buddhism who for five years had been leading a contemplative, if not entirely unworldly, life in a settlement inside the gates of Kyoto's Nishi-Honganji Temple. The notion of a person's retiring from the world to lead a spiritual existence—an Oriental one, at that—made Brando's face become still, in a dreaming way. He listened with surprising attention to what I could tell him about the young man's present life, and was puzzled—chagrined, really—that it was not at all, or at all, a matter of withdrawal, of silence and prayer-sore knees. On the contrary, behind

Nishi-Honganji's walls my Buddhist friend occupied three snug, sunny rooms brimming with books and phonograph records; along with attending to his prayers and performing the tea ceremony, he was quite capable of mixing a martini; he had two servants, and a Chevrolet in which he often conveyed himself to the local cinemas. And speaking of that, he had read that Marlon Brando was in town, and longed to meet him. Brando was little amused. The puritan streak in him, which has some width, had been touched; his conception of the truly devout could not encompass anyone as *du monde* as the young man I'd described. "It's like the other day on the set," he said. "We were working in a temple, and one of the monks came over and asked me for an autographed picture. Now, *what* would a monk want with my autograph? A picture of me?"

He stared questioningly at his scattered books, so many of which dealt with mystical subjects. At his first Tokyo press conference, he had told the journalists that he was glad to be back in Japan, because it gave him another chance to "investigate the influence of Buddhism on Japanese thought, the determining cultural factor." The reading matter on display offered proof that he was adhering to this scholarly, if somewhat obscure, program. "What I'd like to do," he presently said, "I'd like to talk to someone who *knows* about these things. Because—" But the explanation was deferred until the maid, who just then skated in balancing vast platters, had set the lacquer table and we had knelt on cushions at either end of it.

"Because," he resumed, wiping his hands on a small steamed towel, the usual preface to any meal served in Japan, "I've seriously considered—I've very *seriously* thought about—throwing the whole thing up. This business of being a successful actor. What's the point, if it doesn't evolve into anything? All right, you're a success. At last you're *accepted*, you're welcome everywhere. But that's it, that's all there is to it, it doesn't lead anywhere. You're just sitting on a pile of candy gathering thick layers of —of *crust*." He rubbed his chin with the towel, as though removing stale make-up. "Too much success can ruin you as surely as too much failure." Lowering his eyes, he looked without appetite at the food that the maid, to an accompaniment of constant giggles, was distributing on the plates. "Of course," he said hesitantly, as if he were slowly turning over a coin to study the side that seemed to be shinier, "you can't *always* be a failure. Not and survive. Van Gogh! There's an example of what can happen when a person never receives any recognition. You stop relating; it puts you outside. But I guess success does that, too. You know, it took me a long time before I was aware that that's what I was—a big success. I was so absorbed in myself, my own problems, I never looked around, took account. I used to walk in New York, miles and miles, walk in the streets late at night, and never *see* anything. I was never sure about acting, whether that was what I really wanted to do; I'm still not. Then, when I was in

Streetcar, and it had been running a couple of months, one night—dimly, dimly—I began to hear this roar. It was like I'd been asleep, and I woke up here sitting on a pile of candy."

Before Brando achieved this sugary perch, he had known the vicissitudes of any unconnected, unfinanced, only partly educated (he has never received a high-school diploma, having been expelled before graduation from Shattuck Military Academy, in Faribault, Minnesota, an institution he refers to as "the asylum") young man who arrives in New York from more rural parts—in his case, Libertyville, Illinois. Living alone in furnished rooms, or sharing underfurnished apartments, he had spent his first city years fluctuating between acting classes and a fly-by-night enrollment in Social Security; Best's once had him on its payroll as an elevator boy.

A friend of his, who saw a lot of him in those pre-candy days, corroborates to some extent the rather somnambulistic portrait Brando paints of himself. "He was a brooder, all right," the friend has said. "He seemed to have a built-in hideaway room and was always rushing off to it to worry over himself, and gloat, too, like a miser with his gold. But it wasn't all Gloomsville. When he wanted to, he could rocket right out of himself. He had a wild, kid kind of fun thing. Once he was living in an old brownstone on Fifty-second Street, near where some of the jazz joints are. He used to go up on the roof and fill paper bags with water and throw them down at the stiffs coming out of the clubs. He had a sign on the wall of his room that said 'You Ain't Livin' If You Don't Know It.' Yeah, there was always something jumping in that apartment—Marlon playing the bongos, records going, people around, kids from the Actors' Studio, and a lot of down-and-outers he'd picked up. And he could be sweet. He was the least opportunistic person I've ever known. He never gave a damn about anybody who could help him; you might say he went out of his way to avoid them. Sure, part of that—the kind of people he didn't like and the kind he did, both—stemmed from his insecurities, his inferiority feelings. Very few of his friends were his equals—anybody he'd have to *compete* with, if you know what I mean. Mostly they were strays, idolizers, characters who were dependent on him one way or another. The same with the girls he took out. Plain sort of somebody's-secretary-type girls—nice enough but nothing that's going to start a stampede of competitors." (The last-mentioned preference of Brando's was true of him as an adolescent, too, or so his grandmother has said. As she put it, "Marlon always picked on the cross-eyed girls.")

The maid poured *sake* into thimble-sized cups, and withdrew. Connoisseurs of this palely pungent rice wine pretend they can discern variations in taste and quality in over fifty brands. But to the novice all *sake* seems to have been brewed in the same vat—a toddy, pleasant at first, cloying afterward, and not likely to echo in your head unless it is devoured by the quart, a habit many of Japan's *bons vivants* have adopted. Brando ignored the *sake* and went straight for his filet. The steak was excellent; Japanese take a just pride in the quality of their beef. The spaghetti, a dish that is very popular in Japan, was not; nor was the rest—the conglomeration of peas, potatoes, beans. Granted that the menu was a queer one, it is on the whole a mistake to order Western-style food in Japan, yet there arise those moments when one retches at the thought of more raw fish, sukiyaki, and rice with seaweed, when, however temptingly they may be prepared and however prettily presented, the unaccustomed stomach revolts at the prospect of eel broth and fried bees and pickled snake and octopus arms.

As we ate, Brando returned to the possibility of renouncing his movie-star status for the satisfactions of a life that "led somewhere." He decided to compromise. "Well, when I get back to Hollywood, what I *will* do, I'll fire my secretary and move into a smaller house," he said. He sighed with relief, as though he'd already cast off old encumbrances and entered upon the simplicities of his new situation. Embroidering on its charms, he said, "I won't have a cook or maid. Just a cleaning woman who comes in twice a week. But"—he frowned, squinted, as if something were blurring the bliss he envisioned—"wherever the house is, it has to have a *fence*. On account of the people with pencils. You don't know what it's like. The people with pencils. I need a fence to keep them out. I suppose there's nothing I can do about the telephone."

"Telephone?"

"It's tapped. Mine is."

"Tapped? Really? By whom?"

He chewed his steak, mumbled. He seemed reluctant to say, yet certain it was so. "When I talk to my friends, we speak French. Or else a kind of bop lingo we made up."

Suddenly, sounds came through the ceiling from the room above us—footfalls, muffled voices like the noise of water flowing through a pipe. "Sh-h-h!" whispered Brando, listening intently, his gaze alerted upward. "Keep your voice down. *They* can hear everything." They, it appeared, were his fellow actor Red Buttons and Buttons's wife, who occupied the suite overhead. "This place is made of paper," he continued in tiptoe tones, and with the absorbed countenance of a child lost in a very earnest game —an expression that half explained his secretiveness, the looking-over-his-shoulder, coded-bop-for-telephones facet of his personality that occasionally causes conversation with him to assume a conspiratorial quality, as though one were discussing subversive topics in perilous political territory. Brando said nothing; I said nothing. Nor did Mr. and Mrs. Buttons—not anything distinguishable.

During the siege of silence, my host located a letter buried among the dinner plates, and read it while he ate, like a gentleman perusing his breakfast newspaper. Presently, remembering me, he remarked, "From a friend of mine. He's making a documentary, the life of James Dean. He wants me to do the narration. I think I might." He tossed the letter aside and pulled his apple pie, topped with a melting scoop of vanilla ice cream, toward him. "Maybe not, though. I get excited about something, but it never lasts more than seven minutes. Seven minutes exactly. That's my limit. I never know why I get up in the morning." Finishing his pie, he gazed speculatively at my portion; I passed it to him. "But I'm really considering this Dean thing. It could be important."

James Dean, the young motion-picture actor killed in a car accident in 1955, was promoted throughout his phosphorescent career as the all-American "mixed-up kid," the symbol of misunderstood hot-rodding youth with a switchblade approach to life's little problems. When he died, an expensive film in which he had starred, *Giant*, had yet to be released, and the picture's press agents, seeking to offset any ill effects that Dean's demise might have on the commercial prospects of their product, succeeded by "glamorizing" the tragedy, and in ironic consequence, created a Dean legend of rather necrophilic appeal. Though Brandon was seven years older than Dean, and professionally more secure, the two actors came to be associated in the collective movie-fan mind. Many critics reviewing Dean's first film, *East of Eden*, remarked on the well-nigh plagiaristic resemblance between his acting mannerisms and Brando's. Off-screen, too, Dean appeared to be practicing the sincerest form of flattery; like Brando, he tore around on motorcycles, played bongo drums, dressed the role of rowdy, spouted an intellectual rigmarole, cultivated a cranky, colorful newspaper personality that mingled, to a skillfully potent degree, plain bad boy and sensitive sphinx.

"No, Dean was never a friend of mine," said Brando, in response to a question that he seemed surprised to have been asked. "That's not why I may do the narration job. I hardly knew him. But he had an *idée fixe* about me. Whatever I did he did. He was always trying to get close to me. He used to call up." Brando lifted an imaginary telephone, put it to his ear with a cunning, eavesdropper's smile. "I'd listen to him talking to the answering service, asking for me, leaving messages. But I never spoke up. I never called him back. No, when I—"

The scene was interrupted by the ringing of a real telephone. "Yeah?" he said, picking it up. "Speaking. From where? . . . Manila? . . . Well, I don't know anybody in Manila. Tell them I'm not here. No, when I finally met Dean," he said, hanging up, "it was at a party. Where he was throwing himself around, acting the madman. So I spoke to him. I took him aside and asked him didn't he know he was sick? That he needed help?" The memory evoked an intensified version of Brando's familiar look of enlightened compassion. "He listened to me. He knew he was sick. I gave him the name of an analyst, and he went. And at least his *work* improved. Toward the end, I think he was beginning to find his own way as an actor. But this glorifying of Dean is all wrong. That's why I believe the documentary could be important. To show he wasn't a hero; show what he really was—just a lost boy trying to find himself. That ought to be done, and I'd like to do it—maybe as a kind of expiation for some of my own sins. Like making *The Wild One.*" He was referring to the strange film in which he was presented as the Führer of a tribe of Fascist-like delinquents. "But. Who knows? Seven minutes is my limit."

From Dean the conversation turned to other actors, and I asked which ones, specifically, Brando respected. He pondered; though his lips shaped several names, he seemed to have second thoughts about pronouncing them. I suggested a few candidates—Laurence Olivier, John Gielgud, Montgomery Clift, Gérard Philipe, Jean-Louis Barrault. "Yes," he said, at last coming alive, "Philipe is a good actor. So is Barrault. Christ, what a wonderful picture that was—*Les Enfants du Paradis*! Maybe the best movie ever made. You know, that's the only time I ever fell in love with an actress, somebody on the screen. I was mad about Arletty." The Parisian star Arletty is well remembered by international audiences for the witty, womanly allure she brought to the heroine's part in Barrault's celebrated film. "I mean, I was really in *love* with her. My first trip to Paris, the thing I did right away, I asked to meet Arletty. I went to see her as though I were going to a shrine. My ideal woman. Wow!" He slapped the table. "Was that a mistake, was that a disillusionment! She was a tough article."

The maid came to clear the table; *en passant,* she gave Brando's shoulder a sisterly pat, rewarding him, I took it, for the cleaned-off sparkle of his plates. He again collapsed on the floor, stuffing a pillow under his head. "I'll tell you," he said, "Spencer Tracy is the kind of actor I like to watch. The way he holds back, *holds* back—then darts in to make his point, darts back. Tracy, Muni, Cary Grant. They know what they're doing. You can learn something from them."

Brando began to weave his fingers in the air, as though hoping that gestures would describe what he could not precisely articulate. "Acting is such a tenuous thing," he said. "A fragile, shy thing that a sensitive director can help lure out of you. Now, in movie-acting, the important, the *sensitive* moment comes around the third take of a scene; by then you just need a whisper from the director to crystallize it for you. Gadge"—he was using Elia Kazan's nickname—"can usually do it. He's wonderful with actors."

Another actor, I suppose, would have understood at once what Brando was saying, but I found him difficult to follow. "It's what happens inside you on the third take," he said, with a careful emphasis that did not lessen my incomprehension. One of the most memorable film scenes Brando has played occurs in the Kazan-directed *On the Waterfront;* it is the car-ride scene in which Rod Steiger, as the racketeering brother, confesses he is leading Brando into a death trap. I asked if he could use the episode as an example, and tell me how his theory of the "sensitive moment" applied to it.

"Yes. Well, no. Well, let's see." He puckered his eyes, made a humming noise. "That was a seven-take scene, and I didn't like the way it was written. Lot of dissension going on there. I was fed up with the whole picture. All the location stuff was in New Jersey, and it was the dead of winter—the cold, Christ! And I was having problems at the time. Woman trouble. That scene. Let me see. There were seven takes because Rod Steiger couldn't stop crying. He's one of those actors loves to cry. We kept doing it over and over. But I can't remember just when, just how it crystallized itself for me. The first time I saw *Waterfront*, in a projection room with Gadge, I thought it was so terrible I walked out without even speaking to him."

A month earlier, a friend of Brando's had told me, "Marlon always turns against whatever he's working on. Some element of it. Either the script or the director or somebody in the cast. Not always because of anything very rational—just because it seems to comfort him to be dissatisfied, let off steam about something. It's part of his pattern. Take *Sayonara*. A dollar gets you ten he'll develop a hoss on it somewhere along the line. A hoss on Logan, maybe. Maybe against Japan—the whole damn country. He loves Japan *now*. But with Marlon you never know from one minute to the next."

I was wondering whether I might mention this supposed "pattern" to Brando, ask if he considered it a valid observation about himself. But it was as though he had anticipated the question. "I ought to keep my mouth shut," he said. "Around here, around *Sayonara*, I've let a few people know the way I feel. But I don't always feel the same way two days running."

It was ten-thirty, and Murray called on the dot.

"I went out to dinner with the girls," he told Brando, his telephone voice so audible that I could hear it, too; it spoke above a blend of dance-band rumble and barroom roar. Obviously he was patronizing not one of the more traditional, cat-quiet Kyoto restaurants but, rather, a place where the customers wore shoes. "We're just finishing. How about it? You through?"

Brando looked at me thoughtfully, and I, in turn, at my coat. But he said, "We're still yakking. Call me back in an hour."

"Okay. Well . . . okay. Listen. Miiko's here. She wants to know did you get the flowers she sent you?"

Brando's eyes lazily rolled toward the glassed-in sun porch, where a bowl of asters was centered on a round bamboo table. "Uh-huh. Tell her thanks very much."

"Tell her yourself. She's right here."

"No! Hey, wait a minute! Christ, *that's* not how you do it." But the protest came too late. Murray had already put down the phone, and Brando, reiterating "*That's* not how you do it," blushed and squirmed like an embarrassed boy.

The next voice to emanate from the receiver belonged to his *Sayonara* leading lady, Miss Miiko Taka. She asked about his health.

"Better, thanks. I ate the bad end of an oyster, that's all. Miiko? . . . Miiko, that was very *sweet* of you to send me the flowers. They're beautiful. I'm looking at them right now. Asters," he continued, as though shyly venturing a line of verse, "are my favorite flowers . . ."

I retired to the sun porch, leaving Brando and Miss Taka to conduct their conversation in stricter seclusion. Below the windows, the hotel garden, with its ultra-simple and *soigné* arrangements of rock and tree, floated in the mists that crawl off Kyoto's waterways—for it *is* a watery city, crisscrossed with shallow rivers and cascading canals, dotted with pools as still as coiled snakes and mirthful little waterfalls that sound like Japanese girls giggling. Once the imperial capital and now the country's cultural museum, such an aesthetic treasure house that American bombers let it go unmolested during the war, Kyoto is surrounded by water, too; beyond the city's containing hills, thin roads run like causeways across the reflecting silver of flooded rice fields. That evening, despite the gliding mists, the blue encircling hills were discernible against the night, for the upper air had purity; a sky was there, stars were in it, and a scrap of moon. Some portions of the town could be seen. Nearest was a neighborhood of curving roofs, the dark façades of aristocratic houses fashioned from silky wood yet austere, northern, as secret-looking as any stone Siena palace. How brilliant they made the street lamps appear, and the doorway lanterns casting keen kimono colors—pink and orange, lemon and red. Farther away was a modern flatness—wide avenues and neon, a skyscraper of raw concrete that seemed less enduring, more perishable, than the papery dwellings stooping around it.

Brando completed his call. Approaching the sun porch, he looked at me looking at the view. He said, "Have you been to Nara? Pretty interesting."

I had, and yes, it was. "Ancient, old-time Nara," as a local cicerone unfailingly referred to it, is an hour's drive from Kyoto—a postcard town set in a show-place park. Here is the apotheosis of the Japanese genius for hypnotizing nature into unnatural behavior. The great shrine-infested park is a green salon where sheep graze, and herds of tame deer wander under trim pine trees and, like Venetian pigeons, gladly pose with honeymoon couples; where children yank the beards of unretaliating goats; where old men wearing black capes with mink collars squat on the shores of lotus-quilted lakes and, by clapping their hands, summon swarms of fish, speckled and scarlet carp, fat, thick as trout, who allow their snouts to be tickled, then gobble the crumbs that the old men sprinkle. That this serpentless Eden should strongly appeal to Brando was a bit surprising. With his liberal taste for the off-trail and not-overly-trammeled, one might have thought he would be unresponsive to so ruly, subjugated a landscape. Then, as though apropos of Nara, he said, "Well, I'd like to be married. I want to have children." It was not, perhaps, the *non sequitur* it seemed; the gentle safety of Nara just could, by the association of ideas, suggest marriage, a family.

"You've got to have love," he said. "There's no other reason for living. Men are no different from mice. They're born to perform the same function. Procreate." ("Marlon," to quote his friend Elia Kazan, "is one of the gentlest people I've ever known. Possibly the gentlest." Kazan's remark had meaning when one observed Brando in the company of children. As far as he was concerned, Japan's youngest generation—lovely, lively, cherry-cheeked kids with bowlegs and bristling bangs—was always welcome to lark around the *Sayonara* sets. He was good with the children, at ease, playful, appreciative; he seemed, indeed, their emotional contemporary, a co-conspirator. Moreover, the condoling expression, the slight look of dispensing charitable compassion, peculiar to his contemplation of some adults was absent from his eyes when he looked at a child.)

Touching Miss Taka's floral offering, he went on, "What other reason is there for living? Except love? That has been my main trouble. My inability to love anyone." He turned back into the lighted room, stood there as though hunting something—a cigarette? He picked up a pack. Empty. He slapped at the pockets of trousers and jackets lying here and there. Brando's wardrobe no longer smacks of the street gang; as a dresser, he has graduated, or gone back, into an earlier style of outlaw chic, that of the prohibition sharpie—black snap-brim hats, striped suits and somber-hued George Raft shirts with pastel ties. Cigarettes were found; inhaling, he slumped on the pallet bed. Beads of sweat ringed his mouth. The electric heater hummed. The room was tropical; one could have grown orchids. Overhead, Mr. and Mrs. Buttons were again bumping about, but Brando appeared to have lost interest in them. He was smoking, thinking. Then, picking up the stitch of his thought, he said, "I can't. Love anyone. I can't trust anyone enough to give myself to them. But I'm ready. I want it. And I may, I'm almost on the point, I've really got to . . ." His eyes narrowed, but his tone, far from being intense, was indifferent, dully objective, as though he were discussing some character in a play—a part he was weary of portraying yet was trapped in by contract. "Because—well, what else is there? That's all it's all about. To love somebody."

(At this time Brando was, of course, a bachelor, who had, upon occasion, indulged in engagements of a quasi-official character—once to an aspiring authoress and actress, by name Miss Blossom Plumb, and again, with more public attention, to Mlle. Josanne Mariani-Bérenger, a French fisherman's daughter. But in neither instance were banns ever posted. One day last month, however, in a sudden and somewhat secret ceremony at Eagle Rock, California, Brando was married to a dark, sari-swathed young minor actress who called herself Anna Kashfi. According to conflicting press reports, either she was a Darjeeling-born Buddhist of the purest Indian parentage or she was the Calcutta-born daughter of an English couple named O'Callaghan, now living in Wales. Brando has not yet done anything to clear up the mystery.)

"Anyway, I have *friends*. No. No, I don't," he said, verbally shadowboxing. "Oh, sure I do," he decided, smoothing the sweat on his upper lip. "I have a great many friends. Some I don't hold out on. I let them know what's happening. You have to trust somebody. Well, not all the way. There's nobody I rely on to tell *me* what to do."

I asked if that included professional advisers. For instance, it was my understanding that Brando very much depended on the guidance of Jay Kanter, a young man on the staff of the Music Corporation of America, which is the agency that represents him. "Oh, Jay," Brando said now. "Jay does what I tell *him* to. I'm alone like that."

The telephone sounded. An hour seemed to have passed, for it was Murray again. "Yeah, still yakking," Brando told him. "Look, let *me* call *you* . . . Oh, in an hour or so. You be back in your room? . . . Okay."

He hung up, and said, "Nice guy. He wants to be a director—eventually. I was saying something, though. We were talking about friends. Do you know how I make a friend?" He leaned a little toward me, as though he had an amusing secret to impart. "I go about it very gently. I circle around and around. I circle. Then, gradually, I come nearer. Then I reach out and touch them—ah, so gently . . ." His fingers stretched forward like insect feelers and grazed my arm. "Then," he said, one eye half shut, the other, à la Rasputin, mesmerically wide and shining, "I draw back. Wait awhile. Make them wonder. At just the right moment, I move in again. Touch them. Circle." Now his hand, broad and blunt-fingered, traveled in a rotating pattern, as though it held a rope with which he was binding an invisible presence. "They don't know what's happening. Before they realize it, they're all entangled, involved. I have them. And suddenly, sometimes, I'm all *they* have. A lot of them, you see, are people who don't fit anywhere; they're not accepted, they've been hurt, crippled one way or another. But I want to help them, and they can focus on me; I'm the duke. Sort of the duke of my domain."

(A past tenant on the ducal preserve, describing its seigneur and his subjects, has said, "It's as though Marlon lived in a house where the doors are never locked. When he lived in New York, the door always *was* open. Anybody could come in, whether Marlon was there or not, and everybody did. You'd arrive and there would be ten, fifteen characters wandering around. It was strange, because nobody seemed to really know anybody else. They were just there, like people in a bus station. Some type asleep in a chair. People reading the tabs. A girl dancing by herself. Or painting her toenails. A comedian trying out his night-club act. Off in a corner, there'd be a chess game going. And drums—bang, boom, bang, boom! But there was never any drinking—nothing like that. Once in a while somebody would say, 'Let's go down to the corner for an ice-cream soda.' Now, in all this Marlon was the common denominator, the only connecting link. He'd move around the room drawing individuals aside and talking to them alone. If you've noticed, Marlon can't, *won't,* talk to two people simultaneously. He'll never take part in a *group* conversation. It always has to be a cozy tête-à-tête—one person at a time. Which is necessary, I suppose, if you use the same kind of charm on everyone. But even when you know that's what he's doing, it doesn't matter. Because when *your* turn comes, he makes you feel you're the only person in the room. In the world. Makes you feel that you're under his protection and that your troubles and moods concern him deeply. You have to believe it; more than anyone I've known, he radiates *sincerity*. Afterward you may ask yourself, 'Is it an act?' If so, what's the point? What have you got to give him? Nothing except—and this *is* the point—affection. Affection that lends him authority over you. I sometimes think Marlon is like an orphan who later on in life tries to compensate by becoming the kindly head of a huge orphanage. But even outside this institution he wants everybody to love him." Although there exist a score of witnesses who might well contradict the last opinion, Brando himself is credited with having once informed an interviewer, "I can walk into a room where there are a hundred people—if there is *one* person in that room who doesn't like me, I know it and have to get out." As a footnote, it should be added that within the clique over which Brando presides he is esteemed as an intellectual father, as well as an emotional big brother. The person who probably knows him best, the comedian Wally Cox, declares him to be "a creative philosopher, a very deep thinker," and adds, "He's a real liberating force for his friends."

Brando yawned; it had got to be a quarter past one. In less than five hours he would have to be showered, shaved, breakfasted, on the set, and ready for a make-up man to paint his pale face the mulatto tint that Technicolor requires.

"Let's have another cigarette," he said as I made a move to put on my coat.

"Don't you think you should go to sleep?"

"That just means getting up. Most mornings, I don't know why I do. I can't face it." He looked at the telephone, as though remembering his promise to call Murray. "Anyway, I may work later on. You want something to drink?"

Outside, the stars had darkened and it had started to drizzle, so the prospect of a nightcap was pleasing, especially if I should have to return on foot to my own hotel, which was a mile distant from the Miyako. I poured some vodka; Brando declined to join me. However, he subsequently reached for my glass, sipped from it, set it down between us, and suddenly said, in an offhand way that nonetheless conveyed feeling, "My mother. She broke apart like a piece of porcelain."

I had often heard friends of Brando's say, "Marlon worshipped his mother." But prior to 1947, and the première of *A Streetcar Named Desire*, few, perhaps none, of the young actor's circle had met either of his parents; they knew nothing of his background except what he chose to tell them. "Marlon always gave a very colorful picture of home life back in Illinois," one of his acquaintances told me. "When we heard that his family were coming to New York for the opening of *Streetcar*, everybody was very curious. We didn't know what to expect. On opening night, Irene Selznick gave a big party at '21.' Marlon came with his mother and father. Well, you can't imagine two more attractive people. Tall, handsome, charming as they could be. What impressed me—I think it amazed everyone—was Marlon's attitude toward them. In their presence, he wasn't the lad we knew. He was a model son. Reticent, respectful, very polite, considerate in every way."

Born in Omaha, Nebraska, where his father was a salesman of limestone products, Brando, the family's third child and only son, was soon taken to live in Libertyville, Illinois. There the Brandos settled down in a rambling house in a countrified neighborhood; at least, there was enough country around the house to allow the Brandos to keep geese and hens and rabbits, a horse, a Great Dane, twenty-eight cats and a cow. Milking the cow was the daily chore that belonged to Bud, as Marlon was then nicknamed. Bud seems to have been an extroverted and competitive boy. Everyone who came within range of him was at once forced into some variety of contest: Who can eat fastest? Hold his breath longest? Tell the tallest tale? Bud was rebellious, too; rain or shine, he ran away from home every Sunday. But he and his two sisters, Frances and Jocelyn, were devotedly close to their mother. Many years later Stella Adler, Brando's former drama coach, described Mrs. Brando, who died in 1954, as "a very beautiful, a heavenly, lost, girlish creature." Always, wherever she lived, Mrs. Brando had played leads in the productions of local dramatic societies, and always she had longed for a more brightly footlighted world than her surroundings provided. These yearnings inspired her children. Frances took to painting;

Jocelyn, who is at present a professional actress, interested herself in the theater. Bud, too, had inherited his mother's theatrical inclinations, but at seventeen he announced a wish to study for the ministry. (Then, as now, Brando searched for a belief. As one Brando disciple once summed it up, "He needs to find something in life, something in himself, that is permanently true, and he needs to lay down his life for it. For such an intense personality, nothing less than that will do.") Talked out of his clerical ambitions, expelled from school, rejected for military service in 1942 because of a trick knee, Brando packed up and came to New York. Whereupon Bud, the plump, towheaded, unhappy adolescent, exits, and the man-sized and very gifted Marlon emerges.

Brando has not forgotten Bud. When he speaks of the boy he was, the boy seems to inhabit him, as if time had done little to separate the man from the hurt, desiring child. "My father was indifferent to me," he said. "Nothing I could do interested him, or pleased him. I've accepted that now. We're friends now. We get along." Over the past ten years the elder Brando has supervised his son's financial affairs; in addition to Pennebaker Productions, of which Mr. Brando, Sr., is an employee, they have been associated in a number of ventures, including a Nebraska grain-and-cattle ranch, in which a large percentage of the younger Brando's earnings was invested. "But my mother was everything to me. A whole world. I tried so hard. I used to come home from school . . ." He hesitated, as though waiting for me to picture him: Bud, books under his arm, scuffling his way along an afternoon street. "There wouldn't be anybody home. Nothing in the icebox." More lantern slides: empty rooms, a kitchen. "Then the telephone would ring. Somebody calling from some bar. And they'd say, 'We've got a lady down here. You better come get her.' " Suddenly Brando was silent. In the silence the picture faded, or, rather, became fixed: Bud at the telephone. At last the image moved again, leaped forward in time. Bud is eighteen, and: "I thought if she loved me enough, trusted me enough, I thought, then we can be together, in New York; we'll live together and I'll take care of her. Once, later on, that really happened. She left my father and came to live with me. In New York, when I was in a play. I tried so hard. But my love wasn't enough. She couldn't care enough. She went back. And one day"—the flatness of his voice grew flatter, yet the emotional pitch ascended until one could discern, like a sound within a sound, a wounded bewilderment—"I didn't care anymore. She was there. In a room. Holding on to me. And I let her fall. Because I couldn't take it anymore—watch her breaking apart, in front of me, like a piece of porcelain. I stepped right over her. I walked right out. I was indifferent. Since then, I've been indifferent."

The telephone was signaling. Its racket seemed to rouse him from a daze; he stared about, as though he'd wakened in an unknown room, then smiled wryly, then whispered, "Damn, damn, damn," as his hand lurched toward the telephone. "Sorry," he told Murray. "I was just going to call you . . . No, he's leaving now. But look, man, let's call it off tonight. It's after one. It's nearly two o'clock . . . Yeah . . . Sure thing. Tomorrow."

Meanwhile, I'd put on my overcoat and was waiting to say good-night. He walked me to the door, where I put on my shoes. "Well, *sayonara,* " he mockingly bade me. "Tell them at the desk to get you a taxi." Then, as I walked down the corridor, he called, "And listen! Don't pay too much attention to what I say. I don't always feel the same way."

In a sense, this was not my last sight of him that evening. Downstairs, the Miyako's lobby was deserted. There was no one at the desk, nor, outside, were there any taxis in view. Even at high noon the fancy crochet of Kyoto's streets had played me tricks; still, I set off through the marrow-chilling drizzle in what I hoped was a homeward direction. I'd never before been abroad so late in the city. It was quite a contrast to daytime, when the central parts of the town, carousel by crowds of fiesta massiveness, jangle like the inside of a *pachinko* parlor, or to early evening—Kyoto's most exotic hours, for then, like night flowers, lanterns wreathe the side streets, and resplendent geishas, with their white ceramic faces and their ballooning lacquered wigs strewn with silver bells, their hobbled wiggle-walk, hurry among the shadows toward meticulously tasteful revelries. But at two in the morning these exquisite grotesques are gone, the cabarets are shuttered; only cats remained to keep me company, and drunks and red-light ladies, the inevitable old beggar-bundles in doorways, and, briefly, a ragged street musician who followed me playing on a flute a medieval music. I had trudged far more than a mile when, at last, one of a hundred alleys led to familiar ground—the main-street district of department stores and cinemas. It was then that I saw Brando. Sixty feet tall, with a head as huge as the greatest Buddha's, there he was, in comic-paper colors, on a sign above a theater that advertised *The Teahouse of the August Moon.* Rather Buddha-like, too, was his pose, for he was depicted in a squatting position, a serene smile on a face that glistened in the rain and the light of a street lamp. A deity, yes; but more than that, really, just a young man sitting on a pile of candy.

From
Observations

(with Richard Avedon)

(1959)

RICHARD AVEDON

RICHARD AVEDON IS A MAN WITH gifted eyes. An adequate description; to add is sheer flourish. His brown and deceivingly normal eyes, so energetic at seeing the concealed and seizing the spirit, pursuing the flight of a truth, a mood, a face, are the important features: those, and his born-to-be absorption in his craft, photography, without which the unusual eyes, and the nervously sensitive intelligence supplying their power, could not dispel what they distillingly imbibe. For the truth is, though loquacious, an unskimping conversationalist, the sort that zigzags like a bee ambitious to depollen a dozen blossoms simultaneously, Avedon is not, not very, articulate: he finds his proper tongue in silence, and while maneuvering a camera —his voice, the one that speaks with admirable clarity, is the soft sound of the shutter forever freezing a moment focused by his perception.

He was born in New York, and is thirty-six, though one would not think it: a skinny, radiant fellow who still hasn't got his full growth, animated as a colt in Maytime, just a lad not long out of college. Except that he never went to college, never, for that matter, finished high school, even though he appears to have been rather a child prodigy, a poet of some talent, and already, from the time he was ten and the owner of a box camera, sincerely embarked on his life's labor: the walls of his room were ceiling to floor papered with pictures torn from magazines, photographs by Muncaczi and Steichen and Man Ray. Such interests, special in a child, suggest that he was not only precocious but unhappy; quite happily he says he was: a veteran at running away from home. When he failed to gain a high-school diploma, his father, sensible man, told him to "Go ahead! Join the army of illiterates." To be contrary, but not altogether disobedient, he instead joined the Merchant Marine. It was under the auspices of this organization that he encountered his first formal photographic training. Later, after the war, he studied at New York's New School for Social Research, where Alexey Brodovitch, then Art Director of the magazine *Harper's Bazaar*, conducted a renowned class in experimental photography. A conjunction of worthy teacher with worthy pupil: in 1945, by way of his editorial connection, Brodovitch arranged for the professional debut of his exceptional student. Within the year the novice was established; his work, now regularly appearing in *Harper's Bazaar* and *Life* and *Theatre Arts*, as well as on the walls of exhibitions, was considerably discussed, praised for its inventive features, its tart insights, the youthful sense of movement and blood-coursing aliveness he could insert in so still an entity as a photograph: simply, no one had seen anything exactly comparable, and so, since he had staying power, was a hard worker, was, to sum it up, seriously gifted, very naturally he evolved to be, during the next decade, the most generously remunerated, by and large successful American photographer of his generation, and the most, as the excessive number of Avedon imitators bears witness, aesthetically influential.

"My first sitter," so Avedon relates, "was Rachmaninoff. He had an apartment in the building where my grandparents lived. I was about ten, and I used to hide among the garbage cans on his back stairs, stay there hour after hour listening to him practice. One day I thought I must: must ring his bell. I asked could I take his picture with my box camera. In a way, that was the beginning of this book."

Well, then, this book. It was intended to preserve the best of Avedon's already accomplished work, his observations, along with a few of mine. A final selection of photographs seemed impossible, first because Avedon's portfolio was too richly stocked, secondly because he kept burdening the problem of subtraction by incessantly thinking he must: must hurry off to ring the doorbell of latter-day Rachmaninoffs, persons of interest to him who had by farfetched mishap evaded his ubiquitous lens. Perhaps that implies a connective theme as regards the choice of personalities here included, some private laurel-awarding system based upon esteem for the subject's ability or beauty; but no, in that sense the selection is arbitrary, on the whole the common thread is only that these are some of the people

Avedon happens to have photographed, and about whom he has, according to his calculations, made valid comment.

However, he does appear to be attracted over and again by the mere condition of a face. It will be noticed, for it isn't avoidable, how often he emphasizes the elderly; and, even among the just middle-aged, unrelentingly tracks down every hard-earned crow's-foot. In consequence there have been occasional accusations of malice. But, "Youth never moves me," Avedon explains. "I seldom see anything very beautiful in a young face. I do, though: in the downward curve of Maugham's lips. In Isak Dinesen's hands. So much has been written there, there is so much to be read, if one could only read. I feel most of the people in this book are earthly saints. Because they are obsessed. Obsessed with work of one sort or another. To dance, to be beautiful, tell stories, solve riddles, perform in the street. Zavattini's mouth and Escudero's eyes, the smile of Marie-Louise Bousquet: they are sermons on bravado."

One afternoon Avedon asked me to his studio, a place ordinarily humming with hot lights and humid models and harried assistants and haranguing telephones; but that afternoon, a winter Sunday, it was a spare and white and peaceful asylum, quiet as the snow-made marks settling like cat's paws on the skylight.

Avedon was in his stocking-feet, wading through a shiny surf of faces, a few laughing and fairly afire with fun and devil-may-care, others straining to communicate the thunder of their interior selves, their art, their inhuman handsomeness, or faces plainly mankindish, or forsaken, or insane: a surfeit of countenances that collided with one's vision and rather stunned it. Like immense playing cards, the faces were placed in rows that spread and filled the studio's vast floor. It was the final collection of photographs for the book; and as we gingerly paraded through this orchard of prunings, warily walked up and down the rows (always, as though the persons underfoot were capable of crying out, careful not to step on a cheek or squash a nose), Avedon said: "Sometimes I think all my pictures are just pictures of me. My concern is, how would you say, well, the human predicament; only what I consider the human predicament may be simply my own." He cupped his chin, his gaze darting from Dr. Oppenheimer to Father Darcy: "I hate cameras. They interfere, they're always in the way. I wish: if I just could work with my eyes alone!" Presently he pointed to three prints of the same photograph, a portrait of L⸺ asked which I preferred; to me they were triplets u⸺ their differences, indicated how one was a degree d⸺ while from the third a shadow had been removed. "⸺ print," he said, his voice tight with that intensity p⸺ "one that contains all you intended, is very often mor⸺ ous than the sitting itself. When I'm photographing⸺

when I've got the image I really want. But to get the image out of the camera and into the open is another matter. I make as many as sixty prints of a picture, would make a hundred if it would mean a fraction's improvement, help show the invisible visible, the inside outside."

We came to the end of the last row, stopped, surveyed the gleaming field of black and white, a harvest fifteen years on the vine. Avedon shrugged. "That's all. That's it. The visual symbols of what I want to tell are in these faces. At least," he added, beginning a genuine frown, the visual symbol of a nature too, in a fortunate sense, vain, too unrequited and questing to ever experience authentic satisfaction, "at least I hope so."

JOHN HUSTON

Of course, at their best, movies are anti-literature and, as a medium, belong not to writers, not to actors, but to directors, some of whom, to be sure —for one, John Huston—served their apprenticeship as studio scribblers. Huston has said: "I became a director because I couldn't watch any longer how my work as a writer was ruined." Though that could not have been the only reason: this lanky, drawling dandy, who might be a cowboy as imagined by Aubrey Beardsley, has in abundance that desire to command Zavattini disavows.

Huston's work and the manner of man he happens to be are inseparably related, his films silhouette the contours of his private mindscape (as do Eisenstein's, Ingmar Bergman's, Jean Vigo's) in a way not usual to the profession, movies being, the majority of them, objective operations unrevealing of their maker's subjective preoccupations; therefore it is perhaps permissible to mention in personal style Huston's stylized person—his riverboat-gambler's suavity overlaid with roughneck buffooning, the hearty mirthless laughter that rises toward but never reaches his warmly crinkled and ungentle eyes, eyes bored as sunbathing lizards; the determined seduction of his confidential gazes and man's man camaraderie, all intended as much for his own benefit as that of his audience, to camouflage a refrigerated void of active feeling, for, as is true of every classic seducer, or charmer if you prefer, the success of the seduction depends upon himself never feeling, never becoming emotionally inserted: to do so would mean forfeiting control of the situation, the "picture"; thus, he is a man of obsessions rather than passions, and a romantic cynic who believes that all endeavor, virtuous or evil or simply plodding, receives the same honorarium: a check in the amount of zero. What has this to do with his ... Something. Consider the plot of the first, still best, Huston-directed ... he Maltese Falcon, in which the motivation is contributed by a ... iou in the shape of a falcon, a treasure for which the principal participants betray each other and murder and die—only to discover the falcon not to be the jeweled and genuine item but a solid lead fake, a cheat. This happens to be the theme, the dénouement, of most of Huston's films, of *The Treasure of the Sierra Madre*, in which the prospector's hoard of killed-over gold is blown away by the wind, of *The Asphalt Jungle*, *The Red Badge of Courage*, *Beat the Devil*, and, of course, of *Moby Dick*, that dead-end statement on man's defeat. Indeed, Huston seems seldom to have been attracted to material that did not accept human destiny as an unhappy joke, a confidence ploy with no pea under any pod; even the scripts he wrote as a young man—by example, *High Sierra* and *Juarez*—confirm his predilection. Like much art, his art, and he can be an artist when he chooses, is in great degree the compensatory result of a flaw in the man: that emotional lacuna that causes him to see life as a cheat (because the cheater is cheated, too) is the irritant that births the pearl; and his payment has been to be, in human terms, himself something of a maltese falcon.

CHARLIE CHAPLIN

Shortly before Chaplin departed from America in 1952, a leave-taking of deplorable permanence, he asked Avedon to make his passport portrait, a chore Chaplin proceeded, in the midst of the sitting, to satirize, and the product of his clowning, a horned Pan-sprite mocking the spoilsport universe of governmental borders (in territory and thought), is surely the sort of picture the lovable tramp would have pasted inside *his* passport: a nice eyebugger for boresome officials. It does amuse to remember the fadeout road of Chaplin's silent days, the empty dusty vista down which, at the end of every adventure, the little bum recedingly sashayed, knapsack aboard: remember, and realize now where the road was awinding: of all places, to Switzerland! and that sorry knapsack, why, it was full of greenbacks! bullion to buy a marbled king-of-the-mountain abode above a lake blue as bluebirds, a Happy Ending bower where the revamped tramp, surrounded by the dotings of a beautiful waif-bride and seven beautiful waif-children, moseys about sniffing his beloved flowers. Which is as it should be (the person responsible for *City Lights*, *The Gold Rush*, *Modern Times*, creations final and perfect as a lion, as water, is perfectly final, deserves—on this earth here and now—bliss), and is almost, but isn't: because, in recent years, Chaplin has permitted petulance to absorb him—he believes himself, perhaps rightly, to have been maltreated by America, its press, State Department, and so paces his villa garrulously fuming: which is his privilege, still it is regrettable, for it is wasteful: his last film, *A King in New York*, an irritable poking at things U.S.A., was entirely waste-motion—was. it served to drain the gall out of his craw.

Chaplin has had access to genius, and another advantage rarer than that: the benefit of being sole proprietor of his own shop—financier, producer, director, writer, star. One father to a baby is nature's requirement; the necessity of collaborative seeding is the oddity-making curse of film-art, that blasted heath upon which few giants, and as few middling grown men, stride: those who do, all honor to them.

A GATHERING OF SWANS

From the journal of a Mr. Patrick Conway, aged seventeen, during the course of a visit to Bruges in the year 1800: "Sat on the stone wall and observed a gathering of swans, an aloof armada, coast around the curves of the canal and merge with the twilight, their feathers floating away over the water like the trailing hems of snowy ball-gowns. I was reminded of beautiful women; I thought of Mlle. de V., and experienced a cold exquisite spasm, a chill, as though I had heard a poem spoken, fine music rendered. A beautiful woman, beautifully elegant, impresses us as art does, changes the weather of our spirit; and that, is that a frivolous matter? I think not."

The intercontinental covey of swans drifting across our pages boasts a pair of cygnets, fledglings of the prettiest promise who may one day lead the flock. However, as is generally conceded, a beautiful girl of twelve or twenty, while she may merit attention, does not deserve admiration. Reserve that laurel for decades hence when, if she has kept buoyant the weight of her gifts, been faithful to the vows a swan must, she will have earned an audience all-kneeling; for her achievement represents discipline, has required the patience of a hippopotamus, the objectivity of a physician combined with the involvement of an artist, one whose sole creation is her perishable self. Moreover, the area of accomplishment must extend much beyond the external. Of first importance is voice, its timbre, how and what it pronounces; if stupid, a swan must seek to conceal it, not necessarily from men (a dash of dumbness seldom diminishes masculine respect, though it rarely, regardless of myth, enhances it); rather from clever women, those witch-eyed brilliants who are simultaneously the swan's mortal enemy and most convinced adorer. Of course the perfect Giselle, she of calmest purity, i̶s̶ ̶n̶o̶t̶ a clever woman. The cleverest are easily told; and not by any ̶o̶p̶i̶n̶i̶o̶n̶ ̶o̶n̶ politics or Proust, any smartly placed banderillas of wit; not, ̶b̶y̶ ̶t̶he presence of *any* positive factor, but the absence of one: ̶p̶a̶s̶s̶i̶o̶n̶. The very nature of her attainment presupposes a certain ̶d̶e̶v̶o̶t̶ion; nonetheless, if one can remark on her face or in her ̶m̶a̶n̶n̶e̶r̶ ̶a̶ ̶f̶a̶l̶s̶e̶n̶e̶s̶s̶ of the impression she makes, it is as though, attending ̶a̶ ̶b̶a̶n̶q̶u̶e̶t̶,̶ ̶o̶n̶e̶ ̶h̶a̶d̶ ̶t̶he misfortune to glimpse the kitchen.

To pedal a realistic chord—and it must be sounded, if only out of justice to their cousins of coarser plumage—authentic swans are almost never women that nature and the world has deprived. God gave them good bones; some lesser personage, a father, a husband, blessed them with that best of beauty emollients, a splendid bank account. Being a great beauty, and *remaining* one, is, at the altitude flown here, expensive: a fairly accurate estimate on the annual upkeep could be made—but really, why spark a revolution? And if expenditure were all, a sizable population of sparrows would swiftly be swans.

It may be that the enduring swan glides upon waters of liquefied lucre; but that cannot account for the creature herself—her talent, like all talent, is composed of unpurchasable substances. For a swan is invariably the result of adherence to some aesthetic system of thought, a code transposed into a self-portrait; what we see is the imaginary portrait precisely projected. This is why certain women, while not truly beautiful but triumphs over plainness, can occasionally provide the swan-illusion: their inner vision of themselves is so fixed, decorated with such clever outer artifice, that we surrender to their claim, even stand convinced of its genuineness: and it *is* genuine; in a way the *manqué* swan (our portfolio contains two excellent examples) is more beguiling than the natural (of which, among present company, the classic specimens are Mme. Agnelli, the European swan *numero uno,* and America's superb unsurpassable Mrs. William S. Paley): after all, a creation wrought by human nature is of subtler human interest, of finer fascination, than one nature alone has evolved.

A final word: the advent of a swan into a room starts stirring in some persons a decided sense of discomfort. If one is to believe these swan "allergics," their hostility does not derive from envy, but, so they suggest, from a shadow of "coldness" and "unreality" the swan casts. Yet isn't it true that an impression of coldness, usually false, accompanies perfection? And might it not be that what the critics actually feel is fear? In the presence of the very beautiful, as in the presence of the immensely intelligent, terror contributes to our over-all reaction, and it is as much fright as appreciation which causes the stabbed-by-an-icicle chill that for a moment murders us when a swan swims into view.

PABLO PICASSO

In 1981 our world, granted it is still orbiting, will celebrate Picasso's centenary. Of course, because he has that kind of luck, the great man will be on hand; and available, as usual, to all mediums of publicity: very likely on this occasion television will display him in the buff, as befits a god-creature quite beyond the laws of human decorum. Born in Malaga, a country of figs and stone and guitars, Picasso was a child-prodigy who stayed one: that is, remained a prodigy and something of a child, a man inhabited by a boy's fooling-around impatience, hatred of system, fresh-eyed curiosity: "Pablo," to quote his oldest friend, Jaime Sabartes, "is preeminently a sum of curiosities. He has more curiosity than a thousand million women." When Picasso was thirteen his father, an acrimonious Andalusian art-teacher who ground out greeting-card still lifes for the Barcelona bourgeoi-sie, gave over to his son his palette and brushes and never painted again; which was, in its way, Picasso's first conquest—he went on to strew the century with painters overshadowed by him or altogether put to pasture. Queer, come to think of it, why some of these fellows have not united to assassinate this octopus of art; for, though not the master of Matisse and unpossessed by Braque's compositional strength, Picasso has, via vivacious gall and a bottomless plethora of inventional surprises, outrun them all: he is *the* winner.

COCO CHANEL

Chanel, a spare spruce sparrow voluble and vital as a woodpecker, once, midflight in one of her nonstoppable monologues, said, referring to the very costly *pauvre* orphan appearance she has lo these decades modeled: "Cut off my head, and I'm thirteen." But her head has always remained attached, definitely she had it perfectly placed way back yonder when she *was* thirteen, or scarcely more, and a moneyed "kind gentleman," the first of several grateful and well-wishing patrons, asked petite "Coco," daughter of a Basque blacksmith who had taught her to help him shoe horses, which she preferred, black pearls or white? Neither, she answered—what she preferred, *Chéri*, were the stakings to start a little shop. Thus emerged Chanel, the fashion-visionary. Whether or not the productions of a dress-maker can be called important "cultural" contributions (and perhaps they can: a Mainbocher, a Balenciaga, are men of more authentic creative signifi-cance than several platoons of poets and composers who rise to mind) is uninteresting; but a career woman impure and simple like Chanel arouses a documentary interest, the sum of which is partially totaled in these photographs of her changeling's face, at one angle a darling dangling in a heartshaped locket, at another an arid and avid go-getter—observe the striving in the taut stem of her neck: one thinks of a plant, an old hardy perennial still pushing toward, though now a touch parched by, the sun of success that, for those talented inconsolables primed with desire and fueled with ego and whose relentless energy propels the engine that hauls along the lethargic rest of us, invariably flourishes in the frigid sky of ambition. Chanel lives alone in an apartment across the street from the Ritz.

MARCEL DUCHAMP

Duchamp, born in Rouen, the third son of a multi-membered middle-class family, many of whom were artistically inclined, has lived in New York since 1915. During these forty-four years of American residence he has dabbled away at only one painting (*Bride Stripped Bare by Her Bachelors, Even*—an oil, on transparent glass, the size of a church window), and finished none; for all practical purposes, he abandoned painting in 1913, the year his *Nude Descending a Staircase* (of which a contemporary critic remarked, "Whirl around three times, bump your head twice against the wall, and if you bump hard enough the meaning will be perfectly obvious") was the drunkmaking sensation of some sixteen hundred forerunner experiments on view at the historic Armory show. "But," protests Duchamp, "not to paint doesn't mean I've given up art. All good painters have only about five masterpieces to their name. The others are not vital. The five have the force of shock. Shock is good. If I've done five good things, it's enough. Or you might say that instead of dying like Seurat at thirty-one, I am a man whose inspiration for painting stopped, eh?" His inspiration, at all events his talent, for playing games with art, wherein resides the kindergartenish and nowadays altogether shockless charm of his paintings, has not lain entirely fallow: in his infinite spare time he has concocted surrealist perfume bottles, made a pioneer abstract film, involved himself in interior decoration (ceilings swathed in coal sacks), devised a portable Duchamp museum fitted with miniatures of his best-known works (also a phial containing "Parisian Air"), and invented for himself other fraudulent forms of art-toy; but what seems to concern him sincerely is chess, a more serious style of fun, a subject around which he has improvised the most *recherché* volume possible: a thousand copies were printed in three languages, and (hold on to your berets) the title goes *Opposition et Cases Conjuguées, Opposition und Schwesterfelder, Opposition and Sister Squares.* Duchamp explains that "It all has to do with blocked pawns, when your only means of winning is by moves of kings. This happens only once in a thousand times. And why," he adds, "why isn't my chess playing an art activity? A chess game is very plastic. You construct it. It's mechanical sculpture and with chess one creates beautiful problems and that beauty is made with the heads and hands. Besides, it's purer, socially, than painting, for you can't make money out of chess, eh?"

And supposing you could, undoubtedly Duchamp wouldn't: he has often expressed anti-lucre sentiments amounting to a financial allergy ("No! Painting shouldn't become a fashionable thing. And money, money, money comes in, and it becomes a Wall Street office"); certainly very little about his living quarters, a fourth-floor walkup in a soiled and sullen brownstone on an unprepossessing Manhattan sidestreet, implies limousine standards; the flat, done up in a sort of flapper-period of modern artiness, boasts nothing rain might harm, except a small Matisse and a large Miró: as a sanctuary, it speaks of a man who would be himself, reasonably free and unbeholden. Downstairs, there is on the mailbox a nameplate dingy but dazzling; it reads: "Matisse-Duchamp-Ernst." Because, you see, the present Madame Duchamp is the former Madame Matisse, wife of the great man's son Pierre; as for Ernst, that is boyishly pink and silvery Surrealist Max, the apartment's onetime tenant. The order of the names, the billing, as it were, seems an appropriate artistic judgment.

JEAN COCTEAU AND ANDRÉ GIDE

André Gide, that moralizing immoralist, a writer favored with sincerity but denied imagination, quite disapproved of Jean Cocteau, whose gifts the mischievous muses had reversed, making of him, both as man and artist, a creature vastly imaginative but vivaciously insincere. It is interesting, then, that Gide should have authored the most accurate, and for that reason most sympathetic, description of our eldest terrible child.

Gide is writing in his journal; the time is August, 1914. "Jean Cocteau had arranged to meet me in an 'English tearoom' on the corner of the rue de Ponthieu and the avenue d'Antin. I had no pleasure in seeing him again, despite his extreme kindness; but he is incapable of seriousness, and all his thoughts, his witticisms, his sensations, all the extraordinary brilliance of his customary conversation shocked me like a luxury article displayed in a period of famine and mourning. He is dressed almost like a soldier, and the fillip of the present events has made him look healthier. He is relinquishing nothing, but simply giving a martial twist to his usual liveliness. When speaking of the slaughter of Mulhouse he uses amusing adjectives and mimicry; he imitates the bugle call and the whistling of the shrapnel. Then, changing subjects since he sees he is not amusing me, he claims to be sad; he wants to be sad with the same kind of sadness as you, and suddenly he adopts your mood and explains it to you. Then he talks of Blanche, mimics Mme. R. and talks of the lady at the Red Cross who shouted on the stairway, 'I was promised fifty wounded men for this morning; I want my fifty wounded men.' Meanwhile he is crushing a piece of plum cake in his plate and nibbling it; his voice rises suddenly and has odd twists; he laughs, leans forward, bends toward you and touches you. The odd thing is that I think he would make a good soldier. He asserts that he would and that he would be brave too. He has the carefree attitude of the street urchin; it is in his company that I feel the most awkward, the most heavy, the most gloomy."

In the spring of 1950, in the piazza of a Sicilian town where Gide was vacationing (it was the last year of his life), he had another meeting with Cocteau, a farewell encounter which the writer of these notes happened to observe. It was Gide's custom to dream away the morning hours propped in the piazza sun; there he sat sipping from a bottle of salt-water brought fresh from the sea, a motionless mandarin shrouded in a woolly wintry black cape and with a wide-brimmed dark fedora casting a shadow the length of his stern, brimstone countenance: an idle idol-saint (of sorts) unspeaking and unspoken to except for occasional consultations with those of the village Ganymedes who snagged his fancy. Then one morning Cocteau, whirling a cane, sauntered upon the piazza-scene and proceeded to interrupt the steely-eyed reveries of Il Vecchio (as the local *ragazzi* called the distinguished octogenarian). Thirty-five years had gone by since the wartime tea party, yet nothing in the attitude of the two men toward each other had altered. Cocteau was still anxious to please, still the rainbow-winged and dancing dragonfly inviting the toad not merely to admire but perhaps devour him. He jigged about, his jingling merriment competed with the bell-music of passing donkey carts, he scattered rays of bitter wit that stung like the Sicilian sun, he effused, enthused, he fondled the old man's knee, caressed his hands, squeezed his shoulders, kissed his parched Mongolian cheeks—nay, nothing would awaken Il Vecchio: as though his stomach turned at the thought of digesting such fancy-colored fodder, he remained a hungerless frog upon a thorny frond; until at last he croaked, "Do be still. You are disturbing the view."

Very true: Cocteau was disturbing the view. He has been doing so since his debut as an opium-smoking prodigy of seventeen. For more than four decades this eternal gamin has conducted a fun-for-all vaudeville, with many flashing changes of attire: poet, novelist, playwright, journalist, designer, painter, inventor of ballets, film maker, professional conversationalist. Most of these costumes have fit well, a few brilliantly. But it is in the guise of catalytic agent that he has been most capable: as an innovator for, and propagandist of, other men's ideas and gifts—from Radiguet to Genet, Satie to Auric, Picasso to Bérard, Worth to Dior. Cocteau has lived absolutely inside his time, and more than anyone else, formed French taste in the present century. It is Cocteau's kinship with his own epoch, his exclusive concern with the modern, that lay at the root of Il Vecchio's aversion. "I do not seek to be of my epoch; I seek to overflow my epoch" was Gide's declared ambition; a commendable one, too. But isn't it possible that a man who has so enlivened our today will, if not overflow, at least trickle into somebody's tomorrow?

MAE WEST

Once upon a time an outrageous young man of wide acquaintance thought to give an unusual tea party. It was to honor Miss Mae West, then appearing in a Manhattan night club. Dame Edith Sitwell was invited to pour, a task the Dame, always a devotee of *outré* incident, accepted. New York illuminati, titillated at the prospect of an interview between two ladies of such differently composed distinction, begged bids.

"My dear," the young man was congratulated in advance, "it's *the* camp of the season."

But—everything went awry. At four the Dame, pleading laryngitis, telephoned her regrets. By six, with the party at midpoint, it seemed Miss West would disappoint, too. Muttering guests mentioned hoax; at seven the host retired to a private chamber. Ten minutes later the guest of honor arrived, and what remained of the assemblage were not sorry they had waited. Not sorry, but strangely confused. The familiar appurtenances were there: the brass wig, the scimitar eyes with sword-length lashes, the white skin, white as a cottonmouth's mouth, the shape, that Big Ben of hour-glass figures, that convict's dream—nothing was absent; except Miss West.

For surely this was not the real Mae. Yet it was indeed Miss West: an uneasy, a shy and vulnerable, an unclassifiably virginal woman whose tardy entrance was conceivably due to having lingered on the street before summoning the courage to ring the bell. As one watched her, a jittery moth of a smile leaping about her lips but never alighting, huskily whisper "Sopleastameetya," and, as though too bashful to proceed, at once abandon her seat on the seesaw of any potential conversation, the *tour de force* nature of her theater-self, its eerie and absolute completeness, struck with force. Removed from the protecting realm of her hilarious creation, her sexless symbol of uninhibited sexuality, she was without defense: her long lashes fluttered like the feelers of a beetle on its back.

Only once did the tougher Mae reveal herself. The display was occasioned by an intense young girl who, approaching the actress, announced, "I saw *Diamond Lil* last week; it was wonderful."

"Didja, honey? Wheredja see it?"

"At the Museum. The Modern Museum."

And a dismayed Miss West, seeking shelter in the sassy drawl of her famous fabrication, inquired, "Just whaddya mean, honey? A *museum?*"

LOUIS ARMSTRONG

Surely the Satch has forgotten, still, he was one of this writer's first friends, I met him when I was four, that would be around 1928, and he, a hard-plump and belligerently happy brown Buddha, was playing aboard a pleasure steamer that paddled between New Orleans and St. Louis. Never mind why, but I had occasion to take the trip very often, and for me the sweet anger of Armstrong's trumpet, the froggy exuberance of his come-to-me-baby mouthings, are a piece of Proust's madeleine cake: they make Mississippi moons rise again, summon the muddy lights of river towns, the sound, like an alligator's yawn, of river horns—I hear the rush of the mulatto river pushing by, hear, always, stomp! stomp! the beat of the grinning Buddha's foot as he shouts his way into "Sunny Side of the Street" and the honeymooning dancers, dazed with bootleg brew and sweating through their talcum, bunny-hug around the ship's saloony ballroom. The Satch, he was good to me, he told me I had talent, that I ought to be in vaudeville; he gave me a bamboo cane and a straw boater with a peppermint headband; and every night from the stand announced: "Ladies and gentlemen, now we're going to present you one of America's nice kids, he's going to do a little tap dance." Afterward I passed among the passengers, collecting in my hat nickels and dimes. This went on all summer, I grew rich and vain; but in October the river roughened, the moon whitened, the customers lessened, the boat rides ended, and with them my career. Six years later, while living at a boarding school from which I wanted to run away, I wrote my former, now famous, benefactor, and said if I came to New York, couldn't he get me a job at the Cotton Club or somewhere? There was no reply, maybe he never got the letter, it doesn't matter, I still loved him, still do.

HUMPHREY BOGART

If one listens attentively to any man's vocabulary, it will be noticed that certain key-to-character words recur. With Bogart, whose pungent personal thesaurus was by and large unspeakably unprintable, "bum" and "professional" were two such verbal signposts. A most moral—by a bit exaggerating you might say *"prim"*—man, he employed "professional" as a platinum medal to be distributed among persons whose behavior he sanctioned; "bum," the reverse of an accolade, conveyed, when spoken by him, almost scarifying displeasure. "My old man," he once remarked of his father, who had been a reputable New York doctor, "died ten thousand dollars in debt, and I had to pay off every cent. A guy who doesn't leave his wife and kids provided for, he's a bum." Bums, too, were guys who cheated on their wives, cheated on their taxes, and all whiners, gossipists, most politicians, most writers, women who Drank, women who were scornful of men who Drank; but the bum true-blue was any fellow who shirked his job, was not, in meticulous style, a "pro" in his work. God knows he was. Never mind that he might play poker until dawn and swallow a brandy for breakfast; he was always on time on the set, in make-up and letter-perfect in his part (forever the same part, to be sure, still there is nothing more difficult to interestingly sustain than repetition). No, there was never a mite of bum-hokum about Bogart; he was an actor without theories (well, one: that he should be highly paid), without temper but not without temperament; and because he understood that discipline was the better part of artistic survival, he lasted, he left his mark.

EZRA POUND

Born 1885, an Idaho boy. Taught school; was tossed out for being "too much the Latin Quarter type." Soon sought solace amid similar souls abroad. Aged twenty-three, while starving himself fat on a potato diet in Venice, he published *A Lume Spento*, a first book of poems which instigated a fierce friendship with Yeats, who wrote of him: "A rugged and head-strong nature and he is always hurting people's feelings, but he has I think some genius and great goodwill." Goodwill: to say it slightly!—between 1909 and 1920, while living first in London, then Paris, he steadily champi-oned the careers of others (it was to Pound that Eliot dedicated *The Wasteland;* it was Pound who raised the money that enabled Joyce to complete *Ulysses*). His generosity in this sphere is a matter on which even Hemingway, who does not often celebrate the kindness of others, has offered testimony: "So then, so far," he wrote, writing in 1925, "we have Pound the major poet devoting, say, one fifth of his time to his poetry. With the rest of his time he tries to advance the fortunes, both material and artistic, of his friends. He defends them when they are attacked, he gets them into magazines and out of jail. He loans them money. He sells their pictures. He arranges concerts for them. He writes articles about them. He introduces them to wealthy women. He gets publishers to take their books. He sits up all night with them when they claim to be dying and witnesses their wills. He advances them hospital expenses and dissuades them from suicide. And in the end a few of them refrain from knifing at the first opportunity."

Nevertheless, he managed to regularly issue pamphlets, roar out his Cantos ("the epic of the farings of a literary mind," so Marianne Moore, evidencing her customary exactness, defined them) and to give both sculpture and painting a serious if unavailing try. But it was the study of economics that became increasingly his intensest interest ("History that omits economics is sheer bunk"); he developed odd notions on the subject, and some of them led to his ruin: in 1939, by now a long-term mussolinized Italophile, he began broadcasting via Rome radio a sequence of fascist-tempered discourses which culminated in his being indicted as an American traitor; units of the American army advancing into Italy caught up with him in 1945. For several weeks, like a zoo-beast mangy and rabid, he was imprisoned in an open-air cage at Pisa. Some months later, on the eve of his treason trial, he was declared insane, as might be any poet in his right artistic mind; and so he spent the next twelve years sealed away in the District of Columbia's St. Elizabeths Hospital. While there, he published *The Pisan Cantos* and won the Bollingen Prize, an award excessively censured in dough-headed circles.

However, one rainy Washington April day in 1958, Pound, an old man of seventy-two, his once flaming beard gone ashen and his satyr-saint's face scribbled with lines that spelled out a disconsolate tale, stood before a certain Judge Bolitha J. Laws and heard himself declared "incurably insane." Incurable, but "harmless" enough to go free. Whereupon Pound announced, "Any man who could live in America is insane," and prepared to depart for Italy.

Photographs were taken of him a few days before he sailed. Arrogant, mocking, his eyes squeezed shut as he burst into snatches of senseless song, he strode back and forth, as though still pacing a Pisan cage; or, rather, a cage that had become life itself.

SOMERSET MAUGHAM

Says young and opinionated Holden Caulfield, the Huckleberry Finn of upper Park Avenue who narrates J. D. Salinger's *The Catcher in the Rye:* "What really knocks me out is a book that, when you're all done reading it, you wish the author that wrote it was a terrific friend of yours and you could call him up on the phone whenever you felt like it. You take that book 'Of Human Bondage' by Somerset Maugham—I wouldn't want to call Somerset Maugham up. I don't know. He just isn't the kind of guy I'd want to call up, that's all. I'd rather call old Thomas Hardy up. I like that Eustacia Vye." Well, old Holden has a point—but he misses it: Mr. Maugham doesn't wish to be phoned, he wants to be read; though his prose is rebuffingly impersonal, too clear and sensible to generate audience-affection, he achieves his intention: quite recently a team of auditors estimated that for every minute of every hour he earns in royalties thirty-two dollars. Which doesn't mean he's any good; but he is. If Holden were a novice author, it would be well worth his while to ring up the old boy, he might learn a lot, for few have kept the foxy rules of story making in severer focus, and it is advisable to know those rules, especially if, like most novices, you mean to dismantle them.

Over the past twenty years, Mr. Maugham has made more farewell appearances than Sir Harry Lauder: each new book is announced as his swan song contribution; and today, aged eighty-five, he constantly threatens to embark on the last and most distinguished of experiences. If he must make the journey, then all we can do is gather at the dock and, grateful for the pleasure he has given us, bid him a fond *bon voyage*.

ISAK DINESEN

Rungsted is a sea town on the coast road between Copenhagen and Elsinore. Among eighteenth-century travelers the otherwise undistinguished village was well known for the handsomeness of its Inn. The Inn, though it no longer obliges coachmen and their passengers, is still renowned: as the home of Rungsted's first citizen, the Baroness Blixen, alias Isak Dinesen, alias Pierre Andrezel.

The Baroness, weighing a handful of feathers and fragile as a *coquillage* bouquet, entertains callers in a sparse, sparkling parlor sprinkled with sleeping dogs and warmed by a fireplace and a porcelain stove: a room where she, an imposing creation come forward from one of her own Gothic tales, sits bundled in bristling wolfskins and British tweeds, her feet fur-booted, her legs, thin as the thighs of an ortolan, encased in woolen hose, and her neck, round which a ring could fit, looped with frail lilac scarves. Time has refined her, this legend who has lived the adventures of an iron-nerved man: shot charging lions and infuriated buffalo, worked an African farm, flown over Kilimanjaro in the perilous first planes, doctored the Masai; time has reduced her to an essence, as a grape can become a raisin, roses an attar. Quite instantly, even if one were deprived of knowing her dossier, she registers as *la vraie chose*, a true somebody. A face so faceted, its prisms tossing a proud glitter of intelligence and educated compassion, which is to say wisdom, cannot be an accidental occurrence;

nor do such eyes, smudges of kohl darkening the lids, deeply set, like velvet animals burrowed in a cave, fall into the possession of ordinary women.

If a visitor is invited to tea, the Baroness serves a very high one: sherry before, afterward a jamboree of toast and varied marmalades, cold pâtés, grilled livers, orange-flavored crêpes. But the hostess cannot partake, she is unwell, she eats nothing, nothing at all, oh, perhaps an oyster, one strawberry, a glass of champagne. Instead, she talks; and like most artists, certainly all old beauties, she is sufficiently self-centered to enjoy herself as conversational subject.

Her lips, just touched with paint, twist in a sideways smile of rather paralytic contour, and speaking an English brushed with British inflections, she might say, "Ah, well, yes, what a lot of stories this old Inn could tell. It belonged to my brother, I bought it from him; *Last Tales* paid the last installment. Now it is mine, absolutely. I have plans for it after I die. It will be an aviary, the grounds, the park, will be a bird sanctuary. All the years in Africa, when I had my highland farm, I never imagined to make my home again in Denmark. When I knew, was certain, the farm was slipping away, saw I'd lost it, that is when I began writing my stories: to forget the unendurable. During the war, too; the house was a way station for Jews escaping to Sweden. Jews in the kitchen and Nazis in the garden. I had to write to save my mind, I wrote *The Angelic Avengers*, which was not a political parable, though it amused me how many decided it to be so. Extraordinary men, the Nazis. I often argued with them, spoke back very sharply. Oh, don't think I mean to seem brave, I risked nothing; they were such a masculine society, they simply didn't care what a woman thought. Another muffin? Please do. I enjoy dining vicariously. I waited for the postman today; I'd hoped he'd bring a new parcel of books. I read so quickly, it's difficult to keep me supplied. What I ask of art is air, an atmosphere. That is very meager on the menu nowadays. I never weary of books that I like, I can read them twenty times—can, and have. *King Lear*. I always judge a person by what he thinks of *King Lear*. Of course, one does want a new page; a different face. I have a talent for friendship, friends are what I have enjoyed most: to stir, to get about, to meet new people and attach them."

Periodically the Baroness does stir. Leaning on the affectionate arm of forlornly cheerful Miss Clara Svendsen, her long-in-service secretary-companion ("Dear Clara. Originally I hired her as a cook. After three wretched meals I accused her, 'My dear, you are an imposter. Speak the truth!' She wept, and told me she was a schoolteacher from the north of Denmark who loved my books. One day she'd seen an advertisement I'd placed for a kitchen wench. So she came; and she wanted to stay. Since she couldn't cook, we arranged she should be secretary. I regret the decision exceedingly. Clara is an appalling tyrant"), she sets forth for Rome or

London, going usually by ship ("One does not travel in a plane; one is merely sent, like a parcel"). Last January, the winter of 1959, she made her initial visit to America, a country to which she is grateful because it provided the first publisher and audience for her work. Her reception was comparable to Jenny Lind; at least out-distanced anything accorded a literary dignitary since Dickens and Shaw. She was televised and *Life* ized, the one public "reading" for which she was scheduled developed into a marathon of ticket-scalper, standing-ovation events, and no one, heaven knows, has ever been guest of honor at so numbing a number of parties ("It was delicious. New York: ah! *That* is where things are happening! Lunches and dinners, champagne, champagne; everyone was too kind. I arrived weighing sixty-five pounds and came home an even fifty-three; the doctors didn't know why I was alive, they insisted I ought to be dead, but oh, I've known that for years, Death is my oldest flirt. No, we *lived*, and Clara—Clara gained a stone").

Her acceptance of immense age and its consequences is not stoically final; notes of healthy hope intrude: "I want to finish a book, I want to see next summer's fruit, and Rome again, Gielgud at Stratford, perhaps America. If only. *Why* am I so weak?" she asks, twitching at her lilac scarves with a brown bony hand; and the question, accompanied by the chimings of a mantel clock and a murmur from Miss Svendsen, invites the guest to depart, permitting the Baroness to doze on a couch next to the fire.

As the visitor goes he may be presented a copy of her favorite of her books ("Because it is about real things"), the beautiful *Out of Africa*. A souvenir inscribed "*Je repondrai*—Karen Blixen."

"*Je repondrai*," she explains, standing at the door and, in farewell, offering her cheek to be kissed, "I answer—a lovely motto. I borrowed it from the Finch-Hatton family. I like it because I believe every one of us has an answer in him."

Her own answer has been a yes to life, an affirmation her art echoes with an echo that will echo.

Jane
Bowles

(1966)

I T MUST BE SEVEN OR EIGHT YEARS
since I last saw the modern legend named
Jane Bowles; nor have I heard from her, at least not directly. Yet I am sure
she is unchanged; indeed, I am told by recent travelers to North Africa,
who have been or sat with her in some dim Casbah café, that this is true,
and that Jane, with her dahlia-head of cropped, curly hair, her tilted nose
and mischief-shiny, just a trifle mad eyes, her very original voice (a husky
soprano), her boyish clothes and schoolgirl's figure and slightly limping
walk, is more or less the same as when I first knew her more than twenty
years ago: even then she had seemed the eternal urchin, appealing as the
most appealing of nonadults, yet with some substance cooler than blood
invading her veins and with a wit, an eccentric wisdom no child, not the
strangest *Wunderkind*, ever possessed.

When I first met Mrs. Bowles (1944? 1945?), she was already, within
certain worlds, a celebrated figure: though only in her twenties, she had
published a most individual and much remarked novel, *Two Serious Ladies;*
she had married the gifted composer and writer Paul Bowles, and was,
together with her husband, a tenant in a glamorous boardinghouse established on Brooklyn Heights by the late George Davis. Among the
Bowleses' fellow boarders were Richard and Ellen Wright, W. H. Auden,
Benjamin Britten, Oliver Smith, Carson McCullers, Gypsy Rose Lee and
(I seem to remember) a trainer of chimpanzees who lived there with one

563

of his star performers. Anyway, it was one hell of a household. But even amid such a forceful assembly, Mrs. Bowles, by virtue of her talent and the strange visions it enclosed, and because of her personality's startling blend of playful-puppy candor and feline sophistication, remained an imposing, stage-front presence.

Jane Bowles is an authoritative linguist; she speaks, with the greatest precision, French and Spanish and Arabic—perhaps this is why the dialogue of her stories sounds, or sounds to me, as though it has been translated into English from some delightful combination of other tongues. Moreover, these languages are self-learned, the product of Mrs. Bowles's nomadic nature: from New York she wandered on to and all over Europe, traveled away from there and the impending war to Central America and Mexico, then alighted awhile in the historic ménage on Brooklyn Heights. Since 1947 she has been almost continuously resident abroad: in Paris or Ceylon, but largely in Tangier—in fact, both Jane and Paul Bowles may now safely be described as permanent Tangerinos, so total has their adherence become to that steep, shadowy-white seaport. Tangier is composed of two mismatching parts, one of them a dull, modern area stuffed with office buildings and tall, gloomy dwellings, and the other a Casbah descending through a medieval puzzlement of alleys and alcoves and kif-odored, mint-scented piazzas down to the crawling-with-sailors, ship-horn-hollering port. The Bowleses have established themselves in both sectors—have a sterilized, *tout confort* apartment in the new quarter and also a refuge hidden away in the darker Arab neighborhood: a native house that must be one of the city's tiniest habitations—ceilings so low that one had almost literally to move on hands and knees from room to room; but the rooms themselves are like a charming series of postcard-sized Vuillards —Moorish cushions spilling over Moorish-patterned carpets, all cozy as a raspberry tart and illuminated by intricate lanterns and windows that allow the light of sea-skies and views that encompass minarets and ships and the blue-washed rooftops of native tenements, receding like a ghostly staircase to the clamorous shoreline. Or that is how *I* remember it on the occasion of a single visit made at sunset on an evening, oh, fifteen years ago.

A line from Edith Sitwell: *Jane, Jane, the morning light creaks down again* —This from a poem I've always liked without, as so often with the particular author, altogether understanding it. Unless "morning light" is an image signifying memory(?). My own most satisfying memories of Jane Bowles revolve around a month spent in side-by-side rooms in a pleasantly shabby hotel on the rue du Bac during an icy Paris winter—January, 1951. Many a cold evening was spent in Jane's snug room (fat with books and papers and foodstuffs, and a snappy white Pekingese puppy bought from a Spanish sailor); long evenings spent listening to a phonograph and drinking warm applejack while Jane built sloppy, marvelous stews atop an electric burner: she is a good cook, yessir, and kind of a glutton, as one might suspect from her stories, which abound in accounts of eating and its artifacts. Cooking is but one of her extracurricular gifts; she is also a spooky accurate mimic, and can re-create with nostalgic admiration the voices of certain singers—Helen Morgan, for example, and her close friend Libby Holman. Years afterward I wrote a story called *Among the Paths to Eden*, in which, without realizing it, I attributed to the heroine several of Jane Bowles's characteristics: the stiff-legged limp, her spectacles, her brilliant and poignant abilities as a mimic. ("She waited, as though listening for music to cue her; then, *'Don't ever leave me, now that you're here! Here is where you belong. Everything seems so right when you're near. When you're away it's all wrong.'* And Mr. Belli was shocked, for what he was hearing was exactly Helen Morgan's voice, and the voice, with its vulnerable sweetness, refinement, its tender quaver toppling high notes, seemed not to be borrowed, but Mary O'Meaghan's own, a natural expression of some secluded identity.") I did not have Mrs. Bowles in mind when I invented Mary O'Meaghan—a character she in no essential way resembles; but it is a measure of the potent impression Jane has always made on me that some fragment of her should emerge in this manner.

That winter Jane was working on *In the Summer House*, the play that was later so sensitively produced in New York.

I'm not all that keen on the theater: cannot sit through most plays once; nevertheless, I saw *In the Summer House* three times, and not out of loyalty to the author, but because it had a thorny wit, the flavor of a newly tasted, refreshingly bitter beverage—the same qualities that had initially attracted me to Mrs. Bowles's novel *Two Serious Ladies*.

My only complaint against Mrs. Bowles is not that her work lacks quality, merely quantity. The volume in hand constitutes her entire shelf, so to say. And grateful as we are to have it, one could wish that there was more. Once, while discussing a colleague, someone more facile than either of us, Jane said, "But it's so easy for him. He has only to turn his hand. Just *turn* his hand." Actually, writing is never easy: in case anyone doesn't know, it's the hardest work around, and for Jane, I think it is difficult to the point of true pain. And why not?—when both her language and her themes are sought after along tortured paths and in stony quarries: the never-realized relationships between her people, the mental and physical discomforts with which she surrounds and saturates them—every room an atrocity, every urban landscape a creation of neon-dourness. And yet, though the tragic view is central to her vision, Jane Bowles is a very funny writer, a humorist of sorts—but *not*, by the way, of the Black School. Black Comedy, as its perpetrators label it, is, when successful, all lovely artifice and lacking any hint of compassion. Her subtle comprehension of eccentricity and human apartness as revealed in her work requires us to accord Jane Bowles high esteem as an artist.

Cecil
Beaton

(1969)

To CALL A BOOK *The Best of Beaton*
is catchy enough, but inaccurate—unless some one book could contain fine specimens of Beaton's many facets:
his stage décors, his costume designs, sketches and paintings, pages reprinted from his very remarkable journals and at least several verbatim
samples of his conversational gifts, for surely Cecil is one of the few
surviving artists in this increasingly obsolete area.

I don't know, I've never asked him, but I suspect Cecil would prefer to
be remembered for his talents in mediums other than photography—a
phenomenon quite common with persons who develop multiple gifts: they
often prefer to rather slight the original one. It might be said that Beaton
was without any central talent until, as a very ambitious but unsensible
young man of great sensibility, he started using a camera: it was the camera,
curiously enough, that released all the subtler creative strains.

And for all the documented brilliance of his other muses, it is as a
photographer that Beaton attains cultural importance—not only because of
the individual excellence of his own work, but because of its influence on
the work of the finest photographers of the last two generations: whether
or not they admit it, or are even conscious of it, there is almost no first-rate
contemporary photographer of any nationality who is not to some degree
indebted to Cecil Beaton. Why? Look at the pictures. Even the earliest ones
presage future influence on a multitude of camera-artists. For instance, the

portraits of Lady Oxford and Edith Sitwell made in the twenties: no one had photographed faces in quite this manner before, surrounded them with such neoromantic, stylized décor (spun glass, masked statues, pastry molds and extravagant costumes: all the appurtenances of Beaton's own surrealism) or lighted them with such lacquered luminosity. And the thing is, these portraits have not "dated," not even, in a technical sense, the so-called "fashion" photographs. (The attitude of photographers toward fashion photography, and the position it holds in their careers, is an ambiguous business. With the exception of Cartier-Bresson, a man of independent means, I can't offhand recall a single photographer seriously making a livelihood out of his trade who doesn't work extensively for either fashion magazines or advertising agencies. And why not? It disciplines the artist and forces his invention. Beaton, like many others, owes a number of his most interesting photographs to the limitations imposed by purely commercial factors. But photographers as a breed seem not to gain much satisfaction from their labors in such vineyards—I don't mean Beaton: he is too much a craftsman and too unpretentious not to be grateful for the merit of his work in whatever style.)

But again, this question of unyellowing, of the timeless quality in these pictures. Of course, in some instances Beaton has already pre-aged his portraits by setting them in the past—for example, the various pastiche of Victorian daguerreotype: the combination of modern with long-ago creates its own time—suspension. But when one speaks of the timeless, this is not what one means. Then what *does* one mean? Well, any in the series Beaton calls Time Sequences—subjects he has had the opportunity to photograph over periods extending as much as four decades. One observes a slowly thickening, but ever lustrous, rather maniacal-eyed Picasso; an Auden, starting off like a duly wrinkled bloodhound pup and ending looking like the hound's sagging, tobacco-stained sire; or Cocteau, fragile and fresh and expensive as a sprig of muguet in January, then later, with his jeweled fingers, seeming an animated Proustian souvenir. None of these studies is dependent for its effect upon its relation to the rest of the sequence; separated, any one of them seems an ageless and definitive image of the man. Yet how eerie, and sad, yet how exhilarating to see these faces as they flow through time—frozen by sensitively manipulated light and shadow.

It is not difficult to discern Beaton's influence in the work of others: a harder task is to identify those who have influenced him. Obviously he is indebted to Baron de Meyer, that original and tragic artist who contributed photographs of a pioneer stylishness to the earlier issues of *Vanity Fair*. Beaton, with his own sense of elegance, was the first direct descendant of the late Baron. And Beaton admired Steichen; but name a photographer not obliged to Steichen. To my mind, Beaton's work does not reflect artistic sources as much as it does his private social interests and the temperaments of his times. For example, in 1938 and 1939 Beaton photographed a contingent of personalities not amid flowers and the sleek apparatus of the studios, but through the broken windows of abandoned sinister houses and factories. These photographs are like fever charts of the future, a prediction of the bombs soon to explode.

Speaking of which, one of Beaton's most distinguished and versatile achievements is his war photographs, these smoky pictures of London asunder, of violent skies and bandaged children: here the artist produces a brutal poignance, a harsher color, than the viewer usually associates with his photographic palette. This is also true of Beaton's photographs of India and China, countries in which he served during the war. A pity, for though these are not military pictures in the sense that Cim's or Capa's were, they are nevertheless war documents of painful poetic insight which illustrate a side of Beaton insufficiently recognized. Nowadays a professional photographer is by necessity almost a professional traveler: editors with commissions hustle them on to jets that hustle them around the world in pursuit of Lord knows what. Even the feeblest talents are subsidized in this manner (and may I say in passing that ninety percent—make that ninety-five—of fully employed photographers are feeble indeed: an amazing racket, really, and even a few of the very few genuinely gifted photographers secretly consider themselves racketeers). But Cecil has always been a determined roamer, and as a youth wandered by cargo boat from Haiti to Morocco. Myself, also a footloose fellow, I've run into Mr. B. in the damnedest places. On the beach at Waikiki—with hula music in the background. In a Sicilian olive grove, in a Greek monastery, in the lobby of the Barcelona Ritz, by the pool at the Bel Air Hotel, at a café table in the Tangier Casbah, on a junk in the Hong Kong bay, backstage at a Broadway musical, on a *téléphérique* climbing a Swiss alp, in a geisha house in Kyoto, among the ruins of Angkor Wat, the temples of Bangkok, aboard Daisy Fellowes's yacht *Sister Ann,* in a Harlem night club, a Venetian palazzo, a Parisian *antiquaire,* a London shoeshop, and so forth on and on. The point is, I've observed Beaton in all climates, mental and otherwise, and have often had the privilege of watching him work with a camera—actually, we have once in a while collaborated: my text accompanying his photographs. I've had that sort of experience with other photographers, particularly Henri Cartier-Bresson and Richard Avedon—both of whom I respect extremely: with Beaton added, I consider that they ought to occupy the first three places in any list of the world's superior photographers. But how differently each man operates! Avedon is primarily a studio photographer; at any rate, he seems at his most creative ease in the midst of perfectly functioning machinery and attentive assistants. Rather recently I worked with Avedon, under primitive conditions, on a story in the American Midwest; he had no assistant and was using a newfangled Japanese camera that was capable of taking a hundred-odd exposures before the film needed changing. We slaved the whole of one morning, drove many a mile through heat and dust, and then, when we returned to the motel where we were staying, Avedon, with a jittery little laugh, suddenly announced that all our labor was for naught: it had been so many years since he had worked without assistants, who always prepared his cameras, that he had forgot to put any film in the Japanese job.

Cartier-Bresson is another *tasse de thé* entirely—self-sufficient to a fault. I remember once watching Bresson at work on a street in New Orleans —dancing along the pavement like an agitated dragonfly, three Leicas swinging from straps around his neck, a fourth one hugged to his eye: click-click-click (the camera seems a part of his own body), clicking away with a joyous intensity, a religious absorption. Nervous and merry and dedicated, Bresson is an artistic "loner," a bit of a fanatic.

But not Beaton. This man, with his cool (sometimes cold) blue eyes and palely lifted eyebrows, is as casual and detached as he seems: with a camera in his hand, he just knows what he is doing, that's all, has no need for a lot of temper and attitudinizing. Unlike many of his colleagues, I've never heard Cecil talk about Technique or Art or Honesty. He simply takes pictures and hopes to be paid for them. But the way in which he works is very special to him. One of the immediately striking things about Beaton's personal behavior is the manner in which he creates an illusion of time-without-end. Though he is apparently always under the pressure of a disheartening schedule, one would never suppose he wasn't a gentleman of almost tropical leisure: if he has ten minutes to catch a plane, and yet is speaking with you on the telephone, he does nothing to shorten the call but continues to indulge in a luxury of marvelous manners. Nevertheless, you can be damn sure he will make that plane. As with the caller, so it is with the sitter: a person sitting for Beaton has a sense of slightly drifting in space—of not being photographed but painted, and painted by a casual, barely visible presence. But Beaton is there, oh yes. For all his quiet tread he is one of the most on-the-spot people alive: his visual intelligence is genius—the camera will never be invented that could capture or encompass all that he actually sees. To listen to Beaton describe in strictly visual terms a person or room or landscape is to hear a recitation that can be hilarious or brutal or very beautiful, but will always certainly be brilliant. And that—the remarkable visual intelligence infiltrating his pictures, however diluted—is what makes Beaton's work unusually separate, the preservative for which our next-century historians will be even more grateful than we are now.

Elizabeth
Taylor

(1974)

S OME YEARS AGO, RATHER MORE THAN
fifteen, a friend and I decided to install,
among the New York social curriculum, a series of surprise-guest lunch
parties; the idea seemed amusing enough for February, the dreariest month
in New York, so my friend and I invited four other friends to join us for
lunch at a private apartment. The idea was that the six of us would,
individually, supply an additional guest, a "mystery" guest—preferably
someone interesting and well-known and yet not known personally to any
or at least all of us. My choice was Dr. J. Robert Oppenheimer, but he
wasn't available that day; now I can't remember *who* I brought.

But I do remember the selection made by Lady Keith, who was then
Mrs. Leland Hayward. Lady Keith, whom her friends call Slim, is a tall,
coltish, California-bred aristocrat (northern California, need one add) with
the most beautiful legs, ankles and feet extant. Her "surprise," Elizabeth
Taylor, was rather a runt by comparison—like Mrs. Onassis, her legs are
too short for the torso, the head too bulky for the figure in toto; but the
face, with those lilac eyes, is a prisoner's dream, a secretary's self-fantasy:
unreal, nonobtainable, at the same time shy, overly vulnerable, very
human, with the flicker of suspicion constantly flaring behind the lilac
eyes.

We had met once before—one summer afternoon on the farm of a
mutual friend in Connecticut. At the time, her third husband, the tough

and short and sexy Mike Todd, still had his plane crash ahead of him, was still alive and married to this beautiful child who seemed besotted by him.

Often, when couples make oozing displays of themselves, always kissing, gripping, groping—well, often one imagines their romance must be in serious difficulties. Not so with these two. I remember them, that afternoon, sprawled in the sun in a field of grass and daisies holding hands and kissing while a litter of six or eight fat Newfoundland puppies tumbled over their stomachs, tangled in their hair.

But it was not until I encountered her as Slim Hayward's guest that Elizabeth Taylor made an impression on me, at least as a person; as an actress I'd always liked her—from *National Velvet* straight on, but especially as the rich girl in *A Place in the Sun*.

In the years since our first meeting, much had happened to her, but the two worst things were that Mike Todd had died and that she had married the "singer" Eddie Fisher—an event almost as unsuitable as Mrs. Kennedy's Grecian nuptials. Still, neither of these occurrences had dimmed the hectic allure Taylor radiates like a rather quivery light.

The lunch was long, we talked a lot. My first discovery about her was that despite an amusing abundance of four-lettered profanity, she was in various areas a moralist, quite a strict one, almost Calvinistic. For instance, she was agitated at the thought of playing the ill-starred, hedonistic heroine of John O'Hara's *Butterfield 8*; she had an unbreakable legal obligation to do the role (for which she later won an Academy Award), but she wished she could get out of it because "I don't like that girl. I don't like what she stands for. The sleazy emptiness of her. The men. The sleeping around."

At this point I recalled a conversation I'd once had with Marilyn Monroe (not that I'm making a comparison between Taylor and Monroe; they were different birds, the first being a take-or-leave-it professional, the other a morbidly uncertain, naturally gifted primitive). But Monroe's moral attitude was similar: "I don't believe in casual sex. Right or wrong, if I go for a guy, I feel I ought to marry him. I don't know why. Stupid, maybe. But that's just the way I feel. Or if not that, then it should have meaning. Other than something only physical. Funny, when you think of the reputation I have. And maybe deserve. Only I don't think so. Deserve it, I mean. People just don't understand what can happen to you. Without your real consent at all. Inside consent."

The second surprise was how well-read Taylor seemed to be—not that she made anything of it, or posed as an intellectual, but clearly she cared about books and, in haphazard style, had absorbed a large number of them. And she discussed them with considerable understanding of the literary process; all in all, it made one wonder about the men in her life—with the exception of Mike Todd, who had had a certain flashbulb-brightness, a certain neon-savvy, her husbands thus far had not been a whiplash lot:

Nicky Hilton, Michael Wilding, Mr. Fisher—what on earth did this very alert and swift-minded young woman find to talk to them about? "Well, one doesn't always fry the fish one wants to fry. Some of the men I've really liked really didn't like women."

And so we began to discuss a mutual friend, Montgomery Clift, the young actor with whom she had starred in *A Place in the Sun,* and toward whom she felt an affectionate protectiveness. She said, "You know, it happened at my house. Or rather, just after he'd left my house. He'd had a lot to drink, and he lost control of his car. He was really all right before that—before the accident. Well, he always drank too much—but it was after the accident, getting hooked on all those pills and pain-killers. Nobody beats that rap forever. I haven't seen him for over a year. Have you?"

And I said yes, I had. He called a few days before Christmas, and he sounded fine. He wanted to know what I was doing for lunch, and I wasn't doing anything, I was going Christmas shopping, so he said he'd buy me lunch at Le Pavillon if I'd take him shopping. He had a couple of martinis at lunch, but he was rational, very amusing; but on the way he stopped in the gents, and while he was in there he must have taken something, because about twenty minutes later he was flying.

We were in Gucci, and he had picked out and piled on the counter perhaps two dozen very expensive sweaters. Suddenly, he grabbed up all the sweaters and sauntered outside, where it was pouring rain. He threw the sweaters into the street and began kicking them around.

The Gucci personnel took it calmly. One of the attendants produced a pen and sales pad and asked me, "To whom shall I charge these sweaters?" The thing was he really didn't know. He said he wanted some identification. So I went out into the street, where Monty was still kicking the sweaters around (observed by amassing voyeurs), and asked him if he had a charge card. He looked at me with the most manic, far-gone hauteur, and said, "My face is my charge card!"

Taylor, her eyes always so liquid with life, acquired an additional mistiness. "He can't go on like that. It will kill him." She was right; it did. But not before, greatly because of her sympathy and insistence at a time when producers were reluctant to use Clift, they worked together in *Suddenly, Last Summer*—which contained Clift's last worthy performance, and one of Taylor's best—except, many years later, the subtlety and shrewish, constrained hysteria with which she pigmented the role of the alcoholic wife in Albee's *Who's Afraid of Virginia Woolf?*

Some years went by before we met again, on this occasion in London, where she was biding time before heading for Rome and the start of the doomed *Cleopatra* production. She and "The Busboy," as Mr. Fisher was called by many of Mrs. Fisher's friends, were living in a penthouse at the Dorchester.

I'd visited that same penthouse often, as another friend had once lived there. Oliver Messel had tarted it up, and it was rather pretty, or had been: during the Taylor residency, the rooms were so crowded with shedding cats and unhousebroken dogs and a general atmosphere of disorderly paraphernalia that one could not easily espy the Messel touch.

On the first evening I saw Taylor in this particular surrounding, she tried her best to give me a charming calico cat she had gathered up off some street. "No? That's really very mean of you. I can't cart all *this* . . ." she extended her arms, indicating the vastness of her burdens—enough animals to stock a pet shop, a male secretary serving drinks, a maid whisking in and out of the room displaying newly arrived dresses ("All from Paris. But I'll have to send most of them back. I can't afford it. I really haven't any money. *He* doesn't have any either. Debbie Reynolds—if you'll pardon the expression—got it all"), not to mention "The Busboy," who sat on the couch rubbing his eyes as if trying to rouse himself from a nap.

She said to him, "What's the matter? Why do you keep rubbing your eyes?"

"It's all that reading!" he complained.

"All *what* reading?"

"That *thing* you tell me I gotta read. I've tried. I can't get through it somehow."

Her gaze disdainfully glided away from him. "He means *To Kill a Mockingbird*. Have you read it? It just came out. I think it's a really lovely book."

Yes, I'd read it; as a matter of fact, I told her, the author, Harper Lee, was a childhood friend. We'd grown up together in a small Alabama town, and her book was more or less autobiographical, a *roman à clef;* indeed, Dill, one of the principal characters, was supposed to be me.

"You *see,*" she told her husband, "I may not have had a particular education, but somehow I knew that book was true. I like the truth."

"The Busboy" regarded her oddly. "Oh, yeah?"

A few mornings later I rang her up, and was informed by her secretary that she was in the hospital, a circumstance the London evening press confirmed: LIZ CRITICAL.

When I got Mr. Fisher on the phone, he was already balanced on the precipice of mourning: "It looks like I'm going to lose my girl." He was so destined, though not in the style he presumed.

Then I heard she hadn't died after all, so I stopped by the hospital to leave her some books, and to my surprise, was ushered straightaway to her room. I was so impressed by the smallness of it; at least she wasn't in a ward, but this claustrophobic closet, entirely stuffed by one narrow iron bed and one wooden chair, did not seem an appropriate arena for the life-death struggles of a Flick Queen.

She was very lively, though one could see she had undergone a massive ordeal. She was whiter by far than the hospital's bedsheets; her eyes, without make-up, seemed bruised and swollen, like a weeping child's. What she was recovering from was a form of pneumonia. "My chest and lungs were filled with a sort of thick black fire. They had to cut a hole in my throat to drain out the fire. You see," she said, pointing at a wound in her throat that was stopped with a small rubber plug. "If I pull this out my voice disappears," and she pulled it out, and indeed her voice did disappear, an effect which made me nervous, which made her merry.

She was laughing, but I didn't hear her laughter until she had reinserted the plug. "This is the second time in my life that I felt—that I *knew*—I was dying. Or maybe the third. But this was the most real. It was like riding on a rough ocean. Then slipping over the edge of the horizon. With the roar of the ocean in my head. Which I suppose was really the noise of my trying to breathe. No," she said, answering a question, "I wasn't afraid. I didn't have time to be. I was too busy fighting. I didn't want to go over that horizon. And I never will. I'm not the type."

Perhaps not; not like Marilyn Monroe and Judy Garland, both of whom had yearned to go over the horizon, some darker rainbow, and before succeeding, had attempted the voyage innumerable times. And yet there was some common thread between these three, Taylor, Monroe, Garland —I knew the last two fairly well, and yes, there *was* something. An emotional extremism, a dangerously greater need to be loved than to love, the hotheaded willingness of an incompetent gambler to throw good money after bad.

"Would you like some champagne?" she said, indicating a bottle of Dom Perignon cooling in a bucket beside the bed. "I'm not supposed to have any. But—that. I mean when you've been through what I've been through. . . ." She laughed, and once more uncorked the throat incision, sending her laughter into soundless oblivion.

I opened the champagne, and filled two ugly white plastic hospital glasses.

She sighed. "Hmm, that's good. I really like only champagne. The trouble is, it gives you permanently bad breath. Tell me, have you ever thought you were dying?"

"Yes. Once I had a burst appendix. And another time, when I was wading in a creek, I was bitten by a cottonmouth moccasin."

"And were you afraid?"

"Well, I was only a child. Of course I was afraid. I don't know whether I would be now."

She pondered, then, "My problem is I can't afford to die. Not that I have any great artistic commitments (before Mike, before what happened to him, I'd been planning to get the hell out of movies; I thought I'd had enough of the whole damn thing). Just financial commitments, emotional: what would become of my children? Or my dogs, for that matter?" She'd finished her champagne, I poured her another glass, and when she spoke again she seemed, essentially, to be addressing herself. "Everyone wants to live. Even when they *don't* want to, *think* they don't. But what I really believe is: Something is going to happen to me. That will change everything. What do you suppose it might be?"

"Love?"

"But what kind of love?"

"Well. Ah. The usual."

"This can't be anything usual."

"Then perhaps a religious vision?"

"Bull!" She bit her lip, concerned. But after a while she laughed and said, "How about love *combined* with a religious vision?"

It was years before we met again, and then it seemed to me that I was the one undergoing a religious vision. This was one winter night in New York, and I was in a limousine together with Taylor and Richard Burton, the gifted coal-miner's son who had replaced "The Busboy."

The Burtons' chauffeur was driving away from, or attempting to drive away from, a Broadway theater where Burton was appearing in a play. But the car couldn't move because of the thousands, really thousands, of people carousing the streets, cheering and shouting and insisting on a glimpse of the most celebrated lovers since Mrs. Simpson deigned to accept the King. Damp, ghostly faces were flattened against the car's windows; hefty girls, in exalted conditions of libidinous excitement, pounded the roof of the car; hundreds of ordinary folk, exiting from other theaters, found themselves engorged among the laughing, weeping Burton-Taylor freaks. The whole scene was like a stilled avalanche nothing could budge, not even a squad of mounted policemen badgering the mob, in a rather good-natured way, with their clubs.

Burton, a light-eyed man with a lilting, Welsh-valley voice and an acne-rough complexion you could scratch a match on, visibly relished the carrying-on. "It's just a phenomenon," he said, grinning a good grin full of expensive teeth. "Every night Elizabeth comes to pick me up after the show, and there are always these . . . these . . . these . . ."

"Sex-maniacs," his wife interposed coolly.

"These *enthusiastic* crowds," he corrected her a little scoldingly, "waiting . . . waiting . . ."

"To see a pair of sinful freaks. For God's sake, Richard, don't you realize the only reason all this is happening is because they think we're sinners and freaks."

An old man who had climbed onto the hood of the car shouted obscenities as the car suddenly started an abrupt escape, and he slid off the hood under the hooves of prancing horses.

Taylor was upset. "That's the thing that always bothers me. That someone is going to get hurt."

But Burton seemed unconcerned. "Sinatra was with us the other night. He couldn't get over it. He said he'd never seen anything like it. He was really impressed."

Well, it *was* impressive. And depressing. Taylor was depressed by it, and as soon as we eventually arrived at the hotel where they were staying, and where there was another group to greet their arrival, she fixed herself a sort of triple vodka. So did Burton.

Champagne followed vodka, and from room service appeared a not very exciting after-midnight buffet. Burton and Taylor wolfed it down: I've noticed that actors and dancers always seem to have uncontrollable hungers—yet their weight stays at some strange, ethereal level (even Taylor, who never, off-camera, appears as plumpish as she occasionally does in photographs: the camera has a habit of adding thirty pounds—even Audrey Hepburn is no exception).

Gradually, one became aware of an excessive tension between the two: constant contradictions in dialogue, a repartee reminiscent of the husband and wife in *Who's Afraid of Virginia Woolf?* Yet it was the tension of romance, of two people who had made a physical, psychological commitment to one another. Jane Austen once said that all literature revolved around two themes: love and money. Burton, an exceptional conversationalist, encompassed the first theme ("I love this woman. She is the most interesting and exciting woman I've ever known"), and the second ("I care about money. I've never had any, and now I do, and I want—well, I don't know what you consider rich, but that's what I want to be"). Those two subjects, and literature—not acting, writing: "I never wanted to be an actor. I always wanted to be a writer. And that's what I will be if this circus ever stops. A writer."

When he said this, Taylor's eyes had a particularly prideful glow. Her enthusiasm for the man illuminated the room like a mass of Japanese lanterns.

He left the room to uncork another bottle of champagne.

She said, "Oh, we quarrel. But at least he's worth quarreling with. He's really brilliant. He's read everything and I can talk to him—there's nothing I can't talk to him about. All his friends . . . Emlyn Williams told him he was a fool to marry me. He was a great actor. Could *be* a great actor. And I was *nothing*. A *movie* star. But the most important thing is what happens between a man and a woman who love each other. Or any two people who love each other."

She walked to the window and pushed back the curtain. It had started to rain and the rain was puttering against the window. "Rain makes me sleepy. I really don't want any more champagne. No. No. Don't go. We'll drink it anyway. And then either everything will be wonderful or we'll have a real fight. He thinks I drink too much. And I *know* he does. I'm just trying to stay in the mood. Keep up. I always want to be *where* he is. Remember, a long time ago, I told you there was something I wanted to live for?"

She closed the curtains against the rain, and looked at me sightlessly—Galatea surveying some ultimate horizon.

"Well, what do you think?" But it was a question with an answer already prepared. "What do you suppose will become of us? I guess, when you find what you've always wanted, that's not where the beginning begins, that's where the end starts."

A Beautiful
Child

(1979)

*T*ime: 28 April 1955.
　　Scene: The chapel of the Universal Funeral Home at Lexington Avenue and Fifty-second Street, New York City. An interesting galaxy packs the pews: celebrities, for the most part, from an international arena of theater, films, literature, all present in tribute to Constance Collier, the English-born actress who had died the previous day at the age of seventy-five.

Born in 1880, Miss Collier had begun her career as a music-hall Gaiety Girl, graduated from that to become one of England's principal Shakespearean actresses (and the longtime fiancée of Sir Max Beerbohm, whom she never married, and perhaps for that reason was the inspiration for the mischievously unobtainable heroine in Sir Max's novel *Zuleika Dobson*). Eventually she emigrated to the United States, where she established herself as a considerable figure on the New York stage as well as in Hollywood films. During the last decades of her life she lived in New York, where she practiced as a drama coach of unique caliber; she accepted only professionals as students, and usually only professionals who were already "stars"—Katharine Hepburn was a permanent pupil; another Hepburn, Audrey, was also a Collier protégée, as were Vivien Leigh and, for a few months prior to her death, a neophyte Miss Collier referred to as "my special problem," Marilyn Monroe.

Marilyn Monroe, whom I'd met through John Huston when he was directing her in her first speaking role in *The Asphalt Jungle,* had come under Miss Collier's wing at my suggestion. I had known Miss Collier perhaps a half-dozen years, and admired her as a woman of true stature, physically, emotionally, creatively; and, for all her commanding manner, her grand cathedral voice, as an adorable person, mildly wicked but exceedingly warm, dignified yet *gemütlich.* I loved to go to the frequent small lunch parties she gave in her dark Victorian studio in mid-Manhattan; she had a barrel of yarns to tell about her adventures as a leading lady opposite Sir Beerbohm Tree and the great French actor Coquelin, her involvements with Oscar Wilde, the youthful Chaplin, and Garbo in the silent Swede's formative days. Indeed she was a delight, as was her devoted secretary and companion, Phyllis Wilbourn, a quietly twinkling maiden lady who, after her employer's demise, became, and has remained, the companion of Katharine Hepburn. Miss Collier introduced me to many people who became friends: the Lunts, the Oliviers, and especially Aldous Huxley. But it was I who introduced her to Marilyn Monroe, and at first it was not an acquaintance she was too keen to acquire: her eyesight was faulty, she had seen none of Marilyn's movies, and really knew nothing about her except that she was some sort of platinum sex-explosion who had achieved global notoriety; in short, she seemed hardly suitable clay for Miss Collier's stern classic shaping. But I thought they might make a stimulating combination.

They did. "Oh yes," Miss Collier reported to me, "there is something there. She is a beautiful child. I don't mean that in the obvious way—the perhaps too obvious way. I don't think she's an actress at all, not in any traditional sense. What she has—this presence, this luminosity, this flickering intelligence—could never surface on the stage. It's so fragile and subtle, it can only be caught by the camera. It's like a hummingbird in flight: only a camera can freeze the poetry of it. But anyone who thinks this girl is simply another Harlow or harlot or whatever is *mad.* Speaking of mad, that's what we've been working on together: Ophelia. I suppose people would chuckle at the notion, but really, she could be the most exquisite Ophelia. I was talking to Greta last week, and I told her about Marilyn's Ophelia, and Greta said yes, she could believe that because she had seen two of her films, very bad and vulgar stuff, but nevertheless she had glimpsed Marilyn's possibilities. Actually, Greta has an amusing idea. You know that she wants to make a film of *Dorian Gray?* With her playing Dorian, of course. Well, she said she would like to have Marilyn opposite her as one of the girls Dorian seduces and destroys. Greta! So unused! Such a gift—and rather like Marilyn's, if you consider it. Of course, Greta is a consummate artist, an artist of the utmost control. This beautiful child is without any concept of discipline or sacrifice. Somehow I don't think she'll make old bones. Absurd of me to say, but somehow I feel she'll go young.

I hope, I really pray, that she survives long enough to free the strange lovely talent that's wandering through her like a jailed spirit."

But now Miss Collier had died, and here I was loitering in the vestibule of the Universal Chapel waiting for Marilyn; we had talked on the telephone the evening before, and agreed to sit together at the services, which were scheduled to start at noon. She was now a half-hour late; she was *always* late, but I'd thought just for once! For God's sake, goddamnit! Then suddenly there she was, and I didn't recognize her until she said . . .

MARILYN: Oh, baby, I'm so sorry. But see, I got all made up, and then I decided maybe I shouldn't wear eyelashes or lipstick or anything, so then I had to wash all that off, and I couldn't imagine what to wear . . .

(What she had imagined to wear would have been appropriate for the abbess of a nunnery in private audience with the Pope. Her hair was entirely concealed by a black chiffon scarf; her black dress was loose and long and looked somehow borrowed; black silk stockings dulled the blond sheen of her slender legs. An abbess, one can be certain, would not have donned the vaguely erotic black high-heeled shoes she had chosen, or the owlish black sunglasses that dramatized the vanilla-pallor of her dairy-fresh skin.)

TC: You look fine.

MARILYN (gnawing an already chewed-to-the-nub thumbnail): Are you sure? I mean, I'm so jumpy. Where's the john? If I could just pop in there for a minute—

TC: And pop a pill? No! Shhh. That's Cyril Ritchard's voice: he's started the eulogy.

(Tiptoeing, we entered the crowded chapel and wedged ourselves into a narrow space in the last row. Cyril Ritchard finished; he was followed by Cathleen Nesbitt, a lifelong colleague of Miss Collier's, and finally Brian Aherne addressed the mourners. Through it all, my date periodically removed her spectacles to scoop up tears bubbling from her blue-gray eyes. I'd sometimes seen her without make-up, but today she presented a new visual experience, a face I'd not observed before, and at first I couldn't perceive why this should be. Ah! It was because of the obscuring head scarf. With her tresses invisible, and her complexion cleared of all cosmetics, she looked twelve years old, a pubescent virgin who has just been admitted to an orphanage and is grieving over her plight. At last the ceremony ended, and the congregation began to disperse.)

MARILYN: Please, let's sit here. Let's wait till everyone's left.

TC: Why?

MARILYN: I don't want to have to talk to anybody. I never know what to say.

TC: Then you sit here, and I'll wait outside. I've got to have a cigarette.

MARILYN: You can't leave me alone! My God! Smoke here.

TC: *Here?* In the chapel?

MARILYN: Why not? What do you want to smoke? A reefer?

TC: Very funny. Come on, let's go.

MARILYN: Please. There's a lot of shutterbugs downstairs. And I certainly don't want them taking my picture looking like this.

TC: I can't blame you for that.

MARILYN: You said I looked fine.

TC: You do. Just perfect—if you were playing the Bride of Frankenstein.

MARILYN: Now you're laughing at me.

TC: Do I look like I'm laughing?

MARILYN: You're laughing inside. And that's the worst kind of laugh. (Frowning; nibbling thumbnail) Actually, I could've worn make-up. I see all these other people are wearing make-up.

TC: I am. Globs.

MARILYN: Seriously, though. It's my hair. I need color. And I didn't have time to get any. It was all so unexpected, Miss Collier dying and all. See? (She lifted her kerchief slightly to display a fringe of darkness where her hair parted.)

TC: Poor innocent me. And all this time I thought you were a bona-fide blonde.

MARILYN: I am. But nobody's *that* natural. And incidentally, fuck you.

TC: Okay, everybody's cleared out. So up, up.

MARILYN: Those photographers are still down there. I know it.

TC: If they didn't recognize you coming in, they won't recognize you going out.

MARILYN: One of them did. But I'd slipped through the door before he started yelling.

TC: I'm sure there's a back entrance. We can go that way.

MARILYN: I don't want to see any corpses.

TC: Why would we?

MARILYN: This is a funeral parlor. They must keep them somewhere. That's all I need today, to wander into a room full of corpses. Be patient. I'll take us somewhere and treat us to a bottle of bubbly.

(So we sat and talked and Marilyn said: "I hate funerals. I'm glad I won't have to go to my own. Only, I don't want a funeral—just my ashes cast on waves by one of my kids, if I ever have any. I wouldn't have come today except Miss Collier cared about me, my welfare, and she was just like a granny, a tough old granny, but she taught me a lot. She taught me how to breathe. I've put it to good use, too, and

I don't mean just acting. There *are* other times when breathing is a problem. But when I first heard about it, Miss Collier cooling, the first thing I thought was: Oh, gosh, what's going to happen to Phyllis?! Her whole life was Miss Collier. But I hear she's going to live with Miss Hepburn. Lucky Phyllis; she's going to have fun now. I'd change places with her pronto. Miss Hepburn is a terrific lady, no shit. I wish she was my friend. So I could call her up sometimes and . . . well, I don't know, just call her up."

We talked about how much we liked New York and loathed Los Angeles ("Even though I was born there, I still can't think of one good thing to say about it. If I close my eyes, and picture L.A., all I see is one big varicose vein"); we talked about actors and acting ("Everybody says I can't act. They said the same thing about Elizabeth Taylor. And they were wrong. She was great in *A Place in the Sun*. I'll never get the right part, anything I really want. My looks are against me. They're too specific"); we talked some more about Elizabeth Taylor, and she wanted to know if I knew her, and I said yes, and she said well, what is she like, what is she *really* like, and I said well, she's a little bit like you, she wears her heart on her sleeve and talks salty, and Marilyn said fuck you and said well, if somebody asked me what Marilyn Monroe was like, what was Marilyn Monroe *really* like, what would I say, and I said I'd have to think about that.)

TC: Nòw do you think we can get the hell out of here? You promised me champagne, remember?

MARILYN: I remember. But I don't have any money.

TC: You're always late and you never have any money. By any chance are you under the delusion that you're Queen Elizabeth?

MARILYN: Who?

TC: Queen Elizabeth. The Queen of England.

MARILYN (frowning): What's that cunt got to do with it?

TC: Queen Elizabeth never carries money either. She's not allowed to. Filthy lucre must not stain the royal palm. It's a law or something.

MARILYN: I wish they'd pass a law like that for me.

TC: Keep going the way you are and maybe they will.

MARILYN: Well, gosh. How does she pay for anything? Like when she goes shopping.

TC: Her lady-in-waiting trots along with a bag full of farthings.

MARILYN: You know what? I'll bet she gets everything free. In return for endorsements.

TC: Very possible. I wouldn't be a bit surprised. By Appointment to Her Majesty. Corgi dogs. All those Fortnum & Mason goodies. Pot. Condoms.

MARILYN: What would she want with condoms?

TC: Not her, dopey. For that chump who walks two steps behind. Prince Philip.

MARILYN: Him. Oh, yeah. He's cute. He looks like he might have a nice prick. Did I ever tell you about the time I saw Errol Flynn whip out his prick and play the piano with it? Oh well, it was a hundred years ago, I'd just got into modeling, and I went to this half-ass party, and Errol Flynn, so pleased with himself, he was there and he took out his prick and played the piano with it. Thumped the keys. He played *You Are My Sunshine*. Christ! Everybody says Milton Berle has the biggest schlong in Hollywood. But who *cares*? Look, don't you have *any* money?

TC: Maybe about fifty bucks.

MARILYN: Well, that ought to buy us some bubbly.

(Outside, Lexington Avenue was empty of all but harmless pedestrians. It was around two, and as nice an April afternoon as one could wish: ideal strolling weather. So we moseyed toward Third Avenue. A few gawkers spun their heads, not because they recognized Marilyn as *the* Marilyn, but because of her funeral finery; she giggled her special little giggle, a sound as tempting as the jingling bells on a Good Humor wagon, and said: "Maybe I should always dress this way. Real anonymous."

As we neared P. J. Clarke's saloon, I suggested P.J.'s might be a good place to refresh ourselves, but she vetoed that: "It's full of those advertising creeps. And that bitch Dorothy Kilgallen, she's always in there getting bombed. What is it with these micks? The way they booze, they're worse than Indians."

I felt called upon to defend Kilgallen, who was a friend, somewhat, and I allowed as to how she could upon occasion be a clever funny woman. She said: "Be that as it may, she's written some bitchy stuff about me. But all those cunts hate me. Hedda. Louella. I know you're supposed to get used to it, but I just can't. It really hurts. What did I ever do to those hags? The only one who writes a decent word about me is Sidney Skolsky. But he's a guy. The guys treat me okay. Just like maybe I was a human person. At least they give me the benefit of the doubt. And Bob Thomas is a gentleman. And Jack O'Brian."

We looked in the windows of antique shops; one contained a tray of old rings, and Marilyn said: "That's pretty. The garnet with the seed pearls. I wish I could wear rings, but I hate people to notice my hands. They're too fat. Elizabeth Taylor has fat hands. But with those eyes, who's looking at her hands? I like to dance naked in front of mirrors and watch my titties jump around. There's nothing wrong with them. But I wish my hands weren't so fat."

Another window displayed a handsome grandfather clock, which prompted her to observe: "I've never had a home. Not a real one with all my own furniture. But if I ever get married again, and make a lot of money, I'm going to hire a couple of trucks and ride down Third Avenue buying every damn kind of crazy thing. I'm going to get a dozen grandfather clocks and line them all up in one room and have them all ticking away at the same time. That would be real homey, don't you think?")

MARILYN: Hey! Across the street!

TC: What?

MARILYN: See the sign with the palm? That must be a fortune-telling parlor.

TC: Are you in the mood for that?

MARILYN: Well, let's take a look.

(It was not an inviting establishment. Through a smeared window we could discern a barren room with a skinny, hairy gypsy lady seated in a canvas chair under a hellfire-red ceiling lamp that shed a torturous glow; she was knitting a pair of baby-booties, and did not return our stares. Nevertheless, Marilyn started to go in, then changed her mind.)

MARILYN: Sometimes I want to know what's going to happen. Then I think it's better not to. There's two things I'd like to know, though. One is whether I'm going to lose weight.

TC: And the other?

MARILYN: That's a secret.

TC: Now, now. We can't have secrets today. Today is a day of sorrow, and sorrowers share their innermost thoughts.

MARILYN: Well, it's a man. There's something I'd like to know. But that's all I'm going to tell. It really *is* a secret.

(And I thought: That's what you think; I'll get it out of you.)

TC: I'm ready to buy that champagne.

(We wound up on Second Avenue in a gaudily decorated deserted Chinese restaurant. But it did have a well-stocked bar, and we ordered a bottle of Mumm's; it arrived unchilled, and without a bucket, so we drank it out of tall glasses with ice cubes.)

MARILYN: This is fun. Kind of like being on location—if you like location. Which I most certainly don't. *Niagara*. That stinker. Yuk.

TC: So let's hear about your secret lover.

MARILYN: (Silence)

TC: (Silence)

MARILYN: (Giggles)

TC: (Silence)

MARILYN: You know so many women. Who's the most attractive woman you know?

TC: No contest. Barbara Paley. Hands down.

MARILYN (frowning): Is that the one they call "Babe"? She sure doesn't look like any Babe to me. I've seen her in *Vogue* and all. She's so elegant. Lovely. Just looking at her pictures makes me feel like pig-slop.

TC: She might be amused to hear that. She's very jealous of you.

MARILYN: Jealous of *me?* Now there you go again, laughing.

TC: Not at all. She *is* jealous.

MARILYN: But why?

TC: Because one of the columnists, Kilgallen I think, ran a blind item that said something like: "Rumor hath it that Mrs. DiMaggio rendezvoused with television's toppest tycoon and it wasn't to discuss business." Well, she read the item and she believes it.

MARILYN: Believes *what?*

TC: That her husband is having an affair with you. William S. Paley. TV's toppest tycoon. He's partial to shapely blondes. Brunettes, too.

MARILYN: But that's batty. I've never met the guy.

TC: Ah, come on. You can level with me. This secret lover of yours—it's William S. Paley, *n'est-ce pas?*

MARILYN: No! It's a writer. He's a writer.

TC: That's more like it. Now we're getting somewhere. So your lover is a writer. Must be a real hack, or you wouldn't be ashamed to tell me his name.

MARILYN (furious, frantic): What does the "S" stand for?

TC: "S." What "S"?

MARILYN: The "S" in William S. Paley.

TC: Oh, *that* "S." It doesn't stand for anything. He sort of tossed it in there for appearance sake.

MARILYN: It's just an initial with no name behind it? My goodness. Mr. Paley must be a little insecure.

TC: He twitches a lot. But let's get back to our mysterious scribe.

MARILYN: Stop it! You don't understand. I have so much to lose.

TC: Waiter, we'll have another Mumm's, please.

MARILYN: Are you trying to loosen my tongue?

TC: Yes. Tell you what. We'll make an exchange. I'll tell you a story, and if you think it's interesting, then perhaps we can discuss your writer friend.

MARILYN (tempted, but reluctant): What's your story about?

TC: Errol Flynn.

MARILYN: (Silence)

TC: (Silence)

MARILYN (hating herself): Well, go on.

TC: Remember what you were saying about Errol? How pleased he was with his prick? I can vouch for that. We once spent a cozy evening together. If you follow me.

MARILYN: You're making this up. You're trying to trick me.

TC: Scout's honor. I'm dealing from a clean deck. (Silence; but I can see that she's hooked, so after lighting a cigarette . . .) Well, this happened when I was eighteen. Nineteen. It was during the war. The winter of 1943. That night Carol Marcus or maybe she was already Carol Saroyan, was giving a party for her best friend, Gloria Vanderbilt. She gave it in her mother's apartment on Park Avenue. Big party. About fifty people. Around midnight Errol Flynn rolls in with his alter ego, a swashbuckling playboy named Freddie McEvoy. They were both pretty loaded. Anyway, Errol started yakking with me, and he was bright, we were making each other laugh, and suddenly he said he wanted to go to El Morocco, and did I want to go with him and his buddy McEvoy. I said okay, but then McEvoy didn't want to leave the party and all those debutantes, so in the end Errol and I left alone. Only we didn't go to El Morocco. We took a taxi down to Gramercy Park, where I had a little one-room apartment. He stayed until noon the next day.

MARILYN: And how would you rate it? On a scale of one to ten.

TC: Frankly, if it hadn't been Errol Flynn, I don't think I would have remembered it.

MARILYN: That's not much of a story. Not worth mine—not by a long shot.

TC: Waiter, where is our champagne? You've got two thirsty people here.

MARILYN: And it's not as if you'd told me anything new. I've always known Errol zigzagged. I have a masseur, he's practically my sister, and he was Tyrone Power's masseur, and he told me all about the thing Errol and Ty Power had going. No, you'll have to do better than that.

TC: You drive a hard bargain.

MARILYN: I'm listening. So let's hear your best experience. Along those lines.

TC: The best? The most memorable? Suppose you answer the question first.

MARILYN: And *I* drive hard bargains! Ha! (Swallowing champagne) Joe's not bad. He can hit home runs. If that's all it takes, we'd still be married. I still love him, though. He's genuine.

TC: Husbands don't count. Not in this game.

MARILYN (nibbling nail; really thinking): Well, I met a man, he's related to Gary Cooper somehow. A stockbroker, and nothing much to look at—sixty-five, and he wears those very thick glasses. Thick as jellyfish. I can't say what it was, but—

TC: You can stop right there. I've heard all about him from other girls. That old swordsman really scoots around. His name is Paul Shields. He's Rocky Cooper's stepfather. He's supposed to be sensational.

MARILYN: He is. Okay, smart-ass. Your turn.

TC: Forget it. I don't have to tell you damn nothing. Because I know who your masked marvel is: Arthur Miller. (She lowered her black glasses: Oh boy, if looks could kill, wow!) I guessed as soon as you said he was a writer.

MARILYN (stammering): But how? I mean, nobody . . . I mean, hardly anybody—

TC: At least three, maybe four years ago Irving Drutman—

MARILYN: Irving *who*?

TC: Drutman. He's a writer on the *Herald Tribune*. He told me you were fooling around with Arthur Miller. Had a hang-up on him. I was too much of a gentleman to mention it before.

MARILYN: Gentleman! You bastard. (Stammering again, but dark glasses in place) You don't understand. That was long ago. That ended. But this is new. It's all different now, and—

TC: Just don't forget to invite me to the wedding.

MARILYN: If you talk about this, I'll murder you. I'll have you bumped off. I know a couple of men who'd gladly do me the favor.

TC: I don't question that for an instant.

(At last the waiter returned with the second bottle.)

MARILYN: Tell him to take it back. I don't want any. I want to get the hell out of here.

TC: Sorry if I've upset you.

MARILYN: I'm not upset.

(But she was. While I paid the check, she left for the powder room, and I wished I had a book to read: her visits to powder rooms sometimes lasted as long as an elephant's pregnancy. Idly, as time ticked by, I wondered if she was popping uppers or downers. Downers, no doubt. There was a newspaper on the bar, and I picked it up; it was written in Chinese. After twenty minutes had passed, I decided to investigate. Maybe she'd popped a lethal dose, or even cut her wrists. I found the ladies' room, and knocked on the door. She said: "Come in." Inside, she was confronting a dimly lit mirror. I said: "What are you doing?" She said: "Looking at Her." In fact, she was coloring her lips with ruby lipstick. Also, she had removed the somber head scarf and combed out her glossy fine-as-cotton-candy hair.)

MARILYN: I hope you have enough money left.

TC: That depends. Not enough to buy pearls, if that's your idea of making amends.

MARILYN (giggling, returned to good spirits. I decided I wouldn't mention Arthur Miller again): No. Only enough for a long taxi ride.

TC: Where are we going—Hollywood?

MARILYN: Hell, no. A place I like. You'll find out when we get there.

(I didn't have to wait that long, for as soon as we had flagged a taxi, I heard her instruct the cabby to drive to the South Street Pier, and I thought: Isn't that where one takes the ferry to Staten Island? And my next conjecture was: She's swallowed pills on top of that champagne and now she's off her rocker.)

TC: I hope we're not going on any boat rides. I didn't pack my Dramamine.

MARILYN (happy, giggling): Just the pier.

TC: May I ask why?

MARILYN: I like it there. It smells foreign, and I can feed the sea gulls.

TC: With what? You haven't anything to feed them.

MARILYN: Yes, I do. My purse is full of fortune cookies. I swiped them from that restaurant.

TC (kidding her): Uh-huh. While you were in the john I cracked one open. The slip inside was a dirty joke.

MARILYN: Gosh. Dirty fortune cookies?

TC: I'm sure the gulls won't mind.

> (Our route carried us through the Bowery. Tiny pawnshops and blood-donor stations and dormitories with fifty-cent cots and tiny grim hotels with dollar beds and bars for whites, bars for blacks, everywhere bums, bums, young, far from young, ancient, bums squatting curbside, squatting amid shattered glass and pukey debris, bums slanting in doorways and huddled like penguins at street corners. Once, when we paused for a red light, a purple-nosed scarecrow weaved toward us and began swabbing the taxi's windshield with a wet rag clutched in a shaking hand. Our protesting driver shouted Italian obscenities.)

MARILYN: What is it? What's happening?

TC: He wants a tip for cleaning the window.

MARILYN (shielding her face with her purse): How horrible! I can't stand it. Give him something. Hurry. Please!

> (But the taxi had already zoomed ahead, damn near knocking down the old lush. Marilyn was crying.)

I'm sick.

TC: You want to go home?

MARILYN: Everything's ruined.

TC: I'll take you home.

MARILYN: Give me a minute. I'll be okay.

> (Thus we traveled on to South Street, and indeed the sight of a ferry moored there, with the Brooklyn skyline across the water and careening, cavorting sea gulls white against a marine horizon streaked with thin fleecy clouds fragile as lace—this tableau soon soothed her soul.
>
> As we got out of the taxi we saw a man with a chow on a leash, a prospective passenger, walking toward the ferry, and as we passed them, my companion stopped to pat the dog's head.)

THE MAN (firm, but not unfriendly): You shouldn't touch strange dogs. Especially chows. They might bite you.

MARILYN: Dogs never bite me. Just humans. What's his name?

THE MAN: Fu Manchu.

MARILYN (giggling): Oh, just like the movie. That's cute.

THE MAN: What's yours?

MARILYN: My name? Marilyn.

THE MAN: That's what I thought. My wife will never believe me. Can I have your autograph?

(He produced a business card and a pen; using her purse to write on, she wrote: *God Bless You—Marilyn Monroe.*)

MARILYN: Thank you.

THE MAN: Thank *you*. Wait'll I show this back at the office.

(We continued to the edge of the pier, and listened to the water sloshing against it.)

MARILYN: I used to ask for autographs. Sometimes I still do. Last year Clark Gable was sitting next to me in Chasen's, and I asked him to sign my napkin.

(Leaning against a mooring stanchion, she presented a profile: Galatea surveying unconquered distances. Breezes fluffed her hair, and her head turned toward me with an ethereal ease, as though a breeze had swiveled it.)

TC: So when do we feed the birds? I'm hungry, too. It's late, and we never had lunch.

MARILYN: Remember, I said if anybody ever asked you what I was like, what Marilyn Monroe was *really* like—well, how would you answer them? (Her tone was teaseful, mocking, yet earnest, too: she wanted an honest reply) I bet you'd tell them I was a slob. A banana split.

TC: Of course. But I'd also say . . .

(The light was leaving. She seemed to fade with it, blend with the sky and clouds, recede beyond them. I wanted to lift my voice louder than the sea gulls' cries and call her back: Marilyn! Marilyn, why did everything have to turn out the way it did? Why does life have to be so fucking rotten?)

TC: I'd say . . .

MARILYN: I can't hear you.

TC: I'd say you are a beautiful child.

Remembering
Tennessee

(1983)

TENNESSEE WILLIAMS DEAD AT 71.
So announced the headline on the
front page of *The New York Times*. He had strangled, it turned out, while
using a plastic bottle cap to take barbiturates; incredibly, the cap had
popped down his throat and choked him to death. All of this had happened
at the Elysée, a curious little hotel located in the East Fifties. Actually,
Tennessee had an apartment in New York. But when he was in the city,
he always stayed at the Elysée. The apartment, a small jumble of sparsely
furnished rooms "conveniently" located on West 42nd Street, was reserved
for the entertainment of kind strangers.

It was a strange end for a man obsessed with a rather poetic concept of
death. Even as a young man, he was convinced that the next day would
be his last. The only serious quarrel we ever had involved his hypochon-
driac sensitivity to this subject. At the time, he had a play in rehearsal:
Summer and Smoke. We were having dinner together, and to amuse him
(I thought), I began to tell him stories I had heard from members of the
cast about the play's director, a woman from Texas. It seemed that at every
rehearsal, she would assemble the cast and tell them what an effort they
must make, how hard they must work, "because this flower of genius is
Tenn's last. He is dying. Yes, he is a dying man with only months left to
live. He told me so himself. Of course, he's always claiming to be dying.
But this time I'm afraid it's true. Even his agent believes it."

Far from amusing my old friend, the anecdote enraged him. First he broke glasses and plates, then he turned over the entire table and stalked out of the restaurant, leaving me amazed—and also to pay for the destruction.

I was sixteen years old when I met him. He was thirteen years older than I was, a waiter at the Greenwich Village Café and a would-be playwright. We became great friends—it really was a sort of intellectual friendship, though people inevitably thought otherwise. In those early days he used to give me all of his short, one-act plays to read, and we would act them out together. Gradually, over the years, we built up *The Glass Menagerie*. I would play the daughter.

With his tendency toward around-the-clock sex and gin and general carousing, Tennessee, who was not a born survivor, probably would not have lasted beyond the age of forty if it hadn't been for Frank Merlo. Frank was a sailor, a wartime discovery of mine. Some five years after I met him, and when he was no longer involved with the Navy, Tennessee saw us lunching in a cozy Italian restaurant. I never saw him so excited, either before or since. He deserted his own luncheon companion—his agent, Audrey Wood—and swiftly, without any invitation, sat himself at our table. After I had introduced him to my friend, not two minutes passed before he said, "Could you have dinner with me tonight?"

The invitation clearly did not include me. But Frank was embarrassed; he didn't know what to say. I answered for him: "Yes," I said, "of course he'd like to have dinner with you."

So he did. They were together for fourteen years, and those were the happiest years of Tennessee's life. Frank was like a husband, a lover, a business agent to him. He also had a great gift for parties, which suited Tennessee just fine. When Yukio Mishima, the brilliant Japanese writer—the one who formed an army and confronted the Japanese military commander and ended up committing hara-kiri—when he came to New York in 1952, Tennessee told Frank that he wanted to throw a party in Mishima's honor. So Frank rounded up every geisha girl between New York and San Francisco, but he didn't stop at that. *Then* he outfitted about a hundred drag geishas. It was the most fantastic party I'd ever seen in my entire life. And Tennessee dressed up as a great geisha dame and they drove through the park all night till dawn, drinking champagne. This was Mishima's first taste of life in the Western world, and he said, "I'm *never* going back to Japan."

When Frank died of cancer in 1962, Tennessee died a little, too. I remember all too well the last hours of Frank's life. He lived them in a New York hospital room, where crowds of friends drifted in and out. Finally, a stern doctor ordered the room rid of all visitors, including Tennessee. But he refused to leave. He knelt by the narrow bed and clutched Frank's hand, pressing it against his cheek.

Nevertheless, the doctor told him he must go. But suddenly Frank whispered, "No. Let him stay. It can't do me any harm. After all, I'm used to him."

The doctor sighed and left them alone.

Tennessee was never the same after that. He had always drunk a good deal, but he started combining drugs and alcohol. He was also meeting some very strange people. I think he lived the last two decades of his life alone—with the ghost of Frank.

But now when I remember Tennessee, I think of the good times, the funny times. He was a person who, despite his inner sadness, never stopped laughing. He had a remarkable laugh. It wasn't coarse or vulgar or even especially loud. It just had an amazing sort of throaty Mississippi-riverman ring to it. You could always tell when he had walked into a room, no matter how many people were there.

As for his sense of humor, normally it was pretty raucous. But when he got into a fury, he seemed to swing between two things: either very sick humor—laughing nonstop during those five-martini lunches of his—or deep bitterness, about himself, about his father, about his family. His father never understood him, his family seemed to blame him for his sister's insanity, and Tennessee himself—well, I think he thought he was not very sane. You could see all of this in his eyes, which had a changing in them, like a Ferris wheel of merriment and bitterness.

This isn't to say that he wasn't fun to be with. We used to go to the movies together, and I guess I've been thrown out of more movie houses with him than with anybody else in my life. He would always start reciting lines, making fun, doing Joan Crawford. Before long, the manager would come down and tell us to get out.

My funniest memory, though, is of four or five years ago, when I was staying with Tennessee in Key West. We were in a terrifically crowded bar—there were probably three hundred people in it, both gays and straights. A husband and wife were sitting at a little table in the corner, and they were both quite drunk. She had on a pair of slacks and a halter top, and she approached our table and held out an eyebrow pencil. She wanted me to autograph her belly button.

I just laughed and said, "Oh, no. Leave me alone."

"How can you be so cruel?" Tennessee said to me, and as everyone in the place watched, he took the eyebrow pencil and wrote *my* name around her navel. When she got back to her table, her husband was furious. Before we knew it, he had grabbed the eyebrow pencil out of her hand and walked over to where we were sitting, whereupon he unzipped his pants and pulled out his cock and said—to me—"Since you're autographing everything today, would you mind autographing *mine*?"

I had never heard a place with three hundred people in it get that quiet. I didn't know what to say—I just looked at him.

Then Tennessee reached up and took the eyebrow pencil out of the stranger's hand. "I don't know that there's room for Truman to autograph it," he said, giving me a wink, "but I'll initial it."

It brought down the house.

The last time I saw him was a few weeks before he died. We had dinner together at a very private little place called Le Club, and Tennessee was fine physically, but sad. He said he had no friends anymore, that I was one of the few people in his life who really knew him. He wished we could be close the way we were in the old days.

And as he talked and the fireplace blazed, I thought, Yes, I *did* know him. And I remembered a night many, many years before when I first realized that that was true.

The year was 1947, and the opening night of *A Streetcar Named Desire* was a hauntingly dazzling event. As the lights dimmed on the final scene and Blanche DuBois, reaching out in the darkness for the guiding hands of a nurse and a doctor, whispered, "Whoever you are—I have always depended on the kindness of strangers," a thrilling silence immobilized the audience. Terror and beauty had stopped their hearts. Even long after the curtain had descended, the hush continued. Then it was as if a cascade of balloons had exploded. The magnificent applause, the momentous rising of the audience to its feet, was as sudden and as breathtaking as a cyclone.

The stars, Jessica Tandy and Marlon Brando, took sixteen curtain calls before the "Author! Author!" demands were met. He was reluctant to be led onstage, this young Mr. Williams. He blushed as though it were the first time he had ever been kissed, and by strangers at that. Certainly, he had not splurged on the evening (he had an overpowering fear of money, one so severe that even an occasion such as this could not make him succumb to thoughts of a new suit), so he was dressed in a dark blue that many a subway seat had shined; and his tie had become loosened; and one of the buttons on his shirt was dangling. But he was beguiling: short but trim, sturdy, healthy-colored. He held up two smallish plowman's hands and quietened the ecstasy long enough to say, "Thank you. Thank you very, very, very . . ." in a voice as sluggish and Southern as the Mississippi if the river were polluted with gin. What he felt, one felt, was joy, not happiness; joy is cocaine brief, but happiness has at least a little longer-lasting languor.

Tennessee was an unhappy man, even when he was smiling the most, laughing his loudest. And the truth was, at least to me, that Blanche and her creator were interchangeable; they shared the same sensitivity, the same insecurity, the same wistful lust. And suddenly, as one was thinking that and was watching his bows to the deafening clamor, he seemed to recede on the stage, to fade through the curtains—led by the same doctor who had guided Blanche DuBois toward undesirable shadows.

ESSAYS

A House
on the Heights

(1959)

I LIVE IN BROOKLYN. BY CHOICE.
Those ignorant of its allures are enti-
tled to wonder why. For, taken as a whole, it *is* an uninviting community.
A veritable veldt of tawdriness where even the *noms des quartiers* aggravate:
Flatbush and Flushing Avenue, Bushwick, Brownsville, Red Hook. Yet,
in the greenless grime-gray, oases do occur, splendid contradictions, hearty
echoes of healthier days. Of these seeming mirages, the purest example is
the neighborhood in which I am situated, an area known as Brooklyn
Heights. Heights, because it stands atop a cliff that secures a sea gull's view
of the Manhattan and Brooklyn bridges, of lower Manhattan's tall dazzle
and the ship-lane waters, breeding river to bay to ocean, that encircle and
seethe past posturing Miss Liberty.

I'm not much acquainted with the proper history of the Heights. However, I *believe* (but please don't trust me) that the oldest house, the oldest
still extant and functioning, belongs to our backyard neighbors, Mr. and
Mrs. Philip Broughton. A silvery-gray, shingle-wood Colonial shaded by
trees robustly leafed, it was built in 1790, the home of a sea captain. Period
prints, dated 1830, depict the Heights area as a cozy port bustling with
billowed sails; and, indeed, many of the section's finer houses, particularly
those of Federal design, were first intended to shelter the families of ship-
masters. Cheerfully austere, as elegant and other-era as formal calling cards,
these houses bespeak an age of able servants and solid fireside ease; of horses

in musical harness (old rose-brick carriage houses abound hereabouts; all now, naturally, transformed into pleasant, if rather doll-pretty, dwellings); invoke specters of bearded seafaring fathers and bonneted stay-at-home wives: devoted parents to great broods of future bankers and fashionable brides. For a century or so that is how it must have been: a time of tree-shrouded streets, lanes limp with willow, August gardens brimming with bumblebees and herbaceous scent, of ship horns on the river, sails in the wind, and a country-green meadow sloping down to the harbor, a cow-grazing, butterflied meadow where children sprawled away breezy summer afternoons, where the slap of sleds resounded on December snows.

Is that how it was? Conceivably I take too Valentine a view. However it be, my Valentine assumes the stricter aspect of a steel engraving as we mosey, hand in hand, with Henry Ward Beecher, whose church once dominated the spiritual life of the Heights through the latter half of the last century. The great Bridge, opened in 1883, now balanced above the river; and the port, each year expanding, becoming a more raucous, big-business matter, chased the children out of the meadow, withered it, entirely whacked it away to make room for black palace-huge warehouses tickly with imported tarantulas and reeking of rotten bananas.

By 1910 the neighborhood, which comprises sly alleys and tucked-away courts and streets that sometimes run straight but also dwindle and bend, had undergone fiercer vicissitudes. Descendants of the Reverend Beecher's stiff-collared flock had begun removing themselves to other pastures; and immigrant tribes, who had first ringed the vicinity, at once infiltrated en masse. Whereupon a majority of what remained of genteel old stock, the sediment in the bottom of the bottle, poured forth from their homes, leaving them to be demolished or converted into eyesore-seedy rooming establishments.

So that, in 1925, Edmund Wilson, allowing a paragraph to what he considered the dead and dying Heights, disgustedly reported: "The pleasant red and pink brick houses still worthily represent the generation of Henry Ward Beecher; but an eternal Sunday is on them now; they seem sunk in a final silence. In the streets one may catch a glimpse of a solitary well-dressed old gentleman moving slowly a long way off; but in general the respectable have disappeared and only the vulgar survive. The empty quiet is broken by the shouts of shrill Italian children and by incessant mechanical pianos in dingy apartment houses, accompanied by human voices that seem almost as mechanical as they. At night, along unlighted streets, one gives a wide berth to drunkards that sprawl out across the pavement from the shadow of darkened doors; and I have known a dead horse to be left in the road—two blocks from the principal post office and not much more from Borough Hall—with no effort made to remove it, for nearly three weeks."

Gothic as this glimpse is, the neighborhood nevertheless continued to possess, cheap rents aside, some certain appeal that brigades of the gifted —artists, writers—began to discover. Among those riding in on the initial wave was Hart Crane, whose poet's eye, focusing on his window view, produced *The Bridge*. Later, soon after the success of *Look Homeward, Angel*, Thomas Wolfe, noted prowler of the Brooklyn night, took quarters: an apartment, equipped with the most publicized icebox in literature's archives, which he maintained until his "overcrowded carcass" was carried home to the hills of Carolina. At one time, a stretch of years in the early forties, a single, heaven knows singular, house on Middagh Street boasted a roll call of residents that read: W. H. Auden, Richard Wright, Carson McCullers, Paul and Jane Bowles, the British composer Benjamin Britten, impresario and stage designer Oliver Smith, an authoress of murder entertainments—Miss Gypsy Rose Lee, and a Chimpanzee accompanied by Trainer. Each of the tenants in this ivory-tower boardinghouse contributed to its upkeep, lights, heat, the wages of a general cook (a former Cotton Club chorine), and all were present at the invitation of the owner, that very original editor, writer, *fantaisiste*, a gentleman with a guillotine tongue, yet benevolent and butter-hearted, the late, the justly lamented George Davis.

Now George is gone, and his house too; the necessities of some absurd civic project caused it to be torn down during the war. Indeed, the war years saw the neighborhood slide to its nadir. Many of the more substantial old houses were requisitioned by the military, as lodgings, as jukebox canteens, and their rural-reared, piney-woods personnel treated them quite as Sherman did those Dixie mansions. Not that it mattered; not that anyone gave a damn. No one did; until, soon after the war, the Heights commenced attracting a bright new clientele, brave pioneers bringing brooms and buckets of paint: urban, ambitious young couples, by and large midrung in their Doctor-Lawyer-Wall Street-Whatever careers, eager to restore to the Heights its shattered qualities of circumspect, comfortable charm.

For them, the section had much to offer: roomy big houses ready to be reconverted into private homes suitable for families of old-fashioned size; and such families are what these young people either had made or were making at stepladder rates. A good place to raise children, too, this neighborhood where the traffic is cautious and the air has clarity, a seaside tartness; where there are gardens for games, quiet stoops for amusing; and where, above all, there is the Esplanade to roller-skate upon. (Forbidden: still the brats do it.) While far from being a butterflied meadow, the Esplanade, a wide terracelike walk overlooking the harbor, does its contemporary best to approximate that playing pasture of long-gone girls and their brothers.

So, for a decade and longer, the experiment of reviving the Heights has proceeded: to the point where one is tempted to term it a *fait accompli*.

Window boxes bloom with geraniums; according to the season, green foliated light falls through the trees or gathered autumn leaves burn at the corner; flower-loaded wagons wheel by while the flower seller sings his wares; in the dawn one occasionally hears a cock crow, for there is a lady with a garden who keeps hens and a rooster. On winter nights, when the wind brings the farewell callings of boats outward bound and carries across rooftops the chimney smoke of evening fires, there is a sense, evanescent but authentic as the firelight's flicker, of time come circle, of ago's sweeter glimmerings recaptured.

Though I'd long been acquainted with the neighborhood, having now and then visited there, my closer association began two years ago when a friend bought a house on Willow Street. One mild May evening he asked me over to inspect it. I was most impressed; exceedingly envious. There were twenty-eight rooms, high-ceilinged, well proportioned, and twenty-eight workable marble-manteled fireplaces. There was a beautiful staircase floating upward in white, swan-simple curves to a skylight of sunny amber-gold glass. The floors were fine, the real thing, hard lustrous timber; and the walls! In 1820, when the house was built, men knew how to make walls —thick as a buffalo, immune to the mightiest cold, the meanest heat.

French doors led to a spacious rear porch reminiscent of Louisiana. A porch canopied, completely submerged, as though under a lake of leaves, by an ancient but admirably vigorous vine weighty with grapelike bunches of wisteria. Beyond, a garden: a tulip tree, a blossoming pear, a perched black-and-red bird bending a feathery branch of forsythia.

In the twilight, we talked, my friend and I. We sat on the porch consulting martinis—I urged him to have one more, another. It got to be quite late, he began to see my point: Yes, twenty-eight rooms *were* rather a lot; and yes, it seemed only *fair* that I should have some of them.

That is how I came to live in the yellow brick house on Willow Street.

Often a week passes without my "going to town," or "crossing the bridge," as neighbors call a trip to Manhattan. Mystified friends, suspecting provincial stagnation, inquire, "But what do you *do* over there?" Let me tell you, life can be pretty exciting around here. Remember Colonel Rudolf Abel, the Russian secret agent, the biggest spy ever caught in America, head of the whole damned apparatus? Know where they nabbed him? Right here! smack on Fulton Street! Trapped him in a building between David Semple's fine-foods store and Frank Gambuzza's television-repair shop. Frank, grinning as though he'd done the job himself, had his picture in *Life;* so did the waitress at the Music Box Bar, the colonel's favorite watering hole. A peevish few of us couldn't fathom why our pictures weren't in *Life* too. Frank, the Music Box Bar girl—they weren't the only people who knew the colonel. Such a gentlemanlike gentleman: one would never have *supposed* . . .

I confess, we don't catch spies every day. But most days are supplied with stimulants: in the harbor some exotic freighter to investigate; a bird of strange plumage resting among the wisteria; or, and how exhilarating an occurrence it is, a newly arrived shipment at Knapp's. Knapp's is a set of shops, really a series of storerooms resembling caverns, clustered together on Fulton near Pineapple Street. The proprietor—that is too modest a designation for so commanding a figure—the czar, the Aga Khan of these paradisaic emporiums is Mr. George Knapp, known to his friends as Father.

Father is a world traveler. Cards arrive: he is in Seville, now Copenhagen, now Milan, next week Manchester, everywhere and all the while on a gaudy spending spree. Buying: blue crockery from a Danish castle. Pink apothecary jars from an old London pharmacy. English brass, Barcelona lamps, Battersea boxes, French paperweights, Italian witch balls, Greek icons, Venetian blackamoors, Spanish saints, Korean cabinets; and junk, glorious junk, a jumble of ragged dolls, broken buttons, a stuffed kangaroo, an aviary of owls under a great glass bell, the playing pieces of obsolete games, the paper moneys of defunct governments, an ivory umbrella cane *sans* umbrella, crested chamber pots and mustache mugs and irreparable clocks, cracked violins, a sundial that weighs seven hundred pounds, skulls, snake vertebrae, elephants' hoofs, sleigh bells and Eskimo carvings and mounted swordfish, medieval milkmaid stools, rusted firearms and flaking waltz-age mirrors.

Then Father comes home to Brooklyn, his treasures trailing after him. Uncrated, added to the already perilous clutter, the blackamoors prance in the marvelous gloom, the swordfish glide through the store's Atlantic-depth dusk. Eventually they will go: fancier *antiquaires*, and anonymous mere beauty lovers, will come, cart them away. Meanwhile, poke around. You're certain to find a plum; and it may be a peach. That paperweight —the one imprisoning a Baccarat dragonfly. If you want it, take it now: tomorrow, assuredly the day after, will see it on Fifty-seventh Street at quintuple the tariff.

Father has a partner, his wife Florence. She is from Panama, is handsome, fresh-colored and tall, trim enough to look well in the trousers she affects, a woman of proud posture and, vis-à-vis customers, of nearly eccentric curtness, take-it-or-go disdain—but then, poor soul, she is under the discipline of not being herself permitted to sell, even quote a price. Only Father, with his Macaulayan memory, his dazzling ability to immediately lay hold of any item in the dizzying maze, is so allowed. Brooklyn-born, waterfront-bred, always hatted and usually wearing a wet cold cigar, a stout, short, round powerhouse with one arm, with a strutting walk, a rough-guy voice, shy nervous sensitive eyes that blink when irritation makes him stutter, Father is nevertheless an aesthete. A tough aesthete who takes no guff, will not quibble over his evaluations, just declares: "Put it down!" and, "Get it Manhattan half the money, I give it yuh free." They are an excellent couple, the Knapps. I explore their museum several times a week, and toward October, when a Franklin stove in the shape of a witch hut warms the air and Florence serves cider accompanied by a damp delicious date-nut bread she bakes in discarded coffee cans, never miss a day. Occasionally, on these festive afternoons, Father will gaze about him, blink-blink his eyes with vague disbelief, then, as though his romantic accumulations were closing round him in a manner menacing, observe: "I got to be crazy. Putting my heart in a fruitcake business like this. And the *investment*. The money alone! Honest, in your honest opinion, wouldn't you say I'm crazy?"

Certainly not. If, however, Mrs. Cornelius Oosthuizen were to beg the question—

It seems improbable that someone of Mrs. Oosthuizen's elevation should have condescended to distinguish me with her acquaintance. I owe it all to a pound of dog meat. What happened was: the butcher's boy delivered a purchase of mine which, by error, included hamburger meant to go to Mrs. O. Recognizing her name on the order slip, and having often re-marked her house, a garnet-colored château in mood remindful of the old Schwab mansion on Manhattan's Riverside Drive, I thought of taking round the package myself, not dreaming to meet the fine lady, but, at most, ambitious for a moment's glance into her fortunate preserve. Fortunate, for it boasted, so I'd had confided to me, a butler and staff of six. Not that this is the Height's sole *maison de luxe*: we are blessed with several exponents of limousine life—but unarguably, Mrs. O. is *la regina di tutti*.

Approaching her property, I noticed a person in Persian lamb very vexedly punching the bell, pounding a brass knocker. "God damn you, Mabel," she said to the door; then turned, glared at me as I climbed the steps—a tall, intimidating replica of frail unforbidding Miss Marianne Moore (who, it may be recalled, is a Brooklyn lady too). Pale lashless eyes, razor lips, hair a silver fuzz. "Ah, *you*. I know you," she accused me, as behind her the door was opened by an Irish crone wearing an ankle-length apron. "So. I suppose you've come to sign the petition? Very good of you, I'm sure." Mumbling an explanation, muttering servile civilities, I con-veyed the butcher's parcel from my hands to hers; she, as though I'd tossed her a rather rotten fish, dangled it gingerly until the maid remarked, "Ma'am, 'tis Miss Mary's meat the good lad's brought."

"Indeed. Then don't stand there, Mabel. Take it." And, regarding me with a lessening astonishment that I could not, in her behalf, reciprocate: "Wipe your boots, come in. We will discuss the petition. Mabel, send Murphy with some Bristol and biscuit. . . . Oh? At the dentist's! When I *asked* him *not* to tamper with that tooth. What hellish nonsense," she swore as we passed into a hatrack-vestibule. "Why didn't he go to the hypnotist, as I told him? Mary! Mary! Mary," she said when now appeared a friendly nice dog of cruel pedigree: a spaniel *cum* chow attached to the legs of a dachshund, "I believe Mabel has your lunch. Mabel, take Miss Mary to the kitchen. And we will have our biscuits in the Red Room."

The room, in which red could be discerned only in a bowl of porcelain roses and a basket of marzipan strawberries, contained velvet-swagged windows that commanded a pulse-quickening prospect: sky, skyline, far away a wooded slice of Staten Island. In other respects, the room, a heavy confection, cumbersome, humorless, a hunk of Beidermeier pastry, did not recommend itself. "It was my grandmother's bedroom; my father preferred it as a parlor. Cornelius, Mr. Oosthuizen, died here. Very suddenly: while listening at the radio to the Roosevelt person. An attack. Brought on by anger and cigars. I'm sure you won't ask permission to smoke. Sit down. . . . Not there. There, by the window. Now here, it *should* be here, somewhere, in this drawer? Could it be upstairs? Damn Murphy, horrid man always meddling with my— No, I have it: the petition."

The document stated, and objected to, the plans of a certain minor religious sect that had acquired a half-block of houses on the Heights which they planned to flatten and replace with a dormitory building for the benefit of their Believers. Appended to it were some dozen protesting signatures; the Misses Seeley had signed, and Mr. Arthur Veere Vinson, Mrs. K. Mackaye Brownlowe—descendants of the children in the meadow, the old-guard survivors of *their* neighborhood's evilest hours, those happy few who regularly attended Mrs. O.'s black-tie-sit-downs. She wasted no eloquence on the considerable merit of their complaint; simply, "Sign it," she ordered, a Lady Catherine de Bourgh instructing a Mr. Collins.

Sherry came; and with it an assembly of cats. Scarred battlers with leprous fur and punch-drunk eyes. Mrs. O., motioning toward the least respectable of these, a tiger-striped marauder, told me, "This is the one you may take home. He's been with us a month, we've put him in splendid condition, I'm sure you'll be devoted. Dogs? What *sort* of dogs have you? Well, I don't approve the pure breeds. Anyone will give *them* a home. I took Miss Mary off the street. And Lovely Louise, Mouse and Sweet William—my dogs, all my cats, too, came off the streets. Look below, there in the garden. Under the heaven tree. Those markings: graves are what you see, some as old as my childhood. The seashells are goldfish. The yellow coral, canaries. That white stone is a rabbit; that cross of pebbles: my favorite, the first Mary—angel girl, went bathing in the river and caught a fatal chill. I used to tease Cornelius, Mr. Oosthuizen, told him, ha-ha, told him I planned to put him there with the rest of my darlings. Ha-ha, he wasn't amused, not at all. So, I mean to say, your having dogs doesn't signify: Billy here has such spirit, *he* can hold his own. No, I insist you have him. For I can't keep him much longer, he's a disturbing influence; and if I let him loose, he'll run back to his bad old life in the St. George alley. I wouldn't want *that* on my conscience if I were you."

Her persuasions failed; in consequence our parting was cool. Yet at Christmas she sent me a card, a Cartier engraving of the heaven tree protecting the bones in its sad care. And once, encountering her at the bakery, where we both were buying brownies, we discussed the impudent disregard her petition had received: alas, the wreckers had wrecked, the brethren were building. On the same occasion, she shame-on-you informed me that Billy the cat, released from her patronage, had indeed returned to the sinful ways of the St. George alley.

The St. George alley, adjoining a small cinema, is a shadowy shelter for vagrants: wino derelicts wandered over the bridge from Chinatown and the Bowery share it with other orphaned, gone-wild creatures; cats, as many as minnows in a stream, who gather in their greatest numbers toward nightfall; for then, as darkness happens, strange-eyed women, not unlike those black-clothed fanatics who haunt the cat arenas in Rome, go stealing through the alley with caressing hisses and sacks of crumbled salmon. (Which isn't to suggest that Mrs. O. is one who indulges in this somehow unhealthy hobby: regarding animals, her actions, while perhaps a bit overboard, are kindly meant, and not untypical of the Heights, where a high percentage of the pet population has been adopted off the streets. Astonishing, really, the amount of lost strays who roam their way into the neighborhood, as though instinct informed them they'd find someone here who couldn't abide being followed through the rain, but would, instead, lead them home, boil milk and call Dr. Wasserman, Bernie, our smart-as-they-come young vet whose immaculate hospital resounds with the music of Bach concertos and the barkings of mending beasts.)

Just now, in connection with these notes, I was hunting through a hieroglyphic shambles I call my journal. Odd, indeed the oddest, jottings —a majority of which conceal from me their meanings. God knows what "Thunder on Cobra Street" refers to. Or "A diarrhea of platitudes in seventeen tongues." Unless it is intended to describe a most tiresome local person, a linguist terribly talkative in many languages though articulate in none. However, "Took T&G to G&T" does make sense.

The first initials represent two friends, the latter a restaurant not far away. You must have heard of it, Gage & Tollner. Like Kolb's and Antoine's in New Orleans, Gage & Tollner is a last-century enterprise that has kept in large degree its founding character. The shaky dance of its gaslight chandeliers is not a period-piece hoax; nor do the good plain marble-topped tables, the magnificent array of gold-edged mirrors, seem sentimental affectations—rather, it is a testament to the seriousness of the proprietors, who have obliged us by letting the place stay much as it was that opening day in 1874. One mightn't suppose it, for in the atmosphere there is none of the briny falderal familiar to such aquariums, but the specialty is sea food. The best. Chowders the doughtiest Down Easter must approve. Lobsters that would appease Nero. Myself, I am a soft-shelled-crab *aficionado:* a plate of sautéed crabs, a halved lemon, a glass of chilled Chablis—most satisfactory. The waiters, too, dignified but swift-to-smile Negroes who take pride in their work, contribute to the goodness of Gage & Tollner; on the sleeves of their very laundered jackets they sport military-style chevrons awarded according to the number of years each has served; and, *were* this the Army, some would be generals.

Nearby, there is another restaurant, a fraction less distinguished, but of similar vintage and virtually the same menu: Joe's—Joe being, by the way, an attractive young lady. On the far fringes of the Heights, just before Brooklyn becomes Brooklyn again, there is a street of gypsies, with gypsy cafés (have your future foretold and be tattooed while sipping tankards of Moorish tea); there is also an Arab-Armenian quarter sprinkled with spice-saturated restaurants where one can buy, hot from the oven, a crusty sort of pancake frosted with sesame seed—once in a while I carry mine down to the waterfront, intending to share with the gulls; but gobbling as I go, none is ever left. On a summer's evening a stroll across the bridge, with cool winds singing through the steel shrouds, with stars moving about above and ships below, can be intoxicating, particularly if you are headed toward the roasting-pork, sweet-and-sour aromas of Chinatown.

Another journal notation reads: "At last a face in the ghost hotel!" Which means; after months of observation, in all climates at all hours, I'd sighted someone in a window of a haunted-seeming riverfront building that stands on Water Street at the foot of the Heights. A lonely hotel I often make the destination of my walks: because I think it romantic, in aggravated moments imagine retiring there, for it is as secluded as Mt. Athos, remoter than the Krak Chevalier in the mountains of wildest Syria. Daytimes the location, a dead-end Chiricoesque piazza facing the river, is little disturbed; at night, not at all: not a sound, except foghorns and a distant traffic whisper from the bridge which bulks above. Peace, and the shivering glow of gliding-by tugs and ferries.

The hotel is three-storied. Sunstruck scraps of reflected river-shine, and broken, jigsaw images of the bridge waver across the windows; but beyond the glass nothing stirs: the rooms, despite contradictory evidence, milk bottles on sills, a hat on a hook, unmade beds and burning bulbs, appear unoccupied: never a soul to be seen. Like the sailors of the *Marie Celeste,* the guests, hearing a knock, must have opened their doors to a stranger who swallowed them whole. Could it be, perhaps it *was,* the stranger himself that I saw?—"At last a face in the ghost hotel!" I glimpsed him just the once, one April afternoon one cloudless blue day; and he, a balding man in an undershirt, hurled up a window, flexed hairy arms, yawned hugely, hugely inhaled the river breeze—was gone. No, on careful second thought, I will never set foot in that hotel. For I should either be devoured or have my mystery dispelled. As children we are sensitive to mystery: locked boxes, whisperings behind closed doors, the what-thing that lurks yonder in the trees, waits in every stretch between street lamps; but as we grow older all is too explainable, the capacity to invent pleasurable alarm recedes: too bad, a pity—throughout our lives we ought to believe in ghost hotels.

Close by the hotel begins a road that leads along the river. Silent miles of warehouses with shuttered wooden windows, docks resting on the water like sea spiders. From May through September, *la saison pour la plage*, these docks are diving boards for husky ragamuffins—while perfumed apes, potentates of the waterfront but once dock-divers themselves, cruise by steering two-toned (banana-tomato) car concoctions. Crane-carried tractors and cotton bales and unhappy cattle sway above the holds of ships bound for Bahia, for Bremen, for ports spelling their names in Oriental calligraphy. Provided one has made waterfront friends, it is sometimes possible to board the freighters, carouse and sun yourself: you may even be asked to lunch—and I, for one, am always quick to accept, embarrassingly so if the hosts are Scandinavian: they always set a superior table from larders brimming with smoked "taste thrills" and iced aquavit. Avoid the Greek ships, however: very poor cuisine, no liquor served except ouzo, a sickly licorice syrup; and, at least in the opinion of this panhandler, the grub on French freighters by no means meets the standards one might reasonably expect.

The tugboat people are usually good for a cup of coffee, and in wintry weather, when the river is tossing surf, what joy to take refuge in a stove-heated tug cabin and thaw out with a mug of the blackest Java. Now and again along the route minuscule beaches occur, and once, it was around sunset on a quiet Sunday, I saw on one of them something that made me look twice, and twice more: still it seemed a vision. Every kind of sailor is common enough here, even saronged East Indians, even the giant Senegalese, their onyx arms afire with blue, with yellow tattooed flowers, with saucy torsos and garish *graffiti* (Je t'aime, Hard Luck, Mimi Chang, Adios Amigo). Runty Russians, too—one sees them about, flap-flapping in their pajamalike costumes. But the barefooted sailors on the beach, the three I saw reclining there, profiles set against the sundown, seemed mythical as mermen: more exactly, mermaids—for their hair, striped with albino streaks, was lady-length, a savage fiber falling to their shoulders; and in their ears gold rings glinted. Whether plenipotentiaries from the pearl-floored palace of Poseidon or mariners merely, Viking-tressed seamen out of the Gothic North languishing after a long and barberless voyage, they are included permanently in my memory's curio cabinet: an object to be revolved in the light that way and this, like those crystal lozenges with secretive carvings sealed inside.

After consideration, "Thunder on Cobra Street" does become decipherable. On the Heights there is no Cobra Street, though a street exists that suits the name, a steep downhill incline leading to a dark sector of the dockyards. Not a true part of the Heights neighborhood, it lies, like a serpent at the gates, on the outmost periphery. Seedy hangouts, beer-sour bars and bitter candy stores mingle among the eroding houses, the multifamily dwellings that architecturally range from time-blackened brownstone to magnified concepts of Mississippi privy.

Here, the gutters are acrawl with Cobras; that is, a gang of "juvenile" delinquents: COBRA, the word is stamped on their sweatshirts, painted, sometimes in letters that shine with a fearful phosphorescence, across the backs of their leather jackets. The steep street is within their ugly estate, a bit of their "turf," as they term it; an infinitesimal bit, for the Cobras, a powerful cabala, cast owning eyes on acres of metropolitan terrain. I am not brave—*au contraire;* quite frankly, these fellows, may they be twelve years old or twenty, set my heart thumping like a sinner's at Sunday meeting. Nevertheless, when it has been a matter of convenience to pass through this section of their domain, I've compelled my nerves to accept the challenge.

On the last venture, and perhaps it will remain the last, I was carrying a good camera. The sun was unseen in a sky that ought to either rumble or rain. Rackety children played skip-rope, while a lamppost-lot of idle elders looked on, dull-faced and drooping: a denim-painted, cowboy-booted gathering of Cobras. Their eyes, their asleep sick insolent eyes, swerved on me as I climbed the street. I crossed to the opposite curb; then *knew*, without needing to verify it, that the Cobras had uncoiled and were sliding toward me. I heard them whistling; and the children hushed, the skip-rope ceased swishing. Someone—a pimpled purple-birthmark bandit-masked the lower half of his face—said, "Hey yuh, Whitey, lemmeseeduh-camra." Quicken one's step? Pretend not to hear? But every alternative seemed explosive. "Hey, Whitey, hey yuh, takemuhpitchawantcha?"

Thunder salvaged the moment. Thunder that rolled, crashed down the street like a truck out of control. We all looked up, a sky ripe for storm stared back. I shouted, "Rain! Rain!" and ran. Ran for the Heights, that safe citadel, that bourgeois bastion. Tore along the Esplanade—where the nice young mothers were racing their carriages against the coming disaster. Caught my breath under the thrashing leaves of troubled elms, rushed on: saw the flower-wagon man struggling with his thunder-frightened horse. Saw, twenty yards ahead, then ten, five, then none, the yellow house on Willow Street. Home! And happy to be.

Lola

(1964)

YES, IT SEEMED IN EVERY RESPECT
a curious gift. An appalling one, really.
For I had already a sufficiency of pets: two dogs, an English bulldog and
a Kerry blue terrier. Moreover, I have never been partial to birds; indeed,
I've had always rather an aversion to them: when, on a beach, sea gulls
swoop and dive, I am (for example) very liable to panic and run. Once
when I was five or six, a sparrow, having flown through the window of
my room, became trapped there: flew about till I was almost faint from an
emotion in which pity figured but fear predominated. And so it was with
some dismay that I received Graziella's Christmas present: an ugly young
raven with wings cruelly clipped.

Now more than twelve years have gone by, for that was Christmas
morning, 1952. I was living then in Sicily on a mountainside; the house,
placed amid a silvery olive orchard, was made of pale pink stone; it had
many rooms, and a terrace with a view of Etna's snowcapped summit. Far
below one saw, on sunlit days, a sea blue as a peacock's eye. It was a
beautiful house, though not very comfortable, especially in winter when
north winds sang, shouted, when one drank wine for warmth and even so
the touch of the stone floors was cold as a dead man's kiss. Whatever the
weather, winter-withered or sun-scorched, the house would not have been
quite habitable without Graziella, a servant girl from the village who
appeared early each morning and stayed until after supper. She was seven-

teen, a stocky young lady too sturdily built: she had the legs of a Japanese wrestler—slightly bowed, with bulging calves. Her face, however, was pretty as could be: eyes brown and gold as the local home-brewed brandy; rosy cheeks; rosier lips; a fine dark brow; and black hair brushed smooth to the skull, then secured in that austere position by a little pair of Spanish combs. She had a hard life, and in an amused, uncomplaining fashion, complained of it constantly: a father who was the village drunk, at any rate one of them; her mother, a religious hysteric; and Paolo, her elder brother —she adored him, though he every week beat her and robbed her of her wages. We were good friends, Graziella and I, and it was natural that at Christmas we should exchange gifts. I gave her a sweater, a scarf and a necklace of green beads. And she, to repeat, presented me with a raven.

I have said it was ugly. It was. An object both dreadful and pathetic. No matter the risk of outraging Graziella, I would have set it free at once had it been capable of fending for itself. But the wings had been very closely cut and it could not fly; it could only wobble about, its black beak agape like the jaws of an idiot, its eyes flat and bleak. Graziella, having climbed high into the dour volcanic slopes above Bronte, had captured it in a ravine where ravens thrive, a valley of stones and thorns and deformed trees. She said, "I caught it with a fishing net. I ran among the birds. When I threw the net in the air two of them tangled. One I let go. The other, this one, I put in a shoebox. I took it home and cut its wings. Ravens are very clever. Smarter than parrots. Or horses. If we split its tongue, we can teach it to talk." It was not that Graziella was unkind; she simply shared the indifference of Mediterraneans to the sufferings of animals. She grew quite cross when I refused to let her mutilate the bird's tongue; in fact, she lost all interest in the poor creature, the well-being of which now became my own unhappy burden.

I kept it shut away in a spare, unfurnished room; kept it locked there like a mad relative. I thought, Well, its wings will soon grow out, then it can go away. But the New Year came and went, weeks passed, and presently Graziella confessed it would be six months before my Christmas gift could once again ascend the skies.

I loathed it. I loathed visiting it; the room was the coldest in the cold house, and the bird so forlorn, so impeccably sad a sight. Yet awareness of its loneliness forced me there—though at the start it seemed to enjoy my visits rather less than I did: it would stalk into a corner and turn its back on me, a silent prisoner hunched between a bowl of water and a bowl of food. In time, however, I came to feel my presence was not unwelcome; it ceased to avoid me, it stared me in the eye and, in a rough, unmusical voice, produced friendly-seeming noises: muted cawings. We began to make discoveries concerning one another: I found it liked to have its head scratched, it realized how much its playful peckings amused me. Soon it learned to balance on the rim of my hand, then to sit upon my shoulder. It grew fond of kissing me—that is, gently, with its beak nipping at my chin, cheeks, an earlobe. Nevertheless, I remained, or imagined I did, somewhat repelled by it: the funereal coloring, the bird-feel of its feathers —distasteful (to me) as fish skin, snake hide.

One morning—it was late January, but spring comes early to Sicily, and the almond trees were in flower: a mist of scent and bloom drifting across the landscape—one morning I arrived to find the raven had absconded. The room in which it lived contained French doors leading into a garden; during the night the doors had somehow come undone; perhaps the sirocco, which was blowing then (bringing with it gritty bits of African desert), had pushed them open. The bird, anyway, was gone. I combed the garden; Graziella climbed the mountainside. The morning ended, and the afternoon. By nightfall we had searched "everywhere": the prickly interior of a wild cactus grove, among the graves of a cemetery close by, inside a cave reeking of bat urine. Gradually, in the course of our pursuit, a certain fact at last penetrated: I very much liked—Lola. Lola! The name emerged like the new moon overhead, unbidden but inevitable; until then I'd not wanted to give her a name: to do so, I felt, would be to admit she was a permanent belonging.

"Lola?"

I called to her from my window. Finally I went to bed. Of course I could not sleep. Visions intervened: Lola, her neck clasped between cat teeth; a red tom racing with her toward the feasting hall of some bloodstained, feather-strewn lair. Or Lola, earthbound and helpless, somewhere hiding until hunger and thirst felled her forever.

"Lo-o-o-la-a-a?"

We had not looked through the house. Possibly she had never left it, or departed by one door and reentered by another. I lighted a candle (our electricity seldom functioned); I traveled from room to room; and in one, an unused parlor, the candlelight illuminated a familiar pair of eyes.

"Ah, Lola."

She stepped aboard my hand; back in the bedroom I transferred her to the foot-railing of a brass bed. She clutched it with her claws and tucked a tired head under one of her disfigured wings. Soon she was asleep, so was I, so were the dogs (curled together in front of a fireplace vaguely aglow with the aromatic flames of a eucalyptus fire).

The dogs had never met Lola, and it was with some anxiety that I next morning introduced them, for they both, and particularly the Kerry blue, were capable of cranky behavior. But if she meant to make her home with us, it must be done. I put her on the floor. The bulldog sniffed at her with his squashed, trufflelike nose, then yawned, not from boredom but embarrassment; all dogs yawn when they are embarrassed. Clearly he did not know what she was. Food? A plaything? The Kerry decided Lola was the latter. He tapped her with his paw. He chased her into a corner. She fought back, pecked his snout; her cawings were coarse and violent as the harshest curse words. It frightened the bulldog; he ran from the room. Even the Kerry retreated—sat down and gazed at her, marveling.

From then on, the dogs had great respect for Lola. They showed her every consideration; she showed them very few. She used their water bowl as a splash bath; at mealtimes, never content with her own dish, she always raided theirs, taking what she pleased. The bulldog she turned into a private mount; perched on his broad rump, she trotted around the garden like a bareback circus rider. At night, camping by the hearth, she huddled between the dogs, and if they threatened to stir, or otherwise disturb her comfort, she stabbed them with her beak.

Lola must have been very young when Graziella caught her—hardly more than a fledgling. By June she had tripled in size, grown big as a chicken. Her wings had come back, or almost. But still she did not fly. Indeed, she refused to. She preferred to walk. When the dogs went for a hike she hopped along beside them. One day it occurred to me that Lola did not know she was a bird. She thought she was a dog. Graziella agreed with me, and we both laughed; we considered it a delightful quirk, neither one foreseeing that Lola's misconception was certain to end in tragedy: the doom that awaits all of us who reject our own natures and insist on being something else than ourselves.

Lola was a thief; otherwise she might never have used her wings at all. However, the sort of articles she was fond of stealing—shiny things, grapes and fountain pens, cigarettes—were situated usually in elevated areas; so, to reach a tabletop, she occasionally took a (quite literally) flying jump. Once she stole a set of false teeth. The teeth belonged to a guest, a difficult and elderly friend, a lady. She said she thought it not the least funny and burst into tears. Alas, we did not know where Lola hid her loot (according to Graziella, all ravens are robbers and invariably keep a secret storage den for stolen treasure). The only sensible course was to try to trick Lola into revealing where she had taken the teeth. She admired gold: a gold ring I sometimes wore constantly excited her greedy gaze. We (Graziella and I) therefore baited our trap with the ring: left it on the luncheon table, where Lola was cleaning up crumbs, and hid behind a door. The instant she imagined herself unobserved, she snatched the ring and rushed out of the dining room and along a hall to the "library"—a small, gloomy room stuffed with cheap paperback editions of the classics, the property of a former tenant. She leaped from floor to chair to bookshelf; then, as though it were a cleft in a mountainside leading to an Ali Baba's cavern, she squeezed between two books and disappeared behind them: evaporated, rather like Alice through the looking glass. *The Complete Jane Austen* concealed her cache, which, when we found it, consisted, in addition to the purloined dentures, of the long-lost keys to my car (I'd not blamed Lola: I thought I'd lost them myself), a mass of paper money—thousands of lire torn into tiny scraps, as though intended for some future nest, old letters, my best cuff links, rubber bands, yards of string, the first page of a short story I'd stopped writing because I couldn't find the first page, an American penny, a dry rose, a crystal button—

Early that summer Graziella announced her engagement to a young man named Luchino, a slim-waisted waiter with oily, curly hair and a film-star profile. He spoke a little English, a little German; he wore green suede shoes and drove his own Vespa. Graziella had reason to think him a formidable catch; still, I was not happy about it. I felt she was too plain and healthy, simply too nice, for a sharp fellow like Luchino (who had a reputation as a semiprofessional gigolo catering to solitary tourists: Swedish spinsters, German widows and widowers), though, to be fair, such activities were far from uncommon among the village youth.

But Graziella's joy was difficult to resist. She pinned photographs of Luchino all over the kitchen, above the stove, above the sink, inside the icebox door and even on the trunk of a tree that grew outside the kitchen window. Romance, of course, interfered with her care of me: now, in the Sicilian fashion, she had her fiancé's socks to mend, laundry to do (and such a lot of it!), not to mention the hours she spent preparing a trousseau, embroidering underwear, fitting a wedding veil. Often at lunch I was handed a plate of ice-hard spaghetti, then given cold fried eggs for supper. Or perhaps nothing at all; she was forever hurrying off to meet her lover in the piazza for a twilight promenade. Yet in retrospect I do not begrudge her that happiness: it was but the prelude to the bitterest bad luck.

One August night her father (much beloved despite his drunkenness) was offered (by an American tourist) a tall glass of straight gin, told to drink it at one go, did so and underwent a stroke that left him paralyzed. And the very next day even starker misfortune struck; Luchino, streaking along a country road aboard his Vespa, rounded a corner, ran into and instantly killed a three-year-old girl. I drove Luchino and Graziella to the child's funeral; afterward, on the way home, Luchino was dry-eyed but Graziella moaned and wept as though her heart had been halved: I assumed she was grieving for the dead baby. No, it was for herself, the dark prospect before her: Luchino faced possible imprisonment and certainly a huge indemnity payment—there would be no marriage now, not for years (if ever).

The poor girl was prostrated. A doctor confined her to bed. One day I went to see how she was getting on. I took Lola with me, meaning to cheer the invalid. Instead, the sight of the bird horrified her; she screamed. She said Lola was a witch, she said Lola had the *malocchio*, the evil eye, and that the double tragedy, her father's stroke and Luchino's accident, was

Lola's work, a punishment inflicted for having caught her and clipped her wings. She said, Yes, yes, it's true: every child knows ravens are the embodiment of black and wicked spirits. And, "I will never come to your house again."

Nor did she. Nor did any other servant girl. For out of Graziella's accusations, a myth grew that mine was a house of the evil eye: that not merely Lola, but I myself, possessed a potent *malocchio*. Nothing worse can be said of one in Sicily. Moreover, it is a charge against which there is no defense. In the beginning I joked about it, though it was not in the least a humorous adventure. Persons meeting me in the street crossed themselves; or, as soon as I had passed, arranged one hand in the shape of a bull's head with horns—a dark-magic gesture meant to dispel the power of my malevolent, spell-casting, tortoise-shell-rimmed eye.

I woke one night around midnight and decided (snap!) to clear out. Leave before dawn. Rather a decision, for I'd lived there two years, and did not altogether relish being suddenly homeless. Homeless with two large dogs and an uncaged, peculiar bird. Nevertheless, I stuffed the car: it looked like a rolling cornucopia: shoes and books and fishing gear spilling out the windows; with a few rough shoves I contrived to fit the dogs inside. But there was no room left for Lola. She had to sit on my shoulder, which was not ideal, for she was a nervous passenger, and any abrupt twist or turn made her either squawk or relieve herself.

Across the Straits of Messina, across Calabria, on to Naples and Rome. It is a journey pleasant to look back upon: sometimes, when balanced on the edge of sleep, I see pictures of it slide past. A picnic in the Calabrian mountains: a hard blue sky, a herd of goats below, the thin sweet pipings of the goatherder on a bamboo whistle—and Lola gobbling bread crumbs soaked in red wine. Or Cape Palinuro, a remote, forest-fringed Calabrian beach where we all were sunning ourselves under a still-warm October sun when a wild pig charged out of the woods and raced toward us, as though to attack. I was the only one intimidated: I ran into the sea. The dogs stood their ground and Lola stood with them, flapped about, shouting encouragements in her rusty voice; together, in concert, they chased the pig back into the forest. The evening of the same day we traveled as far as the ruins at Paestum: a brilliant evening, the sky like another sea, the half-moon like an anchored ship rocking in a surf of stars, and all around us the moon-brightened marble, the broken temples of a distant time. We slept on the beach that borders the ruins; or they did—Lola and the dogs: I was tormented by mosquitoes and thoughts of mortality.

We settled for the winter in Rome, first at a hotel (the management of which expelled us after five days, and it was not even a first-class establishment), then in an apartment at 33 Via Margutta, a narrow street often painted by bad painters and renowned for the number of cats who dwell there, unowned cats sheltering in the overgrown patios and existing on the charity of half-mad elderly women, crones who every day tour the cat jungles with sacks of scrap food.

Our apartment was a penthouse: to reach it one climbed six flights of steep dark stairs. We had three rooms and a balcony. It was because of the balcony that I rented it; after the vastness of the view from the Sicilian terrace, the balcony offered, in contrast, a miniature scene tranquil and perfect as firelight: several Roman rooftops, faded orange, faded ocher, and a few across-the-way windows (behind which episodes of family life could be observed). Lola loved the balcony. She was scarcely ever off it. She liked to sit perched on the edge of the stone balustrade and study the traffic on the cobbled street below: the old ladies feeding the Margutta cats; a street musician who came each afternoon and played bagpipes, until, feeling throughly blackmailed, one tossed him a coin; a handsome knife-grinder advertising his services with a song sung in the most bull-like of baritones (housewives hurried!).

When the sun was out Lola always took her bath on the balcony balustrade. Her tub was a silver soup dish; after a moment of sprightly immersion in the shallow water, she would spring up and out, and as though casting off a crystal cloak, shake herself, swell her feathers; later, for long, bliss-saturated hours, she drowsed in the sun, her head tilted back, her beak ajar, her eyes shut. To watch her was a soothing experience.

Signor Fioli seemed to think so. He sat at his window, which was exactly opposite the balcony, and played attentive audience to Lola as long as she was visible. Signor Fioli interested me. I had taken the trouble to learn his name and something of his story. He was ninety-three years old, and in his ninetieth year he had lost the ability to speak: whenever he wished to attract the attention of his family (a widowed granddaughter and five grown great-grandsons), he rang a small supper bell. Otherwise, and even though he never left his bedroom, he appeared to be in complete command of himself. His eyesight was excellent: he saw everything Lola did, and if she did anything especially foolish or lovely, a smile sweetened his sour, very virile old face. He had been a cabinetmaker, and the business he had founded still operated on the ground floor of the building in which he lived; three of his great-grandchildren worked there.

One morning—it was the week before Christmas, almost a year to the day that Lola had entered my life—I filled Lola's soup bowl with mineral water (she preferred to bathe in mineral water, the bubblier the better), carried it out to her on the balcony, waved at Signor Fioli (who, as usual, was settled at his window waiting to attend Lola's toilette), then went inside, sat down at my desk and started to write letters.

Presently I heard the summoning tinkle of Signor Fioli's supper bell: a well-known noise, one heard it twenty times a day; but it had never sounded just like this: a ringing rapid as the beat of an excited heart. I wondered why, and went to see, and saw: Lola, a stupefied sun worshiper squatting on the balustrade—and behind her an immense ginger cat, a cat that had crept across the rooftops and was now crawling on its belly along the balustrade, green eyes aglitter.

Signor Fioli shook his bell. I shouted. The cat leaped, claws unfurled. But it was as if at the last moment Lola sensed her peril. She jumped off the balustrade, fell outward into space. The disgruntled cat, Signor Fioli and I watched her extraordinary descent.

"Lola! Fly, Lola, fly!"

Her wings, though spread, remained motionless. Slowly, gravely, as though attached to a parachute, she drifted downward; down and down.

A small pickup truck was passing in the street below. At first I thought Lola would fall in front of it: that seemed dangerous enough. But what happened was worse, was eerie and awful: she landed on top of some sacks stacked on the back of the truck. And stayed there. And the truck kept going: turned the corner and drove out of the Via Margutta.

"Come back, Lola! Lola!"

I ran after her; skidded down the six flights of slippery stone stairs; fell; skinned my knees; lost my glasses (they flew off and smashed against a wall). Outside, I ran to the corner where the truck had turned. Far off, through a haze compounded of myopia plus tears of pain, I saw the little truck stopped at a traffic light. But before I could reach it, long before, the light changed and the truck, bearing Lola away, taking her forever from me, blurred into the traffic swirling about the Piazza di Spagna.

Not many minutes had elapsed since the cat had lunged, only four or five. Yet it took an hour to retrace my route, climb the stairs, pick up and pocket the broken glasses. And all the while Signor Fioli had been sitting at his window, waiting there with an expression of grieved astonishment. When he saw that I had returned he rang his bell, calling me to the balcony.

I told him, "She thought she was something else."

He frowned.

"A dog."

The frown thickened.

"She's gone."

That he understood. He bowed his head. We both did.

A Voice
from a Cloud

(1969)

O *ther Voices, Other Rooms* (my own title:
it is not a quotation) was published in
January, 1948. It took two years to write and was not my first novel, but
the second. The first, a manuscript never submitted and now lost, was
called *Summer Crossing*—a spare, objective story with a New York setting.
Not bad, as I remember: technically accomplished, an interesting enough
tale, but without intensity or pain, without the qualities of a private vision,
the anxieties that then had control of my emotions and imagination. *Other
Voices, Other Rooms* was an attempt to exorcise demons: an unconscious,
altogether intuitive attempt, for I was not aware, except for a few incidents
and descriptions, of its being in any serious degree autobiographical. Re-
reading it now, I find such self-deception unpardonable.

Surely there were reasons for this adamant ignorance, no doubt protective ones: a fire curtain between the writer and the true source of his
material. As I have lost contact with the troubled youth who wrote this
book, since only a faded shadow of him is any longer contained inside
myself, it is difficult to reconstruct his state of mind. However, I shall try.

At the time of the appearance of *Other Voices, Other Rooms*, critics,
ranging from the warmest to the most hostile, remarked that obviously I
was much influenced by such Southern literary artists as Faulkner and
Welty and McCullers, three writers whose work I knew well and admired.
Nevertheless, the gentlemen were mistaken, though understandably. The
American writers who had been most valuable to me were, in no particular

order, James, Twain, Poe, Cather, Hawthorne, Sarah Orne Jewett; and, overseas, Flaubert, Jane Austen, Dickens, Proust, Chekhov, Katherine Mansfield, E. M. Forster, Turgenev, De Maupassant and Emily Brontë. A collection more or less irrelevant to *Other Voices, Other Rooms;* for clearly no one of these writers, with the conceivable exception of Poe (who was by then a blurred childhood enthusiasm, like Dickens and Twain), was a necessary antecedent to this particular work. Rather, they *all* were, in the sense that each of them had contributed to my literary intelligence, such as it was. But the real progenitor was my difficult, subterranean self. The result was both a revelation and an escape: the book set me free, and, as in its prophetic final sentence, I stood there and looked back at the boy I had left behind.

I was born in New Orleans, an only child; my parents were divorced when I was four years old. It was a complicated divorce with much bitterness on either side, which is the main reason why I spent most of my childhood wandering among the homes of relatives in Louisiana, Mississippi and rural Alabama (off and on, I attended schools in New York City and Connecticut). The reading I did on my own was of greater importance than my official education, which was a waste and ended when I was seventeen, the age at which I applied for and received a job at *The New Yorker* magazine. Not a very grand job, for all it really involved was sorting cartoons and clipping newspapers. Still, I was fortunate to have it, especially since I was determined never to set a studious foot inside a college classroom. I felt that either one was or wasn't a writer, and no combination of professors could influence the outcome. I still think I was correct, at least in my own case; however, I now realize that most young writers have more to gain than not by attending college, if only because their teachers and classroom comrades provide a captive audience for their work; nothing is lonelier than to be an aspiring artist without some semblance of a sounding board.

I stayed two years at *The New Yorker,* and during this period published a number of short stories in small literary magazines. (Several of them were submitted to my employers, and none accepted, though once one was returned with the following comment: "Very good. But romantic in a way this magazine is not.") Also, I wrote *Summer Crossing.* Actually, it was in order to complete the book that I took courage, quit my job, left New York and settled with relatives, a cotton-growing family who lived in a remote part of Alabama: cotton fields, cattle pastures, pinewoods, dirt roads, creeks and slow little rivers, jaybirds, owls, buzzards circling in empty skies, distant train whistles—and, five miles away, a small country town: the Noon City of the present volume.

It was early winter when I arrived there, and the atmosphere of the roomy farmhouse, entirely heated by stoves and fireplaces, was well suited to a fledgling novelist wanting quiet isolation. The household rose at four-thirty, breakfasted by electric light, and was off about its business as the sun ascended—leaving me alone and, increasingly, in a panic. For, more and more, *Summer Crossing* seemed to me thin, clever, unfelt. Another language, a secret spiritual geography, was burgeoning inside me, taking hold of my night-dream hours as well as my wakeful daydreams.

One frosty December afternoon I was far from home, walking in a forest along the bank of a mysterious, deep, very clear creek, a route that led eventually to a place called Hatter's Mill. The mill, which straddled the creek, had been abandoned long ago; it was a place where farmers had brought their corn to be ground into cornmeal. As a child, I'd often gone there with cousins to fish and swim; it was while exploring under the mill that I'd been bitten in the knee by a cottonmouth moccasin—precisely as happens to Joel Knox. And now as I came upon the forlorn mill with its sagging silver-gray timbers, the remembered shock of the snakebite returned; and other memories too—of Idabel, or rather the girl who was the counterpart of Idabel, and how we used to wade and swim in the pure waters, where fat speckled fish lolled in sunlit pools; Idabel was always trying to reach out and grab one.

Excitement—a variety of creative coma—overcame me. Walking home, I lost my way and moved in circles round the woods, for my mind was reeling with the whole book. Usually when a story comes to me, it arrives, or seems to, *in toto:* a long sustained streak of lightning that darkens the tangible, so-called real world, and leaves illuminated only this suddenly seen pseudo-imaginary landscape, a terrain alive with figures, voices, rooms, atmospheres, weather. And all of it, at birth, is like an angry, wrathful tiger cub; one must soothe and tame it. Which, of course, is an artist's principal task: to tame and shape the raw creative vision.

It was dark when I got home, and cold, but I didn't feel the cold because of the fire inside me. My Aunt Lucille said she had been worried about me, and was disappointed because I didn't want any supper. She wanted to know if I was sick; I said no. She said, "Well, you *look* sick. You're white as a ghost." I said good night, locked myself in my room, tossed the manuscript of *Summer Crossing* into a bottom bureau drawer, collected several sharp pencils and a fresh pad of yellow lined paper, got into bed fully clothed, and with pathetic optimism, wrote: "*Other Voices, Other Rooms*—a novel by Truman Capote." Then: "Now a traveller must make his way to Noon City by the best means he can . . ."

It is unusual, but occasionally it happens to almost every writer that the writing of some particular story seems outer-willed and effortless; it is as though one were a secretary transcribing the words of a voice from a cloud. The difficulty is maintaining contact with this spectral dictator. Eventually it developed that communication ran highest at night, as fevers are known to do after dusk. So I took to working all night and sleeping all day, a routine that distressed the household and caused constant disapproving comment: "But you've got everything turned upside down. You're ruining your health." That is why, in the spring of the year, I thanked my exasperated relatives for their generosity, their burdened patience, and bought a ticket on a Greyhound bus to New Orleans.

There I rented a bedroom in the crowded apartment of a Creole family who lived in the French Quarter on Royal Street. It was a small hot bedroom almost entirely occupied by a brass bed, and it was noisy as a steel mill. Streetcars racketed under the window, and the carousings of sightseers touring the Quarter, the boisterous whiskey brawlings of soldiers and sailors made for continuous pandemonium. Still, sticking to my night schedule, I progressed; by late autumn the book was half finished.

I need not have been as lonely as I was. New Orleans was my hometown and I had many friends there, but because I did not desire that familiar world and preferred to remain sealed off in the self-created universe of Zoo and Jesus Fever and the Cloud Hotel, I called none of my acquaintances. My only company was the Creole family, who were kindly working-class people (the father was a dock hand and his wife a seamstress), or encounters with drugstore clerks and café folk. Curiously, for New Orleans is not that sizable a town, I never saw a soul I knew. Except, by accident, my father. Which was ironic, considering that though I was unaware of it at the time, the central theme of *Other Voices, Other Rooms* was my search for the existence of this essentially imaginary person.

I seldom ate more than once a day, usually when I finished work. At that dawn hour I would walk through the humid, balconied streets, past St. Louis Cathedral and on to the French Market, a square crammed in the murky early morning with the trucks of vegetable farmers, Gulf Coast fishermen, meat vendors and flower growers. It smelled of earth, of herbs and exotic, gingery scents, and it rang, clanged, clogged the ears with the sounds of vivacious trading. I loved it.

The market's chief gathering place was a café that served only bitter-black chicory coffee and the crustiest, most delicious fresh-fried doughnuts. I had discovered the place when I was fifteen, and had become addicted. The proprietor of the café gave all its habitués a nickname; he called me the Jockey, a reference to my height and build. Every morning as I plowed into the coffee and the doughnuts, he would warn me with a sinister chuckle, "Better watch it, Jockey. You'll never make your weight."

It was in this café that five years earlier I'd met the prototype of Cousin Randolph. Actually, Cousin Randolph was suggested by two people. Once, when I was a very young child, I had spent a few summer weeks in an old house in Pass Christian, Mississippi. I don't remember much about it, except that there was an elderly man who lived there, an asthmatic invalid who smoked medicinal cigarettes and made remarkable scrap-quilts. He had been the captain of a fishing trawler, but illness had forced him to retire to a darkened room. His sister had taught him to sew; in consequence, he had found in himself a beautiful gift for designing cloth pictures. I often used to visit his room, where he would spread his tapestry-like quilts on the floor for me to admire: rose bouquets, ships in full sail, a bowl of apples.

The other Randolph, the character's spiritual ancestor, was the man I met in the café, a plump blond fellow who was said to be dying of leukemia. The proprietor called him the Sketcher, for he always sat alone in a corner drawing pictures of the clientele, the truckers and cattlemen, in a large looseleaf notebook. One night it was obvious that I was his subject; after sketching for a while, he moseyed over to the counter where I was sitting and said, "You're a *Wunderkind*, aren't you? I can tell by your hands." I didn't know what it meant—*Wunderkind*; I thought that either he was joking or making a dubious overture. But then he defined the word, and I was pleased: it coincided with my own private opinion. We became friends; afterward I saw him not only at the café, but we also took lazy strolls along the levee. We did not have much conversation, for he was a monologist obsessed with death, betrayed passions and unfulfilled talent.

All this transpired during one summer. That autumn I went to school in the East, and when I returned in June and asked the proprietor about the Sketcher, he said, "Oh, he died. Saw it in the *Picayune*. Did you know he was rich? Uh-huh. Said so in the paper. Turned out his family owned half the land around Lake Pontchartrain. Imagine that. Well, you never know."

The book was completed in a setting far removed from the one in which it was begun. I wandered and worked in North Carolina, Saratoga Springs, New York City and, ultimately, in a rented cottage on Nantucket. It was there at a desk by a window with a view of sky and sand and arriving surf that I wrote the last pages, finishing them with disbelief that the moment had come, a wonder simultaneously regretful and exhilarated.

I am not a keen rereader of my own books: what's done is done. Moreover, I am always afraid of finding that my harsher detractors are correct and that the work is not as good as I choose to think it. Until the subject of the present reissue arose, I never again really examined *Other Voices, Other Rooms*. Last week I read it straight through.

And? And, as I have already indicated, I was startled by its symbolic subterfuges. Also, while there are passages that seem to me accomplishments, others arouse uneasiness. On the whole, though, it was as if I were reading the fresh-minted manuscript of a total stranger. I was impressed by him. For what he had done has the enigmatic shine of a strangely colored prism held to the light—that, and a certain anguished, pleading intensity like the message of a shipwrecked sailor stuffed into a bottle and thrown into the sea.

Ghosts in Sunlight:
The Filming of
In Cold Blood

(1967)

ONE HOT AFTERNOON LAST MARCH IN a courthouse on the high wheat plains of western Kansas, Richard Brooks turned to me, between takes of the movie he was directing, and rather reproachfully asked, "What are you laughing at?"

"Oh, nothing," I said, but the truth was that I'd remembered a long-ago question by Perry Smith, one of the two murderers whose trial was being reenacted here. He had been captured a few days before, and his question was, "Were there any representatives of the cinema there?" I wondered what he would have thought of the present scene: the huge arc lights arranged inside the courtroom where he and Richard Hickock had been tried, the jury box filled with the very same men who had convicted them, the purring generators, whirring cameras, the whispering technicians dancing in and out among thick coils of electric cable.

The first conversation I ever had with Perry Smith was at the beginning of January, 1960. It was a cold day, glittery as an icicle; Smith and I talked together at the sheriff's office in a room where prairie winds pressed against the windows, sucked the glass, rattled it. I was fairly rattled myself, for I had been working for more than a month on a book about the murder of Herbert Clutter and his family, *In Cold Blood*, and unless I could establish close contact with this half-Irish, half-Indian young man, I would have to abandon the project. His court-appointed attorney had persuaded him to speak to me; but it was soon obvious that Smith regretted having granted the interview. He was remote, suspicious, sullenly sleepy-eyed: It took years, hundreds of letters and conversations, before I slipped all the way past this façade. At the moment, nothing I said interested him. He rather arrogantly began to question my credentials. What kind of writer was I, and what had I written? Well, he said, after I'd provided a dossier, he'd never heard of me or any of my books; but—had I written any movies? Yes, one: *Beat the Devil*. Now the sleepy eyes somewhat wakened. "Uh-huh. I remember. Only saw it because Humphrey Bogart was in it. Did you, uh, uh, *know* Bogart? Personally?" When I answered that Bogart had been a close friend of mine, he smiled in the flustered, fragile way I came to know very well. "Bogart," he said, his voice so soft one could scarcely hear it above the wind. "I've always had this thing about him. He was my favorite actor. I saw *Treasure of the Sierra Madre*—oh, over and over. One of the reasons I liked that picture so much was—the old man in it, Walter Huston? that played the crazy gold prospector?—he was just like my father. Tex Smith. *Just* like him. I couldn't get over it. It really hit me." Then he said, "Were you there last night? When they brought us in?"

He was referring to the previous evening when the two handcuffed murderers, escorted by a regiment of state troopers, had arrived by car from Las Vegas, where they were arrested, to be arraigned at the Finney County courthouse in Garden City, Kansas. Hundreds of people had waited for hours in the dark and zero-cold to glimpse them; the crowd, orderly, almost awesomely hushed, had filled the square. The press, too, had been heavily represented by newsmen from all over the West and Midwest; there were also several television crews.

I told him yes, I'd been present—and had minor pneumonia to prove it. Well, he said, he was sorry about that: "Pneumonia is nothing to fool around with. But tell me—I was so scared I couldn't see what was happening. When I saw that crowd, I thought, Jesus, these people are going to tear us limb from limb. To hell with the public hangman. They were going to hang us on the spot. Which maybe wouldn't have been the worst idea. I mean, what's the use of going through this whole ordeal? Trial and everything. It's such a farce. These prairie-billies, they'll hang us in the long run." He chewed his lip; something shy and bashful happened to his face—the aw-gee expression of a kid digging his toe into the ground. "What I wanted to know is—were there any representatives of the cinema there?"

This was typical of Perry—of his pathetic linguistic pretensions (the careful insertion of words like "cinema"), and of the kind of vanity that made him welcome "recognition" regardless of its nature. He tried to disguise it, shrug it off, but nevertheless he was undeniably gratified when I informed him that indeed the event had been recorded by motion-picture cameras.

Now, seven years later, I laughed to myself at the recollection, but I avoided answering Brooks's query because the young men who were playing Perry and Dick were standing nearby, and I felt extremely uneasy in their presence. Self-conscious. I had seen photographs of Robert Blake (Perry) and Scott Wilson (Dick) before they were selected for the roles. But it wasn't until I went to Kansas to follow the progress of the film that I met them. And meeting them, having to be around them, was not an experience I care to repeat. This has nothing to do with my reaction to them as private individuals: they both are sensitive, seriously gifted men. It's simply that despite the clear physical resemblance to the original pair, their photographs had not prepared me for the mesmerizing reality.

Particularly Robert Blake. The first time I saw him I thought a ghost had sauntered in out of the sunshine, slippery-haired and sleepy-eyed. I couldn't accept the idea that this was someone pretending to be Perry, he was Perry—and the sensation I felt was like a free fall down an elevator shaft. Here were the familiar eyes, placed in a familiar face, examining me with the detachment of a stranger. It was as though Perry had been resurrected but was suffering from amnesia and remembered me not at all. Shock, frustration, helplessness—these emotions, combined with impending flu, sent me home to a motel on the outskirts of Garden City. The Wheat Lands Motel, a place I had often stayed during the years I worked on *In Cold Blood.* An accumulated remembrance of those years, the loneliness of the endless wintry nights with forlorn salesmen coughing next door, seized me like a sudden Kansas cyclone and threw me on the bed.

To quote from my day-to-day journal: "Presently passed out, having drunk a pint of Scotch in less than thirty minutes. Woke in the morning with fever, television still going and total lack of knowledge of where I was or why. All unreal because too real, as reality's reflections tend to be. Called Dr. Maxfield, who gave me an injection and several prescriptions. But the trouble is in my mind (?)."

That phrase "reality's reflections" is self-explanatory, but perhaps I ought to clarify my own interpretation of it. Reflected reality is the essence of reality, the truer truth. When I was a child I played a pictorial game. I would, for example, observe a landscape: trees and clouds and horses wandering in grass; then select a detail from the overall vision—say, grass bending in the breeze—and frame it with my hands. Now this detail became the essence of the landscape and caught, in prismatic miniature, the true atmosphere of a panorama too sizable to encompass otherwise. Or if I was in a strange room, and wanted to understand the room and the nature of its inhabitants, I let my eye wander selectively until it discovered something—a shaft of light, a decrepit piano, a pattern in the rug—that seemed of itself to contain the secret. All art is composed of selected detail, either imaginary or, as in *In Cold Blood*, a distillation of reality. As with the book, so with the film—except that I had chosen my details from life, while

Brooks had distilled his from my book: reality twice transposed, and all the truer for it.

As soon as the book was published, many producers and directors expressed a desire to make a film of it. Actually, I had already decided that if a film was to be made, I wanted the writer-director Richard Brooks to act as intermediary between book and screen. Aside from my long-standing respect for his imaginative professionalism, he was the only director who agreed with—and was willing to risk—my own concept of how the book should be transferred to film. He was the one person who entirely accepted two important points: I wanted the film made in black and white, and I wanted it played by a cast of unknowns—that is, actors without "public" faces. Although Brooks and I have different sensibilities, we both wanted the film to duplicate reality, to have the actors resemble their prototypes as much as possible, and to have every scene filmed in its real locale: the house of the murdered Clutter family; the same Kansas variety store where Perry and Dick bought the rope and tape used to bind their four victims; and certain courthouses, prisons, filling stations, hotel rooms and highways and city streets—all those places that they had seen in the course of their crime and its aftermath. A complicated procedure, but the only possible one by which almost all elements of fantasy could be removed and reality thereby achieve its proper reflection.

I felt this particularly strongly when Brooks and I went into the Clutter house while Brooks was preparing to film the murder sequence. To quote from my journal again: "Spent the afternoon at the Clutter farm. A curious experience to find myself once more in this house where I have so often been, and heretofore under such silent circumstances: the silent house, the plain rooms, the hardwood floors that echo every footstep, the windows that look out on solemn prairies and fields tawny with wheat stubble. No one has really lived there since the murders. The property was bought by a Texan who farms the land, and who has a son who occasionally stays there. Certainly it has not gone to ruin; nevertheless it seems abandoned, a scarecrow without crows to frighten. The present owner gave Brooks permission to film there; a considerable amount of the original furniture was still on hand, and Brooks's chief assistant, Tom Shaw, has done an extraordinary job of tracking down and retrieving the departed pieces. The rooms looked precisely the same as they had when I examined them in December, 1959—that is, soon after the crime was discovered. Mr. Clutter's Stetson hanging on a wall hat rack. Nancy's sheet music open at the piano. Her brother's spectacles resting on a bureau, the lenses shimmering in sunlight.

"But it was the Venetian blinds that I noticed—that I, as it were, 'framed.' The blinds cover the windows of Mr. Clutter's office, the room by which the murderers entered the house. Upon entering, Dick had parted the Venetian slats and peered through them to see if any witnesses were lurking in the moonlit night; again, on departing, and after the immense noise of the shootings, Dick's eyes had explored the landscape through the slats, his heart pounding for fear that the crash of four shotgun blasts might have roused the countryside. And now the actor who is impersonating Dick, and who is so uncannily like Dick, is on the verge of repeating these actions. Yet eight years have passed, the Clutter family are gone and Dick is dead, but the Venetian blinds still exist, still hang at the same windows. Thus reality, via an object, extends itself into art; and that is what is original and disturbing about this film: reality and art are intertwined to the point that there is no identifiable area of demarcation.

"Almost the whole of the murder sequence is being photographed in total darkness—except for the use of flashlights. This has never been done before, because ordinarily a flashlight is incapable of producing light sufficiently powerful to register a scene without the aid of extra illumination. In the present case, however, the production's technicians have invented flashlights fixed with special batteries that generate solid shafts of white blaze—extremely effective as the beams wander in the darkness, crossing and crisscrossing.

"Brooks's attention to detail can occasionally be comic. Today he noticed that between takes inside the Clutter house several of the crew were smoking cigarettes. Suddenly he clapped his hands and shouted, 'All right! Cut that out! Mr. Clutter never allowed anyone to smoke in this house, so I'm not going to allow it either.' "

Presently undermined by flu and the strain of reliving painful events, I left Brooks and his company to get on with their work free of my critical surveillance. No director can abide an author staring over his shoulder; and, agreeable as our relationship was, I sensed that Brooks felt my presence made everyone edgy, himself included. He was not unhappy to see me go.

Returning to New York, I was surprised to find that few people asked me how the film was progressing. Rather, they were curious to know what the reaction of the townspeople was to the fact of the film's being made in their midst: Was the atmosphere antagonistic? Cooperative? What? To answer the question, I have to refer to my own experiences during the years I spent roaming around Finney County, accumulating material.

When I arrived there in 1959 I knew no one, and no one, except the local librarian and several schoolteachers, had ever heard of me. As it happened, the first person I interviewed turned out to be the only genuine enemy I made there—at least the only one both openly and covertly hostile (a contradiction in terms, but nevertheless accurate). This fellow was, and is, the editor of the local daily paper, the Garden City *Telegram*, and therefore in a position to constantly publicize his belligerent attitude toward me and the work I was attempting to do. His columns are signed Bill Brown, and he is as plain as his name: a thin, rumpled man with mud-colored eyes and a beige complexion. Of course, I understood his resentment, and at first sympathized with it: here was this "New York" writer, as he often drawlingly described me, invading his terrain and presuming to write a book about a "sordid" subject that was best swept away and forgotten. His continuous theme was: "We want to forget our tragedy, but this New York writer isn't going to let us." Therefore, it came as no surprise when Brown started a campaign to prevent Brooks from filming the Kansas scenes in Garden City and Holcomb. Now his theme was that the advent of these "Hollywood people" would attract "undesirable elements," and everything in Finney County would go to hell. Huffed and puffed, did Mr. Brown, but his efforts failed. For the simple reason that most of the people I met in western Kansas are reasonable and helpful; I couldn't have survived if it hadn't been for their consistent kindness, and I made friends among them that will last a lifetime.

That was in March of last year. In September, I traveled to California to see a rough cut of the finished film. On arrival, I had a meeting with Brooks, who was screening the picture for me the following day. Brooks is a very secretive man; he hoards his scripts, locks them up at night and never lets anyone read a complete version. Shooting on *In Cold Blood* had ended in June, and since that time Brooks had worked only with a cutter and a projectionist, not allowing anyone else to view a foot of the film. As we talked he seemed under the kind of whitened strain one does not associate with so assertive and vigorous a man. "Of course I'm nervous," he said. "Why shouldn't I be? It's *your* book—and suppose you don't like it?"

And suppose you don't like it? Excellent question; and, strangely, one I'd never asked myself, principally because I had chosen the ingredients, and I always have faith in my own judgment.

The next day, when I arrived at Columbia studios around noon, Brooks was even more nervous. My God, he was glum! He said, "I've had some rough moments with this picture. But today's the roughest." On that note we walked into the screening room, and the sensation was not unlike entering a death cell.

Brooks picked up a telephone connected with the projectionist's booth. "All right. Let's go."

The lights dimmed. The white screen turned into a highway at twilight: Route 50 winding under draining skies through a countryside empty as a cornhusk, woebegone as wet leaves. In the far horizon a silvery Greyhound bus appears, enlarges as it hummingly approaches, streaks by. Music: solitary guitar. Now the credits start as the image changes, dissolves into the Greyhound's interior. Slumber hangs heavily. Only a weary little girl roams the aisle, gradually wandering toward the darkened rear, lured there by the lonely, disconnected plunk-plunk-plunk of a guitar. She finds the player, but we do not see him; she says something to him, but we cannot quite hear what it is. The guitarist strikes a match to light a cigarette, and the flame partially illuminates his face—Perry's face, Perry's eyes, sleepy, remote. Dissolve to Dick, then to Dick and Perry in Kansas City, then to Holcomb, and Herbert Clutter breakfasting on the final day of his life, then back to his future executioners: the contrapuntal technique I used in writing the book.

The scenes move with striking fluidity, but I am increasingly gripped by a sense of loss; and a ring forms around my heart, like the frosty haze around a harvest moon. Not because of what is on the screen, which is fine, but because of what isn't. Why has such-and-such been omitted? Where is Bobby Rupp? Susan Kidwell? The postmistress and her mother? In the midst of my dilemma of not being able to concentrate appreciatively on what was there because of what wasn't, the film caught fire—literally. One could see the tiny fire burning on the screen, a zipper of flame that separated the images and crisped them. In the silence following the abrupt halt, Brooks said, "Nothing serious. Just an accident. It's happened before. We'll have it fixed in a minute."

A lucky accident, for during the time it took the projectionist to repair the damage and resume the screening, I managed to resolve the quarrel I was having with myself. Look, an inner voice said, you're being unrealistic, unfair. This picture is two hours long, and that is as long as it can reasonably be. If Brooks included everything you would like to have shown, every nuance you're grieving over, it would last nine hours! So stop worrying. Watch it for what it is: judge from that.

I did, and it was like swimming into a familiar sea only to be surprised by a muscular wave of sinister height, trapped in a hurtling current that carried me downward to ocean-floor depths, escorted me, pummeled raw and groggy, onto a beach uniquely desolate—not, unfortunately, the victim of a bad dream, or of "just a movie," but of reality.

The screen returned to its pristine state; overhead lighting resumed. But again, as in the motel room in Garden City, I seemed to wake up not knowing where I was. A man was sitting near me. Who was he, and why did he look at me so intently, as if expecting me to say something? Ah, Brooks. Finally I said, "By the way, thank you."

The
White Rose

(1970)

A SILVERY JUNE AFTERNOON. A JUNE afternoon in Paris twenty-three years ago. And I am standing in the courtyard of the Palais Royal scanning its tall windows and wondering which of them belong to the apartment of Colette, the *Grande Mademoiselle* of French letters. And I keep consulting my watch, for at four o'clock I have an appointment with this legendary artist, an invitation to tea obligingly obtained for me by Jean Cocteau after I had told him, with youthful maladroitness, that Colette was the only living French writer I entirely respected—and *that* included Gide, Genet, Camus and Montherlant, not to mention M. Cocteau. Certainly, without the generous intervention of the latter, I would never have been invited to meet the great woman, for I was merely a young American writer who had published a single book, *Other Voices, Other Rooms,* of which she had never heard at all.

Now it was four o'clock and I hastened to present myself, for I'd been told not to be late, and not to stay long, as my hostess was an elderly partial invalid who seldom left her bed.

She received me in her bedroom. I was astonished. Because she looked precisely as Colette ought to have looked. And that was astonishing indeed. Reddish, frizzly, rather African-looking hair; slanting, alley-cat eyes rimmed with kohl; a finely made face flexible as water . . . rouged cheeks . . . lips thin and tense as wire but painted a really brazen hussy scarlet.

628

And the room reflected the cloistered luxury of her worldlier work—say, *Chéri* and *La fin de Chéri*. Velvet curtains were drawn against the June light. One was aware of silken walls. Of warm, rosy light filtering out of lamps draped with pale, rosy scarves. A perfume—some combination of roses and oranges and limes and musk—hovered in the air like a mist, a haze.

So there she lay, propped up by layers of lace-edged pillows, her eyes liquid with life, with kindness, with malice. A cat of peculiar gray was stretched across her legs, rather like an additional comforter.

But the most stunning display in the room was neither the cat nor its mistress. Shyness, nerves, I don't know what it was, but after the first quick study I couldn't really look at Colette, and was somewhat tongue-tied to boot. Instead, I concentrated on what seemed to me a magical exhibition, some fragment of a dream. It was a collection of antique crystal paper-weights.

There were perhaps a hundred of them covering two tables situated on either side of the bed: crystal spheres imprisoning green lizards, salamanders, *millefiori* bouquets, dragonflies, a basket of pears, butterflies alighted on a frond of fern, swirls of pink and white and blue and white, shimmering like fireworks, cobras coiled to strike, pretty little arrangements of pansies, magnificent poinsettias.

At last Madame Colette said, "Ah, I see my snowflakes interest you?"

Yes, I knew what she meant: these objects were rather like permanent snowflakes, dazzling patterns frozen forever. "Yes," I said. "Beautiful. Beautiful. But what are they?"

She explained that they were the utmost refinement of the crystal-maker's art: glass jewels contrived by the premier craftsmen of the greatest French crystal factories—Baccarat and St. Louis and Clichy. Selecting at random one of the weights, a big beauty exploding with thousand-flower colors, she showed where the date of creation, 1842, was concealed inside one of the tiny buds. "All the finest weights," she told me, "were made between 1840 and 1880. After that the whole art disintegrated. I started collecting them about forty years ago. They were out of fashion then and one could find great prizes in the flea market and pay very little for them. Now, of course, a first-class weight costs the earth. There are hundreds of collectors, and all in all only perhaps three or four thousand weights in existence worth a glance. This one, for instance." She handed me a piece of crystal about the size of a baseball. "It's a Baccarat weight. It's called the White Rose."

It was a faceted weight of marvelous, bubble-free purity with a single decoration: a simple white rose with green leaves sunk dead-center.

"What does it remind you of? What thoughts run through your mind?" Madame Colette asked me.

"I don't know. I like the way it feels. Cool and peaceful."

"Peaceful. Yes, that's very true. I've often thought I would like to carry them with me in my coffin, like a pharaoh. But what *images* occur to you?"

I turned the weight this way and that in the dim, rosy light. "Young girls in their communion dresses."

She smiled. "Very charming. Very apt. Now I can see what Jean told me is true. He said. 'Don't be fooled, my dear. He looks like a ten-year-old angel. But he's ageless, and has a very wicked mind.' "

But not as wicked as my hostess, who tapped the weight in my hand and said, "Now I want you to keep that. As a souvenir."

By so doing she arranged for a financially ruinous destiny, for from that moment I became a "collector," and over the years have done arduous duty searching out fine French weights everywhere, from the opulent sales-rooms at Sotheby's to obscure antiquaries in Copenhagen and Hong Kong. It is an expensive pastime (currently the cost of these *objets*, depending on quality and rarity, runs between $600 and $15,000), and in all the while that I have pursued it I have found only two bargains, but these both were staggering coups and more than compensated for many cruel disappoint-ments.

The first was in a huge and dusty junkshop in Brooklyn. I was looking at a bunch of odds and bits in a dark glass cabinet when I saw a St. Louis flower weight with a tomato-colored porcelain overlay. When I sought out the proprietor and asked him about it, it was obvious he had no idea of what it was or what it was worth, which was about $4,000. He sold it to me for $20, and I did feel slightly crooked, but what the hell, it was the first and last time I ever got the best of a dealer.

My second great coup was at an auction in East Hampton on Long Island. I just happened to wander into it, not expecting much, and indeed it was mostly bad paintings and indifferent furniture culled from an old Long Island sea house. But suddenly, just sitting there amid a lot of pottery and boring plates was an electrifying spectacle: an absolutely spectacular *millefiori* weight made in the form of an inkwell. I knew it was the real thing, and by searching carefully I found the date, 1840, and signature of the maker, J.C., deep inside the lower bouquet. It was about eleven o'clock in the morning when I made this discovery, and the inkwell did not appear on the auctioneer's podium until three that afternoon. While waiting, I walked around in a daze of anxiety, wondering if the auctioneer or any of his customers had any notion of the inkwell's rarity and value, which was enough to finance a pair of Siamese twins through college. If all this sounds rather unattractive, and I suppose it does, I can only say that that's what collecting does to you.

Anyway, the auctioneer opened the bidding on the inkwell-weight at $25, so I knew right away *he* didn't know what he was selling; the question was, did anyone in the audience? There were perhaps three hundred people there, a great many of them with very sophisticated eyes. As it turned out, there *was* one who had an inkling: a young dealer from New York who had come to bid on furniture and knew very little about paperweights, but was shrewd enough to realize this was something special. When we reached $300 the others in the auditorium began to whisper and stare; they couldn't fathom what it was that made this hunk of glass worth that kind of money. When we arrived at $600 the auctioneer was fairly excited himself, and my rival was sweating; he was having second thoughts, he wasn't really sure. In a faltering voice he bid $650 and I said $700, and that finished him. Afterward he came over and asked if I thought it worth $700, and I said, "No, seven thousand."

Some people, when traveling, carry with them photographs of friends and family, of loves; I do, too. But I also take along a small black bag that will hold six weights, each wrapped in flannel, for the weights, despite their seeming solidity, are quite fragile, and also, like a crowd of quarrelsome siblings, inimical; one of the easiest ways to chip or shatter a weight is to have it collide with another. So why do I cart them around on, say, a two-day trip to Chicago or Los Angeles? Because, when spread about, they can for me make the most sinisterly anonymous hotel room seem warm and personal and secure. And because, when it's a quarter to two and sleep hasn't come, a restfulness arises from contemplating a quiet white rose until the rose expands into the whiteness of sleep.

Occasionally I have given a weight as a gift to some very particular friend, and always it is from among those I treasure most, for as Colette said that long-ago afternoon, when I protested that I couldn't accept as a present something she so clearly adored, "My dear, really there is no point in giving a gift unless one also treasures it oneself."

Self-Portrait

(1972)

Q: IF YOU HAD TO LIVE IN JUST ONE place—without ever leaving—where would it be?

: Oh, dear. What a devastating notion. To be grounded in just one place. fter all, for thirty years I've lived everywhere and had houses all over the orld. But curiously, no matter where I lived, Spain or Italy or Switzernd, Hong King or California, Kansas or London, I *always* kept an artment in New York. That must signify something. So, if really forced choose, I'd say New York.

: But *why?* It's dirty. Dangerous. In every way difficult.

: Hmmm. Yes. But though I can live for long stretches in mountainous r seaside solitude, primarily I am a city fellow. I like *pavement*. The sound f my shoes on pavement; stuffed windows; all-night restaurants; sirens in e night—sinister but alive; book and record shops that, on impulse, you an visit at midnight.

And in that sense, New York is the world's only city *city*. Rome is noisy d provincial. Paris is sullen, insular, and, odd to say, extraordinarily uritanical. London? All my American friends who have gone to live there ore one so by saying, "But it's so civilized." I don't know. To be totally ead, utterly dull—is that civilized? And to top it all, London is also highly rovincial. The same people see the same people. Everybody knows your usiness. At most, it is only possible to lead *two* separate lives there.

And that is the great advantage of New York, why it is *the* city. One can be a multiple person there: ten different people with ten different sets of friends, none overlapping.

Q: Do you prefer animals to people?

A: I like them about equally. Still, I've usually found there is something secretively cruel about people who really feel more warmly toward dogs and cats and horses than people.

Q: Are *you* cruel?

A: Occasionally. In conversation. Let's put it this way: I'd rather be a friend of mine than an enemy.

Q: Do you have many friends?

A: About seven or so whom I can entirely rely upon. And about twenty more I more or less trust.

Q: What qualities do you look for in friends?

A: Firstly, they mustn't be stupid. I've once or twice been in love with persons who were stupid, indeed very much so; but that is another matter —one can be in love with someone without feeling the least in communication with that person. God, that's how most people get married and why most marriages are unhappy.

Usually, I can tell quite early on whether it is possible for someone and myself to be friends. Because one doesn't have to finish sentences. I mean, you start to say something, then realize, midway, that he or she has already understood. It is a form of mental-emotional conversational shorthand.

Intelligence apart, attention is important: I pay attention to my friends, am concerned about them, and expect the same in return.

Q: Are you often disappointed by a friend?

A: Not really. I've sometimes formed dubious attachments (don't we all?); I've always done it with my eyes open. The only hurt that hurts is one that takes you by surprise. I am seldom surprised. Though I have a few times been outraged.

Q: Are you a truthful person?

A: As a writer—yes, I think so. Privately—well, that is a matter of opinion; some of my friends think that when relating an event or piece of news, I am inclined to alter and overelaborate. Myself, I just call it making something "come alive." In other words, a form of art. Art and truth are not necessarily compatible bedfellows.

Q: How do you like best to occupy your spare time?

A: Not sexually, though I have had my enthusiastic periods. But, as more than a casual pastime, it is too heart-scalding and costly, however you interpret the latter adjective.

Really, I like to read. Always have. There are not many contemporary writers I like too well. Though I have admired, among our own Americans, the late Flannery O'Connor, and Norman Mailer, William Styron,

633

Eudora Welty, Katherine Anne Porter, the early Salinger. And oh, really, a number of others. I've never liked Gore Vidal's fiction, but I think his nonfiction is first-class. James Baldwin, ditto. But for the last decade or so I prefer to read writers I've already read. Proven wine. Proust. Flaubert. Jane Austen. Raymond Chandler (one of the *great* American artists). Dickens (I had read all of Dickens before I was sixteen, and have just now completed the full cycle again).

I am partial to films, too—though I leave in the middle quite a lot. But I only like to go to films alone, and only in the daytime when the theater is mostly empty. That way I can concentrate on what I'm seeing, and depart when I feel like it without having to discuss the merits of the project with someone else: with me, such discussions always lead to argument and irritation.

I prefer to work in the mornings, usually for about four or five hours, and then, if I'm alone in a city, any city, I meet a friend for lunch at some favorite restaurant (in New York: Lafayette, La Côte Basque, Orsini's, the Oak Room at The Plaza, and, until its unhappy demise, the Colony). Many people say they hate to lunch; it fattens them, fatigues them, altogether spoils their day. It makes mine. There are some men I enjoy lunching with, but by and large I prefer beautiful, or at least extremely attractive, alert, and *au courant* women. I count in this category several very young ladies (Lally Weymouth, Amanda Burden, Penelope Tree, Louise Melhado—the latter, alas, married to a very square stockbroker). But I don't consider that any woman deserves full marks until she attains and maintains qualities of style and appearance and amusing good sense beyond the point of easy youthful beguilement: this, a partial list, and a prejudicial one, would have to include Barbara Paley, Gloria Guinness, Lee Radziwill, Oona Chaplin, Gloria Cooper, Slim Keith, Phyllis Cerf, Kay Meehan, Viola Loewy, D. D. Ryan, Evelyn Avedon, Pamela Harriman, Kay Graham—well, one could go on for quite a while, though certainly the names would not top fifty. Notice, the persons I mention are private citizens, not public; after all, for certain public characters—Garbo (an ultimately selfish and tiresome woman) or Elizabeth Taylor (a sensitive, self-educated lady with a tough but essentially innocent attitude—if you sleep with a guy, gosh, that means you have to marry him!)—*allure* is their trade.

Though I know I'm supposed to be very sociable, and though some of the above statements would seem to testify to that, I like to be alone. I like fast, finely made cars, I like lonely motels with their ice machines and eerie anonymity; so sometimes I get behind the wheel and, without warning, without particular destination, drive all alone as far as a thousand miles. I've only once consulted a psychiatrist; instead, I should have gone for a drive with the top down and a wind blowing and a sun shining.

Q: Of what are you most afraid?

A: Not death. Well, I don't want to *suffer*. But if one night I went to sleep and failed to wake, that thought doesn't trouble me much. At least it would be something different. In 1966 I was nearly killed in an auto accident—was flung through the windshield head-on, and though seriously wounded and certain that what Henry James called The Distinguished Thing (death) was nearby, lay fully conscious in pools of blood reciting to myself the telephone numbers of various friends. Since then, I've had a cancer operation, and the only altogether upsetting part was that I had to loiter around an aimless week between the day of diagnosis and the morning of the knives.

Anyway, it strikes me as absurd and rather obscene, this whole cosmetic and medical industry based on lust for youth, age-fear, death-terror. Who the hell wants to live forever? Most of us, apparently; but it's idiotic. After all, there *is* such a thing as life-saturation: the point when everything is pure effort and total repetition.

Poverty? Fanny Brice said, "I've been rich and I've been poor. Believe me, rich is better." Well, I disagree; at least I don't think money makes any ultimate difference to anyone's personal adjustment or (moronic word) "happiness." I know very well a considerable number of very rich people (I don't count anyone rich who can't quite quickly summon up fifty million dollars in hard currency); and there are some who say, when feeling in a bitchy mood, that I don't know anybody else (to which one can best reply, at least they sometimes pick up the check, and never ask for a loan). But the point is: I can't think of a single rich person who, in terms of contentment, or a lessening of the general human anxiety, has it easier than the rest of us. As for me, I can accept it either way: a furnished room on some side street in Detroit or Cole Porter's old apartment in the Waldorf Towers, which the decorator Billy Baldwin transformed into such an island of sublime and subtle luxury. What I couldn't survive is the middle ground: the sound of lawn mowers and water sprinklers outside a two-car-garage ranch split-level in Scarsdale or Shaker Heights. Well, I never said I wasn't a snob. I only said I wasn't afraid of being poor.

Failure? Failure is the condiment that gives success its flavor. No, I've drunk that special hemlock, bit that bullet (especially working in the theater) enough to now scorn it. Honestly, I don't give a damn what anybody says about me, either privately or in print. Of course, that was not true when I was young and first began to publish. And it is not true now on one count—a betrayal of affection can still traumatically disturb me. Otherwise, defeat and criticism are matters of indifference, remote as the mountains of the moon.

Q: Then what does frighten you?

A: The thought that I might lose my sense of humor. Become a mind without a soul, start down the path to madness, and thereby, as the Zen riddle runs, spend the rest of a ruined life listening to the sound of one hand clapping.

Q: What shocks you? If anything?

A: Deliberate cruelty. Cruelty for its own sake, verbal or physical. Murder. Capital punishment. Child-beaters. Animal-baiters.

Once, long ago, I discovered that my best friend, aged eighteen, was having a fully realized love affair with his stepmother. At the time I was shocked; needless to add, I'm not now, and thinking back, can see that it was probably a positive benefit to them both. Since then, I've never been surprised, not to say shocked, by any sexual-moral arrangement. If so, I'd have to lead the parade of our nation's million-upon-million hypocrites.

Q: It is now six years since you published *In Cold Blood*. What have you been working on since then?

A: Published as a book a long short story, "The Thanksgiving Visitor." Collaborated on a film, *Trilogy*, based on three of my short stories ("A Christmas Memory," "Miriam," "Among the Paths to Eden"); made a documentary film about capital punishment, *Death Row U.S.A.*, which was commissioned by ABC but never shown in this country (others, yes; Canada, for one) for reasons still mysterious and unexplained. Have also recently completed a screenplay of Fitzgerald's *The Great Gatsby*—a nearly perfect short novel (or, really, long short story), but hell to dramatize because it consists almost entirely of long-ago exposition and, as it were, offstage scenes. Personally, I like my adaptation, but the producers, Paramount Pictures, are of a different opinion; my pity to whoever attempts a rewrite.

It took five years to write *In Cold Blood*, and a year to recover—*if* recovery is the word; not a day passes that some aspect of that experience doesn't shadow my mind.

However, prior to beginning *In Cold Blood*, in fact soon after finishing *Breakfast at Tiffany's* in 1957, I began to prepare the notes and structure for an ambitious novel then entitled, and entitled now, *Answered Prayers*, which derives from a remark of St. Theresa's: "More tears are shed over answered prayers than unanswered ones." I think that's true: no matter what desires are requited, they are always replaced by another. It's like those racing greyhounds and the mechanical rabbit—one can never catch it. It makes for the worst and best in life. I remember a friend at Robert Kennedy's funeral, someone very close to him, and she said: "It was such a hot day. Sweltering. And there was the grave waiting in the grass under this great cool green tree. And suddenly I envied him. Envied him all that green peacefulness. I thought, Bless you, Bobby, you don't have to fight anymore. You're safe."

Answered Prayers is complicated technically and much the longest work I've done—indeed, triple the length of all my other books combined.

During the past year or so I've been under great pressure to finish it; but literature has its own life, and insists on dancing to its own measure. *Answered Prayers* is like a wheel with a dozen spokes; the fuel that spins the wheel is an extraordinary young woman who has had fifty affairs, could have married virtually anyone, but for twelve years has loved an "older" man who can't marry because he is married, and *won't* divorce because he expects, with reasonable cause, to be the next President of the United States.

q: If you hadn't decided on writing, a creative life, what would you have done?

a: Become a lawyer. I often considered it, and many lawyers, including one attorney general and a Supreme Court justice, have told me I would have made a first-class trial lawyer, though my voice, often described as "high and childish" (*among* other things), might have been a detriment.

Also, I wouldn't have minded being kept, but no one has ever wanted to keep me—not more than a week or so.

q: Do you take any form of exercise?

a: Yes. Massage.

q: Can you cook?

a: Not for company. For myself, I always dish up the same cuisine. Crackers and cream of tomato soup. Or a baked potato stuffed with fresh caviar.

q: If *Reader's Digest* ever commissioned from you an "Unforgettable Character" article, whom would you write about?

a: God forbid that such a degrading assignment should ever come my way. But if it did—ahem, let's see. Robert Frost, America's Poet Laureate, was fairly memorable. An old bastard, if ever there was one. I met him when I was eighteen; apparently he didn't consider me a sufficiently humble worshiper at the altar of his ego. Anyway, by writing a scurrilous letter to Harold Ross, the late editor of *The New Yorker*, where I was then employed, he got me fired from my first and last time-clock job. Perhaps he did me a favor; because then I sat down and wrote my first book, *Other Voices, Other Rooms*.

As a child, I lived until I was ten or so with an elderly spinster relative in a rural, remote part of Alabama. Miss Sook Faulk. She herself was not more than twelve years old mentally, which is what accounted for her purity, timidity, her strange, unexpected wisdom. I have written two stories about her, "A Christmas Memory" and "The Thanksgiving Visitor"—both of which were filmed for television with Geraldine Page portraying Miss Faulk with an uncanny beauty and accuracy.

Miss Page is rather unforgettable, come to consider: a Jekyll and Hyde; Dr. Jekyll on stage, Mr. Hyde off. It is purely a matter of appearance; she has better legs than Dietrich and as an actress can project an illusion of infinite allure—but in private she insists, Lord knows why, in disguising herself under witchlike wigs and costumes of consummate eccentricity.

Of course, I don't care much for actresses *or* actors. A friend, I can't remember just now who, said, "All actresses are more than women, and all actors are less than men. A half-true observation; still, true enough to be, in my opinion, the root cause of the prevailing theatrical neurosis. But the trouble with most actors (*and* actresses) is that they are dumb. And, in many instances, the dumbest are the most gifted. Sir John Gielgud, the kindest man alive, an incomparable technician, brilliant voice; but, alas, all his brains are in his voice. Marlon Brando. No actor of my generation possesses greater natural gifts; but none other has transported intellectual falsity to higher levels of hilarious pretension. Except, perhaps, Bob Dylan: a sophisticated musical (?) con man pretending to be a simple-hearted (?) revolutionary but sentimental hillbilly.

But enough of this question. It was stupid to start with.

Q: What is the most hopeful word in any language?

A: Love.

Q: And the most dangerous?

A: Love.

Q: Have you ever wanted to kill anybody?

A: Haven't you? No? Cross your heart? Well, I still don't believe you. Everybody at one time or another has wanted to kill someone. The true reason why many people commit suicide is because they are cowards who prefer to murder themselves rather than murder their tormentor. As for me, if desire had ever been transferred into action, I'd be right up there with Jack the Ripper. Anyway, it's amusing to think about: the plotting, the planning, the surprise and regret imprinting the face of the villain-turned-victim. Very relaxing. Better than counting sheep.

Not long ago my doctor suggested that I adopt some healthier hobby other than wine-tasting and fornication. He asked if I could think of anything. I said, "Yes, murder." He laughed, we both did, except I wasn't laughing. Poor man, little did he know what a painful and perfect demise I'd planned for him when, after eight days abed with something closely resembling black cholera, he still refused to pay me a house call.

Q: What are your political interests?

A: I've known a few politicians whom I liked, and a more surrealist montage could not be imagined. Adlai Stevenson was a friend, and always a generous one; we were staying as guests in the same house when he died, and I remember watching a manservant pack his belongings, and then, when the suitcases were so pathetically filled, but still unclosed, I walked in and helped myself to one of his ties—a sort of sentimental theft, because the night before I'd complimented him on the tie and he'd promised to give it to me. On the other hand, I like Ronald Reagan, too. Many of my friends think I'm teasing them when I say that. I'm not. Though Governor Stevenson and Governor Reagan are quite different spirits, the latter shares with the former a modesty, an "I'm looking you in the eye and I mean what I say" directness that is rare enough among us folk, not to mention politicians. I suppose New York's Senator Jacob Javits and Governor Reagan, for purely reflex reasons, feel antipathetical toward each other. Actually, I think they would get along fine, and would make an interesting political combination. (Of course, the real reason I always speak well of Governor Reagan and Senator Javits is that I like both their wives, though they are even less alike than their husbands, Mrs. Javits being a lacquered but still untamed city urchin, a smoochy-voiced and sexy-eyed child-woman with a vocabulary as fresh and salty and Brooklyn-bred as the waves that spank the beaches at Coney Island. As for Mrs. Reagan—I don't know, there is about her something so small-town American and nostalgia-making: the homecoming queen riding past on a throne of roses.)

The two politicians I've known best were President Kennedy and his brother Robert. They, too, were quite unalike, and not as close as generally believed; at any rate, the younger brother was very much afraid of the elder—

Q: Do we really have to hear *any* more about *any* Kennedy? Moreover, you're sidestepping the question, which wasn't about politicians but your own interest in politics.

A: I have none. I've never voted. Though, if invited, I suppose I might join almost anyone's protest parade: Antiwar, Free Angela, Gay Liberation, Ladies' Lib, etc.

Q: If you could be anything, what would you most like to be?

A: Invisible. To be visible or invisible at will. I mean, think of the possibilities: the power, the riches, the constant erotic amusement.

Q: What are your chief vices? And virtues?

A: I have no vices. The concept doesn't exist in my vocabulary. My chief virtue is gratitude. So far as I know, I've never betrayed anyone who was kind to me. But as art is life's compensation for the flawed delights of living, I reserve my greatest gratitude for those poets, painters, composers who have compensated me most. A work of art is the one mystery, the one extreme magic; everything else is either arithmetic or biology. I think I understand a considerable lot about writing; nevertheless, when I read something good, in fact, a work of art, my senses sail away into a universe of wonder: How did he do it? How is it possible?

Q: Looking back, it would seem as though some of your answers are rather inconsistent. Deliberate cruelty, you say, is the one unforgivable sin. Then you confess to occasional verbal cruelty, and later on admit that you have contemplated prepared murder.

A: Anyone consistently consistent has a head made of biscuit. My head, the interior, may be made of something odd, but it isn't biscuit.

Q: Suppose you were drowning. What images, in the classic tradition, do you envision rolling across your mind?

A: A hot Alabama day in, oh, 1932, so I must be eight, and I am in a vegetable garden humming with bees and heat waves, and I am picking and putting into a basket turnips and slushy scarlet tomatoes. Then I am running through a pine and honeysuckle woods toward a deep cool creek, where I bathe and wash the turnips, the tomatoes. Birds, bird-music, leaf-light, the stringent taste of raw turnip on my tongue: pleasures everlasting, hallelujah. Not far away a snake, a cottonmouth moccasin, writhes, ripples across the water; I'm not afraid of it.

Ten years later. New York. A wartime jazz joint on West 52nd Street: The Famous Door. Featuring my most beloved American singer—then, now, forever: Miss Billie Holiday. *Lady Day.* Billie, an orchid in her hair, her drug-dimmed eyes shifting in the cheap lavender light, her mouth twisting out the words: *Good mornin', Heartache—You're here again to stay—*

June, 1947. Paris. Having a *fine l'eau* at a sidewalk café with Albert Camus, who tells me I must learn to be less sensitive to criticism. (Ah! If he could have lived to see me now.)

Standing at the window of a *pension* on a Mediterranean island watching the afternoon passenger boat arrive from the mainland. Suddenly, there on the wharf carrying a suitcase is someone I know. Very well. Someone who had said good-bye to me, in what I took to be final tones, not many days prior. Someone who had apparently had a change of mind. So: is it the real turtle soup?—or only the mock? Or is it at long last love? (It was.)

A young man with black cowlicked hair. He is wearing a leather harness that keeps his arms strapped to his sides. He is trembling; but he is speaking to me, smiling. All I can hear is the roar of blood in my ears. Twenty minutes later he is dead, hanging from the end of a rope.

Two years later. Driving down from the April snows of the Alps into the valleys of an Italian spring.

Visiting, at Père-Lachaise in Paris, the grave of Oscar Wilde—overshadowed by Epstein's rather awkward rendition of an angel; I don't think Oscar would have cared for it much.

Paris. January, 1966. The Ritz. An unusual friend comes to call, bringing as gifts masses of white lilac and a baby owl in a cage. The owl, it seems, must be fed live mice. A waiter at the Ritz very kindly sent it to live with his farm-family in Provence.

Oh, but now the mental slides are moving very fast. The waves are closing over. Picking apples on an autumn afternoon. Nursing to life a bulldog puppy ill-to-death with distemper. And she lives. A garden in the

California desert. The surf-sound of wind in the palm trees. A face, close by. Is it the Taj Mahal I see? Or merely Asbury Park? Or is it at long last love? (It wasn't—God no, was it ever not.)

Suddenly, everything is again spinning backward; my friend Miss Faulk is making a scrap-quilt, the design is of roses and grapes, and now she is drawing the quilt up to my chin. There is a kerosene lamp by the bed; she wishes me happy birthday, and blows out the light.

And at midnight when the church-bell chimes I'm eight.

Once more, the creek. The taste of raw turnip on my tongue, the flow of summer water embracing my nakedness. And there, *just* there, swiveling, tangoing on the sun-dappled surface, the exquisitely limber and lethal cottonmouth moccasin. But I'm not afraid; am I?

Preface to
The Dogs Bark

(1973)

IT MUST HAVE BEEN THE SPRING OF 1950 or 1951, since I have lost my notebooks detailing those two years. It was a warm day late in February, which is high spring in Sicily, and I was talking to a very old man with a mongolian face who was wearing a black velvet Borsalino and, disregarding the balmy, almond-blossom-scented weather, a thick black cape.

The old man was André Gide, and we were seated together on a sea wall overlooking shifting fire-blue depths of ancient water.

The postman passed by. A friend of mine, he handed me several letters, one of them containing a literary article rather unfriendly toward me (had it been friendly, of course no one would have sent it).

After listening to me grouse a bit about the piece, and the unwholesome nature of the critical mind in general, the great French master hunched, lowered his shoulders like a wise old . . . shall we say buzzard?, and said, "Ah, well. Keep in mind an Arab proverb: 'The dogs bark, but the caravan moves on.'"

I've often remembered that remark—occasionally in a gaga romantic way, thinking of myself as a planet wanderer, a Sahara tourist approaching through darkness desert tents and desert campfires where dangerous natives lurk listening to the warning barkings of their dogs. It seems to me that I've spent a great bit of time taming or eluding natives and dogs, and the contents of this book rather prove this. I think of them, these descriptive paragraphs, these silhouettes and souvenirs of places and persons, as a prose map, a written geography of my life over the last three decades, more or less from 1942 to 1972.

Everything herein is factual, which doesn't mean that it is the truth, but it is as nearly so as I can make it. Journalism, however, can never be altogether pure—nor can the camera, for after all, art is not distilled water: personal perceptions, prejudices, one's sense of selectivity pollute the purity of germless truth.

The earliest pieces in the present volume, youthful impressions of New Orleans and Tangier, Ischia, Hollywood, Spanish trains, Moroccan festivals, et al., were collected in *Local Color*, a slim limited edition published in 1951 and now long out-of-print. I use the present occasion to reissue its contents for two reasons: the first being nostalgia, a reminder of a time when my eye was less narrowed and more lyric; the second, because these small impressions are the opening buds, the initial thrust of an interest in nonfiction writing, a genre I invaded in a more ambitious manner five years later with *The Muses Are Heard*, which also has appeared separately as a small book.

The Muses Are Heard is the one work of mine I can truly claim to have enjoyed writing, an activity I've seldom associated with pleasure. I imagined it as a brief comic novel; I wanted it to be very Russian, not in the sense of being reminiscent of Russian writing, but rather of some Czarist *objet*, a Fabergé contrivance, one of his music boxes, say, that trembled with some glittering, precise, mischievous melody.

Many in the cast of characters, Americans as well as Soviets, considered *The Muses Are Heard* just plain mischievous. However, in my journalistic experience it would seem that I've *never* described anyone to his or her satisfaction; or if, initially, some person was not unhappy with my revelations or small portraits, friends and relatives soon talked the subject into nit-picking misgivings.

Of all my sitters, the one most distressed was the subject of *The Duke in His Domain*, Marlon Brando. Though not claiming any inaccuracy, he apparently felt it was an unsympathetic, even treacherous intrusion upon the secret terrain of a suffering and intellectually awesome sensibility. My opinion? Just that it is a pretty good account, and a sympathetic one, of a wounded young man who is a genius, but not markedly intelligent.

However, the Brando profile interests me for literary reasons; indeed, that was why I wrote it—to accept a challenge and underline a literary point. It was my contention that reportage could be as groomed and elevated an art as any other prose form—the essay, short story, novel—a theory not so entrenched in 1956, the year the piece was printed, as it is today, when its acceptance has become perhaps a bit exaggerated. My thinking went: What is the lowest level of journalistic art, the one most difficult to turn from a sow's ear into a silk purse? The movie star "interview," *Silver Screen* stuff: surely nothing could be less easily elevated than that! After selecting Brando as the specimen for the experiment, I checked my equipment (the main ingredient of which is a talent for mentally recording lengthy conversations, an ability I had worked to achieve while researching *The Muses Are Heard,* for I devoutly believe that the taking of notes—much less the use of a *tape recorder!*—creates artifice and distorts or even destroys any naturalness that might exist between the observer and the observed, the nervous hummingbird and its would-be captor). It was a lot to remember, that long stretch of hours of Brando muttering and meandering, but I wrote it all out the morning after the "interview," then spent a month shaping it toward the ultimate result. What I learned most from it was how to control "static" writing, to reveal character and sustain mood unaided by a narrative line—the latter being, to a writer, what a rope and pickaxe are to a mountain climber.

In *The Dogs Bark* two pieces especially demonstrate the difference between narrative and "static" writing. *A Ride Through Spain* was a lark; buoyed along by its anecdotal nature, it skimmed off the end of a Black Wing pencil in a matter of hours. But something like *A House on the Heights,* where all the movement depends on the writing itself, is a matter of how the sentences sound, suspend, balance and tumble; a piece like that can be red hell, which is why I have more affection for it than *A Ride Through Spain,* even though I know the latter is better, or at least more effective.

Much of the substance of this book appeared over the years in various publications, but they have never before found shelter under one roof. One of them, *Lola,* has a curious history. Written to exorcise the ghost of a lost friend, it was bought by an American magazine, where for years it reposed unprinted because the magazine's editor decided he loathed it; he said he didn't know what it was about, and moreover, found it forbidding, black. I disagree; still, I can see what he meant, for instinctively he must have seen through the sentimental disguises of this true tale and realized, without altogether recognizing, what it in fact concerned: the perils, the dooms of not perceiving and accepting the limits of one's supposed identity, the classifications imposed by others—a bird that believes it is a dog, Van Gogh insisting that he was an artist, Emily Dickinson a poet. But without such misjudgments and such faiths, the seas would sleep, the eternal snows remain untracked.

A Day's
Work

(1979)

S cene: A RAINY APRIL MORNING, 1979.
I am walking along Second Avenue in
New York City, carrying an oilcloth shopping satchel bulging with house-
cleaning materials that belong to Mary Sanchez, who is beside me trying
to keep an umbrella above the pair of us, which is not difficult as she is
much taller than I am, a six-footer.

Mary Sanchez is a professional cleaning woman who works by the hour,
at five dollars an hour, six days a week. She works approximately nine
hours a day, and visits on the average twenty-four different domiciles
between Monday and Saturday: generally her customers require her services just once a week.

Mary is fifty-seven years old, a native of a small South Carolina town
who has "lived North" the past forty years. Her husband, a Puerto Rican,
died last summer. She has a married daughter who lives in San Diego, and
three sons, one of whom is a dentist, one who is serving a ten-year sentence
for armed robbery, a third who is "just gone, God knows where. He called
me last Christmas, he sounded far away. I asked where are you, Pete, but
he wouldn't say, so I told him his daddy was dead, and he said good, said
that was the best Christmas present I could've given him, so I hung up the
phone, slam, and I hope he never calls again. Spitting on Dad's grave that
way. Well, sure, Pedro was never good to the kids. Or me. Just boozed and
rolled dice. Ran around with bad women. They found him dead on a bench

645

in Central Park. Had a mostly empty bottle of Jack Daniel's in a paper sack propped between his legs; never drank nothing but the best, that man. Still, Pete was way out of line, saying he was *glad* his father was dead. He owed him the gift of life, didn't he? And I owed Pedro something too. If it wasn't for him, I'd still be an ignorant Baptist, lost to the Lord. But when I got married, I married in the Catholic church, and the Catholic church brought a *shine* to my life that has never gone out, and never will, not even when I die. I raised my children in the Faith; two of them turned out fine, and I give the church credit for that more than me."

Mary Sanchez is muscular, but she has a pale round smooth pleasant face with a tiny upturned nose and a beauty mole high on her left cheek. She dislikes the term "black," racially applied. "I'm not black. I'm brown. A light-brown colored woman. And I'll tell you something else. I don't know many other colored people that like being called blacks. Maybe some of the young people. And those radicals. But not folks my age, or even half as old. Even people who really are black, they don't like it. What's wrong with Negroes? I'm a Negro, and a Catholic, and proud to say it."

I've known Mary Sanchez since 1968, and she has worked for me, periodically, all these years. She is conscientious, and takes far more than a casual interest in her clients, many of whom she has scarcely met, or not met at all, for many of them are unmarried working men and women who are not at home when she arrives to clean their apartments; she communicates with them, and they with her, via notes: "Mary, please water the geraniums and feed the cat. Hope this finds you well. Gloria Scotto."

Once I suggested to her that I would like to follow her around during the course of a day's work, and she said well, she didn't see anything wrong with that, and in fact, would enjoy the company: "This can be kind of lonely work sometimes."

Which is how we happen to be walking along together on this showery April morning. We're off to her first job: a Mr. Andrew Trask, who lives on East Seventy-third Street.

TC: What the hell have you got in this sack?

MARY: Here, give it to me. I can't have you cursing.

TC: No. Sorry. But it's heavy.

MARY: Maybe it's the iron.

TC: You iron their clothes? You never iron any of mine.

MARY: Some of these people just have no equipment. That's why I have to carry so much. I leave notes: get this, get that. But they forget. Seems like all my people are bound up in their troubles. Like this Mr. Trask, where we're going. I've had him seven, eight months, and I've never seen him yet. But he drinks too much, and his wife left him on account of it, and he owes bills everywhere, and if ever I answered his phone, it's somebody trying to collect. Only now they've turned off his phone.

> (We arrive at the address, and she produces from a shoulder-satchel a massive metal ring jangling with dozens of keys. The building is a four-story brownstone with a midget elevator.)

TC (after entering and glancing around the Trask establishment—one fair-sized room with greenish arsenic-colored walls, a kitchenette, and a bathroom with a broken, constantly flowing toilet): Hmm. I see what you mean. This guy has problems.

MARY (opening a closet crammed and clammy with sweat-sour laundry): Not a clean sheet in the house! And look at that bed! Mayonnaise! Chocolate! Crumbs, crumbs, chewing gum, cigarette butts. Lipstick! What kind of woman would subject herself to a bed like that? I haven't been able to change the sheets for weeks. Months.

> (She turns on several lamps with awry shades; and while she labors to organize the surrounding disorder, I take more careful note of the premises. Really, it looks as though a burglar had been plundering there, one who had left some drawers of a bureau open, others closed. There's a leather-framed photograph on the bureau of a stocky swarthy macho man and a blond hoity-toity Junior League woman and three tow-headed grinning snaggletoothed suntanned boys, the eldest about fourteen. There is another unframed picture stuck in a blurry mirror: another blonde, but definitely not Junior League—perhaps a pickup from Maxwell's Plum; I imagine it is her lipstick on the bed sheets. A copy of the December issue of *True Detective* magazine is lying on the floor, and in the bathroom, stacked by the cease-lessly churning toilet, stands a pile of girlie literature—*Penthouse, Hustler, Oui;* otherwise, there seems to be a total absence of cultural possessions. But there are hundreds of empty vodka bottles everywhere—the miniature kind served by airlines.)

TC: Why do you suppose he drinks only these miniatures?

MARY: Maybe he can't afford nothing bigger. Just buys what he can. He has a good job, if he can hold on to it, but I guess his family keeps him broke.

TC: What does he do?

MARY: Airplanes.

TC: That explains it. He gets these little bottles free.

MARY: Yeah? How come? He's not a steward. He's a pilot.

TC: Oh, my God.

> (A telephone rings, a subdued noise, for the instrument is submerged under a rumpled blanket. Scowling, her hands soapy with dishwater, Mary unearths it with the finesse of an archeologist.)

MARY: He must have got connected again. Hello? (Silence) Hello?

A WOMAN'S VOICE: Who *is* this?

MARY: This is Mr. Trask's residence.

WOMAN'S VOICE: Mr. Trask's *residence?* (Laughter; then, hoity-toity) To whom am I speaking?

MARY: This is Mr. Trask's maid.

WOMAN'S VOICE: So Mr. Trask has a maid, has he? Well, that's more than *Mrs.* Trask has. Will Mr. Trask's maid please tell Mr. Trask that Mrs. Trask would like to speak to him?

MARY: He's not home.

MRS. TRASK: Don't give me that. Put him on.

MARY: I'm sorry, Mrs. Trask. I guess he's out flying.

MRS. TRASK (bitter mirth): Out flying? He's always flying, dear. Always.

MARY: What I mean is, he's at work.

MRS. TRASK: Tell him to call me at my sister's in New Jersey. Call the instant he comes in, if he knows what's good for him.

MARY: Yes, ma'am. I'll leave that message. (She hangs up) Mean woman. No wonder he's in the condition he's in. And now he's out of a job. I wonder if he left me my money. Uh-huh. That's it. On top of the fridge.

(Amazingly, an hour or so afterward she has managed to somewhat camouflage the chaos and has the room looking not altogether ship-shape but reasonably respectable. With a pencil, she scribbles a note and props it against the bureau mirror: "Dear Mr. Trask yr. wive want you fone her at her sistar place sinsirly Mary Sanchez." Then she sighs and perches on the edge of the bed and from her satchel takes out a small tin box containing an assortment of roaches; selecting one, she fits it into a roach-holder and lights up, dragging deeply, holding the smoke down in her lungs and closing her eyes. She offers me a toke.)

TC: Thanks. It's too early.

MARY: It's never too early. Anyway, you ought to try this stuff. *Mucho cojones.* I get it from a customer, a real fine Catholic lady; she's married to a fellow from Peru. His family sends it to them. Sends it right through the mail. I never use it so's to get high. Just enough to lift the uglies a little. That heaviness. (She sucks on the roach until it all but burns her lips) Andrew Trask. Poor scared devil. He could end up like Pedro. Dead on a park bench, nobody caring. Not that I didn't care none for that man. Lately, I find myself remembering the good times with Pedro, and I guess that's what happens to most people if ever they've once loved somebody and lose them; the bad slips away, and you linger on the nice things about them, what made you like them in the first place. Pedro, the young man I fell in love with, he was a beautiful dancer, oh he could tango, oh he could rumba, he taught me to dance and danced me off my feet. We were regulars at the old Savoy Ballroom. He was clean, neat—even when the drink got to him his fingernails were always trimmed and polished. And he could cook up a storm. That's how he made a living, as a short-order cook. I said he never did anything good for the children; well, he fixed their lunchboxes to take to school. All kinds of sandwiches wrapped in wax paper. Ham, peanut butter and jelly, egg salad, tuna fish, and fruit, apples, bananas, pears, and a thermos filled with warm milk mixed with honey. It hurts now to think of him there in the park, and how I didn't cry when the police came to tell me about it; how I never did cry. I ought to have. I owed him that. I owed him a sock in the jaw, too.

I'm going to leave the lights on for Mr. Trask. No sense letting him come home to a dark room.

(When we emerged from the brownstone the rain had stopped, but the sky was sloppy and a wind had risen that whipped trash along the gutters and caused passers-by to clutch their hats. Our destination was four blocks away, a modest but modern apartment house with a uniformed doorman, the address of Miss Edith Shaw, a young woman in her mid-twenties who was on the editorial staff of a magazine. "Some kind of news magazine. She must have a thousand books. But she doesn't look like no bookworm. She's a very healthy kind of girl, and she has lots of boyfriends. Too many—just can't seem to stay very long with one fellow. We got to be close because . . . Well, one time I came to her place and she was sick as a cat. She'd come from having a baby murdered. Normally I don't hold with that; it's against my beliefs. And I said why didn't you marry this man? The truth was, she didn't know who to marry; she didn't know who the dad was. And anyway, the last thing she wanted was a husband or a baby.")

MARY (surveying the scene from the opened front door of Miss Shaw's two-room apartment): Nothing much to do here. A little dusting. She takes good care of it herself. Look at all those books. Ceiling to floor, nothing but library.

(Except for the burdened bookshelves, the apartment was attractively spare, Scandinavianly white and gleaming. There was one antique: an old roll-top desk with a typewriter on it; a sheet of paper was rolled into the machine; and I glanced at what was written on it).

> Zsa Zsa Gabor is
> 305 years old
> I know
> Because I counted
> Her Rings

And triple-spaced below that, was typed:

> Sylvia Plath, I hate you
> And your damn daddy.
> I'm glad, do you hear,

> *Glad* you stuck your head
> In a gas-hot oven!

TC: Is Miss Shaw a poet?

MARY: She's always writing something. I don't know what it is. Stuff I see, sounds like she's on dope to me. Come here, I want to show you something.

> (She leads me into the bathroom, a surprisingly large and sparkling chamber. She opens a cabinet door and points at an object on a shelf: a pink plastic vibrator molded in the shape of an average-sized penis.)

Know what that is?

TC: Don't you?

MARY: I'm the one asking.

TC: It's a dildo vibrator.

MARY: I know what a vibrator is. But I never saw one like that. It says "Made in Japan."

TC: Ah, well. The Oriental mind.

MARY: Heathens. She's sure got some lovely perfumes. If you like perfume. Me, I only put a little vanilla behind my ears.

> (Now Mary began to work, mopping the waxed carpetless floors, flicking the bookshelves with a feather duster; and while she worked she kept her roach-box open and her roach-holder filled. I don't know how much "heaviness" she had to lift, but the aroma alone was lofting me.)

MARY: You sure you don't want to try a couple of tokes? You're missing something.

TC: You twisted my arm.

> (Man and boy, I've dragged some powerful grass, never enough to have acquired a habit, but enough to judge quality and know the difference between ordinary Mexican weed and luxurious contraband like Thai-sticks and the supreme Maui-Wowee. But after smoking the whole of one of Mary's roaches, and while halfway through another, I felt as though seized by a delicious demon, embraced by a mad marvelous merriment: the demon tickled my toes, scratched my itchy head, kissed me hotly with his red sugary lips, shoved his fiery tongue down my throat. Everything sparkled; my eyes were like zoom lenses; I could read the titles of books on the highest shelves: *The Neurotic Personality of Our Time* by Karen Horney; *Eimi* by e.e. cummings; *Four Quartets: The Collected Poems of Robert Frost.*)

TC: I despise Robert Frost. He was an evil, selfish bastard.

MARY: Now, if we're going to curse—

TC: Him with his halo of shaggy hair. An egomaniacal double-crossing sadist. He wrecked his whole family. Some of them. Mary, have you ever discussed this with your confessor?

MARY: Father McHale? Discussed what?

TC: The precious nectar we're so divinely devouring, my adorable chick-adee. Have you informed Father McHale of this delectable enterprise?

MARY: What he don't know won't hurt him. Here, have a Life Saver. Peppermint. It makes that stuff taste better.

> (Odd, she didn't seem high, not a bit. I'd just passed Venus, and Jupiter, jolly old Jupiter, beckoned beyond in the lilac star-dazzled planetary distance. Mary marched over to the telephone and dialed a number; she let it ring a long while before hanging up.)

MARY: Not home. That's one thing to be grateful for. Mr. and Mrs. Berkowitz. If they'd been home, I couldn't have took you over there. On account of they're these real stuffy Jewish people. And you know how stuffy *they* are!

TC: Jewish people? Gosh, yes. Very stuffy. They all ought to be in the Museum of Natural History. All of them.

MARY: I've been thinking about giving Mrs. Berkowitz notice. The trouble is, Mr. Berkowitz, he was in garments, he's retired, and the two of them are always home. Underfoot. Unless they drive up to Greenwich, where they got some property. That's where they must have gone today. Another reason I'd like to quit them. They've got an old parrot—makes a mess everywhere. And stupid! All that dumb parrot can say is two things: "Holy cow!" and *"Oy vey!"* Every time you walk in the house it starts shouting *"Oy vey!"* Gets on my nerves something terrible. How about it? Let's toke another roach and blow this joint.

> (The rain had returned and the wind increased, a mixture that made the air look like a shattering mirror. The Berkowitzes lived on Park Avenue in the upper Eighties, and I suggested we take a taxi, but Mary said no, what kind of sissy was I, we can walk it, so I realized that despite appearances, she, too, was traveling stellar paths. We walked along slowly, as though it were a warm tranquil day with turquoise skies, and the hard slippery streets ribbons of pearl-colored Caribbean beach. Park Avenue is not my favorite boulevard; it is rich with lack of charm; if Mrs. Lasker were to plant it with tulips all the way from Grand Central to Spanish Harlem, it would be of no avail. Still, there are certain buildings that prompt memories. We passed a building where Willa Cather, the American woman writer I've most admired, lived the last years of her life with her companion, Edith Lewis; I often sat in front of their fireplace and drank Bristol Cream and observed the firelight enflame the pale prairie-blue of Miss Cather's serene genius-eyes. At Eighty-fourth Street I recognized an apartment house where I had once attended a small black-tie dinner given by Senator and Mrs. John F. Kennedy, then so young and insouciant. But despite the agreeable efforts of our hosts, the evening was not as enlightening

as I had anticipated, because after the ladies had been dismissed and the men left in the dining room to savor their cordials and Havana cigars, one of the guests, a rather slope-chinned dressmaker named Oleg Cassini, overwhelmed the conversation with a travelogue account of Las Vegas and the myriad showgirls he'd recently auditioned there: their measurements, erotic accomplishments, financial requirements—a recital that hypnotized its auditors, none of whom was more chucklingly attentive than the future President.

When we reach Eighty-seventh Street, I point out a window on the fourth floor at 1060 Park Avenue, and inform Mary: "My mother lived there. That was her bedroom. She was beautiful and very intelligent, but she didn't want to live. She had many reasons—at least she thought she did. But in the end it was just her husband, my stepfather. He was a self-made man, fairly successful—she worshipped him, and he really was a nice guy, but he gambled, got into trouble and embezzled a lot of money, and lost his business and was headed for Sing Sing."

Mary shakes her head: "Just like my boy. Same as him."

We're both standing staring at the window, the downpour drenching us. "So one night she got all dressed up and gave a dinner party; everybody said she looked lovely. But after the party, before she went to bed, she took thirty Seconals and she never woke up."

Mary is angry; she strides rapidly away through the rain: "She had no right to do that. I don't hold with that. It's against my beliefs.")

SQUAWKING PARROT: Holy cow!

MARY: Hear that? What did I tell you?

PARROT: *Oy vey! Oy vey!*

(The parrot, a surrealist collage of green and yellow and orange moulting feathers, is ensconced on a mahogany perch in the relentlessly formal parlor of Mr. and Mrs. Berkowitz, a room suggesting that it had been entirely made of mahogany: the parquet floors, the wall paneling, and the furniture, all of it costly reproductions of grandiose period-piece furniture—though God knows what period, perhaps early Grand Concourse. Straight-back chairs; settees that would have tested the endurance of a posture professor. Mulberry velvet draperies swathed the windows, which were incongruously covered with mustard-brown Venetian blinds. Above a carved mahogany mantelpiece a mahogany-framed portrait of a jowly, sallow-skinned Mr. Berkowitz depicted him as a country squire outfitted for a fox hunt: scarlet coat, silk cravat, a bugle tucked under one arm, a riding crop under the other. I don't know what the remainder of this rambling abode looked like, for I never saw any of it except the kitchen.)

MARY: What's so funny? What you laughing at?

TC: Nothing: It's just this Peruvian tobacco, my cherub. I take it Mr. Berkowitz is an equestrian?

PARROT: *Oy vey! Oy vey!*

MARY: Shut up! Before I wring your damn neck.

TC: Now, if we're going to curse . . . (Mary mumbles; crosses herself) Does the critter have a name?

MARY: Uh-huh. Try and guess.

TC: Polly.

MARY (truly surprised): How'd you know that?

TC: So she's a female.

MARY: That's a girl's name, so she must be a girl. Whatever she is, she's a bitch. Just look at all that crap on the floor. All for me to clean it up.

TC: Language, language.

POLLY: Holy cow!

MARY: My nerves. Maybe we better have a little lift. (Out comes the tin box, the roaches, the roach-holder, matches) And let's see what we can locate in the kitchen. I'm feeling real munchie.

(The interior of the Berkowitz refrigerator is a glutton's fantasy, a cornucopia of fattening goodies. Small wonder the master of the house has such jowls. "Oh yes," confirms Mary, "they're both hogs. Her stomach. She looks like she's about to drop the Dionne quintuplets. And all his suits are tailor-made: nothing store-bought could fit him. Hmm, yummy, I sure do feel munchie. Those coconut cupcakes look desirable. And that mocha cake, I wouldn't mind a hunk of that. We could dump some ice cream on it." Huge soup bowls are found, and Mary masses them with cupcakes and mocha cake and fist-sized scoops of pistachio ice cream. We return to the parlor with this banquet and fall upon it like abused orphans. There's nothing like grass to grow an appetite. After finishing off the first helping, and fueling ourselves with more roaches, Mary refills the bowls with even heftier portions.)

MARY: How you feel?

TC: I feel good.

MARY: How good?

TC: Real good.

MARY: Tell me exactly how you feel.

TC: I'm in Australia.

MARY: Ever been to Austria?

TC: Not Austria. Australia. No, but that's where I am now. And everybody always said what a dull place it is. Shows what they know! Greatest surfing in the world. I'm out in the ocean on a surfboard riding a wave high as a, as a—

MARY: High as you. Ha-ha.

TC: It's made of melting emeralds. The wave. The sun is hot on my back, and the spray is salting my face, and there are hungry sharks all around me. *Blue Water, White Death*. Wasn't that a terrific movie? Hungry white man-eaters everywhere, but they don't worry me—frankly, I don't give a fuck . . .

MARY (eyes wide with fear): Watch for the sharks! They got killer teeth. You'll be crippled for life. You'll be begging on street corners.

TC: Music!

MARY: Music! That's the ticket.

(She weaves like a groggy wrestler toward a gargoyle object that had heretofore happily escaped my attention: a mahogany console combining television, phonograph and a radio. She fiddles with the radio until she finds a station booming music with a Latin beat.

Her hips maneuver, her fingers snap, she is elegant yet smoothly abandoned, as if recalling a sensuous youthful night, and dancing with a phantom partner some remembered choreography. And it is magic, how her now-ageless body responds to the drums and guitars, contours itself to the subtlest rhythm: she is in a trance, the state of grace saints supposedly achieve when experiencing visions. And I am hearing the music, too; it is speeding through me like amphetamine—each note ringing with the separate clarity of cathedral chimings on a silent winter Sunday. I move toward her, and into her arms, and we match each other step for step, laughing, undulating, and even when the music is interrupted by an announcer speaking Spanish as rapid as the rattle of castanets, we continue dancing, for the guitars are locked in our heads now, as we are locked in our laughter, our embrace: louder and louder, so loud that we are unaware of a key clicking, a door opening and shutting. But the parrot hears it.)

POLLY: Holy cow!

WOMAN'S VOICE: What is this? What's happening here?

POLLY: *Oy vey! Oy vey!*

MARY: Why, hello there, Mrs. Berkowitz. Mr. Berkowitz. How ya doin'?
(And there they are, hovering in view like the Mickey and Minnie Mouse balloons in a Macy's Thanksgiving Day parade. Not that there's anything mousey about this twosome. Their infuriated eyes, hers hot behind harlequin spectacles with sequined frames, absorb the scene: our naughty ice-cream mustaches, the pungent roach smoke polluting the premises. Mr. Berkowitz stalks over and stops the radio.)

MRS. BERKOWITZ: Who is this man?

MARY: I din't think you was home.

MRS. BERKOWITZ: Obviously. I asked you: Who is this man?

MARY: He's just a friend of mine. Helping me out. I got so much work today.

MR. BERKOWITZ: You're drunk, woman.

MARY (deceptively sweet): How's that you say?

MRS. BERKOWTIZ: He said you're drunk. I'm shocked. Truly.

MARY: Since we're speaking truly, what I have truly to say to you is: today is my last day of playing nigger around here—I'm giving you notice.

MRS. BERKOWITZ: You are giving *me* notice?

MR. BERKOWITZ: Get out of here! Before we call the police.

(Without ado, we gather our belongings. Mary waves at the parrot: "So long, Polly. You're okay. You're good girl. I was only kidding." And at the front door, where her former employers have sternly stationed themselves, she announces: "Just for the record, I've never touched a drop in my life."

Downstairs, the rain is still going. We trudge along Park Avenue, then cut across to Lexington.)

MARY: Didn't I tell you they were stuffy.

TC: Belong in a museum.

(But most of our buoyancy has departed; the power of the Peruvian foliage recedes, a letdown has set in, my surfboard is sinking, and any sharks sighted now would scare the piss out of me.)

MARY: I still got Mrs. Kronkite to do. But she's nice; she'll forgive me if I don't come till tomorrow. Maybe I'll head on home.

TC: Let me catch you a cab.

MARY: I hate to give them my business. Those taxi people don't like coloreds. Even when they're colored themselves. No, I can get the subway down here at Lex and Eighty-sixth.

(Mary lives in a rent-controlled apartment near Yankee Stadium; she says it was cramped when she had a family living with her, but now that she's by herself, it seems immense and dangerous: "I've got three locks on every door, and all the windows nailed down. I'd buy me a police dog if it didn't mean leaving him by himself so much. I know what it is to be alone, and I wouldn't wish it on a dog.")

TC: Please, Mary, let me treat you to a taxi.

MARY: The subway's a lot quicker. But there's someplace I want to stop. It's just down here a ways.

(The place is a narrow church pinched between broad buildings on a side street. Inside, there are two brief rows of pews, and a small altar with a plaster figure of a crucified Jesus suspended above it. An odor of incense and candle wax dominates the gloom. At the altar a woman is lighting a candle, its light fluttering like the sleep of a fitful spirit; otherwise, we are the only supplicants present. We kneel together in the last pew, and from the satchel Mary produces a pair of rosary beads —"I always carry a couple extra"—one for herself, the other for me, though I don't know quite how to handle it, never having used one before. Mary's lips move whisperingly.)

MARY: Dear Lord, in your mercy. Please, Lord, help Mr. Trask to stop boozing and get his job back. Please, Lord, don't leave Miss Shaw a bookworm and an old maid; she ought to bring your children into this world. And, Lord, I beg you to remember my sons and daughter and my grandchildren, each and every one. And please don't let Mr. Smith's family send him to that retirement home; he don't want to go, he cries all the time . . .

(Her list of names is more numerous than the beads on her rosary, and her requests in their behalf have the earnest shine of the altar's candleflame. She pauses to glance at me.)

MARY: Are you praying?

TC: Yes.

MARY: I can't hear you.

TC: I'm praying for you, Mary. I want you to live forever.

MARY: Don't pray for me. I'm already saved. (She takes my hand and holds it) Pray for your mother. Pray for all those souls lost out there in the dark. Pedro. Pedro.

Dazzle

(1979)

S HE FASCINATED ME.
        She fascinated everyone, but most
people were ashamed of their fascination, especially the proud ladies who
presided over some of the grander households of New Orleans' Garden
District, the neighborhood where the big plantation owners lived, the
shipowners and oil operators, the richest professional men. The only persons not secretive about their fascination with Mrs. Ferguson were the
servants of these Garden District families. And, of course, some of the
children, who were too young or guileless to conceal their interest.

I was one of those children, an eight-year-old boy temporarily living
with Garden District relatives. However, as it happened, I did keep my
fascination to myself, for I felt a certain guilt: I had a secret, something that
was bothering me, something that was really worrying me very much,
something I was afraid to tell anybody, *any*body—I couldn't imagine what
their reaction would be, it was such an odd thing that was worrying me,
that had been worrying me for almost two years. I had never heard of
anyone with a problem like the one that was troubling me. On the one hand
it seemed maybe silly; on the other . . .

I wanted to tell my secret to Mrs. Ferguson. Not *want* to, but felt I had
to. Because Mrs. Ferguson was said to have magical powers. It was said,
and believed by many serious-minded people, that she could tame errant
husbands, force proposals from reluctant suitors, restore lost hair, recoup

squandered fortunes. In short, she was a witch who could make wishes come true. I had a wish.

Mrs. Ferguson did not seem clever enough to be capable of magic. Not even card tricks. She was a plain woman who might have been forty but was perhaps thirty; it was hard to tell, for her round Irish face, with its round full-moon eyes, had few lines and little expression. She was a laundress, probably the only white laundress in New Orleans, and an artist at her trade: the great ladies of the town sent for her when their finest laces and linens and silks required attention. They sent for her for other reasons as well: to obtain desires—a new lover, a certain marriage for a daughter, the death of a husband's mistress, a codicil to a mother's will, an invitation to be Queen of Comus, grandest of the Mardi Gras galas. It was not merely as a laundress that Mrs. Ferguson was courted. The source of her success, and principal income, was her alleged abilities to sift the sands of daydreams until she produced the solid stuff, golden realities.

Now, about this wish of my own, the worry that was with me from first thing in the morning until last thing at night: it wasn't anything I could just straight out ask her. It required the right time, a carefully prepared moment. She seldom came to our house, but when she did I stayed close by, pretending to watch the delicate movements of her thick ugly fingers as they handled lace-trimmed napkins, but really attempting to catch her eye. We never talked; I was too nervous and she was too stupid. Yes, stupid. It was just something I sensed; powerful witch or not, Mrs. Ferguson was a stupid woman. But now and again our eyes did lock, and dumb as she was, the intensity, the *fascination* she saw in my gaze told her that I desired to be a client. She probably thought I wanted a bike, or a new air rifle; anyway, she wasn't about to concern herself with a kid like me. What could I give her? So she would turn her tiny lips down and roll her full-moon eyes elsewhere.

About this time, early December in 1932, my paternal grandmother arrived for a brief visit. New Orleans has cold winters; the chilly humid winds from the river drift deep into your bones. So my grandmother, who was living in Florida, where she taught school, had wisely brought with her a fur coat, one she had borrowed from a friend. It was made of black Persian lamb, the belonging of a rich woman, which my grandmother was not. Widowed young, and left with three sons to raise, she had not had an easy life, but she never complained. She was an admirable woman; she had a lively mind, and a sound, sane one as well. Due to family circumstances, we rarely met, but she wrote often and sent me small gifts. She loved me and I wanted to love her, but until she died, and she lived beyond ninety, I kept my distance, behaved indifferently. She felt it, but she never knew what caused my apparent coldness, nor did anyone else, for the reason was part of an intricate guilt, faceted as the dazzling yellow stone dangling from a slender gold-chain necklace that she often wore. Pearls would have suited her better, but she attached great value to this somewhat theatrical gewgaw, which I understood her own grandfather had won in a card game in Colorado.

Of course the necklace wasn't valuable; as my grandmother always scrupulously explained to anyone who inquired, the stone, which was the size of a cat's paw, was not a "gem" stone, not a canary diamond, nor even a topaz, but a chunk of rock-crystal deftly faceted and tinted dark yellow. Mrs. Ferguson, however, was unaware of the trinket's true worth, and when one afternoon, during the course of my grandmother's stay, the plump youngish witch arrived to stiffen some linen, she seemed spellbound by the brilliant bit of glass swinging from the thin chain around my grandmother's neck. Her ignorant moon eyes glowed, and that's a fact: they truly glowed. I now had no difficulty attracting her attention; she studied me with an interest absent heretofore.

As she departed, I followed her into the garden, where there was a century-old wisteria arbor, a mysterious place even in winter when the foliage had shriveled, stripping this leaf-tunnel of its concealing shadows. She walked under it and beckoned to me.

Softly, she said: "You got something on your mind?"

"Yes."

"Something you want done? A favor?"

I nodded; she nodded, but her eyes shifted nervously: she didn't want to be seen talking to me.

She said: "My boy will come. He will tell you."

"*When?*"

But she said hush, and hurried out of the garden. I watched her waddle off into the dusk. It dried my mouth to think of having all my hopes pinned on this stupid woman. I couldn't eat supper that night; I didn't sleep until dawn. Aside from the thing that was worrying me, now I had a whole lot of new worries. If Mrs. Ferguson did what I wanted her to do, then what about my clothes, what about my name, where would I go, who would I be? Holy smoke, it was enough to drive you crazy! Or was I already crazy? That was part of the problem: I must be crazy to want Mrs. Ferguson to do this thing I wanted her to do. That was one reason why I couldn't tell anybody: they would think I was crazy. Or something worse. I didn't know what that something worse could be, but instinctively I felt that people saying I was crazy, my family and their friends and the other kids, might be the least of it.

Because of fear and superstition combined with greed, the servants of the Garden District, some of the snobbiest mammies and haughtiest housemen who ever tread a parquet floor, spoke of Mrs. Ferguson with respect. They also spoke of her in quiet tones, and not only because of her peculiar gifts, but because of her equally peculiar private life, various details of which I had gradually collected by eavesdropping on the tattletale of these elegant blacks and mulattoes and Creoles, who considered themselves the real royalty of New Orleans, and certainly superior to any of their employers. As for Mrs. Ferguson—she was not a madame, merely a mamselle: an unmarried woman with a raft of children, at least six, who came from East Texas, one of those redneck hamlets across the border from Shreveport. At the age of fifteen she had been tied to a hitching post in front of the town post office and publicly flogged with a horsewhip by her own father. The reason for this terrible punishment was a child she had borne, a boy with green eyes but unmistakably the product of a black father. With the baby, who was called Skeeter and was now fourteen and said to be a devil himself, she came to New Orleans and found work as a housekeeper for an Irish Catholic priest, whom she seduced, had a second baby by, abandoned for another man, and went on from there, living with a succession of handsome lovers, men she could only have succeeded in acquiring through potions poured into their wine, for after all, without her particular powers, who was she? White trash from East Texas who carried on with black men, the mother of six bastards, a laundress, a servant herself. And yet they respected her; even Mme. Jouet, the head mammy of the Vaccaro family, who owned the United Fruit Company, always addressed her civilly.

Two days after my conversation with Mrs. Ferguson, a Sunday, I accompanied my grandmother to church, and as we were walking home, a matter of a few blocks, I noticed that someone was following us: a well-built boy with tobacco-colored skin and green eyes. I knew at once that it was the infamous Skeeter, the boy whose birth had caused his mother to be flogged, and I knew that he was bringing me a message. I felt nauseated, but also elated, almost tipsy, enough so to make me laugh.

Merrily, my grandmother asked: "Ah, you know a joke?"

I thought: No, but I know a secret. However, I only said: "It was just something the minister said."

"Really? I'm glad you found some humor. It struck me as a very dry sermon. But the choir was good."

I refrained from making the following comment: "Well, if they're just going to talk about sinners and hell, when they don't know what hell is, they ought to ask me to preach the sermon. I could tell them a thing or two."

"Are you happy here?" my grandmother asked, as if it were a question she had been considering ever since her arrival. "I know it's been difficult. The divorce. Living here, living there. I want to help; I don't know how."

"I'm fine. Everything's hunky-dory."

But I wished she'd shut up. She did, with a frown. So at least I'd got one wish. One down and one to go.

When we reached home my grandmother, saying she felt the start of a migraine and might try to ward it off with a pill and a nap, kissed me and went inside the house. I raced through the garden toward the old wisteria arbor and hid myself inside it, like a bandit in a bandit's cave waiting for a confederate.

Soon Mrs. Ferguson's son arrived. He was tall for his age, just shy of six feet, and muscular as a dockworker. He resembled his mother in no respect. It wasn't only his dark coloring; his features were nicely defined, the bone structure quite precise—his father must have been a handsome man. And unlike Mrs. Ferguson, his emerald eyes were not dumb comic-strip dots, but narrow and mean, weapons, bullets threateningly aimed and primed to explode. I wasn't surprised when, not many years later, I heard he'd committed a double murder in Houston and died in the electric chair at Texas State Prison.

He was natty, dressed like the adult sharp-guy hoodlums who lounged around the waterfront hangouts: Panama hat, two-toned shoes, a tight stained white linen suit that some much slighter man must have given him. An impressive cigar jutted from his handkerchief pocket: a Havana Castle Morro, the connoisseur's cigar Garden District gentlemen served along with their after-dinner absinthe and framboise. Skeeter Ferguson lit his cigar with movie-gangster showmanship, constructed an impeccable smoke ring, blew it straight into my face, and said: "I've come to get you."

"*Now?*"

"Just as soon as you bring me the old lady's necklace."

It was useless to stall, but I tried: "What necklace?"

"Save your breath. Go get it and then we'll head somewhere. Or else we won't. And you'll never have another chance."

"But she's wearing it!"

Another smoke ring, professionally manufactured, effortlessly projected. "How you get it ain't none of my beeswax. I'll just be right here. Waiting."

"But it may take a long time. And suppose I can't do it?"

"You will. I'll wait till you do."

The house sounded empty when I entered through the kitchen door, and except for my grandmother, it was; everyone else had driven off to visit a newly married cousin who lived across the river. After calling my grandmother's name, and hearing silence, I tiptoed upstairs and listened at her bedroom door. She must be asleep. Accepting the risk, I inched the door open.

The curtains were drawn and the room dark except for the hot shine of coal burning inside a porcelain stove. My grandmother was lying in bed with covers drawn up to her chin; she must have taken the headache pill, for her breathing was deep and even. Still, I drew back the quilt covering her with the meticulous stealth of a robber tumbling the dials of a bank safe. Her throat was naked; she was wearing only an undergarment, a pink slip.

I found the necklace on a bureau; it was lying in front of a photograph of her three sons, one of them my father. I hadn't seen him for so long that I'd forgotten what he looked like—and after today, I'd probably never see him again. Or if I did, he wouldn't know who I was. But I had no time to think about that. Skeeter Ferguson was waiting for me, standing inside the wisteria arbor tapping his foot and sucking on his millionaire's cigar. Nevertheless, I hesitated.

I had never stolen anything before; well, some Hershey bars from the candy counter at the movies, and a few books I'd not returned to the public library. But this was so important. My grandmother would forgive me if she knew why I had to steal the necklace. No, she wouldn't forgive me; nobody would forgive me if they knew *exactly* why. But I had no choice. It was like Skeeter said: if I didn't do it now, his mother would never give me another chance. And the thing that was worrying me would go on and on, maybe forever and forever. So I took it. I stuffed it in my pocket and fled the room without even closing the door. When I rejoined Skeeter, I didn't show him the necklace, I just told him I had it, and his green eyes grew greener, turned nastier, as he issued one of his big-shot smoke rings and said: "Sure you do. You're just a born rascal. Like me."

First we walked, then we took a trolley car down Canal Street, usually so crowded and cheerful but spooky now with the stores closed and a Sabbath stillness hovering over it like a funeral cloud. At Canal and Royal we changed trolleys and rode all the way across the French Quarter, a familiar neighborhood where many of the longer-established families lived, some with purer lineage than any names the Garden District could offer. Eventually we started walking again; we walked miles. The stiff churchgoing shoes I was still wearing hurt, and now I didn't know where we were, but wherever it was I didn't like it. It was no use questioning Skeeter Ferguson, for if you did, he smiled and whistled, or spit and smiled and whistled. I wonder if he whistled on his way to the electric chair.

I really had no idea where we were; it was a section of the city I'd not seen before. And yet there was nothing unusual about it, except that there were fewer white faces around than one was accustomed to, and the farther we walked the scarcer they became: an occasional white resident surrounded by blacks and Creoles. Otherwise it was an ordinary collection of humble wooden structures, rooming houses with peeling paint, modest family homes, mostly poorly kept but with some exceptions. Mrs. Ferguson's house, when at last we reached it, was one of the exceptions.

It was an old house but a *real* house, with seven or eight rooms; it didn't look as though the first strong breeze from the Gulf would blow it away. It was painted an ugly brown, but at least the paint was not sun-blistered and flaking. And it stood inside a well-tended yard that contained a big shade tree—a chinaberry tree with old rubber tires, several of them, suspended on ropes from its branches: swings for children. And there were other playthings scattered around the yard: a tricycle, buckets, and little shovels for making mud pies—evidence of Mrs. Ferguson's fatherless brood. A mongrel puppy held captive by a chain attached to a stake began bouncing about and yapping the second he glimpsed Skeeter.

Skeeter said: "Here we are. Just open the door and walk in."

"Alone?"

"She's expectin' you. Do what I tell you. Walk right in. And if you catch her in the middle of a hump, keep your eyes open: that's how I got to be a champion humper."

The last remark, meaningless to me, ended with a chuckle, but I followed his instructions, and as I started toward the front door, glanced back at him. It didn't seem possible, but he was already gone, and I never saw him again—or if I did, I don't remember it.

The door opened directly into Mrs. Ferguson's parlor. At least it was furnished as a parlor (a couch, easy chairs, two wicker rocking chairs, maplewood side tables), though the floor was covered with a brown kitchen linoleum that perhaps was meant to match the color of the house. When I came into the room Mrs. Ferguson was tilting to and fro in one of the rocking chairs, while a good-looking young man, a Creole not many years older than Skeeter, rocked away in the other. A bottle of rum rested on a table between them, and they were both drinking from glasses filled with the stuff. The young man, who was not introduced to me, was wearing only an undershirt and somewhat unbuttoned bell-bottom sailor's trousers. Without a word he stopped rocking, stood up, and swaggered down a hall, taking the rum bottle with him. Mrs. Ferguson listened until she heard a door close.

Then all she said was: "Where is it?"

I was sweating. My heart was acting funny. I felt as though I had run a hundred miles and lived a thousand years in just the last few hours.

Mrs. Ferguson stilled her chair, and repeated herself: "Where is it?"

"Here. In my pocket."

She held out a thick red hand, palm up, and I dropped the necklace into it. Rum had already done something to alter the usual dullness of her eyes; the dazzling yellow stone did more. She turned it this way and that, staring at it; I tried not to, I tried to think of other things, and found myself wondering if she had scars on her back, lash marks.

"Am I expected to guess?" she asked, never removing her gaze from the bijou dangling from its fragile gold chain. "Well? Am I supposed to tell you why you are here? What it is you want?"

She didn't know, she couldn't, and suddenly I didn't want her to. I said: "I like to tap-dance."

For an instant her attention was diverted from the sparkling new toy.

"I want to be a tap dancer. I want to run away. I want to go to Hollywood and be in the movies." There was some truth in this; running away to Hollywood was high on my list of escape-fantasies. But that wasn't what I'd decided not to tell her, after all.

"Well," she drawled. "You sure are pretty enough to be in picture shows. Prettier than any boy ought to be."

So she *did* know. I heard myself shouting: "Yes! Yes! That's it!"

"That's what? And stop hollering. I'm not deaf."

"I don't want to be a boy. I want to be a girl."

It began as a peculiar noise, a strangled gurgling far back in her throat that bubbled into laughter. Her tiny lips stretched and widened; drunken laughter spilled out of her mouth like vomit, and it seemed to be spurting all over me—laughter that sounded like vomit smells.

"Please, please. Mrs. Ferguson, you don't understand. I'm very worried. I'm worried all the time. There's something wrong. Please. You've got to understand."

She went on rocking with laughter and her rocking chair rocked with her.

Then I said: "You *are* stupid. Dumb and stupid." And I tried to grab the necklace away from her.

The laughter stopped as though she had been struck by lightning; a storm overtook her face, total fury. Yet when she spoke her voice was soft and hissing and serpentine: "You don't know what you want, boy. I'll show you what you want. Look at me, boy. Look here. I'll show you what you want."

"Please. I don't want anything."

"Open your eyes, boy."

Somewhere in the house a baby was crying.

"Look at me, boy. Look here."

What she wanted me to look at was the yellow stone. She was holding it above her head, and slightly swinging it. It seemed to have gathered up all the light in the room, accumulated a devastating brilliance that plunged everything else into blackness. Swing, spin, dazzle, dazzle.

"I hear a baby crying."

"That's you you hear."

"Stupid woman. Stupid. Stupid."

"Look here, boy."

Spindazzlespinspindazzledazzledazzle.

It was still daylight, and it was still Sunday, and here I was back in the Garden District, standing in front of my house. I don't know how I got there. Someone must have brought me, but I don't know who; my last memory was the noise of Mrs. Ferguson's laughter returning.

Of course, a huge commotion was made over the missing necklace. The police were not called, but the whole household was upside down for days; not an inch was left unsearched. My grandmother was very upset. But even if the necklace had been of high value, a jewel that could have been sold and assured her of comfort the rest of her life, I still would not have accused Mrs. Ferguson. For if I did, she might reveal what I'd told her, the thing I never told anyone again, not ever. Finally it was decided that a thief had stolen into the house and taken the necklace while my grandmother slept. Well, that was the truth. Everyone was relieved when my grandmother concluded her visit and returned to Florida. It was hoped that the whole sad affair of the missing jewel would soon be forgotten.

But it was not forgotten. Forty-four years evaporated, and it was not forgotten. I became a middle-aged man, riddled with quirks and quaint notions. My grandmother died, still sane and sound of mind despite her great age.

A cousin called to inform me of her death, and to ask when I would be arriving for the funeral; I said I'd let her know. I was ill with grief, inconsolable; and it was absurd, out of all proportion. My grandmother was not someone I had loved. Yet how I grieved! But I did not travel to the funeral, nor even send flowers. I stayed home and drank a quart of vodka. I was very drunk, but I can remember answering the telephone and hearing my father identify himself. His old man's voice trembled with more than the weight of years; he vented the pent-up wrath of a lifetime, and when I remained silent, he said: "You sonofabitch. She died with your picture in her hand." I said "I'm sorry," and hung up. What was there to say? How could I explain that all through the years any mention of my grandmother, any letter from her or thought of her, evoked Mrs. Ferguson? Her laughter, her fury, the swinging, spinning yellow stone: spindazzledazzle.

Hidden
Gardens

(1979)

*S*cene: JACKSON SQUARE, NAMED AFTER
Andrew Jackson—a three-hundred-
year-old oasis complacently centered inside New Orleans' old quarter: a
moderate-sized park dominated by the gray towers of St. Louis Cathedral,
and the oldest, in some ways most somberly elegant, apartment houses in
America, the Pontalba Buildings.

Time: 26 March 1979, an exuberant spring day. Bougainvillaea descends,
azaleas thrust, hawkers hawk (peanuts, roses, horse-drawn carriage rides,
fried shrimp in paper scoops), the horns of drifting ships hoot on the
close-by Mississippi, and happy balloons, attached to giggling skipping
children, bounce high in the blue silvery air.

"Well, I do declare, a boy sure do get around"—as my uncle Bud, who
was a traveling salesman when he could pry himself away from his porch
swing and gin fizzes long enough to travel, used to complain. Yes, indeed,
a boy sure do get around; in just the last several months I've been in
Denver, Cheyenne, Butte, Salt Lake City, Vancouver, Seattle, Portland,
Los Angeles, Boston, Toronto, Washington, Miami. But if somebody
asked, I'd probably say, and really think: Why, I haven't been anywhere,
I've just been in New York all winter.

Still, a boy do get around. And now here I am back in New Orleans, my birthplace, my old hometown. Sunning myself on a park bench in Jackson Square, always, since schoolboy days, a favorite place to stretch my legs and look and listen, to yawn and scratch and dream and talk to myself. Maybe you're one of those people who never talk to themselves. Aloud, I mean. Maybe you think only crazies do that. Personally, I consider it's a healthy thing. To keep yourself company that way: nobody to argue back, free to rant along, getting a lot of stuff out of your system.

For instance, take those Pontalba Buildings over there. Pretty fancy places, with their grillwork façades and tall dark French-shuttered windows. The first apartment houses ever built in the U.S.A.; relatives of the original occupants of those high airy aristocratic rooms are still living in them. For a long time I had a grudge against the Pontalba. Here's why. Once, when I was nineteen or so, I had an apartment a few blocks away on Royal Street, an insignificant, decrepit, roach-heaven apartment that erupted into earthquake shivers every time a streetcar clickety-clacked by on the narrow street outside. It was unheated; in the winter one dreaded getting out of bed, and during the swampy summers it was like swimming inside a bowl of tepid consommé. My constant fantasy was that one excellent day I would move out of that dump and into the celestial confines of the Pontalba. But even if I had been able to afford it, it could never have happened. The usual way of acquiring a place there is if a tenant dies and wills it to you; or, if an apartment should become vacant, generally it is the custom of the city of New Orleans to offer it to a distinguished local citizen for a very nominal fee.

A lot of fey folk have strolled about this square. Pirates. Lafitte himself. Bonnie Parker and Clyde Barrow. Huey Long. Or, moseying under the shade of a scarlet parasol, the Countess Willie Piazza, the proprietress of one of the ritzier *maisons de plaisir* in the red-light neighborhood: her house was famous for an exotic refreshment it offered—fresh cherries boiled in cream sweetened with absinthe and served stuffed inside the vagina of a reclining quadroon beauty. Or another lady, so unlike the Countess Willie: Annie Christmas, a female keelboat operator who was seven feet tall and was often observed toting a hundred-pound barrel of flour under either arm. And Jim Bowie. And Mr. Neddie Flanders, a dapper gentleman in his eighties, maybe nineties, who, until recent years, appeared in the square each evening, and accompanying himself on a harmonica, tap-danced from midnight until dawn in the most delicate, limber-puppet way. The *characters*. I could list hundreds.

Uh-oh. What's this I hear across the way? Trouble. A ruckus. A man and a woman, both black: the man is heavyset, bull-necked, smartly coiffed but withal weak-mannered; she is thin, lemon-colored, shrill, but almost pretty.

. . .

HER: Sombitch. What you mean—hold out bread?! I ain't hold out no bread. Sombitch.

HIM: Hush, woman. I seen you. I counted. Three guys. Makes sixty bucks. You onna gimme thirty.

HER: Damn you, nigger. I oughta take a razor on your ear. I oughta cut out your liver and feed the cats. I oughta fry your eyes in turpentine. Listen, nigger. Let me hear you call me a liar again.

HIM (placating): Sugar—

HER: *Sugar.* I'll sugar you.

HIM: Miss Myrtle, now I knows what I seen.

HER (slowly: a serpentine drawl): Bastard. Nigger bastard. Fact is, you never had no mother. You was born out of a dog's ass.

(She slaps him. Hard. Turns and walks off, head high. He doesn't follow, but stands with a hand rubbing his cheek.)

For a while I watch the prancing spring-spry balloon children and see them greedily gather around a pushcart salesman selling a concoction known as Sweetmouth: scoops of flaked ice flavored with a rainbow-variety of colored syrups. Suddenly I recognize that I am hungry, too, and thirsty. I consider walking over to the French Market and filling up on deep-fried doughnuts and that bitter delicious chicory-flavored coffee peculiar to New Orleans. It's better than anything on the menu at Antoine's—which, by the way, is a lousy restaurant. So are most of the city's famous eateries. Gallatoire's isn't bad, but it's too crowded; they don't accept reservations, you always have to wait in long lines, and it's not worth it, at least not to me. Just as I've decided to amble off to the Market, an interruption occurs.

Now, if there is one thing I hate, it's people who sneak up behind you and say—

VOICE (whiskey-husky, virile, but female): Two guesses. (Silence) Come on, Jockey. You know it's me. (Silence; then, removing her blindfolding hands, somewhat petulantly) Jockey, you mean you didn't know it was *me?* Junebug?

TC: As I breathe—Big Junebug Johnson! *Comment ça va?*

BIG JUNEBUG JOHNSON (giggling with merriment): Oh, don't let me *commence.* Stand up, boy. Give old Junebug a hug. My, you're skinny. Like the first time I saw you. How much you weigh, Jockey?

TC: One twenty-five. Twenty-six.

(It is difficult to get my arms around her, for she weighs double that; more. I've known her going on forty years—ever since I lived alone at the gloomy Royal Street address and used to frequent a raucous waterfront bar she owned, and still does. If she had pink eyes, one might call her an albino, for her skin is white as calla lilies; so is her curly, skimpy hair. [Once she told me her hair had turned white overnight, before she was sixteen, and when I said *"Overnight?"* she said: "It was the roller-coaster ride and Ed Jenkins's peter. The two things coming so close together. See, one night I was riding on a roller-coaster out at the lake, and we were in the last car. Well, it came uncoupled, the car ran wild, we damn near fell off the track, and the next morning my hair had gray freckles. About a week later I had this experience with Ed Jenkins, a kid I knew. One of my girl friends told me that her brother had told her Ed Jenkins had the biggest peter anybody ever saw. He was nice-looking, but a scrawny fellow, not much taller than you, and I didn't believe it, so one day, joking him, I said, 'Ed Jenkins, I hear you have one helluva peter,' and he said, 'Yeah, I'll show you,' and he did, and I screamed; he said, 'And now I'm gonna put it in you,' and I said, 'Oh no you ain't!'—it was big as a baby's arm holding an apple. Lord's mercy! But he did. Put it in me. After a terrific tussle. And I was a virgin. Just about. Kind of. So you can imagine. Well, it wasn't long after that my hair went white like a witch."]

B.J.J. dresses stevedore-style: overalls, men's blue shirts rolled up to the elbow, ankle-high lace-up workman's boots, and no make-up to relieve her pallor. But she is womanly, a dignified figure for all her down-to-earth ways. And she wears expensive perfumes, Parisian smells bought at the Maison Blanche on Canal Street. Also, she has a glorious gold-toothed smile; it's like a heartening sunburst after a cold rainfall. You'd probably like her; most people do. Those who don't are mainly the proprietors of rival waterfront bars, for Big Junebug's is a popular hangout, if little known beyond the waterfront and that area's denizens. It contains three rooms—the big barroom itself with its mammoth zinc-topped bar, a second chamber furnished with three busy pool tables, and an alcove with a jukebox for dancing. It's open right around the clock, and is as crowded at dawn as it is at twilight. Of course, sailors and dockworkers go there, and the truck farmers who bring their produce to the French Market from outlying parishes, cops and firemen and hard-eyed gamblers and harder-eyed floozies, and around sunrise the place overflows with entertainers from the Bourbon Street tourist traps. Topless dancers, strippers, drag queens, B-girls, waiters, bartenders, and the hoarse-voiced doormen-barkers who so stridently labor to lure yokels into *vieux carré* sucker dives.

As for this "Jockey" business, it was a nickname I owed to Ginger Brennan. Forty-some years ago Ginger was the chief counterman at the old original all-night doughnuts-and-coffee café in the Market;

that particular café is gone now, and Ginger was long ago killed by a bolt of lightning while fishing off a pier at Lake Pontchartrain. Anyway, one night I overheard another customer ask Ginger who the "little punk" was in the corner, and Ginger, who was a pathological liar, bless his heart, told him I was a professional jockey: "He's pretty hot stuff out at the race track." It was plausible enough; I was short and featherweight and could easily have posed as a jockey; as it happened, it was a fantasy I cottoned to: I liked the idea of people mistaking me for a wise-guy race-track character. I started reading *Racing Form* and learned the lingo. Word spread, and before you could say Boo! everybody was calling me "The Jockey" and soliciting tips on the horses.)

BIG JUNEBUG JOHNSON: I lost weight myself. Maybe fifty pounds. Ever since I got married, I been losing weight. Most ladies, they get the ring, then start swelling up. But after I snagged Jim, I was so happy I stopped cleaning out my icebox. The blues, that's what makes you fat.

TC: Big Junebug Johnson married? Nobody wrote me that. I thought you were a devout bachelor.

BIG JUNEBUG JOHNSON: Can't a gal change her mind? Once I got over the Ed Jenkins incident, once I got that view out of my noggin, I was partial as the next lady for men. 'Course, that took years.

TC: Jim? That's his name?

BIG JUNEBUG JOHNSON: Jim O'Reilly. Ain't Irish, though. He comes from Plaquemine, and they're mostly Cajun, his people. I don't even know if that's his right name. I don't know a whole lot about him. He's kind of quiet.

TC: But some lover. To catch you.

BIG JUNEBUG JOHNSON (eyes rotating): Oh, honey, don't let me *commence.*

TC (laughs): That's one of the things I remember best about you. No matter what anybody said, whether it was the weather or whatever, you always said: "Oh, honey, don't let me *commence.*"

BIG JUNEBUG JOHNSON: Well. That kind of covers it all, wouldn't you say?
(Something I ought to have mentioned: she has a Brooklyn accent. If this sounds odd, it's not. Half the people in New Orleans don't sound Southern at all; close your eyes, and you would imagine you were listening to a taxi driver from Bensonhurst, a phenomenon that supposedly stems from the speech patterns idiosyncratic to a sector of the city known as the Irish Channel, a quarter predominantly populated by the descendants of Emerald Isle immigrants.)

TC: Just how long have you been Mrs. O'Reilly?

BIG JUNEBUG JOHNSON: Three years next July. Actually, I didn't have much choice. I was real confused. He's a lot younger than me, maybe twenty years. And good-looking, my goodness. Catnip to the ladies. But he was plain crazy about me, followed my every footstep, every minute begging me to hitch up, said he'd jump off the levee if I didn't. And presents every day. One time a pair of pearl earrings. Natural-born pearls: I bit them and they didn't crack. And a whole litter of kittens. He didn't know cats make me sneeze; make my eyes swell up, too. Everybody warned me he was only after my money. Why else would a cutie like him want an old hag like me? But that didn't altogether figure 'cause he has a real good job with the Streckfus Steamship Company. But they said he was broke, and in a lot of trouble with Red Tibeaux and Ambrose Butterfield and all those gamblers. I asked him, and he said it was a lie, but it could've been true, there was a lot I didn't know about him, and still don't. All I do know is he never asked me for a dime. I was so confused. So I went to Augustine Genet. You recall Madame Genet? Who could read the spirits? I heard she was on her deathbed, so I rushed right over there, and sure enough she was sinking. A hundred if she was a day, and blind as a mole; couldn't hardly whisper, but she told me: Marry that man, he's a good man, and he'll make you happy—marry him, promise me you will. So I promised. So that's why I had no choice. I couldn't ignore a promise made to a lady on her deathbed. And I'm soooo glad I didn't. *I am happy.* I am a happy woman. Even if those cats do make me sneeze. And you, Jockey. You feel good about yourself?

TC: So-so.

BIG JUNEBUG JOHNSON: When was the last time you got to Mardi Gras? TC (reluctant to reply, not desiring to evoke Mardi Gras memories: they were not amusing events to me, the streets swirling with drunken, squalling, shrouded figures wearing bad-dream masks; I always had nightmares after childhood excursions into Mardi Gras melees): Not since I was a kid. I was always getting lost in the crowds. The last time I got lost they took me to the police station. I was crying there all night before my mother found me.

BIG JUNEBUG JOHNSON: The damn police! You know we didn't have any Mardi Gras this year 'cause the police went on strike. Imagine, going on strike at a time like that. Cost this town millions. Blackmail is all it was. I've got some good police friends, good customers. But they're all a bunch of crooks, the entire shebang. I've never had no respect for the law around here, and how they treated Mr. Shaw finished me off for good. That so-called District Attorney *Jim* Garrison. What a sorry sonofagun. I hope the devil turns him on a slooow spit. And he will. Too bad Mr. Shaw won't be there to see it. From up high in *heaven,* where I know he is, Mr. Shaw won't be able to see old Garrison rotting in hell.

(B.J.J. is referring to Clay Shaw, a gentle, cultivated architect who was responsible for much of the finer-grade historical restoration in New Orleans. At one time Shaw was accused by James Garrison, the city's

abrasive, publicity-deranged D.A., of being the key figure in a purported plot to assassinate President Kennedy. Shaw stood trial twice
on this contrived charge, and though fully acquitted both times, he
was left more or less bankrupt. His health failed, and he died several
years ago.)

TC: After his last trial, Clay wrote me and said: "I've always thought I was
a little paranoid, but having survived this, I know I never was, and know
now I never will be."

BIG JUNEBUG JOHNSON: What is it—paranoid?

TC: Well. Oh, nothing. Paranoia's nothing. As long as you don't take it
seriously.

BIG JUNEBUG JOHNSON: I sure do miss Mr. Shaw. All during his trouble,
there was one way you could tell who was and who wasn't a gentleman
in this town. A gentleman, when he passed Mr. Shaw on the street, tipped
his hat; the bastards looked straight ahead. (Chuckling) Mr. Shaw, he was
a card. Every time he come in my bar, he kept me laughing. Ever hear his
Jesse James story? Seems one day Jesse James was robbing a train out West.
Him and his gang barged into a car with their pistols drawn, and Jesse
James shouts: "Hands up! We're gonna rob all the women and rape all the
men." So this one fellow says: "Haven't you got that wrong, sir? Don't you
mean you're gonna rob all the men and rape all the women?" But there
was this sweet little fairy on the train, and he pipes up: "Mind your own
business! Mr. James knows how to rob a train."

(Two and three and four: the hour-bells of St. Louis Cathedral toll:
. . . five . . . six . . . The toll is grave, like a gilded baritone voice reciting,
echoing ancient episodes, a sound that drifts across the park as solemnly as the oncoming dusk: music that mingles with the laughing
chatter, the optimistic farewells of the departing, sugar-mouthed, bal-
loon-toting kids, mingles with the solitary grieving howl of a far-off
shiphorn, and the jangling springtime bells of the syrup-ice peddler's
cart. Redundantly, Big Junebug Johnson consults her big ugly Rolex
wristwatch.)

BIG JUNEBUG JOHNSON: Lord save us. I ought to be halfway home. Jim has
to have his supper on the table seven sharp, and he won't let anybody fix
it for him 'cept me. Don't ask why. I can't cook worth an owl's ass, never
could. Only thing I could ever do real good was draw beer. And . . . Oh
hell, that reminds me: I'm on duty at the bar tonight. Usually now I just
work days, and Irma's there the rest of the time. But one of Irma's little
boys took sick, and she wants to be home with him. See, I forgot to tell
you, but I got a partner now, a widow gal with a real sense of fun, and
hardworking, too. Irma was married to a chicken farmer, and he up and
died, leaving her with five little boys, two of them twins, and her not thirty
yet. So she was scratching out a living on that farm—raising chickens and

wringing their necks and trucking them into the market here. All by herself. And her just a mite of a thing, but with a scrumptious figure, and natural strawberry hair, curly like mine. She could go up to Atlantic City and win a beauty contest if she wasn't cockeyed: Irma, she's so cockeyed you can't tell what she's looking at or who. She started coming into the bar with some of the other gal truckers. First off I reckoned she was a dyke, same as most of those gal truckers. But I was wrong. She likes men, and they dote on her, cockeyes and all. Truth is, I think my guy's got a sneaker for her; I tease him about it, and it makes him *soooo* mad. But if you want to know, I have more than a slight notion that Irma gets a real tingle when Jim's around. You can tell who she's looking at *then*. Well, I won't live forever, and after I'm gone, if they want to get together, that's fine by me. I'll have had my happiness. And I know Irma will take good care of Jim. She's a wonderful kid. That's why I talked her into coming into business with me. Say now, it's great to see you again, Jockey. Stop by later. We've got a lot to catch up on. But I've got to get my old bones rattling now.

Six . . . six . . . six . . . : the voice of the hour-bell tarries in the greening air, shivering as it subsides into the sleep of history.

Some cities, like wrapped boxes under Christmas trees, conceal unexpected gifts, secret delights. Some cities will always remain wrapped boxes, containers of riddles never to be solved, nor even to be seen by vacationing visitors, or, for that matter, the most inquisitive, persistent travelers. To know such cities, to unwrap them, as it were, one has to have been born there. Venice is like that. After October, when Adriatic winds sweep away the last American, even the last German, carry them off and send their luggage flying after them, another Venice develops: a clique of Venetian *élégants*, fragile dukes sporting embroidered waistcoats, spindly contessas supporting themselves on the arms of pale, elongated nephews; Jamesian creations, D'Annunzio romantics who would never consider emerging from the mauve shadows of their palazzos on a summer's day when the foreigners are abroad, emerge to feed the pigeons and stroll under the Piazza San Marco's arcades, sally forth to take tea in the lobby of the Danieli (the Gritti having closed until spring), and most amusing, to swill martinis and chew grilled-cheese sandwiches within the cozy confines of Harry's American Bar, so lately and exclusively the watering hole of loud-mouthed hordes from across the Alps and the seas.

Fez is another enigmatic city leading a double life, and Boston still another—we all understand that intriguing tribal rites are acted out beyond the groomed exteriors and purple-tinged bow windows of Louisburg Square, but except for what some literary, chosen-few Bostonians have divulged, we don't know what these coded rituals are, and never will.

However, of all secret cities, New Orleans, so it seems to me, is the most secretive, the most unlike, in reality, what an outsider is permitted to observe. The prevalence of steep walls, of obscuring foliage, of tall thick locked iron gates, of shuttered windows, of dark tunnels leading to overgrown gardens where mimosa and camellias contrast colors, and lazing lizards, flicking their forked tongues, race along palm fronds—all this is not accidental décor, but architecture deliberately concocted to camouflage, to mask, as at a Mardi Gras Ball, the lives of those born to live among these protective edifices: two cousins, who between them have a hundred other cousins spread throughout the city's entangling, intertangling familial relationships, whispering together as they sit under a fig tree beside the softly spilling fountain that cools their hidden garden.

A piano is playing. I can't decide where it's coming from: strong fingers playing a striding, riding-it-on-out piano: "I want, I want . . ." That's a black man singing; he's good—"I want, I want a mama, a big fat mama, I want a big fat mama with the meat shakin' on her, yeah!"

Footfalls. High-heeled feminine footsteps that approach and stop in front of me. It is the thin, almost pretty, high-yeller who earlier in the afternoon I'd overheard having a fuss with her "manager." She smiles, then winks at me, just one eye, then the other, and her voice is no longer angry. She sounds the way bananas taste.

HER: How you doin'?

TC: Just taking it easy.

HER: How you doin' for time?

TC: Let's see. I think it's six, a little after.

HER (laughs): I mean how you doin' for *time?* I got a place just around the corner here.

TC: I don't think so. Not today.

HER: You're cute.

TC: Everybody's entitled to their opinion.

HER: I'm not playing you. I mean it. You're cute.

TC: Well, thanks.

HER: But you don't look like you're having any fun. Come on. I'll show you a good time. We'll have fun.

TC: I don't think so.

HER: What's the matter? You don't like me?

TC: No, I like you.

HER: Then what's wrong? Give me a reason.

TC: There's a lot of reasons.

HER: Okay. Give me one, just one.

TC: Oh, honey, don't let me *commence.*

Hello, Stranger

(1979)

*T*ime: DECEMBER 1977.
Place: A New York restaurant, The
Four Seasons.

The man who had invited me to lunch, George Claxton, had suggested
we meet at noon, and made no excuse for setting such an early hour. I soon
discovered the reason, however; in the year or more since I had last seen
him, George Claxton, heretofore a man moderately abstemious, had become a two-fisted drinker. As soon as we were seated he ordered a double
Wild Turkey ("Just straight, please; no ice"), and within fifteen minutes
requested an encore.

I was surprised, and not just by the urgency of his thirst. He had gained
at least thirty pounds; the buttons of his pinstripe vest seemed on the verge
of popping loose, and his skin color, usually ruddy from jogging or tennis,
had an alien pallor, as though he had just emerged from a penitentiary.
Also, he was sporting dark glasses, and I thought: How theatrical! Imagine
good old plain George Claxton, solidly entrenched Wall Street fellow
living in Greenwich or Westport or wherever it was with a wife named
Gertrude or Alice or whatever it was, with three or four or five children,
imagine this guy chugging double Wild Turkeys and wearing dark glasses!

It was all I could do not to ask straight out: Well, what the hell happened
to you? But I said: "How are you, George?"

. . .

GEORGE: Fine. Fine. Christmas. Jesus. Just can't keep up with it. Don't expect a card from me this year. I'm not sending any.

TC: Really? Your cards seemed such a tradition. Those family things, with dogs. And how is your family?

GEORGE: Growing. My oldest daughter just had her second baby. A girl.

TC: Congratulations.

GEORGE: Well, we wanted a boy. If it had been a boy, she would have named him after me.

TC (thinking: Why am I here? Why am I having lunch with this jerk? He bores me, he's always bored me): And Alice? How is Alice?

GEORGE: Alice?

TC: I mean Gertrude.

GEORGE (frowning, peevish): She's painting. You know our house is right there on the Sound. Have our own little beach. She stays locked in her room all day painting what she sees from the window. Boats.

TC: That's nice.

GEORGE: I'm not so sure. She was a Smith girl; majored in art. She did a little painting before we were married. Then she forgot about it. Seemed to. Now she paints all the time. *All the time.* Stays locked in her room. Waiter, could you send the maître d' over with a menu? And bring me another of these things. No ice.

TC: That's very British, isn't it? Neat whiskey without ice.

GEORGE: I'm having root-canal. Anything cold hurts my teeth. You know who I got a Christmas card from? Mickey Manolo. The rich kid from Caracas? He was in our class.

> (Of course, I didn't remember Mickey Manolo, but I nodded and pretended yes, yes. Nor would I have remembered George Claxton if he hadn't kept careful track of me for forty-odd years, ever since we had been students together at an especially abysmal prep school. He was a straight-arrow athletic kid from an upper-middle-class Pennsylvania family; we had nothing in common, but we stumbled into an alliance because in exchange for my writing all his book reports and English compositions, he did my algebra homework and during examinations slipped me the answers. As a result, I had been stuck for four decades with a "friendship" that demanded a duty lunch every year or two.)

TC: You very seldom see women in this restaurant.

GEORGE: That's what I like about it. Not a lot of gibbering broads. It has a nice masculine look. You know, I don't think I'll have anything to eat. My teeth. It hurts too much to chew.

TC: Poached eggs?

GEORGE: There's something I'd like to tell you. Maybe you could give me a little advice.

TC: People who take my advice usually regret it. However . . .

GEORGE: This started last June. Just after Jeffrey's graduation—he's my youngest boy. It was a Saturday and Jeff and I were down on our little beach painting a boat. Jeff went up to the house to get us some beer and sandwiches, and while he was gone I suddenly stripped down and went for a swim. The water was still too cold. You can't really swim in the Sound much before July. But I just felt like it.

I swam out quite a ways and was lying there floating on my back and looking at my house. It's really a great house—six-car garage, swimming pool, tennis courts; too bad we've never been able to get you out there. Anyway, I was floating on my back feeling pretty good about life when I noticed this bottle bobbing in the water.

It was a clear-glass bottle that had contained some kind of soda pop. Someone had stoppered it with a cork and sealed it with adhesive tape. But I could see there was a piece of paper inside, a note. It made me laugh; I used to do that when I was a kid—stuff messages in bottles and throw them in the water: *Help! Man Lost at Sea!*

So I grabbed the bottle and swam ashore. I was curious to see what was inside it. Well, it was a note dated a month earlier, and it was written by a girl who lived in Larchmont. It said: *Hello, stranger. My name is Linda Reilly and I am twelve years old. If you find this letter please write and let me know when and where you found it. If you do I will send you a box of homemade fudge.*

The thing is, when Jeff came back with our sandwiches I didn't mention the bottle. I don't know why, but I didn't. Now I wish I had. Maybe then nothing would have happened. But it was like a little secret I wanted to keep to myself. A joke.

TC: Are you sure you aren't hungry? I'm only having an omelette.

GEORGE: Okay. An omelette, very soft.

TC: And so you wrote this young lady, Miss Reilly?

GEORGE (hesitantly): Yes. Yes, I did.

TC: What did you say?

GEORGE: On Monday, when I was back in my office, I was checking through my briefcase and I found the note. I say "found" because I don't remember putting it there. It had vaguely crossed my mind I'd drop the kid a card—just a nice gesture, you know. But that day I had lunch with a client who likes martinis. Now, I never used to drink at lunch—nor much any other time, either. But I had two martinis, and I went back to the office feeling swivel-headed. So I wrote this little girl quite a long letter; I didn't dictate it, I wrote it in longhand and told her where I lived and how I'd found her bottle and wished her luck and said some dumb thing like that though I was a stranger, I sent her the affectionate wishes of a friend.

TC: A two-martini missive. Still, where's the harm?

GEORGE: Silver Bullets. That's what they call martinis. Silver Bullets.

TC: How about that omelette? Aren't you even going to touch it?

GEORGE: Jesus Christ! My teeth *hurt*.

TC: It's really quite good. For a restaurant omelette.

GEORGE: About a week later a big box of fudge arrived. Sent to my office. Chocolate fudge with pecans. I passed it around the office and told everybody my daughter had made it. One of the guys said: "Oh, yeah! I'll bet old George has a secret girl friend."

TC: And did she send a letter with the fudge?

GEORGE: No. But I wrote a thank-you note. Very brief. Have you got a cigarette?

TC: I stopped smoking years ago.

GEORGE: Well, I just started. I still don't buy them, though. Just bum one now and then. Waiter, could you bring me a pack of cigarettes? Doesn't matter what brand, as long as it isn't menthol. And another Wild Turkey, please?

TC: I'd like some coffee.

GEORGE: But I got an answer to my thank-you note. A long letter. It really threw me. She enclosed a picture of herself. A color Polaroid. She was wearing a bathing suit and standing on a beach. She may have been twelve, but she looked sixteen. A lovely kid with short curly black hair and the bluest eyes.

TC: Shades of Humbert Humbert.

GEORGE: Who?

TC: Nothing. A character in a novel.

GEORGE: I never read novels. I hate to read.

TC: Yes, I know. After all, I used to do all your book reports. So what did Miss Linda Reilly have to say?

GEORGE (after pausing a full five seconds): It was very sad. Touching. She said she hadn't been living in Larchmont very long, and that she had no friends, and that she had tossed dozens of bottles into the water, but that I was the only person who had found one and answered. She said she was from Wisconsin, but that her father had died and her mother had married a man who had three daughters of his own and that none of them liked her. It was a ten-page letter, no misspellings. She said a lot of intelligent things. But she sounded really miserable. She said she hoped I'd write again, and maybe I could drive over to Larchmont and we could meet someplace. Do you mind listening to all this? If you do . . .

TC: Please. Go ahead.

GEORGE: I kept the picture. In fact, I put it in my wallet. Along with snaps of my other kids. See, because of the letter, I started to think of her as one of my own children. I couldn't get the letter out of my mind. And that night, when I took the train home, I did something I'd done only a very few times. I went into the club car and ordered myself a couple of stiff drinks and read the letter over and over. Memorized it, practically. Then when I got home I told my wife I had some office work to do. I shut myself in my den and started a letter to Linda. I wrote until midnight.

TC: Were you drinking all this time?

GEORGE (surprised): Why?

TC: It might have some bearing on what you wrote.

GEORGE: Yes, I was drinking, and I guess maybe it was a pretty emotional letter. But I felt so upset about this kid. I really wanted to help her. I wrote her about some of the troubles my own kids had had. About Harriet's acne and how she never had a single boyfriend. Not till she had her skin-peel. I told her about the hard times I'd had when I was growing up.

TC: Oh? I thought you'd enjoyed the ideal life of an ideal American youth.

GEORGE: I let people see what I wanted them to see. Inside was a different story.

TC: Had me fooled.

GEORGE: Around midnight my wife knocked on the door. She wanted to know if anything was wrong, and I told her to go back to bed, I had an urgent business letter to finish, and when it was finished I was going to drive down to the post office. She said why couldn't it wait until morning, it's after twelve. I lost my temper. Married thirty years, and I could count on ten fingers the times I've lost my temper with her. Gertrude is a wonderful, wonderful woman. I love her heart and soul. I do, goddamnit! But I shouted at her: No, it can't wait. It has to go tonight. It's very important.

(A waiter handed George a pack of cigarettes already opened. He stuck one in his mouth, and the waiter lit it for him, which was just as well, for his fingers were too agitated to hold a match without endangering himself.)

And Jesus Christ, it *was* important. Because I felt if I didn't mail the letter that night, I never would. Maybe, sober, I'd think it was too personal or something. And here was this lonely unhappy kid who'd shown me her heart: how would she feel if she never heard one word from me? No. I got in my car and drove down to the post office and as soon as I'd mailed the letter, dropped it into the slot, I felt too tired to drive home. I fell asleep in the car. It was dawn when I woke up, but my wife was asleep and she didn't notice when I came in.

I just about had time to shave and change my clothes before rushing off to catch the train. While I was shaving, Gertrude came into the bathroom. She was smiling; she hadn't mentioned my little temper tantrum. But she had my wallet in her hand, and she said, "George, I'm going to have Jeff's graduation picture enlarged for your mother," and with that she started shuffling through all the pictures in my wallet. I didn't think anything about it until suddenly she said: "Who is this girl?"

TC: And it was the young lady from Larchmont.

GEORGE: I should have told her the whole story right then. But I . . . Anyway, I said it was the daughter of one of my commuter friends. I said he'd been showing it to some of the guys on the train, and he'd forgot and left it on the bar. So I'd put it in my wallet to return the next time I saw him.

Garçon, un autre de Wild Turkey, s'il vous plaît.

TC (to the waiter): Make that a single.

GEORGE (in a tone unpleasantly pleasant): Are you telling me I've had too much to drink?

TC: If you have to go back to the office, yes.

GEORGE: But I'm not going back to my office. I haven't been there since early November. I'm supposed to have had a nervous breakdown. Overwork. Exhaustion. I'm supposed to be resting quietly at home, tenderly cared for by my adoring wife. Who is locked in her room painting pictures of boats. A boat. The same damn boat over and over.

TC: George, I've got to take a leak.

GEORGE: Not running out on me? Not running out on your old school buddy that sneaked you all the algebra answers?

TC: And even so, I flunked! Be back in a jiffy.

(I didn't need to take a leak; I needed to collect my thoughts. I didn't have the nerve to steal out of there and hide in a quiet movie somewhere, but I sure as hell didn't want to go back to that table. I washed my hands and combed my hair. Two men came in and stationed themselves at urinals. One said: "That guy that's so loaded. For a moment I thought it was somebody I know." His friend said: "Well, he's not a complete stranger. That's George Claxton." "You're kidding!" "I ought to know. He used to be my boss." "But my God! What happened?" "There are different stories." Then both men fell silent, perhaps out of deference to my presence. I returned to the dining room.)

GEORGE: So you *didn't* cut out?

(Actually, he seemed more subdued, less intoxicated. He was able to strike a match and light a cigarette with reasonable competence.)

Are you ready to hear the rest of this?

TC: (Silent, but with an encouraging nod)

GEORGE: My wife didn't say anything, just tucked the picture back in my wallet. I went on shaving, but cut myself twice. It had been so long since I'd had a real hangover, I'd forgotten what it was like. The sweat; my stomach—it felt like I was trying to shit razor blades. I stuffed a bottle of bourbon in my briefcase, and as soon as I got on the train I headed straight for the john. The first thing I did was to tear up the picture and drop it in the toilet. Then I sat down on the toilet and opened up that bottle. At first it made me gag. And it was hot as hell in there. Like Hades. But after a while I began to calm down, and to wonder: Well, what am I in such a stew about? I haven't done anything wrong. But when I stood up I saw that the torn-up Polaroid was still floating in the toilet bowl. I flushed it, and the pieces of the picture, her head and legs and arms, started churning around, and it made me dizzy: I felt like a killer who had taken a knife and cut her up.

By the time we got to Grand Central, I knew I was in no state to handle the office, so I walked over to the Yale Club and took a room. I called my secretary and said I had to go to Washington and wouldn't be in till the next day. Then I called home and told my wife that something had come up, a business thing, and I'd be staying overnight at the club. Then I got into bed, and thought: I'll sleep all day; I'll have one good long drink to relax me, stop the jitters, and go to sleep. But I couldn't—not until I'd downed the whole bottle. Boy, did I sleep then! Until around ten the next morning.

TC: About twenty hours.

GEORGE: About that. But I was feeling fairly okay when I woke up. They have a great masseur at the Yale Club, a German, hands strong as a gorilla's. That guy can really fix you up. So I had some sauna, a real storm-trooper massage, and fifteen minutes under a freezing shower. I stayed on and ate lunch at the club. No drinks, but boy, did I wolf it down. Four lamb chops, two baked potatoes, creamed spinach, corn-on-the-cob, a quart of milk, two deep-dish blueberry pies . . .

TC: I wish you'd eat something now.

GEORGE (a sharp bark, startlingly rude): Shut up!

TC: (Silence)

GEORGE: I'm sorry. I mean, it was like I was talking to myself. Like I'd forgotten you were here. And your voice . . .

TC: I understand. Anyway, you had a hearty lunch and you were feeling good.

GEORGE: Indeed. Indeed. The condemned man had a hearty lunch. Cigarette?

TC: I don't smoke.

GEORGE: That's right. Don't smoke. Haven't smoked for years.

TC: Here, I'll light that for you.

GEORGE: I'm perfectly capable of coping with a match without blowing up the place, thank you.

Well now, where were we? Oh yes, the condemned man was on his way to his office, subdued and shining.

It was Wednesday, the second week in July, a scorcher. I was alone in my office when my secretary rang through and said a Miss Reilly was on the phone. I didn't make the connection right off, and said: Who? What does she want? And my secretary said she says it's personal. The penny dropped. I said: Oh yes, put her on.

And I heard: "Mr. Claxton, this is Linda Reilly. I got your letter. It's the nicest letter I've ever had. I feel you really are a friend, and that's why I decided to take a chance on calling you. I was hoping you could help me. Because something has happened, and I don't know what I'll do if you can't help me." She had a sweet young-girl's voice, but was so breathless, so excited, that I had to ask her to speak more slowly. "I don't have much time, Mr. Claxton. I'm calling from upstairs and my mother might pick up the phone downstairs any minute. The thing is, I have a dog. Jimmy. He's six years old but frisky as can be. I've had him since I was a little girl, and he's the only thing I have. He's a real gent, just the cutest little dog you ever saw. But my mother is going to have him put to sleep. I'll die! I'll just die. Mr. Claxton, please, can you come to Larchmont and meet me in front of the Safeway? I'll have Jimmy with me, and you can take him away with you. Hide him until we can figure out what to do. I can't talk any more. My mother's coming up the stairs. I'll call you first chance I get tomorrow and we can make a date—"

TC: What did *you* say?

GEORGE: Nothing. She'd hung up.

TC: But what *would* you have said?

GEORGE: Well, as soon as she hung up, I decided that when she called back I'd say yes. Yes, I'd help the poor kid save her dog. That didn't mean I had to take it home with me. I could have put it in a kennel, or something. And if matters had turned out differently, that's what I would have done.

TC: I see. But she never called back.

GEORGE: Waiter, I'll have another one of these dark things. And a glass of Perrier, please. Yes, she called. And what she had to say was very brief. "Mr. Claxton, I'm sorry; I sneaked into a neighbor's house to phone, and I've got to hurry. My mother found your letters last night, the letters you wrote me. She's crazy, and her husband's crazy, too. They think all kinds of terrible things, and she took Jimmy away first thing this morning, but I can't talk any more; I'll try to call later."

But I didn't hear from her again—at least, not personally. My wife phoned a few hours later; I'd say it was about three in the afternoon. She said: "Darling, please come home as soon as you can," and her voice was so calm that I knew she was in extreme distress; I even half-knew why, although I acted surprised when she told me: "There are two policemen here. One from Larchmont and one from the village. They want to talk to you. They won't tell me why."

I didn't bother with the train. I hired a limousine. One of those limousines with a bar installed. It's not much of a drive, just over an hour, but I managed to knock down quite a few Silver Bullets. It didn't help much; I was really scared.

TC: Why, for Christ's sake? What had you done? Play Mr. Good Guy, Mr. Pen Pal.

GEORGE: If only it were that neat. That tidy. Anyway, when I got home the cops were sitting in the living room watching television. My wife was serving them coffee. When she offered to leave the room, I said no, I want you to stay and hear this, whatever it is. Both the cops were very young and embarrassed. After all, I was a rich man, a prominent citizen, a churchgoer, the father of five children. I wasn't frightened of them. It was Gertrude.

The Larchmont cop outlined the situation. His office had received a complaint from a Mr. and Mrs. Henry Wilson that their twelve-year-old daughter, Linda Reilly, had been receiving letters of a "suspicious nature" from a fifty-two-year-old man, namely, me, and the Wilsons intended to bring charges if I couldn't explain myself satisfactorily.

I laughed. Oh, I was just as jovial as Santa Claus. I told the whole story. About finding the bottle. Said I'd only answered it because I liked chocolate fudge. I had them grinning, apologizing, shuffling their big feet, and saying well, you know how parents get nutty ideas nowadays. The only one not taking it all as a dumb joke was Gertrude. In fact, without my realizing it, she'd left the room before I'd finished talking.

After the cops left, I knew where I'd find her. In that room, the one where she does her painting. It was dark and she was sitting there in a straight-back chair staring out at the darkness. She said: "The picture in your wallet. That was the girl." I denied it, and she said: "Please, George. You don't have to lie. You'll never have to lie again."

And she slept in that room that night, and every night ever since. Keeps herself locked in there painting boats. A boat.

TC: Perhaps you did behave a bit recklessly. But I can't see why she should be so unforgiving.

GEORGE: I'll tell you why. That wasn't our first visit from the police.

Seven years ago we had a sudden heavy snowstorm. I was driving my car, and even though I wasn't far from home, I lost my way several times. I asked directions from a number of people. One was a child, a young girl. A few days later the police came to the house. I wasn't there, but they talked to Gertrude. They told her that during the recent snowstorm a man answering my description and driving a Buick with my license plate had got out of his car and exposed himself to a young girl. Spoken lewdly to her. The girl said she had copied down the license number in the snow under a tree, and when the storm had stopped, it was still decipherable. There was no denying that it was my license number, but the story was untrue. I convinced Gertrude, and I convinced the police, that the girl was either lying or that she had made a mistake concerning the number.

But now the police have come a second time. About another young girl.

And so my wife stays in her room. Painting. Because she doesn't believe me. She believes that the girl who wrote the number in the snow told the truth. I'm innocent. Before God, on the heads of my children, I am innocent. But my wife locks her door and looks out the window. She doesn't believe me. Do you?

> (George removed his dark glasses and polished them with a napkin. Now I understood why he wore them. It wasn't because of the yellowed whites engraved with swollen red veins. It was because his eyes were like a pair of shattered prisms. I have never seen pain, a suffering, so permanently implanted, as if the slip of a surgeon's knife had left him forever disfigured. It was unbearable, and as he stared at me my own eyes flinched away.)

Do *you* believe me?

TC (reaching across the table and taking his hand, holding it for dear life): Of course, George. Of course I believe you.

Derring-do

(1979)

Time: NOVEMBER, 1970.
Place: Los Angeles International Airport.

I am sitting inside a telephone booth. It is a little after eleven in the morning, and I've been sitting here half an hour, pretending to make a call. From the booth I have a good view of Gate 38, from which TWA's nonstop noon flight to New York is scheduled to depart. I have a seat booked on that flight, a ticket bought under an assumed name, but there is every reason to doubt that I will ever board the plane. For one thing, there are two tall men standing at the gate, tough guys with snap-brim hats, and I know both of them. They're detectives from the San Diego Sheriff's Office, and they have a warrant for my arrest. That's why I'm hiding in the phone booth. The fact is, I'm in a real predicament.

The cause of my predicament had its roots in a series of conversations I'd conducted a year earlier with Robert M., a slender, slight, harmless-looking young man who was then a prisoner on Death Row at San Quentin, where he was awaiting execution, having been convicted of three slayings: his mother, a sister, both of whom he had beaten to death, and a fellow prisoner, a man he had strangled while he was in jail awaiting trial for the two original homicides. Robert M. was an intelligent psychopath; I got to know him fairly well, and he discussed his life and crimes with me freely—with the understanding that I would not write about or repeat anything that he told me. I was doing research on the subject of multiple murderers, and Robert M. became another case history that went into my files. As far as I was concerned, that was the end of it.

Then, two months prior to my incarceration in a sweltering telephone booth at Los Angeles airport, I received a call from a detective in the San Diego Sheriff's Office. He had called me in Palm Springs, where I had a house. He was courteous and pleasant-voiced; he said he knew about the many interviews I'd conducted with convicted murderers, and that he'd like to ask me a few questions. So I invited him to drive down to the Springs and have lunch with me the following day.

The gentleman did not arrive alone, but with three other San Diego detectives. And though Palm Springs lies deep in the desert, there was a strong smell of fish in the air. However, I pretended there was nothing odd about suddenly having four guests instead of one. But they were not interested in my hospitality; indeed, they declined lunch. All they wanted to talk about was Robert M. How well did I know him? Had he ever admitted to me any of his killings? Did I have any records of our conversations? I let them ask their questions, and avoided answering them until I asked my own question: Why were they so interested in my acquaintance with Robert M.?

The reason was this: due to a legal technicality, a federal court had overruled Robert M.'s conviction and ordered the state of California to grant him a new trial. The starting date for the retrial had been set for late November—in other words, approximately two months hence. Then, having delivered these facts, one of the detectives handed me a slim but exceedingly legal-looking document. It was a subpoena ordering me to appear at Robert M.'s trial, presumably as a witness for the prosecution. Okay, they'd tricked me, and I was mad as hell, but I smiled and nodded, and they smiled and said what a good guy I was and how grateful they were that my testimony would help send Robert M. straight to the gas chamber. That homicidal lunatic! They laughed, and said good-bye: "See ya in court."

I had no intention of honoring the subpoena, though I was aware of the consequences of not doing so: I would be arrested for contempt of court, fined, and sent to jail. I had no high opinion of Robert M., or any desire to protect him; I knew he was guilty of the three murders with which he was charged, and that he was a dangerous psychotic who ought never to be allowed his freedom. But I also knew that the state had more than enough hard evidence to reconvict him without my testimony. But the main point was that Robert M. had confided in me on my sworn word that I would not use or repeat what he told me. To betray him under these circumstances would have been morally despicable, and would have proven to Robert M., and the many men like him whom I'd interviewed, that they had placed their trust in a police informer, a stool pigeon plain and simple.

I consulted several lawyers. They all gave the same advice: honor the subpoena or expect the worst. Everyone sympathized with my quandary, but no one could see any solution—*unless I left California.* Contempt of court was not an extraditable offense, and once I was out of the state, there was nothing the authorities could do to punish me. Yes, there was one thing: I could never *return* to California. That didn't strike me as a severe hardship, although, because of various property matters and professional commitments, it was difficult to depart on such short notice.

I lost track of time, and was still tarrying in Palm Springs the day the trial began. That morning my housekeeper, a devoted friend named Myrtle Bennett, rushed into the house hollering: "Hurry up! It's all on the radio. They've got a warrant out for your arrest. They'll be here any minute."

Actually, it was twenty minutes before the Palm Springs police arrived full-force and with handcuffs at the ready (an overkill scene, but believe me, California law enforcement is not an institution one toys with lightly). However, though they dismantled the garden and searched the house stem to stern, all they found was my car in the garage and the loyal Mrs. Bennett in the living room. She told them I'd left for New York the previous day. They didn't believe her, but Mrs. Bennett was a formidable figure in Palm Springs, a black woman who had been a distinguished and politically influential member of the community for forty years, so they didn't question her further. They simply sent out an all-points alarm for my arrest.

And where *was* I? Well, I was tooling along the highway in Mrs. Bennett's old powder-blue Chevrolet, a car that couldn't do fifty miles an hour the day she bought it. But we figured I'd be safer in her car than my own. Not that I was safe anywhere; I was jumpy as a catfish with a hook in its mouth. When I got to Palm Desert, which is about thirty minutes out of Palm Springs, I turned off the highway and onto the lonely curving careening little road that leads away from the desert and up into the San Jacinto mountains. It had been hot in the desert, over a hundred, but as I climbed higher in the desolate mountains the air became cool, then cold, then colder. Which was okay, except that the old Chevy's heater wouldn't work, and all I had to wear were the clothes I had on when Mrs. Bennett had rushed into the house with her panic-stricken warnings: sandals, white linen slacks, and a light polo sweater. I'd left with just that and my wallet, which contained credit cards and about three hundred dollars.

Still, I had a destination in mind, and a plan. High in the San Jacinto mountains, midway between Palm Springs and San Diego, there's a grim little village named Idylwyld. In the summer, people from the desert travel there to escape the heat; in the winter it's a ski resort, though the quality of both the snow and the runs is threadbare. But now, out of season, this grim collection of mediocre motels and fake chalets would be a good place to lie low, at least until I could catch my breath.

It was snowing when the old car grunted up the last hill into Idylwyld: one of those young snows that suffuse the air but dissolve as it falls. The village was deserted, and most of the motels closed. The one I finally stopped at was called Eskimo Cabins. God knows, the accommodations were icy as igloos. It had one advantage: the proprietor, and apparently the only human on the premises, was a semi-deaf octogenarian far more interested in the game of solitaire he was playing than he was in me.

I called Mrs. Bennett, who was very excited: "Oh, honey, they're looking for you everywhere! It's all on the TV!" I decided it was better not to let her know where I was, but assured her I was all right and would call again tomorrow. Then I telephoned a close friend in Los Angeles; he was excited, too: "Your picture is in the *Examiner!*" After calming him down, I gave specific instructions: buy a ticket for a "George Thomas" on a nonstop flight to New York, and expect me at his house by ten o'clock the next morning.

I was too cold and hungry to sleep; I left at daybreak, and reached Los Angeles around nine. My friend was waiting for me. We left the Chevrolet at his house, and after wolfing down some sandwiches and as much brandy as I could safely contain, we drove in his car to the airport, where we said good-bye and he gave me the ticket for the noon flight he had booked for me on TWA.

So that's how I happen now to be huddled in this forsaken telephone booth, sitting here contemplating my predicament. A clock above the departure gate announces the hour: 11:35. The passenger area is crowded; soon the plane will be ready for boarding. And there, standing on either side of the gate through which I must pass, are two of the gentlemen who had visited me in Palm Springs, two tall watchful detectives from San Diego.

I considered calling my friend, asking him to return to the airport and pick me up somewhere in the parking lot. But he'd already done enough, and if we were caught, he could be accused of harboring a fugitive. That held true for all the many friends who might be willing to assist me. Perhaps it would be wisest to surrender myself to the guardians at the gate. Otherwise, what? Only a miracle, to coin a phrase, was going to save me. And we don't believe in miracles, do we?

Suddenly a miracle occurs.

There, striding past my tiny glass-doored prison, is a haughty, beautiful black Amazon wearing a zillion dollars' worth of diamonds and golden sable, a star surrounded by a giddy, chattering entourage of gaudily dressed chorus boys. And who is this dazzling apparition whose plumage and presence are creating such a commotion among the passers-by? A friend! An old, old friend!

. . .

TC (opening the booth's door; shouting): *Pearl!* Pearl Bailey! (A miracle! She *hears* me. All of them do, her whole entourage) Pearl! Please come here . . .

PEARL (squinting at me, then erupting into a radiant grin): Why, baby! What you doing hiding in there?

TC (beckoning her to come closer; whispering): Pearl, listen. I'm in a terrific jam.

PEARL (immediately serious, for she is a very intelligent woman, and at once understood that whatever this was, it wasn't funny): Tell it to me.

TC: Are you on that plane to New York?

PEARL: Yeah, we all are.

TC: I've got to get on it, Pearl. I have a ticket. But there're two guys waiting at the gate to stop me.

PEARL: Which guys? (I pointed them out) How can they stop you?

TC: They're detectives. Pearl, I haven't got time to explain all this . . .

PEARL: You don't have to explain nothing.

(She surveyed her troupe of handsome young black chorus boys; she had a half-dozen—Pearl, I remembered, always liked to travel with a lot of company. She motioned to one of them to join us; he was a sleek number sporting a yellow cowboy hat, a sweatshirt that said SUCK DAMMIT, DONT BLOW, a white leather windbreaker with an ermine lining, yellow jitterbug pants [circa 1940], and yellow Wedgies.)

This is Jimmy. He's a little bigger than you, but I think it'll all fit. Jimmy, take my friend here to the men's room and change clothes with him. Jimmy, don't flap your yap, just do like Pearlie-Mae say. We'll wait right here for you. Now hurry up! Ten more minutes and we'll miss that plane.

(The distance between the telephone booth and the men's room was a ten-yard dash. We locked ourselves into a pay toilet and started our wardrobe exchange. Jimmy thought it was a riot: he was giggling like a schoolgirl who's just puffed her first joint. I said: "Pearl! That really was a miracle. I've never been so happy to see someone. Never." Jimmy said: "Oh, Miss Bailey's got spirit. She's all heart, know what I mean? All heart."

There was a time when I would have disagreed with him, a time when I would have described Pearl Bailey as a heartless bitch. That was when she was playing the part of Madame Fleur, the principal role in *House of Flowers*, a musical play for which I had written the book and, with Harold Arlen, co-authored the lyrics. There were many gifted men attached to that endeavor: the director was Peter Brook; the choreographer, George Balanchine; Oliver Messel was responsible for the legendarily enchanting décor and costumes. But Pearl Bailey was so strong, so determined to have her way, that she dominated the entire production, much to its ultimate detriment. However, live and learn, forgive and forget, and by the time the play ended its Broadway run, Pearl and I were friends again. Aside from her skill as a performer, I'd come to respect her character; it might occasionally be unpleasant to deal with, but certainly she had it: she was a woman of character—one knew who she was and where she stood.

As Jimmy was squeezing into my trousers, which were embarrassingly too tight for him, and as I was slipping on his white leather ermine-lined windbreaker, there was an agitated knock at the door.)

MAN'S VOICE: Hey! What's goin' on in there?

JIMMY: And just *who* are *you*, pray tell?

MAN'S VOICE: I'm the attendant. And don't sass me. What's going on in there is against the law.

JIMMY: No shit?

ATTENDANT: I see four feet in there. I see clothes comin' off. You think I'm too stupid I don't know what's goin' on? It's against the law. It's against the law for two men to lock themselves in the same toilet at the same time.

JIMMY: Aw, shove it up your ass.

ATTENDANT: I'll get the cops. They'll hand you an L and L.

JIMMY: What the hell's an L and L?

ATTENDANT: Lewd and lascivious conduct. Yessir. I'll get the cops.

TC: Jesus, Joseph, and Mary—

ATTENDANT: Open that door!

TC: You've got it all wrong.

ATTENDANT: I know what I see. I see four feet.

TC: We're changing our costumes for the next scene.

ATTENDANT: Next scene what?

TC: The movie. We're getting ready to shoot the next scene.

ATTENDANT (curious and impressed): They're making a movie out there?

JIMMY (catching on): With Pearl Bailey. She's the star. Marlon Brando, he's in it, too.

TC: Kirk Douglas.

JIMMY (biting his knuckles to keep from laughing): And Shirley Temple. She's making her comeback.

ATTENDANT (believing, yet not believing): Yeah, well, who are you?

TC: We're just extras. That's why we don't have a dressing room.

ATTENDANT: I don't care. Two men, four feet. It's against the law.

JIMMY: Look outside. You'll see Pearl Bailey in person. Marlon Brando. Kirk Douglas. Shirley Temple. Mahatma Gandhi—she's in it, too. Just a cameo.

ATTENDANT: Who?

JIMMY: Mamie Eisenhower.

TC (opening the door, having completed the transference of clothing; my stuff doesn't look too bad on Jimmy, but I suspect that his outfit, as worn by me, will produce a galvanizing effect, and the expression on the attendant's face, a bristling short black man, confirms this expectation): Sorry. We didn't realize we were doing anything against the rules.

JIMMY (regally sweeping past the attendant, who seems too befuddled to budge): Follow us, sweetheart. We'll introduce you to the gang. You can get some autographs.

(At last we were in the corridor, and an unsmiling Pearl wrapped her sable-soft arms around me; her companions closed about us in a concealing circle. There were no jokes or jesting. My nerves sizzled like a cat just hit by lightning, and as for Pearl, the qualities about her that had once alarmed me—that strength, that self-will—were flowing through her like power from a waterfall.)

PEARL: From now on keep quiet. Whatever I say, don't you say anything. Tuck the hat more over your face. Lean on me like you're weak and sick. Lean your face against my shoulder. Close your eyes. Let me lead you.

All right. We're moving now toward the counter. Jimmy has all the tickets. They've already announced the last boarding call, so there aren't too many people around. Those gumshoes haven't moved an inch, but they seem tired and kind of disgusted. They're looking at us now. Both of them. When we pass between them the boys will distract them and start jabbering. Here comes somebody. Lean closer, groan a little—it's one of those VIP guys from TWA. Watch Mama go into her act . . . (Changing voice, impersonating her theatrical self, simultaneously droll and drawling and slightly flaky) Mr. Calloway? Like in Cab? Well, aren't you just an angel to help us out. And we surely could use some help. We need to get on that plane just as fast as possible. My friend here—he's one of my musicians— he's feeling something terrible. Can't hardly walk. We've been playing Vegas, and maybe he got too much sun. Sun can addle your brain and your stomach both. Or maybe it's his diet. Musicians eat funny. Piano players in particular. He won't eat hardly anything but hot dogs. Last night he ate ten hot dogs. Now, that's just not healthy. I'm not surprised he feels poisoned. Are you surprised, Mr. Calloway? Well, I don't suppose very much surprises you, being in the airplane business. All this hijacking that's going on. Criminals afoot all over the place. Soon as we get to New York, I'm taking my friend straight to the doctor. I'm going to tell the doctor to tell him to stay out of the sun and stop eating hot dogs. Oh, thank you, Mr. Calloway. No, I'll take the aisle. We'll put my friend in the window seat. He'll be better off by the window. All that fresh air.

Okay, Buster. You can open your eyes now.

TC: I think I'll keep them closed. It makes it seem more like a dream.

PEARL (relaxed, chuckling): Anyway, we made it. Your friends never even saw you. As we went by, Jimmy goosed one, and Billy stomped on the other guy's toes.

TC: Where is Jimmy?

PEARL: All the kids go economy. Jimmy's duds do something for you. Pep you up. I like the Wedgies especially—just love 'em.

STEWARDESS: Good morning, Miss Bailey. Would you care for a glass of champagne?

PEARL: No, honey. But maybe my friend could use something.

TC: Brandy.

STEWARDESS: I'm sorry, sir, but we only serve champagne until after takeoff.

PEARL: The man wants brandy.

STEWARDESS: I'm sorry, Miss Bailey. It's not permitted.

PEARL (in a smooth yet metallic tone familiar to me from *House of Flowers* rehearsals): Bring the man his brandy. The whole bottle. Now.

(The stewardess brought the brandy, and I poured myself a hefty dose with an unsteady hand: hunger, fatigue, anxiety, the dizzying events of the last twenty-four hours were presenting their bill. I treated myself to another drink and began to feel a bit lighter.)

TC: I suppose I ought to tell you what this is all about.

PEARL: Not necessarily.

TC: Then I won't. That way you'll have a free conscience. I'll just say that I haven't done anything a sensible person would classify as criminal.

PEARL (consulting a diamond wristwatch): We should be over Palm Springs by now. I heard the door close ages ago. Stewardess!

STEWARDESS: Yes, Miss Bailey?

PEARL: What's going on?

STEWARDESS: Oh, there's the captain now—

CAPTAIN'S VOICE (over loudspeaker): Ladies and gentlemen, we regret the delay. We should be departing shortly. Thank you for your patience.

TC: Jesus, Joseph, and Mary.

PEARL: Have another slug. You're shaking. You'd think it was a first night. I mean, it can't be *that* bad.

TC: It's worse. And I can't stop shaking—not till we're in the air. Maybe not till we land in New York.

PEARL: You still living in New York?

TC: Thank God.

PEARL: You remember Louis? My husband?

TC: Louis Bellson. Sure. The greatest drummer in the world. Better than Gene Krupa.

PEARL: We both work Vegas so much, it made sense to buy a house there. I've become a real homebody. I do a lot of cooking. I'm writing a cookbook. Living in Vegas is just like living anywhere else, as long as you stay away from the undesirables. *Gamblers.* Unemployeds. Any time a man says to me he'd work if he could find a job, I always tell him to look in the phone book under G. G for gigolo. He'll find work. In Vegas, anyways. That's a town of desperate women. I'm lucky; I found the right man and had the sense to know it.

TC: Are you going to work in New York?

PEARL: Persian Room.

CAPTAIN'S VOICE: I'm sorry, ladies and gentlemen, but we'll be delayed a few minutes longer. Please remain seated. Those who care to smoke may do so.

PEARL (suddenly stiffening): I don't like this. They're opening the door.

TC: What?

PEARL: *They're opening the door.*

TC: Jesus, Joseph—

PEARL: I don't like this.

TC: Jesus, Joseph—

PEARL: Slump down in the seat. Pull the hat over your face.

TC: I'm scared.

PEARL (gripping my hand, squeezing it): Snore.

TC: Snore?

PEARL: Snore!

TC: I'm strangling. I *can't* snore.

PEARL: You'd better start trying, 'cause our friends are coming through that door. Looks like they're gonna roust the joint. Clean-tooth it.

TC: Jesus, Joseph—

PEARL: Snore, you rascal, snore.

(I snored, and she increased the pressure of her hold on my hand; at the same time she began to hum a low sweet lullaby, like a mother soothing a fretful child. All the while another kind of humming surrounded us: human voices concerned with what was happening on the plane, the purpose of the two mysterious men who were pacing up and down the aisles, pausing now and again to scrutinize a passenger. Minutes elapsed. I counted them off: six, seven. Tickticktick. Eventually Pearl stopped crooning her maternal melody, and withdrew her hand from mine. Then I heard the plane's big round door slam shut.)

TC: Have they gone?

PEARL: Uh-huh. But whoever it is they're looking for, they sure must want him bad.

They did indeed. Even though Robert M.'s retrial ended exactly as I had predicted, and the jury brought in a verdict of guilty on three counts of first-degree murder, the California courts continued to take a harsh view of my refusal to cooperate with them. I was not aware of this; I thought that in due time the matter would be forgotten. So I did not hesitate to return to California when a year later something came up that required at least a brief visit there. Well, sir, I had no sooner registered at the Bel Air Hotel than I was arrested, summoned before a hard-nosed judge who fined me five thousand dollars and gave me an indefinite sentence in the Orange County jail, which meant they could keep me locked up for weeks or months or years. However, I was soon released because the summons for my arrest contained a small but significant error: it listed me as a legal resident of California, when in fact I was a resident of New York, a fact which made my conviction and confinement invalid.

But all that was still far off, unthought of, undreamed of when the silver vessel containing Pearl and her outlaw friend swept off into an ethereal November heaven. I watched the plane's shadow ripple over the desert and drift across the Grand Canyon. We talked and laughed and ate and sang. Stars and the lilac of twilight filled the air, and the Rocky Mountains, shrouded in blue snow, loomed ahead, a lemony slice of new moon hovering above them.

TC: Look, Pearl. A new moon. Let's make a wish.

PEARL: What are you going to wish?

TC: I wish I could always be as happy as I am at this very moment.

PEARL: Oh, honey, that's like asking miracles. Wish for something real.

TC: But I believe in miracles.

PEARL: Then all I can say is: don't ever take up gambling.

Nocturnal
Turnings

or How Siamese Twins Have Sex

(1979)

TC: Shucks! Wide awake! Lawsamercy, we ain't been dozed off a minute. How long we been dozed off, honey?

TC: It's two now. We tried to go to sleep around midnight, but we were too tense. So you said why don't we jack off, and I said yes, that ought to relax us, it usually does, so we jacked off and went right to sleep. Sometimes I wonder: Whatever would we do without Mother Fist and her Five Daughters? They've certainly been a friendly bunch to us through the years. Real pals.

TC: A lousy two hours. Lawd knows when we'll shut our eyes agin. An' cain't do nothin' 'bout it. Cain't haf a lil old sip of sompin 'cause dats a naw-naw. Nor none of dem snoozy pills, dat bein' also a naw-naw.

TC: Come on. Knock off the Amos 'n' Andy stuff. I'm not in the mood tonight.

TC: You're never in the mood. You didn't even want to jack off.

TC: Be fair. Have I ever denied you that? When you want to jack off, I always lie back and let you.

TC: Y'all ain't got de choice, dat's why.

TC: I much prefer solitary satisfaction to some of the duds you've forced me to endure.

TC: 'Twas up to you, we'd never have sex with anybody except each other.

TC: Yes, and think of all the misery *that* would have saved us.

TC: But then, we would never have been in love with people other than each other.

TC: Ha ha ha ha ha. Ho ho ho ho ho. "Is it an earthquake, or only a shock? Is it the real turtle soup, or merely the mock? Is it the Lido I see, or Asbury Park?" Or is it at long last shit?

TC: You never could sing. Not even in the bathtub.

TC: You really are bitchy tonight. Maybe we could pass some time by working on your Bitch List.

TC: I wouldn't call it a *Bitch* List. It's more sort of what you might say is a Strong Dislike List.

TC: Well, who are we strongly disliking tonight? Alive. It's not interesting if they're not alive.

TC: Billy Graham
    Princess Margaret
    Billy Graham
    Princess Anne
    The Reverend Ike
    Ralph Nader
    Supreme Court Justice Byron "Whizzer" White
    Princess Z
    Werner Erhard
    The Princess Royal
    Billy Graham
    Madame Gandhi
    Masters and Johnson
    Princess Z
    Billy Graham
    CBSABCNBCNET
    Sammy Davis, Jr.
    Jerry Brown, Esq.
    Billy Graham
    Princess Z
    J. Edgar Hoover
    Werner Erhard

TC: One minute! J. Edgar Hoover is dead.

TC: No, he's not. They cloned old Johnny, and he's everywhere. They cloned Clyde Tolson, too, just so they could go on goin' steady. Cardinal Spellman, cloned version, occasionally joins them for a partouze.

TC: Why harp on Billy Graham?

TC: Billy Graham, Werner Erhard, Masters and Johnson, Princess Z— they're all full of horse manure. But the Reverend Billy is just *so* full of it.

TC: The fullest of anybody thus far?

TC: No, Princess Z is more fully packed.

TC: How so?

TC: Well, after all, she *is* a horse. It's only natural that a horse can hold more horse manure than a human, however great his capacity. Don't you remember Princess Z, that filly that ran in the fifth at Belmont? We bet on her and lost a bundle, practically our last dollar. And you said: "It's just like Uncle Bud used to say—'Never put your money on a horse named Princess.' "

TC: Uncle Bud was smart. Not like our old cousin Sook, but smart. Anyway, who do we Strongly Like? Tonight, at least.

TC: Nobody. They're all dead. Some recently, some for centuries. Lots of them are in Père-Lachaise. Rimbaud isn't there; but it's amazing who is. Gertrude and Alice. Proust. Sarah Bernhardt. Oscar Wilde. I wonder where Agatha Christie is buried—

TC: Sorry to interrupt, but surely there is someone alive we Strongly Like?

TC: Very difficult. A real toughie. Okay. Mrs. Richard Nixon. The Empress of Iran. Mr. William "Billy" Carter. Three victims, three saints. If Billy Graham was Billy Carter, then Billy Graham would be Billy Graham.

TC: That reminds me of a woman I sat next to at dinner the other night. She said: "Los Angeles is the perfect place to live—if you're Mexican."

TC: Heard any other good jokes lately?

TC: That wasn't a joke. That was an accurate social observation. The Mexicans in Los Angeles have their own culture, and a genuine one; the rest have zero. A city of suntanned Uriah Heeps.

However, I *was* told something that made me chuckle. Something D. D. Ryan said to Greta Garbo.

TC: Oh, yes. They live in the same building.

TC: And have for more than twenty years. Too bad they're not good friends, they'd like each other. They both have humor and conviction, but only *en passant* pleasantries have been exchanged, nothing more. A few weeks ago D.D. stepped into the elevator and found herself alone with Garbo. D.D. was costumed in her usual striking manner, and Garbo, as though she'd never truly noticed her before, said: "Why, Mrs. Ryan, you're *beautiful.*" And D.D., amused but really touched, said: "Look who's talkin'."

TC: That's all?

TC: *C'est tout.*

TC: It seems sort of pointless to me.

TC: Look, forget it. It's not important. Let's turn on the lights and get out the pens and paper. Start that magazine article. No use lying here gabbing with an oaf like you. May as well try to make a nickel.

TC: You mean that Self-Interview article where you're supposed to interview yourself? Ask your own questions and answer them?

TC: Uh-huh. But why don't you just lie there quiet while I do this? I need a rest from your evil frivolity.

TC: Okay, scumbag.

TC: Well, here goes.

Q: What frightens you?

A: Real toads in imaginary gardens.

Q: No, but in real life—

A: I'm talking about real life.

Q: Let me put it another way. What, of your own experiences, have been the most frightening?

A: Betrayals. Abandonments.

But you want something more specific? Well, my very earliest childhood memory was on the scary side. I was probably three years old, perhaps a little younger, and I was on a visit to the St. Louis Zoo, accompanied by a large black woman my mother had hired to take me there. Suddenly there was pandemonium. Children, women, grown-up men were shouting and hurrying in every direction. Two lions had escaped from their cages! Two bloodthirsty beasts were on the prowl in the park. My nurse panicked. She simply turned and ran, leaving me alone on the path. That's all I remember about it.

When I was nine years old I was bitten by a cottonmouth water moccasin. Together with some cousins, I'd gone exploring in a lonesome forest about six miles from the rural Alabama town where we lived. There was a narrow, shallow crystal river that ran through this forest. There was a huge fallen log that lay across it from bank to bank like a bridge. My cousins, balancing themselves, ran across the log, but I decided to wade the little river. Just as I was about to reach the farther bank, I saw an enormous cottonmouth moccasin swimming, slithering on the water's shadowy surface. My own mouth went dry as cotton; I was paralyzed, numb, as though my whole body had been needled with Novocaine. The snake kept sliding, winding toward me. When it was within inches of me, I spun around, and slipped on a bed of slippery creek pebbles. The cottonmouth bit me on the knee.

Turmoil. My cousins took turns carrying me piggyback until we reached a farmhouse. While the farmer hitched up his mule-drawn wagon, his only vehicle, his wife caught a number of chickens, ripped them apart alive, and applied the hot bleeding birds to my knee. "It draws out the poison," she said, and indeed the flesh of the chickens turned green. All the way into town, my cousins kept killing chickens and applying them to the wound. Once we were home, my family telephoned a hospital in Montgomery, a hundred miles away, and five hours later a doctor arrived with a snake serum. I was one sick boy, and the only good thing about it was I missed two months of school.

Once, on my way to Japan, I stayed overnight in Hawaii with Doris Duke in the extraordinary, somewhat Persian palace she had built on a cliff at Diamond Head. It was scarcely daylight when I woke up and decided to go exploring. The room in which I slept had French doors leading into a garden overlooking the ocean. I'd been strolling in the garden perhaps half a minute when a terrifying herd of Dobermans appeared, seemingly out of nowhere; they surrounded and kept me captive within the snarling circle they made. No one had warned me that each night after Miss Duke and her guests had retired, this crowd of homicidal canines was let loose to deter, and possibly punish, unwelcome intruders.

The dogs did not attempt to touch me; they just stood there, coldly staring at me and quivering in controlled rage. I was afraid to breathe; I felt if I moved my foot one scintilla, the beasts would spring forward to rip me apart. My hands were trembling; my legs, too. My hair was as wet as if I'd just stepped out of the ocean. There is nothing more exhausting than standing perfectly still, yet I managed to do it for over an hour. Rescue arrived in the form of a gardener, who, when he saw what was happening, merely whistled and clapped his hands, and all the demon dogs rushed to greet him with friendly wagging tails.

Those are instances of specific terror. Still, our real fears are the sounds of footsteps walking in the corridors of our minds, and the anxieties, the phantom floatings, they create.

Q: What are some of the things you can do?

A: I can ice-skate. I can ski. I can read upside down. I can ride a skateboard. I can hit a tossed can with a .38 revolver. I have driven a Maserati (at dawn, on a flat, lonely Texas road) at 170 mph. I can make a soufflé Furstenberg (quite a stunt: it's a cheese-and-spinach concoction that involves sinking six poached eggs into the batter before cooking; the trick is to have the egg yolks remain soft and runny when the soufflé is served). I can tap-dance. I can type sixty words a minute.

Q: And what are some of the things you can't do?

A: I can't recite the alphabet, at least not correctly or all the way through (not even under hypnosis; it's an impediment that has fascinated several psychotherapists). I am a mathematical imbecile—I can add, more or less, but I can't subtract, and I failed first-year algebra three times, even with the help of a private tutor. I can read without glasses, but I can't drive without them. I can't speak Italian, even though I lived in Italy a total of nine years. I can't make a prepared speech—it has to be spontaneous, "on the wing."

Q: Do you have a "motto"?

A: Sort of. I jotted it down in a schoolboy diary: *I Aspire.* I don't know why I chose those particular words; they're odd, and I like the ambiguity—do I aspire to heaven or hell? Whatever the case, they have an undeniably noble ring.

Last winter I was wandering in a seacoast cemetery near Mendocino—a New England village in far Northern California, a rough place where the water is too cold to swim and where the whales go piping past. It was a lovely little cemetery, and the dates on the sea-gray-green tombstones were mostly nineteenth century; almost all of them had an inscription of some sort, something that revealed the tenant's philosophy. One read: NO COMMENT.

So I began to think what I would have inscribed on my tombstone —except that I shall never have one, because two very gifted fortune tellers, one Haitian, the other an Indian revolutionary who lives in Moscow, have told me I will be lost at sea, though I don't know whether by accident or by choice (*comme ça,* Hart Crane). Anyway, the first inscription I thought of was: AGAINST MY BETTER JUDGMENT. Then I thought of something far more characteristic. An excuse, a phrase I use about almost any commitment: I TRIED TO GET OUT OF IT, BUT I COULDN'T.

Q: Some time ago you made your debut as a film actor (in *Murder by Death*). And?

A: I'm not an actor; I have no desire to be one. I did it as a lark; I thought it would be amusing, and it was fun, more or less, but it was also hard work: up at six and never out of the studio before seven or eight. For the most part, the critics gave me a bouquet of garlic. But I expected that; everyone did—it was what you might call an obligatory reaction. Actually, I was adequate.

Q: How do you handle the "recognition factor"?

A: It doesn't bother me a bit, and it's very useful when you want to cash a check in some strange locale. Also, it can occasionally have amusing consequences. For instance, one night I was sitting with friends at a table in a crowded Key West bar. At a nearby table, there was a mildly drunk woman with a very drunk husband. Presently, the woman approached me and asked me to sign a paper napkin. All this seemed to anger her husband; he staggered over to the table, and after unzipping his trousers and hauling out his equipment, said: "Since you're autographing things, why don't you autograph this?" The tables surrounding us had grown silent, so a great many people heard my reply, which was: "I don't know if I can autograph it, but perhaps I can *initial* it."

Ordinarily, I don't mind giving autographs. But there *is* one thing that gets my goat: without exception, every grown man who has ever asked me for an autograph in a restaurant or on an airplane has always been careful to say that he wanted it for his wife or his daughter or his girl friend, but never, *never* just for himself.

I have a friend with whom I often take long walks on city streets. Frequently, some fellow stroller will pass us, hesitate, produce a sort of is-it-or-isn't-it frown, then stop me and ask, "Are you Truman Capote?" And I'll say, "Yes, I'm Truman Capote." Whereupon my friend will scowl and shake me and shout, "For Christ's sake, George —when are you going to stop this? Some day you're going to get into serious trouble!"

Q: Do you consider conversation an art?

A: A dying one, yes. Most of the renowned conversationalists—Samuel Johnson, Oscar Wilde, Whistler, Jean Cocteau, Lady Astor, Lady Cunard, Alice Roosevelt Longworth—are monologists, not conversationalists. A conversation is a dialogue, not a monologue. That's why there are so few good conversations: due to scarcity, two intelligent talkers seldom meet. Of the list just provided, the only two I've known personally are Cocteau and Mrs. Longworth. (As for her, I take it back —she is not a solo performer; she lets you share the air.)

Among the best conversationalists I've talked with are Gore Vidal (if you're not the victim of his couth, sometimes uncouth, wit), Cecil Beaton (who, not surprisingly, expresses himself almost entirely in visual images—some very beautiful and *some* sublimely wicked). The late Danish genius, the Baroness Blixen, who wrote under the pseudonym Isak Dinesen, was, despite her withered though distinguished appearance, a true seductress, a *conversational* seductress. Ah, how fascinating she was, sitting by the fire in her beautiful house in a Danish seaside village, chain-smoking black cigarettes with silver tips, cooling her lively tongue with draughts of champagne, and luring one from this topic to that—her years as a farmer in Africa (be certain to read, if you haven't already, her autobiographical *Out of Africa*, one of this century's finest books), life under the Nazis in occupied Denmark ("They adored me. We argued, but they didn't care what I said; they didn't care what *any* woman said—it was a completely masculine society. Besides, they had no idea I was hiding Jews in my cellar, along with winter apples and cases of champagne").

Just skimming off the top of my head, other conversationalists I'd rate highly are Christopher Isherwood (no one surpasses him for total but lightly expressed candor) and the felinelike Colette. Marilyn Monroe was very amusing when she felt sufficiently relaxed and had had enough to drink. The same might be said of the lamented screen-scenarist Harry Kurnitz, an exceedingly homely gentleman who conquered men, women and children of all classes with his verbal flights. Diana Vreeland, the eccentric Abbess of High Fashion and one-time, longtime editor of *Vogue*, is a charmer of a talker, a snake charmer.

When I was eighteen I met the person whose conversation has impressed me the most, perhaps because the person in question is the one who has most impressed me. It happened as follows:

In New York, on East Seventy-ninth Street, there is a very pleasant shelter known as the New York Society Library, and during 1942 I spent many afternoons there researching a book I intended writing but never did. Occasionally, I saw a woman there whose appearance rather mesmerized me—her eyes especially: blue, the pale brilliant cloudless blue of prairie skies. But even without this singular feature, her face was interesting—firm-jawed, handsome, a bit androgynous. Pepper-salt hair parted in the middle. Sixty-five, thereabouts. A lesbian? Well, yes.

One January day I emerged from the library into the twilight to find a heavy snowfall in progress. The lady with the blue eyes, wearing a nicely cut black coat with a sable collar, was waiting at the curb. A gloved, taxi-summoning hand was poised in the air, but there were no taxis. She looked at me and smiled and said: "Do you think a cup of hot chocolate would help? There's a Longchamps around the corner."

She ordered hot chocolate; I asked for a "very" dry martini. Half seriously, she said, "Are you old enough?"

"I've been drinking since I was fourteen. Smoking, too."

"You don't look more than fourteen now."

"I'll be nineteen next September." Then I told her a few things: that I was from New Orleans, that I'd published several short stories, that I wanted to be a writer and was working on a novel. And she wanted to know what American writers I liked. "Hawthorne, Henry James, Emily Dickinson . . ." "No, living." Ah, well, hmm, let's see: how difficult, the rivalry factor being what it is, for one contemporary author, or would-be author, to confess admiration for another. At last I said, "Not Hemingway—a really dishonest man, the closet-everything. Not Thomas Wolfe—all that purple upchuck; of course, he isn't living. Faulkner, sometimes: *Light in August.* Fitzgerald, sometimes: *Diamond as Big as the Ritz, Tender Is the Night.* I really like Willa Cather. Have you read *My Mortal Enemy*?"

With no particular expression, she said, "Actually, I wrote it."

I had seen photographs of Willa Cather—long-ago ones, made perhaps in the early twenties. Softer, homelier, less elegant than my companion. Yet I knew instantly that she *was* Willa Cather, and it was one of the *frissons* of my life. I began to babble about her books like a schoolboy—my favorites: *A Lost Lady, The Professor's House, My Ántonia.* It wasn't that I had anything in common with her as a writer. I would never have chosen for myself her sort of subject matter, or tried to emulate her style. It was just that I considered her a great artist. As good as Flaubert.

We became friends; she read my work and was always a fair and helpful judge. She was full of surprises. For one thing, she and her lifelong friend, Miss Lewis, lived in a spacious, charmingly furnished Park Avenue apartment—somehow, the notion of Miss Cather living in an apartment on Park Avenue seemed incongruous with her Nebraska upbringing, with the simple, rather elegiac nature of her novels. Secondly, her principal interest was not literature, but music. She went to concerts constantly, and almost all her closest friends were musical personalities, particularly Yehudi Menuhin and his sister Hepzibah.

Like all authentic conversationalists, she was an excellent listener, and when it was her turn to talk, she was never garrulous, but crisply pointed. Once she told me I was overly sensitive to criticism. The truth was that she was more sensitive to critical slights than I; any disparaging reference to her work caused a decline in spirits. When I pointed this out to her, she said: "Yes, but aren't we always seeking out our own vices in others and reprimanding them for such possessions? I'm alive. I have clay feet. Very definitely."

Q: Do you have any favorite spectator sport?

A: Fireworks. Myriad-colored sprays of evanescent designs glittering the night skies. The very best I've seen were in Japan—these Japanese masters can create fiery creatures in the air: slithering dragons, exploding cats, faces of pagan deities. Italians, Venetians especially, can explode masterworks above the Grand Canal.

Q: Do you have many sexual fantasies?

A: When I do have a sexual fantasy, usually I try to transfer it into reality—sometimes successfully. However, I do often find myself drifting into erotic daydreams that remain just that: daydreams.

I remember once having a conversation on this subject with the late E. M. Forster, to my mind the finest English novelist of this century. He said that as a schoolboy sexual thoughts dominated his mind. He said: "I felt as I grew older this fever would lessen, even leave me. But that was not the case; it raged on through my twenties, and I thought: Well, surely by the time I'm forty, I will receive some release from this torment, this constant search for the perfect love object. But it was not to be; all through my forties, lust was always lurking inside my head. And then I was fifty, and then I was sixty, and nothing changed: sexual images continued to spin around my brain like figures on a carrousel. Now here I am in my *seventies,* and I'm still a prisoner of my sexual imagination. I'm stuck with it, just at an age when I can no longer do anything about it."

q: Have you ever considered suicide?

a: Certainly. And so has everyone else, except possibly the village idiot. Soon after the suicide of the esteemed Japanese writer Yukio Mishima, whom I knew well, a biography about him was published, and to my dismay, the author quotes him as saying: "Oh yes, I think of suicide a great deal. And I know a number of people I'm certain will kill themselves. Truman Capote, for instance." I couldn't imagine what had brought him to this conclusion. My visits with Mishima had always been jolly, very cordial. But Mishima was a sensitive, extremely intuitive man, not someone to be taken lightly. But in this matter, I think his intuition failed him; I would never have the courage to do what he did (he had a friend decapitate him with a sword). Anyway, as I've said somewhere before, most people who take their own lives do so because they really want to kill someone else—a philandering husband, an unfaithful lover, a treacherous friend—but they haven't the guts to do it, so they kill themselves instead. Not me; anyone who had worked me into that kind of a position would find himself looking down the barrel of a shotgun.

q: Do you believe in God, or at any rate, some higher power?

a: I believe in an afterlife. That is to say, I'm sympathetic to the notion of reincarnation.

q: In your own afterlife, how would you like to be reincarnated?

a: As a bird—preferably a buzzard. A buzzard doesn't have to bother about his appearance or ability to beguile and please; he doesn't have to put on airs. Nobody's going to like him anyway; he is ugly, unwanted, unwelcome everywhere. There's a lot to be said for the sort of freedom that allows. On the other hand, I wouldn't mind being a sea turtle. They can roam the land, and they know the secrets of the ocean's depths. Also, they're long-lived, and their hooded eyes accumulate much wisdom.

q: If you could be granted one wish, what would it be?

a: To wake up one morning and feel that I was at last a grown-up person, emptied of resentment, vengeful thoughts, and other wasteful, childish emotions. To find myself, in other words, an adult.

tc: Are you still awake?

tc: Somewhat bored, but still awake. How can I sleep when you're not asleep?

tc: And what do you think of what I've written here? So far?

tc: Wellll . . . since you *ask*. I'd say Billy Grahamcrackers isn't the only one familiar with horse manure.

tc: Bitch, bitch, bitch. Moan and bitch. That's all you ever do. Never a kind word.

tc: Oh, I didn't mean there's anything *very* wrong. Just a few things here and there. Trifles. I mean, perhaps you're not as honest as you pretend to me.

TC: I don't pretend to be honest. I *am* honest.

TC: Sorry. I didn't mean to fart. It wasn't a comment, just an accident.

TC: It was a diversionary tactic. You call me dishonest, compare me to Billy Graham, for Christ's sake, and now you're trying to weasel out of it. Speak up. What have I written here that's dishonest?

TC: Nothing. Trifles. Like that business about the movie. Did it for a lark, eh? You did it for the moola—and to satisfy that clown side of you that's so exasperating. Get rid of that guy. He's a jerk.

TC: Oh, I don't know. He's unpredictable, but I've got a soft spot for him. He's part of me—same as you. And what are some of these other trifles?

TC: The next thing—well, it's not a trifle. It's how you answered the question: Do you believe in God? And you skipped right by it. Said something about an afterlife, reincarnation, coming back as a buzzard. I've got news for you, buddy, you won't have to wait for reincarnation to be treated like a buzzard; plenty of folks are doing it already. Multitudes. But that's not what's so phony about your answer. It's the fact that you don't come right out and say that you *do* believe in God. I've heard you, cool as a cucumber, confess things that would make a baboon blush blue, and yet you won't admit that you believe in God. What is it? Are you afraid of being called a Reborn Christian, a Jesus Freak?

TC: It's not that simple. I did believe in God. And then I didn't. Remember when we were very little and used to go way out in the woods with our dog Queenie and old Cousin Sook? We hunted for wildflowers, wild asparagus. We caught butterflies and let them loose. We caught perch and threw them back in the creek. Sometimes we found giant toadstools, and Sook told us that was where the elves lived, under the beautiful toadstools. She told us the Lord had arranged for them to live there just as He had arranged for everything we saw. The good and the bad. The ants and the mosquitoes and the rattlesnakes, every leaf, the sun in the sky, the old moon and the new moon, rainy days. And we believed her.

But then things happened to spoil that faith. First it was church and itching all over listening to some ignorant redneck preacher shoot his mouth off; then it was all those boarding schools and going to chapel every damn morning. And the Bible itself—nobody with any sense could believe what it asked you to believe. Where were the toadstools? Where were the moons? And at last life, plain living, took away the memories of whatever faith still lingered. I'm not the worst person that's crossed my path, not by a considerable distance, but I've committed some serious sins, deliberate cruelty among them; and it didn't bother me one whit, I never gave it a thought. Until I had to. When the rain started to fall, it was a hard black rain, and it just kept falling. So I started to think about God again.

I thought about St. Julian. About Flaubert's story *St. Julien, L'Hospita-*

lier. It had been so long since I'd read that story, and where I was, in a sanitarium far distant from libraries, I couldn't get a copy. But I remembered (at least I thought this was more or less the way it went) that as a child Julian loved to wander in the forests and loved all animals and living things. He lived on a great estate, and his parents worshipped him; they wanted him to have everything in the world. His father bought him the finest horses, bows and arrows, and taught him to hunt. To kill the very animals he had loved so much. And that was too bad, because Julian discovered that he liked to kill. He was only happy after a day of the bloodiest slaughter. The murdering of beasts and birds became a mania, and after first admiring his skill, his neighbors loathed and feared him for his bloodlust.

Now, there's a part of the story that was pretty vague in my head. Anyway, somehow or other Julian killed his mother and father. A hunting accident? Something like that, something terrible. He became a pariah and a penitent. He wandered the world barefoot and in rags, seeking forgiveness. He grew old and ill. One cold night he was waiting by a river for a boatman to row him across. Maybe it was the River Styx? Because Julian was dying. While he waited, a hideous old man appeared. He was a leper, and his eyes were running sores, his mouth rotting and foul. Julian didn't know it, but this repulsive evil-looking old man was God. And God tested him to see if all his sufferings had truly changed Julian's savage heart. He told Julian He was cold, and asked to share his blanket, and Julian did; then the leper wanted Julian to embrace Him, and Julian did; then He made a final request—He asked Julian to kiss His diseased and rotting lips. Julian did. Whereupon Julian and the old leper, who was suddenly transformed into a radiant shining vision, ascended together to heaven. And so it was that Julian became St. Julian.

So there I was in the rain, and the harder it fell the more I thought about Julian. I prayed that I would have the luck to hold a leper in my arms. And that's when I began to believe in God again, and understand that Sook was right: that everything was His design, the old moon and the new moon, the hard rain falling, and if only I would ask Him to help me, He would.

TC: And has He?

TC: Yes. More and more. But I'm not a saint yet. I'm an alcoholic. I'm a drug addict. I'm homosexual. I'm a genius. Of course, I could be all four of these dubious things and still be a saint. But I shonuf ain't no saint yet, nawsuh.

TC: Well, Rome wasn't built in a day. Now let's knock it off and try for some shut-eye.

TC: But first let's say a prayer. Let's say our *old* prayer. The one we used to say when we were real little and slept in the same bed with Sook and

Queenie, with the quilts piled on top of us because the house was so big and cold.

TC: Our old prayer? Okay.

TC and TC: Now I lay me down to sleep, I pray the Lord my soul to keep. And if I should die before I wake, I pray the Lord my soul to take. Amen.

TC: Good night.

TC: Good night.

TC: I love you.

TC: I love you, too.

TC: You'd better. Because when you get right down to it, all we've got is each other. Alone. To the grave. And that's the tragedy, isn't it?

TC: You forget. We have God, too.

TC: Yes. We have God.

TC: Zzzzzzz

TC: Zzzzzzzzz

TC and TC: Zzzzzzzzzzz

Mr. Jones

(1980)

D URING THE WINTER OF 1945 I LIVED
for several months in a rooming house
in Brooklyn. It was not a shabby place, but a pleasantly furnished, elderly
brownstone kept hospital-neat by its owners, two maiden sisters.

Mr. Jones lived in the room next to mine. My room was the smallest in
the house, his the largest, a nice big sunshiny room, which was just as well,
for Mr. Jones never left it: all his needs, meals, shopping, laundry, were
attended to by the middle-aged landladies. Also, he was not without visitors; on the average, a half-dozen various persons, men and women, young,
old, in-between, visited his room each day, from early morning until late
in the evening. He was not a drug dealer or a fortune teller; no, they came
just to talk to him and apparently they made him small gifts of money for
his conversation and advice. If not, he had no obvious means of support.

I never had a conversation with Mr. Jones myself, a circumstance I've
often since regretted. He was a handsome man, about forty. Slender,
black-haired, and with a distinctive face; a pale, lean face, high cheekbones,
and with a birthmark on his left cheek, a small scarlet defect shaped like
a star. He wore gold-rimmed glasses with pitch-black lenses: he was blind,
and crippled, too—according to the sisters, the use of his legs had been
denied him by a childhood accident, and he could not move without
crutches. He was always dressed in a crisply pressed dark gray or blue

three-piece suit and a subdued tie—as though about to set off for a Wall Street office.

However, as I've said, he never left the premises. Simply sat in his cheerful room in a comfortable chair and received visitors. I had no notion of why they came to see him, these rather ordinary-looking folk, or what they talked about, and I was far too concerned with my own affairs to much wonder over it. When I did, I imagined that his friends had found in him an intelligent, kindly man, a good listener in whom to confide and consult with over their troubles: a cross between a priest and a therapist.

Mr. Jones had a telephone. He was the only tenant with a private line. It rang constantly, often after midnight and as early as six in the morning.

I moved to Manhattan. Several months later I returned to the house to collect a box of books I had stored there. While the landladies offered me tea and cakes in their lace-curtained "parlor," I inquired of Mr. Jones.

The women lowered their eyes. Clearing her throat, one said: "It's in the hands of the police."

The other offered: "We've reported him as a missing person."

The first added: "Last month, twenty-six days ago, my sister carried up Mr. Jones's breakfast, as usual. He wasn't there. All his belongings were there. But he was gone."

"It's odd—"

"—how a man totally blind, a helpless cripple—"

Ten years pass.

Now it is a zero-cold December afternoon, and I am in Moscow. I am riding in a subway car. There are only a few other passengers. One of them is a man sitting opposite me, a man wearing boots, a thick long coat and a Russian-style fur cap. He has bright eyes, blue as a peacock's.

After a doubtful instant, I simply stared, for even without the black glasses, there was no mistaking that lean distinctive face, those high cheek-bones with the single scarlet star-shaped birthmark.

I was just about to cross the aisle and speak to him when the train pulled into a station, and Mr. Jones, on a pair of fine sturdy legs, stood up and strode out of the car. Swiftly, the train door closed behind him.

A Lamp
in a Window

(1980)

Once I was invited to a wedding;
the bride suggested I drive up from
New York with a pair of other guests, a Mr. and Mrs. Roberts, whom I
had never met before. It was a cold April day, and on the ride to Connecticut the Robertses, a couple in their early forties, seemed agreeable enough
—no one you would want to spend a long weekend with, but not bad.

However, at the wedding reception a great deal of liquor was consumed,
I should say a third of it by my chauffeurs. They were the last to leave the
party—at approximately 11 P.M.—and I was most wary of accompanying
them; I knew they were drunk, but I didn't realize *how* drunk. We had
driven about twenty miles, the car weaving considerably, and Mr. and Mrs.
Roberts insulting each other in the most extraordinary language (really, it
was a moment out of *Who's Afraid of Virginia Woolf?*), when Mr. Roberts,
very understandably, made a wrong turn and got lost on a dark country
road. I kept asking them, finally begging them, to stop the car and let me
out, but they were so involved in their invectives that they ignored me.
Eventually the car stopped of its own accord (temporarily) when it swiped
against the side of a tree. I used the opportunity to jump out the car's back
door and run into the woods. Presently the cursed vehicle drove off,
leaving me alone in the icy dark. I'm sure my hosts never missed me; Lord
knows I didn't miss them.

But it wasn't a joy to be stranded out there on a windy cold night. I started walking, hoping I'd reach a highway. I walked for half an hour without sighting a habitation. Then, just off the road, I saw a small frame cottage with a porch and a window lighted by a lamp. I tiptoed onto the porch and looked in the window; an elderly woman with soft white hair and a round pleasant face was sitting by a fireside reading a book. There was a cat curled in her lap, and several others slumbering at her feet.

I knocked at the door, and when she opened it I said, with chattering teeth: "I'm sorry to disturb you, but I've had a sort of accident; I wonder if I could use your phone to call a taxi."

"Oh, dear," she said, smiling. "I'm afraid I don't have a phone. Too poor. But please, come in." And as I stepped through the door into the cozy room, she said: "My goodness, boy. You're freezing. Can I make coffee? A cup of tea? I have a little whiskey my husband left—he died six years ago."

I said a little whiskey would be very welcome.

While she fetched it I warmed my hands at the fire and glanced around the room. It was a cheerful place occupied by six or seven cats of varying alley-cat colors. I looked at the title of the book Mrs. Kelly—for that was her name, as I later learned—had been reading: it was *Emma* by Jane Austen, a favorite writer of mine.

When Mrs. Kelly returned with a glass of ice and a dusty quarter-bottle of bourbon, she said: "Sit down, sit down. It's not often I have company. Of course, I have my cats. Anyway, you'll spend the night? I have a nice little guest room that's been waiting such a long time for a guest. In the morning you can walk to the highway and catch a ride into town, where you'll find a garage to fix your car. It's about five miles away."

I wondered aloud how she could live so isolatedly, without transportation or a telephone; she told me her good friend, the mailman, took care of all her shopping needs. "Albert. He's really so dear and faithful. But he's due to retire next year. After that I don't know what I'll do. But something will turn up. Perhaps a kindly new mailman. Tell me, just what sort of accident did you have?"

When I explained the truth of the matter, she responded indignantly: "You did exactly the right thing. I wouldn't set foot in a car with a man who had sniffed a glass of sherry. That's how I lost my husband. Married forty years, forty happy years, and I lost him because a drunken driver ran him down. If it wasn't for my cats . . ." She stroked an orange tabby purring in her lap.

We talked by the fire until my eyes grew heavy. We talked about Jane Austen ("Ah, Jane. My tragedy is that I've read all her books so often I have them memorized"), and other admired authors: Thoreau, Willa Cather, Dickens, Lewis Carroll, Agatha Christie, Raymond Chandler, Hawthorne, Chekhov, De Maupassant—she was a woman with a good and varied mind; intelligence illuminated her hazel eyes like the small lamp shining on the table beside her. We talked about the hard Connecticut winters, politicians, far places ("I've never been abroad, but if ever I'd had the chance, the place I would have gone is Africa. Sometimes I've dreamed of it, the green hills, the heat, the beautiful giraffes, the elephants walking about"), religion ("Of course, I was raised a Catholic, but now, I'm almost sorry to say, I have an open mind. Too much reading, perhaps"), gardening ("I grow and can all my own vegetables; a necessity"). At last: "Forgive my babbling on. You have no idea how much pleasure it gives me. But it's way past your bedtime. I know it is mine."

She escorted me upstairs, and after I was comfortably arranged in a double bed under a blissful load of pretty scrapquilts, she returned to wish me good night, sweet dreams. I lay awake thinking about it. What an exceptional experience—to be an old woman living alone here in the wilderness and have a stranger knock on your door in the middle of the night and not only open it but warmly welcome him inside and offer him shelter. If our situations had been reversed, I doubt that I would have had the courage, to say nothing of the generosity.

The next morning she gave me breakfast in her kitchen. Coffee and hot oatmeal with sugar and tinned cream, but I was hungry and it tasted great. The kitchen was shabbier than the rest of the house; the stove, a rattling refrigerator, everything seemed on the edge of expiring. All except one large, somewhat modern object, a deep-freeze that fitted into a corner of the room.

She was chatting on: "I love birds. I feel so guilty about not tossing them crumbs during the winter. But I can't have them gathering around the house. Because of the cats. Do you care for cats?"

"Yes, I once had a Siamese named Toma. She lived to be twelve, and we traveled everywhere together. All over the world. And when she died I never had the heart to get another."

"Then maybe you will understand this," she said, leading me over to the deep-freeze, and opening it. Inside was nothing but cats: stacks of frozen, perfectly preserved cats—dozens of them. It gave me an odd sensation. "All my old friends. Gone to rest. It's just that I couldn't bear to lose them. *Completely.*" She laughed, and said: "I guess you think I'm a bit dotty."

A bit dotty. Yes, a bit dotty, I thought as I walked under gray skies in the direction of the highway she had pointed out to me. But radiant: a lamp in a window.

Hospitality

(1980)

ONCE UPON A TIME, IN THE RURAL South, there were farmhouses and farm wives who set tables where almost any passing stranger, a traveling preacher, a knife-grinder, an itinerant worker, was welcome to sit down to a hearty midday meal. Probably many such farm wives still exist. Certainly my aunt does, Mrs. Jennings Carter. Mary Ida Carter.

As a child I lived for long periods of time on the Carters' farm, small then, but today a considerable property. The house was lighted by oil lamps in those days; water was pumped from a well and carried, and the only warmth was provided by fireplaces and stoves, and the only entertainment was what we ourselves manufactured. In the evenings, after supper, likely as not my uncle Jennings, a handsome, virile man, would play the piano accompanied by his pretty wife, my mother's younger sister.

They were hardworking people, the Carters. Jennings, with the help of a few sharecropping field hands, cultivated his land with a horse-drawn plow. As for his wife, her chores were unlimited. I helped her with many of them: feeding the pigs, milking the cows, churning milk into butter, husking corn, shelling peas and pecans—it was fun, except for one assignment I sought to avoid, and when forced to perform, did so with my eyes shut: I just plain hated wringing the necks of chickens, though I certainly didn't object to eating them afterward.

This was during the Depression, but there was plenty to eat on Mary

Ida's table for the principal meal of the day, which was served at noon and to which her sweating husband and his helpers were summoned by clanging a big bell. I loved to ring the bell; it made me feel powerful and beneficent.

It was to these midday meals, where the table was covered with hot biscuits and cornbread and honey-in-the-comb and chicken and catfish or fried squirrel and butter beans and black-eyed peas, that guests sometimes appeared, sometimes expected, sometimes not. "Well," Mary Ida would sigh, seeing a footsore Bible salesman approaching along the road, "we don't need another Bible. But I guess we'd better set another place."

Of all those we fed, there were three who will never slip my memory. First, the Presbyterian missionary, who was traveling around the countryside soliciting funds for his Christian duties in unholy lands. Mary Ida said she couldn't afford a cash contribution, but she would be pleased to have him take dinner with us. Poor man, he definitely looked as though he needed one. Arrayed in a rusty, dusty, shiny black suit, creaky black undertaker shoes, and a black-greenish hat, he was thin as a stalk of sugar cane. He had a long red wrinkled shirt. I thought he was nice, we all did; he had a flower tattooed on his wrist, his eyes were gentle, he was gently spoken. He said his name was Bancroft (which, as it turned out, *was* his true name). My uncle Jennings asked him: "What's your line of work, Mr. Bancroft?"

"Well," he drawled, "I'm just lookin' for some. Like most everybody else. I'm pretty handy. Can do most anythin'. You wouldn't have somethin' for me?"

Jennings said: "I sure could use a man. But I can't afford him."

"I'd work for most nothin'."

"Yeah," said Jennings. "But nothing is what I've got."

Unpredictably, for it was a subject seldom alluded to in that household, crime came into the conversation. Mary Ida complained: "Pretty Boy Floyd. And that Dillinger man. Running around the country shooting people. Robbing banks."

"Oh, I don't know," said Mr. Bancroft. "I got no sympathy with them banks. And Dillinger, he's real smart, you got to hand him that. It kinda makes me laugh the way he knocks off them banks and gets clean away with it." Then he actually laughed, displaying tobacco-tinted teeth.

"Well," Mary Ida countered, "I'm slightly surprised to hear you say that, Mr. Bancroft."

Two days later Jennings drove his wagon into town and returned with a keg of nails, a sack of flour, and a copy of the *Mobile Register*. On the front page was a picture of Mr. Bancroft—"Two-Barrels" Bancroft, as he was colloquially known to the authorities. He had been captured in Evergreen, thirty miles away. When Mary Ida saw his photo, she rapidly fanned her face with a paper fan, as though to prevent a fainting fit. "Heaven help me," she cried. "He could have killed us all."

Jennings said sourly: "There was a reward. And we missed out on it. *That's* what gets my goat."

Next, there was a girl called Zilla Ryland. Mary Ida discovered her bathing a two-year-old baby, a red-haired boy, in a creek that ran through the woods back of the house. As Mary Ida described it: "I saw her before she saw me. She was standing naked in the water bathing this beautiful little boy. On the bank there was a calico dress and the child's clothes and an old suitcase tied together with a piece of rope. The boy was laughing, and so was she. Then she saw me, and she was startled. Scared. I said: 'Nice day. But hot. The water must feel good.' But she snatched up the baby and scampered out of the creek, and I said: 'You don't have to be frightened of me. I'm only Mrs. Carter that lives just over yonder. Come on up and rest a spell.' Then she commenced to cry; she was only a little thing, no more than a child herself. I asked what's the matter, honey? But she wouldn't answer. By now she had pulled on her dress and dressed the boy. I said maybe I could help you if you'd tell me what's wrong. But she shook her head, and said there was nothing wrong, and I said well, we don't cry over nothing, do we? Now you just follow me up to the house and we'll talk about it. And she did."

Indeed she did.

I was swinging in the porch swing reading an old *Saturday Evening Post* when I noticed them coming up the path, Mary Ida toting a broken-down suitcase and this barefooted girl carrying a child in her arms.

Mary Ida introduced me: "This is my nephew, Buddy. And—I'm sorry, honey, I didn't catch your name."

"Zilla," the girl whispered, eyes lowered.

"I'm sorry, honey. I can't hear you."

"Zilla," she again whispered.

"Well," said Mary Ida cheerfully, "that sure is an unusual name."

Zilla shrugged. "My mama give it to me. Was her name, too."

Two weeks later Zilla was still with us; she proved to be as unusual as her name. Her parents were dead, her husband had "run off with another woman. She was real fat, and he liked fat women, he said I was too skinny, so he run off with her and got a divorce and married her up in Athens, Georgia." Her only living kin was a brother: Jim James. "That's why I come down here to Alabama. The last I heard, he was located somewhere around here."

Uncle Jennings did everything in his power to trace Jim James. He had good reason, for, although he liked Zilla's little boy, Jed, he'd come to feel quite hostile toward Zilla—her thin voice aggravated him, and her habit of humming mysterious tuneless melodies.

Jennings to Mary Ida: "Just the hell how much longer is our boarder going to hang around?" Mary Ida: "Oh, Jennings. Shhh! Zilla might hear you. Poor soul. She's got nowhere to go." So Jennings intensified his labors. He brought the sheriff into the case; he even *paid* to place an ad in the local paper—and that was really going far. But nobody hereabouts had ever heard of Jim James.

At last Mary Ida, clever woman, had an idea. The idea was to invite a neighbor, Eldridge Smith, to evening supper, usually a light meal served at six. I don't know why she hadn't thought of it before. Mr. Smith was not much to look at, but he was a recently widowed farmer of about forty with two school-aged children.

After that first supper Mr. Smith got to stopping by almost every twilight. After dark we all left Zilla and Mr. Smith alone, where they swung together on the creaking porch swing and laughed and talked and whispered. It was driving Jennings out of his mind because he didn't like Mr. Smith any better than he liked Zilla; his wife's repeated requests to "Hush, honey. Wait and see" did little to soothe him.

We waited a month. Until finally one night Jennings took Mr. Smith aside and said: "Now look here, Eldridge. Man to man, what are your intentions toward this fine young lady?" The way Jennings said it, it was more like a threat than anything else.

Mary Ida made the wedding dress on her foot-pedaled Singer sewing machine. It was white cotton with puffed sleeves, and Zilla wore a white silk ribbon bow in her hair, especially curled for the occasion. She looked surprisingly pretty. The ceremony was held under the shade of a mulberry tree on a cool September afternoon, the Reverend Mr. L. B. Persons presiding. Afterward everybody was served cupcakes and fruit punch spiked with scuppernong wine. As the newlyweds rode away in Mr. Smith's mule-drawn wagon, Mary Ida lifted the hem of her skirt to dab at her eyes, but Jennings, eyes dry as a snake's skin, declared: "Thank you, dear Lord. And while You're doing favors, my crops could use some rain."

Preface to
Music for
Chameleons

(1980)

Y LIFE—AS AN ARTIST, AT LEAST
—can be charted as precisely as a
fever: the highs and lows, the very definite cycles.

I started writing when I was eight—out of the blue, uninspired by any example. I'd never known anyone who wrote; indeed, I knew few people who read. But the fact was, the only four things that interested me were: reading books, going to the movies, tap-dancing and drawing pictures. Then one day I started writing, not knowing that I had chained myself for life to a noble but merciless master. When God hands you a gift, he also hands you a whip; and the whip is intended solely for self-flagellation.

But of course I didn't know that. I wrote adventure stories, murder mysteries, comedy skits, tales that had been told me by former slaves and Civil War veterans. It was a lot of fun—at first. It stopped being fun when I discovered the difference between good writing and bad, and then made an even more alarming discovery: the difference between very good writing and true art; it is subtle, but savage. And after that, the whip came down!

As certain young people practice the piano or the violin four and five hours a day, so I played with my papers and pens. Yet I never discussed my writing with anyone; if someone asked what I was up to all those hours, I told them I was doing my school homework. Actually, I never did any homework. My literary tasks kept me fully occupied: my apprenticeship at the altar of technique, craft; the devilish intricacies of paragraphing, punctuation, dialogue placement. Not to mention the grand overall design, the great demanding arc of middle-beginning-end. One had to learn so much, and from so many sources: not only from books, but from music, from painting, and just plain everyday observation.

In fact, the most interesting writing I did during those days was the plain everyday observations that I recorded in my journal. Descriptions of a neighbor. Long verbatim accounts of overheard conversations. Local gossip. A kind of reporting, a style of "seeing" and "hearing" that would later seriously influence me, though I was unaware of it then, for all my "formal" writing, the stuff that I polished and carefully typed, was more or less fictional.

By the time I was seventeen I was an accomplished writer. Had I been a pianist, it would have been the moment for my first public concert. As it was, I decided I was ready to publish. I sent off stories to the principal literary quarterlies, as well as to the national magazines, which in those days published the best so-called "quality" fiction—*Story, The New Yorker, Harper's Bazaar, Mademoiselle, Harper's, Atlantic Monthly*—and stories by me duly appeared in those publications.

Then, in 1948, I published a novel: *Other Voices, Other Rooms.* It was well received critically, and was a best seller. It was also, due to an exotic photograph of the author on the dust jacket, the start of a certain notoriety that has kept close step with me these many years. Indeed, many people attributed the commercial success of the novel to the photograph. Others dismissed the book as though it were a freakish accident: "Amazing that anyone so young can write that well." Amazing? I'd only been writing day in and day out for fourteen years! Still, the novel was a satisfying conclusion to the first cycle in my development.

A short novel, *Breakfast at Tiffany's,* ended the second cycle in 1958. During the intervening ten years I experimented with almost every aspect of writing, attempting to conquer a variety of techniques, to achieve a technical virtuosity as strong and flexible as a fisherman's net. Of course, I failed in several of the areas I invaded, but it is true that one learns more from a failure than one does from a success. I know I did, and later I was able to apply what I had learned to great advantage. Anyway, during that decade of exploration I wrote short-story collections (*A Tree of Night, A Christmas Memory*), essays and portraits (*Local Color, Observations,* the work contained in *The Dogs Bark*), plays (*The Grass Harp, House of Flowers*), film scripts (*Beat the Devil, The Innocents*), and a great deal of factual reportage, most of it for *The New Yorker.*

In fact, from the point of view of my creative destiny, the most interesting writing I did during the whole of this second phase first appeared in *The New Yorker* as a series of articles and subsequently as a book entitled

The Muses Are Heard. It concerned the first cultural exchange between the U.S.S.R. and the U.S.A.: a tour, undertaken in 1955, of Russia by a company of black Americans in *Porgy and Bess.* I conceived of the whole adventure as a short comic "nonfiction novel," the first.

Some years earlier, Lillian Ross had published *Picture,* her account of the making of a movie, *The Red Badge of Courage;* with its fast cuts, its flash forward and back, it was itself like a movie, and as I read it I wondered what would happen if the author let go of her hard linear straight-reporting discipline and handled her material as if it were fictional—would the book gain or lose? I decided, if the right subject came along, I'd like to give it a try: *Porgy and Bess* and Russia in the depths of winter seemed the right subject.

The Muses Are Heard received excellent reviews; even sources usually unfriendly to me were moved to praise it. Still, it did not attract any special notice, and the sales were moderate. Nevertheless, that book was an important event for me: while writing it, I realized I just might have found a solution to what had always been my greatest creative quandary.

For several years I had been increasingly drawn toward journalism as an art form in itself. I had two reasons. First, it didn't seem to me that anything truly innovative had occurred in prose writing, or in writing generally, since the 1920s; second, journalism as art was almost virgin terrain, for the simple reason that very few literary artists ever wrote narrative journalism, and when they did, it took the form of travel essays or autobiography. *The Muses Are Heard* had set me to thinking on different lines altogether: I wanted to produce a journalistic novel, something on a large scale that would have the credibility of fact, the immediacy of film, the depth and freedom of prose, and the precision of poetry.

It was not until 1959 that some mysterious instinct directed me toward the subject—an obscure murder case in an isolated part of Kansas—and it was not until 1966 that I was able to publish the result, *In Cold Blood.*

In a story by Henry James, I think *The Middle Years,* his character, a writer in the shadows of maturity, laments: "We live in the dark, we do what we can, the rest is the madness of art." Or words to that effect. Anyway, Mr. James is laying it on the line there; he's telling us the truth. And the darkest part of the dark, the maddest part of the madness, is the relentless gambling involved. Writers, at least those who take genuine risks, who are willing to bite the bullet and walk the plank, have a lot in common with another breed of lonely men—the guys who make a living shooting pool and dealing cards. Many people thought I was crazy to spend six years wandering around the plains of Kansas; others rejected my whole concept of the "nonfiction novel" and pronounced it unworthy of a "serious" writer; Norman Mailer described it as a "failure of imagination"—

meaning, I assume, that a novelist should be writing about something imaginary rather than about something real.

Yes, it was like playing high-stakes poker; for six nerve-shattering years I didn't know whether I had a book or not. Those were long summers and freezing winters, but I just kept on dealing the cards, playing my hand as best I could. Then it turned out I *did* have a book. Several critics complained that "nonfiction novel" was a catch phrase, a hoax, and that there was nothing really original or new about what I had done. But there were those who felt differently, other writers who realized the value of my experiment and moved swiftly to put it to their own use—none more swiftly than Norman Mailer, who has made a lot of money and won a lot of prizes writing nonfiction novels (*The Armies of the Night, Of a Fire on the Moon, The Executioner's Song*), although he has always been careful never to describe them as "nonfiction novels." No matter; he is a good writer and a fine fellow and I'm grateful to have been of some small service to him.

The zigzag line charting my reputation as a writer had reached a healthy height, and I let it rest there before moving into my fourth, and what I expect will be my final, cycle. For four years, roughly from 1968 through 1972, I spent most of my time reading and selecting, rewriting and indexing my own letters, other people's letters, my diaries and journals (which contain detailed accounts of hundreds of scenes and conversations) for the years 1943 through 1965. I intended to use much of this material in a book I had long been planning: a variation on the nonfiction novel. I called the book *Answered Prayers,* which is a quote from Saint Thérèse, who said: "More tears are shed over answered prayers than unanswered ones." In 1972 I began work on this book by writing the last chapter first (it's always good to know where one's going). Then I wrote the first chapter, "Unspoiled Monsters." Then the fifth, "A Severe Insult to the Brain." Then the seventh, "La Côte Basque." I went on in this manner, writing different chapters out of sequence. I was able to do this only because the plot—or rather plots—was true, and all the characters were real: it wasn't difficult to keep it all in mind, for I hadn't invented anything. And yet *Answered Prayers* is not intended as any ordinary roman à clef, a form where facts are disguised as fiction. My intentions are the reverse: to remove disguises, not manufacture them.

In 1975 and 1976 I published four chapters of the book in *Esquire* magazine. This aroused anger in certain circles, where it was felt I was betraying confidences, mistreating friends and/or foes. I don't intend to discuss this; the issue involves social politics, not artistic merit. I will say only that all a writer has to work with is the material he has gathered as the result of his own endeavor and observations, and he cannot be denied the right to use it. Condemn, but not deny.

However, I did stop working on *Answered Prayers* in September 1977, a fact that had nothing to do with any public reaction to those parts of the book already published. The halt happened because I was in a helluva lot of trouble: I was suffering a creative crisis and a personal one at the same time. As the latter was unrelated, or very little related, to the former, it is only necessary to remark on the creative chaos.

Now, torment though it was, I'm glad it happened; after all, it altered my entire comprehension of writing, my attitude toward art and life and the balance between the two, and my understanding of the difference between what is true and what is *really* true.

To begin with, I think most writers, even the best, overwrite. I prefer to underwrite. Simple, clear as a country creek. But I felt my writing was becoming too dense, that I was taking three pages to arrive at effects I ought to be able to achieve in a single paragraph. Again and again I read all that I had written of *Answered Prayers,* and I began to have doubts—not about the material or my approach, but about the texture of the writing itself. I reread *In Cold Blood* and had the same reaction: there were too many areas where I was not writing as well as I could, where I was not delivering the total potential. Slowly, but with accelerating alarm, I read every word I'd ever published, and decided that never, not once in my writing life, had I completely exploded all the energy and aesthetic excitements that material contained. Even when it was good, I could see that I was never working with more than half, sometimes only a third, of the powers at my command. Why?

The answer, revealed to me after months of meditation, was simple but not very satisfying. Certainly it did nothing to lessen my depression; indeed, it thickened it. For the answer created an apparently unsolvable problem, and if I couldn't solve it, I might as well quit writing. The problem was: how can a writer successfully combine within a single form —say the short story—all he knows about every other form of writing? For this was why my work was often insufficiently illuminated; the voltage was there, but by restricting myself to the techniques of whatever form I was working in, I was not using everything I knew about writing—all I'd learned from film scripts, plays, reportage, poetry, the short story, novellas, the novel. A writer ought to have all his colors, all his abilities available on the same palette for mingling (and, in suitable instances, simultaneous application). But how?

I returned to *Answered Prayers.* I removed one chapter and rewrote two others. An improvement, definitely an improvement. But the truth was, I had to go back to kindergarten. Here I was—off again on one of those grim gambles! But I was excited; I felt an invisible sun shining on me. Still, my first experiments were awkward. I truly felt like a child with a box of crayons.

From a technical point, the greatest difficulty I'd had in writing *In Cold Blood* was leaving myself completely out of it. Ordinarily, the reporter has to use himself as a character, an eyewitness observer, in order to retain credibility. But I felt that it was essential to the seemingly detached tone of that book that the author should be absent. Actually, in all my reportage, I had tried to keep myself as invisible as possible.

Now, however, I set myself center stage, and reconstructed, in a severe, minimal manner, commonplace conversations with everyday people: the superintendent of my building, a masseur at the gym, an old school friend, my dentist. After writing hundreds of pages of this simpleminded sort of thing, I eventually developed a style. I had found a framework into which I could assimilate everything I knew about writing.

Later, using a modified version of this technique, I wrote a nonfiction short novel *(Handcarved Coffins)* and a number of short stories. The result is the present volume: *Music for Chameleons*.

And how has all this affected my other work-in-progress, *Answered Prayers?* Very considerably. Meanwhile, I'm here alone in my dark madness, all by myself with my deck of cards—and, of course, the whip God gave me.

READ MORE IN PENGUIN

In every corner of the world, on every subject under the sun, Penguin represents quality and variety – the very best in publishing today.

For complete information about books available from Penguin – including Puffins, Penguin Classics and Arkana – and how to order them, write to us at the appropriate address below. Please note that for copyright reasons the selection of books varies from country to country.

In the United Kingdom: Please write to *Dept. EP, Penguin Books Ltd, Bath Road, Harmondsworth, West Drayton, Middlesex UB7 0DA*

In the United States: Please write to *Consumer Services, Penguin Putnam Inc., 405 Murray Hill Parkway, East Rutherford, New Jersey 07073-2136.* VISA and MasterCard holders call 1-800-631-8571 to order Penguin titles

In Canada: Please write to *Penguin Books Canada Ltd, 10 Alcorn Avenue, Suite 300, Toronto, Ontario M4V 3B2*

In Australia: Please write to *Penguin Books Australia Ltd, 487 Maroondah Highway, Ringwood, Victoria 3134*

In New Zealand: Please write to *Penguin Books (NZ) Ltd, Private Bag 102902, North Shore Mail Centre, Auckland 10*

In India: Please write to *Penguin Books India Pvt Ltd, 11 Community Centre, Panchsheel Park, New Delhi 110017*

In the Netherlands: Please write to *Penguin Books Netherlands bv, Postbus 3507, NL-1001 AH Amsterdam*

In Germany: Please write to *Penguin Books Deutschland GmbH, Metzlerstrasse 26, 60594 Frankfurt am Main*

In Spain: Please write to *Penguin Books S. A., Bravo Murillo 19, 1°B, 28015 Madrid*

In Italy: Please write to *Penguin Italia s.r.l., Via Vittorio Emanuele 45la, 20094 Corsico, Milano*

In France: Please write to *Penguin France, 12, Rue Prosper Ferradou, 31700 Blagnac*

In Japan: Please write to *Penguin Books Japan Ltd, Iidabashi KM-Bldg, 2-23-9 Koraku, Bunkyo-Ku, Tokyo 112-0004*

In South Africa: Please write to *Penguin Books South Africa (Pty) Ltd, P.O. Box 751093, Gardenview, 2047 Johannesburg*

READ MORE IN PENGUIN

A CHOICE OF TWENTIETH-CENTURY CLASSICS

The Golden Bough James Frazer

James George Frazer (1854–1941) caught the popular imagination with his vast and enterprising comparative study of the beliefs and institutions of mankind. This edition is Frazer's own single-volume abridgement of 1922.

The Slave Isaac Bashevis Singer

'*The Slave* – the finest, most lyrical of his novels – is replete with the sounds and smells of the Polish countryside ... the best of his writing warms the heart and reaffirms one's beleaguered faith in pitiful humanity' – Paul Bailey

The Quiet American Graham Greene

The Quiet American is a terrifying portrait of innocence at large. While the French Army in Indo-China is grappling with the Vietminh, back at Saigon a young and high-minded American begins to channel economic aid to a 'Third Force'. 'There has been no novel of any political scope about Vietnam since Graham Greene wrote *The Quiet American*' – *Harper's*

Letters 1931–1966 Jean Rhys

The publication of *Wide Sargasso Sea* finally brought Jean Rhys to fame at the age of seventy-six. These letters span the period of the completion of her masterpiece and make exhilarating as well as painful reading, providing a frank self-portrait of a fascinating, complex, tormented personality striving to know herself.

The Desert of Love François Mauriac

Two men, father and son, share a passion for the same woman. Maria Cross is attractive, intelligent and proud, but her position as a 'kept woman' makes her an outcast from society. Many years later, in very different circumstances, the two men encounter Maria again and once more feel the power of this enigmatic woman who has indelibly marked their lives.

READ MORE IN PENGUIN

A CHOICE OF TWENTIETH-CENTURY CLASSICS

Ulysses James Joyce

Ulysses is unquestionably one of the supreme masterpieces, in any artistic form, of the twentieth century. 'It is the book to which we are all indebted and from which none of us can escape' – T. S. Eliot

The Heart of the Matter Graham Greene

Scobie is a highly principled police officer in a war-torn West African state. When he is passed over for promotion he is forced to borrow money to send his despairing wife on holiday. With a duty to repay his debts and an inability to distinguish between love, pity and responsibility to others and to God, Scobie moves inexorably towards his final damnation.

The Age of Innocence Edith Wharton

To the rigid world of propriety, of which Old New York is composed, returns the Countess Olenska. Separated from her European husband and displaying an independence and impulsive awareness of life, she stirs the educated sensitivity of Newland Archer, who is engaged to be married to young May Welland.

Mr Noon D. H. Lawrence

This Penguin edition is the first annotated paperback publication of Lawrence's autobiographical and strikingly innovative unfinished novel. Abandoning a promising academic career, Gilbert Noon becomes embroiled in an affair which causes him to flee to Germany, there to find true passion with the unhappily married wife of an English doctor.

Black List, Section H Francis Stuart

This astonishingly powerful novel follows H on a spiritual quest for revelation and redemption, from his disastrous marriage to Iseult Gonne, the Irish Civil War and internment, to his life as a writer, poultry farmer, racehorse owner and Bohemian in 1930s London, and his arrival in Hitler's Germany in 1940.

READ MORE IN PENGUIN

A CHOICE OF TWENTIETH-CENTURY CLASSICS

Orlando Virginia Woolf

Sliding in and out of three centuries, and slipping between genders, Orlando is the sparkling incarnation of the personality of Vita Sackville-West as Virginia Woolf saw it.

Selected Poems Patrick Kavanagh

One of the major figures in the modern Irish poetic canon, Patrick Kavanagh (1904–67) was a post-colonial poet who released Anglo-Irish verse from its prolonged obsession with history, ethnicity and national politics. His poetry, written in an uninhibited vernacular style, focused on the 'common and banal' aspects of contemporary life.

More Die of Heartbreak Saul Bellow

'One turns the last pages of *More Die of Heartbreak* feeling that no image has been left unexplored by a mind not only at constant work but standing outside itself, mercilessly examining the workings, tracking the leading issues of our times and the composite man in an age of hybrids' – *New York Book Review*

Tell Me How Long the Train's Been Gone James Baldwin

Leo Proudhammer, a successful Broadway actor, is recovering from a near-fatal heart attack. Talent, luck and ambition have brought him a long way from the Harlem ghetto of his childhood. With Barbara, a white woman who has the courage to love the wrong man, and Christopher, a charismatic black revolutionary, Leo faces a turning-point in his life.

Memories of a Catholic Girlhood Mary McCarthy

Blending memories and family myths, Mary McCarthy takes us back to the twenties, when she was orphaned in a world of relations as colourful, potent and mysterious as the Catholic religion. 'Superb . . . so heartbreaking that in comparison Jane Eyre seems to have got off lightly' – Anita Brookner

BY THE SAME AUTHOR

Answered Prayers

Truman Capote's great unfinished novel blisters with scandal and malice. His candid exposé of the exclusive world of the very rich teems with beautiful, spiteful women, psychotic and sadistic husbands and other thinly disguised friends and acquaintances of the author.

'A master writer ... Between the cloudbursts of malice there are flashes of prose that bring the aching reminder of a more whole writer, prose that makes the heart sing and the narrative fly' – *The New York Times*

In Cold Blood

On a November night in 1959 a wealthy Kansas farmer, his wife and their two teenage children were shot and killed. The two young men who had murdered them were eventually hanged for the crime. In the six-year interim, Truman Capote researched and wrote *In Cold Blood*, an investigative classic which raises as many compelling and horrifying questions as it answers.

'One of the stupendous books of the decade' – *Sunday Express*

also published in separate volumes:

Breakfast At Tiffany's
Music for Chameleons